Spring-Heel'd Jack

The Terror of London (1863)

The Spring-Heeled Jack Library: Volume 1

Alfred Coates

Edited with a New Introduction by

J.S. Mackley

The Spring-Heeled Jack Library

Spring Heel'd Jack: The Terror of London (1863)*

Spring Heeled Jack: The Terror of London (2 vols.) (1886)

Spring-Heeled Jack: Articles and Short fiction (1838–1897)
The Resident of Peckham letter (1838)
The Spring Jack (1838)
Springheel Jack: The Terror of London (The Origin Story) (1878)
From *Chums* by Harleigh Severne (1878)
Spring-Heeled Jack, from *All the Year Round* (9 August 1884)
Spring Heel Jack, *or* the Masked Mystery of the Tower (1885)
Spring-Heeled Jack (The Dialect Story) (1888)
The Mystery of Spring Heel Jack, *or* The Haunted Grange (1897)

Spring-Heeled Jack: The Human Bat
The Human Bat (1899–1901)
The Black Phantom (1901)

Dandy Dick, *or* The King's Highway**
Dandy Dick (1900)
Dandy Dick's Double (1900-1901)

Spring-Heeled Jack: Man or Fiend (1904)*

The Winged Man; *or* 'Twixt Midnight and Dawn (1913)***

* Complete for the first time
** A story featuring Spring-Heeled Jack as an ancillary character
*** A story influenced by The Human Bat series

First published in Great Britain in 2020

New Edition 2024 Published by Isengrin Publishing

Paperback: ISBN: 978-1-917130-00-4
eBook ISBN: 978-1-917130-54-7
www.jonmackley.com

For Mike Dash
In appreciation

SPRING-HEEL'D JACK:

THE TERROR OF LONDON.

SPRING-HEEL'D JACK'S DARING LEAP.

CHAPTER I.

SPRING-HEELED JACK—THE OFFICER'S FRIGHT— CATCH IF YOU CAN.

It is now a little over a quarter of a century since the inhabitants of London and its suburbs were kept in a continual state of terror by a man who, under various disguises, and in different shapes and forms, would suddenly appear before the unsuspecting pedestrian, and, after having nearly frightened the traveller out of his or her senses, would as suddenly disappear, with terrific bounds, from his side, leaving for a time the impression upon his affrighted victim that his Satanic Majesty had paid a visit to the earth, and especially favoured them with his presence.

Evening was generally the time chosen by this eccentric character for his strange conduct; and doubtless there are many living who can recollect—but not without a shudder—the pang of fear which shot through their hearts when, leaping from some dark corner, out of a doorway, or over a thickset hedge, he stood before them.

What his true object could be none have been able to conjecture. Certain it is that robbery was not the cause, for he was never known to take a single coin from his victims, even when fright had rendered them almost insensible; nor did he ever practise any other degree of cruelty beyond affrighting them.

But this was bad enough—so bad, that in some cases the victims of his eccentricities never thoroughly recovered the shock their nerves sustained; and, indeed, in one or two instances, death was ultimately the result.

As may be supposed, his capture was ardently desired both by those whose path he had crossed and those who had not even seen him, and not a few attempts were made to render him powerless to continue his course for some time to come.

It was at the time that the terror he caused was at its height—when the husband, on his return home, cast suspicious glances behind him, and clutched nervously at his walking-stick; and the wife waited anxiously, with barred door, her husband's return, fearful even to open it to his well-known knock, lest it should be Spring-heeled Jack—that that worthy one evening entered a public-house in the neighbourhood of the Liverpool-road, Islington.

He was tall and well formed, which even the large dark Spanish cloak he wore did not disguise.

He called for refreshments for himself, and, addressing two or three persons standing at the bar, he likewise requested the landlord to serve them with whatever they required, adding, that he would pay the bill.

This, of course, drew all eyes towards him, and a policeman, who at the moment entered the bar, was solicited to partake of his kindness.

Nothing loth, the officer accepted, and his glass being filled, the stranger remarked—

"Yours is a dreary beat, officer, this dark night."

"You may well say that, sir," replied the officer. "But I don't mind much."

"You are not afraid, then, of this Spring-heeled Jack there is such a talk about just now?" said the man in the cloak, in an offhand manner.

"Not a bit of it!" said the policeman, supping the hot rum and water with which he had been supplied.

"And yet I think he'd frighten you, if you met him," continued the man in the cloak.

"He might frighten an old woman, but he wouldn't frighten me!" said the officer. "I should like to be as sure of a five-pound note to-morrow morning, as I am now, that if he comes across me to-night I'll lodge him in the station-house!"

"Nonsense!" said the stranger, coolly.

"Good sense! sir. All I hope is, I may get the chance, for I believe, if any of our men take him, he's certain of promotion," said the officer.

"That won't be you, bobby," said a tall, ostler-looking man, winking over the rim of a quart pot out of which he was drinking.

"Why not?" asked the policeman, indignantly.

"Because you'd be frightened to death!"

"Should I?"

"Yes, you would?"

"I tell you what I'll do with you," said the officer, indignantly, "I'll bet you a glass of brandy and water that I take him if he comes on my beat."

"And I'll bet you that you don't!" said the ostler, placing the pot down on the bar, and extending his hand to the policeman.

"Done!" said the officer, shaking the man's hand.

"That's a fair bet," said the man in the cloak; "and now I'll bet you both the same, that Spring-heeled Jack will be on this officer's beat to-night."

"To-night?" exclaimed the officer and the others.

"Yes, to-night."

"How do you know?" said the ostler, looking at him suspiciously.

"Because I have seen him."

"When?"

"Just now."

"Where?" asked the policeman, turning pale a little.

"Just up the road."

"The devil!" stammered the officer.

"Well, I can't say whether it is the devil or not," said the man in the cloak; "but I believe he is the devil and no one else."

"Do you really think so, sir?" said the officer.

"Yes; but I may be mistaken. However, you are sure to know if you catch him."

"I'll do that," said the policeman, "never fear. Devil or no devil, if I get a sight of him I'll have him."

The stranger shook his head.

"I fear your courage would fail you at the moment you most needed it," he said.

"No fear, sir; I ain't so easily frightened," said the policeman.

"You are not?"

"No."

"Well, it is certainly worthy of the trial, if you would get promoted for it," said the stranger.

"And I mean to make it."

"Perhaps you had better not."

"Why so?"

"The shock might be too much for you."

"No fear of that."

"And if you did not succeed you would be laughed at."

"I'd chance that," said the officer. "He had better not come near me, nor even let me see him. I'd take some of the spring out of his heels."

"Well, you've got a chance, bobby," said the ostler, "for this gentleman says he's on your beat to-night."

"And I spoke truly, my friend."

INTRODUCTION

Spring-Heeled Jack – History and Fiction

There was a time towards the mid-nineteenth century when the name of Spring-Heeled Jack would have been spoken in whispers and would have instilled terror in all who heard it. In early 1838, newspaper columns were filled with reports of Jack's alleged "pranks" which led him to be known as the "Terror of London". Jack's reputation developed from "suburban ghost stories" such as the Hammersmith Ghost of 1803, where it was easy for a man to hide in the foggy, gas-lit streets of London and to then leap out and frighten someone. However, the legend of Spring-Heeled Jack is an intriguing mix of fact and fiction, and there are four groups of historical sightings of Jack that were investigated: three appearances in London (1838), scaring soldiers at Aldershot Barracks (March and August 1877), leaping the Newport Arch in Lincoln (November 1877) and jumping across roofs in Everton, Liverpool (1904).[1] This introduction will consider the early sightings of Spring-Heeled Jack and how the character became woven into popular culture until the publication of the first serial novel in 1863. The later sightings will be covered in the introductions to subsequent volumes.

The First Reports of Spring-Heeled Jack

In January 1838, Sir John Cowan, the Lord Mayor of London, received a letter signed by "A Resident of Peckham", but the "odd nature" of the letter "had induced him to withhold it from the public for some days".

---

[1] Recent studies of Jack's antics have been published by Mike Dash (1996), Karl Bell (2012), John Mathews (2016) and J.S. Mackley (2016 and 2021). Notably, Dash's study, published in *Fortean Studies*, has collated primary source material from the newspapers which is invaluable to anyone interested in Spring-Heeled Jack and is the foundation of any contemporary scholars' work on Jack. Less reliable is the 1977 study by Peter Haining which, as Dash has demonstrated and discussed through this series, often proves to be exaggerated at best, and often contains downright fabrications with suggestions that cannot be substantiated.

The letter, published in *The Times*, complained that "some individuals (of … the higher ranks of life) have laid a wager … [to] take upon himself of visiting many villages near London in three disguises—a ghost, a bear and a devil" and, furthermore, "this affair has now been going on for some time, and … the papers are still silent on the subject" (9 January 1838; Dash 44). The Lord Mayor received many responses to the publication of this letter some of which detailed further examples of earlier sightings: "many persons, believed to be a member of a certain band of aristocrats [had] … in the shape of a large white bull" attacked several people on Barnes Common in South London (*The Morning Chronicle*, 10 January 1838; Dash 45). Sometimes this figure appeared wearing armour, and sometimes he was a leaping man or wearing a pair of spring boots which enabled him to vault over a ten-feet wall. Although a correspondent named numerous villages across London where these strange sightings occurred, when reporters were sent to these locations to investigate, they found no first-hand witnesses of the attacks (*Kentish Mercury*, 13 January 1838). These early incidents are attributed to "the ghost", although by 13 January he is named as "Spring Jack" in the *Greenwich, Woolwich and Deptford Gazette* when the report including the letter from the "Resident of Peckham'" was published.

By the end of January, a short morality story appeared in *Franklin's Miscellany* (27 January 1838). Written by "Peter Piper", it is accompanied by an illustration of "The Spring Jack". Here Jack is depicted as wearing a devilish mask with curling horns, a cape, a pair of boots and a close-fitting costume displaying his muscular body. Beneath him, residents in a house are seen to be crying out in terror. The article speaks of Jack introducing himself to a pub landlord as "the Devil", before melting a pewter mug, the result of which is that the landlord regularly attends Church and gives exact measures to his customers. In effect, the appearance of the "Spring Jack" scares the landlord into living an honourable, Christian life and becoming an honest member of his profession. This feature appears in Volume 3 of this library: *Spring-Heeled Jack: Articles and Short Fiction* (1838–1897).

The following month, however, complaints were made to the police: on 20 February 1838, Jane Alsop, the 18-year old daughter of a banker, was attacked outside her home in Bearbinder Lane, in a remote location between the villages of Bow and Old Ford. A figure who she thought was a policeman, but who became a terrifying apparition, called her outside claiming to have caught Spring-Heeled Jack. Jane described her attacker as wearing "a very large helmet; and his dress, which appeared to fit him very tight, appeared to resemble white oil-skin". During this attack, where her assailant "used considerable violence", Jane was slashed by metallic claws, which ripped through her dress and skin, and her hair was torn out. This was no prank of a suburban ghost leaping out and shouting "boo", this was a violent assault, although later Jane was dragged inside by her sister, and they screamed for help from the top window of their house, before the assailant fled across the fields. The press jumped on this story, heading it as an "OUTRAGE ON A YOUNG LADY", and this was also the first occasion that the name "Spring-Heeled Jack" was employed, although Jane's response to the "policeman's" call suggested the name had be circulated orally (*The Times*, 22 February 1838; Dash 53). Jane and her ailing father went to Lambeth Street police station to report the incident, although the police claimed, "in her fright the young lady had much mistaken the appearance of her assailant" and believed that the incident was "the result of a drunken frolic" which was investigated. Two men named Payne and Millbank were questioned in relation to the attack, and it was argued that "the two men knew more about the affair than they wished to acknowledge. The eye-witness testimony in court from a wheelwright named James Smith claimed "I have no doubt but that the man Millbank was the person who had so frightened the Misses Alsop" (*Bell's New Weekly Messenger*, 4 March 1838). The testimony of the proprietor of the Pavilion Theatre named Farrell pointed out that the effects of fire that Jack was seen to produce could be achieved by "the dropping of certain strong acids on a sponge charged with spirits of wine" and that "the colour of flame emitted would depend on the peculiar quality or description of acid (*London Evening Standard*, 3 March 1838),

However, despite "strong suspicion" and because of "solemn and repeated assertions of respectable individuals on oath and … without any earthly assignable motive" they were released without charge. No one was ever prosecuted. (*Bell's New Weekly Messenger*, 4 March 1838) The investigating officer suggested "in consequence of the notoriety which the gambols of "Spring-heeled Jack" had gained, the character was now assumed by many thoughtless young men, who considered it "a good lark" (*Morning Post*, 28 February 1838). By 5 March 1838 a play about Spring-Heeled Jack was performed alongside two other plays at the Royal Pavilion Theatre in Whitechapel, London, thus demonstrating the popular interest in the circulating stories (*Morning Advertiser*, 5 March 1838).

On 28 February, a young woman named Lucy Scales was attacked, along with her sister, as they walked home from visiting their brother, a butcher in Limehouse. The women were set upon by an attacker who "spurted a large quantity of blue flame" into her face, although when Lucy fainted, her attacker left her, despite her being prone and vulnerable. The similarities between the attacks on Jane Alsop and Lucy Scales led the police to conclude that "those disgraceful outrages were committed by the same individual and not by several" (*London Evening Standard*, 8 March 1838). *Bell's Life in London and Sporting Chronicle* reported that "'Spring-heeled Jack,' or some fool who assumes this character, has been again charged at Lambeth-street with frightening almost to death Miss Scales, the daughter of a butcher at Limehouse" (11 March 1838).

Something about the Spring-Heeled Jack legend had caught the public imagination which led to a series of imitators. Just a few days after the attack on Jane Alsop, the *Bell's New Weekly Messenger* described an "outrage committed by a miscreant, who has been nicknamed 'Spring-heeled Jack'" and "no doubt he is some aristocratical ruffian" who "has been committing similar outrages in the neighbourhood of the metropolis for some time past" (25 February 1838). In one report, also on 25 February, a young man answered the door of the house belonging to Mr Thomas Ashworth, a cabinet maker.[2] The young man—one of Ashworth's 15-year old twins—asked for Ashworth by name, but then he threw off his cloak and "presented a most hideous appearance". The young man's screams before he had even opened the door meant that Jack was "unable to accomplish any further mischief" (*London Courier and Evening Gazette*, 1 March 1838) The three incidents in Bearbinder Lane, Green Dragon Alley and Turner Street were all within about two miles of each other.

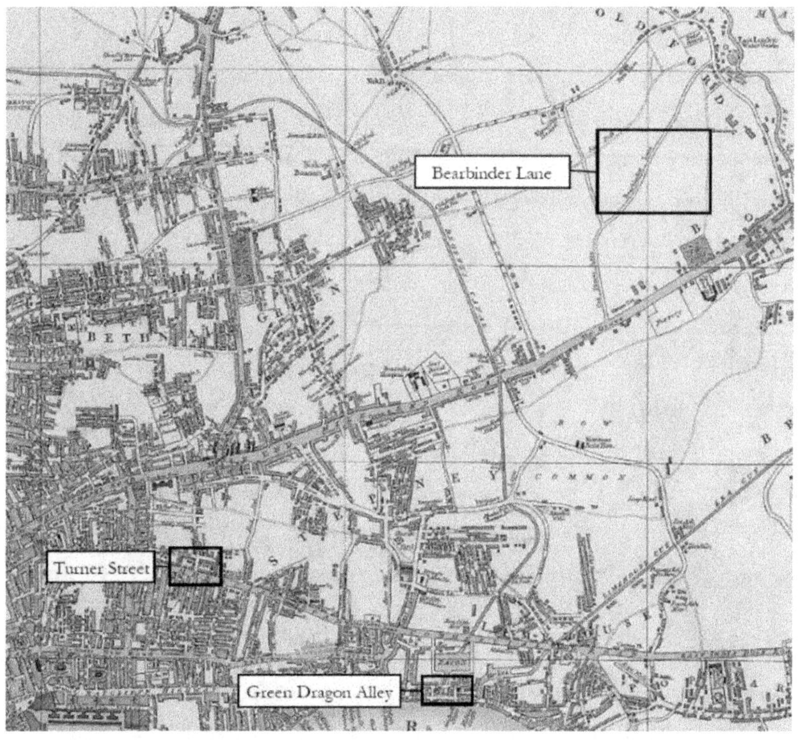

---

[2] The Newspaper reports the address as 2 Turner Street, Commercial Road, (in Whitechapel). Pigot's directory (and other sources), list this as 1 Great Turner Street.

Payne and Millbank investigation

In another incident, Charles Grenville, a young man of "weak mind" was taken to court after scaring his neighbours. He was warned by the magistrate not to do it again. (*Bell's New Weekly Messenger*, 25 March 1838). An example of the general societal anxiety is demonstrated through newspaper reports of one Thomas Bush, "a simple-looking sailor" who was taken into custody by police after he was seen in the streets having, "for a lark", put on a bonnet and cloak belonging to "his woman". He was told "silly as the trick was, it might prove serious in the present times, when so many females and children were frightened into fits by the 'Spring-heeled-Jack' adventurers (*Morning Advertiser*, 29 March 1838).

Rather vaguely, *The Globe* reports that "having left London and its neighbourhood, [Spring-heeled Jack] is now visiting more distant parts of the country" (5 June 1838), while all that the *Kentish Mercury* has to say is that "there is an idle report abroad that Spring-heeled Jack has found his way to Ramsgate and Margate" (17 March 1838). In Kilburn, an 18-year old youth named James Painter was fined £4 for scaring women dressed as a ghost. He was told "if fellows like you think they can frighten respectable females with impunity by imitating the scandalous pranks of Spring-heeled Jack they will be convinced of their mistakes by finding themselves within the walls of Newgate (*Morning Post*, 4 April 1838). Further afield, in Carshalton, Surrey, a fourteen-year old named Thomas Worth was jumped upon by "a scoundrel in some awful disguise" who was "personating the character of Spring-heeled Jack", and the incident left him "bereft of reason" (*John Bull*, 28 May 1838), while Falmouth, Cornwall, a Miss Symonds was attached by "some miscreants [who] caught hold of her dress, which terrified her to such a degree that on entering the house she became seriously ill (*Cornwall Gazette*, reported in the *London Dispatch* 28 October 1838). However, as Clarke (2006) notes, after the "initial panic" caused by Jack's antics, the newspapers "lost interest" (48), and, despite imitators exploiting the prevailing fears caused by the reports, a reader of the *Newcastle Chronicle* notes that "after April, 1838, he was seen no more" (3 November 1894). Decades after the initial assaults, the *Illustrated Police News* reported somewhat cynically, "Spring-heeled Jack—the most vulgar and unromantic ghost imaginable—took to playing pranks in one quarter of

London, to the great alarm of its feminine inhabitants. But its success brought into the field who were speedily found out, and the originator of the deception retired from business in disgust" (17 September 1881).

So, who was Spring-Heeled Jack? There were plenty of suspicions circulating at the time, but Jennifer Westwood and Jaqueline Simpson suggest he is simply an "imaginary bogeyman" and a general epithet for unidentifiable criminals at the time (Westwood and Simpson 343). In the *South Shields Daily Gazette and Shipping Telegraph* (15 November 1886) he is described as "nothing more than a footpad with unusual dexterity of limb, [who] was executed at Tyburn in or about the year 1777" (15 November 1886). Other critics described him as being "a ghost, created by your own imagination" (*Bell's Life in London and Sporting Chronicle*, 22 July 1838). The *Lancashire Daily Post* suggests that the name was used "to scare naughty children", and also "given to a community of gentlemen in the West Country … who gained a precarious living" (22 October 1929). This latter example is perhaps linked to the stories claiming that Jack haunted the lanes near Maidencombe simply to keep the villagers indoors so that smugglers could carry out their work undisturbed as cited by Kevin Dixon in an online article. The name appears to be in common use as a metaphor for something more generally frightening: in a play entitled *The Wife* by James Sheridan Knowles, Julian St Pierre is a character from whom "all young women would run, as from an ogre or Spring-heeled Jack" (*Morning Chronicle*, 9 May 1838).

However, as noted above, there was a popular suggestion of linking a reckless aristocratic youth to these crimes and one individual whose name was frequently associated with the Spring-Heeled Jack incidents was Henry de la Poer Beresford, the 3rd Marquis of Waterford (1811–1859). Such was the reputation of the "Mad Marquis" that he quite literally "painted the town red"; he may be the intended focus of the finger pointing to the "higher ranks of life" as mentioned in the Resident of Peckham letter, and certainly there was early speculation as to his "supposed implication in the Spring-heel'd Jack blackguardism" (*The Satirist*, 29 April 1838). This association may come from an early report on the Lord Mayor's response to the Resident of Peckham letter entitled "The Ghost at the Mansion House" which begins "Some persons of the Waterford class appear to have been amusing themselves for the past week or two at the expense of decency and humanity" (*The Examiner*, 14 January 1838); consequently, it is a *comparison* with Beresford's reputation that has forged this very early link between the Marquis and Jack, rather than any actual evidence; however, as the Marquis had been connected with the urban terror so early in the investigation, so the association became woven into the legend.

This relationship with the Marquis was underscored by Peter Haining in his 1977 publication *The Legend and Bizarre Crimes of Spring-Heeled Jack*, where in addition to entirely fictitious assaults and incidents, Haining adds fabricated detail—an ancestral crest and the embroidered letter "W" on the hem of the visitor's cloak (Haining 53). The sole purpose of this fabrication seems to have been introduced only to support the suggestion that Henry Beresford and Spring-Heeled Jack were one and the same, even though this had been dismissed by writers such as Charles Dickens who noted that "not a shadow of proof could ever be adduced to support this theory" almost a century before Haining was writing (*All the Year Round*, 9 August 1884, 346). It is unlikely that someone who had disguised himself would also have carried items by which he could easily be identified. That said, the connection between the Marquis and Spring-Heeled Jack is also suggested in the 1863 serial story, and will be discussed below.

Most likely – the early sightings about which the Resident of Peckham were indeed a prank

This was then taken up – probably by Payne and Millbank. They weren't responsible for the early attacks, but the three assaults in February and March were within two miles of their locality – two targets and one opportunistic.

While the panic about Spring-Heeled Jack and his attacks subsided, there was a rise of interest in society more generally. As noted above, a hurriedly-penned play was performed just days after the attack on Jane Alsop. There was also a racehorse named Spring-Heeled Jack, "whose name aptly describes him, [he] is a speedy horse but not over-gifted with stoutness. His race for the Liverpool Autumn Leger has made him a great favourite … He will be a very forward horse on this occasion, and should the field be contracted, may actually be the winner" (*Manchester Courier and Lancashire General Advertiser*, 17 October 1840). In 1848, a production of a "New Comic Ballet entitled Spring Heel Jack" was performed at the Theatre-Royal in Hull (*Hull Packet*, 4 August 1848; Bell 182). A further four-act drama was performed in the Royal Grecian Theatre in 1863 entitled *Spring-Heel'd Jack, or the Felon's Wrongs*, written by Frederick Hazelton (*Morning Advertiser*, 4 July 1863). Such productions must have rekindled an interest in the legend of Spring-Heeled Jack, as 1863 saw the publication of a 40-issue "Penny Dreadful" story called *Spring-Heel'd Jack: The Terror of London* (reprinted in 1867–68). This was the first of many serial stories featuring Jack published between 1863 and 1913. While there was an outcry about the content of the Penny novels and their effect on the morality of the readership, a commentator in the London *Daily News* accepted that, compared with the other publications, "'Spring-heeled Jack, the Terror of London' is, we believe, to be distinguished from many of these as having in all its eccentricities the saving motive of a reform of manners" (17 April 1886).

After the first publication of the 1863 story, further plays were performed, including a production entitled *Spring-Heeled Jack, or The Flying Highwayman* performed at the Royal Queen's Theatre in Hull (*The Hull Packet and East Riding Times*, 13 October 1865. Most notably, however, is the production which was heavily based on the serial story, which corresponded with the reprinting in 1867. A theatre notice in *The Era* notes that the author, W. Travers, wrote the play "expressly for this theatre … taken from a Popular Work now Publishing." The announcements list the characters' names and the actors and, except for Richard Clavering whose name is changed to Richard Clancy, the names are all the same as those in the serial (*The Era*, 31 May 1868; Bell, 185).

The title page of the 1867 reprint attributes authorship to "The author of the 'Confederate's Daughter'" which is a two-act drama written by Colin Henry Hazelwood adapted from the "popular work" by Alfred Coates and performed in the Britannia Theatre in August 1865 (*Clerkenwell News*, 5 August 1865; original manuscript in the Pettingell Collection at the University of Kent). Thus, we can reasonably ascribe authorship to Coates.

The 1863 story

Written for a newly-literate audience of working-class men, the Newsagents' Publishing Company published *Spring-Heel'd Jack: The Terror of London* in weekly instalments in 1863. Each issue was eight pages long, and contained a cover illustration with a few lines of the story at the bottom of the page, followed by seven complete pages of text in two columns, running to a total of 312 pages. As is often the case with serial publications, they often ended mid-sentence and then resumed in the next issue. There is no summary for new readers. The copy contained in the British Library is incomplete – missing the fourteenth issue (pages 105–112 in the original, 196–210 in this volume and marked with ** at the start and end of the text). This has been supplied for this volume by the University of California in Los Angeles.

The narrative style of this serial novel is intriguing. Jack is often seen observing the events; this observation leads him to action, as a repentance for what he has done before. The story may leave Jack in a dangerous situation at the end of one chapter, and then "fast forward" to another moment, normally providing the background to another victim of cruelty on whose behalf Jack intervenes, before revealing how Jack extracted himself from the previous encounter.

In particular, the 1863 version of the story reads like a novel. It is a complete and coherent narrative with a structured plot, although some of the pranks that Jack plays feel like diversions from the main plot. That said, there are surprising twists along the way. It is never certain that Jack will be successful in defending those susceptible to the machinations of evil men, it becomes clear that saving people is not easy, and there are some occasions when he doesn't succeed. However, the continuity of the narrative is unlike some of the other stories featuring Spring-Heeled Jack which have clearly been written by different authors, and these authors are often not familiar with the material that has gone before, and in one case it is left on a cliff-hanger while new issues were promised, which were never forthcoming.

The narrative begins by placing Spring-Heeled Jack in the context of the historically attested exploits:

IT IS now a little over a quarter of a century since the inhabitants of London and its suburbs were kept in a continual state of terror by a man who, under various disguises, and in different shapes and forms, would suddenly appear before the unsuspecting pedestrian, and, after having nearly frightened the traveller out of his or her senses, would as suddenly disappear, with terrific bounds, from his side, leaving for a time the impression upon his affrighted victim that his Satanic Majesty had paid a visit to the earth, and especially favoured them with his presence.

Furthermore, his aim is not to rob his victims (1) in fact, on many occasions, Jack says that he is looking for adventure which causes him "to overstep the bounds of imprudence" (330), and perhaps seeking some restitution for his previous pranks. Jack explains "I can almost forgive myself some of the pranks I have played" (261). While Jack continues with his mayhem and misrule, the focus has changed. Although he still engages in the occasional trick for its amusement value, he is no longer targeting vulnerable young women as seen in the attacks on Jane Alsop and Lucy Slater. In addition, such occurrences are to startle and confuse his victims, rather than being a violent assault. Instead, his attacks are more sinister and aggressive, when he targets the proud, the boasters and the corrupt. In fact, he becomes a champion for the vulnerable and the oppressed, and especially for women.

Jack's adversaries have wonderfully onomatopoeic names, such as the morally repugnant Grasper, the thieving Filcher, the indignant and garrulous Frump, the aggressive Slogger, the miserly Scrivener, and the "libertine" Clavering: like pantomime villains we know who to "boo" during the chapters. The villains earn the loathing that is due to them, and the story threads come together in the final chapters so that the repentant redeem themselves, and the wicked receive their comeuppance. In the opening chapter, Jack torments a boasting policeman who claims that Spring-Heeled Jack would never frighten him: "Let him but come within reach of me, and I'll make him my prisoner before he knows where he is" (4); then Jack slips on his mask to terrify him, thus demonstrating Jack's *modus operandi*. On the other hand, he attempts to defend and protect Jane Slater, a woman being blackmailed for sexual favours by her husband's employer, Ralph Grasper: in his desperation, James Slater forged a cheque in his employer's name and faces transportation. Here we see the link between the historical Jack and the protagonist in this story as he acknowledges when seeing Jane Slater's plight: "I may be able to do a good turn in part payment for the many bad ones I've had a hand in" (5).

Other women Jack attempts to defend include Ellen Folder, a poor seamstress, who is driven to suicide by her hypocritical landlord, who chases her for rent when he has not paid his own (instead spending it on alcohol, and it is revealed that he has not paid his own bar tab); Martha Scrivener, who is being defrauded of her inheritance by her uncle; and Jessie Bolton, a ballet dancer who is enticed from poverty by the cruel aristocratic "libertine", Richard Clavering, who views women as "a toy [which] had pleased him for a time then he wearied of it" (74) and attempts to force his wife into a terrible and humiliating role. As Jack intervenes on behalf of these women, he describes how he "felt an inward gratification at being the means of saving both these poor women …and in that feeling he found his reward" (487), and furthermore, the narrator intrudes into the text itself and speaks to Jack directly: by doing good, he has "atoned for many a thoughtless deed" (487). By contrast, however, as Jack watches the "Reward" posters displayed in London, he realises "my little games are becoming intolerable in this vast emporium" (557).

The story presents an interesting, although somewhat romanticised of the daily strife of the common people of mid-Victorian Britain, and this is seen through the eyes of an aristocrat. Jack observes that in this society there are "fools and rogues in gilded chambers, wisdom and talent in a wretched hovel" (176). A starving old woman tells Jack "it's the way of the world, to hurt the poor and the starving. Once down, you're kept down—kicked down—trampled down. Who cares for the wretch without home, food, or friends?" (177). This leads Jack to conclude that there is no justice for poor people: "that's only for those who can pay for it" (178).

Spring-Heeled Jack in the 1863 story

Again, one might ask "Who is Spring-Heeled Jack?" in relation to this serial. Essentially, he is a man in a mask, or, as Jess Nevins describes him, "a dual-identity costumed vigilante" (108). Like many vigilantes, Jack operates beyond the boundaries of the law, normally chased by policemen and the general population who want to claim the reward for his capture, but there are occasions when he works alongside the police, for example when saving the wealthy but naïve Tobias Bacon from being defrauded (505).

Of his private life, we know that he is an aristocrat and a gentleman who has not married (431) and that Spring-Heeled Jack is the only name he wishes to be known by (475). The physical descriptions of Jack are vague: "He was tall and well formed, which even the large dark Spanish cloak he wore did not disguise" (1). His hands are "long" with "finger-nails … which resembled more the claws of a wild animal than anything else" (119). He has a "spectre face and demon form" (337) and a "white mask" (338). This mask is described as a "hideous face, ears, and horns on its forehead" (119). However, Jack does not only use the mask to conceal his identity: on other occasions his disguise is "a thick pair of bushy whiskers, which gave him the appearance of being some years older than he really was" (302), At times, when he appears, his "head and body glowered with a blue, phosphorescent fire" (41). There are occasions when, viewing him in disguise for the first time, Jack is believed to be the devil, and he happily plays this role by threatening to drag miscreants to Hell, and noting "superstition is inherent in the hearts of all to a less or greater degree" (51). However, Jack's mask is so much a part of Jack's identity that he often forgets that he's wearing it, which sometimes leads him to scare people unintentionally.

The most remarkable thing about Jack in these stories, however, is his ability to leap great distances, but it is never explained how he can achieve this; however, at one point, he deters a man from burgling a house and when he asks to go with Jack to apprehend his former partners in crime, Jack explains that the thief cannot go with him, "Because I can escape where you could not," and at this point Jack looks "significantly" at his heel (100). His mischief is often aimed at people who boast about how they would face Spring-Heeled Jack, or authority figures who are unable to perform their duties. In one occasion, Jack terrifies a thief to death: in this instance, Jack feels remorse for his actions and explains "the poor wretch is dead…and though he deserves his fate, I cannot help feeling more like a murderer than an executioner" (50). But Jack's principal concern is to defend the vulnerable – generally women who find themselves as victims of oppressive men. Some of these characters are truly vicious and, faced with these, Jack observes "People look upon me as a villain, but they know not what villainy is" (7). In doing these good deeds he restores his own reputation, if only by the few who witness his noble actions. One of the women saved by Jack notes that, while men will "speak of Spring-Heeled Jack as a wretch who deserves no pity … while I live, I shall ever remember with thankfulness and gratitude the service he has rendered me and mine" (10).

It soon becomes clear that Spring-Heeled Jack is the *alter ego* of an aristocrat: when he confronts Richard Clavering, the "libertine". Despite his initial appearance as a common thief, Jack tells Richard "'tis yours to obey, mine to command in this house" (78), and when Richard complains that he "will do nothing … at the bidding of a fellow who dare not show his face" (80). Jack removes his mask; at this point Richard observes that he is in the company of "the Mar—"; Jack silences him with his comment "Suffice it that you know me" (80). Likewise, Clavering's housemaid, Lizzie, when confronted by Jack, also names him as the "Mar—", but again, Jack silences her, stating "You recognise me as a friend of your master's" (88) and that is enough for her to remain silent. Indeed, on the four occasions that Jack's *alter ego* is recognised, all that the character manages to exclaim is the three letters "mar" before they are silenced. The suggestion, of course, builds on the speculation noted above of the link between Spring-Heeled Jack's "pranks" and the antics of Henry de la Poer Beresford, 3rd Marquis of Waterford, even though Beresford has been dead four years before the publication of this story.

The Missing Issue

In issue 14 of this serial, which has, until now, been lost from this story, there are three principal narrative threads. The first is the conclusion of a narrative strand featuring Peggy Mittern who is first confronted by her employers for stealing food and gives it to Johnny Bristles, "the model policeman"; Peggy is then vindicated against the man who spied on her. The second strand concerns Jane Slater, wife of the forger, who returns to Ralph Grasper to submit to his desires (although the reader, by this stage, knows that her actions are in vain), but when she returns home she is faced with a horrendous sight. The third strand is the poor seamstress,

Ellen Folder, safely removed from Bill Jackson's lodgings. Of particular note is that she opposes and stands resolute against the avaricious (and, unfortunately, unpleasantly stereotypical) Jewish clothier, Isaac Levy, who attempts to extort twice the value of the cloths stolen from her during Bill Jackson's drunken rampage. This is an important section as we see how Jack's influence helps the characters to regain their confidence. However, what this chapter shows is that, despite his best efforts, Jack cannot save everyone.

Spring-Heeled Jack Sightings and Further Fiction after the 1863 story

While the Spring-Heeled Jack serial stories may have rekindled some public interest in the urban legend that was circulating at the time, and such was the popularity of the 1863 story that it was republished in 1867, they are unlikely to have inspired the sightings at Aldershot Barracks and the sighting of Jack leaping the Newport Arch in Lincoln which occurred in 1877. In fact, the "Origin Story", published in 1878, may well have been a response to the sudden reinterest in Jack because of these incidents. It is not until 1890 that the lengthy 48-issue story is published. This, along with the subsequent serials and stories, is unlikely to have inspired the events of 1904 except by witnesses or reporters associating. These events will be discussed in the introductions to subsequent Spring-Heeled Jack volumes.

The Spring-Heeled Jack Library

Until recently, the only nineteenth-century story about Spring-Heeled Jack available was the 1885 novella (around 26,000 words, referred to in this series as the "Origin Story") which has been in the public domain through Project Guttenberg, and published in John Matthew's *The Legend of Spring-Heeled Jack: From Victorian Legend to Steampunk Hero*. While this novella is interesting in terms of how the legend of Jack developed in popular fiction, it is focused on Jack's origins, rather than his role as "The Terror of London". In fact, there are seven serial novels or novellas that either feature Spring-Heeled Jack or were directly influenced by works written about him. Some of these are *very* long (one of the serials runs to over 500,000 words!). A fragment of a story written in the local dialect appears in the *Wigan and*

District Advertiser in February and March 1888, a further standalone novel-length story was published in the USA in 1895 by *Beadle's Dime Library*, and an extended short story, "The Haunted Grange" appeared in the *Halfpenny Marvel* in 1897. Most of these stories are only found in specialist libraries, and the collection is sometimes incomplete. Other serials were published in newspapers and their condition is delicate to say the least. The aim of the Spring-Heeled Jack Library is to make accessible all the stories about Jack and to restore the episodes missing from a collection.

J.S. Mackley
April 2020

Bibliography

Bell, Karl. *The Legend of Spring-Heeled Jack: Victorian Urban Folklore and Popular Cultures.* Woodbridge: The Boydell Press, 2012.

Brewer, E. Cobham. *The Reader's Handbook of Allusions, References, Plots and Stories.* Philadelphia: J.B. Lippincott Company, 1895.

Clarke, David. "Unmasking Spring-heeled Jack: A case study of a 19th century ghost panic". *Contemporary Legend.* N.S. 9 (2006): 28–52.

Dash, Mike. 'Spring-Heeled Jack: To Victorian Bugaboo from Suburban Ghost'. Steve Moore (ed.). *Fortean Studies.* Vol. 3. London: John Brown Publishing, 1996. 7–125.

Dickens, Charles. *All the Year Round,* A weekly journal conducted by Charles Dickens. New Series, Volume XXXIV: 9th August 1884. 346.

Dixon, Kevin. "Spring-Heel Jack Terrifies Torquay". *We Are South Devon.* https://wearesouthdevon.com/spring-heel-jack-terrifies-torquay/. 19 April 2018. [Accessed 07 June 2020]

Haining, Peter. *The Legend and Bizarre Crimes of Spring-Heeled Jack.* London: Frederick Muller Ltd, 1977.

Mackley, J. S. Spring-heeled Jack: the Terror of London. *Aeternum: the Journal of Contemporary Gothic Studies.* 3(2), 2016. 1-20.

Mackley, J.S. "Penny Dreadfuls and Spring-heeled Jack" in *The Palgrave Handbook of Steam Age Gothic.* Ed. Clive Bloom. London: Palgrave, 2021.

Matthews, John. *The Legend of Spring-Heeled Jack: From Victorian Legend to Steampunk Hero.* Rochester, Vermont: Destiny Books, 2016.

Nevins, Jess, *The Evolution of the Costumed Avenger: The 4,000-Year History of the Superhero.* Santa Barbara, California: Praeger, 2017.

Westwood, Jennifer and Simpson, Jacqueline. *The Lore of the Land: A Guide to English Legends, from Spring-heeled Jack to the Witches of Warboys.* London: Penguin Books, 2005.

READ THIS STARTLING TALE.

SPRING-HEEL'D JACK,

THE TERROR OF LONDON.

SPRING-HEEL'D JACK'S DARING LEAP.

Spring-Heeled Jack will, in type, perform over again his midnight freaks and daring adventures.

WITH ILLUSTRATIONS EVERY WEEK OF HIS DOINGS.

NEWSAGENTS' PUBLISHING COMPANY, 147, FLEET STREET, LONDON, E.C.

CHAPTER I.

SPRING-HEELED JACK—THE OFFICER'S FRIGHT—CATCH IF YOU CAN.

IT IS now a little over a quarter of a century since the inhabitants of London and its suburbs were kept in a continual state of terror by a man who, under various disguises, and in different shapes and forms, would suddenly appear before the unsuspecting pedestrian, and, after having nearly frightened the traveller out of his or her senses, would as suddenly disappear, with terrific bounds, from his side, leaving for a time the impression upon his affrighted victim that his Satanic Majesty had paid a visit to the earth, and especially favoured them with his presence.

Evening was generally the time chosen by this eccentric character for his strange conduct; and doubtless there are many living who can recollect—but not without a shudder—the pang of fear which shot through their hearts when, leaping from some dark corner, out of a doorway, or over a thickset hedge, he stood before them.

What his true object could be, none have been able to conjecture. Certain it is that robbery was not the cause, for he was never known to take a single coin from his victims, even when fright had rendered them almost insensible; nor did he ever practise any other degree of cruelty beyond affrighting them.

But this was bad enough—so bad, that in some cases the victims of his eccentricities never thoroughly recovered the shock their nerves sustained; and, indeed, in one or two instances, death was ultimately the result.

As may be supposed, his capture was ardently desired both by those whose path he had crossed and those who had not even seen him, and not a few attempts were made to render him powerless to continue his course for some time to come.

It was at the time that the terror he caused was at its height—when the husband, on his return home, cast suspicious glances behind him, and clutched nervously at his walking-stick; and the wife waited anxiously, with barred door, for her husband's return, fearful even to open it to his well-known knock, lest it should be Spring-heeled Jack—that that worthy one evening entered a public-house in the neighbourhood of the Liverpool-road, Islington.

He was tall and well formed, which even the large dark Spanish cloak he wore did not disguise.

He called for refreshments for himself, and, addressing two or three persons standing at the bar, he likewise requested the landlord to serve them with whatever they required, adding, that he would pay the bill.

This, of course, drew all eyes towards him, and a policeman, who at the moment entered the bar, was solicited to partake of his kindness.

Nothing loth, the officer accepted, and his glass being filled, the stranger remarked—

"Yours is a dreary beat, officer, this dark night."

"You may well say that, sir," replied the officer. "But I don't mind much."

"You are not afraid, then, of this Spring-heeled Jack there is such a talk about just now?" said the man in the cloak, in an offhand manner.

"Not a bit of it!" said the policeman, supping the hot rum and water with which he had been supplied.

"And yet I think he'd frighten you, if you met him," continued the man in the cloak.

"He might frighten an old woman, but he wouldn't frighten me!" said the officer. "I should like to be as sure of a five-pound note to-morrow morning, as I am now, that if he comes across me to-night I'll lodge him in the station-house!"

"Nonsense!" said the stranger, coolly.

"Good sense! sir. All I hope is, I may get the chance, for I believe, if any of our men take him, he's certain of promotion," said the officer.

"That won't be you, bobby,"[1] said a tall, ostler-looking man,[2] winking over the rim of a quart pot out of which he was drinking.

"Why not?" asked the policeman, indignantly.

"Because you'd be frightened to death!"

"Should I?"

"Yes, you would!"

"I tell you what I'll do with you," said the officer, indignantly, "I'll bet you a glass of brandy and water that I take him if he comes on my beat."

"And I'll bet you that you don't!" said the ostler, placing the pot down on the bar, and extending his hand to the policeman.

"Done!" said the officer, shaking the man's hand.

"That's a fair bet," said the man in the cloak; "and now I'll bet you both the same, that Spring-heeled Jack will be on this officer's beat to-night."

"To-night?" exclaimed the officer and the others.

"Yes, to-night."

"How do you know?" said the ostler, looking at him suspiciously.

"Because I have seen him."

"When?"

"Just now."

"Where?" asked the policeman, turning pale a little.

"Just up the road."

"The devil!" stammered the officer.

"Well, I can't say whether it is the devil or not," said the man in the cloak; "but I believe he is the devil and no one else."

"Do you really think so, sir?" said the officer.

"Yes; but I may be mistaken. However, you are sure to know if you catch him."

"I'll do that," said the policeman, "never fear. Devil or no devil, if I get a sight of him I'll have him."

The stranger shook his head.

"I fear your courage would fail you at the moment you most needed it," he said.

"No fear, sir; I ain't so easily frightened," said the policeman.

"You are not?"

"No."

"Well, it is certainly worthy of the trial, if you would get promoted for it," said the stranger.

---

[1] "Bobby" or "Peeler" general names for a policeman after the founder of the police force, Sir Robert Peel.

[2] A man employed to look after the horses of people staying at an inn.

"And I mean to make it."

"Perhaps you had better not."

"Why so?"

"The shock might be too much for you."

"No fear of that."

"And if you did not succeed you would be laughed at."

"I'd chance that," said the officer. "He had better not come near me, nor even let me see him. I'd take some of the spring out of his heels."

"Well, you've got a chance, bobby," said the ostler, "for this gentleman says he's on your beat to-night."

"And I spoke truly, my friend."

"Then I'll just go home," said a man who had been listening to all that had passed, "for if my old woman was to see him she'd about go into fits. I hope he'll soon be collared, for I feel half afraid to go out into my back garden after dark."

"You wouldn't do for the police," said the officer, contemptuously.

"Perhaps I've got as much pluck in me as other people," said the individual thus contemptuously addressed. "Yes, quite as much when the time comes for it to be wanted."

"Humph!" said the man in the cloak, "I must be going. Now, landlord, what's to pay?"

The host having reckoned up, the stranger flung a sovereign down on the bar, and received his change.

"By-the-bye," he said, turning suddenly to the officer, "you did not accept the wager, did you?"

"What wager?"

"That Spring-heeled Jack would not be on your beat tonight."

"I took your word for that, sir; so it ain't worth betting on."

"No more it ain't. But, come; I'll make you a bet that he will appear before you in less than an hour, and that not only will you not take him, but that you'll start back in terror."

"I'll take you; and wish it was for fifty-pound," said the policeman. "Frighten me! I should like to see him do it! Let him but come within reach of me, and I'll make him my prisoner before he knows where he is."

The man dropped a coin on to the floor, and stooped as if to pick it up, but as he did so he thrust a hideous mask over his face.

Then springing up, and turning to the officer, at the same time flinging back the large folds of his cloak, and revealing its white lining, he exclaimed—

"Boaster! I am Spring-heeled Jack!"

With a cry of terror the officer sprang backwards on to the steps which led up to the house.

"Ha! ha! ha!" laughed Jack. "Follow me if you can—take me if you dare!"

With a terrific bound he sprang up and over the head of the officer right into the centre of the roadway.

Here he paused, and gave vent to a loud laugh, then bounded back again to the officer's side.

"Why don't you do your duty?" he exclaimed, leaping on to the policeman's shoulders and forcing his hat over his eyes.

Then with another laugh he bounded across the road as the men who had partaken of his treat rushed from the house towards him.

"I'll have a shy[3] for him," exclaimed the man who had made no secret of his nervousness.

"Come on, my friend," cried Jack. "You are what I thought, after all—the bravest of the lot."

The man ran towards him, and even succeeded in catching hold of his cloak.

But he was unable to retain it, for with a spring Jack bounded away over a hedge into the field beyond, and was lost to view, while in the centre of the road stood the officer, his battered hat in one hand, shouting at the top of his voice, till those who had been with him at the bar were out of sight, and he was left alone.

"Stop him!—stop him! Don't be frightened! Don't let him get away! Stop him!—stop him!"

"That's your duty, my friend; but you are such a coward," exclaimed a voice behind him.

The officer turned, uttered a cry, and fled at the top of his speed, whilst the loud laughter of Spring-heeled Jack rang out on the night air.

CHAPTER II.
THE SHADOW ON THE BLIND—THE FIGURE AT THE WINDOW—THE SCOUNDREL AND HIS VICTIM—A FRIEND IN NEED—THE LEAP—THE SHOT.

IT was about eleven o'clock, and silence reigned in almost every street. Here and there a light, streaming with subdued lustre through the drawn blind out into the roadway, bespoke the fact that the inhabitants had not yet retired to rest, but these were few and far between. The generality of the occupiers of the houses in the neighbourhood of Islington had closed their eyes in slumber, and darkness reigned throughout their dwellings.

In a turning out of the Liverpool-road a faint light flickered in the front garret of a small house. The blind was down over the window, and on this every now and then appeared the shadow of a female as she stood between the window and the light, which rested on a small table in the centre of the room.

It could plainly be seen from the street that she was in grief, for the shadow wrung its hands, then extended them, clasped together in a supplicating attitude, to some person on the opposite side of the room.

Then it would pass hurriedly to and fro across the blind as the female paced the narrow limits of the chamber.

This had been going on a few minutes, when a tall, dark figure, springing out from a doorway, stood on the edge of the pavement opposite to the house in question, and gazed up intently at the blind.

"Humph!" he muttered. "There's something going on there which I should much like to understand—something, perhaps, which my presence might greatly tend to settle to the benefit of the woman, whoever she may be, who seems in great grief. Maybe it's only a domestic quarrel. Husband come home drunk—but, no; the attitudes of that

---

[3]Have a shy - "Have a go" (in the context of a "coconut shy" where shy means to "throw").

woman are rather those of supplication than anger. I have frightened not a few lately, and now who knows but I might save one from some ill or other? However, be what it may, it will provide food for my adventurous spirit. If I can't do no good, I at least may give them a fright, for there is more than one in that room, unless the figure whose shadow now rests on the blind is some half-mad creature amusing herself by her strange antics."

He strolled across the road and examined the house narrowly. There was a small fore-court, the sides of which were bounded by a brick wall.

Taking a spring, he alighted on this as easily as if it had only been a foot high, and then, once more minutely inspecting the house, he took off his cloak, and, turning it, appeared enveloped in a white garment.

Then he took from his coat pocket a repulsive-looking mask, which he placed over his face, and a pair of gloves made of the hide of some animal, at the tips of the fingers of which were nails tapering to a point at the end and very long.

Having drawn these over his hands, he took another bound upwards, and alighted on a small balcony before the windows of the first floor.

Into the window he peered, but the darkness which reigned in the room, albeit the blinds were not drawn, prevented him from examining the interior; so he cast his eyes upwards once more.

"I must be careful not to miss my hold of the coping-stone," he muttered, "or I may get a fall that will break my bones."

Throwing his cloak back, so as to leave him free liberty of his arms, he stood upon the very edge of the balcony, took one bound upwards, and caught at the coping-stone with his gloved hands.

For a moment, and a moment only, he hung suspended thus, then drew himself up till his body rested on the ledge. Rolling his legs quietly over into the gutter just under the window, he sat upon the stone and listened.

A woman's tones came in pleading accents to his ears, but in such a low and tremulous voice did she speak, that he was unable to hear a word.

He shifted his position a little, and endeavoured to peer into the room through the edge of the blind.

On one side it lay so close to the frame that he could not discover a chink of the breadth of a pin; on the other he could only gaze upon the soiled paper of the side wall of the room.

In disappointment, he placed his ear to the window and strove once more to catch the sounds which emanated from within.

Suddenly, the tones of a man's voice broke upon his ears.

They were harsh and discordant.

"Your choice?" was all that he said, but there was such deep meaning in the tones that the disguised figure at the window fairly started.

"There's foul play going on in there," he muttered. "I'm sure of it. I thought so from the attitudes of the shadow when I stood in the street. Well, I may be able to do a good turn in part payment for the many bad ones I've had a hand in. Confound that blind! I wish there was a hole in it, that I might see into the room."

Then drawing the glove from his right hand, he doubled his fist and softly drew the back of it down the glass, and a slight scratching sound was produced.

So slight, however, that it was almost imperceptible.

This he repeated two or three times, then holding his left hand under the right, a square piece of glass fell upon the glove.

"I thought my ring would do that nicely," he muttered, as he laid the glass upon the coping-stone at his side.

The voice of the woman now came more clearly to his ears.

"Oh! sir, have pity on me, have pity, for heaven's sake," she said, still in those imploring accents which had before riveted the attention of the strange figure on the outside of the window.

"There's something wrong going on here," murmured the cloaked figure, "and I must see as well as hear."

He took a penknife from his pocket, and opening it, he thrust the point of the small blade through the hole in the window into the blind, and then swiftly drawing it downwards inflicted a long rent therein.

The action of the wind rushing through the square hole widened the slit, and he could see into the room.

At the opposite side of the apartment was a bed, the curtains of which were tied round the ornamental posts, a short distance from it was a small toilet table, and between the bed and this sat a man about fifty years of age, holding in his hand a slip of paper.

On the opposite side of the table, near to the window, stood a young female, apparently about five-and-twenty years of age, poorly, but neatly dressed.

Her face was pale as that of a corpse, her eyes red, and swollen with weeping—the dark lashes fringed with tears. Her hands were clasped supplicatingly together, and her whole air was dejected and sorrowful.

For an instant the figure at the window took in all that was going on in the apartment, and he ground his teeth together as he drew on his glove, and adjusted his mask more tightly to his face.

"You are obstinate," said the man, addressing the woman, who stood trembling before him—"foolishly obstinate—you see this cheque." He held up the paper which he had in his grasp.

"I do, I do!" sobbed the woman.

"It is drawn on the bank, my name, my signature forged, and by your husband— transportation is the penalty of the crime—transportation, do you hear, if I appear against him?"

"Oh! sir, but you will not, your heart is not all stone, you will have mercy, mercy on him, on me!" cried the young woman, raising her clasped hands, then dropping them with a deep sigh.

"It was because I wished to do," said the man, looking hard in her face, "that I requested you to come to me to-night. I am willing to have mercy on him, more willing than you are."

"Oh! no! no!" cried the woman.

"Oh! yes!" said the man. "Here is that which will tear him from you—send him across the seas with the brand of traitor upon him—to associate and work with men of the most base and degraded passions; this will blast his reputation, consign him to a gaol—the bulks; make his wife a thing at which the finger of scorn is pointed. Will you see him dragged from you to infamy and disgrace? Will you make yourself a thing of pity, of contempt, when by that little word yes, you may gain possession of this paper, and defy the law to touch him?"

"Oh! God!" exclaimed the woman, "what, what shall I do?"

"What?" said the man, and his grey eyes twinkled as he spoke; "what would a sensible woman do, but consent?"

"But the shame, the disgrace, the injury to the man I have sworn to love!"

"Bah!" said the old man, "he did not hesitate to disgrace you by this act; he did not stop to think of the pain and injury he would inflict on you."

"No—no; but"—

"But he did it; he rushed into the crime. Will you be worse than he if you consent to my wishes? No, better a thousand times, for you will save him."

"Is there no other way? Oh! there is, there must be," she cried.

"None—emphatically none!" said the man. "Consent, and I place this forged cheque in your hand—refuse, and, by all the devils in hell, I will prosecute him with the utmost rigour of the law. Take your choice. Be mine for one short hour, or be widowed for years by your accursed obstinacy."

"Mercy, sir—mercy!"

"I have said, consent, or reject my proposals; I give you one minute to decide whether you will save or destroy your husband."

And the hoary headed old sinner took his gold watch from his pocket, and held it in his hand.

To and fro before that little table, wringing her hands in agony, paced that trembling woman, the tears streaming copiously from her eyes, and her bosom rising and falling like a stormy sea.

And through the slit in the blind gazed the masked figure on the coping stone, but his hands were clutching the framework of the window, and his breath came thick and short through his repulsive mask.

"Damn him!" he muttered to himself, "people look upon me as a villain,[4] but they know not what villainy is. The hoary-headed scoundrel! But I'll spoil his play as sure as I am called Spring-heeled Jack."

The minute passed away, and the man at the table placed the watch in his pocket, and leaped to his feet.

"Your answer!" he exclaimed; "yes or no?"

The woman turned towards him, pale as death, and with a look so imploring that none but a fiend could have resisted that mute appeal.

"Spare me—spare him!" she gasped.

"Have you decided?"

"For the love of heaven!" she pleaded.

But the man stopped her by an impatient gesture.

"For the last time," he said, "I ask you, have you decided? I ask no more, and on your answer depends his fate."

There was that in the tones of the speaker that assured both the agonized woman and

---

[4] Low or base person – from the French *villain* –peasant; particularly insulting to an aristocrat.

the anxious listener that he was determined, and that no appeal, no prayer, could alter his resolve.

The woman shuddered, looked into his face, dropped her eyes to the floor, and gasped forth in tones so piteous, so yearning, that it seemed as if her heart's strings burst with the effort—

"To save him I must—I must consent!"

Then a groan broke from her lips, and she staggered and would have fallen, but the arms of the now smiling libertine encircled her waist.

"You are mine!" he said.

And with a grin of devilish triumph on his face, he bore her towards the bed.

But a crash caused him to pause and turn, and with a shriek of horror, he let go his hold of the young woman, who fell insensible to the floor.

There, before him, stood a figure which caused his heart to almost stand still, every drop of blood in his veins to run through their channels like icy water; his iron-gray hair fairly stood on end, whilst his eyeballs, distorted by terror, seemed about to burst from their sockets.

With such terror was he seized that his knees knocked together, and the cry upon his lips was stifled by his tongue cleaving with horror to his mouth, whilst large drops of perspiration stood in beads upon his now colourless face.

"Villain! villain!" came in hollow tones from that hideous mouth.

The next moment the long claws of the terrible visitor seized his throat, and lacerated the flesh.

Then a shriek of horror escaped the man's lips, a shriek so wild and piercing, that it almost caused his strange visitor to relax his hold, and then down he fell upon his knees on the floor, beside the insensible woman.

"Mer—mer—mercy!" he gasped.

"As much as you showed to her," said the fearful looking stranger.

"Mercy! I—I meant no harm, I"—

"Liar!"

"Upon my!"—

"Hold! wretch! give me that cheque, or I will"—

"No, no," gasped the terror-stricken wretch—"spare me—spare me. There—there is the cheque—take it, but spare me—oh! spare me."

With trembling hands the man took the cheque from his waistcoat pocket, and held it up to Jack, who in an instant tore it from his hold, and thrust it into his breast.

Then, with an exclamation of contempt, he kicked the man aside, and stooped over the insensible woman.

"Poor thing!" he muttered; "I am not so bad after all."

The shivering wretch crawled towards the door of the apartment on perceiving that his strange and fearful visitor was paying no heed to him, by an effort he sprung to his feet, and opening the door, bounded from the room, screaming for help with all his might.

Jack seized the girl in his arms, and raised her from the floor.

"Curse the fellow," he said, "I wish I had choked him."

There was the quick opening of doors, and voices were heard inquiring what was the matter.

"It's Spring-heeled Jack!" exclaimed a voice. "I was told he was about—where is he?"

"In my room!"

"I'll have a shot at him!" said the other.

"Will you, my fine fellow!" muttered Jack, bearing the girl to the window, and tearing down the blind.

Thrusting the window back (which opened inwards) to its full extent, he sprung with her upon the coping-stone, and cast one look below.

He could hear the footsteps of two persons hurriedly ascending the stairs, and one of them exclaiming—

"He has robbed me, shoot him—shoot him!"

Grasping the young woman firmly in his arms, he sprang from the parapet, and alighted on the footpath in front of the house, as the report of a pistol broke the stillness of the night, and a bullet flew harmlessly over his head.

"I'll mark you for that," he said to himself, as he tore away at a rapid pace, bearing the girl in his arms.

The report of the pistol he knew would arouse the whole neighbourhood; and he sped on till the houses gave place to fields and hedgerows.

"It is not so easy a matter to leap up with a woman in your arms as it is to leap down," he muttered. "I have saved her from that villain's wiles, and her husband from a gaol if I am not mistaken; but I must not leave her till she recovers, so that I can place the cheque in her hand, and make the heart, which a few minutes since was bowed with grief, pant with hope and joy. Hillo! there is some one in pursuit. I must not be taken with the accusation of robbery."

He lifted the woman over a low portion of the hedge, and let her form slip quietly down on the opposite side, then hounded over after her.

"Stop him—stop thief!" came in a shout to his ears; and he crouched down under the hedge, tore off his gloves and mask, and turned his cloak.

The footsteps came nearer and nearer, then passed him, and were soon lost in the distance.

A sigh broke from the woman's lips.

"Are you better?" he asked.

The woman sprang to her feet.

"Who are you? Where am I?" she asked, in terror.

"Where you are safe, and with one who saved you from that scoundrel. Yes, and saved your husband, too; for here is the cheque— destroy it. Make your way home as quick as you can!"

"Oh! heaven!" gasped the woman, quietly, "who are you, my preserver?"

"One who is not so black as he is painted— Spring-heeled Jack."

And pressing the cheque into her hand, he sprung over the hedge into the road.

CHAPTER III.

SPRING-HEELED JACK'S REVENGE ON THOSE WHO SOUGHT HIS CAPTURE.

SURPRISE, hope, and joy, intermingled together, leapt into that poor woman's heart, as the words of her saviour fell upon her ears, and she crumpled in her hand the cheque which her husband, in a moment of temptation, had forged upon the man whose base whose base soul had prompted him to seek her ruin by fears for her husband's safety.

But soon her joy was surmounted by a fresh terror.

Where was she?

She could not tell.

She gazed around.

All was dark.

On one side a thickset hedge.

On the other a large black space which she knew must be a field.

As she stood half-bewildered, a distant clock struck twelve.

"Great heavens! What shall I do? How shall I find my way home to him—him. I came to save. Oh! heaven! what a trial have I passed through. What should I be now but for that stranger, whose name ere this night has struck so much terror to my soul? Alas! I must not—dare not—think of it. May heaven reward him for saving me from worse than death—my husband from a felon's doom! Let men speak of Spring-heeled Jack as a wretch who deserves no pity; but while I live, I shall ever remember with thankfulness and gratitude the service he has rendered me and mine. Bless him—bless him!"

"By my faith, it's little else than curses I have received," said a voice on the other side of the hedge; "and doubtless I have deserved them. Do not fear, I will not harm you."

And as he finished speaking, he bounded over the hedge to her side.

"Now," he said, "you are doubtless anxious to reach home?"

"Indeed I am."

"And doubly so, perhaps, to bear welcome tidings to one you love," he added, tapping her hand with his finger.

The woman sighed.

"You are right, sir," she said, in a low, choking tone.

"That old rascal little thought there was one listening at the window to his base and dishonourable proposition," continued Jack.

The woman answered not.

She averted her face to hide the blush of shame which mantled her cheeks.

There was no need for her to do so, for the night was dark—so dark that the outline of her face could scarcely be traced by the cloaked figure, much less the lineaments of her countenance.

"Yes, I heard all—saw all," he continued, after a pause. "Saw the fearful struggle that was going on in your heart. Oh! it is a sad thing when man stoops to crime—forgets the misery his thoughtless acts may inflict upon others. But there, we are none of us faultless—none can throw the first stone. You have saved him this time. Let that be a warning to him to sin no more."

"Oh! sir, could he but know the agony I have endured"—

"He would beg—starve, before he forgot that an honest name is dearer than all else in the world," interrupted the man. "But there—the subject is painful. You wish to bear home the good tidings that your husband is safe. "Where do you live?"

"Britannia fields."

"Come this way, then," said the stranger, taking her arm. "Fear not, I will not harm you. To take the high road may be dangerous. The neighbourhood is alarmed, and those accursed villains might do you some mischief yet. Do you fear me?"

JACK ESCAPES CAPTURE.

"Fear you?"

"Ay."

"No," said the woman boldly. "The man who can save me from a wretch, will not harm me when powerless to protect myself."

"You are right. Spring-heeled Jack is bad enough, but he is not lost to every sense of manhood. Come."

She took his arm, and walked out at a quick pace with him across the dark field till they had reached a stile at the centre of the hedge.

Assisting her over this, he held her hand in his own an instant, and said—

"Yonder lies your way, you will doubtless now meet with no molestation. Hurry on your road, and forget not to destroy that cheque after you have shown it to your husband, who, I trust, will prove he is in future worthy of the wife who would sacrifice all for his sake. Farewell, and if ever you think of this night, you will perhaps remember with kindness Spring-heeled Jack."

He shook her hand warmly, and ere she could utter a word of thanks, he had disappeared over the hedge again into the field, and the woman, with tearful eyes, and grateful heart, hurried on her way home.

"Wonder how the old man is," he muttered, as he strode slowly along back over the field. "By my faith, but I not only disappointed him and spoilt his game, but gave him a fright he'll not get over in a hurry—ha! ha! ha!"

And he rubbed his hands together in high glee at the thought of the abject terror of the aged villain.

Suddenly he paused, and shaded his eyes with his hands.

"Hilloa, what's that?" he said, half aloud, as he fancied he perceived two dark objects coming over the field towards him. With his hand still shading his eyes, he looked in their direction for several moments.

"Two of my pursuers, I take it, unable to find me in the road, have taken the field for it," he continued, after a pause, "let them come."

So saying, he laid himself down at full length upon the grass, and kept his eyes still riveted upon the approaching forms.

Nearer and nearer they came, and at length their voices smote his ears.

"I tell you he is nowhere about here," said one.

"But I tell you that I am sure he is," said the other. "Why, I could swear that I saw the figure of a man hereabouts, a little while since."

"So you said, but it was all imagination," remarked his companion. "Let us get back to the high road."

"I tell you I won't till I am certain he is not here in this field, and if he is I mean to have a pop at him," said the other in a determined tone.

"Be careful, or you may get in for manslaughter!"

"I don't care!"

"But I do!"

"Well, I don't. He frightened my sister nearly to death the other night, and it is high time some one put a stop to his career. It's shameful that people can't go out after dark without running the risk of being driven mad by his antics. I've kept this pistol loaded ever since, and he shall have a bullet in his legs that will take the spring out of them if I come across him."

"Much obliged to you, very much," muttered Jack to himself.

On they came, till they were within about half a dozen yards of the prostrate man, when they stopped suddenly, and one of them asked—

"What's that?"

"What?"

"There!"

"Where?"

"There, on the ground, yonder?"

"I see—it's"—

"What?"

"Blessed if I know!"

"It's something dark!"

"Yes, it's"—

"Who?"

"Him."

"What, Spring-heeled Jack?"

"Yes."

"The devil! Here goes then."

"Hold!"

"What for?"

"In case it ain't him. Challenge him first."

"Hi! there; who are you?" said the man, holding the pistol towards the object on the ground.

There was no answer.

"Speak, or I fire!" Still no answer.

"Let us go a little nearer," said his cautious companion. "It's so dark, one can hardly tell what it is."

"I'm sure it's a man."

"I think it is; but perhaps it's only some poor devil asleep."

"You go and see."

"No, you go."

"What, are you frightened?"

"No; only you've got the pistol," said his companion.

"Yes, but if you go and find it's him, I can stand here and fire, you know."

"You could hit him better if you was nearer," said his companion, afraid to take another step. "Besides you might miss him and hit me. Let's both go."

The two men now moved forward slowly towards Jack, who, the moment they had got up to him, and were just in the act of stooping down to examine him more minutely, gave a sudden bound upwards between them, and extending his arm at the same time hurled them both to the earth.

"Murder! mur—murder!" shouted the man, as the pistol was hurled from his grasp, and he rolled over, clutching in terror at his companion.

"Help! thieves!" shouted the other, loudly. "Baker, why don't you fire? He's choking me—he's choking me!"

And in his terror, the cautious man fairly believed that it was Spring-heeled Jack who had got hold of his throat instead of his companion, whilst the other was unable to tell whether it was his friend's throat he was clutching or Jack's.

With a loud laugh Jack picked up the pistol which had struck his foot, and waited till the two friends should gain sufficient composure to know the true state of affairs.

This they quickly did, and both sprang to their feet.

"Stand!" said Jack, in a loud authoritative voice, "or I'll send a bullet through each of your brains."

"Oh!" gasped one.

"Murder!" cried the other.

"Silence, and listen to me," said Jack. "You seek my capture, or my death?"

"I didn't," said one.

"Well, your friend did, that's all the same," said Jack; "and I mean to punish you both for it. No resistance, or I'll make dead meat of you in no time. I want your clothes."

"Our clothes?" stammered both together.

"Your clothes."

The two men huddled together in terror and surprise.

"Do you hear?" said Jack.

And he sprang close up to them, and laid the cold barrel of the pistol against the forehead of one.

"For God's sake, don't!" shouted the man, springing back a pace.

"Obey then."

"But, sir"—

"Quick."

"Sir, I"—

"Another word—the least hesitation, and I'll lay you dead on the grass."

This was said in a tone that struck such conviction of his determination, that he hurriedly took off his coat and handed it to Jack.

"Throw it down," said that personage.

His order was obeyed.

"Now, then, yours," he added.

"Are you a robber?" said the man.

"What's that to you?" said Jack. "Off with it at once."

"I thought"—

"You'd no right to think," interrupted Jack; "quick, or it's all up with you!"

"No—no—no!" cried the man; "you—you shall have my coat! yes, you shall have it!"

And trembling, he drew off his coat, tearing the cuff nearly from the sleeve in his terror.

"Down with it!"

This order was obeyed.

"Glad to see you are sensible men," said Jack, ironically. "Now your waistcoats."

"No—no!" cried both in a breath.

"Yes—yes!" said Jack, decidedly. "Off with them, if you wish ever to return to the bosoms of your families. No trifling!"

Off came the waistcoats with a bad grace, and very slowly. These were flung down upon the coats at his feet.

"Well done, gentlemen!" said Jack. "There is yet another favour I have to ask!"

"Another?"

"Exactly!"

"What?"

"Only your trousers."

"Our trousers?"

"Just so!"

"Take them off!" gasped one.

"That's it!"

"If I do, I'm"—

"Silence, sir!" exclaimed Jack. "No swearing, if you please, in my presence!"

"But I say I won't be robbed and insulted in this manner!" cried the man. "I'll have the law on you—I'll"—

"Close your mouth," interrupted Jack, "or I'll open it a little wider for you with the bullet you placed in this pistol for me. Come, no more hesitation—I'm a desperate man, and so you'll find if you attempt to thwart me. Off with them!"

"But!"

"But me, no buts!" said Jack. "Your trousers, quick, or I'll shoot you first, and have them afterwards!"

Again the pistol barrel was thrust against his perspiring brow, and with a cry of terror the man flung his braces over his shoulders.

"It takes you a long time to undress!" said Jack, becoming impatient at the space occupied to pull off their nether garments.

Finding all appeals useless, the two men took off their trousers and laid them on their other garments.

Jack stood gazing upon them, as they stood trembling: before him arrayed only in their shirts, for some moments, with difficulty suppressing his laughter, then suddenly exclaimed—

"Halloa! who's this coming?"

The two men turned quickly, and as they did so Jack clutched at their clothing, and with a loud shout of laughter, sped away over the field.

Recovering themselves in a moment, the men darted after him, imploring him to restore their clothes.

But he only laughed the louder, and gaining the hedge, he sprang over it into the high road, across the road, and over the opposite hedge into another field, shouting out at the top of his voice—

"Go home, and tell your friends how you captured Spring-heeled Jack."

CHAPTER IV.

NETTING THE WRONG BIRD—THE PROFFERED REWARD—OFF AGAIN.

RUNNING wildly backwards and forwards, the two men endeavoured to find out a gap in the hedge through which they might pass, to follow Spring-heeled Jack, but no gap could they discover.

The hedge was not high, but to attempt to surmount it was impossible, when they took into consideration its prickly nature, and their almost perfect nudity, and, in utter despair, they stood still and gazed at each other.

The more cautious of the two now commenced upbraiding his companion for his obstinacy in not returning before they encountered Jack; and vexed at himself, he in turn accused his friend of cowardice, till at length words ran high, and each in his turn cursed and swore at the other.

But to stay in that field in the state they were till morning was impossible, and they once more started off in the hope of discovering a gap or a gate, which would enable them to pass into the high road.

Whilst thus engaged, Jack walked quietly along by the side of the hedge of the opposite field, till he came to where it was parted by a ditch, but which at the time was dry, and into this he threw the garments of the men, together with the pistol, then leapt the hedge again into the road.

He could hear, in the still night air, the voices of those on whom he had played such a trick far away in the opposite field, and, after listening to them for some few moments, he hurried off in a different direction along the high road.

Suddenly he imagined he heard a heavy footfall; and as he paused to listen, another smote his ear.

"That is the step of a policeman," he muttered. "There are two of them. I heard something about doubling them on the dreary roads, so as to effect my capture if they should meet me. I will seek them."

So saying, he walked hurriedly in the direction whence he had heard their slow measured step.

In a short time he could see them coming slowly down the road, in close conversation.

Hurrying towards them, he called out loudly—

"Hi! police!"

The men started at his voice, and came on to meet him.

"Oh! dear!" said Jack, assuming a frightened tone. "I'm so glad I've met you—so glad, you don't believe."

"What's the matter?" asked one of the men.

"Spring-heeled Jack!"

"What of him?"

"Oh! he's nearly frightened the life out of me," said Jack.

"Where?" said the officer who had before spoken.

"Down the road."

"The devil he has!"

"Yes; as I was walking along—not being able to get a conveyance at this late hour of the night—a man all in white leaped over the hedge from a field on the left."

"What, that field yonder?"

"Yes."

"Then that's where he gave us the slip before," said the policeman, turning to his companion.

"Have you seen him, then?" asked Jack.

"We didn't see him; but we heard he had robbed a gentleman down the road, and gave pursuit, but the fellow got away. However, we'll see if we can't have him this time. All in white, is he? Ah! the gentleman said he was all in white, didn't he?"

"Yes," said the other.

"Thank you, sir," said the officer who had before spoken. "We are looking out for him, and, depend upon it, he won't frighten anybody again in a hurry if we once get hold of him."

"You'll try, won't you?"

"I should say we would."

"I don't wish to insult you," said Jack, "but here's a sovereign for you; and if you can only lodge him in prison to-night I shall be glad to give you another when I see you again on your beat."

"Thank you, sir; much obliged, I'm sure. You will not be molested by him again, you may depend upon it. Come on, Dick. If he's in that field, we'll have him."

"I'm sure he is there, or was there, a few minutes ago. You are sure to know him by his white dress."

"All right, sir. Good night. Come on, Dick; we'll have a shy for him, anyhow."

"Good night," said Jack, turning away with a smile, as the officers quickened their pace to a run.

When the policemen had got some distance down the road Jack turned, and, keeping close within the shadow of the hedges, followed.

Gaining access to the field by a gate, the officers were not slow in perceiving a white figure walking close under the hedge which skirted the road, and standing close to the hedge themselves to prevent being seen, they waited for what they believed to be Spring-heeled Jack coming up near enough for them to make a sudden spring and effect his capture.

While they stood there, with their staves firmly grasped in their hands, they were more surprised by the appearance of a second figure just behind the first, and similarly attired.

This not a little perplexed the functionaries of the law, who began to whisper to each other.

"I tell you what it is, Dick," said one, "there's two Spring-heeled Jacks, and that accounts for his appearance in different places so quickly. Keep back till they are close upon us, then make a spring and collar. I'll have the first—you the second. Don't stand any nonsense. Let him have the staff on his head if he tries to get away. It's promotion, you know—a sergeant's stripes and a sergeant's pay. Now, stand ready."

Dispirited and in silence, shivering, too, with the cold, damp dews, the two men came along the hedge looking in vain for a gap, and just as they reached the spot where the two officers stood concealed they perceived an opening, through which they attempted to pass into the road.

Baker had just forced his head and shoulders through the gap, when he received a blow on the head from the staff of Dick, which sent him down as if shot, while a blow aimed by the other policeman at the head of Baker's unfortunate companion met with a resistance by falling on the hedge.

With a loud cry, the man leaped back.

"Murder!" he yelled, as loud as he could bawl. "Thieves! fire! murder!"

Then, as the officer advanced towards him, he made a quick bolt for the gap in which Baker was lying stunned from the effect of the blow he had received, and in endeavouring to leap over his friend, caught his shirt in the prickly branches, and slit it in a dozen places.

Despite his struggles he was unable to accomplish his object, for he was held so tightly by the twigs that he could not extricate himself, and the hand of Dick clutched his throat as in a vice.

"Hold hard, comrade!" he cried, addressing his brother officer, who had raised his staff again. "I've got him tight enough—he can't get away."

And so saying, the officer forced him back from the hedge, tearing his shirt to ribbons as he did so.

"For heaven's sake let me go!" cried the unlucky man.

"Caught you at last, my fine fellows," said Dick, shaking his prisoner till the poor fellow's teeth chattered together, and he experienced a suffocating sensation from the pressure of his captor's fingers on his windpipe. "It's all over with your springing now. No resistance, or down you go, like your friend there."

"Mer—mer—mercy!" gasped the half-strangled man, struggling to free himself from the officer's hold. "I won't run away, upon my soul I won't!"

"Don't try it on," said Dick. "Would you resist? You would, would you? I'll split your head open if you try to get away from me."

Thus warned and threatened, and so bewildered as scarcely to know what to do or say, he quietly suffered himself to be handcuffed.

By this time Baker showed signs of recovery, and the attention of the officers was immediately centred upon him.

"Oh! you're coming to, are you?" said Dick. "Mind what you are after, old chap, or you'll get another taste of our staves. I reckon I took the spring out of you that time."

"Oh!" groaned Baker.

"Pull him out by his legs, Bill," said Dick.

This order Bill stooped down to obey, but as he caught hold of Baker's foot, that gentleman kicked out so fiercely, that, striking the officer in the pit of the stomach, for a moment completely doubled him up, and caused him to drop the staff from his hand—a fortunate circumstance for Baker, who thereby escaped a severe blow, which in his rage the officer would doubtless have inflicted upon him.

Dick came instantly to his brother officer's aid, and seizing the leg of the still prostrate man, dragged him into the field.

"Get up, will you?" he said; "or shall I give you one that will keep you there till we fetch a stretcher for you?"

Releasing his hold of Baker's leg, Dick seized his arm, and jerked him to his feet.

"Are you going to murder me?" cried Baker, looking bewildered from one to the other.

"It would serve you right if we did," said Bill, grasping him by the shoulder, and shaking him violently. "Here, Dick, slip the darbies[5] on him."

Dick seized his hands, and the next moment the click of the handcuffs broke the momentary silence.

Baker was so thunderstruck at finding himself handcuffed, that he could only glare for several moments upon his manacled hands; then dropping them despairingly, he turned to the officer, saying—

"What does all this mean?"

---

[5]Darbies – handcuffs. Refers to a notorious money lender, Father Derby, it subsequently refers to a bond by which a debtor was bound and put within the power of a money lender.

"You'll find out time enough," said the man who had him in custody. "Dick, hit him on the head with your staff if he tries to give me the go-by."

Thus saying, the officer mounted the bars of the gate, still keeping a firm hold of the man's arm.

"But, policeman, there is some mistake—let me explain!"

"You can do that at the station."

"No, no," said the other. "For mercy's sake, listen to us!"

"Shut up!"

"I tell you we've been robbed of our clothes by that confounded rascal, Spring-heeled Jack."

"All very fine. Come on!"

"But don't you see we are naked?"

The officers for the first time now became cognisant of the fact that their prisoners were habited only in their shirts and stockings.

"Blowed if they ain't," said one.

"This is a rum go," said the other.

"It is, indeed," said Baker. "There is some mistake. Myself and a friend hearing an alarm raised that Spring-heeled Jack was about, determined to try and effect his capture. We found him in this field, but when we believed we had him secure he presented a pistol at our heads, and threatened, if we did not strip ourselves, to blow our brains out. There was no alternative! so we obeyed; and then, before we could look round, the fellow sprang off with our things and disappeared."

"What do you think, Bill?" asked his brother officer.

"That it's all a lie," was the reply. "It won't do. We ain't to be fiddled. We've got 'em, and we'll keep 'em. So move on, my fine fellows."

"Where to?" asked Baker.

"The station-house, to be sure."

"Oh! no. Pray don't take us there. We are honest, respectable men."

"To be sure you are," sneered Dick.

"We are—upon my soul, we are!" cried the other.

"Well, you can say all you've got to say at the station," said Bill,

"You dare not take us there," said Baker, plucking up a little spirit. "I'll have the coats off your backs if you attempt to take us through the streets in this state."

"We can't have them off yours, can we?" said Bill. "Now, move on; and if you try any games with us, you'll repent it."

And he shook his staff menacingly in Baker's face.

The unfortunate man looked at his companion in distress, heaved a deep sigh, suffered his head to fall on his breast, and moved slowly away from the gate down the road.

Shivering with cold, smarting from the treatment of the officers, and the scratches they had received from the prickly hedge, the two unfortunate men and their captors had got about a quarter of a mile from the scene of their capture when a hurried footstep behind them caused all to turn, and Baker to utter a cry of joy, as his eyes rested on the form of a gentleman hurrying along towards them.

"Mr. Bittern! Mr. Bittern!" he cried. "Oh! sir, you can prove I'm not Spring-heeled Jack! You can prove I'm a respectable man—a husband, and the father of a family!"

As the words left the lips of Baker, the gentleman addressed as Mr. Bittern arrived at his side.

"Why, what, in heaven's name, does this mean!" cried the newcomer, looking in surprise from one to the other of the party.

"Means, sir? Means that we have been robbed and nearly murdered, and then taken for Spring-heeled Jack, and being taken like felons through the streets to jail."

"There's some mistake here," said Mr. Bittern. "Pray let me understand all this strange affair correctly."

Dick immediately put him in possession of the information he desired, and when he had concluded, the gentleman said—

"These persons are friends of mine. I have no wish to interfere with you in the execution of your duty, but if you keep them prisoners any longer you will have cause to repent it. I tell you I can vouch for their respectability, and assure you that you are mistaken in supposing either of them to be the person you imagine."

"Blowed if I don't believe you," said Dick, after a pause.

"You may. They are respectable men, and live about half a mile down the road, at Camp-town Villas."

The officers released their hold of the men, and rubbed their chins thoughtfully.

"This is a rum do," said Dick, after a pause.

"Very," said his brother officer.

"What do you think of it?"

"Why, that we've been sold."

"So do I."

"What dress did he wear?" asked the policeman of the shivering men.

"A large, dark, Spanish cloak.

"Whew! Dick, the fellow that sent us here was the chap himself, I do believe, after all."

"And so do I."

"Sold!"

"To rights."

"Did he have our clothes?" asked Baker.

"He had nothing, that I could see," said Dick; "in fact, I'm sure he hadn't. He's dropped them somewhere, no doubt, for I don't believe the fellow, whoever he is, is a prig."

"Then what can be his object?"

"A spree."[6]

"Curse his sprees," said Baker, savagely.

"Well, you get away home, sir, as quick as you can," said Dick, "and we'll lend you our great coats."

The men were profuse in their thanks as the officers divested themselves of their large coats and flung them over their shivering forms.

"Policeman," said Baker, "if you can lodge that scoundrel in jail, I'll give you five pounds."

"And I'll make it ten," said the other.

"We will do our best to do so, sir," said Dick. "But you'd better hurry home. I dare

---

[6]A lively or boisterous frolic.

say we shall light upon your clothes at daybreak somewhere hereabout."

"Yes—yes," said Baker, "we will get home. Curse the fellow! I only wish he stood before me now—I only do."

"At your service, sir," exclaimed a voice behind him. "Spring-heeled Jack is here! "

All turned in surprise; but with a loud laugh Jack cleared the hedge ere a hand could be put forth to stay him.

CHAPTER V.
THE NEIGHBOURHOOD DISTURBED—NO CAPTIVE—DEFEATED.

FOAMING with rage at the trick played upon them, and also at the quickness with which Jack eluded their grasp, the officers bounded over the gate in pursuit, leaving Baker and his companion standing wrapped up in the policemen's great coats, shivering with fear and cold.

"We had better get home," said Baker, his teeth chattering together loudly; "we can't aid the policemen attired as we are."

"I don't want to try," growled his companion. "I've had quite enough of Spring-heeled Jack to last me for a lifetime, and hope I shall never see him again, unless it is in Newgate."[7]

"Let me hear he is there, and I'll soon put in a word to make his punishment the heavier."

"Come on."

Baker was nothing loth, and after thanking his friend Bittern for the service he had rendered them, and bidding him good-night, turned to make his way homewards.

"Don't you think we had better take the middle of the road for it?" he asked, looking anxiously back over his shoulder.

"Why?"

"Because the fellow's just as likely as not to spring over the hedge upon us at any moment."

"So he is," replied the other, taking a quick step into the road, whither he was as quickly followed by his companion.

Half-ashamed, half-annoyed, the two men walked on at a brisk pace, ever and anon casting furtive glances behind them, and starting at the slightest sound, till at length they arrived at the row of villas, in two of which they lived.

"Thank God! we have got back," said Baker, laying one hand on the latch of the gate, whilst with the other he seized the bell knob, which projected from a little hollow in its side-post; "but, I say, don't you think it would be better for us not to say too much about what has happened to-night!"

"Why so?" asked his companion.

"People are so ungenerous, you know," said Baker, and would only laugh at us."

"They'd cry," said his companion, "if it had been them instead. Yes, we had better put the best face on it, and swear that we had a desperate struggle with Spring-heel Jack and half-a-dozen of his companions. It would seem strange to others that one man could rob us both of our clothes. People don't know what they'd do till they are put to it."

"I wish I could get in without being seen."

---

[7]Newgate Prison.

"So do I."

"But I can't."

"No more can I."

"I'm ashamed to bring anyone to the door to see me in this plight," said Baker, shivering with cold, but still hesitating to ring the bell. "It's true the coat comes down to my ankles, but— but—oh! what a pair of fools we shall look. There's no help for it, I suppose." And with a deep sigh Baker pulled the bell.

"Good night," said the other, turning away to reach his own door.

"Good night. Oh, dear! here's somebody. I hope it's my wife. What will she think when she sees me half-naked?"

At this moment the door opened, and Mrs. Baker stood on the threshold.

"Who's that?" asked the lady, in no very amiable tone of voice.

"Me, my dear."

"Sir, don't dear me," cried the lady, who, not having brought a light to the door, and perceiving what she believed to be a policeman standing at the gate, considered it a great piece of impudence to be addressed in such affectionate terms by a strange man. "How dare you—I'll report you!"

"It's me, my dear, do come and open the gate. I've been waylaid, and robbed, and nearly murdered by a desperate band of ruffians, who have taken away my clothes, and, but for the kindness of a policeman, who lent me his greatcoat, I should now appear before you in a state of nudity."

"Oh! mercy on us," cried the lady, recognising the voice of her husband, and stepping along the little garden to the gate. "Dear me, I must go and fetch the key, for I locked it lest Spring-heeled Jack should get in."

"Damn Spring-heeled Jack!" roared Baker.

"Well, you've no need to be angry with me for protecting your house in your absence!" exclaimed Mrs. Baker; "but if you are vexed at the treatment you have received, I don't think it right to blame me for doing all I can to make the place secure."

"Make haste and fetch the key, I'm shivering with cold!" cried Baker.

Away went the woman back into the house for the key of the gate, as the door of the next villa closed on the form of his no less fortunate companion.

Never did the moments seem to Baker to pass so slowly away. His impatience to get into his own home was very great, for he feared that Spring-heeled Jack might yet again stand before him.

And this fear was realized.

As he stood grasping a rail of the gate in either hand, and looking anxious into the dark passage for his wife's return, he felt a heavy slap on his shoulder, and turned, with a cry of terror, to see his tormentor at his side.

"The—the devil!" he gasped.

"No, sir, your servant, Spring-heeled Jack. I could not resist the pleasure of again seeing you; in fact, I was anxious to learn from your own lips how this coat fits you."

And as he spoke he seized a lappet[8] of the garment in either hand, and by a sudden jerk, unfastened every one of the buttons.

---

[8]A loose or overlapping part of a garment, forming a flap or fold.

"Murder—murder!" cried Baker. "Mary—Mary—make haste, I'm being murdered!"

"You snivelling cur!"[9] cried Jack. "You deserve to be dragged through a horse-pond!"

His cries quickly brought his wife to the door, who uttered a low scream as she perceived Jack bound away, half across the road at a single leap.

"Let me in—let me in!" gasped the trembling man. "He's frightened me to death."

Jack was by no means frightened at the appearance of Mrs. Baker, but at that moment he perceived the two policemen whom he had passed, and afterwards evaded, making quickly towards the spot, and felt it necessary for his safety to place a little distance between himself and them as quickly as possible.

Trembling as violently as her husband, and screaming loud enough to wake the dead, the lady endeavoured to open the gate to admit her spouse, but her agitation was so great that she dropped the key, and was unable to find it.

"Get over Baker, get over, for goodness sake!" cried his wife. "I can't find the key."

This advice Baker soon availed himself of, and placing one foot on the lock, flung his other leg over the top of the railings.

But his troubles were not yet ended.

The long tails of the policeman's great coat caught on the spear tops of the iron railings, and as he leapt down to his wife's side left him attired, except his shoulders, in only his torn shirt.

Imagining in his fright that Jack had once more got hold of him, he kicked and bellowed for mercy, whilst Mrs. Baker covered her face with her hands as if to hide her blushes, and screamed and bellowed in such a tone that the windows of the neighbouring houses were flung up quickly, and night-capped heads protruded over their sills.

Lights were held out of some of the windows, and their glare was cast upon the strange figure of Baker, as he stood on the little pathway of the garden, seemingly held by the top of the iron railings.

"Shame—shame!" yelled an old lady in a cracked tone from a neighbouring house. "Disgraceful for people to be disturbed in the dead of the night by a drunken, dirty fellow. Send for the police—lock him up, the nasty, indecent, rude, unmannerly wretch. Oh! ugh! to have no more respect for decent people than to expose himself in his shirt in the open streets!"

"Go in, old woman," said a young man at another window, who appeared greatly to enjoy the fun, "or you'll set the curtains on fire with your blushes. I say, Baker, don't kick like that, you see there is a modest young damsel looking at you."

"For God's sake, somebody come and help me!" cried Baker.

"Get your missus!" cried one.

"Go in!" roared another.

"Why don't you wear longer shirts?" exclaimed a third.

"Mrs. Baker, why don't you sew a piece on the tail?"

"Shocking! horrible! disgraceful! villainous!" cried the old lady.

"Why the devil don't you do it, then!" said Baker, waxing wroth, "instead, of stopping there looking at me? You ain't got no shame in you."

"You vile, drunken rascal! What do you mean?" yelled the old lady.

---

[9] Coward or base born person.

"Means? why he means that you can't take your eyes off him," said the young man. "For it's a sight you don't see every day."

"You blackguard young monkey! I wish I was there, I'd—I'd"—

"Give the world to be, wouldn't you?" cried the youth. "I say, Miss Frump, why don't you get married? You wouldn't mind it then."

With a howl of rage, the old lady and her immense frilled night-cap disappeared, and the window was flung down violently.

Mrs. Baker, by this time, had released her husband, who, no sooner found himself free, than he dashed into the house, followed by his amiable dame, and quickly closed the door behind them.

Meantime, Spring-heeled Jack had bounded away at terrific speed, followed by the officers.

No longer were there any hedgerows over which he could spring to avoid their grasp, and therefore he had to trust entirely to his speed of foot.

Away they went, Jack and the two policemen, at one time the former gaining considerably upon them, at another, finding them almost at his heels.

"Give it up, Jack," gasped one of the men, speaking with difficulty from want of breath. "We shall run you down to a certainty."

"Try it," said Jack, taking one of his terrific springs forward.

"Knock under, old fellow, or we must bring you down with our staves," said the other. "Your game's up now."

"Not quite," said Jack. "It would take a dozen of you to make me prisoner."

"None of your boasting, for I've got you safe now," cried the man who had rejoiced in the name of Dick, as he grasped our hero by the shoulder, just as they arrived opposite a newly built public-house at the corner of the roads.

"Hold tight, then!" said Jack, with a quick and sudden blow knocking the officer over on to the ground.

With a cry of rage the other policeman bounded towards him, but Jack eluded his grasp, and summoning up all his strength for a spring, bounded high up and far off at the same time.

"Follow if you dare!" said Jack. "Take me if you can!"

And as the man stood hesitating whether to stay with his fellow-comrade or follow, Spring-heeled Jack dashed quickly away in the darkness, and was soon lost to sight.

CHAPTER VI.

TREACHERY—THE ARREST—BLIGHTED HOUSES.

TWO O'CLOCK had sounded from a hundred steeples in the great metropolis, and died away over the vast and slumbering city, which echoed only to the monotonous tread of the policeman as he went his measured round, or the rude song of the drunken brawler, who had spent his last shilling in the low public,[10] as he reeled home to his bed.

Sleep had closed the eyes of thousands of the weary sons of toil, but some there were who still laboured, watched or wept.

---

[10]A "low public house", a lower class drinking establishment.

And among the latter was the poor young creature whom Jack had rescued from a fate more horrible than death a few short hours before.

In a small room of a little cottage standing in the Britannia Fields—now a thickly inhabited town—sat Jane Slater, the wife of a clerk, who, forgetful of the advice of kind and indulgent parents, forgetful of his own character and his wife's love, in an evil hour had forged his employer's name to a cheque for fifty pounds.

The forgery had been discovered—the signature of the forger traced, and infamy, disgrace, and shame had fallen upon that small but hitherto happy abode.

The employer, as we have seen, was a man of unflinching resolve, and cruel and heartless nature.

He had been poor—abjectly poor—in his youth, and it would seem that poverty had steeled his heart and warped his soul.

Cool, calculating, and designing, he no sooner commenced to earn money, than he found means to double it, if not morally honest, at least legally so.

Mean in his dealings with others, he was also mean to himself; everything, save absolute necessaries, he abjured, and lived in the garret of a house in a second-rate neighbourhood, when his position would have enabled him to live in style and be surrounded by every comfort.

But money was his god, and dearly did he worship it. No wife or child shared his love: that was centred alone in his gold.

No wonder, then, that the poor foolish forger dared not hope for mercy at the hands of such a man—no wonder that surprise almost held James Slater spell-bound, when a note requesting the presence of his wife was placed in his hands, at the moment he was about to flee to escape the penalty of his crime.

What could he think of this request from his miserly employer, Ralph Grasper?

What could it mean from one he knew to be of an unforgiving nature, of a cruel heart, and firm resolves?

He could not divine.

But the woman, with her forgiving nature, believed she could perceive the clue to the mystery.

Ralph Grasper had seen her on more than one occasion, when on a fine evening she had gone to the warehouse to meet her beloved husband, and accompany him home.

She at once leapt to the conclusion that the iron nature of the man was not, after all, so hard and unfeeling that, though he felt bound to threaten the forger, he could yet forgive him through his wife.

"He pities me," she said, "and will forgive you, James! I will see him—go at once. My tears, my prayers, my supplications will melt his stubborn heart, and all will yet be well."

As drowning men grasp at straws, so did James Slater grasp at this hope, and urged his wife to go and see the man whom he had so basely injured, promising to await her return, and then seek safety in flight if she failed to obtain for him forgiveness.

With a beating, yet hopeful heart, the young wife sped on her errand, leaving her guilty husband to await her return with mingled feeling of hope, fear, and shame.

But ere she had left the house five minutes he heard heavy footsteps ascending the stairs.

He sprang to his feet pale with terror and dismay.

He judged whose those footsteps were.

He grasped his hat and sprang to the window.

To fling it up was but the work of a moment; the distance to leap to the ground was not more than ten feet, but he recoiled with a cry of despair.

In front of the house stood two policemen.

What should he do?

Ere he could answer the question he had asked himself, the door of the room was flung open.

He turned quickly.

Two officers stood before him.

He recoiled till his back touched the wall, then covering his face with his hands, groaned in agony—

"Oh! God! Lost—lost!"

"Not quite, my fine fellow," said one. "You should say found—found—for you are our prisoner!"

"Your prisoner!" gasped Slater.

"That's it," said the man, coolly drawing a pair of handcuffs from his pocket.

"For what?"

"Lor' don't you know!"

"No, no!" half shrieked Slater.

"How green you are," said the man, approaching with the handcuffs.

"Keep off—keep off!" cried Slater. "I won't be taken—I won't be taken"

"Oh! won't you, I'll see about that," said the officer, adroitly slipping the manacles on to his wrists and locking them in a moment. "You won't be taken, won't you, and blessed if you don't hold your hands up for the cuffs."

"What—what does all this mean?" cried Slater, dropping his arms in utter despair.

"It means that you won't have a chance, at least for some time, of forging other people's names. Now do you understand?" said the policeman, coolly surveying the blanched cheeks and trembling limbs of the forger.

"Oh! heaven!" gasped Slater, "and hope had only just beamed in my heart. He will not forgive me—not forgive me!"

"Not likely!" said the officer. "Now come along."

And he placed his hand on the forger's shoulder.

"Where—where?"

"To jail!"

With a deep sigh, the head of the agonized and guilty man sank upon his bosom.

"My wife—oh! my wife!" he groaned.

"You should have thought of her before," said the officer, coldly, leading him across the room to the door. "Where is she—out?"

"Yes, yes."

"A good job too," said the man. "It will save her one pang."

"Thank God! gasped Slater. "Thank God!"

But what would have been his agony had he known the purpose of the guilty wretch whose name he had forged, of the indignities and insults the poor heartbroken woman had gone to receive at the hands of the treacherous Ralph Grasper!

But he knew it not, guessed it not, and feeling very grateful that she was not present to see him borne away from her side by the officers of the law, he bowed his head still lower, and between the two policemen descended the stairs to the street.

It was dark, but still Slater requested that his hat might be pulled lower down over his forehead, lest anyone should recognise him on his way to jail.

This request was instantly granted by one of the policemen, who drew the hat of the guilty man down so as to shade his face.

It was a request the officer could not refuse.

And this, with his head still bent upon his heaving chest, with an officer on either side, and two following closely behind him, James Slater was escorted to the station, and while he sat sobbing in the cold, dark cell, his wife, with clasped hands and tearful eyes, listened to the base proposals of the man who had placed him there.

After leaving Spring-heeled Jack at the field gate, with a beating heart Jane Slater hurried on her way home.

In her right hand she grasped the fatal evidence of her husband's first and only crime.

Little heeded she the pain which had seized her in her side, from the rapid pace at which she ran rather than walked in the direction of her once happy dwelling, for her heart was bounding with joy and gratitude.

Joy at having possession of that which could transport the man she loved, in spite of the misery his act had inflicted upon her—gratitude to her preserver who had saved her from a fate so disgusting and loathsome.

But when she reached the door of her home, and held the knocker in her trembling grasp, a strange, an indefinable terror assailed her—a something seemed to whisper in her ears, "Thy sufferings are not yet ended."

The knocker slipped from her fingers, and as it echoed through the silent street, the sound appeared to her like a death-blow to her happiness.

She leaned against the door-post, and strained every nerve to catch the footfall of her husband, as he came to answer the summons. Oh, how anxiously she did listen!

But not a sound broke the silence.

She staggered rather than walked backwards a few paces, and gazed up at the window.

The apartment was in darkness.

She sprang to the door.

She seized the knob in one hand and the knocker in the other.

She raised the latter, but as she brought it down the door gave way before her.

A cold perspiration broke out in every pore.

Her limbs trembled till she could scarcely retain an upright position, and still grasping at the knob in the centre of the door, she staggered into the passage.

"James! James!" she cried.

Echo alone answered her.

By an effort she closed the door behind her, went along the dark passage, up the stairs to the room where she had left him.

The candle had burned down in the socket, and a piece of the smouldering wick alone remained.

She cast her eyes around the apartment.

She called her husband by name.

She staggered to the bed.

She clutched at its coverlet, and with a wild, despairing cry, fell forward upon it!

"Gone! Gone!" she gasped, in agony. "Oh, God! and I could save him!"

Then a bursting sob, which seemed to tear the stretched heartstrings asunder, escaped her bosom, and for a time her sorrows and her sufferings were buried in oblivion.

Heaven, in its infinite mercy, had taken some compassion upon her, and plunged her into insensibility.

A light shot up for a moment from the smouldering wick in the candlestick on the mantel shelf, and then went out, leaving darkness throughout the apartment.

What could be more emblematical of the last few hours of that poor woman's existence?

Hope had lighted her soul and cheered her heart for a short time, but despair had extinguished the bright gleam, and left her prey to the darkest misery.

The minutes flew by, and with their flight came returning sense to the forger's wife.

Once more alive to all that had passed, she dragged her wearied body from the bed, and tottered to a chair, into which she sank.

"Gone—gone!" she muttered. "They have torn him from me—borne him away to a felon's cell! He would not have left the house by his own accord till my return. They have borne him to jail—to prison—to a felon's cell, and I am left alone in my misery, to mourn his fate—his disgrace—his shame. God help me! For I am sorely tried—widowed in heart and soul! Covering her face with her hands, she sobbed aloud, the sounds of her grief mingling with the tick of the clock, which seemed to mock at her misery.

CHAPTER VII.

FRESH TROUBLES—THE ACCUSATION—A GEM IN THE ROUGH—A VILLAIN DEFEATED BY AN UN-LOOKED-FOR FRIEND.

THROUGHOUT that night Jane Slater sat a prey to the most poignant grief, nor did the cold morning air, which struck a chill to her shivering form, induce her to retire to her own bed.

The first streak of dawn, the rays of the rising sun, the hurried step of the artisan as he went to his daily toil, and the busy hum of the new day—all broke upon her senses, yes she moved not from her seat, but still clasped her tear-bedewed face in her hands, and wept and sobbed as if the well-springs of her lacerated heart would never dry up.

Seven o'clock and the busy hum of life had taken the place of silence and slumber, when a loud knock at the street door caused the palpitating heart of Jane Slater to throb with fearful violence, and she bounded from her chair.

Again the summons sounded through the house, and with feelings indescribable she tottered from the room down the stairs to the door.

Trembling with agitation, she drew back the lock and staggered to the wall of the passage, as the door was thrust violently open and revealed to her the forms of two policemen on its threshold.

"Are you Mrs. Slater?" asked one of the men.

Jane made no reply.

She could but gaze in horror upon the man.

The question was repeated in a more surly tone.

JACK LEAPS INTO THE THAMES AFTER THE SEAMSTRESS.

Jane strove to reply, but her tongue refused its office, and the tears which, for a moment had ceased to flow burst forth afresh.

Observing this, the other officer, who seemed less rough than his companion, laid his hand gently on her arm, and in a low, mild tone, said—

"Don't be alarmed, my good woman, but tell us, is your name Slater?"

"It is," she sighed.

"Then it becomes our painful duty to inform you—although, doubtless, you are aware of the fact—that your husband is in custody on the charge of forgery."

"My heart told me so," she sobbed, "when I found him gone."

"We have no wish to wound your feelings," continued the man, "but we have a duty to perform."

And as he spoke he walked into the passage, followed by his companion, who immediately closed the door behind him.

"A duty?" cried Jane. "Oh! what duty?"

"To search your house," replied the man. "You can see our warrant if you desire it."

"No," she said, sorrowfully. "Do as you please. The worst has come to pass."

"We have no wish to cause you unnecessary pain," said the man, "but you will not be allowed to leave this house till we depart."

"You will find nothing here but what is honestly come by," sobbed Jane.

"I hope not."

"Indeed you will not!"

"Still we must obey orders."

"I shall make no attempt to go."

"Very good, then. We will just look over this room first," said the man, opening the door of this little parlour.

Jane staggered to the stairs and sat down upon them.

She cared not what the officers did, or how they displaced the things in that room she loved to keep so neat and tidy.

The man having looked around, opened the two little sideboard cupboards and gazed into every corner, came to the passage again."

"We daresay you have got nothing but what belongs to you," said one, "but we will take a peep upstairs, if you please."

"Go where you like—do what you like!" sobbed Jane, rising to let them pass.

"There—there! Don't take on so, my good woman; things may turn out better than you think for, after all."

"Alas! alas! hope is dead within me," sighed the forger's wife.

"Be of good cheer. It's not every fellow that does wrong gets punished for it, especially if he gets good counsel. A dozen things stand in the way of a conviction. A flaw in the indictment, or something else may turn up; so don't be downhearted; while there's life there's hope, you know."

"Not for me—not for me!"

The two officers went up the stairs, leaving her standing on the little mat at the bottom, and entered the room where her husband had been made prisoner the night before.

Certainly they did not expect to find anything for they just glanced around the apartment, and turned to descend again to the passage, when the eye of him who had spoken so brusquely lighted upon a crumpled piece of paper lying on the floor.

He kicked it with the toe of his boot, then stooped and picked it up.

"What's up?" was the question.

"Blessed if it ain't"—

"What?" interrupted the other.

"A cheque."

"A cheque!" said his companion in surprise.

"Yes, and drawn on the same bank, and signed by the same name as this fellow's in quod[11] for."

"The devil!"

"Look!"

The man cast his eyes over the paper.

"Whew!" he whistled; "it's a rum go."

"Ruin for him."

"Seems so."

"He's been trying it more than once."

"Looks like it."

"We better look a little closer about this crib."

Rat-tat-tat thundered at the knocker.

"What's up now?" said the mild officer.

"You go and see."

"All right."

The man bounded from the room, and reached the passage, as Jane opened the door.

Before it stood Ralph Grasper and a policeman.

The woman uttered a piercing cry, and started back, and then Grasper and his companion strode in.

"I give that woman into custody," said Grasper, turning to the officer, who had followed him, "for robbing me last night, with the aid of another person, of the cheque which was forged by her husband."

The policeman caught Jane Slater by the wrist.

"You are my prisoner," he said.

"Prisoner!" cried the woman, with a bewildered gaze from one to the other.

"Yes, a prisoner!" exclaimed Grasper. "You and your husband shall stand at a criminal bar together."

"Scoundrel!" cried the woman.

"Officer, do your duty," said Grasper.

"Scoundrel—I say!" cried Jane, her indignation and disgust rising above her sorrows and fears. "Dare you come here and accuse the woman you so basely insulted and strove to outrage! Can you come here without a blush of shame on your face, and charge me with a crime of which you know I was never guilty! Ah, villain—villain!"

"I will have justice," said Grasper.

"Heaven, in its own good time, will mete it out to you," said Jane, heaving a deep sigh.

"Where's your bonnet and shawl?" asked the officer who had hold of her arm.

---

[11] Prison.

"Upstairs!"

"Just bring them down with you," said the man to the policeman, who had come down to see the cause of the knock, and who had stood beside him, listening to all that passed, but never said a word; "I suppose she don't want to go without them."

"Take her off—don't wait!" said Grasper.

"Why not?" asked the man who had been requested to obtain the walking garments.

"Because she is a thief!"

"Oh!" said the officer; "but I suppose she is a woman, ain't she?"

"What of that?" growled Grasper.

"We are not in the habit of treating women like brutes—that's all," was the sarcastic reply.

"Who are you presuming to talk to, Sir?" said Grasper.

"Not to a man," was the reply. "That's evident!"

"What do you mean, fellow?"

"I mean that you are no man to wish to inflict unnecessary pain upon the poor devil who even in an unguarded moment stoops to crime. She may be guilty of what you lay to her charge, but there are many more deserving of punishment than those who get it—and a good many, too, I reckon, who are anxious to make it hard for others."

Jane Slater raised her eyes with a look of gratitude to the speaker's face.

"Fellow—I will report you!" replied Grasper. "I'll have that coat off your back in a very short time. You're a disgrace to the force!"

"And you are a disgrace to humanity," said the man.

"He is—he is!" cried Jane. "Last night he invited me to his house. I went there in the hope that he would extend mercy to my misguided husband. Oh, God! at what price did he offer it at—that of a wife's honour! He held the fatal cheque before my eyes, and told me how I could obtain it to save my husband. I did not steal the cheque from him—it was taken by one whom I never saw before nor since—one whom heaven must have sent to save me from his villainy!"

"When did you say that was?" asked the man who had hold of her arm.

"Last night."

"Why, that's when he gave your husband in custody."

"Yes, the perfidious villain," cried Jane. "He lured me by false hopes to his house, and would have ruined the wife under pretence of forgiving her husband at the very hour he knew he had placed the officers of justice on his track."

"All lies—all lies!" yelled Grasper.

"'Tis true—true as heaven," sobbed Jane.

"Do your duty—lock her up," roared Grasper, foaming with rage.

But the man released his hold of her arm and turned towards him.

"I do not believe she stole the cheque," he said, "and I would warn you to be careful how you proceed in this business."

"I tell you she did—a cheque forged by her husband, drawn on the County Bank, and dated June the 7th."

"This cheque bears that date," said the officer, who had picked it up from the floor, and now leaned over the stair balustrades, holding it open in his hand. "Is this the one you mean?"

"Let me see—let me see," exclaimed Grasper, bounding up a couple of the stairs and taking it from the man's hand. "Yes, this is it; this is the one," he cried, leaping back to the side of the policeman he had brought with him; "look, there's the date. I had it safe last night—she stole it from me. But I will punish her for the deed. There is my signature forged by my clerk—by her husband."

"You must come with me," said the man; "I must take you, so come quietly."

"Drag her along if she won't," cried Grasper; "Show her no mercy. She shall go to prison, and this cheque—this evidence—shall transport them both."

Jane cast one imploring look at the officers, and then, with a spasmodic gasp, her head fell upon her bosom, and she suffered herself to be led from the house by the officers, while Ralph Grasper, crumpling the cheque in revengeful glee in his hands, strode after the prisoner, with his head as erect as if no black spot rested on his heart—as if no qualm of conscience smote his soul for his base and wicked work.

CHAPTER VIII.

A FRESH LOCALITY—THE PIGEON FANCIER AND THE SEAMSTRESS—
THE FACE IN THE TRAP.

IN ONE of those dirty streets which run out of the Bethnal Green Road stood a small four-roomed house in a very dilapidated condition, surmounted by a large structure of laths[12] and rotten boards, yclept[13] a pigeon-dormer.

Many of the windows were broken, and filled up with bundles of dirty rags, or pasted over with paper.

The shutters were broken, and through the centre of the door a hole had been bored, and a piece of dirty, greasy cord attached to the handle of the lock inside, passed through it, so that the knocker was seldom used by the inmates, as a pull at the cord instantly obtained them admission.

The front room upstairs of this habitation, if such it could be called, was occupied by a poor seamstress, and a cheerless, miserable apartment it indeed was, its wretchedness being greatly enhanced in wet weather by the rain finding its way through the roof, which was sadly destroyed by the numerous pigeons kept there by the owner of the house.

Directly opposite was a small, low, dirty beer-shop, called the Pigeon Flyers, a place of resort for those whose tastes led them to keep birds in such quantities in that locality.

From this house the voices of several men in loud conversation issued, and broke the silence which otherwise would have reigned in the street at the hour at which we visit it, and caused a tall, well-dressed, gentlemanly-looking man to pause in his rather hurried walk, and cast a glance in upon those assembled before the bar.

"What a den!" he muttered; "but for such places as these, many a sickly wife would be a happy woman, and many a starving child well fed and clad. 'Tis a pity when men waste their hard-earned money thus! Bah! hard-earned did I say? Well, perhaps I am

---

[12]A thin narrow strip of wood used to fasten slates or tiles of a roof or the plaster of a wall or ceiling, and in the construction of lattice or trellis work and Venetian blinds.
[13] Called.

right; for money ill-got is hard-got, and then wasted in such houses as this."

He turned as he finished speaking, and his eyes rested upon the faint glimmer of a candle as it played upon a dirty blind over the window of the upstairs room of the house we have noticed opposite and then upon the lath-work which protruded over the coping-stone, and with a shrug of the shoulders, he was about to continue his walk, when the angry conversation of those at the bar of the Pigeon Flyers arrested his attention.

"I tell you I ain't got no money," said a rough-looking fellow, bringing the quart-pot, out of which he had been drinking, with a loud bang on the counter, "and you won't get it—there!"

"Now, look here, Bill," said the man addressed, whose bleared eyes and swaying body betokened that he had been drinking pretty freely, as indeed had most of the party, "you've owed me that half-a-crown for more nor[14] a fortnight, and he won't trust me a pot; so shell out, and I'll pay for one."

"Who won't trust you a pot?" said Bill, staggering forward, and catching at the bar. "Who won't trust you a pot?"

"I won't," said the landlord. "I won't trust no more beer till I've been paid for what you've had."

"You won't?" said Bill, in drunken accents; "you won't? Then will you trust me?"

"No. If you pay Bob that half-bull, he'll do it."

"I ain't got it."

"Go and rob the old woman for it," said Bob.

"She?—she's never got any money," said Bill; "and that's what makes me so thundering wild with her. I'm a jolly sight too easy, I am, and ought to stick to it all myself!"

"So you ought," said Bob.

"And so I will for the future."

"And then you'd be able to pay your debts," said Bob, sarcastically.

"I was obliged to lick[15] her the other night, because she'd spent all the five bob and hadn't left me any money for half an ounce of 'bacca.[16] Yes, I'm a thundering sight too easy! I let everybody impose on me. But I mean to alter, I do, now. People won't let me owe them anything, and I won't let them owe me; if I do"—

"Shut up, Bill," said one of the party. "It's devilish little that's owing you, and a devilish lot you owe, and are likely to. I'd bet a crown that half a sov[17] would cover the lot you could ask for anywhere."

"And I'll have it, whatever it is, or there'll be a thundering row, and that afore long too, you'll see! You shall have your money, Bob, you shall have your money," he added, moving towards the door, as the listener strode away from before the window of the Pigeon Flyers, with a smile on his face, and a contemptuous curl of the lip.

The stranger did not go far, however, for when he had got about a dozen doors past the beer-shop, he crouched in the shadow of the wall, and kept his gaze fixed upon the house where he had observed the rushlight dimly burning in the up-stairs room.

It was evident that he had some purpose in view, with regard to the house on which

---

[14] Than.

[15] Beat.

[16] Tobacco.

[17] Sovereign.

his gaze was so intently fixed, for his glance roving upwards to the network of laths, he struck his hands together with an exclamation of satisfaction.

The gaslight in the beer-shop was flaring away—for it was eleven o'clock at night— and lighting up the front of the house with the broken shutters, bringing out in strong relief the dirty bundles of rags in the upper windows, and completely putting into the shade the sickly glimmer of a halfpenny rushlight, whose feeble rays in vain endeavoured to force themselves through the skirt of an old cotton gown which served the purpose of a blind, when Bill Jackson—for such was the name by which the owner of the dwelling was familiarly called—staggered rather than walked out of the Pigeon Flyers, and after steadying himself on the cellar-flap, crossed the road to his own door.

Here he amused himself for some moments by drawing his dirty hand over the panels in search of the greasy cord; and whether the flickering of the gaslight opposite, or a certain wandering of the mind to which he was subject, rendered him forgetful of its exact position or not, we cannot say, but it is a fact that when, after about a minute's searching for it, and making sure he had found it at last, he grasped only at its shadow, and, staggering back to the kerb, fell into a sitting posture in the gutter, and consequently Bill fired up furiously, and staggered to his feet, consigning his soul to a certain warm place with a sulphury savour about it, and rushed like a savage, as he was, at the door, this time succeeding in grasping the greasy cord, which the knot at the end prevented from slipping through his closed fist.

With a jerk at the cord the door flew open, and Bill dashed it back to its full extent against the wall of the passage, which had long lost its covering—to wit, the paper with which it had once been graced, and rolled into the narrow slip which parted the little parlour from the next house.

"Why don't you bring a light, you lazy varmints?" he cried out, supporting his tottering limbs by still clinging to the cord.

"Why don't you keep sober, and then I might have money to buy candles with, you nasty, unfeeling wretch?" cried a woman from the back room. "You may break your neck for all I care, and the sooner you do it the better for me and the children. What with your pigeons and you"—

"Shut up!" exclaimed Bill. "I am not in any humour for any of your jaw, I can tell you to-night, and I won't stand it, I won't; if I do, I may be"—

Ere the indignant Bill could finish the sentence the greasy cord slipped from his grasp, and he fell heavily in the passage, striking his head against the door, which, rebounding against the wall, made so great a noise and brought down such a quantity of the plaster, as not only to bring a poor, thin, sickly-looking woman, who rejoiced in the proud title of Bill's wife, from the little back room, but also was the cause of the dim flicker of the rushlight suddenly disappearing from the room above and making its appearance in the passage below, held by the trembling hand of a wan-featured, but not unhandsome young woman of some twenty-two years of age.

"Mercy on us, what is the matter, Mrs. Jackson?" asked this latter personage, as she held the light high up above her head, and gazed down tremblingly upon the heap of humanity at her feet.

"He's drunk again, that Bill of mine," replied the wife, "drunk again."

"That's a lie," roared Bill, making several ineffectual struggles to regain his equilibrium, which he did by grasping at the door.

"Look at the beast, Miss Folder, only look at the beast!" cried the wife; "he's not drunk—why, he can't stand."

"You're a thundering"—

Bill Jackson had just got fairly upon his legs, when away went the rickety door from his grasp, and over again he went on to the floor, drowning the last word in the clatter of the panels against the dilapidated wall.

This second fall rendered Bill furious, and, like the dog that turns and bites the stone which strikes him, Jackson struck frantically at the door with his clenched fist, swearing fearfully all the while.

The young woman gazed on with a shudder of horror; but Mrs. Jackson paid but little heed to his antics.

She had got used to them long since.

"For heaven's sake, Mr. Jackson," said the girl, "do pray get up. You will do yourself some injury, if you allow your passions to master your feelings in this way."

"Oh, let him alone," said the wife, in a whisper. "If the door didn't get it, I should. He must hit somebody or something when he's like this; and while he's fighting the door he's not ill-using me. Let him go on."

But Bill evidently did not seem disposed to go on long. Drunk as he was, he had still the sense of feeling—if not in his heart, at least in his hands—and he therefore desisted from his stupid attack, and again managed to struggle to his feet.

For a moment he glared with his bloodshot eyes upon his wife and the young lodger, and then stretching out his brawny hand, he seized the tin candlestick which contained the rushlight, and rudely tore it from her grasp.

"What's that for, Bill?" asked his wife.

"What's it for?"

"Yes."

"You say you ain't got no light, because you ain't got no light, because you ain't got no money. Well, then, I'm not a going to go without one, while people as owes me rent has, that's what it's for."

The young woman heaved a deep sigh, and the water rose to her eyes.

"I'm blowed if I mean to wait any longer for the rent," continued Bill, staggering, and nearly making his wife's eye an extinguisher for the now guttering rush. "I want my money, and I mean to have it, or out she goes."

"There, talk about that to-morrow, Bill," said his wife, coaxingly.

"I'll talk about it to-night. I'm not a going to be badgered for what I owe, when people owe me a lot of rent.

"But, Mr. Jackson"—began the young woman.

"Shut up with your misters," growled Bill. "I ain't so drunk but I know when people comes the mister with me they are trying the soft-soap. I tell you my name's Bill Jackson and I want the rent you owe me, and mean to have it too, or out you goes."

Bill made a stooping, staggering movement towards the young woman, as he gave expression to his resolves, and as with a sigh the poor creature stepped aside, Bill ran his head and the rushlight at the same moment against the wall and extinguished it in an instant.

"What did you blow the light out for?" he cried, savagely flinging the candlestick at his wife's head.

Fortunately, however, for the poor woman, the missile missed its mark, and struck the dirty, greasy panelling of the passage.

"I didn't blow it out," quietly replied his wife.

"I say you did," growled the surly ruffian.

"No, indeed she did not," said Ellen Folder, in a meek, coaxing tone.

"Then it was you."

"No, you staggered against the wall, and extinguished it," she replied.

"Did I?"

"You did indeed, Mr. Jackson."

"Well, I mean to extinguish you as well, unless you dub up the money you owe me," said Bill, ferociously.

"Mr. Jackson, I'm very sorry"—

"Blow your sorrows! Are you going to pay me my rent?" said Bill, raising his voice to a pitch sufficient to he heard in the bar of the Pigeon Flyers, on the opposite side of the road.

"I assure you"—

"I don't want that, I want my rent," interrupted Bill.

"For goodness sake, Mr. Jackson, don't talk so loud," pleaded Ellen.

"What have I got to be ashamed of?" said Bill, steadying himself by placing his hands against the wall? "I ain't a-going to rob anybody. I'm only asking for my own."

"Don't holler, Bill—don't holler," said his wife.

"You shut up, and mind your own business, or I'll make you holler," he replied, brutally.

The poor woman was silent.

She understood the threat, and trembled for her safety.

"Believe me, Mr. Jackson, I am extremely sorry that I am unable to comply with your demands to-night," said Ellen, in a low choking voice. "I have not been able to go to the warehouse, but will work all night to get the shirts finished and taken them in to-morrow, and I promise you I will then give you some."

"I don't want some, I want all," growled Bill, "and what's more, I want all and will have it before you go upstairs."

"But I've not got it. The last halfpenny I had in the world I laid out for the rushlight to work by."

"You've no right to buy rushlights with my money," cried Bill. "You ain't paid me no rent for three weeks, and there's five owing, and I want it, and will have it, that's that."

"You cannot have what I have not got."

"Then I'll take what you have," growled Bill. "I won't wait any longer, if I do I'm!"—

And the drunken ruffian thrust the poor seamstress violently aside and staggered towards the stairs.

"Oh! Mr. Jackson, to-morrow you shall"—

"To-night I will have some money—I can get it at the dolly shop for some of the stuff you're working on, and you must find out how to get them back. I'm not going to be put off any longer. Light that candle, d'ye hear, you lazy varmint?" he added, addressing his wife, "and let's see what she's got upstairs."

With a half shriek Ellen Folder sprang to the foot of the stairs and seized the arm of the intoxicated man.

"For heaven's sake do not touch the work entrusted to me. The property is not mine."

"You ain't paid no rent, and it's mine," said Bill, shaking off her hold, "and I'll do as I like with it. You'd better bring me a light, missus, or I'll knock out one of your eyes to see my way upstairs with."

Knowing from experience the brutal nature of her husband, and dreaded the putting into practice his threats, Mrs. Jackson went into the little back room, and procuring a light from a small cinder fire in the grate, returned to the passage, and searched for the candlestick, by the light of a piece of paper she held in her hand.

This she had little difficulty in finding; but as to the rushlight, that had been broken and flattened against the wall, and to ignite its battered wick became a work of impossibility.

"Look alive!" yelled the enraged and impatient Bill, swaying to and fro by the handrails of the bannisters.

"It's broke to pieces and won't light," said his wife. "Wait till the morning, Bill—wait till the morning."

"You won't light it, won't you?" yelled Bill leaving his hold of the handrail, and leaping towards her.

"I can't."

Then take that, you obstinate varmint!" he exclaimed, striking his wife a blow on the cheek, and causing her to let fall the candlestick.

"You drunken wretch! You beast! you brute!" cried his wife, bursting into tears, and retreating to the back room.

"What did you say?" yelled Bill, rushing after her, with his unmanly fists closed.

But as he reached the door of the room, the affrighted woman shut it quickly against his face; and the drunken bully, dashing against it, fell across the passage.

The poor girl, who, in the meantime, had stood wringing her hands in agony and fear, now sprang quickly over the prostrate body of Bill, and scarce touching the rickety stairs, flew up them two at a time, reached her own room, closed the door behind her and locked it, then with a sob sank down upon the single chair—the rush bottom of which was fast disappearing—and burying her face in her hands, listened with a beating heart for the sound of the drunkard's footsteps.

"Oh, heavens!" she gasped, "what shall I do!—what shall I do? If he takes my work, I am ruined! They will drag me to a prison—my character will be blasted—my bread gone, and the workhouse alone open to me! Oh, that I had the money to pay him! But now not even a part shall I be able to get to-morrow, for I have no light to work by. Poverty—poverty, what a curse thou art! What indignities, insults, and outrages are not heaped upon thee! Merciful heavens! He is coming up-stairs! He will break the door, and take my work. Oh! what shall I do? What shall I do?"

She sprang from her seat, and wrung her hands in agony.

At this moment there was a noisy commotion among the pigeons in the dormer above her head, and had the door of her room been open, she might have seen a frightful looking-face in the centre of a small trap in the ceiling of the little landing outside.

CHAPTER IX.

THE WORKGIRL'S STRATAGEM—THE STRANGE APPEARANCE—THE BULLY COWED—THE AGREEMENT AND DISAPPEARANCE.

THE HEAVY footfall of the drunken man as he staggered up the stairs, rolling from handrail to wall, and vice versa, sank into the poor girl's heart with terrible force, and seemed to paralyse her every energy.

She did not fear for herself so much as for the safety of the goods entrusted to her to make up, and the loss of which, she felt would not only deprive her of the few pence she could earn, but bring down upon her all the wrath of Mr. Abraham Levy, the great clothier of Whitechapel.

She strove to think what course was best for her to pursue, but to no avail, and she stood in the centre of the little dark room a picture of most abject misery and despair, till she was aroused from the painful attitude by the sound of Bill Jackson's burly body rolling against the panels of her room-door.

"Open the door, you swindling varmint!" he roared out in drunken accents, as he rattled the loosened handle of the half worn-out lock. "Open this door, or I'll break it down!"

But so far from complying with this request, Ellen stretched forth her hands and pushed against it with all her might.

Thump, thump came furiously against the panels, each blow causing them to jar against the palms of the poor seamstress.

"Oh! heaven! what shall I do?" she mentally ejaculated. "To appeal to the feelings of this brute would be vain, and his wife dare not aid me lest he beat her, as he has often done before. Oh! the window. I will tie the work in a bundle and hang it outside, he will not think to look for it there. Yes, yes, that may save it from his clutches."

She sprang lightly across the room, and tore down the old skirt which served as a blind, and thereby let into her apartment light sufficient from the gas in the Pigeon Flyers to enable her quickly to gather together her work, which lay strewed over a rickety deal table in the centre of the room.

Tying the shirts, made and unmade, with nervous hands, in the old skirt, and holding the bundle out over the sill, softly as possible shut it down on the ends of the bows, there being nothing by which she could suspend it.

Having done so, she returned to the door, on which Bill was thumping with all his might, and threatening every moment to burst it open.

A moment she hesitated, and then seizing the key she turned it quickly, and sprang back to the centre of the apartment.

Hearing the key turn, Bill tried the handle, and thrust the door open with a violent jerk.

A little scream escaped Ellen's lips as Bill staggered into the room.

"Now where's my rent?" he said. "I don't want none of your palaver. I want money, and have it I will, either in coin or goods."

"As I told you before, I have no money," replied the girl. "and your foolishness will prevent me obtaining it for you as early as I should have done."

"A fool am I?" said Bill. "Well, I think I am to let you keep this room, and not make you pay your rent. But I won't be a fool any longer, I'll have it now, or its worth, and out you go."

"But you can have neither to-night."

"We'll see."

He went to the table and search for the work entrusted to her to make up.

Oh course he found it not.

Turning to the trembling girl, he inquired where it was.

"What is that to you?" she replied by an effort, making a show of some spirit.

"I want it."

"You will not have it."

"Won't I!"

"No."

"Sal, bring a light up here, will you?" he called out to his wife.

There was no reply.

"I'll have a light," he cried furiously, "if I have the house down to get it. Go and borrow a candle next door, or over at the Pigeons—d'ye hear?"

"Come down, Bill—come down," called his wife from the bottom of the stairs. "You get yourself into trouble!"

"I'll see about that—I'll have some money to-night, or the devil seize me if I don't—oh-oh—oh!"

Bill, who had gone to the door of the room for the purpose of making his demand on his wife, happened to cast his bleared eyes up at the little trap before mentioned, and what he there saw called forth from his lips an exclamation of horror, as he shrank back into the room occupied by the poor seamstress.

In an instant there was a wonderful change in the appearance and manner of the drunken bully.

The fumes of the drink seemed to have disappeared as if by magic, and he was seized with a violent trembling.

He clutched frantically at the door, and slammed it close to, and held it shut with both hands.

"The—the—de—de—devil!" he gasped. "The—the—de—devil!"

Ellen Folder became terribly alarmed at the change, and believing that he was seized with a fit of delirium tremens, and fearful that he might offer her some personal violence, shrieked aloud—

"Help! Help!"

"For God's sake, don't!" cried the man, all the cowardice of his brutal nature at once revealing itself. "There's the devil!—there's the devil!"

"Oh! dear!" cried Ellen, shrinking towards the window; "he's mad—he's mad."

"No—no!" I'm not mad!" exclaimed Bill.

And he turned towards her.

By the light of the gas lamp she could perceive his usually red face had become of a pallid hue.

There was a strange look, too, in his eyes, and his limbs shook as with the palsy.

Back close to the window shrank the girl in terror.

And as if for protection Bill sprang to her side.

But the fears of violence at his hands increased, and Ellen uttered another shriek.

"Don't—oh! don't! He'll hear you and come in here!" cried Bill, catching her arm and grasping it as in a vice.

"Help! Murder!" cried Ellen making an effort and freeing herself from his grasp. "Help! Mrs. Jackson! Help!"

With the speed of terror she crossed the little room and flung open the door.

"For God's sake, don't leave me here!" roared Bill, rushing after her.

But alarmed beyond measure, Ellen pulled the door to after her and sped quickly down the rickety stairs, screaming all the way.

The frightened ruffian in his abject terror could not immediately find the handle to open the door, and when he did so, his hand shook so violently that he was unable for some moment to accomplish his object.

"Oh! bring a light—bring a light!" he yelled as he flung open the door. "Here's the de—Murder! Murder!"

As the last words rang from his lips Bill Jackson recoiled in horror back to the centre of the room, where he clasped his hands over his eyes, and sank upon his knees.

On the threshold of the doorway stood an object that might well have appalled a stouter heart than Bill's—a form that would have shaken more powerful nerves than those which had already been weakened by drink, as were the now trembling and affrighted bully's.

It was that of a tall form, whose head and body glowered with a blue, phosphorescent fire, from the back of which hung, in graceful folds, a long striped cloak, like a tiger skin.

It stood with its arms extended, thus throwing the cloak open in front, and revealing the fore part of the figure, over which the blue flames played, and appeared to curl upwards to the crown of the head.

"Mer—mer—mercy, Mr. Devil!" cried the kneeling man, still keeping his hands pressed over his eyes, to shut out the horrible form which now had the effect of completely sobering him.

The figure took a step towards him, extending its arms still wider, and then paused.

"Mortal," it said.

"Mer—mer—!" began Bill.

"Silence."

"Yes—yes!"

You did not expect to see me?"

"No—no! Do go away, Sa—sa—rah!"

"Call not on her," said the horrible shape, in a deep guttural tone. "She can aid you not. You are mine."

"Have mercy!" cried Bill; "I ain't fit to die!"

"That's the first time you ever spoke the truth," said the apparent demon. "You are not fit to die."

"No—no, not yet!" gasped Bill, slightly removing his hand from before his eyes, but replacing it with a cry, as he perceived the terrible form was bending over him.

"Why should I suffer you to live?" asked the demon. "Answer me that."

"Be—because I'm a sinner!" cried Bill—"A great sinner."

"A liar?"

Bill was silent.

"Answer me."

"Yes—yes!"

"A rogue?"

"Yes."

"A callous-hearted scoundrel, who beats his wife, starves his children, and insults defenceless and unprotected women? Answer or"—

"Yes—yes—yes!" exclaimed Bill, fearful that if he did not quickly reply the demon would bear him away to the place he so often consigned his own eyes and limbs.

"You are all these?"

"I am."

"And yet you would ask mercy of me," said the demon, "and for what?"

"That I may repent."

"Repent?"

"Yes."

"Take your hands from your eyes, and look upon me."

Bill tremblingly obeyed.

"Now answer me."

"I will."

"Truly?"

"So help me"—

"Hold! Mention that name, and"—

"Mercy!" yelled Bill, shrinking even lower as the figure stretched forth its flaming hand towards him.

"Beware how you tempt me to consign you to a place that should be nameless," said the demon.

"I will—upon my soul, I will."

"Enough. What do you in this room?"

"I came for my rent."

"Do you pay your own?"

"Sometimes."

"Not always?"

"No."

"How much is owing you?"

"Five weeks; seven and sixpence," answered Bill.

"And how much do you owe?"

Bill again trembled.

"Quick, and speak truly. You cannot deceive me," said the figure, again raising its hand.

"Seven months," cried Bill, in a low voice.

"Can you pay it?"

"No."

"Do you ever intend to pay it?"

"Yes."

"The truth—or tremble!"

"No."

"And yet you would take goods entrusted to your lodger for the paltry sum she is unable to pay. You would deprive her of her livelihood, and perhaps her liberty, to obtain a few shillings to squander in debauchery, while your wife and children ask for bread. Are you a man? No, you are but a foul blot upon the title—a disgrace to this world—a thing unworthy of even a place in my regions. But in consideration of the benefit it will confer upon your wife and family in particular, and on society in general, I will rid them of your presence. And bear you to a place where—"

"Murder—mur—help! Sarah—Miss Folder, everybody, help! Oh, don't! For mercy's sake do have pity on me!" shrieked Jackson, flinging himself flat on the floor, and rolling about in an agony of terror.

"Come," said the horrible form, stooping down, and laying one hand on Bill's shoulder.

"It burns! it burns!" shrieked Bill. "Mercy! oh, have mercy on me! and I will be a good man. I will—I mean it!"

At this moment the door, which the figure had partially closed behind him, was pushed wide open, and Mrs. Jackson and Ellen stood on the threshold.

The supposed demon turned, and revealed to their gaze his phosphorous-covered face and chest, they uttered a low cry and hurried down the stairs to the passage, where Mrs. Jackson fairly fainted away, and the poor seamstress had to cling for support to the handrails of the banisters.

"Silence!" said the demon, quickly, turning to Bill; "and if you would have me spare you for a time, swear to do as I bid you."

"I—I will! Upon my soul I will."

"Then forgive this poor woman every farthing of the rent she owes you."

"I will."

"And never more molest, insult, or annoy her, either by act or deed."

"I won't forget it—I won't!"

"Never more strike your wife."

"Never."

"Work for her livelihood, like an honest, upright man. And devote the wages of your labours to your wife and children. Forsake drink, and seek to make your wife not only comfortable, but happy."

"I will," said Jackson, "I assure you I will."

"Swear it."

"I do, so help"—

"Hush! Enough. Remember your promise."

"I won't forget it—upon my soul I won't."

"And remember also that to break it, will summon me to your side, when no appeal can save you from my clutches. Remember! Beware—beware."

As the demon spoke, he held his arms wide apart, and backed from the room. As he crossed the threshold he dropped his arms, gave a quick and sudden bound, and disappeared.

With a shriek of relief, Bill sprang to his feet out of the room and down the stairs, as Spring-heeled Jack emerged from the pigeon dormer on the roof, and looked with a smiling face on the star-spangled sky.

CHAPTER X.

THE ROBBERY—A SCENE IN A VAULT—A TERRIBLE DOOM.

THE SHRIEKS of the poor seamstress reached the bar of the Pigeon Flyers, and caused not only the landlord of that establishment, but four or five unshaven, villainous-looking fellows, customers at the bar, to make their way to the door, and look inquiringly over at Bill Jackson's and hence the bleared eyes of the men were unable to penetrate the passage where Ellen was, so each looked at the other, and then turned to look after the beer they had left on the counter.

"Bill and his old woman having a shine, I suppose," said one. "It's no business of our'n, mates."

"None at all," said the landlord. "Ah! She's enough to aggravate a saint, she is, and I ain't got no pity for her. I don't like to see a woman always coming after her old man when he sits down to enjoy a pot and a smoke. It don't look well, it don't; and I know if it was me, I shouldn't stand it, that's all."

"'Taint right," chimed in the others. "Serve her right all she gets."

"I reckon that sanctified sort of girl as is a-lodging there puts her up to doing it; for the old woman's been a sight worse since she had Bill's front room up-stairs," said one who rejoiced in the name of Filcher. "She's a stuck-up bit of goods, I can tell you."

"She ain't got much to be proud on, I reckon," said the landlord, contemptuously.

"Proud on!—no; but she had the cheek to tell me she'd call the police if I didn't sheer off one night when I seed her standing at the door, and paid her the compliment of telling her I was a mind to kiss her. Lor'! You should have seen her; she was about a foot taller in a minute, and she turns up her noise at me as if I warn't as good as her. I should think I was, for I don't starve on shirt-making by a half-penny rushlight. Hallo!" he added, looking over at the window occupied by Ellen, "blowed if she ain't joined the early closing movement. Why, what's that a-hanging out of the window?"

This remark caused the others to look also, and eventually Joe walked out of the house and across the road, to examine the object more minutely.

His curiosity was aroused to know what the bundle contained, and he beckoned over one of his companions, induced him to stand with his face close to the wall of Jackson's dwelling, and permit him to mount on to his shoulders in order to enable Joe to obtain possession of the strangely situated bundle.

"Halves, of course," said the fellow, as he placed himself in the desired position.

"Of course, Tommy," was the reply as Joe, with great agility, commenced to clamber up his friend's body. "Don't shrink, and I'll have it in a jiffy."

Almost as soon as he had concluded speaking, Joe had mounted to the other's shoulders and grasped the bundle.

"Look alive, or I shall drop you."

Joe had firm hold of the bundle, but was unable to extricate it from its fastening, although he used every endeavour to do so.

Tommy, unable to longer endure the pressure of Joe's hobnails on his shoulders, shrank beneath his companion's weight; and holding frantically to the bundle to save himself, the rotten shirt gave way, and down Joe came to the ground with the bundle in his hand.

Fortunately for himself he dropped upon his feet without injury.

"Halves!" cried Tommy, laying his hand on the bundle.

"Then you don't have it," said Joe, vexed at the other for giving way beneath him.

"Why not?"

"Because you don't, that's all. You broke down in your half, and ain't entitled to it. Jemima!" he added, as the torn skirt parted and allowed the poor seamstress's work to fall to the ground. "If it ain't the slopwork of that gal, Tommy. Mum's the word, you know. You must be no-fly over the way. Or they'll want to go snacks. There's enough to fetch five bob round Blodger's dolly-shop."[18]

"Fence, you mean."

"Well, it's all the same, or leastways there's very little difference. The blokes ain't twigged us; so shut up, and we'll go snacks."

By the blokes Joe meant his companions at the bar of the Pigeon Flyers, who, after desultory glances at the bundle, as it hung suspended from the window, had turned again to their beer.

"Right you are, Joe; but where will you slum it till to-morrow?"

"Where I've put other things before."

"Where's that?"

"In the vault."

"The vault?"

"Yes, in the churchyard," said Joe. "It's a first-rate crib. No fear of its being overhauled. Ah, I forgot, you don't know it. I'll show it you, if you, if you like to come."

"A vault in a churchyard?" said Tommy, with just a perceptible shudder pervading his form.

"Yes, in Whitechapel churchyard."

"But how can you get in?"

"Why, there's a rail loose on the left-hand side of the gate; I lift that up, and then I goes to the vault that's got a little black door in the middle of the brickwork. It's never fastened, but shuts close to. Oh, it's a stunning place to slum anything it is; but keep it dark."

"Yes, yes," said Tommy. "But ain't you frightened?"

"Frightened of what?"

"The ghosts."

"Ghosts, I should like to see the ghost as could frighten me," said Joe, with a contemptuous curl of the lip.

"You ain't seen one, but you might," said Tommy.

"Go on, there ain't none, and if there was they wouldn't frighten me in a hurry."

"You don't know!"

"Don't I?" said Joe. "I should like to see one there to-night, I'd show it what sort of flesh of blood Joe Filcher is made of, I would."

"Will you go there to-night?"

"Yes—will you come?" and I'll show you the crib—it's a first rate slum."

"No, I'd rather not."

"You ain't half a chap," said Joe contemptuously; "but there, I'll go myself, and you go back to the Flyers. Mum you know, and if anybody asks for me, say I've gone home."

"All right!" said Tommy. "No fiddling!"

---

[18] Unlicensed pawn-broker.

"S'elp me tater![19] Now what do you take me for?" said Joe.

"All right, then, shares in the morning."

"As true as honour."

"Good night, then, only mind the ghosts," said Tommy, as he turned away to seek the bar of the Pigeon Flyers.

Joe Filcher watched him till he had entered the beerhouse, and then gathered up the skirt tightly in his hands, and turned away in the opposite direction, muttering, half aloud—

"The snivelling cur to be frightened of ghosts! Bah! I should just like to see one to-night in the vault—I just should, that's all!"

A tall, gentlemanly figure passed him with a hurried step, and as he drew his long Spanish cloak closer over his form, said with a smile, in a subdued tone—

"Your courage may be put to the test, my fine fellow. The railing to the left of the gate is loose. The vault used as a receptacle for stolen goods is formed of brick, with a small black door. Ah! Ah! we may meet there, my friend—brave friend, I should have said—meet there, and at midnight."

As he hurried along before Joe, the clocks of the churches in the neighbourhood chimed the half-hour after eleven.

Twelve o'clock had struck, and as its echoes died away, a tall figure forced its way through the door of a brick-built vault in Whitechapel churchyard.

It was the same figure which we have noticed pass Joe Filcher on his way to the same place to hide the poor seamstress's bundle, till he could take it to Blodger's fence, which it would not have been prudent for him to have done that night and at that hour, as the reputed dolly-shop—more than suspected of being what it really was—was being already closely watched by the officers.

Having effected an entrance into the vault Spring-heeled Jack—for he it was—struck a light with a phosphorous match, and looked around the gloomy place.

"Humph!" he muttered, as the match burned out, and left the vault again in Stygian darkness. "This is not a very inviting place. It's cold enough, dark enough, and damp enough to strike terror to the heart, and chill the blood in a man's veins, without the knowledge that human beings are festering in their shrouds at his side. Ugh! the place makes me shudder; yet why should it? What harm can there be in a corpse? None. From the living there is much more to fear, ay, much more. But I forget the purpose for which I came hither."

He took off his cloak, turned it, and drawing a hideous mask from his pocket, placed it on his face.

Then he groped his way to where he had seen a coffin standing on a pair of trestles, and placing his hand upon the lid, vaulted up and sat upon the last home of the dead.

"Now let the rascal come," he said, "and he shall receive the reward of his villainy. He must be a daring scoundrel to desecrate the resting-place of the dead, and make the grave a receptacle for his plunder; but courageous as he appears to be, his courage shall fail him to-night!"

Jack, when he emerged from the pigeon-dormer on the roof, had looked down into the street and heard the conversation of Joe and his companion, and saw the theft

---

[19]According to Albert Barrere's 1890 *A Dictionary of Slang, Jargon & Cant*, this was, at the time, an "oath or adjuration in common use, and of no definite signification".

committed on the seamstress's hidden work.

Disgusted at the act, he resolved to give them a fright, but upon Joe mentioning his intention of seeking the churchyard, our hero resolved to defer his purpose till that worthy should be within the precincts of his hiding-place.

The moments flew by, and Jack listened intently for the footfall of Joe, but no sound broke the stillness.

He began to fear that the ruffian would not make his appearance, and not much relishing his own situation, he had placed his hand to his mask to remove it, when he heard a stealthy step just outside the vault.

Jack strained his eyes through the darkness, towards where the little black door was situated, and drew his white cloak closer around him.

The door opened, and the figure of a man could just be traced by Jack in the square opening.

He held his breath, and continued to gaze anxiously.

He had no doubt that it was Joe, though he was unable to trace more than the outline of a human figure.

He had no fear that he would be discovered himself till the man entered the vault, or he revealed himself, for the blackness of the place was so dense, that no object could be seen without the aid of a light.

"But," thought Jack, all at once, "suppose the rascal should throw his ill-gotten gain into the vault, and go away, I shall be balked of my gratification, and he will not get the reward I intended for him, unless I follow and give him a fright among the tombstones."

Jack was about to leap off his seat, when, muttering a long curse at the darkness, Joe stepped over the threshold of the black door, and stood in the vault.

Then, pushing the door partly to behind him, and still holding it with one hand, and looking towards the front light of the churchyard beyond, he struck a phosphorous match on its panels.

The instant the match ignited Joe shut the door close, evidently because the light strengthened his courage for one thing—and for the other, from fear of its glimmer being seen outside the vault. Holding it so as to permit the flame to burn up brightly, he dropped the bundle at his feet, and placed his disengaged hand in his pocket for the purpose of extracting a piece of wax taper to ignite from the match, when he turned his head half-fearfully round, and catching sight of the horrible figure sitting on the coffin, he uttered a loud shriek of terror, dropped the match from his hand, and grasped at the door of the vault, which in his terror he did not succeed in laying hold of, and stumbling against the bundle, fell heavily to the ground.

Jack slipped quietly from the coffin.

In an instant Joe sprang to his feet, but so great was his terror, that he had completely forgotten the position of the door, and in his eagerness to escape, he stretched forth both hands and clutched at the coffin which Jack had just vacated.

With another cry of terror Joe sprang back.

The perspiration had started in cold drops from every pore of his body.

His limbs were trembling as if he had been struck with palsy, and his teeth chattered so loudly, that in the stillness of that vault they sounded like the rattling of a dice-box, and added even to the terrors of the already affrighted man.

Again he sought to find the door, when his coat was clutched from behind, and he was dragged violently back against the side of the coffin.

The blow resounded through the hollow vault like a clap of thunder, and its echoes mingled with the shriek of the terrified man.

A moment he appeared to stand bewildered and horror-struck, then with a bound he again sprung for the door.

As he grasped at it a soft substance struck against his face, and once more he recoiled.

Jack had silently raised the bundle from the ground and thrust it against Joe's cheek.

"Oh! this is horrible!" gasped the guilty wretch, as he once more came in contact with the coffin.

"Ha! ha! ha!" laughed Jack, in a hollow tone.

The sound echoed around the vault, and, to the affrighted senses of Joe, appeared to come from the coffin.

All strength deserted him now, and he staggered back till his shoulder rested against the side of the vault, and holding out his hands before him, he leaned for support against the cold brickwork, and gasped for breath.

Frantically he glared through the darkness with starting eyeballs.

His hair he could feel was stretching out and standing up on his head.

His knees knocked together, and he felt that gradually his limbs were sinking under him. Oh, how he strove to cry for help!

His tongue, however, clove to the roof of his mouth, and he could not utter a sound.

His lips became parched and dry, and his breath came in short gasps.

His heart beat against his side as if it would burst through his bosom, and its throbbing he could plainly hear in the awful stillness.

Truly he was terribly punished, for great indeed was the agony he endured.

Suddenly a strange luminous gleam of blue light played upon the coffin, and, as horror-struck Joe gazed towards it, he could just see the dim outline of a white ghastly figure standing beside it.

With a desperate effort, Joe summoned up all his energies to make once more for the door, and escape from that horrible place.

He reached it, his hands clasped its black panels: he drew it open, but ere he could pass through it, a hand seized his shoulder and held him firm. He turned a quick, fearful glance behind him and as his eyes encountered the fearful mask of Jack—now luminated with phosphorus—he uttered a shriek so loud, so agonising, that Jack released his hold.

Once more Joe sprang forward—his foot touched the threshold, he staggered for a moment, then fell on his face—dead!

CHAPTER XI.
THE ATTEMPTED CAPTURE—JACK'S ESCAPE.

THE FATE of Joe Filcher was a fearful end to a spree, for by such terms were the antics of Spring-heeled Jack called.

That worthy had no idea, in the darkness which prevailed, that his practical joke had deprived a fellow-creature of existence.

JACK PROTECTS THE YOUNG BALLET GIRL.

His idea was that, terror-stricken, he had fainted; and although Jack considered that what suffering he had caused the guilty wretch was a punishment well merited, he was not so callous-hearted as to refuse him assistance.

Therefore, on finding that Filcher did not move from the spot where he had fallen, he turned his cloak, erased the phosphorous marks from his face and person and, stooping down, drew the body of the man into the vault, and closed the door.

Then taking a match from his pocket, he obtained a light.

The pallor of the wretched man's features struck a chill to his heart, and the hand that held the light trembled perceptibly.

"He cannot—surely he cannot be dead!" he muttered, in tone half aloud, but which in that place sounded loud and unearthly, and caused even Jack to cast an anxious glance around him. "No, no," he added, after a pause, "the fellow has only fainted—the cool night air will revive him."

He placed one hand on Filcher's face, then started back in horror.

"Great heaven! he is dead!" he exclaimed.

"Dead!" was the hollow echo of the receptacle for departed humanity.

Jack was a brave man, but he felt his blood curdle in his veins.

The light went out, and left the vault in darkness.

"Yes, I believe the poor wretch is dead!" he said, "and though he deserves his fate, I cannot help feeling more like a murderer than an executioner. I will procure another light, and make sure that he has only fainted. Heaven grant that is the worst!"

He struck another match with a trembling hand.

It burned up, and threw its glare on the now upturned face of Joe Filcher and the cloth-covered coffin in the centre of the vault.

Anxiously, Jack stooped over the rigid body.

He placed his hand on his face.

It was cold—clammy cold.

He tore open the vest and shirt, and laid his hand upon Filcher's bosom.

Did his heart beat?

No; pulsation had ceased for ever.

Jack sprang to his feet.

"Curse this night's work!" he said, in a hollow voice. "But I must away. Hark! What's that?"

He hastily dashed the match to the ground and opened the door of the vault a few inches, and listened.

The sound of voices came plainly to his ears.

He strained his eyes in the direction whence the sounds came, and he could perceive several forms gathered together outside the railings of the churchyard.

Whilst standing with the little black door in his hand he heard one say—

"I tell you it was a fearful screech I heard, and it seemed to come from that vault."

"Then somebody's there," said another. "Where's a constable? It ought to be seen to."

"Perhaps it's a ghost," said another.

"A ghost?"

"Yes."

"Perhaps it is, for it was a horrible screech," said the first speaker. "Oh, here's the constable; we'll get him to go in and see what it was."

As Jack glanced towards the railings he perceived that the little crowd was gradually becoming larger, and that several had clustered around the tall figure of a man who had made his way to the spot.

"Humph, I'm in a pretty mess here," said Jack, "and how to get out of it I don't know. This is likely to be a serious affair, for should I be captured, I shall certainly be taken for the murderer of this man, and then—but no, I must find some means to get away. Ah, superstition is inherent in the hearts of all to a less or greater degree, and may serve me in good stead now. Some already believe the cry of this affrighted fellow emanated from a ghost. I will turn my cloak again, and trust to Providence, and my springs, for escape. Hallo! they are trying to force the gate; there is not a moment to lose. Quick, Jack! You must not be taken, or you'll stand your trial for murder—the murder of that poor devil who, though he deserved his fate, I wish he'd not met it at my hands!"

The crowd, which had now become considerably augmented in numbers, were endeavouring to force their way into the churchyard by pressing with all their might on the iron gates.

They were composed principally of the lowest and most ignorant of persons—wretches whose home was on the streets, whose bed the doorstep, whose coverlid the sky—that class, in fact, whose ignorance made them superstitious; and Jack did not feel so ill at ease as he might otherwise have done.

Finding all attempts to force the gates futile, the mob commenced clamouring for the officer to climb over the railings—a proceeding which he evidently objected to for some time, either from a disinclination to put himself to the trouble, or a fear of encountering something supernatural.

This delay gave Jack ample time to change his costume and make himself as hideous as he could.

At length, however, the clamour of the mob became so great that the officer, assisted by the bystanders, climbed the iron railings and dropped down on the inside of the churchyard.

Jack then left the vault in a crouching position behind a tall tombstone, where he waited in breathless suspense.

The constable, however, though repeatedly informed that the cry had come from the direction of the vault, would persist in making his way to the opposite course, till a voice in the crowd bawled out—

"There's an officer! Blowed if he ain't afraid to do his duty. Hoot[20] him. Yah! yah!"

"Yah! yah!" came from a dozen throats and appeared to have the desired effect—viz., of changing the course of the guardian of the peace, and leading him to make his way, staff in hand, towards the vault.

He had approached very slowly within about half-a-dozen yards of the place, when Jack sprang quickly up from his recumbent position right before him.

The man was thus brought to a sudden stop. For a moment he gazed upon the white cloak, and then, as it again disappeared behind the tall tombstone, he uttered a yell of horror, dropped his staff from his hand, turned, and sped with the greatest alacrity

---

[20] Shout loudly in scorn or disapproval.

towards the gate, yelling out in affrighted accents—

"A ghost! A ghost!"

The cry was taken up by those outside, and Jack, anxious to increase the impression, believing that it would tend to enable him the easier to beat a retreat from the churchyard, sprang up on to the top of the tall headstone, stood there for a moment, and then disappeared behind it.

"There it is! there it is!" exclaimed a number of voices, and a dozen fingers towards the stone.

"Where? where!" exclaimed those whose attention had been otherwise attracted.

"There! Don't you see? That stone. It was a white figure—so tall—such awful eyes and horns!" and numerous other exclamations.

The officer, who had turned to the gates, was now endeavouring to climb over them into the street.

"Why don't you do your duty?" said a weazened-faced, elderly man, who had been summoned to the spot by the clamour. "You're a pretty fellow for a policeman if you run away from a shadow!"

"I tell you it's a ghost," said the officer, fairly out of breath with his exertions.

"Bah!" said the elderly person, contemptuously. "It's some rascal got in there to frighten people, and you ought to arrest him."

"You had better do it yourself," said the officer.

"I am too old, but I help to pay younger men," was the reply. "You ought to be ashamed of yourself, and deserve to be reported. There's a policeman! there's a policeman!"

This remark called forth jeers from the crowd, and ashamed at the cowardly part he was playing, the officer dropped down again into the churchyard, and, looking at those on the other side of the railings, he said—

"Who's afraid? I tell you what, there ain't one of yer got the pluck to come over here."

"Ain't we?" said one, a tall, strapping costermonger, grasping a railing in either hand and drawing himself up them.

"Come on, then, if you have!" said the officer, with a sigh of relief at the prospect of having someone to keep him company. "Come on, then, and let's see what you'll do!"

The man soon succeeded in climbing over and dropping down beside the constable.

"Now, where's the ghost?" he said.

"There," was the reply of the policeman, pointing to the spot where he had seen Jack.

"Then I'll have a shy at him."

Feeling his courage greatly revived by having so powerful a companion at his side, the officer once more made his way among the graves, searching for his staff as he went.

This he saw at last, and, as he stooped to pick it up, Jack sprang from behind a headstone, and alighted on his back.

So sudden and unexpected was this act, that the officer uttered a cry and fell flat on his face, while his brave companion turned and fled at a terrific speed.

He did not go many steps, however, before his foot, striking against one of the grass-covered mounds, sent him sprawling, and as he fell he struck his head with great violence against the footstone, completely stunning himself for the moment.

The instant he recovered from the shock he was up again and off towards the gate, over which he clambered in a manner that could have done credit to an acrobat.

Another shout arose from the assembled mob as once more they caught sight of the white figure, and the excitement became intense, amid which the costermonger slunk away from the scene.

As soon as the officer fell to the earth our hero sprang away, and once more hid himself behind one of the numerous stones.

"Help!" shouted the constable, scrambling to his feet, and looking with horror around him.

He had clutched at his staff, and retained it in his hand, and as he called out he made frantic blows with it at the air.

"There he is again!" shouted the mob as they caught another glimpse of Jack, as he endeavoured to steal away to the opposite side of the churchyard.

The policeman looked around, and seeing nothing, again walked towards the gate.

But he paused ere he had taken half-a-dozen steps.

The mob were again uttering numerous exclamations at his timidity, and he hesitated.

The fact was, he knew not which was best to encounter, the jeers of those outside, or the supposed ghost within the churchyard—the former he could ill brook, the latter he dreaded.

So he looked nervously around him, and utterly bewildered, he placed one hand on the tombstone and panted for breath.

As he thus stood, Jack sprang up behind him, raised his right hand, and brought it down with all his force on the crown of the officer's hat, driving it completely over his face down to his chin.

"Murder!" shrieked the constable, making a desperate blow with his truncheon, and bringing his knuckles into contact with the headstone of a neighbouring grave. "Murder! Help! Help!"

"Ha! ha! ha!" laughed Jack, striking another blow at the officer's hat, and driving it still lower. "My brave fellow, why don't you do your duty!"

Then giving him a kick behind, the officer started forward, and, being unable to see where he was going, ran full butt against the footstone of a grave, and fell over it, hurting himself very considerably.

Jack saw that the man's cries were bringing him assistance, and while the officer lay on the ground, frantically tugging at his hat, and endeavouring to force it up from over his face, and several of the mob had proceeded to climb the iron railings, he darted away as quickly as he could to the opposite side of the churchyard.

Here he crouched down within the shadow of a tomb, hastily changed his cloak, and cast an anxious look along the railings for the best place to escape from the ground.

"There is enough of this for to-night," he said to himself, as he rose and looked around him. "Now I will go."

"No, you won't," said a voice behind him, and a man who had stolen noiselessly to the spot laid his hand upon Jack's shoulder.

"Here he is!" he added, shouting at the top of his voice. "I've got the ghost—I've got him!"

"Hold him tight, then, my fine fellow!" said Jack, giving himself a sudden twist from the man's hold.

"You don't escape—here, some of you, come and help me!" he shouted again, seizing

Jack by the shoulder.

A loud shout arose in answer to the man's call, and several persons hurried over to the graves to his assistance.

At this moment the clock struck one.

"Time's up!" said Jack, dealing the man a blow in the face, and, wrenching himself from his hold, bounded up and over the iron railings.

CHAPTER XII.

JACK MEETS WITH ELLEN—THE SEAMSTRESS'S ERRAND—A STRUGGLE—THE SUICIDE AND ATTEMPT AT RESCUE.

AMID SHOUTS of disappointment and exclamations of surprise, Jack alighted safely on the other side of the railings, at a spot where no one was about. Turning, and uttering a loud laugh of derision at his baffled foes, he hurried away as quickly as possible, keeping to the back streets, in case of pursuit, which he feared would be hot and fierce should the body of Joe Filcher be discovered.

It was about two o'clock when he strolled leisurely along Bishopgate. He had just lighted a cigar, and as he blew the wreaths of smoke from his lips was thinking over his night's work, when a hurried footstep close behind caused him to glance over his shoulder, and an exclamation rise to his lips.

Scarcely was it uttered, when the figure which had called it forth passed him with a nervous hurried gait, and sped along towards London Bridge.

"Surely," he muttered. "I have seen that delicate figure before, and the face, too, or I am much mistaken! It was but a hurried glance I had, either now or a few hours since, yet I am certain it has the same woe-begone features. What can she do here at this hour?"

The female whose step had attracted his notice, and who had hurried by him in such a quick, nervous manner, was none other than the poor seamstress, Ellen Folder.

The wretched girl, as soon as the excitement had somewhat subsided in her miserable dwelling, had returned to her room, and, anxious about her work, had gone to the window, to find that it was no longer suspended over the sill.

The shock of this discovery seemed almost to deprive her of breath; then she hurried into the street, but of course found not the bundle.

"Gone!" she said, in heart-broken accents. "Oh! I am ruined! Undone! Levy will never believe me if I tell him the whole truth! He will accuse me of making away with it— demand its price or send me to jail! I cannot pay him for it, and he will have no mercy! What's to be done—what's to be done!"

Poverty and toil had already weakened her nerves to such a degree that she was unable to bear up against this new misfortune, and alone and friendless in the world, with a dread of a prison and the brand of a felon, she hurriedly put on her bonnet and shawl, and hurried from the house.

Where did she intend to go?

Anywhere—anywhere!

She knew not—cared not—whither her footsteps led her—anywhere from the wrath of him who paid less for honest labour than honest men pay for the support of the criminal.

Her life had long been a wretched one—toiling early and late for a paltry pittance scarcely sufficient to keep soul and body together, and now the cup of misery was full to the brim. It could bear no more.

She reached Bishopsgate church.

This edifice was the first object which had attracted her attention since she left her little room to go she cared not whither.

She paused for a moment, and looked at the tall white stone which marked the last home of the departed and then with a deep sigh turned away, muttering to herself.

"They are at peace! Why should I wish to live, when nothing but misery is before me? What is the use of life to a wretch like me? Better that I rest in the silent grave than live as I have done! Yes, they are at peace! Why should I live—why should I live, with nothing to live for—nobody to care for me, or even give me a kind word! Heaven forgive me! I am sorely tired."

But for the sound of the clock striking the hours, and the sight of the churchyard, she might have returned home to her wretched dwelling when the fever of her brain had abated, and her mind become somewhat more at ease, but now her thoughts ran into another channel, and that was—death!

Relief from all earthly suffering—escape from the vengeance of a hard-handed and hard-hearted employer!

On, then, with seething brain, and quick, tottering, nervous steps—on, over the flags of the London streets in the dead hour of the night with only the sound of her own footfall to jar upon her ears!

On, with beating heart and tearful eye—on, with pale cheeks rendered more ghastly by the flickering lamps, towards where the river wound its serpentine course!

On to the goal she had resolved to reach ere morning dawned upon the slumbering city.

On to rest her wearied soul and body—on, on to the grave.

Her mind was made up—her resolves were formed.

Before her was oblivion—behind her, poverty, insult, and the jail!

She would not hesitate. No, she would hurry forward to reach that "bourne from whence no traveller returns."[21]

No more with aching eyes and bursting heart would she ply the needle by the half-penny rushlight. No more would she tremble at the drunken tones of her landlord, or seek for employment from the hard-fisted Jew. No longer, over-worked and half-starved, would she live on from day to day a life of wretchedness, when one plunge would rid her for ever of all her fears and her sufferings.

And as she drew nearer and nearer to that spot from whence she had resolved to take the fatal leap, her footsteps quickened and her sorrowing heart ached less acutely.

Still she saw nothing as she went along. Her gaze was turned upon her soul, and could spare not a passing glance for outward objects.

She saw not, heeded not, the sudden pause and astonished look of Jack, as she hurried past him. She heard not his quick footfall on the stone flags as he sped after her, so engrossed was she with the act she mediated.

Not was it till his hand was laid upon her shoulder that she became cognizant of the presence of another human being.

---

[21] Hamlet, Act III, Scene, 1, ll. 1772–3.

Then she uttered a cry, and started round.

A lamp cast a flickering light upon his face, and she almost shrieked as she turned and sped away from the spot.

Jack had forgotten to remove his mask when he made good his escape from the churchyard: a circumstance which might have caused him some inconvenience had he met with anyone on his route.

Still the cause of the girl's flight and terror did not strike him, and anxious to inform her of where she might find her stolen work, he rushed after her.

The girl heard his footsteps behind her, and redoubled her speed.

Terror added wings to her flight.

"By heavens! She runs well," muttered Jack; "but what can induce her to fly from me—what brings her here at this hour?

Over the flags they went, the girl ever and anon casting terrified glances behind her, and struggling to increase her speed as she perceived Jack gaining upon her.

"Stop! Stop!" he cried, "I have something to say to you. I will not harm you—I pledge you my word I will not!" he cried, as he stretched forth his hand to stay her flight.

But the girl only bounded on the quicker.

She had eluded his grasp, and placed a greater distance between them.

"Do not seek to avoid me," he cried; "I assure you I am your friend."

"Oh! leave me—let me go!" she answered, without slackening her speed; "I have no friends."

"Listen to me."

"Go. Do not stop me."

"Whither do you fly?" asked Jack, as he again essayed to stop her progress.

"From the cruel world!" she gasped. "Oh! in heaven's name! let me go."

Jack had grasped at her shawl.

She was held by it a moment, but the next she sprang away, leaving it in his hand.

This enabled her to place a good space between them.

Jack stood with the worn shawl in his hand, looking in surprise for some moments after the fleeing figure of Ellen.

"Poor girl," he mentally ejaculated, "what can be her purpose? Why does she thus fly from me—where can she be going? From the cruel world. What do those words portend? Ah!" he added, flinging the shawl to his feet as the truth suddenly flashed across his mind, "does she meditate suicide? Her strange manner, her hurried speed, convinces me that she does. Jack, you have killed one poor wretch to-night; atone for that unintentional deed by saving this poor mortal from herself—from a crime she stops not to think of! Away, Jack! Away! Or she will elude your arm. 'Stop! stop!' 'Tis useless to call, she is deaf to entreaty. Quick, Jack! Quick! Or the dark river will claim its victim!"

He gathered up the folds of his long cloak, in order that they should not impede his progress, and bounded along after the fleeing girl at a speed that was truly surprising.

Gradually he gained upon her.

Her ears now alive to every sound, Ellen heard his quick footfall, and struggled to run even faster.

But her strength was failing her.

Her breath came in short, thick gasps, and a pain in her side, caused by the exertions she made, compelled her to slacken her pace.

Jack saw this and hurried forward.

Again he had reached her.

Again his hand was upon her shoulder.

Once more he had stayed her flight towards the grave.

But, as he held her forcibly, she gave utterance to a shriek so wild and piercing, that Jack let go his hold and started back.

"You shall not go!" he cried, as he quickly recovered himself, and again sprang forward to stay her.

But as he stretched forth his arm it was seized by a man, who, aroused from a doorway where he had been standing by the cry of the half-frantic girl, had sprung forward to her aid, believing her to be one of those unfortunate wretches whom some imagine, because they are fallen, may be insulted or outraged with impunity.

This circumstance enabled Ellen to again rush on, which she did, despite her loss of breath and the pain she endured, the new-comer urging her forward by saying—

"Run—run, and leave this blackguard[22] to me! We are man to man, and though want has weakened a once-powerful frame, I have still sufficient strength left to chastise the scoundrel who can insult a defenceless woman."

Jack had grasped the man's shoulders with the intention of hurling him to the earth, but, as he gave utterance to these words, he released his hold, and, with a look of admiration, which was lost upon the man, on account of our hero's face still being covered by the hideous mask, he said—

"Whoever you be, those sentiments show a noble mind and a good heart; and the utterance of them has saved you a fall, perhaps, that you would have felt for many a long day. Let go your hold!"

"That you may follow and insult that poor girl, whom, perhaps want and villainy have driven to the streets? No, you get not out of my clutches till I can hand you over to an officer."

"On the word of a man, I seek not to harm her," cried Jack.

"On the word of a man, you shall not!" was the quick reply.

"Fool!" said Jack, annoyed now at finding his good intentions were likely to be thwarted, "I seek to save that woman from hurrying to self-destruction."

"All very fine, but fellows who would save another a pang do not go about in the dead of night with hideous masks over their faces to prevent discovery and punishment for their villainies."

"Ah!" said Jack, now recollecting his mask, "but, hark you, I wish to protect that girl, and I am determined to endeavour to do so. I admire the sentiments of your heart, and they do you honour, whoever you may be, but while I suffer you to hold me thus I am, however unwillingly, permitting that poor girl to rush unbidden into the presence of her Maker. Again I ask you to release your hold, for I would not offer violence to one whose words and deeds stamp him as a man."

"Spring-heeled Jack, every man, woman and child in London have cause to dread your being at liberty. It becomes the bounden duty of every man to attempt your

---

[22]Derogatory term referring to servant, criminal or others of a base nature.

capture; and now I have you, you do not get away easily. Your excuses will avail you nothing. Here I hold you till I can place you in the hands of an officer, and make you answer to those laws you have for some time outraged with impunity."

"You know"—

"That mask betrays you."

"Beware, I am stronger than you," said Jack.

"And I a better one than you, though gold may line your pockets, and my form is attenuated by want and suffering!"

"What I have said is true; and now will you take your hands from me, or must I hurl you to the earth, that I may pursue and save that poor girl!"

"I suffer you not to go, while I have strength to detain you," was the determined reply.

"Then thus do I release myself!" said Jack.

And so saying, he grasped the man by either shoulder, and strove to hurl him from him.

But the man clutched at Jack's throat, and thus prevented his intention.

Jack saw in an instant that his victory would not be an easy one, and he summoned up all his strength for a final effort.

The distant footfall of an officer, too, he could now hear distinctly on the flags of the pavement, and he felt that he must obtain his liberty quickly, or all chance of saving Ellen Folder would be lost.

He shifted his hands from his opponent's shoulders to his waist, and by a quick and sudden jerk lifted him off his feet.

"By heaven, I would not harm you willingly!" cried Jack. "Will you permit me to go on my way?"

"I will not release you but by force!" said the man resolutely, and struggling fiercely.

"Then blame me not!" exclaimed our hero, as by one mighty effort he dashed his adversary to the earth, and turning quickly, hurried away as fast as he could in the direction whence Ellen had fled.

The poor fellow was partially stunned by the fall, but he quickly recovered himself, and springing to his feet, bounded after Jack, who had by this time placed as great a distance between himself and his pursuer, as Ellen had between herself and Jack.

Jack did not stop to look behind him, although he could hear his pursuer, who finding that he was unable to gain upon our hero, commenced shouting loudly—

"Stop him!—stop him!"

"Confound the fellow!" muttered Jack. "He'll wake the whole city!"

Still he kept on his way without meeting with any further obstruction, and at length gained the bridge, and a sight of the outline of a female figure, standing on one of the seats.

"'Tis her! 'tis her! And I am too late to save her!" he cried aloud, gathering the folds of his cloak still higher up around his body, and bounding forward with terrific leaps. "Curses on the fellow for the delay."

He ran on.

"Hold! for heaven's sake, hold!" he shrieked as he dashed towards the half-maddened girl.

Ellen heard his voice, turned her head, and caught sight of his form.

With a cry so wild, yet plaintive, she mounted the stonework of the balustrade.

"For God's sake, hold!" shrieked Jack, in a loud, excited voice.

But Ellen flung her arms wildly above her head, and laughed aloud.

Jack was now but half-a-dozen yards from the seat.

His heart beat audibly.

His eyes were fixed with a fascinated glare upon the figure of that girl standing out in the semi-darkness on that narrow ledge, with the black waters running swiftly on, a long, long way beneath her.

A few steps, and he could seize her frail form in his strong arms.

A few steps more, and he could save a soul from destruction.

With bated breath he dashed madly forward, his eyes starting from their sockets, his arms extended before him.

He reached the seat—he uttered a short, sharp cry.

But as his hand was within a few inches of her dress, Ellen sprang away from his grasp, out over the balustrade into the space beyond, and disappeared from his sight.

A moment Jack stood like one transfixed, dashed his hat to the ground, and strove to tear his cloak from his shoulders, which in his anxiety and haste, he was unable to do; so, gathering up its fold, he mounted the balustrade, cast one look down into the black waters beneath, then sprang far, far out from the narrow ledge, resolved to save or perish in the attempt.

CHAPTER XIII.

THE BALLET GIRL AND HER PERSECUTOR—AN OUTRAGE AND A PROTECTOR.

THE CURTAIN had fallen—the house was in all but darkness—the long tiers of boxes had been covered with canvas to save their curtains from the dust, and but a few remained in that home of the drama, which a short time before had been filled from pit to ceiling, and resounded to the shouts of laughter, the loud applause, or the strains of the orchestra.

Yes, the theatre was deserted by all but a few, and that few were the members of the corps de ballet, who had hurried away to their dressing rooms to change the gauze and spangles for the cotton and the stuff—to wash the paint and powder from their faces—those pale, wan cheeks, on which consumption, want and wretchedness, were in far too many instances depicted.

Young girls and matrons were among them—the mother and the courtesan, the innocent and the pure, the lost and the fallen, but all were hurrying to leave the precincts of the building; some to return to their homes and families, some to adjourn to the coffee and oyster-rooms, some to the wash-tub and the needle, and others to—But let us not be uncharitable to a class whose struggles for existence are indeed great and hard to bear, whose calling brings down upon them too often the unmerited contempt of more fortunate sisters, and whose every act, look, and word are misconstrued by those prudish dames who can see no goodness in a public life.

But for the stage, how many a poor girl would starve at her needle, or faint at the ironing board; but for the few shillings obtained by joining the corps de ballet how many a child would ask in vain for food of its mother—how many a poor wretch would find a home in the parish workhouse, or an existence in the public streets!

But there are a few (and where is the calling that will not produce them?) whose natural inclinations lead them into a life of debauchery and sin.

Do not condemn the poor ballet girl as the lowest grade of womanhood, for in every calling and every stage there are fail sisters and unfortunate women.

But with these we have nothing to do—we leave them to the serpent tongues of their own uncharitable sex, and will follow only one—a pure innocent, beautiful girl—out of the room, where she has changed the gauze for the homely muslin-de-laine—the wreath for the little hat and feather—the scarf for the warm, though much-worn jacket. She was anxious to return home, where her mother awaited her presence—that mother she had taken to the stage to assist to keep from the common home of the aged poor—the workhouse; and with a light step she hurried through the stage-door into the street, and, as she perceived the figure of a man, respectably attired, waiting by the wall of the theatre, she averted her gaze, and hurried along at a quick, nervous pace, muttering inwardly—

"There again! Oh! why does he seek to force his presence upon me? Heaven grant he may not see me! and that I may to-night escape his odious advances."

But there was no such good fortune in store for the poor ballet girl.

The man saw her, and instantly stepped forward to oppose her passage.

His appearance and costume betokened that he was at least well-to-do in the world, but the lines on his face, now brought out clearly by the street lamp, stamped him as one to whom debauchery was a portion of his life.

Features that otherwise would have been handsome were defiled by the traces of late hours and over-indulgence—in fact, "libertine" was stamped there as plainly by nature's hand as it was possible to be.

"Well, my dear," he said, familiarly, "you have not kept me waiting so long to-night. Oh! the delight with which I watched you in the ballet! I had not a single glance for another; my whole thoughts were centred upon you!"

"Sir," replied the girl, "pray allow me to pass? my mother will be anxious till I return."

"Why so coy?" Come, now; you know I admire you, and"—

"Night after night you will persist in forcing yourself upon me!" said the girl, as the tears rose to her eyes, and she stepped off the path into the roadway, in order to endeavour to pursue her course. "I cannot understand such conduct. It is unmanly to thus pursue a poor girl who wishes to have nothing to say to you."

"It is because you are poor I take so much interest in you," said the man.

"I thank you; but must decline to hold any conversation with one who to me is a stranger," said the girl.

"That I am so is not my fault," said the young man. "I have long endeavoured to become better acquainted with you."

"I have no desire that such should be the case," was the remark. "And now, sir, be good enough to understand that I cannot listen further to you, and I trust that you have not so far forgotten the meaning of the word 'gentleman' as to molest me further either on this night or any other when returning from my professional duties."

"Suffer me, then, to see you in the daytime," he said, quickly.

"It cannot be."

"Why not?"

"We are strangers."

JACK'S SUDDEN APPEARANCE SAVES A LIFE.

"A few hours in each other's society will remove that barrier."

"But I have no wish for your society," she said.

"Give me a reason."

"Our positions in the world are evidently so different."

"What of that?"

"Much—very much. You are evidently rich; I am poor—very poor."

"That makes no difference to me."

"But to me it does."

"Nonsense! 'Tis a foolish pride that would induce you to scorn the love of the man who could place wealth at your feet, change your poverty-stricken home to one of splendour, and make your life of toil one round of pleasure and happiness."

The girl sighed, and endeavoured to pass on her way.

The libertine, however, shifted his position, and put forth his hand to stay her.

"Do not flee from me thus," he said.

"Nay, sir; I must go."

"Stay but one minute."

"My mother waits anxiously for my return home," she said.

"Not anxiously as I have waited to see you here," he said. "Come, do not flee from me as though I were some terrible monster. Grant me a minute's speech."

"What can you, a stranger, have to say to me? Nothing that I can hear."

"I have. Listen. From the moment I saw you my heart beat with a strange sensation towards you. Then you were habited in your fairy garb, and your natural beauty enhanced by the appliances of the costumier's art—never did I see a being so beautiful as you! Your loveliness had enchained my heart—made it your captive! From that moment I resolved to throw aside all distinction of position, rank, and fortune, and strive to win the love of her who had already won mine. The curtain fell on the fairy group, and I hurried to the stage-door to await your coming. I recognised you in an instant, for the promptings of my breast pointed out, though so changed in garb, the woman I sought! That beauty I had so admired on the stage was still retained when off the boards, and if anything, my heart yearned more strongly towards you than ever!"

"Pray let me pass!" cried the girl.

"Nay, hear me to the end," he continued. "I love you—would take you from this life which I know is distasteful to you—would surround you with wealth and splendour, study your every wish, and make you the envy of thousands. This will I do. Now, will you be mine?"

"Dare I believe you?"

"You may."

"You love me?"

"I do."

"A stranger, whom you know not even by name—a poor girl whom poverty has driven to seek a livelihood by a calling which merits jeers and contempt of half the world."

"Even so; for I heed not that," he replied, taking her hand in his own, and looking into her pale face.

"And you would rescue me from this life—place me in a home of splendour and plenty?"

"I would."

"And what return do you ask for this?" she said, slowly and pointedly, fixing her liquid eye upon his face with a penetrating and inquiring glance.

"What return can I ask?" he said.

"Ay, what?" she replied.

"Your love."

"My love?"

"Yes."

"My heart?"

"Even so."

"And my hand?"

The libertine did not reply.

"Speak, man!" she said, imperiously. "Do you seek to make me your wife?"

"Yes—yes; that is—but"——

"But what?" she cried, tearing her hand from his hold, and drawing herself proudly up before him, her eyes flashing with an indignant fire, and her pale face suffused with a blush of shame.

"My dear!"

"Speak, and speak truly. Do you pursue me with the desire to make me a happy, honourable wife, or only a libertine's mistress?" she cried almost furiously.

The man's features underwent a perceptible change as she spoke, and his tones were low and stammering as he said—

"You do not understand—you"——

"I do understand you. The motive which brought you to persecute me night after night on my way from the theatre to my home—I do understand you, sir. But now understand me. I know the calling I pursue is looked upon as one which hold among its votaries only the lost and fallen of the female sex—poor girls who can be induced to purchase existence and splendour at the price of honour. You are one who believes us all such, but you are mistaken. All are not fallen; all are not purchased by golden promises, or caught by gilded baits. Stand aside and let me pass; I can read your hopes and desires in your face. You have mistaken the poor ballet girl, who scorns your offers, and spurns, with the contempt they deserve, your disgusting promises!"

"My charmer!"

"Begone, sir, and leave me to pursue my way in peace to my poor but honourable home," she said, thrusting him contemptuously aside, and passing on with quick steps.

"Nay, listen a moment!" he exclaimed.

"I have already listened too long."

"You refuse an offer thousands would be proud to accept," he continued, walking on by her side.

"I scorn an offer which every honourable, right-minded woman would look upon with loathing and disgust!" she replied.

"You are mad!"

"I am true."

"The life you now lead cannot last for ever," he said. "Youth and beauty soon fade, and then, what lies before you but the poorhouse?"

"The knowledge that I did not sell happiness, fame—all for a libertine's gold!"

"And your mother—have you no care for her? Would you see her starve or die in a workhouse, when you might administer to her every want, and smooth the declining hours of her existence with all those comforts wealth would bring?" he said, looking with a sidelong glance, to see the effect of his words.

"Do you think she would purchase comfort at the price of her daughter's shame?" asked the girl, in a pained tone.

"She need not know it."

"Need not?"

"No; you could tell her you were wedded," he said.

"And add lies to my other sins?"

"They would be excusable in such a case," said the libertine.

"Think you my looks—my words, would not betray the fearful truth? Oh, man! man! how are you fallen!" she said, sadly, and increasing her speed.

"Oh, girl! how foolish you must be," he said, "to do battle with a life of poverty, because the world says we shall not follow the bent of our inclinations. Those who would condemn the loudest, would the soonest be guilty of that which they blame in others. But what would be the opinions of others to you? Would you lose friends? No, for the wealth would make them for you tenfold. Gold will hide a thousand sins, and make you respected where poverty only brings you contempt!"

"Speak no more, but leave me!"

"I have followed you too long—I cannot lose you now."

"Your words are poison to my ears and daggers to my heart! If you have one spark of manly feeling, you will let me proceed alone," she said, bursting into tears.

"Spurn me not from you! By heaven! I pity as well as love you!" he cried.

"Love! that is impossible."

"Why impossible?"

"Because love is a pure and holy passion," was the reply.

"Then I do love you."

"Would you lead me to the altar?"

"Of love?—yes."

"Would you make me your wife?"

"I would make you mine—wholly mine," he replied, quickly.

"But would you make me a wife, as custom and the law only recognise the term?"

"I would make you that which, if not in the sight of man, at least in the sight of God would be a wife."

"And yet you profess to love me!" cried the girl. "Of shame—shame upon you! I am the poor and wretched, but the position you offer me would but embitter my miseries—plunge me to despair—bow the gray hairs of her who gave me being with same and sorrow to the grace."

"Pshaw! At most t'would be but a momentary pang."

He seized her hand, and held it firmly.

He bent his head down and looked into her flushed face.

He saw the tears trembling on her eyelids—the nervous twitching of the muscles of her mouth.

From these he augured well for his own base course.

He bent his head still lower.

His lips almost touched her ear.

"Girl," he said, in a whisper, "be mine, and I will heap gold at your feet with which you can make a bright existence for her who now waits for the paltry pence you have earned to buy her bread. Away with all prudish thoughts. You shall be my wife in all but name. Hesitate no longer, whisper your consent, and be mine."

Had an adder stung her, she could not have started back with greater terror.

She tore her hand from his grasp with a violent jerk.

She stood gazing on him with frowning brow and compressed lips.

Proudly erect she stood.

Defiantly contemptuous was her mien.

Then her lips parted, and one word alone issued from between them.

It came in a husky, half-hissing whisper, and that word was, "Scoundrel!"

Then she turned and fled.

The libertine stood for several moments gazing after her pretty figure, and then he started off in pursuit.

The streets were comparatively deserted and the bye-ways into which they had penetrated contained no one out of doors.

After about a hurried run of two minutes, the ruffian caught up to the terrified and disgusted ballet girl as she was about to turn the corner of a short, narrow street, the houses of which spoke only too plainly the poverty of its inhabitants.

She felt his hand upon her shoulder, and uttered a short, sharp cry.

"Hark you, girl," he said, as he brought her to a dead stop; "I have condescended to sue for your favours, but now you shall sue to me for mercy! I have marked you out for a victim, and I will humble your proud spirit to the dust. You cannot escape me! May 'tis useless to struggle!"

"Help! help!" cried the poor girl, struggling to release herself from the ruffian's grasp.

"You struggle in vain," he said, forcing her close to him, and endeavouring to imprint a kiss on her lips. "I will make you mine, despite your cries and struggles. You have none to help you here; and now I command, where before I pleased so abjectly."

He drew her to his bosom—he pressed his lips to her cheeks and forehead, while the girl cried aloud for help.

Suddenly his hat was dashed violently from his head, and as he released his hold on the girl, and staggered back, a strong arm encircled the waist of the poor affrighted ballet girl, and a blow, aimed with terrific force at the face of the ruffian, knocked him over as if he had been shot.

As he fell from its force, striking his head against a post at the corner of the street, the girl looked up into the face of her protector, and started back with a cry, as she saw the hideous mask of Spring-heeled Jack!

CHAPTER XIV.

IN THE DARK WATERS—THE BARGEMAN'S TERROR—THE STRUGGLE FOR LIFE—SAVED AT LAST.

DOWN! DOWN! with the folds of his large cloak carried back from his shoulders by the wind caused in his descent from the bridge. Down, like an arrow, into the bosom of the black, though now smooth waters of the Thames, went Spring-heeled Jack after the wretched girl whom grief had led to make an attempt upon her life.

With a loud splash the waters closed over his form, burying him in darkness for a few seconds, during which time he experienced a painful sensation of suffocation, the terrific height from which he had jumped depriving him almost of his breath ere he reached the surface of the river.

Then he felt himself lifted up, and the next instant he perceived above him a black mass, dotted here and there with a faint glimmering light, which momentarily grew brighter as his eyes became accustomed to the gloom.

It was the bridge and the lamps thereon which had first met his vision as he rose out of the murky depths of the stream, consequently he had turned or been forced completely round either in his descent or ascent, and he instantly changed his position and struck out vigorously.

He was sure of the direction in which the body of the unfortunate girl would float, and as the tide was running down it would be carried towards the pool, and the long row of small craft which rode at anchor there.

Ghostly indeed did the vessels look in that dim light, with their dark hulls and bare masts, but Jack saw them not.

His anxious gaze swept around the black surface of the water in search of her who had excited his pity.

His eyes growing accustomed to the blackness, he had little difficulty in making out small objects at a considerable distance.

The boats, moored to the wharfs, rising and falling with the gentle undulations of the water, the buoy rocking to and fro by the action of the stream, or the shadow of any object on the shore, he knew in an instant, and hence he was not deluded into the belief that either were the form of Ellen floating along to eternity.

His cloak greatly impeded his action, and once or twice he essayed to release himself of it, but unable to do so, he looked searchingly around, and kept himself almost in a stationary position in the water.

"She cannot have floated far out from the bridge," he muttered, "for I must have touched the water almost as soon as she did herself. Poor thing, I fear she has struck her head against an abutment and sank never to rise any more, or else her frail form has been driven beneath one of the barges, and if so there is little hope of saving her. By heaven! I feel myself being drawn forcibly towards them," he added, striking out so as to place a greater distance between himself and a couple of barges which lay moored opposite a wharf on the city side of the bridge, and against whose bows the waters broke and parted as they rushed on towards the sea.

He had taken but a couple of strokes when a low, plaintive cry floated to his ears and he turned as quickly as possible in the direction whence the sound had proceeded.

There, close to one of the barges, he could perceive the head and arms, as they were moved wildly about, of a human being, and, despite the risk he knew he ran of being drawn under the flat bottom of the barges, he struck boldly out for the poor girl's side.

It required little exertion on his own part, for the strength of the current, and the magnetic influence exercised upon it by the vessels, hurled him forward with great velocity.

A quarter of a minute could not have elapsed ere he was alongside the object of his search, as he frantically thrust forth his hand to seize one of her arms, which now alone appeared above the surface, it vanished from his gaze and grasp, and he was borne forward over the spot whence the limb had disappeared, close up under the bow of a barge.

Self-preservation is the first law of nature, and Jack could not be blamed, if for the moment now he forgot the poor girl, and thought only of his own danger.

Another moment, and he must have been sucked under the bottom of the vessel, had he not, by a supreme exertion, grasped at its side, and drawn himself up on to it—a task rendered more easy from the fact that the barge was partially loaded, and hence lay deep in the water.

With his legs dangling over the side, and his feet within a foot of the stream, he rested, and panted for breath for a few moments, taking advantage of the time so occupied to search with his eyes for any indication of the whereabouts of Ellen, and cut with his pen-knife the silken cords that secured his cloak, and which had become knotted so tightly as to defy all attempts to undo them.

This accomplished, he flung the garment from his shoulder into the barge, and standing up upon its very edge, shaded his eyes with his hand, as if to concentrate his vision, and peered down into the dark stream, while he strained every nerve to catch the faintest sound.

Again, that low cry—so low, that it might have been mistaken for the sighing of the wind, or the murmur of the water beneath him, broke upon the night air.

This time it was as if it came from the other end of the barge.

"There—there!" cried Jack. "She is out there. She has escaped the fate I had feared she met with, Yes! 'tis her—'tis her!"

He sped along the narrow side of the vessel, heedless of the danger he ran in the darkness of falling into one of the half-emptied rooms of the barge, and was within a few feet of its stern, when a sudden apparition rose up quickly before him, and caused him almost to fall backwards into the water.

It was the form of a stout, rough-looking man, who seemed to have rose as if by magic from the deck, who now stood confronting him, but who, as Jack recovered from his sudden surprise, fell back trembling before him.

"The devil!" he shouted, in a husky tone. "Not a thief, but the devil!"

In an instant Jack saw who and what the man was, and the cause of his sudden appearance, and now trembling agitation.

He knew that he had to watch the barges and protect them from the thieving proclivities of certain gentlemen who had a penchant for appropriating any little article not too heavy to carry away to their own use, and believing that he had caught one of them on board the craft where he was lying in wait, had sprung forward with the intention of arresting him, but catching a glimpse of the hideous mask Jack wore, had found his courage desert him, imagining in the sudden shock he received, that he had confronted the devil.

He was one of those rough-reared, powerful-built men, with a sort of brute courage, which would lead him to face anything human, but of that ignorant superstitious mind, that was ready to acknowledge on the instant the existence of anything superhuman, not having the sense to imagine before he leaped to conclusions.

The moment his eyes rested on Jack's mask, he had come to the conclusion that he stood in the presence of a superhuman being, and terror so great seized upon him, that he retreated hurriedly towards the very edge of the stern of the barge.

Jack saw the man's danger, and stretched forth his hand to save him; but the poor fellow, fearful of his touch, started violently, and, with a cry of horror, fell backwards off the barge into the river.

With a cry which echoed that of the man, and mingled with the loud splash of the waters, as the poor fellow sank within them, Jack sprang forward, and gazed down upon the spot where he had disappeared.

"Curse the mask!" cried Jack, tearing it from his face, and thrusting it savagely into the pocket of his saturated coat. "Curse the mask, I say! It has, indeed, played the devil to-night. But the girl—the girl! I had forgotten her. The fellow will no doubt be able to save himself."

He was about to spring off the barge into the stream, when the man rose to the surface, with a loud, despairing shriek, which caused Jack to hesitate in his purpose.

As the man rose higher up out of the water, Jack saw that his movements were hampered, and that he was endeavouring to shake off some object which clung to his neck.

Shriek after shriek broke from the man's lips, and echoed from shore to shore, and the next instant our hero's heart bounded with joy as he perceived that the arms of Ellen Folder encircled the neck of the affrighted man.

"For God's sake don't shake her off!" cried Jack. "Don't shake her off."

But the man only struggled the more to release himself.

"Fool!" cried Jack, enraged, as he knelt down on the edge of the barge, and bending over it, stretched forth his hand, with the intention of aiding the man and his burthen[23] up on to the vessel; "would you sacrifice the life of a woman to your terrors?"

Either the man did not hear or paid no heed to his words, for he succeeded in releasing the hold of Ellen from his neck, and like a stone she instantly disappeared in the river.

Insensible to everything, in a dying grasp she had clutched at the neck of the man as he sank into the water, and had been drawn up by him to the surface when he arose.

Such a circumstance would no doubt have given a sudden shock to the bravest when unexpected, as it was in the case of the bargeman, and the man's terror may be well accounted for when he was naturally of an illiterate and superstitious nature.

It was the last despairing yet unknown action of the poor girl, that grasp she had made at his neck, and redoubled the terror which the sight of Jack's mask had already inflicted.

The thought that he might save a life never for an instant entered his mind, he only thought of losing his own.

---

[23] Burden.

As Ellen again disappeared, Jack gave vent to an exclamation of disgust and horror, and in his indignation he struck at the fellow as he frantically grasped the cable which moored the barge in the river, and caused him to relax his hold, and once more disappear beneath the surface.

Without waiting to think what might be the consequences of his act, Jack sprang from off the barge into the water, and succeeded in grasping at the form of the poor insensible girl, as the under-current was bearing her away.

He would have uttered an exclamation of joy, had he cared to open his mouth.

However, his heart beat with the feeling as his left arm encircled her waist, and together they shot upwards to the surface.

He had expected to rise just under the rope by which the barge was moored.

In this, however, he was disappointed.

As his anxious glance swept the surface of the river, he found that himself and his insensible burthen had risen at least a dozen yards further towards the centre of the stream.

The tide was now running rapidly out, and Jack struggled hard to swim towards the barge.

This he found, hampered as he was by Ellen, to be a task impossible, and he changed his course, hoping to be enabled to reach the shore a little further down.

"There is no fear of her struggling," he thought. "She is too far gone for that, poor thing. So I need have no fear that any indiscreet action of her own may carry us both to eternity; and every moment is precious, and her life hangs now upon a thread. Come, Jack, you have done enough harm, now is your time to atone for it."

He shifted Ellen, so as to render her weight the more easy to bear, and struck manfully out.

For a time he seemed to get along as he could wish, but the exertions of that night were telling upon him, and every moment his strength sank lower and lower, and the weight of the poor seamstress became greater and greater.

Still he struggled on.

But the strength of the current was too much even for his endurance. His strokes became shorter, he laboured more heavily, his frame was exhausted, and despair now took the place of hope.

Moments flew by, and on, on, the swiftly running stream bore Jack and his insensible burthen nearer and nearer to the lines of trading vessels, which every instant loomed up larger and clearer to his anxious view. On, past wharves and barges—on, on, till faintness and exhaustion made every stroke a work of such arduous labour, that it seemed as if it must be the last. On, till, with a cry of joy, Jack perceived a small boat moored to the stern of a little collier, which, with a cry of gratitude, he grasped at, and thanked heaven they were saved.

CHAPTER XV.

JACK AND THE RIVER POLICE—THE CAPTURE AND ESCAPE— DISCOMFITURE OF THE OFFICER.

WHILE SUPPORTING himself and Ellen Folder by clinging to the boat, a sudden ray of light flashed across Jack's eyes, and a gruff voice saluted his ears.

"Ahoy there! Who the devil are you?"

Jack cast his eyes upwards, and by the light of a lantern held over the stern of the vessel, he perceived a bronzed and bearded face looking down upon him.

"Bear a hand here," said Jack; "I have a woman half-dead in my arms, and the strength of the current will not let me reach the shore with her."

"Hold on a bit, and I'll be by your side in a jiffy. Hi! you sleepy lubber, come and hold the lantern, and throw a glim over her side," he added, turning his head, and addressing someone on board.

"Come and see," was the short answer of the man.

The next moment another bronze-featured man was looking over the stern of the vessel.

"A bloke," he said, taking the lantern from the other's hand; "chuck him a rope. I suppose he's been after nailing something in the pool and got a ducking for his pains. Don't let go of it, though, for those fellows would pinch a copper nail out of a keel—the warmints. Haul him up and give him a taste of cable on his back, then chuck him overboard again."

"Thank you," said Jack, inwardly, "I won't forget your kind intentions, my friend."

"Close your mug," said the other, clambering over the stern of the vessel and dropping into the boat. "The fellow ain't a land pirate. Turn the glim[24] round, will you, Jerry, and let's see how to ease him of the gal."

"A gal!" cried the man above; "so there is. Why, what's up?"

"Bear a hand, and the girl will be saved," said the other, as he leaned over the boat and seized Ellen in his strong arms.

Then, without paying any heed to Jack, he held her drooping form up till Jerry succeeded in grasping it—having laid the lantern down—and then, with a sudden jerk, lifted her over on to the deck of the little vessel.

"Pull yourself up, mate," said the man in the boat, "and we'll give you a glass of grog[25] to keep the cold out of you. There's nothing like getting wet inside when you are wet out. Pull yourself up, old fellow, there's a rope hanging over her stern."

And catching at a tarred rope that dangled from the stern of the ship, he swung himself up, and stood beside his companion and messmate.

"Take her down below, Jerry," he said, "and pour about half-a-pint of rum down her throat. She'll soon come to."

"That'll put her to rights," said Jerry, bearing her away from the gaze of Jack.

Meantime our hero remained clinging to the side of the boat.

No further notice was taken of him. He was left to shift for himself while the two men went down into the cabin to look after Ellen.

"Pull myself up by the rope," muttered Jack, "that's what I'm to do, is it? All right; but now I'm relieved of my burthen and somewhat refreshed, I think I'll take a stroke or two and return to the barge for my cloak. The poor girl will be all right, though she has two rough nurses. I'd rather trust her with them than your mealy-mouthed snobs. Let me look around and take my bearings. All right; I shall know the ship again by the colour of her hull."

Instead of taking advantage of the rope hanging over the stern of the vessel he let go

---

24 Candle or lantern.

25 A drink consisting of spirits (originally rum) and water.

his hold of the boat and struck out at once for the barge.

The tide, which was now upon the turn, offered no resistance to his exertions, and he made good speed towards the object of his labours.

A few minutes brought him alongside the barge.

Taking advantage of the cable by which she was moored he drew himself up on to the black mass of woodwork, and ran along the side of the half-filled rooms, till he arrived at the spot where his cloak still lay.

Soaking wet as it was, he took it up and flung it round his shoulders, then rolled it up and fastened it round his neck so that it should not impede his movements.

This accomplished, he looked around for the poor fellow who had fallen overboard.

He was nowhere to be seen.

Jack was the only occupant of the barge.

"I hope the poor fellow has not sank," he said. "I gave him a blow which sent him down in my indignation at his conduct, but I had no intention of destroying him."

Jack felt some little compunction at what he had done.

"Now for the ship," he said. "I must not leave that girl, though I doubt not she will be well cared for. The tide is on the turn, and I can reach the vessel in a few minutes. I won't forget that fellow, though, who suggested the rope's end on my back. Oh! no—oh! no."

He was about to leap off the barge into the water, when a boat which he had not before seen pulled up close alongside the barge.

"Hallo, you sir, who are you?" asked a voice.

Jack looked down from the barge, but replied not.

"Who are you?"

"What's that to you?" asked Jack, annoyed at the questioner's tones.

"We'll soon show you."

"Come on, then."

Jack dropped his cloak.

He put on his mask.

"Here's a chance for a lark," he said.

The men in the boat, three in number, pulled up close alongside the barge, shipped their oars, and two instantly scrambled up on to the vessel, leaving one man to look after the boat.

"You must give an account of yourself," said one of the men, placing his hand on Jack's shoulder, our hero having turned his back to them as they got upon the barge.

"Indeed!" said Jack, turning quickly.

The man started back and stood glaring upon him in the faint starlight of the night.

Their surprise, if not terror, was very great for a moment, but recovering the sudden shock, one of the men again placed his hand on Jack's arm.

"Who are you?" he asked.

"Spring-heeled Jack!" answered his companion, as the idea struck him.

"Spring-heeled Jack!" echoed the other, releasing his hold on Jack's arm, then added, quickly, "you're wanted."

"Am I?" said Jack, preparing for a spring.

"You are, old fellow. What the land police haven't been able to do the river police will."

"What's that?"

"Arrest you."

And as he spoke, he made a dart forward.

Jack quickly set to one side, and the man pitched head-first into the nearly empty centre room of the barge.

"Seize him, Murray, don't let him escape," shouted the man, as he scrambled to his feet.

Murray essayed to obey this order, but Jack dealt him a blow in the face which sent him after his companion.

"Well, you see the water rats cannot do anything more than the land rats after all," said Jack, addressing the two men, who were groping about the sides of the room for hand and foot hold to get out of their unpleasant position.

This they had little difficulty in finding and the man whom Jack had struck, and who had been called Murray by his companion, commenced clambering up.

As his head appeared above the deck, Jack placed his foot upon it, and pushed him back so suddenly that he fell upon his companion, and they both rolled over each other on the floor of the barge.

While Jack stood laughing and looking down on them he felt himself suddenly seized from behind and his arms securely pinned to his sides.

So firmly was he held that he felt his capture had at last been effected.

His attention being occupied by those in the rooms of the barge, he had not for a moment thought the third officer would attempt to leave the boat and come to his companions' aid.

But he had.

Hearing the scuffle, and judging that his companions required assistance, he had quickly fastened the boat to the cable of the barge and silently clambered on to the deck of the vessel and stolen behind the unsuspecting Jack.

"It's all up with you now, Jack," whispered the man in his ear. "You are too sensible a fellow to offer resistance where it would be of no avail. You will have a fine ride on the river in our company to-night. Now, then, Murray—come on Slipper. I've got him to rights."

"Hold him tight," said Murray.

"Hurrah!" cried Slipper. "Curse the fellow! he's knocked all the bark off my shins."

"You'll have your revenge," said the man who held our hero. "Look sharp!"

"Oh! oh!" roared Murray, in a sharp painful tone, as he suddenly slipped down again into the bottom of the room.

Jack laughed loudly, but made no attempt to release himself from the hold of his captor.

"Damn it!" cried Slipper. "Pull him back, Benson; pull him backwards; the devil's crushing my fingers with his boots!"

If Jack's arms were secured, his legs were not; and feeling that if the two men in the barge room got out all hope of his escape was gone. The moment they placed their hands on the top of the room to assist them up, he planted his foot upon their fingers, and caused them to fall back with a cry of pain.

Benson pulled him backwards on the inside, a feat that he was enabled to accomplish with ease, for, secured as his arms were, Jack could not resist the act.

"Now, pull up," cried Benson. "Don't try that dodge again, Jack, or I shall be compelled to kick your legs to keep you quiet."

"Thank you kindly," exclaimed Jack, "for the suggestion."

Suddenly kicking out behind, Jack dealt such a blow upon the officer's right shin with the heel of his boot, that the man released his hold on Jack's arms.

In an instant, Jack turned, seized the man by the throat, and, swinging him round so suddenly that he was powerful to offer any resistance, hurled him over the side of the barge into the room, beside his companions.

"Now," said Jack, "if you want to lodge me in jail, you'll have to swim for your object. Good night, my friends. I regret that you will have to remain prisoners on board the barge till daylight. The tables are turned, you see. Good night!"

He sprang off the barge into the boat, and hastily slipping its fastening, seized an oar, and pushed the little bark[26] away from the vessel, on which the officers now stood, looking at each other in silent chagrin.

"Ha! ha! ha!" laughed Jack, as he dropped the oars into the water, and bent his body to the stroke. "Come on, my fine fellows! What! Three of you permit one man to escape? For shame! The world will laugh at you tomorrow as I do to-night. Ha! ha! ha!"

"Bring back the boat, Jack," cried Benson, "and we'll let you go."

"Thank you, my friend, but I'm not a bird to be caught by that chaff—oh, no!"

"Upon my soul we will," cried Slipper.

"I prefer to trust to myself," cried Jack.

"You will be prosecuted for robbery as well as resistance to the law, if you take that boat away," cried Benson.

"Very likely, if they catch me," said Jack. "But you will find the boat safely moored at one of the wharves to-morrow."

"Jack!" cried Benson.

"Hallo! my friend."

"Don't be a fool. Come back. "We shall get into trouble when this affair is known."

"Serve you right," said Jack.

"Think of the loss of our berths—of our wives and children," said Slipper.

"Very sorry for them, but I can't help it," said Jack. "Hark ye, you will find your boat in the morning, and a five-pound note in it, perhaps. I must make use of it now, and will pay for its hire. If you keep your own mouths closed nobody will know what three confounded fools you have been. I have no more time to waste, so, once more, good night, and pleasant thoughts to you in your unpleasant position."

Jack now bent over the oars, and the little vessel shot over the almost smooth water like an arrow in the direction of the vessel by the two rough sailors.

He soon reached the ship, and pulled up under its stern, where he fastened the boat alongside the one to which he had clung with his insensible burthen, then seizing the rope that hung over its side, he drew himself up on to the now deserted deck.

CHAPTER XVI.

THE LIBERTINE AND HIS VICTIM—A DARK DEED PREVENTED.

"HARK YOU, Richard Clavering, you are a contemptible villain, and I tell you so—I, whom you lured away from a peaceful home—from friends, who loved me better than their own life."

---

[26] Small boat.

Such were the words uttered in angry and tearful tones by a young girl—for scarce woman had she become in years—as she stood with flushed face and heaving bosom, glaring upon a furnished, brightly lighted apartment, in the west-end of London.

His form was tall and graceful, but the lineaments of his features bespoke him one who gave unbridled licence to his worst passions.

It was evident from the flushed face and expression of his eyes that he had been drinking freely, and a red scar, passing from the temple to the ear, told of injury received in some affray of recent date.

Even in her indignation, his companion was far more beautiful than the ordinary run of her sex; tall in stature, graceful in deportment, with features of regular symmetry, and eyes of matchless brightness, she was one of those whom any man might be pardoned for looking upon with admiration.

But the lovely features were convulsed now with passion—the worst of all passions—jealousy.

A few months before, and she was the pride of her father's house, the hope of a doting mother, the envy of her sex—pure in heart, in mind, in name.

Now she was the wearied mistress of the man before her—the libertine, Richard Clavering.

He had been smitten with her beauty, and she, fascinated by his manner, led away by his plausible tongue, listened to his lying promises, and deserted friends, kindred, home—all for him, only to find, when too late, like the moth that flutters around the alluring flame, "that all that glitters is not gold," and that poverty with purity of soul are richer gifts than splendour allied to dishonour.

The toy had pleased him for a time then he wearied of it—then sought the gratification of his passions in other quarters, and now desired the absence of Jessie Bolton to make room for another—one who had hitherto repulsed him, but over whom he fondly believed gold would triumph.

And she had, from his coldness, suspected his desires, followed and watched him at the theatre door, and the agonies of jealousy tearing at her heart.

She could have rushed upon and upbraided him with his perfidy, but by an effort she had resolved to wait till he returned home.

Yes, she would not let him see her, or allow him to imagine she doubted him; but when she saw him struck down by Spring-heeled Jack, all the old love returned, and she was by his side to aid him.

Home together had they come.

He, annoyed, ashamed, walked before her in silence.

She, with all the passions of jealousy returned, followed him in silence. A step nearer to her.

"Yes, a villain!"

"Beware, you speak not thus to me," he said.

She found it difficult to keep pace with him.

And now they stood face to face in that sumptuous apartment, where night after night she awaited him—where he had whispered eternal love in her ears, and where she afterwards sat in tears at the thought of what she had become and the memory of her past happy life.

"A contemptible villain, am I?" he said, clenching his hand as he spoke, and taking a step nearer to her.

"Yes, a villain!"

"Beware, you speak not thus to me," he said, his flushed face becoming even more purple. "Recollect what you are—a thing living upon my bounty—trusting to my generosity for bread."

"Oh! God!" sighed the girl; "and has it come to this? Wretch—wretch! are you so fallen, so debased, so lost, as to taunt me with what I am—what you have made me?"

"'Twas your own inclination that led you to sin, if sin you call it."

"It was your lying promises—your perjured oaths, Richard."

"Bah! it may have been my wealth, that glittered till it blinded your reason."

"No—no! oh, no!"

"What then?"

"My love."

"Your love?"

"Yes."

"Bah!"

"Ay, scoff at it now that you are tired of it," she said, with a deep sigh and a fresh gush of scalding tears. "It was love which led me to believe you a true man—it was love which blinded me to your true nature, and now where are your promises—where— where?"

"Where I always intended they should be," he sneered.

"Oh! how have you fallen, shameless man, when you can stand there and own yourself a liar."

The young man set his teeth hard together.

"Curse you!" he hissed. "If you would not have me hurl you forth into the streets to starve, taunt me no more."

"Coward!"

"Fool, rather, that ever I looked upon you as worthy a passing glance," he sneered. "But 'tis the reward of men of position when they condescend to stoop to admire rustic beauty. "Place a beggar on horseback and he'll ride to the devil. Smile upon a poor peasant girl, and she aspires to the position of wife, when she is honoured by that of mistress."

The bosom of Jessie rose and fell with the tumultuous emotions that shook her soul.

"Oh! mother, mother, could you see me now!" she gasped forth, in tones of such agony that even that callous-hearted man moderated the contemptuous curl upon his lip.

"It's a great pity she don't," he said, "for then I should be rid of you."

"Is that your hope?"

"It is."

"That you may place another in my position?" she asked.

"Perhaps."

"That you may drag down to ruin and degradation another soul, whom the breath of impurity has not yet stained."

"May be," he said, coldly, and playing with the massive gold chain that hung at his waistcoat button-hole.

"That you may blight another's hopes, ruin her peace of mind for ever, then insult and cast her aside as you would me," she continued, her pale face flashing with shame and indignation, and her bright eyes sparkling in the jealous fore that consumed her.

"It is more than probable," he sneered.

"And you own this to me?"

"Why not?"

"Why not?" she cried fiercely; "why not? Oh! man—wretch—demon!"

"Rail on—rail on!"

"I cannot find words to upbraid you as I would—words to tell you what my heart feels," she said, placing her hand on her bosom, as if she hoped thereby to still its tumultuous beatings.

"I am not sorry for it."

"No; for if you have one spark of feeling, one sense of honour left, every word would sink like heated iron to your black and callous heart."

"Psha! It is not so tender."

"Alas. I know it. Would I had known it before—before"—

"Before what?"

"Before I—oh! God, shame and horror makes me fear to give it utterance."

"'Tis a pity that you had not sense enough to withhold what you have said already; it would have been better for you."

"Better?"

"Yes."

"How so?"

"Because you would have given me no excuse to leave you."

"And such is your intention?"

"I cannot hold further communication with the woman who calls me a liar and a villain," he said.

"You are both."

"Perhaps I am."

"You have been such to me, and will be to another."

"That's very likely, if she is such a fool as you were to believe all that is said."

She raised her eyes to his face.

She fixed them upon him with a fierce and penetrating glance.

"Hark you, Richard Clavering," she said, in a slow and measured tone. "Hark you, villain, liar, libertine, betrayer that you are! I will foil your base intentions—ay, I will foil you."

He turned away with a sneer.

She sprang forward and grasped him by the arm.

"Stay!" she said, imperiously.

"What!" he exclaimed.

"Stay!"

"You forget yourself."

"I do not."

"I say you do."

"I command you stay and hear me," she cried, loudly.

JACK LEAPS OVER THE STAGE COACH.

"You command?"

"Ay—I."

"Methinks 'tis yours to obey, mine to command in this house. Remember, you are here but on sufferance, living upon my bounty."

"You have told me so before."

"And may do so again."

"No, you will not. Because you dare not, after I have spoken what I will say," she exclaimed in pointed tones.

"What will you say?"

"That the poor girl you seek to make your victim, I will warn against you—tell her your true character."

"Do so. She will not believe you," he sneered.

"She will, for she looks not upon you, as I did."

"She loves me to distraction," he said, jauntily and tauntingly.

"Another lie!" Her poverty may lead her to accept your wicked offer, but"—

"But what?"

"When she knows you for a thief, she"—

"Hold!" he cried, turning fiercely upon her, and clutching her arm. "What do you mean?"

His face was livid now.

His hand shook as it rested on her wrist, and the muscles of his mouth moved nervously.

"What! Why, that I have found the dice you have played with are loaded, and that you have systematically robbed your friends and companions at the gaming-table."

"Ah! How did you learn this?"

"I suspected it, and"—

"What?"

"Found my suspicions to be true. I took them that I might"—

"Betray me?"

"No; that I might shield you from the shame of discovery. But now"—

"Now what?"

"Your perfidy shall be your ruin, and the woman you scorn will be bitterly avenged."

"Where are they?" he hissed.

"In safety."

"Give them to me."

"Never."

"By hell! I will have them," he cried, with fearful emphasis.

"By heaven! you shall not. They shall save her from a villain's wiles and avenge a villain's victim."

He flung her round as she spoke, hurling a chair to the ground as he did so; and snatching a dagger-like knife from his breast pocket, held it before her eyes, saying—

"The dice, or you die."

"Villain, would you murder me?" she shrieked, as he forced her back upon a couch.

Then, overcome with anguish and terror, she uttered a sobbing cry and fainted.

Still grasping her arm, his face livid with passion and fear, the libertine bent over her with the knife clutched tightly in his hand; but ere he could raise it the long French window was flung back and a man bounded through it into the room. The libertine dropped the knife, turned, and stood face to face with Spring-heeled Jack.

CHAPTER XVII.
JACK'S INDIGNATION AND RICHARD'S FEARS—THE DICE, AND THE PISTOL-SHOT.

IF RICHARD Clavering was a villain, he was an educated one; so, after the first shock of terror at the sudden appearance of Jack, he stood quietly confronting him.

Certainly, his face was deadly pale, and his limbs trembled, but it was not because he had any superstitious dread of the strange-looking being before him.

He knew that he was standing in the presence of a man and not as the poor and ignorant believed, in that of a fiend; and he likewise knew that it was the same individual who had rescued the poor ballet-girl from his insulting importunities.

Neither spoke for several seconds.

Jack's eyes wandered from the surprised face of the libertine to the insensible form of poor Jessie, then, raising his hand, and pointing to the girl, he said—

"What were you about to do?"

"She had fainted, and I—I was endeavouring to revive her," he stammered out in reply.

"You use strange restoratives for such a purpose," sneered Jack.

As he spoke he pointed to the knife which had fallen from Richard's hand.

The pale cheek flushed crimson, and the eye fell before the steady stare of the intruder.

"I—I was about to cut the lacings of her bodice."

"Indeed!"

"Yes."

"And had the blade penetrated her bosom, of course it would have been an accident," said Jack in an insinuating tone, his eyes glistening fiercely through the mask and causing Richard Clavering to shrink within himself.

Then by an effort the young man drew himself up, and in a haughty tone he cried—

"Who are you, sir?"

"A man," was the short reply. "Can you say as much?"

"How dare you presume to enter my house unbidden?" cried Richard. "Are you a thief?"

"No, sir, I am not," replied Jack, indignantly, "but I regret to say you are."

The young man clenched his hands and sprang forward.

"Villain, dare you force an entrance into my house and talk thus to me?"

"Indeed I dare."

"I will have you hurled from the place or conveyed to the lock-up," angrily cried Richard.

"Richard Clavering, you will do neither the one nor the other," retorted Jack.

"I shall not?"

"No."

"Who shall prevent me?"

"I will."

"You?"

"Yes, me."

"We shall see," cried Richard, foaming with passion, and, springing across the apartment to the fireplace, seized the red-silken bell pulls.

"I will have you kicked from the house like a dog by my servants!" he exclaimed.

"Richard Clavering, take your hand from that string."

There was something in the tones of Jack that caused the libertine to pause ere he summoned his servants.

Something that told him to beware of how he treated Jack.

With his hand still resting on the cord, he turned to our hero.

"Then begone!" he cried; "begone at once!"

"Pardon me, Mr Clavering; you see I know you—but I command here while I remain."

"You?"

"Yes, me, and you will do well to obey. Do you understand the word?"

"No."

"Then I must teach you."

"Teach me?"

"Aye."

"Who are you?"

Spring-heeled Jack."

"I thought as much."

"Now, be pleased to remove your hand from that cord."

"I will do nothing of the kind at the bidding of a fellow who dare not show his face."

"Dare not?"

"Ay, dare not?"

"Richard Clavering, you lie!" cried Jack, indignantly.

And placing his hand to his mask, he tore it from his face.

The young man started, and dropped the cord from his grasp.

"The devil!—the mar—"—

"Silence!" cried Jack. "Suffice it that you know me."

"You here."

"You see I am."

"What brought you hither?—what do you seek?—why do you come?" asked the young man, hurriedly.

"Firstly, to upbraid you for your rascally conduct to that poor girl in the streets to-night; secondly, because I was summoned hither by her cries," and he pointed to the still insensible Jessie.

"The first reason I cannot understand."

"You cannot?"

"No; not when it is yours."

"Why not?"

"Because you are not the man who can boast of over much honour."

"When did I ever stain it?" asked Jack

"The man who can descend to the pranks which you have been playing"—

"Psha! I seek not to defile the young and beautiful. I stoop not to insult defenceless women."

"Bah! what would life be worth if we could not enjoy it? You enjoy it in your fashion, I in mine."

"To embitter the existence of another is but sorry enjoyment, Richard Clavering."

"To frighten people to death is but sorry pleasure," retorted the other. "To the mar—"—

Jack held up his hand depreciatingly.

"To him I might have felt disposed to listen when he preached morality, but to Spring-heeled Jack—bah! If I have sunk in your estimation, truly you have sunk in mine; if my pleasure merits your contempt, yours likewise merits mine."

"I have much, no doubt, to be ashamed of and sorry for," said Jack, but I neither seek to destroy the one body and soul, or rob the other by means of loaded dice."

"Ah!" cried Richard, paling to an ashy hue, and staggering backwards, till the wall permitted him to go no further. "You—you then"—

"Have overheard your character, as I stood beneath that window."

"It was a lie—a lie!"

"I believe it to be true," said Jack, coldly and calmly.

"You are a villain to assert such a thing!" said Richard, his tones trembling as he spoke. "Leave my house; I will not be insulted in my own place by peer or peasant. Begone! Or I will have you hurled forth like a dog."

Again, he seized the bell-pull.

"Summon your servants here," said Jack, "and I will expose the cheat and robber to them."

Clavering dropped the bell-pull from his hand on the instant.

He had not the courage to stand that accusation before his own hirelings.

"Why do you hesitate?" asked Jack, coldly and pointedly.

The young man made no reply.

The muscles of his mouth worked nervously, and, spite of all his endeavours, he could not assume a calm demeanour.

Jack repeated his question in a sneering, contemptuous tone.

"I do not wish you to commit yourself," he stammered.

"Ho! ho!" laughed Jack; "that's good, very good. But I will pull the cord myself, and"—

He had moved forward as he spoke, but ere he could reach the fireplace Richard sprang before him.

"What would you do?" he asked tremblingly.

"Expose a rascal without one spark of honour or truth to his own servants."

"Are you mad?"

Jack took no notice of the words, but continued—

"Denounce the man who by means of loaded dice robs those he calls his friends; hold up to the scorn of every honest man the thing that can heap insult upon injury, as he has done there."

Jack pointed to the now recovering Jessie.

A shade of sadness was on his brow, a feeling of sorrow in his heart, for that poor, shattered girl, who lay so pale on the silken couch before him.

"No, no," cried Clavering; "you must not. It was all a lie of hers—all a lie. We have quarrelled—she is jealous of me, and a jealous woman will say things she knows are not true. It's all false, I tell you—all false, so help"—

"Hold!" cried Jack; "add not perjury to your other vices."

"It is all false, I tell you—all, all false."

"It is true," said Jessie, rising from the couch and staggering towards him.

"You lie, you"—

"Shame!" cried Jack. "This to a woman! Shame—shame!"

The libertine drew back abashed before the indignant look which accompanied the words.

Weakened by the emotion which lacerated her bosom, the poor ill-used, ill-loved girl tottered towards a chair.

Jessie recoiled.

"No, no," she said. "From what I have heard as I lay there on that couch I am aware that you know me as I am, that you have learned I am not the wife of that man, as you and others have hitherto been led to believe I was. You shall not be polluted by the touch of—of—a"—

"Madam," said Jack sorrowfully, "if you are not what until to-night I believed you to be, you are still a woman, and as such must command my respect."

He took her trembling hand in his own, and led her gently to a chair.

There was a look of gratitude in her eyes as she drew her slender fingers out of the palm of his hand.

"Would his heart were like yours," she said; "would it was—would it was!"

"Indeed I pity you," said Jack; "for it pains me to know that your feelings have been abused by one whom till late I looked upon as a friend and an honourable man. But he shall do you justice yet. Where are those dice?"

"In my keeping."

"Place them in mine," said Jack.

"She dare not; I would"—

"Silence!" cried Jack, imperiously. "If you are by word or deed to offer her violence, I will stretch you at my feet and spurn you as I would a worthless cur."

"You shall answer for this language to me," exclaimed Clavering hoarsely and trembling with passion.

"I will do so, but it shall be with a horse-whip," said Jack. "Gentlemen do not stoop to shoot or thrust as cheats and robbers, but whip or duck them as best suits their fancies."

There was a fearful look in Clavering's eyes now, but he uttered not a word.

He bit his lips till the blood streamed down over his chin, and gnashed his teeth like an enraged tiger.

Jack paid no heed to his fury, but turning to Jessie he said—

"In the sight of God you are that man's wife, and you may be so in the sight of man if you will but place those dice in my hands."

"Could I but remove the foul stigma from my name, I"—

"You can," he added. "Place those dice in my hands. If Richard Clavering acts like a man and makes you his wife within a month, they shall be given to him and none know of their existence but ourselves; if not, I expose him as a cheat, liar, and robber, and produce them to the world as evidence of his guilt."

Placing her hand in her bosom, she drew forth the loaded dice and gave them to Jack, who quickly transferred them to his pocket.

As he did so, Clavering flung open a small ornamental box on a side table, and snatching a pistol from it levelled it at his head.

Jessie screamed.

Richard fired, and the room was filled with smoke. As it rose upwards to the ceiling the libertine saw the girl lying on the floor, but no trace of Jack was visible.

CHAPTER XVIII.

JACK IN THE GARDEN—THE HOUSEMAID AND HER LOVER—THE COMMISSION—THE LEAP OVER THE COACH.

JACK HAD seen the danger just in the nick of time. He had turned as the libertine levelled the pistol at his head, when he felt it was too late to rush upon and wrest it from him.

Richard's finger was already on the trigger, when our hero observed his intention, and hurling Jessie to the floor to shield her from the chance of being struck by the ball, he gave one terrific bound and dropped through the still open French window as the flash of the weapon met the gaze of the alarmed Jessie.

So quick had been the motion of Jack, that in his blind fury Richard Clavering did not see him go, the smoke which puffed up before his face doubtless tending much to cover his sudden and unexpected leap.

Jack had not taken the leap a moment too soon.

Had he hesitated but an instant, his career would have been closed for ever.

Bitter was the disappointment of Clavering at his escape.

With an oath, he flung the weapon upon the superb Turkey carpet, and in his blind fury stamped upon it.

"Gone!" he yelled. "Gone! and with those dice in his possession. Curse him!—curse him! He can now destroy me—blast my character—hold me up to infamy! Ah!" he added, as, pale as death, Jessie Bolton rose trembling to her feet, "this is your work—yours!"

The girl staggered to a seat and sank upon it.

"Oh! Richard, Richard," she sighed, "thank God you are not a murderer!"

"Would that I were—would I had stilled his tongue for ever! See what your cursed jealousy has done—placed me in the power of that man. But you shall repent it—you shall suffer for your work. I will hurl you forth to beg, to starve on the streets."

"Remember the dice!" came in a low, clear tone through the window. "Beware, Richard Clavering, you harm not that girl by word or deed! The dice—remember the loaded dice!"

Clavering turned pale, but furious.

His hand sought the fellow weapon in the box to that which he had cast to the floor.

In an instant it was in his hand, and his finger on the trigger.   .

"Jack, I defy you," he cried, hoarse with passion. "She shall go, and go at once."

"Beware what you do, for I hold your character in my hands," said our hero, appearing out-side the window. "Be merciful to her, and so will I be merciful to you. Seek to cause her heart another pang, and you shall soon find your reward."

"Not so soon as you. Take thine at once!" cried Richard.

Clavering levelled the pistol at the open window.

Jessie uttered a shriek, and sprang from her seat.

The libertine discharged the weapon.

There was a loud crash of broken glass, mingled with the report, then, as the noise died away, a loud defiant laugh rose from beneath the window.

"Foiled again!" yelled Clavering; "foiled again!"

"Ha! ha! ha!" came back in mockery.

"Thank God!—thank God!" cried Jessie, clasping her hands.

"For what?" yelled the libertine.

"That your soul is not stained with blood; that—that"—

The door of the room was burst open, and three of the men-servants rushed into the apartment, pale and excited.

"What's the matter, sir? Oh! what's the matter?" they asked, all at once.

Richard averted his face, and stammered forth—

"Only a robber trying to force his way into the room through the window. I fired at him, and he has doubtless fled."

"Perhaps you hit him, sir. We'll go down and see," said one.

"We had better send for the police, hadn't we, sir?" asked another.

"There may be more of them about the house or grounds," remarked the third, looking nervously behind him, as if he expected to see some one who had no right there.

"No—no need to go for the police," said Richard, who now trembled at the name of an officer. "But," he added, suddenly, "the fellow may still be in the grounds. Arm yourselves, and—and shoot him like a dog!"

The servantss hurried away to perform his bidding.

"Curse him!" muttered Richard, as they left the apartment. "I hope they may kill. him; then, then I could laugh again; but while that man lives, I shall never more know peace."

The last sentence was spoken loud enough for Jessie to hear, and she staggered towards him as he sank down upon the couch where she had lain a short time before, and placed her hand upon his arm.

"Richard, do me an act of justice, and you need never fear your character will be exposed."

"Never!" he said. "I might have been fool enough one time, but now you have sealed your own doom."

"Remember the loaded dice!" she said. "Remember the atonement you owe to me, and remember that man's words."

"I will!" he hissed through his clenched teeth; "I will remember them; but I will remember you also. I loved you once, but I hate you now! Go, leave me. I spurn you from me as I would a cur that bit me! Go away to beg—to starve!"

"Richard!"

"Wanton!"

He flung her hand from his arm.

The word had slung her to the quick.

She drew herself up, set her teeth firmly together, and hissed back her reply to his insult through her parted lips—

"Thief! thief!"

He leaped from the couch furious in his wrath, the mingled blush of pain and shame suffusing his passion-distorted features.

He raised his clenched hand with a terrible oath.

In terror Jessie drew back before the furious gesture.

His arm, however, descended not, for at that moment loud cries from beneath the window of the apartment reached the ears of its occupants, and Richard turned and rushed to the window, while, overpowered by her feelings, Jessie, with a heavy sigh, sat upon the couch, and covering her face with her hands, sobbed aloud.

Twice within a few minutes Jack's agility had saved his life.

Upon the second attempt of Clavering to shoot him, our hero had dropped down from the window, the broken glass falling upon him as he reached the ground.

He did not attempt to leave the spot, but crouched down under the wall of the house for a few seconds, as he thought it was likely that Richard might again fire out of the window, as he crossed the grounds.

Finding, however, that he did not, he arose and listened.

He could hear persons hurriedly moving about the house, and perceived lights flashing from windows which up till now had been darkened.

"The fool has woke up the servants!" he said; "and no doubt the report of the pistol will bring others to the spot. I do not like to leave that girl in his power while his passion lasts; but there, the fear of the consequences will prevent him offering her further violence. I have the dice all right. Yes, here they are. They have made many a man act the villain, but these shall make a villain play the man. They have stained many a man's honour, but these shall be the means of removing the slur from that poor girl's name. How everything can be made to play a double purpose, and good often springeth from evil. The world, or the greater portion of it, condemns me for the pranks I play, but there are not a few, I flatter myself, who will remember with gratitude the name of Spring-heeled Jack."

He cast his glance up at the broken window, as the voices of Richard and the servants broke in upon his soliloquy.

A smile passed over his face, as he heard the order given to shoot him by the libertine, whose evil intention he had that night foiled.

"Ah!" said Jack, replacing his mask on his face, "if ever man desired another's death, that man does mine now, for he knows I hold his fame and honour in my grasp. What could I make him to-morrow by a few words? I could change the courted and respected Richard Clavering to the despised and condemned cheat. It would be a just reward for his attempt upon my life, and his cruelty to that girl; but no, my tongue shall never reveal his true character, if he will atone for his wrongs; there are known villains enough in the world without me holding up another to the gaze of mankind."

At this moment there issued from the house, not only the three servants who had sought an explanation of the pistol shots from their master, but four more persons, two men and two women, housemaid and laundress of the establishment.

The men were armed, two with guns and the other three with sticks, and the two young women were clinging fearfully to the arms of two of the latter.

One of the men also carried a lantern, and as they moved forward very slowly, Jack crawled away round an angle of the building and darted swiftly behind a large holly bush, which grew in the centre of a small flower-bed.

Here he saw them all approach the spot beneath the window, and the man with the lantern held the light so as to cause the pieces of broken glass to sparkle in its rays.

"Don't go any further, James! oh, don't!" said the little housemaid, in trembling accents, as she clung to the arm of a tall footman. "You might get murdered, and then—

then, oh! what would become of me?"

"I don't think it's any good looking for him," said James, in a half-whisper, looking first behind him very furtively, and then into the pale, upturned face of the little serving girl. "I'm half a mind to go back to the house. It's so cold; my teeth keep chattering awfully."

"So do mine," said another of the party. "It's a jolly shame to be called out of bed in the middle of the night to look after thieves. I shan't go no further."

"You're frightened," said one who possessed a gun, drawing himself up valiantly. "I should like to get a pop at the rascal; down he'd go, in the twinkling of an eye."

As he finished speaking, he flung the weapon over his shoulder, and in so doing, struck one of his fellow-servants a violent blow on the head with the butt-end.

"Murder!" roared the fellow, believing that be had received the blow from some hidden foe.

This cry caused the greatest consternation in an instant.

The women clung closer to their partners, and the other three men huddled up together in as small a space as possible.

"Oh! do come in—do come in!" cried the housemaid. "There's a thousand of the villains about, and we shall all be killed. There, I think I see one with a dagger, a shining awfully bright out there. Oh! do come in, James!—do, do!"

Jack here gave vent to a deep groan.

"What's that?" cried all in a breath.

Another groan even louder than before.

"Oh! it's awful!" cried the laundry-maid.

"We shall all be murdered!" sobbed out the housemaid.

"Ye—ye—yes!" groaned James, his teeth chattering now more audibly than before. "Let's pretend to go round the house to look for the thief, and get in at the back."

"So we will," whispered the housemaid.

They were close to the bush now, and Jack, gathering up a handful of the soft earth, threw it among the party, striking four of them in the face.

"Oh!" cried the man who held the lantern, dropping the light from his hand.

An exclamation also broke from the lips of the others, which, ere it was scarcely uttered, was echoed by an unearthly sound that appeared to come from the holly bush.

The men started back, and James and the housemaid fairly took to their heels in their fright. They ran against a terra cotta vase at the edge of the path, and rolled over together among a beautiful bed of geraniums.

While they lay there, struggling and crying for help, Jack flung handful after handful of the soft mould into the faces of the men who, left in the dark by the light in the lantern being extinguished in its fall, commenced to beat a hasty retreat towards the house, leaving James and the housemaid to look after themselves.

When they turned the angle of the building, Jack darted from his hiding-place just as the frightened James succeeded in raising the house-maid to her feet, and stretching forth his hand he clutched at the skirt of her dress.

The girl uttered a loud cry.

James turned, stood for a moment as if paralyzed, then dashed madly away after his companions, leaving the servant girl half fainting in the hands of Jack.

"Mer—mer—mercy, Mr. Robber!" she gasped out, at the same time falling on her knees.

"Fear not. I will not harm you," whispered Jack, hurriedly.

"Mur—"—

"Hush!"

"Oh! it's—it's"—

She had got a good sight of the hideous mask now as she looked imploringly up in Jack's face, and the words she was about to utter died away on her tongue, which became paralyzed with terror.

"It's only a man," said Jack, quickly lifting her to her feet. "Fear me not, I say."

"Good Mr. Beelze—"—

"Peace, girl!"

"Good Mr. Beelzebub, I"—

"Girl, be silent, and listen to me," said Jack. "I have no intention of harming you. Listen, I say."

"Yes, yes."

"You love that footman, James!"

"Oh! Mr. Dev—"—

"Foolish girl, I am not the personage you take me for," said Jack, "but one who will make it worth your while to serve me."

"Serve you?"

"Yes."

"Where? Down—down there?" asked the girl, shuddering in horror, as she pointed with her trembling finger to the earth.

"No, you silly girl, up here," said Jack, unable to suppress a grin at the girl's question. "Now, listen to me ere your silly companions return."

"Yes, yes."

"Don't throw yourself away upon that paltry coward of a James. The fellow is unworthy of the love of such a pretty girl as yourself, if he can run away and leave you in this manner. But enough of that. Will you serve me?"

"How?—how?"

"By informing your mistress that the gentleman who had an interview with Mr. Richard Clavering to-night will be at her side if ever she should need his services."

"Yes, sir; yes, sir," cried the girl, attempting to hurry away.

But Jack detained her gently.

"Tell her this," he continued, in a hurried whisper; "but say not a word to your master or your fellow-servants."

"I won't."

"Promise me faithfully."

"I do."

"I shall be sure to learn if you speak of this interview to any but herself."

"I will not, upon my word."

"Very good. I will believe you. Tell your mistress whatever may happen to insist upon the performance of a certain compact; not to allow fear or threats of violence to prevent justice being done; and, above all, not to leave the house till that compact is signed and sealed."

"Yes, I will tell her."

"Alone?"

"Yes, sir; alone."

"Enough."

"May I go now?"

"Yes; but take with you the reward of your labours. I never expect a service without payment."

As he spoke he forced a silk network purse into the girl's hand.

She held it a moment, then dropped it at her feet.

Jack stooped, picked it up, and offered it to her.

But the girl drew back.

"Will you not take it?"

"I cannot. You are the devil, and want me to sell my soul to you," she sobbed. "O my! O my! Do let me go—oh! do let me go! "

"Girl, are you mad?" said Jack, removing his mask. "Now are you satisfied I am a man?"

The girl started, stared hard into his face, then dropped her eyes to the ground.

"The—the mar—"——

"Hush!" cried Jack, catching at her arm quickly. "You recognise me as a friend of your master's. Enough. He must not know I have spoken to you, nor must any one else. Do as I have told you. Take this gold; and when, one day, you find a husband who will protect instead of desert you, I will see if I cannot find a little dowry for you. Now go; but be silent. Hark! the men servants are coming back again. There are no thieves about the grounds, and they may spare themselves the trouble. But I must be off. Remember your promise, and I will not forget mine."

Jack glided quickly away from the girl's side, as shouts of—

"There she is! There she is!" broke from the lips of the approaching servants, who, with lights in their hands, made their way towards her, James being one of the foremost.

"Oh! my dear Lizzie," he cried, "I'm so glad you are safe."

"Don't touch me, you cowardly fellow," said the girl. "Don't speak to me. I won't have nothing more to do with you. To run away and leave me as you did! There, go away, now, or else I'll slap your face."

As the girl suited the action to the word, and repulsed her lover with a ringing slap on the cheek, Jack vaulted up on to the top of the garden wall at the further end of the grounds.

As he reached the top of the brickwork, a shout from the road broke upon his ears, and, as he looked down, he perceived two officers below him.

"Here he is! Here he is!" exclaimed one. "Now, you sir, come down, or we'll fetch you."

Jack fixed his mask quickly on his face, cast a hurried glance behind into the garden and then along the road, where he could hear the sound of coming wheels.

"Confusion!" he exclaimed. "I'm edged in on both sides."

This exclamation was called forth by perceiving the servants hurrying across the grounds towards him.

While debating in his mind the best means to escape, a stage-coach came along the road at a good pace.

"I may give them the skip yet," he muttered, then added aloud to the officers below, "Catch me as I fall."

"All right," was the reply as the men moved close up under the wall of the road side, while the servants neared it from the garden.

The coach was nearly opposite him now, and as Jack made a feint to drop down up he sprang and over the stage-coach he went, to the opposite side of the road. Another bound, and he was lost to sight.

CHAPTER XIX.
OLD CHARACTERS IN A NEW SCENE.

"REMANDED—yes, remanded for a week. The magistrate might as well have sent him for trial to-day. But the woman is discharged. Confound it! But, no! Let me think. Perhaps, after all, justice plays into my hands, and helps me to the consummation of my wishes. Humph! Remanded for a week, and then—why, then, of course, over the herring pond he goes, to a certainty, unless"—

Ralph Grasper—for he it was—who thus soliloquized as he sat alone in his small apartment, where we first made his acquaintance, paused, and rubbed his hands together, while his eyes sparkled with the thoughts that ran through his mind.

"Unless," he continued, after a pause, "unless in that short week the woman who loves him so well may feel disposed to save him. She is at liberty; but what can liberty be to her with her husband a branded felon far away, with the finger of scorn pointed at her at every turn, with her bread-winner no longer able to procure for her the necessaries of life, with all lost to her—all, all, save honour? Honour? Pish! Honour is a commodity the well-provided-for may boast of; but when all else is gone, it is not worth retention. Honour is all very well, but had I clung to it, what should I now have been? A poor, pleading fool, obeying where I now command. Honour? Bah!"

He curled his lip contemptuously, and tossed off a glass of port wine which stood before him.

Placing the glass on the table, and unconsciously toying with its stem, be continued, half aloud—

"A day or two will bring her to my wishes. She will never sacrifice him to her feelings. There is no hope of escape for him if I again appear against him, and she alone can prevent me. I will see her again at her now wretched home. Her spirit, crushed and broken as it is, cannot enable her to resist my appeal."

He refilled the glass, and emptied it three or four times in quick succession.

Then he rose from his seat.

The liquor had fired his blood and flushed his face.

Nay, more; it had drowned every feeling of manliness in his heart.

He smiled as he drew on his overcoat and gloves.

But it was a smile which told plainly that villainy lurked beneath it—that the soul of that man was black and dead within him.

He wiped his silk hat round with his handkerchief, smiling all the while at its glossy nap; but he saw it not.

His glances rested on no outward object; they were turned upon his own evil thoughts.

Slowly, yet erect, he strode from the room and out into the open air.

A moment he halted on the threshold, stared vacantly along the street, and still with that smile upon his harsh features, strode away along the gravel footpath.

So intently absorbed was his mind by the one subject of his thoughts, that even when he looked along the road in the contrary direction to that which he was about to pursue, he saw not the tall form of a gentlemanly attired man leaning languidly against the gatepost of the next house.

No sooner did he start on his journey, than this personage drew himself up, and, as a peculiar light seemed to shoot from his eyes, he commenced following Grasper along the road.

The pace at which he walked was the same as that the merchant felt disposed to adopt.

If Grasper halted for a moment, so did his follower.

If the merchant, following the impulse of his thoughts, redoubled his speed, so did the other.

Twilight was fast giving place to the deeper gloom of night, and few persons were about, albeit the hour was but nine; for scarcely in half a mile did they meet more than two, and those two servant girls who had been sent for the supper beer to the new public-house, which is ever inseparable from a new neighbourhood.

Opposite one of these establishments, which occupied the corner of two roads, and through the modern glass front of which the gaslight streamed out into the street, Grasper paused, and taking his watch from his pocket examined it by the flood of light which made that part more gay than any other for some distance either way.

The tall gentleman in the rear paused also, and drawing back into the shadow watched the rascally merchant intently.

He observed the peculiar smile which still hung upon his features, and a shade of contempt passed across his own, and his fingers twitched nervously at the folds of the long Spanish cloak which hung gracefully from his shoulders, and which he now drew closer around him.

Giving vent to a cough of satisfaction as he returned the time-piece to his fob, Grasper was about to pursue his way, when two persons made their way out of the door of the public-house, evidently engaged in deep conversation.

As the light played upon their features, the cloaked stranger drew still further back into the shadow with a low chuckle.

Perceiving Grasper, the two men ceased their talk and advanced towards him.

"Oh! Mr. Grasper," cried one, "glad to see you. How d'ye do? How d'ye do?"

Grasper started, and by the suddenness with which the smile disappeared from his face, appeared anything but pleased at seeing them.

Still, he held forth his hand towards the extended one of the person who addressed him, and said—

"Oh! it's you, Baker, is it, and your friend Perkins? How do you find yourselves?"

"Can't say very well," said Baker.

"Can't, eh? How's that?"

"Well, you see, Grasper, that confounded policeman's staff last night"—

"Oh!—ah! yes. I heard something of it," said Grasper, in a short, vacant tune, as if his mind was absorbed by other business, and he was anxious to get away.

"You did?" said Perkins.

"Yes. Some little scandal about Baker and yourself being intoxicated and making an exhibition of yourselves in the neighbourhood, attired only in your shirts. But, of course, I am a man of business, gentlemen, and have little time to spare to listen to stories about drunken men."

"Drunken men, sir?" cried Baker, indignantly.

"Insulted and outraged men, you mean, sir!—men who, in seeking to serve their country and ensure the peace of the neighbourhood, were waylaid, robbed, and insulted on the public highway, and afterwards brutally treated by those whose duty it was to protect us."

"Well, well! I have nothing to say in the matter. Pray do not be so warm upon a subject that does not concern me," said Grasper, haughtily.

"It concerns everybody," said Baker.

"Even Miss Frump, your neighbour, perhaps," said Grasper, who had heard of the scene of the previous evening.

Baker blushed scarlet.

"Sir, you do not believe"—

"What?"

"That I"—

"Was outside your garden gate at a late hour, attired only in your linen, and calling forth the indignation of all around. Indeed, I do believe it, sir. for I heard it from good authority."

"But, Mr. Grasper"—

"But, gentlemen, it is past nine o'clock, and I have business of importance on hand to-night, and must wish you good evening," said Grasper, decisively.

"But allow me to explain," pleaded Baker. "I assure you that the affair has positively made Mrs. Baker quite ill."

"No doubt."

"Then I will explain the whole circumstance to you."

"Some other time."

"No, sir, now."

"You must excuse me, indeed," said Grasper. "Oh! there is Miss Frump, with her jug in her hand, coming hither for her beer. You can explain the affair to her perhaps?"

"The devil!" cried Baker, as he turned his gaze in the direction indicated by Grasper.

The eyes of the cloaked stranger also followed those of the unfortunate gentleman, and perceived the lady mentioned within a few yards of the public-house.

"Well, I won't tell you about it now; some other time," said Baker, nervously. "Good night, Mr. Grasper—good night, sir."

Grasper shrugged his shoulder, and walked away, a proceeding which Baker and Perkins were evidently about to quickly follow, but in a contrary direction, being desirous of avoiding the indignant glance of that ancient maiden, Miss Frump.

The light in the public-house, however, played too strongly upon the form and faces of the two gentlemen to suffer them to hide their identity, and the naturally red face of the maiden lady grew redder as her eyes encountered the slinking figure of poor Baker.

"Ah, you nasty man!" she cried, indignantly. "Ain't you ashamed to show yourself in the neighbourhood! You're a disgrace—a—oh! shocking—shocking!"

"My dear Miss Frump," began Baker, in stammering tones, and blushing till his face was almost as red as her own.

The man in the cloak was about to move after Grasper, but when he heard the old lady's remarks, he drew back with a smile, muttering—

"I must watch that rascal; but if I follow him now, I may lose a chance of some fun. Let him go for the present, I can catch him when I please. By Jove, the old lady's indignation does not say much for her good sense. Poor Baker! I pity him. It is hard to have insult heaped upon injury."

Miss Frump became furious.

"Do you dare to dear me, you—you odious rascal?" she fairly screamed.

"My good woman"—

"I'm not a good woman," cried the old lady.

"You ain't a bad one, are you?" said Parkins, coming to his nervous friend's aid.

"Me a bad woman—me? Do you call me a bad woman? I'll have you to know, sir, that I'm a respectable maiden lady. That—that— oh! the viper!"

Here the lady's power of speech failed.

But action took its place.

As she finished speaking, she walked up close to Perkins, and shook her china jug in his face with such a furious gesture, that that gentleman, fearful that the beauty of his own countenance might be spoiled, deemed it best to spoil the beauty of the jug, so raising his walking cane, he dealt the vessel a blow, and smashed it into a dozen fragments, leaving only the handle on the fingers of the irritable and disgusted lady.

This unexpected action seemed for a time to utterly confuse Miss Frump.

She stood for some moments looking upon the handle of the jug, as if unable to realize what had occurred.

Then she turned her gaze upon Perkins, and from him to Baker.

There was a grin of satisfaction upon that gentleman's face. The action of his friend had somewhat avenged him.

"Serve you right," he said.

These words broke the spell which enchained her.

In an instant a wonderful change came over the ancient maiden.

The look of surprise vanished.

Fury took its place.

Her eyes started forward from out of their sockets.

The teeth, or rather the few which remained of a once good set, were ground together, while the nostrils were widely dilated.

"Serve me right, you vampire!" she hissed rather than spoke. "Serve me right! Oh! you monster! You— you."—

"Go it, mother Frump—go it, old girl!" said a laughing voice behind her.

The woman turned like an enraged tigress, and stood face to face with a rollicking-looking young fellow, whom the sound of her voice had called from the bar of the public-house, where, if the truth must be told, he was paying more attention to the pretty barmaid than to his glass of ale.

It was the same individual who had annoyed the maiden lady by his remarks on the night before, while gazing from their different windows at the comical figure which poor Baker cut in his shirt at the door of his own house.

"Oh! it's you, you jackanapes, is it?" she cried; "you nasty little insulting puppy!"

"What's the matter, old dame?" questioned the young man. "Are you wild that Mr. Baker ain't so fascinating to-night as he was last? Or did the sight of him then turn your

THE MODEL POLICEMAN AND SPRING-HEELED JACK.

aged brain? Wouldn't wonder. Bare sights are always pleasing you know, and dwell so much longer in the recollection. I say, Baker, can't you oblige the old lady again, eh?"

"Such goings on may suit his own wife, but they don't me!" exclaimed the lady. "They please such blackguards as you, but not decent and respectable people. He ought to be indicted, and prosecuted, and imprisoned, for standing before a respectable lone woman's house, with nothing on but his shirt! It's shocking—shocking!"

"There, go home," said the young man. "You know you could cut your head off because he wasn't there without any shirt at all, or else because his old woman pulled him indoors before you got a good look at him."

"I'll have him put in prison for it."

"And go up against him?"

"Yes; and so would any other woman who"—

"Had got as little shame in her as you have. Oh! Miss Frump, what a pity it is you are too old to get married."

"Me married? Never!"

"You are only vexed you are not."

"Me vexed?"

"Yes."

"No, sir; but I should be disgusted to think that a drunken, dissipated husband would disgrace me by carrying out such disgusting tricks, and compel every respectable family in the neighbourhood to keep their blinds down."

"Do you keep yours?"

"To be sure I do."

"Shall I tell you what for, Miss Frump!" said the young man, with a wink at Baker.

"What, pray?"

"Why, because you can peep out of the corner without being seen from the street."

"Me peep?"

"Yes, you."

"Oh, you wicked, lying rascal?"

"Why, I've been watching you. Now I tell you what it is, old Mother Frump, don't come the modest too much, or perhaps I shall tell everybody about"—

"What?" shrieked the old lady.

"Oh! Never mind, I know, so do you," said the young man, with another sly wink.

"You, nor nobody else, can say anything against my character. No, never could, and never will be able to do. There, you insulting young rascal, I defy you—I defy you."

"You do?"

"I do."

"Very well; you will see. You've had a good fling at Baker, and now it shall be his turn."

"And I'll help him to it," muttered Jack, as the old woman bounced indignantly away towards her home, and the three men, laughing loudly, turned into the public-house.

CHAPTER XX.
SPRING-HEELED JACK MAKES A COMPACT WITH TWO OF HIS VICTIMS AND REVEALS HIMSELF.

SPRING-HEELED JACK waited till the old lady had got some distance on her way home, and the roar of laughter called forth by the indignant manner in which she had bounced off bad become somewhat moderated, and then he stole out from the shadow of the house where he had stood concealed, and pressing his hat low down over his forehead strolled into the public-house bar humming a merry tune.

He had little fear of being recognised by either Baker or Perkins, who he had served such a trick in reward for his attempted capture, as by wearing his mask on the night before it was absolutely impossible they could identify him as the person who had committed the outrage upon them, and caused them both ill-treatment and indignities at the hands of the constables.

So he strolled up alongside of Baker, and politely wishing him good evening, a very common custom with strangers out of the great thoroughfares of the city, called for a glass of wine, and stood apparently engaged in thought, drumming his fingers on the bar.

"I should like to serve that prudish old maid out," said the young man; "I should indeed."

"She deserves it," said Baker; "but perhaps the better course to adopt is to take no notice of her."

"I should say she had been crossed in love," remarked Perkins, "and so finds a pleasure in vilifying all our sex."

"Lor! how she did go on last night," said the young man; "I wish Spring-heeled Jack had got hold of her instead of you. I'd give a pound to hear he had frightened the life out of her; I would, or my name's not Tom Bedford. I don't think she'd have much to say about decency if he sent the old gal to her own door attired only in her shift, eh, Baker?"

"Lor'! it would be a lark. I'd let her hear my voice out of the window, if I knew she was there. Tit for tat—I'd give her tit for tat!"

"Revenge is sweet," murmured Perkins.

"Yes; but you were precious lucky in getting out of sight of the old girl. Confound her! Now I wonder if she will endeavour to bring up the affair in a police court?"

And Baker positively paled at the idea.

"Not she!" said Bedford.

"I don't know so much about that," remarked Perkins. "These very extraordinary modest females will often do what those whose professions are not near so great would feel ashamed to enter upon."

"That's true!" said Baker. "Confusion! But she would make me, if not the despised, at least the ridicule, of all who know me!"

"No doubt drive you out of the neighbourhood," said Perkins.

"I couldn't stand much about it," said Baker, dolefully.

"Turn the tables on her," said Bedford: "that's the best."

"Oh! but how?" said Baker.

"That's the thing—how?" remarked Perkins.

"Can't we hit upon some idea?" said Bedford, whose eyes sparkled at the thought.

"Yes," said Jack, turning suddenly.

The three men looked up surprised, and retreated a step.

"Sir!" stammered Baker.

"I beg your pardon for my apparent rudeness, but having been witness to the scenes of last night and this evening, and likewise overhearing a part of your conversation, I thought I could make bold to suggest how your desires to turn the tables upon this lady might be carried out."

"How—how?" said Tom Bedford, quickly. "Tell us, there's a good fellow, whoever you are. Nothing would afford us greater pleasure, would it, Baker?"

Baker was a prudent man.

The person before him was a stranger.

He hesitated, ere he replied—

"Perhaps."

"My friend is loth to speak out before a stranger," said Tom.

"A stranger?" repeated Jack.

"Yes," said the young man, looking inquiringly into his face.

"Well, yes, perhaps you are right, though me and these gentlemen, I think, have met before," said Jack.

"I have no recollection," said Baker.

"Nor I," said Perkins.

"Your memories are not good, I should think then," said Jack.

"Pretty fair," replied Baker.

"Can't say I've got a very bad one," rejoined Perkins.

And then both men examined the features of our hero.

Apparently their scrutiny was of no avail, for Baker shook his head, and Perkins shrugged his shoulders.

"Then you do not recognise me?" said Jack, after a pause.

"Indeed, no."

"Well, no matter," said Jack; "I believe we have, and acting upon that belief I made bold to break in upon your conversation; but if it is offensive, I will say no more."

"Offensive, I should say not, if you can do that old woman a good turn, or rather a bad one."

"I could."

"And would?" asked Bedford, quickly.

"On certain conditions, yes," replied Jack, slowly.

"And what are they?" asked Baker.

"First, a promise of secrecy."

"Oh! that of course," replied Tom Bedford, his face brightening up at the prospect of being revenged on Miss Frump.

"And what is the second?" asked Baker.

"Why, that only me and this young man has a hand in the business; that is all."

"I have no wish to," said Perkins.

"Nor I," said Baker.

"It would not be prudent, as you are both married men," said Jack, with a sly glance.

"Of course you meditate no villainy," said Baker, suddenly and suspiciously.

"Sir," said Jack, "I may be a rough, but I am not a ruffian." There was a tone of wounded dignity in the words. "I can enjoy a bit of fun, but not positive outrage. The vindictiveness of the old lady's spirit prompts me to teach her a lesson in charity, if an opportunity offers, and one can easily be made by her neighbours ere long lending their assistance. But as I said before, myself and this young man alone will be held responsible, as, in the event of us getting into trouble, none will suffer but ourselves, for in the eye of the law, a simple freak is sometimes as bad as a crime. For instance, the trick played upon you last night."

"Trick, you call it," said Baker. "It was robbery and violence."

"No, not robbery," said Bedford, "for you had your things returned."

"It was more than a joke though," said Perkins.

"I call it a good one," said Bedford. "Don't you, sir?"

"Assuredly yes."

"You do?" said Baker.

"I do."

"Then I don't; that's all I can say."

"There—there, don't be sore about it," said Jack.

"Sore! Look at my head."

Baker raised his hat, and showed a piece of strapping plaster, with a doleful visage.

"How did you get that?" asked our hero.

"Why, all through that Spring-heeled Jack."

And the poor fellow began to recount the whole story of the previous night's adventure.

Jack listened to him patiently till the end.

"But I do feel more sore against that Miss Frump, after all, than I do against Jack, for I sought to effect his capture, and hence excited him to what he did; but I have never done any harm to this woman, and ought to expect pity, rather than aught else from her."

"It wouldn't take you long to forgive Jack the trick he played upon you, especially if he played one on the old lady, eh?"

"I don't believe it would, positively I don't," said Baker.

"Then he will earn your forgiveness ere long," said Jack.

"How do you know?" asked Baker.

"Are you a friend of his?" inquired Perkins.

Jack turned to the bar, and took the glass of wine therefrom, which he hastily swallowed, then, as he replaced the glass on the bar, he hurriedly slipped the mask on his face, and turned towards them.

"I am the individual himself!" he exclaimed. "Do you recognise me now?"

The three men recoiled, and Baker turned white as a ghost, but recovering himself, he stretched out his hand, saying—

"Jack, give that old woman a fright, and I'll forgive you."

"Your hand on the compact," said Jack, shaking the extended hand. "I may require your assistance," he added, turning to Bedford.

"And you shall have it willingly," was the reply.

"Then meet me at midnight. For the present, good-bye."

And taking the mask from his face, he bowed to Baker and Perkins, and left the house.

CHAPTER XXI.
SPRING-HEELED JACK EFFECTS AN ENTRANCE INTO MISS FRUMP'S HOUSE—THE OLD MAID'S TERROR.

ONE o'clock had struck, and perfect silence reigned throughout the generally quiet neighbourhood in which Grasper, Baker, and Miss Frump resided.

The public-house, to which we have before referred, had closed its doors and turned down its gases quite an hour and a half before, at which time Tom Bedford, who had outstayed his companions some time in order to have a little conversation with the pretty barmaid, took his departure.

The young man, however, did not proceed home immediately, but waited outside the house in order to keep his appointment with Jack, elated at the prospect of a bit of fun with the ill-tempered old lady.

True to his appointment, our hero made his appearance, and after a few moments' conversation, he took the arm of Tom, and together they proceeded to the latter's lodgings.

Tom Bedford was a city clerk—a position obtained for him by his friends, who resided in Yorkshire.

He was alone in London, at least as far as regarded relatives, and lodged at the house of the cashier of the firm where he was employed—a staid, middle-aged man, and the father of a family, who often felt it his duty to rate Tom on his joking propensities and his late hours.

Tom was not a rake, but he was fond of the company of young men of his own age, and, consequently, the bagatelle-room was often a place where he was when he should have been in bed.

But withal, he was a generous-hearted fellow, and so the staid cashier overlooked a great deal, and Tom retained his lodgings next door to the dwelling of Miss Frump, whose querulous nature made her no very great favourite with the cashier and his family.

But if there was anything Tom's fellow-servant and landlord objected to, it was the young man bringing home any of his friends after the family had retired to rest.

This was a difficulty which the young man felt now as he walked arm-in-arm with Jack, but he frankly told his companion so, and likewise intimated that he had no desire to offend the cashier.

Jack mused a moment.

"That is awkward," he said.

"Yes. For Mr. Sinclair has certainly been kind to me, and I should but ill requite that kindness by giving him any annoyance."

"True. But if he has retired to bed, he will know nothing of the circumstance."

"He will hear us both enter the house."

"He need not."

"How can it be avoided? Can you spring up through my window?" asked Bedford.

"I could do so, perhaps; but then I might be seen. You had better take me on your back and carry me up to your room, then there will be but your footstep on passage and stair."

"Good! I can manage that."

Arriving at the house, Tom opened the door with his latch key, and Jack springing upon his back, Tom made his way up the stairs to his own room.

As he turned the handle of the door, a man's voice exclaimed—

"Is that you, Mr. Bedford?"

"Yes, sir," answered Tom.

"You are late?"

"Yes, rather."

"Good night."

"Good night, sir."

Tom closed the door quickly behind him, and dropped Jack softly to the floor.

"The old boy was awake, you see," he said, in a whisper, as he moved a candle from the wash-hand basin, where it had been placed for him in safety, on to the table.

Jack walked silently to the window of the room, and softly raised the sash.

Placing his head out, he examined the premises on either side, and strained his eyes up and down the street.

Not a footfall broke the silence.

Drawing back his head, he said—

"I can easily spring from the sill of this window to that of the old lady's, but"—

"What?"

"Doubtless her window is secured, and she might wake ere I could succeed in opening it."

"And raise an alarm."

"Yes, that would wake the whole neighbourhood," said Jack, "ere I could effect an entrance."

"That's awkward."

"And furthermore, some wakeful neighbour on the opposite side might by chance observe me."

"So they might, although I think everybody is asleep but us two," said Bedford.

"Is this the only apartment you possess?"

"No; I have another."

"Which?"

"The room next this."

"Good. It opens on the back?"

"Yes."

"That will be the best way to get into the old lady's house without disturbing her or running the risk of being seen. Who resides there besides herself?"

"Only an old crabby gentleman, as deaf as a post, who occupies the two parlours. He would never hear you."

"Is that all?"

"Yes. Miss Frump keeps the house, and Mr. Duppy is her lodger. He is about as miserable an old man as she is a woman. He is a bachelor, and a bachelor at fifty-five or sixty ain't up to much."

Jack's eyes twinkled, and a smile passed over his mouth.

"I will take a survey from that window there, if you please. Of course, I could give the old woman a pretty fright from the front, but then discovery would defeat the object I have in view."

"Step softly, then."

"All right."

Tom opened the door of the room, while Jack softly closed the window, lest its being open should excite suspicion.

Taking the candle, the two then proceeded to the next room, and Jack, looking from the window, perceived a small outhouse just beneath him, which served as a lumber or coal cellar for both houses, and whose slated roof reached up almost to the first floor window.

"Capital!" he exclaimed, "capital!"

"What?" asked Bedford, still in a whisper.

"That outhouse."

"Well?"

"By standing on that, I can raise the window of the room, and enter the house, while, at the same time, it will afford me a ready means to get back here."

"So it will."

"Now let me understand the position of the rooms occupied as sleeping apartments," said Jack.

"The old lady sleeps in the first-floor front room."

"Yes."

"And the old gentleman in the back parlour."

"Very well."

"The house is in every respect the same as this," said Bedford, "only there the staircase is to the right of the passage instead of the left."

"Certainly. Now, Mr. Bedford, I will see if I cannot make her more charitable to others in misfortune. Close your window, but do not fasten it, as I shall wish to return this way."

"All right; but I go with you?"

"No."

"Why not?"

"Because I can escape where you could not," said Jack, looking significantly at his heel.

"I understand."

"Put out the light."

"Is that necessary?"

"Yes, for two reasons."

"And what are they?"

"The first, that it may appear you have retired to bed, for you must not be thought to have had any hand in this business, and I would advise you to divest yourself of your coat and waistcoat."

"I see."

"The next reason why it is necessary you put out the light is, because it may not tend to discover me as I either get in or out this window or your neighbour's."

"It might do that."

"There is a probability of its doing so, at least, and my wish is not to be discovered now."

"Then out it goes," said Bedford.

"And so do I," said Jack. "Keep your eyes and ears open, both front and back."

"All right."

Bedford blew out the candle.

Jack sprang over the window-sill, and alighted on the small outbuilding without any noise.

Bedford watched him eagerly and anxiously.

"Shut the window."

"Now?"

"It would be better to do so; only do not. fasten it."

"You may be sure of that."

Tom shut down the window, and took up his position so that he could see Jack's proceedings through the glass.

Our hero first took a good survey of the surroundings, and then turned his attention to the window he wished to enter.

The blind was not drawn down over it, and Jack endeavoured to peer into the room.

But of course in the darkness he could see nothing of what was therein.

Then he tried to rise the sash, but found it fastened.

"Humph!" he muttered. "I must draw my diamond over the glass; but first my mask."

He took this hideous and inseparable companion from his pocket, and adjusted it to his face.

"Now if I have to jump for it, I shall not be recognised. Now to cut the glass."

He drew his ring across the centre pane of the upper sash, producing a slight scratching sound.

Holding his left hand just under his right, he gave the glass a slight tap with his finger near the bottom mark, and a piece about four inches wide fell outwards into his hand.

"A professional burglar could not have removed it easier or more silently," he muttered, as he gently laid it at his feet on the roof of the outhouse.

Then he listened intently.

Still no sound, save the wind as it rustled the leaves of a stunted tree in the garden beneath him.

"All right," he muttered. "Now to business."

He drew back the cuff of his coat, and inserted his hand through the opening in the glass.

Click!

The catch which secured the window was unlatched.

Nothing now barred our hero's progress to the dark room.

He did not, however, immediately raise the sash, but paused and listened, straining every nerve to catch the slightest sound that might indicate others were aware of his presence besides Tom Bedford.

He knew that aged people sleep lightly, and that even the sharp click of a latch might arouse them.

But a few moments assured him that he had not yet awoke either of the sleepers in that house.

He grasped the sash in both hands, and flung the window quickly up.

It creaked not in its ascent, and with a smile of satisfaction, Jack sprang over the sill, and dropped softly on to a sofa placed beneath it.

In the course of a few moments Jack's eyes became so accustomed to the darkness, that he could make out every object in the apartment, and the position of the door was plainly visible to him from where he sat.

Crossing the room, he flung it open, and stood upon the landing.

Here he could hear the loud snore of Miss Frump, as the music of her nasal organ awoke the silence of the house.

Leaning over the banisters, he could hear another person snoring in unison with the old lady.

The sound came from the back parlour, where deaf Mr. Duppy was said to sleep.

"Now," muttered Jack, "how shall I proceed? Shall I frighten the old gentleman up into her room, or the virtuous maiden down into his? The latter I think will be the best course to pursue."

He turned his cloak, made sure that his mask was properly adjusted, then placing his chest across the rail of the banisters, lifted his feet from the stairs, and permitted his body to slide down the balustrades till he reached the passage.

The back parlour door was left open about an inch, and Jack turned instantly to the front room door, and, turning the handle, discovered it was fast.

The key, however, had been left in the lock, and this Jack instantly removed and placed under the mat before the door.

Then he went to the street door, softly drew back the bolts, and slipped the lock, leaving it so that the slightest push would send it open.

Having done this, he again listened.

The breathing of the sleepers was as regular as before, and Jack grasped the handrail, and commenced silently to ascend the stairs, and once more stood before the door of Miss Frump's bedroom.

For the first time he perceived a faint light through the keyhole, and he stooped and peered through the little crevice into the room.

A small night-light was burning on a toilet-table under the window, and he could see the foot of the four-post bedstead on which Miss Frump reclined, also a chair on which that lady's garments lay, surmounted by something that looked like a curly-haired dog, of a brown black colour.

"Confound it!" said Jack; "I wish Bedford had told me she had a dog in the house. The animal will spoil all; The moment I open the door, he will commence barking. What—ay— a dog—no, it's a wig."

And Jack could scarcely keep back the laughter which was about to burst from his lips.

"So the old lady wears a wig. Hurrah! so much the better. She will look a prettier object without it. By my faith, but she will never let Baker have so much of her tongue again, I warrant."

He opened the door softly.

The faint light played upon his white long cloak, and gave him the appearance of a spectre with a horrible face.

The snoring ceased as the door opened.

The old lady turned upon her pillow.

Jack darted quickly behind the long curtains.

But Miss Frump did not awake; the movement of the door had been just sufficient to disturb her snoring, but not to thoroughly arouse her.

In another moment the nasal organ of the old lady was again in full tune, and Jack tiptoed across the room, taking in every object in the apartment as he did so.

He raised the night-light from the table, and held it before him so as to light up his hideous features and strangely attired form. Then in a deep hollow voice, he exclaimed—

"Miss Frump, awake!"

And Miss Frump did awake instantly, half starting up in the bed as she did so, with mouth and eyes open to their utmost width, and her shoulders drawn up to her ears, and completely buried in the frill of her large night-cap.

A picture of such comical horror did she seem, that Jack could with difficulty prevent shrieking with laughter.

"Miss Frump!" he again spoke in a hollow tone, "I have come to fetch you."

He dropped the little night wick to the floor, and placing his foot upon it, extinguished the light, extending his arms as he did so, and bending over the bed.

With a short, gasping half-shriek, half-sob, Miss Frump's head and shoulders sank back, and disappeared under the bedclothes.

"Come," said Jack.

The coverlet of the bed commenced to shake, and even in the gloom of that apartment Jack could see that the old lady was trembling violently with terror.

"Woman, I can't wait! Come!"

Jack placed his hand on the coverlet, and it rested on Miss Frump's shoulder.

A shriek, which, had it not been smothered by the old lady being so low down under the bedclothes, must have aroused the whole neighbourhood, was the answer.

"Miss Frump, you are mine!"

"G-o-o-d h-e-a-ven, s-a-ve me!" cried Miss Frump, wriggling her body down lower and lower in the bed, till her feet and ankles protruded beyond the covering at the foot.

"Old woman, I can wait no longer!" said Jack, catching hold of one of her feet.

With another cry the old lady drew her legs back, till the position of her body in the centre of the bed seemed like that of a ball.

Jack waited a moment, for the old lady was now muttering a prayer.

Then grasping at the bedclothes, Jack gave them a rapid jerk, and flung them onto the floor, leaving the old woman, attired only in her bed-gown and large frilled night-cap, drawn up into a heap in the centre of the bed.

"Oh! for mercy's sake!" she began.

Jack caught hold of the frill of her night-cap, and by a sudden pull broke its string, revealing to his gaze the bald pate of Miss Frump.

"You don't require any garments where I am going to take you to," he said.

The old lady gave a terrific bound, and sprang from the bed to the opposite side of the room from where Jack stood, shrieking in terror as she did so.

Then she paused, as if not knowing how to act.

"'Tis useless, you can never escape me," said Jack, still keeping up the hollow tone.

The old woman stammered something, but it was rendered unintelligible to Jack by her terror.

Jack again extended his arms, and said—

"Come!"

"Go! go!—oh! go away," she gasped.

"With you— yes; without you—no," said Jack. "Your time has come; we want uncharitable women in my regions, and there must you go with me."

He sprang upon the bed.

The old lady flew to the door of the apartment, which Jack had left half open, and ran full butt against it, closing it with a loud bang.

In a moment Jack was by her side.

His hand grasped her arm.

Down dropped Miss Frump on her knees. "I will never be uncharitable again—never, never," she cried, in supplicating tones. "Oh! have mercy on me—a poor, lone woman."

"Your time has come; you have nothing to live for; nobody to care for, so come."

Jack put his arms around her, and lifted her to her feet.

"Mur—mur—oh!"

Terror caused her legs to give way beneath her, and down she went into a sitting position against the door, nearly pulling Jack upon her, who, as he gave a sudden jerk back to save himself, pulled the old lady's bedgown fairly over her head.

Shame and terror combined now caused the old lady to fight most desperately, and succeeding in releasing her arms from the garment, she sprang at the handle of the door, pulled it open, and fled down the stairs at a wonderful speed, while Jack, holding the bedgown in his hand, stood in the doorway, fairly shaking with suppressed laughter.

"Oh my—oh my!" cried the lady, "what shall I do? Where shall I go? Where shall I hide?"

And she rushed wildly and frantically along the passage, evidently in her terror not knowing what to do.

Jack re-entered the bedroom, flung the bed gown upon the bed, and seizing the old lady's clothes, wig and all, from off the chair, sprang down the stairs after Miss Frump, who was pacing the passage and wringing her hands in agony.

The moment she perceived the white figure of Jack on the stairs, she made a desperate effort to enter the front parlour.

This, of course, she was unable to do, and she turned and fled towards the street door.

She reached it, placed her hand on the lock, but the recollection of her scanty attire deterred her from opening it, and she stood upon the mat wringing her hands.

"Now, woman, enough of this," he said, in an angry, though still hollow tone.

He stretched out his hand, as if to grasp her.

With a loud cry she darted past him.

Jack sprang back to the foot of the stairs to prevent her ascending them.

He was resolved to force her to seek refuge in the back parlour.

At this moment the door of that apartment was flung open, and the old deaf bachelor stood on the threshold.

"What's the matter?" he cried.

"Oh! Mr. Duppy, the—the devil's come for me! Oh dear! oh dear!"

"Eh, what? Oh! oh! oh!"

The old gentleman had caught sight of the white figure of Jack, and staggered back into his room.

SPRING-HEELED JACK AND THE WARDER.

"Now," said Jack, clutching the arm of Miss Frump, "now—now you are mine for ever!"

With a shriek that startled Jack himself, she broke from his hold and bounded into the back parlour, our hero flinging her garments in after her just as she turned and closed the door in his face.

"Save me, Mr. Duppy—good Mr. Duppy—kind Mr. Duppy—save me, oh! save me!"

"Don't hold me so tight, woman—go away, woman—you're all undressed," were the words Jack heard as he turned the key, which was in the lock, upon them.

CHAPTER XXII.
THE ALARM —THE NEIGHBOURHOOD AROUSED—THE SCENE IN THE BACK PARLOUR.

AWAY up the stairs bounded Jack, three steps at a time, into the back room and through the window on to the roof of the little coal-shed beneath it.

Here he paused, and held his sides, for laughter which he could not give vent to without the fear of discovery was nearly choking him.

Recovering himself somewhat, he let down the window of Miss Frump's house, and, stepping along the roof of the shed, tapped at that of Tom Bedford's.

Tom, who stood beside his window, instantly flung it wide open, and our hero sprang lightly into the room beside his new found friend.

"Well," exclaimed Tom, breathless with excitement, "what have you done? I heard the old lady scream. I'm all impatience; do tell."

"Hush! do not speak so loud," said Jack. "I've got her into the old man's room, and locked her there with him, together with her clothes."

"Ha! ha! ha!"

"Hush! The old dame left her bedgown in my hand in her struggles, and her frilled cap I pulled off her head before, so that she cuts a pretty figure. You heard her scream?"

"Yes."

"Good."

"How?"

"It will give you an excuse for arousing the people of this house and your neighbours, and leading them into the old lady's dwelling to see what's the matter."

"Bravo! good. But"—

"But what?"

"How are we to get in? We dare not force an entrance through the window," said Bedford, in a disappointed tone of voice.

"I've arranged that."

"How?"

"Opened the front door."

"You have?"

"Yes."

"Capital, but"—

"What?"

"Can she punish us for entering her house? She's a nasty old woman, you know."

"You heard her cry out for help, shriek murder. You know her to be a lone woman, and all that; therefore what man would not rush to her rescue?"

"I see, I see," cried Bedford. "By jingo! it will be a good laugh for Baker."

"Go and rouse them up."

"And you?"

"Had better remain here till all is again quiet. A stranger might excite suspicion."

"So he might."

"Besides, I want to make it appear that the old lady has occupied the same room with the bachelor, and that some quarrel between themselves was the cause of the cries."

"I'll heap the coals on for her—I'll heap them on. Miss Frump—the virtuous and indignant Miss Frump—in the old bachelor's bedroom attired only in her chemise! Hurrah! the whole neighbourhood shall know it to-morrow. Here goes, to commence."

Tom Bedford opened the room door and called out loudly—

"Mr. Sinclair! Mr. Sinclair!"

In a moment the cashier's voice met the ears of Jack as he sat stifling his laughter in Tom's room.

"What's the matter?"

"Oh! sir, do get up at once. There's murder or something!"

"What—where—what?"

And bang open went the door of Mr. Sinclair's bedroom on the second floor.

"Didn't you hear the shrieks?"

"Shrieks! Where?"

"Next door."

"Next door—which way?"

"At Miss Frump's. It was her voice that roused me up. She's been roaring 'Fire—murder—thieves—help!' for more than half an hour," cried Tom.

"God bless my soul!" said Sinclair; "I think I must have heard something too, but I don't hear any voice now."

"That's what makes me so uncomfortable, sir. I'm afraid she's murdered," said Tom in a solemn tone.

It certainly cost him an effort to appear so much concerned.

"Murdered!" cried Sinclair.

"Yes, sir."

"Goodness gracious me!"

"The sounds got fainter and fainter every moment, and now they have ceased altogether."

"Call the police! Rouse the neighbourhood! Goodness me! what's to be done? My hand shakes so I can't get a light. Mrs. Sinclair, my dear, do you hear what Mr. Bedford says?"

"Oh! we shall be murdered too, perhaps! There's thieves about—where's your rattle? Open the window and spring it. Don't go down till the police come; you might get your throat cut! Did you fasten the front door, Mr. Bedford?" added the lady, as she jumped out of bed to assist her husband in obtaining a light and finding his rattle.

"Jack," said Tom, "you're a brick."

"Thank you."

"You are, upon my soul! I don't think anything ever made me feel so pleased at the idea of a lark. Now, I'm off to rouse Baker, while Sinclair lets the rattle have good play out of his window. I hope to goodness the old gal won't be able to get out of deaf Duppy's room."

"She can't; I've made sure of that by locking them in," said Jack in a low tone.

"Ah, but where's the key?"

"In the door."

"And the front open?"

"Yes."

"All right, good-bye. If you don't see you'll hear a row soon. Hurrah! there goes the rattle!"

Up went Sinclair's bedroom window with a bang, and out on the still night air sounded the whirr of a large rattle, which the cashier twirled round at a fearful rate.

In another few moments a thundering knocking at the doors of the adjoining houses told Jack that the young city clerk was at work.

Up went the windows of the adjoining houses, and night-capped heads protruded far out over their sills, while questions innumerable were asked in excited voices by excited people who were scarcely yet awake.

"Thieves! fire! murder! Get up everybody!" cried Tom, as he clung to Baker's knocker and thumped so furiously at the door that it seemed as if he must really split its panels.

"What's the matter?" roared Baker.

"Oh! get up and come down. Miss Frump's shrieking for help fearful. Come all and see what it is; I'm afraid to go in by myself."

"Where's the police?" roared a night-capped old gentleman from a neighbouring house.

"Where indeed?" cried Mr. Perkins. "People may be murdered in their beds for all they care."

"They're never to be found when they are wanted," shrieked another.

"It's a disgrace and a shame we should have to pay to support a set of fellows in idleness, and then when anything's wanted have to do their duty ourselves!" cried the first speaker.

"Come down! come down!" cried Bedford, "and go in with me to see what it is. Perhaps we can save her!"

"Oh! there's a policeman! there's a policeman!" exclaimed Mrs. Baker, who, together with her spouse, filled up the window.

"Spring the rattle louder—police! police!"

And for a few moments the cry of police from a dozen throats rang loudly out over the neighbourhood.

"Hallo! what's the row?" cried a policeman, hurrying to the scene. "Have you got Spring-heeled Jack here again?"

"Oh! go in there and see what's the matter," said Baker, who had now come down, attired in his breeches and slippers, and armed with the pistol which Jack had taken from him the night before.

There was a silence.

A dozen voices also urged the officer to do as Baker requested.

"Are you sure you heard cries of murder?" asked the officer.

"Yes," said Tom. "They woke the whole neighbourhood up."

Tom then drew Baker aside and whispered—

"The old woman's in for it. She won't be down on you again in a hurry."

"You don't mean"—

"Yes, I do," interrupted Tom, "but don't blow the gaff, as the saying is; come on as if you really thought something was wrong instead of a joke."

Here Perkins joined them, and several other of the male and female inhabitants.

One or two bore candles in their hands, and their faint glimmer seemed to make the scene look inexpressibly comic.

Not one save the policeman but were only half attired, and the terrified looks and rumpled hair of the startled sleepers would have raised a peal of laughter under any other circumstances.

"We shall have to break open the door," said the policeman.

"We'll soon do that," cried Bedford, placing his hands on the panels. "Why, it is open!"

This he did not omit to say in a tone of surprise.

"Open?" cried several.

"Yes."

"Then thieves have got in. Mind how you go—knock 'em down, policeman—be sure you don't let 'em escape," and a dozen other exclamations followed.

"Here, give me a light," cried Tom, taking a guttering candle from the hand of a trembling woman. "Let's see if old deaf Duppy is safe, or whether the poor old gentleman has fallen a victim to these midnight assassins."

"Where does he sleep?" asked the policeman.

"In the back parlour."

"Here?"

"Yes."

The officer placed his hand upon the door and turned over the light in his lantern.

"Why it's fast, and the key is on the outside. That's bad."

"Open the door—open the door!" cried Bedford, "and all stand round to prevent the villain escaping if he is in there."

Click, and the lock flew back.

The door was flung open.

The light of the lantern and candle combined lit up the room.

Right in front of the door, attired only in his shirt, stood Mr. Duppy, surprise, terror, and alarm depicted on his features, and staring with wide-open mouth and eyes.

Tom Bedford looked quickly around the apartment.

A shade of disappointment passed rapidly over his face.

Miss Frump was not to be seen.

"What's—what's all this?" stammered the old gentleman, glaring bewilderedly from one to the other.

"There's been cries of murder and help here," said the policeman. "Has any one been in this room?"

Duppy did not answer.

"How came your door locked on the outside?"

The old man only stared in reply.

"Has anyone been in this room—any thieves?" asked the policeman.

"No, no!" gasped Duppy in tremulous tones. "There's been no thieves here."

"They locked him in, I suppose, to keep him secure while they went upstairs," said Sinclair, who now joined the throng on the threshold of the room.

"Go up, policeman, go up," said a voice. "There's nobody here, and the old gentleman would never have heard them even if there had been."

"There is somebody here," cried Tom, whose glances searching around the room had discovered the foot of Miss Frump sticking out from under Duppy's bedstead.

"Where?" cried all in a breath.

"There—under the bed. Pull him out—pull him out!" cried Bedford, nudging Baker in the ribs with his elbow.

"There's a foot—there's a foot!" exclaimed Baker.

"Here, take this light!" cried Tom, forcing the candlestick into Sinclair's hand. "You stand ready, policeman, with your staff, and I'll drag the rascal out."

Tom stooped.

Duppy here rushed before him.

"No, no, no!" he cried, excitedly.

"But the thief is there," said Tom, pushing him back and attempting to seize the foot, which, however, he was unable to do, by it being drawn up out of his reach.

"Throw the light of your lantern under here," said Tom, addressing the policeman.

"Oh! oh—no, don't—oh!—I shall faint—I shall—oh, dear oh!" cried out a voice from under the bed.

But the policeman did throw the glare of his lantern under the bed, and all of those assembled save Mr. Duppy, stooped down to get a glimpse of whatever person it was there.

"Come out," said Tom.

"Go away—oh! go away!"

"If you won't come out you must be dragged out," shouted Tom, crawling partially under the bed, and getting hold of the old lady's ankle, dragged her by main force along the floor.

"Miss Frump—oh! it's Miss Frump!" shouted the little crowd.

No sooner did the old lady find herself dragged out from her place of concealment than she sprang to her feet.

As she did so a loud roar of laughter broke from every lip, and Tom Bedford, pointing at her, exclaimed—

"By jingo, the old gal's bald-headed! There's a guy!"[27]

The old lady clapped her hands to her head, and gave a deep moan.

"The nasty, disgraceful creature," continued Tom. "There, neighbours, you can see it all, now. It's a living shame, a living disgrace, a foul stigma upon our neighbourhood. Oh! Miss Frump, for shame—for shame!"

"Yes," said Baker, anxious to have his fling. "A pretty person, certainly, to speak ill of her neighbours."

"Rather," said Tom. "Why, look, there's her clothes. The whole mystery is soon cleared up, she does not like sleeping alone, and so has shared old Duppy's bed. They've had a bit

---

[27] Someone to ridicule or make fun of.

of a row I suppose, and her screams have exposed her disgraceful conduct. What do you think of her, friends? Look at her—hoot her. There's a virtuous old maid. Ha! ha! ha!"

Miss Frump was wrapping the counterpane of Duppy's bed around her half-nude form, trembling in every limb, and pale as death, gazing upon Tom while he spoke.

"It's all a lie—all a lie!" she shrieked at last. "I am a true virtuous woman."

"Here's a pretty specimen of it," cried Tom. "Baker, she won't halloo at you any more Miss Frump, hadn't you better leave the neighbourhood?"

"Let me go—let me go!" she cried, springing out of the room and up the stairs to her own apartments, amid the derisive laughter of those assembled.

CHAPTER XXIII.
THE MODEL POLICEMAN AND THE MODEL SERVANT GIRL.

JOHNNY BRISTLES had been an ambitious young cobbler; shoemaker he never was, for somehow Johnny never could get further in the art of the trade, to which his father had apprenticed him, than that of patching boots and shoes. He never liked the business, and when the new police were in formation, Johnny solicited a place in their ranks, and got it.

Now was Johnny's time to turn upon those who had made him a butt for a lengthened period.

He had always been a foolish, nervous fellow, and no sooner did he put on the uniform than Bristles was—at least in his own estimation—one of the bravest men in the world.

Those who before had laughed and jeered at him had but to give him the slightest opportunity, and "Move on!" was his cry.

If this order was not obeyed, Bristles had him by the collar and quickly marched him off to the station.

Indeed, it was stated that Johnny had more charges in one week than any two other men in the force had in a twelvemonth.

So gradually Johnny Bristles, instead of meeting jeers and contempt at every turn, began to be looked upon with terror.

Before he entered the force he was slovenly in habit and appearance, and never had a penny in his pocket.

But he had not been long in the force before he was pretty flush of money, and carried a good silver watch, which he took great pains to let everybody see—at least, the large steel chain of it, at the end of which dangled an enormous bunch of seals.

There were some, and not a few either, who were base enough to assert that it once belonged to a man who got tipsy one night, and who Johnny led to the station, although he was only endeavouring to find his own keyhole when taken into custody.

Certainly it was strange that a few minutes before he fell into this model policeman's hands, that the watch was seen in his possession, and that when he arrived at the station it was nowhere to be found.

It was only the next day that a chain and seals were seen hanging from the fob of Johnny Bristles, and his detractors made this circumstance an opportunity for the base insinuation upon his honesty.

It did them no good, however; on the contrary, it only made an inveterate enemy of the ex-cobbler, who watched for the least opportunity to be avenged on the malicious slanderers.

Now, there was some truth in the reports that Johnny did not go his rounds so regularly as he might; that he was often seen lurking about the front gardens of certain inhabitants of the locality where his beat was; but then Bristles, when taxed by his superiors, always asserted his beat was a dreary one, and that thieves were always on the look-out for plunder, and, like a true officer, he was looking after them.

If he did peep down areas, and go through side gates into back gardens, was he not only doing what was right?

And who could give better information as to footsteps and voices about a house or grounds than the servants?

It was no use. Johnny's enemies could do him no harm; on the contrary, they only raised him in the estimation of his superiors, and excited the pity and commiseration of two or three neatly-attired, small-capped servant girls on his beat.

If Johnny was disliked by the men, he certainly was more than liked by the female portion of the community—at least, that portion which scrub and cook, and are more familiar with the kitchen than the parlour.

There had been not a few quarrels between these serving maids as to who should lay claim to the favours of the model policeman, and more than one foolish girl whom the blue coat and metal buttons had fascinated had come under the wrath of her mistress, and been packed off bag and baggage.

Of course, Johnny Bristles felt very indignant at such harsh conduct, and would shake his fist at the area, down which he used to look with longing eyes at the little maid and neatly-spread kitchen table.

Anyone who might have observed him thus would perhaps have doubted where the eyes of Johnny lingered most, whether at the viands or the maiden. But certain it is, that his mouth used to water as he stood, and an audible groan escape his breast as he turned away to pursue his duties.

But Johnny's heart was pretty tough. He did not grieve long. There were more kitchens on his beat, and more servant maids than would satisfy half the division, of which he believed himself the principal ornament.

He had just recovered one of those painful shocks to his feelings—those feelings, we mean, which lay in the stomach—and made the acquaintance of a natty little country girl, who had just put on the badge of servitude at the Misses Snookers' academy, a short distance from Camberwell church.

If Bristles' heart ever beat for another, it did for Peggy Mittern, and she not only gladdened his soul with her sweet smiles, but filled his belly night after night with the little tit-bits which her mistress's kitchen or larder afforded.

Half a cold fowl at one time found its way from the larder into Johnny's pocket. At another, a nice slice of roasted beef or mutton, wrapped in a clean piece of newspaper, would stare him full in the face as he stooped to brush the dirt from the bottom of his trowsers before the garden gate of the academy.

What could Bristles do but pick it up, especially when it was accompanied with a sly wink from a laughing black eye and a smile from two pouting lips.

But somehow or other the Misses Snookers—disagreeable and suspicious old maids—would always look out of the door or window as he neared the house, and gradually the little luxuries disappeared.

Johnny waxed wrath at this, and he felt an inexpressible desire to look up or move on the subjects of his annoyance.

But the Misses Snookers were law-abiding persons, and Johnny Bristles was far too wise a man to commit a breach of the peace himself, although his hand would rest upon the handle of his staff, and a muttered curse escape his lips as he caught sight of one or other of the ladies.

In fact, the model policeman would have grown thin but for the circumstance of meeting Peggy one evening just as he came upon his beat.

She was returning home after enjoying her holiday, and very pretty she looked, decked out in her veil and cuffs, which she had put on after she left the house, and would have to remove ere she again entered it.

Johnny stopped short in his measured walk right before her, and his large goggle eyes started almost from their sockets with admiration.

"What, Peggy! my own dear, darling, duck of a Peggy!" he cried in overjoyed tones.

"Oh! my Johnny," was the reply, as Miss Peggy flung back her veil, and held forward her hand.

Bristles grasped it in his own, and then, looking up and down the road, and finding nobody near, he drew her closer to him, while his head bent low till it touched the veil of the young girl.

Then there was a loud smack, something like the sound of a carter's horse-whip, and a little half-frightened exclamation of—

"Oh! don't do it again."

"A thousand times, my charmer," said Bristles, again looking anxiously up and down the street.

The coast was clear. The face of Bristles again rested near the serving girl's veil, and a continuation of smacks, swift as file-firing, came from between the two heads so close together.

"Oh! don't, don't, there's a dear," cried Peggy, blushing scarlet, and adjusting her bonnet, which had slipped over the back of her bead. "Oh! what if missus was to see you."

"Damn missus!" exclaimed Bristles wrathfully, his whole manner changing in an instant.

"Oh! for shame," said Peggy.

"They ain't worth calling a missus, they ain't," said Johnny. "I should like to scrag 'em, I should."

"What for, Johnny dear?"

"What for!"

"Yes, Johnny."

"For their meanness and 'spiciousness to be sure, the old cats!" cried Johnny.

"Oh, don't call 'em cats."

"I'd like to serve 'em like cats, I would," said the policeman, drawing his staff from his pocket and flourishing it about. "I'd like to top 'em on the head with this and chuck 'em into the river."

"Oh, lor'! you is vicious."

"No, I ain't."

"Yes, you is."

"Well, and ain't it enough to turn the heart of a stone into a lump of iron to know as how they would rather chuck a bit of cold grub into the dust-hole than see anybody else have it?"

"Oh! they were so angry with me for it. Not that they knowed it for certain, but only suspected. I told 'em it was the cat as thieved it, and they said they would keep a watch, so 'tain't my fault you don't get some nice bits for supper now, Johnny dear. You know I'd give 'em you, but then they should see me and I would lose my place."

"Blow' em!" said Johnny, forcing the staff back into his pocket. "What's a little bit of cold scran[28] where there's plenty. Ah, the avaricious old cats—I wish they'd give me a chance, I do. I'd avenge the insult offered to the gal I love and my own tender and susceptible feelings—so help me Bob, I would!"

"Oh, Mr. Bristles, don't talk like that, there's a dear," said Peggy.

"Mister! Oh, don't Mister me. To you I'm Johnny Bristles; to everybody else I'm Mr. Bristles, the crack policeman of the L division."

Peggy looked admiringly up and down the row of metal buttons which graced the chest of the ex-cobbler, then rested on his face with an admiring smile as she exclaimed—

"You is, you is!"

"And who dare say I'm"—

"A confounded ass!" said a voice which seemed to come from the front garden of the house before which they stood.

Bristles drew back.

So did Peggy.

The countenances of both dropped.

They stood glaring upon each other as if for an explanation of the strange voice.

At length Bristles was himself again.

He drew himself proudly up.

His goggle eyes flashed fire.

Bristles stroked his metal buttons with one hand, and drew his staff from his pocket with the other.

Valiantly he looked around.

Majestically he walked to the garden gate, and looked over and among the shrubs which grew there so luxuriously.

Nobody was to be seen.

Bristles was disappointed.

The model policeman, like some knight of old, desired the chance to prove his valour in the eyes of his lady love.

"Come forth," he cried, "whoe'er you be, and to the station you shall go with me."

"Who is it? Oh, who is it?" cried Peggy, anxiously, paying no heed to what Bristles believed a splendid piece of poetical effusion.

"I'm licked," whispered Bristles; "come a little further down the street."

---

[28] Food.

"I must go in. It's past nine, and I promised to be home then," said Peggy. "Oh, I wish missus would let me stay out longer."

"So do I. But she be blowed!" cried Bristles. "Shall anyone enslave the girl I love— my dear—my darling duck—my dove!"

"Oh! don't talk so nice; it makes me feel I don't know how," said Peggy, looking still more lovingly into his face as they moved along.

"'Tis a way I've got. I ought to have been a poet, Peggy. As you see, when a man's in love he can say anything his heart prompts him; and I say this, that you ain't been so kind to me as you ought have been, Peggy. You lets them old catamarans[29] frighten you from doing your duty, you does."

"My duty?"

"Yes."

"What duty?"

"What duty, Peggy? Can you look me in the face and ask the question?"

"I don't know what you mean."

"You don't?"

"No."

"I do."

"What is it?"

Bristles placed his hand beneath his belt, and heaved a deep sigh.

"Don't you tumble?" he asked.

"No."

"Then you is green."

"What do you mean, Mr. Bristles?" asked the girl, in surprise.

"Mean? Oh! dull of comprehension?"

"I know I am."

"You are."

"But 'tain't my fault."

"Not yours; no, no, not all, but part—but part," said Bristles, shaking his head sadly.

"Oh! do explain," said the girl, in a pleading and half-terrified tone. "What can I do? What do you want me to do? What do you ask?"

"Grub—yes, grub. There's plenty in the kitchen. My bowels cry out aloud for vengeance on that leg of mutton bone," exclaimed Bristles.

"Ah me!"

"Why that groan?"

"Missus knows it's there."

"But you keep a cat."

"Yes—we do."

"And cats like mutton: cats will steal. Why, Peggy, dear, what's more natural?"

"But she might see me give it you, you know. But, stop. I tell you what I'll do," said Peggy, quickly. "I shall have to come out again for my half-a-pint of beer which missus allows me for supper, and I'll bring it with me."

"You will?"

"I will. But where can I give it you without being seen, for I should lose my place if

---

[29] Quarrelsome women.

they knowed it."

"Let me see. Why, I'll be just inside the churchyard. The gate is open. Nobody will see you there. Make haste and bring it me, for I've had no grub since my tea. There, give me another kiss. Now, look alive, and I'll await you there in bliss."

Bristles kissed the girl, and she hurried away from his side, and soon disappeared through the gate of the academy. Johnny grinned a broad grin, and with his measured step walked towards the churchyard.

CHAPTER XXIV.

THE THIEF AND THE RECEIVER — BRISTLES AND THE SPECTRE.

PROUDLY erect walked Johnny Bristles, the model police-officer, towards the church.

His mind had no room for any other thought than the supper which he believed was in store for him.

He had completely forgotten all about the voice he had heard while in conversation with the girl he loved for what he could induce her to steal from her mistress's larder.

Never did he feel so good tempered since he had been in the force.

Had an old tormentor crossed his path, it is doubtful if he would have requested him to move on, so elated was he by the promise of the silly little Peggy Mittern.

Nothing but the vision of a leg of mutton bone could he see as he continued his measured tread along the half-gravelled pathway.

No eye had he for the numerous gateways he passed to reach the appointed spot— not one glance did he deign to cast upon the lighted kitchen windows.

If Johnny Bristles had a love greater than another it was for mutton, and the nearer the bone the sweeter the meat he considered, always providing there was a good quantity of meat on it.

Besides, Johnny preferred the bone to a slice, as he took good care to make a halfpenny out of what he could not eat.

So, with the vision of the mutton bone before his eyes, he walked slowly but stately on till he reached the churchyard, and paused before the closed but not fastened gate.

Then he looked around him.

Up and down the street went his glance in search of any person who might be curious enough to observe his movements.

But no one was near, and placing his back against the gate he pushed it open and swung his body into the churchyard, permitting the gate to close to by its own weight.

It shut with a loud clang, which made Johnny start, for the place was awe-inspiring enough by itself, without requiring any sudden and unexpected noise to add to its terror.

Johnny Bristles had always been a coward before he joined the police, and if he had shown a greater amount of bravery since, it must have been that he imagined the blue coat and metal buttons to possess a charm which shielded the wearer from all possible danger or annoyance.

While he was a cobbler, he never could fancy walking along a dark street late at night, and felt constrained to whistle to keep up his spirits. But once he donned the uniform, these ideas and terrors evaporated, and he would penetrate the darkest garden or lane, without any feeling akin to uneasiness.

But there was one place in which he never felt easy.

That was a churchyard.

The silence, the tall white stones, like so many ghosts, reared up on the tops of their own graves, struck a chill to his heart.

There is always a strange feeling even with the bravest, when business or otherwise may lead them among the homes of the dead.

It may not be fear, but still there is a sensation of awe which strikes to the heart.

If, therefore, brave, educated men feel this, we may perhaps excuse poor Johnny Bristles for experiencing the feeling in a greater degree, even though he believed the coat and buttons to be an invulnerable armour.

Certainly he started when the gate clanged to, and broke the almost oppressive silence.

Certainly he looked nervously around the dreary place, and shuddered.

He had no right there, and that may have tended to render his mind uneasy and for a moment he imagined he saw a strange-looking figure glide hurriedly behind a tombstone about the centre of the churchyard.

The right hand of Bristles involuntarily sought the pockets of his tail coat.

His fingers twined around the handle of his staff, and he half drew the weapon.

Then as if ashamed of himself, he pulled his hand away and muttered—

"What a fool I am!"

Hark! There was a hurried footstep coming along the road in the direction where he expected the mutton bone to travel to reach the place where he stood.

Bristles listened intently.

His heart beat high.

His mouth positively watered, and he smacked his lips together.

"'Tis her—'tis her!" he exclaimed, half aloud.

"She comes with the blow-out, and I must let out my belt a hole or two. Ha! ha! ain't it a fine thing to be a handsome bobby."

He strained his eyes through the railings of the gate, and saw the little Peggy hurrying to the rendezvous.

"She's the girl for me," he muttered; "none of your milliners or bonnet builders, but one of all work, with the run of her missus's-larder. God bless her little heart. Lor! how my belly does begin to grumble. It knows what it's going to have. There's Peggy!"

The girl now reached the gate, and was looking half frightened around her in every direction.

She evidently did not like to enter the churchyard, for her hand lingered on the gate without attempting to move it.

"Come on, Peggy—come on," cried Bristles, in a loud whisper. "Don't be frightened. Ain't I here to protect you—me, your own lover, Johnny Bristles, the model policeman."

"Ah, there you are," said Peggy, becoming sprightly in a moment,

"Here I am, my charmer; come in; don't let anybody see you. Come in quick."

"It's such a nasty place."

"What are you afraid of?"

"The ghosts."

"Ghosts?"

"Yes."

"Peggy Mittern, a policeman's sweetheart should be brave as a lion," said Bristles, pompously. "Ghosts!—I'd smash forty ghosts if they come near me."

"Oh! don't talk so wicked," said the girl, as she pushed the gate back, and nervously entered the ground.

"Ah! what's that?" she cried, as the gate closed to and a footstep in the distance smote her ear.

"What?"

"Hark!"

Bristles listened.

"Somebody's coming."

"Oh dear, let me run out."

"Come behind this vault, and give me the bone; my mouth waters—my belly growls, and I'm anxious to devour it!" cried Bristles, taking the unresisting hand of the girl and leading her behind a large vault, so as to hide them from the view of any passer-by.

"There's the mutton," said Peggy, in a tremulous voice; "take it, and I'll get away home again quick, or missus will be wanting to know where I have been so long."

She passed the bone, wrapped up in a sheet of newspaper, and which she took from under her shawl, into the hands of Bristles.

"Blow your missus!"

"Never mind her. Now I must go," said the girl, anxiously looking about her.

"You are a good girl, Peggy. Lor! you don't know how much I love you," cried the enraptured officer. "If there is any two things in the world I do like, it's a pretty little servant and a nice bit of mutton."

"I must go now. Upon my word I must," said Peggy.

"Wait a bit."

"I mustn't."

"Just while I have my supper."

Bristles would not have confessed it, but he did not like to be left alone in the churchyard; he could hardly commence banqueting off a mutton bone in the open street, and it was too large to force into his pockets, which were already occupied by staff and rattle.

"I cannot, must not. Missus will be calling me, and there'll be such a row. Come to the gate with me, there's a dear. I ain't frightened much, only a little—a very little, but do come to the gate with me; I can't hardly open it—it's so heavy."

"Then you won't stop a little bit longer?"

"No."

"Very well, I won't press you, my little charmer; but just give me one kiss, and then I'll protect you."

The girl made no hesitation in complying with the request, but Bristles, though he had only asked for one, took a dozen, and seemed as if he was loath to forego the caresses then.

"Now, do come, or I'll never speak to you any more," said the girl, really afraid that her lengthened absence would be discovered by her mistresses, and fearful to remain in that dismal place with the feeling fresh in her heart that she had brought stolen property there.

"Yes, I will do my duty. It shan't be said that Johnny Bristles could refuse the light of his soul, the joy of his heart, the star of his existence, anything she asked. No, no; I'm not only a model police-officer, but I'm a regular ladies' man. There, come along, and I say, Peggy, what are you going to have for dinner to-morrow?"

"To-morrow?"

"Yes, my dear."

"Rabbit pie, I think, for missus bought some rabbits while I was out for my holiday," replied the girl.

"She did?"

"Yes."

Bristles smacked his lips loudly together, and, laying the mutton bone down upon the tomb, took the arm of Peggy and led her towards the gate.

"Rabbit pie!" he exclaimed. "Rabbit pie! If there's anything I like it's rabbit pie—I'm dead on it. The smell of it makes my mouth water for a month; the sight of it almost puts me into hysterics; and the taste of it—oh! Gemini!—rabbit pie! Peggy, if you love me, collar a lump for me to-morrow night."

"I will," said the girl quickly, laying her hand on the gate, and pulling it open.

"Sweetest of all Peggies in creation, farewell till to-morrow night," said Bristles, enthusiastically. "I shall know no peace till I see you again—none till I sniff the delightful, delicious flavoured pie."

"You shall have a big piece, Johnny, a great big piece. Good night," and, shaking his hand, Peggy ran away towards home at the top of her speed.

"Rabbit pie to-morrow!—hurrah!" cried Bristles. "But now for the mutton bone."

He hurried back to the vault behind which he had stood, and where he had placed the half- consumed joint the stupid girl had brought him from her mistress's kitchen-safe.

But no bone was there.

The paper in which it was wrapped lay on the slab, but the meat was gone.

Bristles looked hard at the paper, then searched about the grass-grown earth at the base of the tomb.

Nowhere could he see the lost treasure.

He heaved a deep sigh.

He shook back his hat from his brow and scratched his head perplexedly.

"Gone!" he exclaimed in tones of anguish. "Gone! gone!"

"Yes, gone," said a loud, hollow voice, and a missile, which was none other than the lost bone, struck the policeman's hat, and knocked it off his head.

"Who's there? What's that!" half shrieked Bristles, tugging desperately at his staff, which he drew from his pocket and flourished about wildly.

"Who are you I—who—the devil! The—the devil!"

Right up before him sprang a fearful figure on to the top of a foot-stone. It was tall and thin, with hideous face, ears, and horns on its forehead; a white cloak, fastened at the shoulders, was held out by long hands, the finger-nails of which resembled more the claws of a wild animal than anything else.

In truth it was a figure sufficient to awe the boldest, and as Bristles saw it rear up before him he dropped his staff, his knees knocked together in terror, and he fell with a shriek of horror at the base of the stone on which it stood.

CHAPTER XXV.
THE TEMPTER AT WORK—JUST IN TIME—THE CAPTURE AND ESCAPE.

JANE SLATER was alone in her now wretched home.

Her head rested on her hands, and the tears forced themselves through her half-closed fingers.

Sobs broke from her bosom—that bosom which was lacerated now with suffering and indignation.

Her cup of sorrow was full to the brim.

Again she had seen the man who held her husband's liberty in his hands.

Grasper had been there, and made his villainous proposals, and he was to return for her final answer.

And now the time had arrived.

Two days had he given Jane to make up her mind.

Two days of what misery had she experienced —what heartrending suffering!

Scarce had she slept a moment—scarce had her tears ceased to flow since that night when Jack had rescued her from the fate to which she was about to consign herself; but poignant as had been her grief before, it had been doubly enhanced since the visit of her tempter on the evening of that day which had her acquitted and her husband sent back to jail.

She rocked her body to and fro on her chair, and shuddered as her moistened eyes for a moment were raised to the little clock in the corner of the room.

"Only another hour and he will be here," she murmured; "only another hour for one to decide. Decide what? Oh, God! can I possess the power to love my husband, and yet refuse to do so! Can I—dare I sacrifice all—all?"

She wrung her hands together, and sprang to her feet.

"Oh! what shall I do? What shall I do?" she cried, as she hurriedly paced the floor. "Alone, with no friend—none, none to guide or save me."

There was a low knock at the door; but soft as it was, it shook like a heavy blow upon the poor woman's breast.

She paused in her walk, flung her hands wildly above her head, and then sank in a heap upon the floor.

"He is here—he is here!" she sobbed. "He has come for his final answer. Help me, heaven!"

Another knock, this time louder than before, and Jane sprang to her feet.

"Shall I save him—shall I save him?" she gasped. "But the means—means, oh! the means!"

She pressed her hands upon her bosom and looked wildly around her, as if she hoped to find something to guide her in that trying moment.

Once more the knocker was raised, and once more that poor woman sank back as the sound reached her ears.

"I must go," she said. "I must again stand before him—again listen to his persuasion—again bear from his lips the vile means by which I can save the man who would give his life for me."

She tottered rather than walked along the little passage, and placed her shaking hand on the handle of the lock.

A moment she hesitated, then, by a violent effort, she drew back the lock, and flung open the door.

And there she stood, with the knob of the lock grasped in her trembling hand, face to face with Ralph Grasper.

"I began to fear you were out," he said; "you kept me so long waiting."

Then striding over the threshold he pushed the door to, and walked unceremoniously into the little parlour.

Jane Slater staggered after him, and sank, with a sob, into a chair which stood near the door.

Grasper looked at her with his cold, gray eyes, and curled his lip, and shrugged his shoulders half contemptuously as he did so.

"Well!" he exclaimed, at last.

Jane looked up into his face, and that look of agony would have sank deep into the soul of any man with more feeling than him who sat before her.

"Well!" she iterated. "Oh! man—man! have you no mercy?"

"Yes! my object in coming here is to be merciful. Have you decided?"

Jane rose slowly, and tottered forward.

Extending her hand she laid it on Grasper's arm, and, looking into his face, she said in a slow, hollow tone—

"Ralph Grasper, there is one who will punish you for your cruelty to me and mine; one who, in his own good time, will avenge the sufferings I have been made to bear. Oh! man! if man you are and not a devil, spare me and save yourself."

Grasper rose steadily from the seat he had taken on entering the room.

"Jane Slater," he said, "I am a man of few words. I am here to receive your reply to the propositions I have made. I offered to spare your husband"—

"But at what price?" she gasped: "at that of his wife's honour?"

Grasper bowed coldly.

"Can you stand there without a blush?"

"Bah!"

"Oh! sir, be merciful to me, to him, to yourself," cried Jane. "Forgive the deed he has done, and leave me in peace. Oh! God! you are not lost to all feeling. Your heart is not so callous, but that my agony must touch it. Here, on my knees, I implore you, save us all."

She sank on her knees at his feet.

"Enough of this," said Grasper. "I am tired of this fooling; yes or no?"

"Oh! listen."

"Again, I say, will you be mine?"

"Think what you ask."

"I have thought."

"Then you will"—

"Transport your husband unless you submit to my desires," said Grasper.

"Can there be no other means?"

"None."

"Then heaven have mercy on your soul," sobbed Jane, rising from her recumbent position.

"Perhaps it will," he sneered.

"And perhaps it will not," said Jane.

"Well, no matter now," said Grasper. "You, at least, are not to blame. If you yield, you do so under the pressure of circumstances. Bah! any one would think you were some romantic school girl."

"I am a woman and a wife," sobbed Jane.

"Then the greater reason why you should not go on in this stupid way."

"Ah! me!"

"Come, now, be sensible; look upon the matter as a business transaction, that's all. I do not ask for your love, for that is a commodity I don't understand much about."

"No, indeed."

"So come to business at once; you know the terms."

"Too well."

"Then they will not require mentioning again," said Grasper. "Now, give your decision."

She cast an appealing glance upon him.

But Grasper remained still the cold, stern man he ever was.

There was not the least trace of mercy in the hard lines of his features.

She read there her fate, her certain fall, if she would save her husband from a felon's doom.

Fearful was the struggle which raged within her bosom.

Could she sacrifice herself to that man?

Could she know that she possessed the power to save her husband, and yet refuse to obtain him his liberty?

Which way should she decide?

To appeal further to Grasper's generosity she knew would be vain.

She clasped her forehead in her hands, and with an effort that almost tore her heart-strings asunder, she gasped forth—

"I must save him; but, oh! God! at what a price! what a price!"

She flung her hands wildly above her head, and then fell forward.

But Grasper caught her in his arms.

"At last," he muttered, as he placed the stiffened and insensible form upon a chair, "at last she is mine!"

"And you are mine!" cried a hollow voice behind him.

Grasper turned quickly, and stood face to face with an apparition that chased every drop of blood from his cheeks, and left him pale as the fainting woman beside him.

His iron-gray hair stiffened up on his head, and he shook like an aspen leaf, then suddenly recovering himself, he gasped out—

"Who are you?"

"One who will thwart your villainous scheme—one who means you not to injure that woman either by word or deed—one who will hang on your footsteps like a shadow, and crush the coward wretch whose soul is lost to pity or remorse."

"I know who you are."

"Spring-heeled Jack!"

"Yes; leave this house," stammered Grasper. "Your presence here will frighten this woman to death."

SURPRISED!

"My presence here may save her from a worse fate. Villain! I have stood in that passage and heard all that has passed."

"You have."

"I have."

The colour, which was returning to the cheeks of Grasper, faded on the instant.

He looked around him, as if anxious to secure some weapon.

Jack guessed his purpose, and stretching forth his hand, he seized Grasper by the throat.

"Would you murder me?" he asked.

"No," said Jack, "you are too pitiful a scoundrel for any man to place his life in jeopardy for. A brute beast should only be treated as such."

And swinging the merchant round, Jack dealt him a severe kick at the hollow of his back, and thrust him out of the room into the passage.

"You shall pay dearly for this," said Grasper, foaming with rage.

Another kick in the same place was the reply vouchsafed by Jack.

"Help; mur"—

The toe of Jack's boot was once more against the person of Ralph Grasper.

"Now, hark you, sir," said Jack, in a pointed tone, "you will do well to leave this place."

"At your bidding?"

"Yes, at mine."

"I will have you dragged to prison."

"And I will drag you through the nearest horse-pond if you don't go quickly," said Jack, again raising his foot.

Grasper saw the movement, and sprang towards the street door.

Foaming with rage and shame, he grasped the handle, and flinging the door open, stood upon the threshold.

"Whoever you are, you shall suffer for this," he exclaimed.

"Mr. Grasper," said Jack, "this is the second time I have saved this poor woman from a terrible fate. Beware of the third. Go, villain! there is pollution in the very air you breathe; go, and thank heaven you are allowed to escape without a severe punishment."

"I will go," said Grasper. "You have kicked the man who never forgets nor forgives. Spring-heeled Jack, we shall meet again!"

"Then beware of our next meeting."

"The law"—

"Begone!"

Again was Jack's foot raised.

Grasper darted out into the street, and Jack shut the door behind him, and returned to the room.

The poor woman was now showing signs of recovery, and Jack tore the mask from his face, and hastily turned his cloak.

"It would startle her did she wake to consciousness," he said, "and I would not add a pang to her sufferings. Poor thing! 'tis hard indeed for her to have to bear the pangs inflicted by her foolish husband's misconduct without having them added to by that scoundrel's baseness. I can do her no good by remaining here. The wretch surely will not return. Well, I have done many bad things, but, thank heaven, I have been instrumental in saving this woman from that villain's wiles. Such an act atones for past deeds to some extent. The base-hearted villain! Curse him! but I will punish him severely for this. Ah! she revives. I will retire. Better she know not I have been here—better that she remain in ignorance of the fact that a stranger has heard and seen all that has passed."

He stepped softly along the passage, and, silently opening the door, passed into the street.

As he drew the door softly to behind him, he was grasped around the body and his arm pinioned close down to his side, while a voice cried in his ear—

"Spring-heeled Jack, you are wanted!"

Jack turned his head, and his gaze rested on the shilling hat of a policeman and the form of Ralph Grasper.

"Ha! ha! ha!" laughed the merchant. "I told you we would meet again, and so we will to-morrow in a court of justice."

"That's a lie!" cried Jack, giving himself a sudden twist out of the officer's grasp, and dealing the merchant a terrific blow in the face, which sent him to the earth as if he had been shot.

Then, ere the officer could recover from his surprise, he bounded off at terrific speed.

CHAPTER XXVI.

IN THE PRISON — JACK AIDS THE FORGER TO ESCAPE—NEARLY CAUGHT.

SOFT, slow, and measured was the warder's step as, with feet encased in list slippers, he wandered up and down the corridor upon which the cells opened, and in one of which James Slater sat upon his truckle bed, the very picture of despair.

It was twelve o'clock, and yet he had not attempted to lie down and court the drowsy god—had not sought to bury his sufferings in a few hours' sleep, that balm of the wearied.

Too much a prey to agonizing thought was his mind.

Not for himself did he care so much, as the darling wife who so fondly loved him.

He was picturing to himself the grief under which she laboured—the agony she endured, and bitterly did lie curse the temptation he was not able to battle with.

"Oh! heaven," he groaned as his frame shook with the emotions of his soul, "why, why was I tempted to sacrifice position, character, happiness, all for a few paltry pounds that never could have brought joy to my heart. What have I done? Oh! God, that I could forget or bury in death the recollection of my first and only crime!"

He rose and paced the narrow limits of his cell.

"Would I had some weapon with which to probe the heart that was too weak to spare me this shame. But no, no; there is nothing here—nothing. Ah! the walls! Why should I then hesitate to dash out my brains? Yes—but—but shall I slay myself, or, only stunned for a while, add to my sufferings? My sufferings! what are they compared to hers? Nothing—nothing!"

He clasped his hands upon his brow and sobbed aloud.

"I have not the courage," he cried; "I have not the courage. Oh! fool as well as coward!"

For a time he walked up and down the narrow limits of his prison, then his thoughts again reverted to his wife.

"Will she come and see me? Oh! how I long to gaze upon her, to throw myself at her feet and ask her forgiveness. Thank God! she is not made to share my prison. Does she hate me now, I wonder? Can she feel anything but scorn for me now? Better for her if she do, for then she may learn to forget as well as despise the wretch who made her a felon's wife."

Quick and hurried were his steps now.

Click, and the little trap in the panel of the door was flung back, and the rays of the warder's bull's-eye streamed in upon him.

James Slater turned his face in the direction of the door, permitting the powerful rays of the lantern to fall upon cheeks pale and haggard—a face on which years of suffering were depicted.

But a few days, and what a change!

The happy features were pinched, pale, and wan, and the glossy black hair had turned to an iron gray.

Had Grasper seen him as he stood in the glare of that light, even his hard heart must have been touched.

The warder, who had observed changes before almost as great as this, felt a touch of pity, despite the fact that his office had rendered him somewhat callous to the sufferings of the inhabitants of that fearful place.

"Why ain't you in bed?" he said in a husky voice, intended to be severe.

"Bed!" answered Slater.

"Yes."

"Would I were in the grave, sleeping the last sleep—at rest for ever," replied the man sorrowfully.

"Come, it's no use making things worse," said the warder.

"That were impossible."

"No, it ain't. Come, pluck up. If you despair like this now before you are tried, what will you do afterwards if things go against you?"

"Dash out my miserable brains against the walls of my cell," cried Slater.

"Psha!"

Slater heaved a deep sigh and looked at the black wall, now lighted up by the lantern.

"It's only a fool talks like that," said the jailer.

"It's only a fool would act as I have done," said Slater.

"Hold on—don't say anything that would criminate yourself. Now, be more calm, and seek a few hours' sleep. You are the most chicken-hearted fellow I've had for some time. You ain't tried yet, you know, and it's better to hope than despair. Why, lor' bless you, the chances are you will come out all right. An alibi, a flaw in the indictment, a confused witness, and a host of things may turn up in your favour.

Slater shook his head.

"Put a bold face on it, man, and take courage. Come, turn in, or you will wear yourself out."

Slater replied not.

The man slipped back the little trap, and pursued his rounds.

Slater listened for his footfall, but heard it not; and flinging himself upon the bed, buried his face in the pillow to stifle the sobs that shook his very frame.

One o'clock struck by the prison bell, and as its echoes died away over the silent prison, a strange noise at the bars of the window above his head caused his heart to beat fiercely.

He raised his eyes, and through the glass, in the dark heavens beyond, he saw one bright twinkling star.

He had watched it there the night before, but now its bright rays seemed to bid him hope.

Fascinated, as it were, his gaze lingered upon the light speck in that black expanse, till it was shut out from his view by some object passing between it and his own vision.

What could it be?

He sprang quickly up on the bed.

He shaded his eyes with his hand, and with difficulty suppressed the cry that rose to his lips.

But he did suppress it, and gazed with straining eyeballs at the little barred window.

A slight scratching sound came now upon his ears—then a click, as a piece of glass was removed, and a face, the lineaments of which he could not make out, appeared above at the opening.

"Slater!"

The voice was whispered; but how eagerly the ears of the poor wretch devoured it.

But he could not reply.

"Slater! hist! I am your friend," again came in a sort of hissing whisper through the bars.

"My God! have I one left in the wide wide world," gasped the prisoner in a low tone.

"Yes."

"Who?"

"Hush! be silent. Would you leave this place?"

"Would I? Oh, could I!"

"Be calm, and you shall."

"When?"

"Now."

"Now?"

"Yes."

"Oh, speak! speak! tell me I am not mad—I do not dream. Tell me this, whoever you be."

"Best assured you are all right if you will be cool and silent," said he at the window.

"Oh! yes, yes."

"Can you reach these bars?"

"Yes."

"Do so, then."

Slater sprang upon his bed, and his fingers clutched the iron rails.

"Take this, and file away at this bar," said the man outside, forcing a little file into his hand.

"Yes," cried Slater, who seemed now as if the weight of a hundred years had been removed from his frame.

"Hush! you will alarm the warder."

In his eagerness to be free once more, he had commenced filing at the bar so desperately, that the noise made by the instrument upon the iron jarred loudly upon their ears.

Slater trembled.

He feared lest the sound had been heard.

Pausing, he strained every nerve to listen.

But all was still.

With a grateful heart he recommenced his work at the bottom of the bar, while the man outside filed silently away at the top.

Slater was anxious to know who it was who thus sought to effect his release, but fearful now to utter a sound, he asked no further questions.

He had said he was his friend, and the poor forger was grateful to whoever it might be.

They were moments of suspense he endured now, and he could hear his own heart beat within his bosom.

But, oh! how slowly did that file appear to him to cut into the iron.

The little instrument did its work bravely, but the anxiety of the worker was so great that moments appeared to him hours. Inwardly he kept muttering——

"Oh! that the warder come not! Oh! that I may escape!"

Suddenly a hand touched his arm, and stayed its further movement.

"Hist! get down! somebody comes! pretend to sleep! Quick, quick! or you are discovered!"

At the same instant the figure disappeared from the window.

With a sigh that was almost a groan, Slater dropped down upon his bed, and, forcing the file under the coverlid, pretended to sleep.

Not one moment too soon was he; for scarce had he done so, than the little trap in the door was opened, and the warder's light flashed upon the bed.

"Gone to sleep at last," muttered the man. "Poor devil! he has got some little relief now."

The next instant the trap was closed, and the cell was once more in darkness.

What a relief to Slater!

He sprang silently up in the bed, crossed the cell, and placed his ear to the door.

"Has he gone?" he muttered to himself; "or is he listening outside? Oh, that I could hear his footstep!"

But, spite of his exertions, he could hear no sound, save the beating of his own heart, which throbbed so violently in his bosom.

He was trembling, too, in every limb with the excitement under which he laboured.

"Hist!"

He turned from the door.

Again was the figure at the window.

To spring upon his bed was the work of a moment.

"Has he gone, or does he listen outside the cell?" said Slater. "What a narrow escape!"

"He has gone further down the corridor."

"Can you see from there?"

"No; but I could see the flash of light from the windows of the other cells as he goes his rounds."

"Thank heaven! for then there is hope."

"Yes; now work with a will, but silently, and a few minutes will unbar the road to freedom."

Slater required no second bidding.

The little instrument cut deeper and deeper into the iron every moment.

"Now leave the rest to me," said the figure outside the window, as he grasped the bar in either hand.

"God give you strength," whispered Slater, in a voice that trembled with emotion.

A sudden jerk and a powerful wrench, and the next moment the bar was snapped, leaving an opening sufficiently large for a man to pass his body through.

"Thank God!" came from the very heart of the forger; and he thrust his arm through the window as if he would clutch at the space beyond.

"Now draw yourself up, and I will help you through."

No second bidding did Slater require, for ere the sentence was finished he had drawn his head and shoulders through the opening.

But as he turned his eyes upon the face of the stranger, he uttered a sharp cry of terror.

Never had he gazed upon a face so hideous, and in surprise and terror Slater would have fallen back, had not the figure outside the window clutched him by the arm.

"Who—who are you?" he gasped.

"A man, who has taken the form of the devil the better to secure your deliverance. Fear not. I am your friend, Spring-heeled Jack."

"Spring-heeled Jack!"

"The same."

"Who befriended my wife, and tried to save me from a felon's doom?" said Slater.

"Yes."

"God bless you—I"—

"Hush!"

"My lasting gratitude"—

"Enough now; moments are precious, cling to this rope. There—now slide down to the court-yard."

"What can I say? How"—

"Go, quick, if you would again meet your heart-broken wife."

"My wife? Oh! what have I made her!"

"You little know what your crime might have made her but for me," muttered Jack to himself.

Then turning to Slater, he said—"The rope is secured to the bars. Go, and fear not. I will follow you, and point out the road to freedom."

The next moment, and the rope slid through the hands of the forger.

Jack steadied it as the man went down, and then, when he could feel he had reached the yard below, he grasped it firmly in either hand, and then followed with the rapidity of an arrow.

"This way," said Jack, as he stood beside the forger.

Seizing Slater's arm he drew him along under the shadow of the prison for a little distance, and then darting hurriedly across the yard, grasped at a rope which hung from the cheveaux de frize[30] on the top of the prison wall, and placed it in the hands of Slater.

"Now, up with you, quick! I can see the moon will burst through the dark clouds, and delay is fraught with danger."

---

[30]Lit. "Frisian horses" – barbed wire or spikes across the top of the wall.

Slater commenced to draw himself up by the rope.

But he hesitated, saying—

"But these spikes. They will bar my passage to liberty."

"No. When you reach them, beware; they revolve. Fling yourself in between them, and by swaying your body over, they will place you safely on the opposite side of the wall."

"And then?"

"Then draw the rope up, and lower it down the other side. There is a good-sized stone secured to the bottom. Once you have reached the street, fling the rope back over the wall, and seek your own safety in flight."

"And you?"

"Fear not for me—look to yourself. Go! Farewell, and remember that honesty is the best policy."

"God bless you, Jack, for such only can I call you, as I know you by no other name. God bless and protect you!"

Slater commenced ascending the rope.

Jack watched him anxiously till he reached the top, and saw him fulfil his injunction with regard to the cheveaux de frize.

"A pretty thing I'm doing by lending assistance to a criminal to escape from prison, but my heart acquits me when I feel by so doing that I may save a woman's honour. Ah! there; he is gone, and my good wishes go with him."

Jack stood anxiously gazing at the wall in the expectation of seeing the rope thrown over to him, when the prison bell commenced ringing loudly out on the still night air.

"Confusion! they have missed him," cried Jack. "The rope—the rope! Confound it! what a time he is. Ah! I must fight for it now."

This last sentence was called forth by seeing a man hurrying into the court-yard.

It was one of the warders.

The man saw our hero, for the moon's rays now bursting through the clouds, lit up the precincts of the prison with a soft, mellow light.

"Here he is—here he is!" shouted the warder, hurrying towards Jack.

Then, as our hero turned to meet him, the fellow uttered a loud cry, and reeled backwards, startled by Jack's mask.

Jack knew his danger was imminent, and that there was not a moment to lose. As the man fell back, Jack rushed forward, and striking out with all the force of his powerful arm, struck the warder a blow which sent him stunned and bleeding to the earth.

At that moment the rope came over the wall, and, with a cry of joy, Jack clutched it eagerly, and drew himself up to the top of the wall. Then, with a bound, he sprang far out into the street beyond.

CHAPTER XXVII.

ON BOARD THE COLLIER—THE SEAMSTRESS RECOVERS—A SHOCK.

"HOLD on, Jerry—hold on, messmate. That arn't the way to bring the gal round, drinking all the grog yourself! You'd make a pretty nurse for a. workhouse, you would!"

These words were uttered by Peter, the seaman in the cabin of the little collier, to his messmate Jerry, who, finding that he could not force about half-a-pint of rum down the throat of the insensible Ellen Folder, was holding the vessel to his own mouth and taking deep gulps of the fiery liquid.

"Must n't waste it, Peter—must n't waste it," said Jerry, as his messmate pulled the vessel from his hold.

"No fear of that. I'll take care not to waste it."

And so saying, Peter finished the remains of the liquor, setting the tin can down upon a sea-chest beside the couch on which Ellen lay so pale and saturated.

"I tell you what it is, Jerry," said Peter. "This is what I calls a very delicate subject to handle. That ere gal oughtn't to lay in her wet togs, and it wouldn't be right for you or I to take 'em off her, and there's no feminine female aboard. Here! run upon deck and call the chap down as brought her here."

Jerry gave his trowsers a hitch, squirted out a mouthful of tobacco juice, and left the little cabin.

"'Shelp me never! she is a beauty," said Peter, looking admiringly upon the poor girl whom he had lain, with the assistance of his shipmate, tenderly as a child upon his cot. "It's a very delicate position for a chap like me to be placed in, and the sooner that fellow as hauled her out of the water shows his figure-head here, the better. What a fool I am not to have left a drop of brandy; she'd take that, I wager, though she won't touch rum."

The rough fellow took Ellen's hands between his own hard palms and chafed them, in the hope of circulating the blood, and he had the satisfaction of seeing her open her eyes, and glare wildly around her.

"Where—where am I?" she cried, at length, struggling to raise her head from the pillow.

"Along of those who won't harm you, my lass; so don't be frightened—there, don't be frightened. You fell in the river, and somebody brought you aboard. Now, don't look so scared—you won't meet any harm here. There! take a pull at this. Oh I oh! I forgot; it's empty. Never mind. I'll soon put a drop of first-rate grog in it, and a swig will put you all to rights in a minute."

"What strange place is this?" asked Ellen, still glaring about her, and evidently unable to realize her position.

"This is the cabin of the Saucy Jane, as tight a little collier as ever traded between London and Newcastle, and I'm Peter Wickham, captain and part owner."

"Yes, yes. I see it all now—the dark water and—oh, heaven! why am I made thus to suffer?" sobbed Ellen, scalding tears coming to her relief, and chasing each other quickly down her pale cheeks.

"There, there! you'll be better soon," said Peter, pouring out some rum into the tin cup. "Just take a good long pull at that. It's over-proof,[31] and fine stuff, I can tell you."

He held the cup to the girl's lips, but she thrust it away with her hand.

"Oh! no, no!" she cried; "my brain is already on fire."

"Then, blowed if you ain't had enough water to put it out," said Peter, as he laid the cup on the chest. "Maybe, ma'am, you'd like to take off your wet togs, so I'll just take a turn on deck, for decency's sake, you know."

"You are evidently a good, feeling man, although your manners are rough; but, if you would indeed render me a kindness, let me go into that stream from which I have been taken."

---

[31] Stronger alcohol content than usual.

"If I do, I'm damned!" cried Peter. "There, I beg your pardon for swearing, but I'd rather leap in a dozen times to drag you out, I can tell you."

"And thus enhance my misery. Oh! sir, you know not how hateful is life to me now; you know not what it is to toil day and night for the paltry pittance of a seamstress—to feel the cruelty of men whose hearts are steeled by drink and crime—to feel yourself alone in the wide, wide world!"

Peter took her hand, and his rough face glowed with pity.

"Have you?" he asked, in a tone that proved, spite his rough exterior, he had a feeling heart.

"Alas! but too well."

"I don't know you, of course, nor what drove you to try and drown yourself—which I suppose you did from what you say—but I guess you was driven to it. Now, tell—did that chap who brought you here cause you to do it? Is he a confounded rascal who has no more pity for a woman than I have for a water rat? Because if he is, say so, and I'll chuck him overboard."

"Who brought me here?"

"A swellish[32]-looking chap."

"I do not know him."

"Well, you'll see him directly; my mate, Jerry, has just gone upon deck to fetch him down," said Peter

At this moment Jerry reappeared.

"There's nobody on deck," he said; "hallo, has the gal come round?"

"Yes, she'll soon be all right now, if she'd only take a swig at the grog."

"Won't she?"

"No."

"Perhaps you don't ask her properly," said Jerry, sidling up to the bedside, and gazing commiseratingly upon Ellen. "How do you feel now? Coming round a bit, glad to hear; just take a pull at this rum, 'tis better than all the medicine in a doctor's chest."

"Would that it were poison," muttered poor Ellen.

"No, it ain't," said Jerry quietly, as he caught only the last word, uttered as they were between sobs. "Do you think we'd give you poison? Oh! no, it's grog: and a better drop can't be found aboard another vessel in the Pool. Now, just take a little drop; only a little—about half-a-pint will save you catching cold."

Thus pressed Ellen suffered the vessel to be held to her lips, and tasted the spirit.

"Swig away, don't be frightened of it," said Jerry, when, after partaking of about a spoonful, she put the can back with her hand.

"I cannot."

"Well, if you can't, you can't," said Jerry, laying the cup down, but not till he had tasted its contents. "It's rare fine stuff this, and would bring a dead man to life if he drank enough of it. I say, Peter, it's a rum go that chap's, ain't it; he's a gone'un, I expect."

"Did you look into the boat?"

"There, I never thought of that," said Jerry. "Perhaps the fellow's too much knocked up, or got a landsman's terror of climbing aboard by a rope."

---

32 Stylish.

"Go and give him a hoist, Jerry, and bring him down here; I'll wager he'll not refuse a pull at the grog."

Jerry once more took his departure from the cabin, leaving Peter to look after the still sobbing Ellen.

He had just reached the deck, when he found himself confronted with a tall figure robed in white, with a face so hideous that Jerry fairly started back, and nearly tumbled down the steps up which he had come.

Now sailors are a superstitious class of men, and certainly Jerry was no exception to the general rule.

In an instant the rough man was pale as a ghost, and trembling in every limb.

His hair stood on end, and the blood stagnated round his heart.

"I want you," said Jack, for he it was, in that hollow tone which he could so well assume.

"Want me?" stammered Jerry. "Oh! lor! it's Davy Jones."

"The same."

"Pe—pe—Peter?" gasped Jerry.

"Silence."

"Pe—"

"Silence, I say. Do you know what you have done?" said Jack.

"No—o—!"

"Then listen."

"I can't."

"Can't—you must; you said that a friend of mine was a land pirate."

"A friend of yours?"

"Yes, he who brought a girl to this ship, and threatened to rope's-end him when he came on board."

"I—I thought he was—but I don't now; oh! no, I don't now."

"Jerry."

"Yes."

"Where is the rope you intended for him? Quick, give it me."

"I don't know."

"Not know?"

"No."

"'Tis false; give it to me."

"What—what for?" asked Jerry.

"You shall see; quick—you know who I am, don't you?"

"Yes, Davy Jones."

"That's right; now the rope."

Jerry looked imploringly, but Jack stamped his foot, and struck such terror to Jerry's soul, that that personage staggered a few paces along the deck, and picked up a piece of rope, and handed it to Jack, starting back instantly, from fear that he would take hold of him.

"Humph!" said Jack. "Do you know what I'm going to do with this?"

"No, no."

"I'm going to serve you as you would have served the gentleman you were wicked enough to call a land pirate."

Jerry winced and trembled more than ever.

"Of course you are sensible enough to know that you can't help yourself?"

Jerry felt that his questioner spoke truly.

The seaman was a powerfully built man, with an arm and hand that could almost have knocked down a bullock, but he was now so terror-stricken that he could not deny to himself that he was powerless as a child.

He did not reply.

Standing with knees knocking together, he could only glare with starting eyeballs upon the strange being before him.

"Jerry, come here."

This order, so far from being obeyed, was quite the reverse, for as Jack raised his arm Jerry retreated, and stumbled headlong backwards down the stairs to the cabin.

"Hallo! what the devil are you after there, messmate?" cried the voice of Peter.

"The devil! the devil!" cried Jerry in affrighted tones.

"You've been and got drunk, you have," cried Peter, coming from the cabin and helping his friend to his feet.

"No, no! Shut the door, shut the door! Oh! lor—oh! lor."

"What's the matter with you, you fool?" said Peter, as Jerry darted into the cabin and slammed the door to.

"The devil!"

"What do you mean?"

"Oh! I've seen him; he'll be coming here— oh! lor—oh! lor."

An awful groan at the top of the steps caused Jerry to fling his broad back against the door.

"What's that?" asked Peter, himself turning pale and looking half-fearfully at the panels of the cabin door.

"It's him—it's him!"

"The devil?"

"Yes."

Peter listened, but all now was silent again.

Peter shook his head.

"Jerry, you are drunk, I say, and have been frightened by your own shadow."

"Upon my soul, no!" said the terrified Jerry. "I see him on the deck; such a face, and all in white."

"It might be some lubber playing you a trick," said Peter, evidently endeavouring to force himself to believe so.

"No—no!"

"It must have been." "I tell you, it wasn't. He called out my name, and was going to give me the rope's end, and when I tumbled down the steps—oh! lor, it's awful, it is! I won't go on deck again till daylight."

"Jerry, you are a coward."

"I ain't afraid of a man, but I can't fight the devil!" said Jerry. "Give us a swig at the grog. I'm all over shaking like a rag in a storm of wind."

Peter did as requested, and Jerry took a deep draught, the tin can playing a tune all the while on his lips, so violently did the hand of the seaman shake.

SPRING-HEELED JACK AND THE BURGLARS.

"Ship, ahoy!"

The two sailors looked at each other in unfeigned surprise.

"It's all owing to having a woman on board," whispered Jerry.

"That's not a devil's voice. I tell you that's the fellow we left to come aboard, and he's in the boat now."

"Ship, ahoy!" came in louder tones from the stem of the vessel.

"Bear a hand here!"

"Go on, Jerry."

"I shan't. You go."

"No! you."

"Then we'll both go," said Peter. "Let's take a marlin-spike a piece."

"It won't be no use."

"Why not?"

"Cos you can't hurt the devil."

"The devil take me, if I don't try, if he runs foul of me," said Peter, bracing up his nerves for the half-dreaded encounter.

Arming themselves with a couple of marlin spikes, the two men went out of the cabin.

But here they paused.

Neither cared to go first, and, as if by mutual agreement, after a time they walked slowly up the stairs together to the deck.

Both looked anxiously around.

"There's where he stood," said Jerry.

And a heartfelt sigh broke from his lips when he found the deck deserted by all but himself and companion.

"Ship ahoy!"

He now ran to the stern of the vessel and looked over.

There was Jack without his mask, and attired in his black cloak, sitting in the boat.

"Ahoy there!" cried Peter.

"Just be kind enough, my friend, to assist me aboard," said Jack. "I am not used to climbing ropes; I have been bawling myself hoarse ever since you left the deck. Not very kind of you to go away and leave a saturated fellow in the boat like this."

"Well, I'm blowed!" said Peter.

"Well, I'm jiggered!" gasped Jerry. "I say, messmate, have you seen the devil while you have been there?"

"Not unless you are he," was Jack's reply.

"No, no, I'm not; but haven't you seen somebody awful looking?"

"Not that I know of; never saw anybody worse than myself. But just hold out your hand and let me go and see the girl. She's all right I suppose?"

"As lively as a rat in the ship's hold," said Peter, finding his courage returning, and glad to have somebody else beside his messmate aboard. "Here, catch hold!"

Jack took the man's hand, ostensibly for assisting himself up, but in reality to make it appear he was unable to get on the deck without assistance, and so give the seamen no room to think that he and the figure who had alarmed Jerry was one and the same.

When he reached the deck, he said—

"I must convey this poor girl to some place where she can be properly attended to. I believe you are kind enough to do all in your power for her, but she requires the aid of one of her own sex. You can aid me to get her ashore, and I will reward you both for the trouble you have been put to."

"No, you won't," said Peter, bluntly. "No, you won't. I might fall overboard myself tomorrow, and its hard luck if we should refuse to another what we should like done to ourselves."

"Very good, my friend. I admire your sentiments. Now lead me to the girl, and perhaps you will give me the glass of grog you promised."

"With all my heart," said Peter. "This way."

The next minute Jack stood beside the woman he had saved from death.

CHAPTER XXVI

THE LIBERTINE AND SPRING-HEELED JACK.

RICHARD CLAVERING sat with a fierce, gloomy look upon his features.

Before him lay an open letter he had been perusing.

Beside it was a plain gold wire hoop.

On these his gaze was fixed.

Not with the happy glance which a symbol of undying love would be supposed to call up, but with a fierce, sullen, gloomy scowl.

The little hoop had fallen from the scented sheet as he broke the seal from that paper of such exquisite tint, but which contained words of such meaning.

"And so she demands that I shall make her my wife," he muttered, at length; "and if I refuse I am to be held up to infamy and scorn. By heavens! she is bold to write thus to me—me, at whose feet she has knelt ere this; me, whose frown could cause her heart to shrink within her bosom, and whose smile was a reward greater than all else in the world, and now she demands—threatens. Fool! fool to leave those dice where her hands could reach them—to trust her with the great secret of my success. Better a man trust his greatest enemy with a secret than the woman who professes to love him!"

He took the paper from the table, and ran his eye over it again.

"'I have made every preparation for our marriage,' she says. By heavens! that is cool. 'As you must desire secrecy, I have chosen the little church near Clapham. I shall await you there at nine o'clock to-morrow morning. I send you the ring. Beware you fail me not!' And these are her words, and to me!"

He tore the tinted paper to shreds, and flung the pieces at his feet.

Then taking up the little ring, he held it, musingly, between his finger and thumb.

"Curse her!" he muttered, after a pause, "but I'll wring her heart as well as ring her finger, for I must do as she bids me; yes, must, or those cursed dice— But who could have urged her to be thus bold, she who has ever been so timid? Who? Why, he—he who holds the evidence of crime; for cheating, I suppose, is a crime among men of my sphere. Well, I will obey her commands. I will wed her. She has chosen the best place she could. And there are to be no witnesses to the ceremony, save the old clerk and Lizzie, the housemaid, whose silence, she tells me, she can depend upon. Good for me—very good. Lizzie's silence may be bought by others besides herself; and old clerks are not over paid. Oh! yes; Jessie Bolton, you shall be my wife. But better for you had you been content to remain my mistress."

He laid the ring down upon the table, and, rising, paced the room with uneven strides.

"Yes, that ring shall be placed on her finger," he muttered, "and I will swear to love and cherish her. I will honour her commands. She has forced me to make her mine, and by heaven she shall learn she has a master! But this girl—this Lizzie. Why has she selected her before her own maid? I am at a loss to divine. No matter! Perhaps it is the better for me. The girl is ignorant and ill-bred; a few golden coins would buy her soul as well as body, and the one who can pay the most will find her of the best service."

He placed the ring in his waistcoat pocket, and walking to the window, looked out upon the pretty flower-garden below.

Dark clouds were floating in the horizon, and every few moments obscuring the moon, which rode high up above them, nearly at its full, throwing fantastic shadows on the earth as the thick vapours careered along at great speed.

As his glance wandered down to one of the flower-beds, he imagined that he saw a dark figure glide hastily past it and turn the angle of the house, but the moon's rays just bursting through the clouds left him in doubt whether or not he had been mistaken.

He kept his eyes fixed upon the spot where it had disappeared, and in a few moments the form of a woman turned the angle, and made its way along beneath the window where he stood.

The moonlight streamed down full upon her, and he recognised in the girl Lizzie the housemaid.

Still, there was nothing unusual in the servants being in the grounds at that hour; so, after a few moments' reflection, he came to the decision that it must have been her he had seen before, if indeed it was not a shadow cast by the clouds gliding over the moon.

He took a cigar from his ease, lit it, and leaning out of the window, fell into a train of thought respecting the ceremony at which he was to be present as principal on the following morning.

"Yes, I will do as she desires," he muttered, half aloud, "and get back those cursed dice. But once they are in my possession, I'll show her the devil she has made—a devil blacker and more cruel than"—

"Your humble servant, Spring-heeled Jack," cried a voice.

And through the window into the apartment, almost hurling Clavering to the floor in his course, came Spring-heeled Jack.

With a cry of surprise, Clavering sprang back. His gaze fixed a long way out over the garden, he had not observed the dark figure glide back round the angle of the house and stand, listening to what he was saying, directly beneath the window.

"You here?" said Richard, as soon as he could recover from his surprise.

"Yes, I am here."

"What is your business?"

"Am I not welcome?"

"Yes, if you come to return me those dice," said Richard.

"And if not?"

"Then you are far from welcome, and your room would please me better than your company," was the reply.

"No doubt. No, Richard Clavering, I have not come to return you those three little pieces of ivory with which you have robbed your friends on more than one occasion."

"Then what have you come for?" asked Richard, fiercely.

"To urge you to act like a man."

"What do you mean?"

"I will tell you."

"Well?"

"You have been talking aloud, and your words have fallen on my ears as I stood beneath that window."

"Indeed!" sneered Richard.

"Yes, indeed."

"And can you stoop so low as to become an eavesdropper?"

"I had no intention of being one."

"Then why were you there?" asked Clavering, sneeringly.

"I came hither to urge you to do justice to the poor lady who has so long been looked upon as your wife," replied Jack, haughtily.

"You take a strange interest in her, to be sure," said Richard.

"I do. I take a strong interest in every woman whose misfortune it is to fall into the hands of a villain."

"Sir? Dare you"—

Jack held up his hand.

"I dare speak as a man, as well as act as one," he said. "I repeat, Richard Clavering, that you are a villain. But enough of that. It is known to me that this lady has asked you to give her back the fair name of which you have robbed her. There are some men, and you are one of them, who imagine that they would be fools did they do an act of justice and reparation; but did they consider themselves rogues if they refused, they would be nearer the truth of their natures."

"You think so?"

"I am sure."

"All men do not think alike," sneered Richard.

"Certainly not. Rogues and villains cannot think as honest men."

Clavering scowled upon him, but made no remark, and Jack continued—

"Our parting on our last interview was a fiery one, and I believe you sincerely regret the unsteadiness of your hand. Richard Clavering, you came nigh to adding murder to robbery."

"Curses! I wish I had."

"No doubt."

"I do."

"The truth is seldom on your lips," said Jack, "and now I find it there, I look upon it as a good omen. When a bad man becomes truthful, we may naturally infer that he will soon forego his other vices."

"Go to the devil!" roared Richard, turning savagely away.

"I hope not, for I should be certain of meeting you there some day or other."

"Sir, the presence of a fool is distasteful to me."

"And the presence of a rogue is the same to me. Your remark may be just, since it is only fools who will seek to give counsel to rogues."

"I need none of yours."

"But you must listen to it," said Jack, pointedly.

"I will not."

"You shall."

"Sir, leave this place."

"When I have done."

"Shall I summon my servants?"

"If you please."

Jack, who had stood near the bell-pull, moved aside for Richard to advance. But the libertine did not.

"Shall I summon them for you?" asked Jack, after a pause.

"Sir, let this fooling cease. I am in no humour for such nonsense," said Clavering.

"With all my heart," said Jack. "And now to common-sense."

"What would you with me?" asked Caverning, desperately.

"Urge you to act as a man."

"In what course?"

"Wed that woman."

"I intend to do so."

"Good."

"What more?"

"When you have wedded her, treat her as a man and a husband," said Jack.

"What right have you to think I shall not?"

"Your own words."

"My words?"

"Yes."

"What words?"

"Those you gave utterance to as I stood beneath the window."

"Bah! they were nothing."

"They were much. I have promised to surrender those loaded dice the instant you become her husband, and thus save you from disgrace, and I will keep my word. Then my power over you will end, and threats prove unavailing; but I would ask you not to disgrace your manhood by cruel spite upon a poor, defenceless woman, who only seeks at your hands that reparation which, were you in her place, you would pray for. Richard Clavering, I cannot respect you after what I have heard and seen, and what has passed between us; but if not as a friend, at least as a man, let me ask you to act as such."

"Your gra—"—[33]

"Hold, I say!" interrupted Jack.

"Are you ashamed of your name?" sneered Richard.

"No, sir. You must not judge me by your own standard. I am not aware that I ever disgraced it. I am neither cheat, robber, nor would-be assassin."

"Nor am I."

"Indeed! Then why did I find you with the knife raised over the bosom of Jessie Bolton? Why did you fire at me?—me, whom you knew to be no midnight marauder."

Richard Clavering was silent.

____

[33] Referring to the suggestion of Jack's *alter ego* as Marquis. "Your Grace" is actually the title of a Duke, a rank higher than Marquis. Clavering should have addressed Jack as "My Lord".

"You cannot answer. Never mind. Let that pass. I forgive you this attempt to take my life, and seek not to be revenged upon you for the dastardly action."

Richard drew a breath of relief.

"No, sir. I am here only for one purpose, that of begging you to act like a man if you cannot feel as one. You say you have decided to grant the request of this poor lady. That is a step in the right direction; but it has been taken only through fear of exposure—of being held up to the scorn of your fellow-men. You will stand before the altar and swear to love and cherish her. Will you perjure yourself, and add another sin to your already sinful soul? You think this woman was only dazzled by your wealth, actuated only by a desire to move in a circle above that to which she has been accustomed, and a desire to be revenged upon you for the slight you have thrown upon her; but do you think that if she did not love you as a wife can love, that she would consent to stand at the altar with the man who would spurn her for another; who would seek her life, heap insult and injury upon her? Weigh this in your mind: and, Richard Clavering, you are a greater villain than I think if you do not resolve to treat kindly the woman who, after all this, is willing to become your bride."

"But the disgrace of marrying a wanton," said Clavering.

"Who made her such?" asked Jack.

He received no reply.

Richard's eye sank beneath the stern yet indignant glance.

"Who lied to bring her to his arms? Who perjured himself by honied words and false promises to lure her from her happy home? Who brought sorrow and shame upon her friends—misery and disgrace upon herself—who? I ask— who?"

Richard spoke not.

Jack took a step nearer, and placed his hand on the other's arm.

"I will tell you who, Richard Clavering: yourself. It was you—you who made her what she is—you who now would hurl her forth, if you dared, to beg—to starve—to die! Shame on you—shame, I say! Is there no green spot in your heart—no chord that can feel for the woman you have so basely injured? Are you lost to all feeling—all remorse—all manhood? What disgrace to make atonement for the wrongs you have done her? Rather would it not be a lasting disgrace to refuse that atonement and that love you swore to cherish for her!"

Never once did Richard Clavering raise his eyes from the floor.

His temples flushed with shame. He felt the truth of Jack's words—felt them deeply.

But he was proud—filled with that false pride which is but a mockery of the noble self-esteem which sits with such grace on those whose merits call it forth—a pride which is not overbearing, but simply a consciousness of superiority.

His pride was hurt at the idea of marrying a woman he had so basely wronged when he should have been proud of the courage to atone for his baseness—proud of the boldness to face the jeers of the unscrupulous, unpitying, and remorseless. "Richard Clavering," said Jack, after a lengthened pause, during which he had waited for him to speak, "I will say no more, but leave you to think of what I have already spoken. The worst of natures are not wholly bad—the hardest of hearts have one tender chord. Man is not irretrievably lost, and there is hope in the darkest hour of despair. You think me your foe; I have spoken as a friend. To-morrow you will stand before God's altar: add not another sin to those you will have to answer for by perjury. Repair the injury you have done that woman, and by future tenderness atone for the past. Now, farewell! "

Jack waved his hand, and while Richard Clavering stood in the centre of the apartment with his eyes fixed on the floor, Jack sprang through the window into the garden.

CHAPTER XXVII.
SACRILEGE—THE REGISTER—THE APPARITION, AND THE COMMAND.

IT was a beautiful moonlight night.

The silver rays streamed in a perfect flood through the little church window, throwing fantastic and coloured shadows upon the tall pews and quaint columns, and bathing the aisles in a strange, unearthly light.

The silence of the grave reigned throughout the edifice.

A silence so deep, so profound, that it struck awe to the soul of one who polluted its sacred precincts.

That one was Richard Clavering.

Yes, the libertine for the second time that day stood beneath the roof dedicated to the worship of God.

Fifteen hours before, he had stood in front of the little altar with cheeks paled, not by excitement, but passions of the worst description. Fifteen hours before he had sworn to love and cherish the woman he had lured from her innocent, happy home, and now he had returned to destroy the proofs of those vows he had taken—to destroy the register of their marriage.

Little effect had the words of Spring-heel'd Jack upon him. They were forgotten, or at least unheeded.

Truly there was no green spot in his callous, unfeeling heart!

He had forced his way into the place through a low side-window, to effect which purpose he had shattered the stained panes, presented as an offering of gratitude by an aged inhabitant, and had made his way, with trembling step, towards the vestry.

He had come bold of heart and firm of purpose.

But he quailed now. The awful silence appalled him. The hollow sounds of his own footfall caused him to tremble, and look round in nervous agitation.

His blood chilled in his veins, and seemed to stagnate round his heart.

His teeth chattered as if with cold, and a clammy perspiration broke out of every pore of his skin.

Fain would he have retreated, but the recollection that Jessie was now his wife, and that within the precincts of that sacred place rested the leaf which could establish her claim, urged him forward.

Struggling hard to stifle the chattering of his teeth, trembling at every step, he made his way to the vestry.

He had trusted to the moonlight to guide him in his unholy work, and hence had brought with him no means of procuring a light.

But the windows of the edifice being stained, the light was mellowed, and the place consequently more gloomy than he had anticipated.

He laid his hand upon the door of the vestry, and entered.

The room was furnished only with a chair and a table, but in one corner was a safe. To that his gaze was directed.

There he knew the register was kept.

He had lingered long enough in that apartment in the morning to learn this fact.

With starting eyes and throbbing heart, he had watched the aged clerk deposit the book there.

He stood with the door of the little room in his hand, and gazed half fearfully along the church.

The shadows of column and cornice fell upon the floor, and light and shadow, mingling with the silence of death, made him hesitate in his work.

"What am I about to do?" he thought; "commit sacrilege. But then shall a wanton enjoy my wealth—bear my name? No! The crime is horrible to contemplate, but that—that is worse. Away with all questions of conscience— all childish fears! I have not come here to commit murder, but save a proud name from derision and scorn. Why should I hesitate when I have been forced into a ceremony that was hateful to me?"

Closing the door of the vestry, he took hold of the chair, and placed it directly under the safe.

Again he paused.

Again he listened intently.

His heart beat with anxiety, fear, and hope combined.

But all was still.

Hushed was every sound, save the wild throbbing of his excited heart.

This he could hear as well as feel, as it beat against his bosom, and chided him for the act he meditated.

Springing lightly upon the chair, he placed his hand on the knob of the safe.

But as it rested there, the thought that most likely it was locked caused him almost to fall from the chair.

Richard had not once thought of this circumstance before.

It struck him with great violence now.

He had come unprepared to force it, and, if fastened, he had run a terrible risk— undergone an agony of fear for no reward.

Then he had not observed the clerk lock it when he placed the book on one of its shelves.

But then, was it probable he had not since done so?

He almost dreaded to confirm or annihilate his suspicions.

It was moments of intense anxiety he suffered now, while the thought ran through his mind.

But he grasped the knob in his hand, and pulled it towards him.

Joy! The door rolled back upon its hinges.

But a creaking sound was produced—a sound that at any other time, and under any other circumstances, would have been unheeded.

Now it grated on his heart, and caused a fresh thrill of horror to run through his system.

Could that sound have aroused anyone to a suspicion of what he was doing—of the guilty work he was about?

He feared it had.

Yet, a moment's reflection told him that it never could have been heard, had a listener stood outside that little room.

More freely he breathed again.

But his heart still beat, and his limbs trembled as if he was smitten with the ague.

The door having rolled back, several books were revealed to his gaze as they reposed upon three shelves of the safe.

But one only he sought.

His eye detected it on the instant.

Its massiveness and black binding pointed out to his strained vision the register in which he had scribbled his name some few hours before.

He stretched out his hand to grasp it, but paused as he imagined he heard a sound in the church beyond.

The hand, which had nearly touched the book, remained extended, and every nerve was strained to catch a repetition of the imagined noise.

Moments flew by, and the silence of the grave reigned throughout the place.

"What a coward I am!" he gasped at length. "There is no one here—none could have suspected this errand. Pshaw! I will not be alarmed."

He seized the book and lifted it from the shelf.

As he drew it forth, it slipped from his trembling hand.

The libertine tried to save it, but it fell with a loud bang to the floor.

The sound of its fall echoed through the hollow church with a noise resembling the banging of doors.

The robber stood fairly appalled.

His hair almost stood on end; his heart sank within him, while a sensation of faintness stole over his frame.

He clutched at the back of the chair for support.

Glaring wildly at the door of the vestry, as if fearful of some one opening it, he sank down into the chair and held his hand to his heart, gasping for breath.

But again, all was still as the grave; and gradually the sensation wore off, and he rose to his feet.

Could he, however, have seen a reflection of his own face in a glass, he would not have recognised it, for it vied with the whiteness of his shirt-front.

"Let me haste and flee from this place!" he cried, half aloud. "This is horrible!"

He raised the book from the floor, and, as if fearful of making another sound, he lowered it gently down on to the table, and silently opened it.

But though the moonlight which streamed into the apartment was sufficient to light up the room, it would not permit him to read a single line, or detect a single leaf.

The window was small and draped, and hence the room was not so light as the sacred edifice beyond.

"I must go out into the church and take the leaf by the flood of light that pours through the large window over the altar," he said. "I have little doubt that I should select other than the right one; but I must be certain, for I could never undergo such another night of misery."

He tiptoed across the room to the door of the apartment and nervously pulled it open.

The shadows were longer than before, and to his troubled mind appeared like phantoms stretched along the aisle.

But he struggled against his fears, and taking the book from the table, carried it into the church.

With trembling steps he made his way to the altar railings, on to which the moonlight streamed full and bright; and resting the book thereon, held it balanced with the left, while with the right hand he turned over the leaves.

By straining his vision he could trace the characters therein and he soon found the leaf on which his name and that of Jessie Bolton had been written.

As he gazed upon it, his fears vanished; he felt only that he could now destroy that woman's claim upon him.

He took the leaf between his finger and thumb and holding it up, he muttered, in a kind of hissing whisper—

"Now, Jessie Bolton—for no other name shall you ever be able to lay claim to—I will snap the chain that binds me. The dice, whose evidence I so much feared, are in my possession, and I can laugh to scorn your threats. Thus do I release myself of your hateful presence—thus do I sever the bonds that bind us together—thus do I hurl you forth to beggary and despair!"

He was about to tear the leaf away, when a loud, hollow voice at his elbow exclaimed—

"Thus do I prevent the sacrilegious act!"

The young man turned with a cry of horror, his hand still upon the book, and confronted a tall, cloaked figure, of hideous and repulsive features, which, standing full in the glare of the moonlight as it streamed through a pane of glass painted of a pale blue colour, gave it an aspect so unearthly that the hair of the libertine rose gradually upon his head till it stood upright; and trembling in every limb, the book fell from beneath his hand to the floor again, awaking the echoes of the hollow church which reverberated from pillar to pillar like a roll of thunder.

Appalled, Richard Clavering clung to the railings of the altar for support, while with affrighted gaze his eyes rested upon the figure before him.

We have said before that Richard was not naturally a superstitious man, but at this moment he fairly believed that a spectre had risen from its grave to confront him.

So powerful were the emotions that had taken possession of his heart, that he reeled like a drunken man, and but for the rail to which he clung he must have fallen.

And thus he stood glaring upon the tall figure in that pale blue light, who, with extended arm, pointed reprovingly at him.

The silence, too, which again reigned was awful in its intensity.

The guilty man would have given worlds had it been broken.

But not a single sound emanated from the lips of the apparition now.

It stood erect, with extended finger pointed at him, the pale blue light playing upon its hideous face and tall cloaked form.

Richard strove to speak.

He could not.

His tongue clove to the roof of his mouth.

The lips of the libertine became parched and dry, and his eyeballs appeared as if they would start from their sockets.

He tried to close his eyes to shut out the terrible vision, but he could not.

He made an effort to flee, but terror had chained him to the spot.

Richard Clavering was powerless now—powerless as a new-born babe.

Gradually his limbs sank beneath him, a dizziness stole over his brain, a film crossed his eyes, and still clutching at the railing, he dropped all of a heap on the cushion where he had that morning knelt and perjured his already blackened soul.

Then the figure drew nearer to him, with a soft, gliding step, which emitted no sound, and paused on the spot where the moonlight, streaming through a blood-red pane of glass, made him look even more hideous than before.

A minute it stood there, and then, in a hollow voice, it exclaimed—

"Man of evil passions, must the house of God be polluted by thy unholy presence?—the records of the holiest of ties severed by thy guilty hand? Must that altar, dedicated to the worship of the Most High, be debased by contact with thy wicked form? No! Follow me!"

The figure took a step nearer, and laid his hand upon the arm of the crouching man.

With a cry of horror and despair, Richard sprang to his feet.

Never for a moment had it struck him that the being before him was human. In his guilty heart he felt convinced that it was some phantom which had risen to upbraid him.

"Follow or tremble!" said the figure again, in a tone that caused the blood of Richard to curdle.

The guilty man felt himself powerless to resist the mandate. In spite of his endeavours to refuse, he felt himself drawn as if by some magnetic influence towards the cloaked figure, which beckoned him from the altar along the centre aisle of the moonlit church.

CHAPTER XXVIII.

RICHARD FINDS HIMSELF PLACED IN A VERY STRANGE POSITION.

IRRESISTIBLY along the aisle of the sacred edifice Richard Clavering followed the strange figure.

It was with a tottering gait he did so, and ever and anon he was compelled to place his hand on the top of the pews on either side to support himself.

It was somewhat strange that he did not recognise in the tall cloaked figure before him the form of his quondam[34] friend, Spring-heel'd Jack.

But he did not; never did that personage once occur to his memory.

The awe with which that silent church had inspired him, the great strain upon his nerves, and the guilty work in which he was engaged, had rendered him forgetful of the man who had been greatly instrumental in forcing him to do an act of justice to a deceived and too willing woman.

Had the unexpected meeting taken place in any other spot than where it did, doubtless he would have resisted the command of this strange confronter, but here he felt that he was wholly powerless to resist the mandate, and he staggered on after him as he preceded his trembling steps along the church.

In the centre of the aisle Jack paused, turned sharply, and pointed to a large opening in the floor.

---

[34] One time.

"Descend!" he said, in a hollow, unearthly voice.

Richard started back from the black orifice, on the verge of which he stood.

"Descend!" repeated Jack.

Richard glared fearfully around him.

"Descend, or you will repent it!" said Jack. "Coward! do you fear the dark?"

"In God's name, who, and what are you?" cried Richard.

"Take not that name in vain. Base mortal, dare you profane that name, and know that sacrilege brought you hither? Come—come!"

"Oh! where—where?"

"There!"

Jack again pointed to the opening in the church floor.

"Heavens! that leads to the vaults!" shuddered the libertine.

"Aye! to the homes of the dead!"

"Mercy! I cannot!"

"You shall!"

"No! no!"

"Follow me, or beware!"

"I dare not."

"You dare not refuse my commands."

"Are you mortal?"

Jack had averted his face from the other's gaze, and now he turned quickly round and suffered the moonlight to shine full upon him.

In that movement he had changed his mask, unperceived by the trembling man.

"Are you answered?" he cried.

Richard Clavering uttered a loud shriek, and fell backwards in terror against the side of the pews.

The moonlight streamed full upon the white marble face of a skeleton.

"Mortal! are you answered?" he asked again, making his voice more hollow than before.

Richard Clavering covered his face with his hands.

He could not bear the horrible sight which had met his gaze.

Satisfied that he was in the presence of a being of another world, he exclaimed—

"Then the grave does give up its dead?"

"To foil villainy at times, it does," answered Jack. "At your peril, disobey. Follow me."

"Spare me!"

"Guilty man"—

"I know I am a guilty wretch!" cried Richard, quickly, in trembling accents. "I acknowledge it here; but I do repent of the crime I meditated, and will sin no more."

"'Tis given to me to read your heart," said Jack. "Mortal! you lie!"

"No—no."

"Seek not to deceive one from the grave. Come!"

"For heaven"—

"Hold, impious wretch!"

"On my soul"—

"Peace! and follow!"

"I cannot."

"Then will I bear you in my arms," said Jack, advancing a step towards the trembling and horrified man.

With a shriek of horror, Richard held his hands before him to keep him off.

"Touch me not," he said, "for contact with thee will kill me."

"Your life is worthless."

"I have a wife to live for."

"A wife?"

"Yes."

"Ha! ha! ha!"

The tones in which this laugh were uttered were so wild and discordant that Richard almost shrieked aloud in horror and dismay.

"Mortal! do you love your wife?" asked Jack, after the echoes had died away.

Richard did not reply.

The phantom had told him he could read his heart, and he dared not answer.

"Come!" said Jack. "We waste time. Come with me."

"I implore you"—

"You implore in vain," cried Jack, taking another step towards Clavering, "come you must, and shall."

"Keep off—keep off!" shrieked Richard. "Do not touch me—I will go—I will go!"

"Beware you seek not to flee from me. In my presence you are as powerless as a child."

He pointed to the opening.

"But how can I descend?" exclaimed Richard, advancing to the edge of the opening.

"By these steps. Go."

Richard hesitated.

The phantom stretched forth his hand towards him.

Clavering gave him one more despairing and imploring look, but was motioned to descend, and with a shudder of horror and despair, the libertine placed one foot on the steps, the top one of which he could trace in the moonlight.

His blood curdled, and his flesh crept; but the spectre waved him on, and with a desperate effort, the guilty man commenced to descend into the darkness of the vaults beneath the church.

He kept his eyes fixed upwards though, upon the skeleton face above him, still with an imploring look, but the spectre only kept his finger pointed down the opening, and uttered the one word—

"On!"

Richard Clavering felt that he must obey— that his safest course to pursue was to be obedient, and he continued his descent.

As his head disappeared beneath the flooring of the chapel, the spectre shifted his position.

Richard paused on the steps, and, perceiving the horrible figure gone, he was about to rush up them again, when the heavy trap was hurled down upon the opening, and he was left in Stygian darkness.

Horrorstruck, he screamed aloud, and back to his ears came a peal of mocking laughter.

He mounted one step, and stretched up his hands to the trap.

Horror! it was fastened.

He exerted all his strength, but was powerless to move the trap from its resting -place.

The darkness of the grave was there; not one ray of light penetrated the place.

A sensation, as of cold water being poured over him, he now experienced, and he imagined he could smell the mouldering corpses of those whom he believed lay around him.

To such a pitch of agony were his feelings now worked that, forgetful of the penalty for sacrilege, he shrieked aloud—

"Help! Help!"

And "help! help!" came back in mockery to his ears, as if screamed by a hundred spectre tongues.

"O my God—my God! how am I punished for my sin!" he cried, as unable to bear the emotions under which he laboured, he sank down upon the steps.

"Oh! that I had never meditated stealing that register!" he muttered, through his chattering teeth. "Oh! that I never had—I never had!"

After a pause, he sprang hurriedly to his feet, and essayed again and again to raise the trap.

But all his exertions were of no avail, and he crept down the steps till he stood upon the floor of the vault.

"Will no one come?" he cried aloud. "No one—oh, God! this fearful agony will drive me mad!"

"Mad!" was the reply in loud echoes, and he glanced round him as if he expected to see a thousand spectres peering at him and mocking his agony.

"Help, help!"

In vain he cried.

Echo only answered him from all sides.

"Oh! Is there no means of escape—none— none!" he shrieked.

"None—none!" was the reply.

He tried again, but now he knew that it was but the echo of that place which answered him.

"There must be some other opening than that above," he continued, talking aloud now. "Yes; there must be—I will search."

"Search!" replied the echo.

"But where?"

"Where!"

"Oh, God! that fearful echo!"

"Echo!"

"This agony of mind will kill me," he continued. "Oh, God! what is that—whatever is that?"

As he moved fearfully along, stretching his hands out before him, they now came in contact with a coffin, and with a shudder of horror he drew back.

"Yes, these are the vaults—the resting-place of the dead. And he—he—who forced me here —where is he?"

"Here," cried a hollow voice at his elbow. Richard recoiled as if a cobra stood in his path.

"You are," said the voice.

"Here!" he gasped. "Oh, have mercy! Let me forth from this fearful place!"

"For what? That you may seek to defile the register?"

"No—no! I swear I will never more harbour such a wicked thought!" he cried.

"That you may treat with cruelty her who stood beside you at the altar to-day?"

"I swear I will be true-to her," said Clavering.

"You swear?"

"I do, most solemnly."

"Of what avail are dicers' oaths?" asked the voice.

"'Tis true; he can read my heart," thought Richard.

"Have you not to-day falsely sworn, and would you not do so to-morrow?" asked the voice beside him.

"No. I will repent—reform. I have been a gay, bad man, but this night has changed me quite," cried Richard, looking imploringly in the direction of his questioner whom he could not see.

Indeed the darkness was so black that had his questioner stood close before him he could not have known it.

"Why, why have you forced me here?" he asked at last.

"To save you from further sin."

"Good heaven! you do not mean to keep me in this fearful place!" he exclaimed, in agony.

"You must not go hence."

"Not go!"

"No."

"I must!—I will!" he shrieked, fear and terror making him desperate. "I will go forth spite of all the spectres or phantoms in the world."

"You are bold."

"I am mad, or soon shall be," said Clavering, beating his forehead with his clenched hand. "I say I will go forth—I will go home!"

"You are there now."

"Where?"

"At home. Your home now is here—here among the festering remains of those who lived and died; here, where the atmosphere you breathe is impregnated with foetid exhalations of the mouldering corpses; here"—

"Hold! In mercy, hold!" cried Richard. "Kill me if you will; but I cannot bear this horrible torture. Slay me, or let me hence. Dash out my brains with your bony hands. I shall go mad—mad—mad!"

"Ha! ha! ha!" laughed the spectral voice; and a dozen more spectral tones appeared to the affrighted man to join in the unearthly laugh.

"Oh, God! I can bear it no longer!" cried Richard Clavering. "Curses on my folly and my wickedness. I am punished — fearfully punished!"

"Then, have mercy!—oh, have mercy on a guilty and repentant wretch!" he cried, in tones of such abject entreaty that Jack felt he could not torture him any more; so, gliding silently away from his side, he turned round a pile of coffins, pushed open a little door in the wall, and stood outside the edifice. Walking round this, he made his way to the

SPRINGHEELED JACK ALARMS THE MISER.

window by which Richard had entered, and crept through it; ran along the aisle to the trap, raised it, and retreated from the church by the way he had come, taking care first to replace the register in the safe from which it had been taken.

CHAPTER XXIX.
ON THE HOUSETOPS—JACK'S ADVENTURE WITH THE BURGLARS.

AS JACK leaped to the ground, he was run against by a policeman, who, having just observed the open window, had drawn back into the shadow to watch if anyone would come through it.

He had passed the spot several times before that night, but had not observed whether the window was open or closed.

It was not certain to his mind whether it had been left open by accident or had been forced open from the outside; so deemed it best to keep out of sight and watch for a time whether any person made their appearance.

He had not waited long—indeed he had only arrived at the spot where he made his discovery a moment after Jack had entered the sacred edifice through it—when he perceived our hero at the opening, and rushed forward, as, all unsuspecting of danger, he leaped to the ground.

Ere Jack could sufficiently recover the shock with which they came together, he found himself a prisoner.

The officer had flung himself upon him behind, and held him by the collar of his cloak and his left arm.

"I've cotched[35] yer, have I?" said the policeman. "After the sacrament plate, eh? But you're done this time, my fine fellow."

Jack made an effort to get away.

He saw how affairs stood in a second, and had made up his mind how to act in an instant.

His face was still covered with the skeleton mask, and to that he trusted rather than to his own strength to release himself from the custody of the policeman.

So, turning his head slowly round, he said, in the deep, hollow tone he found usually so effective—

"Frail mortal, can you bind the dead! Can you stay my passage back to the grave?"

With a howl of terror, the officer released his hold, and leaped backwards several feet.

"Oh, Lord! oh, Lord! it's a skeleton!" he exclaimed.

"And to such will you come some day after you have shuffled off this mortal coil," said Jack. "'Tis one o'clock, and I must away!"

At this moment the clock struck one, and Jack taking advantage of the officer's terror and surprise, gave a terrific bound and disappeared in the angle of the church.

Keeping close to the wall, he slipped off his mask, and peeped round at the officer.

There the man stood in the road where he had left him, evidently believing that he had seen a veritable ghost, and that the spectre had gone back to his grave.

Jack had no fear that the policeman would follow, so he strolled quietly away along the road, wondering how Richard Clavering was faring, and congratulating himself upon

---

[35] Caught.

being instrumental in saving the register from being defiled by the libertine's hand.

"Poor devil, I could almost pity him," he said to himself, "still I do not regret his sufferings. The fright I have given him may tend to make him a better and more feeling man. Hallo! that looks suspicious!"

This last remark was called forth by seeing a man whisk down a narrow street, giving a strange and peculiar whistle as he did so, and at the same time noticing that a light was instantaneously extinguished in a parlour window of a large house nearly opposite to where he was.

The whistle was again repeated, but at a greater distance, and Jack walked quietly over the road and looked up at the house.

It stood a little way back from the road behind a small but neat garden, which was protected by a close paling about four feet high.

The moon, which was still shining brilliantly, lit up every object around, and Jack looked over the paling into the forecourt, and to his surprise perceived near the doorway a large bundle evidently ready to be taken away.

"The sudden disappearance of that man, and the peculiar whistle he gave vent to, made me think all was not right," muttered Jack. "And I'm convinced my suspicions were correct now. That bundle speaks for itself. There are thieves about; and my coming along the road has alarmed them. That light, too—that looks bad. I'll arouse the inmates, and perhaps the rascals may yet be captured."

He vaulted over the paling into the forecourt, and ran along the smoothly-gravelled pathway to the front door. Here he saw what the shrubs in the garden prevented him before observing, namely, that the kitchen window was open.

He rushed to this, and though he saw no one, he fancied he could hear a deadened footfall, which he attributed to the burglar being without his shoes.

"I'll stop you this way," said Jack, seizing the sash, and pulling the window down, then springing to the street-door, he knocked loudly.

"That will alarm the inmates," he said, "and the thieves too. They will fancy the house is surrounded, and make no attempt to escape this way. They, will be forced to escape by the roof or try to do so, any way; but the rascals ought not to get off without a shock, and I fancy, from the build of this place, I can give them one, but I must be sharp, or they will have got away."

He cast his glance upwards.

The door and windows were ornamented by overhanging porches, which stretched out from the walls some distance; and Jack, gathering the folds of his cloak about him, so as not to permit it to impede his motions, vaulted on to the brick wall which parted the grounds of the two houses.

Another bound, and he alighted on the ornamental porch of the door.

Had he hesitated a moment he must have fallen; but springing up quickly, his feet rested on the projecting ornament over the first floor window.

This formed a sufficiently broad ledge for him to stand upon, and placing his hands against the wall to steady himself, he looked upwards.

He was still about twelve feet from the roof, which he desired to reach, and the next projection was only the leaden gutter of the house.

He flung his cloak back from off his shoulders, expanded his chest, stooped, then up he bounded like an arrow, swiftly for the gutter.

This he caught with his hands, and hung suspended by that frail support, which he could feel bend beneath his weight.

But drawing his body quickly up by his arms, he flung himself over on to the roof.

In another moment he was on his feet, and standing beside a small stack of chimneys looking down at a trap-door.

"I'm up first, then," he said. "Now for my mask—which shall it be—the death's-head? no, no! not that; I will wear my usual one—the skeleton must be kept for rare occasions; the demon will serve me best now."

And taking the mask in which we have so often seen him, from his pocket, he readily slipped it over his face.

Hardly had he settled it to his features, than the trap at his feet began to move.

"I guessed that would be their game," he said with a smile, as he drew back behind the stack of chimneys, but still kept his eyes fixed on the trap, which mow rose slowly from its bed.

At this moment, a cloud partially obscured the moon, and Jack seized the folds of his cloak in his hands, intending to hold them out in such a fashion, as he had done when he alarmed the model policeman, but suddenly altering his mind, he coiled his body round one of the taller chimneys, and placed himself in such a position as almost to bide himself among the stack.

Up went the trap-door as far as it would go, and a head and burglarious-looking face appeared in the opening.

But it did not come up higher just then.

The head turned suspiciously each way, and the eyes in that head were evidently engaged in looking if the coast was clear.

Of course, the burglar did not look up at the chimneys, and consequently, satisfied with his scrutiny, the head was followed by the shoulders, and in another few moments the burglar stood upon the roof.

He strode forward a step towards the chimney- stack, looked above, and then turned to the trap.

"All right, Jerry—come on," he said, in a husky whisper.

Jack shot out his right arm between the pots, and caught the fellow so heavy a blow on the nape of the neck, as to cause him to leap quite two yards on one side, when he paused, closed his fists, and looked savagely around him in the greatest surprise.

"Well, I'm jiggered," he muttered, "where did that come from? There's nobody here, and Jerry couldn't have done it, when he ain't up the trap."

Jack stuck close to the chimneys, and hidden completely in the stack, he continued to smother his laughter.

"Oh, I see what it was," he muttered, "I must have been fool enough to shove my head agin one of them 'ere chimneys."

Jack grinned. .

The ruffian again approached the trap. Jack measured his distance. Out went his hand again, and the burglar received a smart blow on the cheek.

Round he sprang like a top. Fury was in his glance. But he saw nothing.

He dropped his upraised hand to his side— staggered back a step, and muttered—

"Well, I'm licked!"

The man was certainly becoming frightened now.

Unable to trace the source from whence the blows came, it was evident that his ignorance was leading him to look upon it as the work of a supernatural being.

"It must have been the devil," he said, scratching his head with one hand, and rubbing his smarting face with the other. "It couldn't have been anybody else, or I must have seen 'em. Jerry—Jerry!"

He had again turned to the trap.

"Confound the fellow, why don't he come— he can't slope[36] off the other way, for the peelers is on the watch—hist, Jerry, all square up here?"

Jack had got down from the chimney-stack, and darting quickly and silently forward, he administered a tremendous kick at the bottom of the burglar's back as he was stooping to call his comrade, which sent him staggering along the roof for several feet.

Ere he had gained his equilibrium, Jack had once more made for his place of concealment, where he crouched, watching the fellow with great amusement.

"Thunder me blue!" roared the burglar, forgetting that silence was a virtue in his situation; "if you'll only show yourself, I'll chuck you off the cursed house."

"Very kind of you, I'm sure," muttered Jack to himself.

"I will—so help me never, I will," continued the excited man, placing himself in a fighting attitude, and squaring at the air.

Jack now picked a piece of loose mortar from behind the chimneys, and with unerring aim, threw it at the eye of the burglar.

The man uttered a horrible curse, and sprang forward.

"I'll find out who it is, I will by—" he yelled.

Another piece, larger than the one before, struck him on the nose.

Unable to trace the spot from where they came, or discover the hand that, hurled them with such precision, the burglar had become utterly bewildered and alarmed, and turned first one way and then the other, anxious to escape yet not knowing which way to fly.

At this moment the aroused inmates commenced bawling for the police loudly from the window, and the burglar once more became alive to his danger, and the prospects of his capture if he did not beat a hasty retreat.

Still, he was evidently loth to go without his pal, who still lingered behind—from some cause or other.

"Jerry—Jerry!" he cried, "if you don't come I must go without you. We shall be nailed if we stop here any longer—cuss the swag, never mind that—let it go to the devil!"

"I don't want it," said Jack, gliding from his concealment, and standing upon the roof, holding the folds of his cloak out at arm's length.

The man turned quickly on the very edge of the trap, and stood face to face with our hero.

His rough visage blanched with terror and dismay.

His eyes and mouth opened till they could stretch no wider.

His short-cropped hair stood up like porcupine's quills, and lifted his cap upon his head.

He trembled as if seized with the palsy, and his cruel heart throbbed as though it

---

[36] Sneak away.

would burst through his bosom.

"Je—Je—Jerry!" he gasped. "Here's the de—de—devil!"

"Glad to see me, are you not?" asked Jack, in his hollow tone, and turning so as to allow the moonlight to fall on his mask.

"No—no—no!" stammered the man.

"Sorry for that, because I've come for you, you see."

"Co—co—come for me?"

"Just so. Are you ready to go?"

"No, no, no!"

"Well, it's all the same, you must come," said Jack.

And he advanced with extended arms, as if to clasp the burglar in his embrace.

The man uttered a short, sharp cry of terror, and stepped back hastily.

That was a fatal step for him, and also for his companion, who was now making his way up the ladder to the roof to join his comrade.

The burglar had found no resting-place for his foot as he fell back before the advance of Jack. He had stepped into the traphole in his terror, and, losing his balance, fell backwards through it on the head of his friend, dashing him to the landing with fearful violence, and, rolling over him, pitched head first down the flight of stairs to the first floor, where he lay groaning with agony, having broken his collar-bone in the fall.

Jerry was more fortunate than his friend and fellow-burglar. That personage had certainly received an injury of the neck, but it did not prevent him rising hastily to his feet and making up the ladder to the roof, in the hopes of escape.

Of course he knew nothing of what had caused his pal to fall back upon him. He doubtless attributed it to accident, and feeling that his best course would be to ensure his own safety and leave his companion to himself, he sped on till he reached the roof.

As he was about getting on the pots through the opening on to the moonlit tiles, he was confronted by Jack, who had again sprung on to the stack of chimneys, and with a shout of terror he turned to retreat down the trap, when our hero jumped down and seized him by the arm, saying—

"Hold!"

Like his companion, his brutish nature was cowed on the instant by the sight of that face and form, and stood trembling in the grasp of our hero.

"No, you don't," said Jack; "you're wanted, my boy."

"Wa—wa—wanted?" stammered the fellow.

"Yes; you've been long enough at this game. Time's up; come!"

And Jack led him unresistingly across the roof to the coping-stone in front of the house.

"Look there," said Jack, pointing over. "Do you see the top of those hats glistening in the moonlight? They are policemen; you're a thief. They are waiting for you."

"Oh!" and the man drew a long breath of relief. "Then it's not you who wants me?"

"Not yet."

"Thank God!" cried Jerry.

If ever man uttered a fervent exclamation, Jerry the burglar did then.

"No, you are too bad for me. But I will give you one chance of escape."

"What is it?"

"Never steal more, and I will let you go. Promise me that," said Jack.

"I will."

"But can I believe you?"

"You can."

"Beware you do not deceive yourself, for you cannot deceive me. Attempt to commit another robbery, and you will find me at your side."

"I swear it, I never will!" gasped Jerry.

"Enough; I'll trust you this once. Now, begone."

He removed his hand.

Jerry required no second bidding.

He darted away over the housetops with the speed of an antelope, the fear of capture lending wings to his flight.

Jack watched him for some moments, when the sound of voices aroused him to the fact that the police were making their way to the roof, and having no desire to be seen by them, Jack stepped along the tiles of the adjoining houses, and finally sprang into a garden at the rear of a house some short distance from the scene of the robbery.

CHAPTER XXX.

MISS FRUMP SEEKS A HUSBAND, AND MEETS A REPULSE.

WITH the counterpane belonging to old deaf Duppy's bed wrapped around her, the old maid reached her own room, where she locked herself in, and then, with an hysterical sob, sank down upon the floor.

Poor lady, her garrulous nature had brought about all she had suffered, but still she did not deserve it.

She had certainly made herself at times very obnoxious to her neighbours by her fussy ways and the bitter spirit she often exhibited against those who had not strictly conformed to her ideas of morality.   .

In her eyes the poor deluded girl was a base, designing hussy, and deserved to be badgered and bated, and held up to scorn and loathing, rather than receive pity. She had no sympathy for those who had strayed, either from inclination or a too trusting heart, from the paths of rectitude and honour.

But then Miss Frump was one of those personages whom males had looked upon but coldly. She had never been in love, from the mere fact that her over-prudish and repelling nature had rather kept away than lured lovers to her side.

On all sides she was slighted, for her heart never beat in unison with another. She was too cold; the fault was nature's perhaps, and not her own.

Had she been a wife and a mother, doubtless she would have been very different in her feelings, but she was neither, and as years passed over her head, and time left its traces on her brow, the cold, unimpulsive heart of her girlhood grew harder and harder, for her bosom seemed only to contain bitterness and gall.

And so she was disliked by all and her society shunned.

She felt she was disliked, and therefore she turned upon others at every chance she could got.

Poor Baker had given her one, and now, out of revenge for her bitterness on that occasion, his friends had turned the tables upon herself, and bitterly did she feel it.

She sat rocking herself to and fro upon the floor, while the remarks of those who had been summoned from their beds in the dead of the night came with no very flattering sentiments to her ears.

Of course she knew that she was not guilty of that which was imputed to her, but who would believe it?

"None."

If she had no real enemies, she certainly had no real friends. She heard not one voice raised in her favour.

But she heard Tom Bedford saying in a very loud tone that poor Duppy was not so much to blame, for Miss Frump never would let the poor old man alone.

Oh! if she could but have reached the speaker's face with her nails—if she could but have twined her fingers in his hair—her wounded heart might have found some relief; but she could not—dared not leave her room to give him the length of her tongue, and so she wrung her hands together, and sobbed violently.

After a time all was still; the house was deserted by all save herself and Duppy.

Then she rose from her crouching position on the floor. She had made up her mind what to do.

She went to her drawers and took out fresh attire, her own being below, and robed herself.

Her wig of course she could not put on, that being with her clothes below.

But she put on a cap, looked at herself in the glass, and turned with a determined step to the door.

"I will do it now," she said. "I will not wait till the morning, lest my courage fail me. He must share with me the disgrace—he shall help me to redeem my character."

She walked down the stairs and tapped at Duppy's door.

"Mr. Duppy! Mr. Duppy!" The old man was too excited to retire to rest, and had dressed himself.

He did not hear her voice, but he saw her form through the partially open door, and he rose and confronted her.

"Mr. Duppy."

"Yes, ma'am."

"Please to walk into the parlour, sir."

Tom Bedford had placed the key in the lock, and there was no difficulty for the old maid to surmount in obtaining an entrance.

Duppy followed her with his candlestick in his hand.

"Please to be seated, Mr. Duppy."

Mr. Duppy complied, after placing the candlestick on the table.

"This has been a sad piece of business, Mr. Duppy."

"Very sad, ma'am."

"Come a little nearer, Mr. Duppy; you will hear better."

Mr. Duppy did as requested, looking rather bashful, and certainly much surprised.

"Mr. Duppy, I'm a lost woman," said Miss Frump, "unless"—

She paused and looked round at him, and then dropped her eyes to the floor. "Unless what, ma'am?"

"You will save me."

"Me, Miss Frump?"

"You, Mr. Duppy!"

"I do not understand you."

"Not?"

"Indeed, no!"

"Can you forget what has passed but a short time since?"

"I wish it never had happened."

"So do I; but"—

She looked down again.

"But," she simpered, "but, Mr. Duppy, the world is so cruel."

"Very, ma'am."

"It will say that you and I have overstepped the bounds of prudence. It has said so."

"It tells a lie, ma'am. You know there was nothing wrong between us. You ought to know that I didn't do any wrong—I should have known it if I did."

"But will the world believe"—

"I don't care what the world says."

"But you are a man."

"I'm old enough to be one."

"I am a woman. You know that I am a woman, Mr. Duppy."

"Well, I suppose you are, ma'am."

"Yes, Mr. Duppy. A man is forgiven by the cruel world if he errs, either by mistake or design. But a woman—oh! Mr. Duppy, for her there is but one escape from its sneers—but one—only one! "

"And what's that, ma'am?"

"Can you ask?"

Miss Frump's hand rested on his arm, and her eyes were turned upon his face.

"Poison?"

"No, sir."

"Drowning?"

"No, sir."

"Cutting her throat?"

"None of those."

"Then I can't tell of any other remedy," said Duppy.

"You can't?"

"No!"

"Shall I whisper it to you?"

"I'm rather deaf. You'd better speak out loud."

"Marriage."

Duppy started.

"Yes, marriage. When a maiden is suspected of wrong she can only silence the cruel taunts of a cold, unfeeling world, by undergoing that ceremony with the man with whom she is suspected of having gone too far."

"Damn it, ma'am, you don't call yourself a maiden, do you?"

"Mr. Duppy, do you doubt it?"

"And you nearly sixty?"

"No, only fifty—only fifty."

"'Then you are about the oldest maiden I know," said Duppy.

"Oh, doubt not my honour because cruel fate flung me into your arms! Oh, sir, if you could have seen my heart—if you could have felt its throbs!"

"Well, ma'am, I felt most damnably annoyed."

"Hurt, Mr. Duppy, you mean?"

"No; you didn't hurt me exactly—only tore my shirt-front, and hugged me round the neck till you nearly choked me; that's all, ma'am."

"Mr. Duppy."

She shifted her chair so close to his own now that her skirts covered the old gentleman's knees.

"Well, ma'am?"

"Do you know, I've been thinking."

"What, ma'am?"

"That—that" —

"Go on, ma'am—go on."

"Shall I speak?"

"Not unless you like, certainly."

"I know a maiden may be blamed for speaking so plainly, but circumstances alter cases, Mr. Duppy."

"Very naturally sometimes, ma'am."

"Then the circumstances of this fatal night—I say fatal, because to you and I they are so—make me forget the natural coyness of my disposition, and speak out boldly. Oh, sir, as I said before, there is but one way to silence the slanderous tongues that will spread what has transpired to-night from one end of London to the other."

"By marriage, didn't you say?"

"Yes; that is the only means."

"Then you had better get married."

"I think so."

"If you can get anyone to have you," said the old gentleman,

"Anybody, Mr. Duppy? There is but one—one who can stop the breath of slander."

"And who's that, ma'am, if I may be so bold?" said Duppy.

"Who?"

"Yes, who?"

"Why, yourself, Mr. Duppy, to be sure; your own dear, darling self."

"Go to the devil!" roared Duppy, jumping up so suddenly that he nearly upset the old lady off her chair. "Me marry you! What the dev— Why the woman's mad! Marry! What! a woman who wears a wig!"

All her gentleness vanished. Up she rose before him. "I'll have you to know, sir, that if I do wear a wig, I'm as good as you, sir—yes, and better, sir—better. I'm a poor lone woman whose character you have assisted to destroy; but I will assert my rights. I have asked for justice. I deserve it at your hands, and, Mr. Duppy, I will have it."

"Damn it, woman, do you mean to say you will marry me whether I will have you or no? You say I've aided to defame your character. Why, it was you who came to my bedroom—not me to yours. If there hadn't been another place in the whole world, curse me if I'd have gone there!"

Miss Frump burst into tears. "Cruel, hard-hearted man!" she cried.

"Foolish old woman," sneered Duppy.

"Where is your heart?"

"In my bosom, I hope, ma'am."

"Where is your manliness? Oh, Mr. Duppy, shall the world say that which is not true? Shall the finger of scorn be pointed at us? Shall"—

"I tell you what they shan't say," interrupted Duppy. "They shan't say that an old ill-tempered woman got some fellow to pretend to frighten her so as to give her a chance of an excuse for entrapping me for her husband."

"Do you think I summoned the devil, sir?"

"The devil? Bah! I tell you it was some trick of your own to get a husband."

"Oh! Mr. Duppy. Oh! you cruel man to suspect me, a virtuous maiden, of such an act."

"It looks like it, ma'am."

"Oh! you—you"—

"There, don't get excited."

"Excited! Who could help getting excited at such words? I tell you, if it wasn't the devil, it must have been that Spring-heeled Jack, and I believe he is the devil himself."

"Whoever it was, he played the devil with my night's rest; and all the harm I wish him is, that he was in hell," said Duppy, waxing warm.

"But as to it being anyone that I had got to do such a thing—. Oh! Mr. Duppy, do you think that if such a thing had been likely, I would have met you attired as I was? My modesty is shocked."

"Well, I certainly thought you did it on purpose when you asked me to marry you."

"I asked you to shield me from the scorn of the world—to save your own name from calumny and contempt."

"Fiddlesticks!" said Duppy. "I care nothing for what people think of me, for I never take the trouble to think or talk of others; and you'll feel the same, Miss Frump, if you let other people alone, and their business to boot. Those who can't speak well and act well to others mustn't be surprised if they are not talked well of themselves. Everybody would pity instead of condemning you if you deserved their sympathy; but you know you don't, and so fear them. So, good night, Miss Frump."

"Mr. Duppy! And have you resolved to spurn me? Will not your heart soften?"

"It's more likely to—. But, there! I thought you had something particular to communicate instead of this nonsense about marrying, and at our age, too! You should be thinking of your shroud at your age, and not a bridal dress; for only think what an old fool you would look entering a church to be married— ha! ha! ha!"

And making a dive at his candlestick, Mr. Duppy left the old maid's room for his own. Miss Frump sprang after him into the passage. She seized his arm.

"Mr. Duppy," she said, in a tone of ill-suppressed passion, "is this your decision? You will not marry me?"

"It is."

"Then you are a nasty, hard-hearted, wicked old man, and you shan't remain in this house. I give you warning to go at the end of the week. Oh! you—you"—

Frump could say no more. She burst into an hysterical fit of sobbing. Duppy looked at her a moment, shrugged his shoulders, then entered his own room.

"The vile, base, wicked man," sobbed Miss Frump, "to refuse to repair the injury he has done me, and then laugh at me for condescending to look at such an ugly, deaf old brute! But, there! I deserve it for lowering myself so much—me, as could find a hundred gentlemen to marry me. Oh! I deserve it for stooping to a paltry, pensioned clerk. But he shall go. I'll let my rooms to somebody else; I'll—I'll Oh! you nasty, wicked, cruel-hearted, deaf old rascal! you—you—. Oh! oh! oh!"

"Go to the devil, you stupid old cat!" roared Duppy; "but put your wig on, or you'll frighten him. Take all your clothes, too, you stupid old woman!"

And Duppy flung first the wig, and then the garments of Miss Frump, out into the passage, and slammed the door of his room in her face.

"The last hope is gone," murmured the lady, as she stooped to raise the things from the floor, "and I shall be the laughing-stock of the whole parish. But I won't; I'll run away; I'll leave the house, and go where nobody will know me. Oh! the unfeeling old brute! I—I could poison myself with vexation, I could!"

And upstairs went Miss Frump, bearing her wig and clothes in her arms, muttering maledictions against her lodger.

When she reached her own room, she opened one of the drawers and took out a half-pint black bottle, the neck of which she applied to her own lips, and then flung herself into a chair to give free vent to her tears.

CHAPTER XXXI.

THE RETURN HOME—THE LETTER—AGONY AND DESPAIR—THE SUICIDE PREVENTED.

LIBERTY!

Who is there can have any idea of the true meaning of the word but those who have been placed in confinement?

None.

The wretched convict or the bedridden alone can know how sweet is the breath of freedom.

James Slater knew it—sighed for it during the days and nights that the dark prison-walls encircled him—tasted it when he fell at the bottom of the outside prison-wall.

As his feet touched the pavement he felt that he was a different man.

He seemed to be endowed with the strength of a lion; his limbs appeared more supple—his bearing more erect.

He felt that he was free; and the weight of fifty years seemed taken from his back.

He clutched at the air as if he would embrace it.

The whole system was exhilarated—the man was a man again.

But hark! what was that which paled his flushed cheeks, and struck like a death-knell to his soul?

It was the prison-bell, announcing to those within and without its walls that a culprit had escaped.

All his strength so lately renewed, appeared to desert him.

Again he was weak, feeble as an infant.

The tones of the bell held him spell-bound for an instant, and he could only glance up and down the road in search of those who came to bear him back to his cell.

Then, like an electric flash, came the thought that he was attired in his own dress, and not the uniform of the prison, and that if he ventured away from its precincts, there was yet hope of avoiding discovery.

He turned and fled.

But ere he had gone fifty yards, he recollected that the man who had served him could not escape without the aid of the rope and nail. He had not flung it over the wall.

A moment he hesitated, whether to return or leave him to his fate.

To return was fraught with danger to himself; to flee was to sacrifice his best of friends.

His mind was made up on the instant, and he hurried back to the spot where the rope hung against the wall.

To grasp the stone at the end, and fling it high in the air, was the work of a moment; and then he took to his heels and fled with all the speed his desperation could summon to his limbs.

But now the prison-bell had been heard and its meaning divined, and anxious eyes and eager hands were waiting for him.

When about a hundred and fifty yards had been passed over by his fleet feet, a figure appeared in his path with extended arms.

He saw them in time to avoid running into their embrace, and he turned aside; but the policeman, who had made sure of his capture, missed his mark, and by a desperate and well-delivered blow, was hurled to the earth.

Slater waited not to see the effect of his blow, but dashed on even faster than before.

Desperation had lent suppleness to his feet, and he was more than half-a-mile from the prison ere he could have believed himself capable of covering a quarter of the distance.

Houses and shops flew past him, till a pain in his side and a shortness of breath warned him he must slacken his speed.

"Free! free!" he gasped. "Oh, God! I'm free!"

There was a footfall behind him, and he turned to defend his liberty as a lioness would turn to defend her young, and stood face to face with Ralph Grasper.

The recognition was mutual.

A cry of surprise broke from the lips of both, but Grasper also uttered another, and that was, "Police!"

But he could not repeat it.

A blow of such tremendous force fell upon his lips, that they were split from the nose to the chin, and he dropped to the earth as if shot.

Fear had called forth Slater's violence, not indignation, for he knew not of the indignities offered to his wife by the ruffian who now lay bleeding and senseless at his feet.

And so again he bounded on, never heeding the pain in his side or the shortness of his breath, till the fields were in sight, and then he paused.

He had panted to see his wife; but now that he was so near the home he had made wretched, he almost dreaded to meet her.

How could he gaze upon the face which he had blanched with sorrow? How could he look into those eyes his guilty deeds had dimmed with tears? How could he press to his bosom the woman he had so cruelly tortured?

Then, the thought of how she would meet him, whether with upbraidings, or the spirit of forgiveness, came with torturing force to his mind, and he slackened his speed, till he stood still a few doors from his once happy home.

After a pause he moved forward again. But his step was slow and tottering now. He reeled like a drunken man. His temples throbbed, and his heart beat violently.

He reached the door, he grasped the knocker in his trembling hand; but he feared to raise it.

The sound, he dreaded, would arouse the neighbours, reveal his presence, and ensure his capture.

How could he announce his presence to her he called wife?

These thoughts caused him an agony almost too great to bear.

Too well he knew the officers of the law would seek him there, and that speedily, too; but could he fly without seeing her, without imprinting a kiss upon her cheek? without asking her forgiveness for the misery he had caused her, and praying her to fly with him?

No!

And yet he dared not announce his presence to her, lest he announced it to others. What was to be done?

He released his hold of the knocker, and sprang to the shutters. Joy! they were unfastened, and so was the window.

One glance around to see that none observed him, and he raised the sash and sprang into the neatly kept parlour. To close it after him and fasten it was the work of a moment, and he made his way to the passage.

On the foot of the stairs he paused, and strained every nerve to catch her breathing.

But he heard it not; and silently, yet tremblingly, he went up the narrow stairway.

His hand shook so violently he could scarcely open the door of the apartment where he knew his wife slept; but he succeeded, and passed into the room.

All was in darkness.

Could he awake his wife without alarming her? could he announce his presence without bringing a cry to her lips?

It was doubtful, but he must try

He approached the bed.

He bent over it, stretched forth his hand, and started back. Cold drops of perspiration oozed out from every pore, and bathed his forehead in a clammy sweat. The bed was empty.

Jane was not there.

He sprang to the mantel-shelf where he knew the matches were always kept, and grasped the tinder-box, then sank back upon the foot of the bed.

The next instant he struck the flint upon the steel, and the sparks of fire ran along the tinder.

To apply a match and procure a light was no easy matter, so violently did he tremble.

But at length he succeeded.

The lighted match revealed a candle on the table beneath the window.

He lit it and looked around.

Everything was as usual, but the bed was empty.

"Where is Jane?" he repeated several times to himself. "Where—where can she be?"

His eyes lighted upon a folded sheet of paper on the table, and he grasped it eagerly, unfolded it, held it to the light, and read—

"Husband! to save you I have sacrificed all that is worth living for—peace of mind, fame, honour! I shall save you, but I destroy myself. We meet no more on earth. God bless you, and farewell for ever.—JANE."

The letter dropped from his hands, and a wild, piercing cry broke from his lips, and he fell forward on to the bed. He slid down upon his knees to the floor, his face buried in the coverlet, and his hands clasped to his heart.

"Oh, God! Oh, God!" burst in agony from his lips. "Surely my sin has found me out!"

Sobs of agony broke from his heaving bosom, and shook the bed against which he leaned.

"Gone! gone!" he cried. "Gone for ever! Great heavens! guide me now. Without her the world is to me a blank, and I care not what becomes of me. Oh! whither has she gone?— whither fled?"

He sprang to his feet.

He dashed aside the tears that overflowed his eyes.

"I will seek her!" he exclaimed. "Seek her even at the farthermost ends of the earth. But— mercy! what do these words portend?"

Seizing the letter, he read and re-read the lines.

"To save me she has sacrificed fame, honour! 'Tis a lie—a base, a wicked lie! She never wrote those words—never—never!" he cried, smiting his breast with his clenched fist. "She, my wife—my love, sacrifice fame and honour—no, no— a thousand times no! Some one has forged this damnable lie—this black, foul, and wicked slander."

He flung the paper from him, and paced the room with quick and nervous strides.

"Hate me she may, despise me she must, but to fall herself—oh, no, no! I will not believe it. I would slay the man who told me such an infamous lie. She is too good, too pure, to do this even for my sake—me whom she loved so well!"

He paused, and clasped his forehead in his trembling hand.

"And how have I repaid that love—how, how?" he continued. "By bringing her to beggary and disgrace, by crushing her noble heart, by—oh, God! let me not think, lest I go mad—mad!'

He flung himself into a chair, and rocked his body to and fro.

His sufferings were more than he could bear.

Surely his sin had found him out—surely he was punished enough by the emotions under which he laboured.

"Why did I leave my cell?" he muttered. "Why did I long to be free? Why pant for the breath of liberty? That I might see her—obtain her forgiveness. But now—now, would the black walls enclosed me; would I had never seen that note! Then I had been happy. Oh! torture, but 'tis a lie—a damned lie—a wicked, black, infernal lie!"

Who could describe the agony of that man's mind—who could paint the wild throes of his throbbing heart?

The misery he had endured in gaol was nothing compared to what he suffered now in that room, where he passed so many happy hours ere he had grasped the pen and traced the characters which stamped him with the brand of a felon.

He strove to believe the note a falsehood, written by other hands than his wife's; yet he knew her calligraphy so well that he could have sworn to it out of a thousand.

Fain would he believe it not hers; yet how could he doubt it?

He struggled hard to persuade himself it was a forgery, but his own heart told him it was not.

If hers—what had he done—what had he become?

Not only was he a forger, but the murderer of his own peace of mind—of his wife's—for ever!

He had brought disgrace upon her, but he had compelled her to bring disgrace upon herself; he had made her a thing loathsome even in her own eyes.

And to save him!

"Disgrace! A felon's doom! Death a thousand times first!" he cried, as he again rose to his feet, and crushed the letter under the heel of his boot. "I could bear anything but this; this I cannot, will not hear!"

He crossed over the room to a small chest of drawers, and drew open the top one.

"If she has fallen, I will not survive her disgrace," he said, in a hollow tone, as he took from the drawer a small leather case. "If she has sacrificed honour and fame to save me, I will sacrifice life to save myself. What have I to live for but her? Could I live and feel daily, hourly, what she had become for my sake? No—not a minute. We meet no more. No, we meet no more!"

He unfastened the case, and took from it a tortoiseshell-handled razor.

He felt the keen edge of the blade, then laid it down beside the little case, and once more picked up the letter from the floor, smoothed it, and read it again.

"Honour, fame—honour, fame!" he said, in slow tones, his eyes fixed upon the words—"sacrificed to save me. But to whom sacrificed?" he added, raising his voice, and looking furiously around. "To whom—to whom? Why does she not write his name, that I might seek him, and tear his heart from his breast? Who— who is he that can save me? But it's all false. I will not believe it. No! no! and, yet—yet— oh, God! let me end this agony!"

He suffered the letter to fall at his feet, and seizing the razor quickly from the drawers, he stropped it upon the palm of his hand.

As he did so, the severe expression of his face relaxed, the look of agony vanished, and one of peace and serenity usurped its place.

"If she have spoken true—if she have not deceived me—if she has sacrificed honour and fame for my sake—she cannot survive the loss, and must die. We meet no more on earth, No! but we will in heaven! Ay, we will meet there. Jane, I come—I haste! Oh, God! forgive me. I come!"

He closed his eyes, and raised the weapon to his throat with a smile upon his face.

Then he hesitated for a moment.

His hand trembled, but still he was fixed in his purpose.

He looked around the room.

It was the last look he was to take upon that once happy home.

"Why do I hesitate?" he muttered; "why do I pause? I will delay no longer. Jane, I come—I come!"

SPRING-HEELED JACK PARTS THE LOVERS.

He pressed the keen blade to his throat.

He drew it along with a sudden jerk, and the crimson fluid gushed forth in a stream, and dyed his shirt and vest.

The razor fell from his hand, he reeled for a moment like a drunken man, and then fell backwards to the floor.

CHAPTER XXXII.

THE ESCAPE FROM THE VAULT—THE CAPTURE—THE BRIBE AND THE LOSS.

THE TERROR-STRICKEN Richard Clavering had fainted.

The strain upon the nerves of the guilty man had been too much for him longer to bear, and the horrors of his situation were for a time forgotten in insensibility.

But for a short time only did he remain unconscious of his true position.

Reason, which appeared tottering from its throne, returned, and once more all the horrors of his situation pressed upon his brain.

He shuddered as the cold, clammy perspiration oozed from every pore of his skin, and the dark, damp vault struck a chill to his very soul.

When insensibility stole over him, he fell, striking his head rather heavily, and his temples throbbed violently under the effect of the blow.

He clasped his brow in his hand and strove to penetrate the darkness around him, moving forward as he did so.

Suddenly a faint streak of light met his gaze.

He uttered a loud cry of joy and sprang towards the aperture, through which Jack had passed out of the vault.

In another moment he stood in the open air, outside the sacred edifice.

Oh! what a sigh of relief broke from his chest! How wildly his heart throbbed as he gazed upon the outer walls of the building! How fervently he clasped his hands together, and muttered—

"Thank God—oh, thank God! I am out of that fearful place."

He turned to flee from the spot, when he recollected that he had no hat on.

That had been left by him in the vestry.

"I dare not return for it," he muttered, "and yet to leave it there will be certain ruin. What's to be done?"

He cared nothing for the loss, so far as regarded its value, but he remembered that his name was marked on its lining.

This was a fresh shock. His sudden joy at his escape was damped again by the fear of his having been in that edifice traced out by means of the hat.

One moment he was prompted to enter the little church by the window, procure the hat, and flee at once, without attempting to again tamper with the register.

But then the dread of encountering that horrible spectre, of being again forced into the vault with the festering remains of humanity was too much for his courage, and he resolved to leave the hat where he had left it, and trust to Providence to shield him from discovery.

"And if they should trace it to me," he said, "what of that? I have not stolen anything.

They can't say I have done that."

True, they could not, but he was none the less guilty. His inclination led him to commit the theft, and defile that register which his terror alone had saved from his polluting grasp.

Still he felt ill at ease as he made his way out of the churchyard into the street.

As he turned round the little edifice he uttered a cry of fear.

The officer stood before him.

It was the same one from whom Jack had escaped a short time before.

The man had scarcely recovered the shock to his feelings when he was surprised by perceiving a second form in the vicinity of the church. At first he thought, as Richard's back was towards him, that it was another denizen of the other world, but as he half turned, and the policeman perceived a human face, he drew back and watched the libertine's movements.

"That's no ghost or skeleton," he muttered, "and I ain't afraid of him. I wonder what he's up to? I'll wager he don't get out of my clutches in a hurry."

And so drawing still further back into the shade of the wall, he kept a sharp look out, without being seen by the object of his curiosity.

As Richard confronted him, all the libertine's strength vanished, and he stood trembling and powerless before the officer.

"Well, my fine fellow," said the man, "what are you after here, eh?"

Clavering felt that he must say something, and he replied—

"Looking at the church."

"Humph!" said the policeman. "You want me to believe that, don't you?"

"Yes—no—that is, you can if you like," stammered Richard.

"I don't like."

"I can't help it if you don't," said the libertine, trying to put on a show of courage.

"Hark, here, my fine fellow, I'd like to know the game you're after," said the officer, sharply.

"The game?" said Clavering.

"Yes, the game. What did you want there at this time of night?"

"I will tell you," said Richard. "I have a fancy for gazing at different buildings by moonlight, and as I had business this way, I thought I'd stop to admire"—

"The communion plate," interrupted the officer. "I dare say you are a downy[37] one, but you don't get over me."

"Scoundrel! do you dare impute dishonesty to me?" cried Clavering, assuming an indignant tone and look. "Do you take me for a thief, sir?"

"That's just what I do take you for," was the reply.

"Sir, you shall suffer for this," cried Clavering. "You shall be taught that such conduct towards a gentleman" —

"Swell mobsman,[38] you mean," interrupted the officer. "You see that window, eh?"

And the man pointed to the window he had been watching when Jack gave him the start.

Clavering looked blank.

"What of it?" he asked.

---

[37] Sharp-witted.
[38] Member of a group of lawbreakers.

"It's been forced for some purpose—to nail the plate, I suppose," said the policeman.

"What is that to me?"

"What to you?"

"Yes."

"Well, I don't know, but it's a good deal to me. Here's a window forced, and a man in the enclosed ground—and what does it mean?"

"How should I know?"

"Of course not; how should you know. Strange, ain't it? What have you got in your pockets?"

And the officer caught hold of the tails of Clavering's coat, as he spoke.

"Insolent rascal! would you rob me?"

"Not exactly; I'm only taking care you don't rob anybody else, that's all," was the sneering reply.

"This is beyond endurance. Am I to submit to be stopped on the public way, and thus treated?"

"I must do my duty. Humph! can't find nothing. But I say, where is your hat? People don't generally stroll about admiring things at night without a hat on, does they?"

"The wind has blown it off, and" —

"There ain't been a breath to move a leaf tonight; and if it had, why didn't you go after it?"

Richard did not reply.

"It won't do, old fellow—it won't do," said the officer, looking very knowing. "I'm up to you chaps. You've left it in the church."

"Oh!" cried Clavering, feeling that all hope of escape was gone.

"Perhaps you'll go to the station with me quietly?"

And the policeman twined his fingers into the cuff of Clavering's coat, at the same time pressing his knuckles slightly into that gentleman's wrist, as an intimation that it would be rather painful for him to try to escape.

For some few moments Richard Clavering stood like one dumbfounded.

What would be thought of him now by his friends and acquaintances?

The thought was maddening.

He felt that he had suffered enough for his attempt to obtain the proof of his marriage, without now finding himself a prisoner in the hands of the police, and the certainty of being publicly charged with sacrilege—a charge which the production of his hat would establish beyond any doubt.

Bitterly did he curse himself for seeking to rob Jessie of the position to which he had raised her —bitterly did he curse the promptings of his own black heart.

"Come on," said the policeman, forcing him away; "and if you don't want a broken head, you'll come quietly."

"For God's sake, man, don't attempt to drag me to a prison. You cannot surely meditate such an act?"

"Can't I, though? Come."

"I shall be ruined," cried Richard— "irretrievably ruined."

"Lor! how people do change their tones, to be sure!" said the officer, with a leer at Richard's face.

"My good man"—

"Only just now you called me a scoundrel."

"Yes, yes—I was incensed."

"And now you're collared. Come, step out, will yer."

"But my hat."

"Oh, that'll be found in the morning. Don't suppose anybody will go into the church to nail it."

"Are you determined to take me to the police-station?" said Richard, almost beside himself with shame and terror.

"Most decidedly," was the reply; and the knuckles sunk a little deeper into the libertine's wrist.

"Oh!" cried Clavering, "you will break my wrist—you will break my wrist."

"That's very likely, if you don't step out," was the cool reply.

Richard sighed despairingly, and moved on by the officer's side.

Suddenly, as if struck by a sudden thought, he said, in an insinuating tone of voice—

"Officer, you are ill-paid for the duties you have to perform."

"Am I?"

"Yes; when I think of the risk you run of being badly treated by your prisoners," remarked Richard.

"What are you driving at," said the man, quickly whipping out his staff. "If you have any idea of trying on any of that sort of game, you'll find it won't pay."

And the policeman held the staff up before Richard's face.

"I have no such intention. Believe me, I never meditated such a thing; for, of course, I well know that you are only doing your duty. You have made a very great mistake—a very great mistake—in this case; and no doubt you will be called upon to account for your conduct. But still I admit, when I come to think, that you are justified in mistaking me for a very different sort of person. Of course I can satisfy any sensible man that I had no dishonourable motives to-night. Still I can't blame you; I am only sorry for you, as perhaps you have a wife and children depending on you for support."

"So I have; but you can't come the hankey-pankey over me[39]—seen too much of it since I've been in the force," said the man.

"Well, you, of course, must not blame me if you get into trouble for this night's work."

"Oh, dear—no! I'm not such a fool."

"I have no wish to hurt your feelings, said Richard; "but you will be a foolish man if you take me to the station on such a ridiculous charge as entering a church with the intention of robbery—a charge which my position and character will at once rebut—a charge which will rebound upon yourself, and lead either to your suspension for some time, or utter dismissal. Still, even the knowledge of that is but a sorry recompense to me for the indignities I am forced to bear. To those who move in the lower grades of society it is nothing to be dragged to the station; but, to a gentleman of wealth and position, it is degrading indeed."

"All right," said the officer.

"Oh, my friend, it is not all right. You will find, ere long, that it is all wrong. But don't

---

[39] Distract me with chatter.

blame me. Go your own course. Me break into a church? Me? Preposterous!—absurd!"

The tone in which these last sentences were uttered really did set the officer thinking whether it was possible he had arrested a man without a faint apology for so doing.

Certainly Richard Clavering's appearance was that of a man moving in a superior grade. And though the officer knew he would be blamed if he did not perform his duty, he would be severely censured indeed if he overstepped it by arresting an innocent man, and one too, who had wealth and position on his side.

He believed he was acting rightly. Yet feared that he had shown too much zeal in the performance of his duty.

This feeling having once taken possession of the officer's heart, it grew stronger every minute, till he began to feel convinced in his own mind that he had gone too far, and pictured to himself his either being suspended or turned out of the force.

The wily libertine watched him keenly, and saw, by his altered countenance, what was transpiring in the officer's mind.

Having assured himself that he had raised a doubt in the officer's mind, he put on a still greater air of injured innocence, and muttered as if to himself, but, in reality, loud enough for the man to hear—

"What fools some men are! They will persist in getting themselves into trouble, despite all the warnings they receive. Well, he can't blame me if he persists in this outrage. The consequences be on his own head. I could pity him but for the indignity offered to myself. Yes, an indignity that would almost induce a gentleman to give a sovereign rather than submit to it. Even though he knows how absurd is the charge, and the certainty of the punishment which will be awarded to the obstinate and stupid fellow who prefers it."

Then suddenly raising his voice, he exclaimed, almost fiercely—

"Now, sir; how much further have we to go to put an end to this farce? How far is it to the station?"

"You are not far from it now," was the reply in extremely modulated tones.

"I am glad of that, for I am sickening of this nonsense. But, there! you must do your duty, of course. Duty—humph! A strange duty, to be sure."

"I hope I am performing my duty, sir. I have no wish to neglect or exceed it," said the man.

"Oh! no; of course not. But it strikes me very forcibly you will find that you have exceeded it very considerably by arresting, as a thief, a gentleman whom curiosity alone drew near a church which had a broken window in it. Ha! Ha! Ha! Truly, I could laugh at the absurdity and ridiculousness of the thing, were it not also annoying to my feelings. I know what I should do as a respecter of law and order, and but for pressing engagements I would, and that is, press hard for a conviction against you for excess of zeal; but, unfortunately, I must leave this part of the country early to-morrow, and would rather have given five pounds to prevent this nonsense; nay, I would now, though I know by so doing that I am paying a man who seeks to injure me, when I should do all that I can to punish him severely for the indignity he offers me."

The officer released his grasp of Clavering's arm.

"I'm sure, sir, I should be very sorry to do anything wrong."

"Then do what's right," said Clavering, quickly; "and to prove to you that I bear you no ill-will for your stupid notions, there is something for you to buy your wife a bonnet

with. None but a madman would act as you have done. But there, let this fooling cease."
He placed two or three golden coins in the officer's hand, and, turning quickly, hurried from the spot, leaving the surprised guardian of the peace with his hand still extended and open, looking after his retreating figure.

"Well, this is a rum go," he exclaimed, after a long pause, looking at the glittering coins in the palm of his hand. "Confound me! for a fool. The fellow's a thief, safe enough, and the devil take me for letting him go like that."

"He'll take the wages off you, sir," cried a voice behind him, and ere the officer could close his fingers over the coins, they were snatched from his hand, and a tall, cloaked figure sprang up on to a high garden wall at his side. "Gold obtained by bribery never does any good. The man who will sell justice deserves to be sold himself. Other and more worthy folks shall have what you so easily obtained, and so quickly lost."

The next moment Jack was gone, and the officer gazed upon the empty wall.

CHAPTER XXXIII.
THE SEAMSTRESS RETURNS HOME—SPRING-HEEL'D JACK AND THE OUTCAST.

AS OUR HERO entered the cabin of the little collier, preceded by Jerry and Peter, the poor young seamstress started up on the couch where she had been reclining, and gazed with a half- frightened stare upon Jack.

In an instant Jack was at her side, and taking her hand in his own, he said, in a commiserating tone—

"I am happy, Miss Folder—for such I have learned your name to be—to see you thus far recovered."

Then, turning to Jerry and his messmate, said—

"My friends, will you leave us alone for a few moments?"

Jerry and Peter looked at each other, and then the latter, spitting out a mouthful of tobacco juice, stepped up in front of Jack, and in reply, said—

"Now, look here, mate. I am a rough sort of fellow, but I got a heart in my bosom. I ain't going to say as you are a bit of a scoundrel, for I don't think you are by your looks; but we don't know each other, and some of your mealy-mouthed chaps ain't worth a stale quid; but I believe you're square and right; and if I didn't, I'd see you darned[40] first before I'd leave you alone with that poor gal, for I'm sure it's been trouble as drove her into the river. You may be her friend, and I won't say you ain't; but I tell you what, if you say anything to her as she don't like, and she can scream out, may I be cussed if I don't chuck you overboard!"

"My friend," said Jack, "did I wish her harm, I had not risked my life to save her. I am not a man to profess what I do not feel, nor am I the man to insult a weak and defenceless woman. I wish to be a friend to her, not a foe. I admire your feelings, and I pledge you my word that I have no intention, either by word or act, to cause her one moment's pain, or add one pang to her sufferings; but if Miss Folder fears to be left alone with me, I will not press you to leave the cabin."

He turned to her for a reply.

---

[40] Damned.

"Who are you?" she asked, "that you know my name, and sought to rob me of the grave which suffering drove me to seek?"

"A friend, believe me," replied Jack; "one who can sympathise with and pity you."

"I will believe you, though friends are few indeed to the poor and suffering."

"I will take a turn on deck, Jerry," said Peter, "and leave 'em alone; but if he acts like a pirate, he'll find my maulers on his biscuit trap 'afore he knows where he is."

Jack merely smiled, and seated himself on a sea-chest as the two men left the cabin, and closed the door after them.

Jack and the seamstress continued to gaze at each other for some few moments in silence, and then Ellen timidly asked—

"Sir, who are you, that evince so much interest in me, an entire stranger?"

"I will tell you," said Jack; "but let not surprise or the mention of my name lead you to utter a sound that would induce those rough, but good-hearted men, to think I intend you harm. We have met before, twice to-night; once in your own wretched habitation, in the deserted streets, and now here. It was I who saved you from violence at the hands of the drunken ruffian you called landlord. I who strove to arrest your course to a suicide's grave. Hush! I am Spring-heeled Jack!"

A cry rose to the girl's lips, but Jack held up his hand deprecatingly, and the poor seamstress stifled it ere it escaped.

"You—you Spring-heeled Jack?" she gasped.

"The same, but fear me not, for I am a man! Ay! and one who can pity the helpless and the suffering. There are those who look upon me as one devoid of all feeling, all respect, but they do me injustice. I have no wish to deny my failings, but among them is not numbered heartlessness. By an accident, I became acquainted with your sufferings, and I determined to aid you all in my power. Do not fear me. Believe me, I would be your friend."

He took her hand in his own, and told her how he had got on to the roof of her wretched dwelling, and what had transpired after she fled frightened down the stairs—the scene in the vault—and every circumstance up to the moment he stood before her.

"The world," he said, "has been cruel to you. I, perhaps, have been cruel to the world, but I would aid you—take you from that life of misery and toil which has worn you to a shadow, and led you to seek a brighter existence in another world. Nay, fear not to accept my offer, for I am rich, and can well afford to be bountiful. I ask nothing in return but your good opinion of me whom many condemn. Now, tell me—how can I serve you."

Ellen burst into tears.

"Kind, generous man," she said, "I deserve not sympathy."

"The poor and the wretched ever deserve it at the hands of their more fortunate fellow-creatures," said Jack.

"Death would be preferable to me to aught else," said Ellen.

"Not so. You are young. The world is before you. The meanest of God's creatures have something to live for—some destiny to fulfil. Pardon me if I say it, but it is wicked to seek to end that life which has been given us—wicked to usurp heaven's prerogative, and fly unbidden before your Maker."

Ellen looked fixedly at the man before her for some minutes.

Could this be Spring-heel'd Jack—this the man who had been the terror of the metropolis and its surroundings? Could this be he who now spoke such words to her?

Surely, then, he was not the wretch he had been represented—not all bad?

There were some redeeming qualities in his heart, and Ellen felt her soul warm towards him.

She could not but acknowledge to herself the wickedness of the act she had meditated, but she excused it by suffering, poverty, and wrong.

"Oh! sir," she said, after a pause, "how can I thank you for the interest you take in one who is unworthy of sympathy—whose poverty has caused her to herd with the lowest?"

"But not whose inclinations," interrupted Jack.

"Indeed, no!"

"You have seen better days—of that I feel assured," said Jack.

Ellen sighed.

"I have, indeed."

"Then make me your confidant. Believe me, I will not abuse it; and tell me how you became so reduced as to be compelled to labour for a pittance scarcely sufficient to keep soul and body together. But I forget you are robed in garments saturated, and will catch a cold that may be fatal to you."

"And you?"

"Oh! never mind me, I will soon change mine. Suffer me to remove you to your lodgings, and to-morrow I will wait upon you."

Ellen shuddered.

"Alas!" she answered, "I fear to return there."

"Wherefore?"

"I dread the fury of that dissipated and lawless man."

"You need have no fear of him."

"Oh! sir, you know him not."

"Indeed, I do. I know him to be a heartless cur, who will not dare ever to molest you again," said Jack.

Ellen shook her head.

"I have given him such a fright to-night, that he will never attempt to molest or annoy you again," said Jack. "He has promised, nay, sworn, not to do so, and his cowardly nature will make him keep this oath, at least, if you never divulge to him the circumstance that it was I who stood before him. He believed me to be the devil himself, and such abject terror did I strike to his soul, that he will never more, by word or deed, annoy you. I would advise your return thither till you have recovered, and then some other and more decent place must be found you."

Ellen replied only with a grateful look.

"I have no doubt one of the seamen will take us ashore in a boat, when I will procure a vehicle to convey you home, for to remain long thus without a change of garments is only to court that fate which, I thank Heaven, I have been instrumental in saving you from. Say, shall I call them hither?"

"If you will; though I care not for life."

"Come, come; talk not thus," said Jack. "To-morrow you will think differently."

"To-morrow I shall have to face a cruel and remorseless employer," said Ellen; "one who will have no pity—one who will demand his goods, or"—

She paused, and burst into tears.

"Or what?"

"Have me conveyed to a prison," she replied.

Jack became thoughtful.

He knew the goods were taken to the vault by Joe Filcher; but was there any prospect of their remaining there?

He doubted it much; for he expected that the vault would be searched at daylight, if not before, and he did not think it policy to go near it again just yet.

So he gave up all idea of being able to restore the goods entrusted to Ellen to make up; but then he knew he could give her their value to hand over to the Jew clothier.

So Jack bade her be of good cheer, and succeeded in calming her apprehensions in that quarter, and, going to the cabin door, called to Jerry and his messmate.

Au arrangement was soon made with Peter to take them ashore in the ship's boat; and after each partaking of a little grog, Ellen was placed in the boat, and landed in safety at the Tower stairs.

Jack persisted in wrapping his large cloak around her shivering form, and having procured a vehicle, ordered the driver to set them down at the corner of the street in which the house of Bill Jackson was situated.

This was done; and in a short time Jack and his charge stood before the door with the greasy cord and dirty panels.

There was no one about, and the street was very dark now, for the Pigeon Flyers was closed, and had been for some hours.

"Will you be able to obtain an entrance without being seen?" asked Jack.

"Oh, yes," she replied, "by pulling the string. There is no fastening on the door save the latch."

Jack took her hand in his, and fixing his eyes upon her face, he whispered—

"Dare I leave you—dare I believe you will not meditate such another crime again?"

"You may," she said. "I pledge you my word, you may."

"Enough! I will believe you. To-morrow I will seek you in your wretched home, when I hope to be enabled to better your circumstances, and save you from a life of misery and want. Farewell!"

He turned to leave her to enter the house, when she sprang towards him, and catching his hand in her own, raised it to her lips.

"God bless you!" she cried.

Then dropping his hand quickly, as if she felt she had gone too far, she seized the greasy cord, silently opened the door, and glided into the dark passage.

Jack remained till the door closed behind her, and shut her from his view, and then he turned, with a slow step and thoughtful brow, away from the spot.

"It's a strange world this," he muttered to himself, as he went along. "A very strange world, and a strange mass of people indeed it is composed of—good and bad, rich and poor. To some it goes merrily as a marriage-bell, to others a death-knell is borne upon every moment of time as it passes on to eternity. What a record it would make could the lives and doings of every soul within it be chronicled!—a stupendous one indeed! of hopes and joys, miseries and sorrows, want and plenty, good and evil. There we should read wealth and plenty allied to sin, shame, and degradation; poverty and want to honour, truth, and integrity; sin rewarded by affluence, honesty by poverty. Fools and rogues in gilded chambers, wisdom and talent in a wretched hovel. 'Tis strange, but true; has been for years and will be for years to come—a strange world, truly! But I forget my garments are soaked, and that a chill is striking to my very bones," he added, increasing his speed, and hurrying towards the west.

As he turned quickly round the corner of the dark street, he ran against what appeared to him to be a large bundle of dirty clothes, but which was indeed a poor, ill-clad woman, who had fallen asleep in a doorway, and who was hurled off the step on to the pavement by the force of the concussion.

Jack paused on the moment, and, stooping, lifted the wretched being to her feet, as she uttered a frightened cry of pain and terror.

"My good woman," said Jack, "I sincerely regret my carelessness, and hope I have not hurt you."

The poor creature tore herself rudely from his hold.

"Hurt me!" she said; "what does it matter who hurts me?"

"I should be sorry to do so," said Jack; "and if in my hurry I caused you pain I am sorry for it."

"I dare say you are," said the other, bitterly. "But it's the way of the world, to hurt the poor and the starving. Once down, you're kept down—kicked down—trampled down. Who cares for the wretch without home, food, or friends? They are obstructions in the way, that may be hurled aside by the foot of the more fortunate."

As the woman spoke, she moved out of the shadow into the dim glare of a dirty gas-lamp, and Jack fairly started as his eye fell upon a form so wasted, and a face so wan, that starvation and misery were imprinted in every feature.

"Oh, God!" he muttered, "what a sight!— what an object!"

"Yes, what an object!" echoed the woman, bitterly; "only fit to be hurled about till death relieves her sufferings!"

"Woman," said Jack, "tell me what I can do for you."

"Begone, and leave me to die in peace upon that stone bed."

She pointed to the step from which Jack had so unintentionally hurled her.

"What suffering and want must have reduced you to this!" said Jack. "You are starving—dying—and that in the midst of plenty."

"Yes," she replied, in a kind of hissing whisper; "starving, with food around me, and not suffered to rest my weakened frame even on the cold stones."

"This must not be," cried Jack. "I see that want has embittered your heart against humanity. But you are unjust. You must not, shall not be suffered to starve in the streets, whatever may have brought you to such depths of wretchedness. Sorry indeed am I that I threw you from the step, but glad indeed I am that it gives me an opportunity of relieving your wants.

He thrust his hand into his pocket, and took out a few coins.

"Here, take these, and get food and lodging," he said, forcing them into the wretched woman's hand.

The poor wretch seemed dumbfounded at this unexpected generosity, and stood glaring with her sunken eyes, first upon the coins, and then upon Jack, and finally bursting into an hysterical but hollow laugh.

"Gold!" she cried. "Gold! Oh! but is it gold? Is it good money, or"—

"Of what injustice do you complain?" said Jack.

She paused as her eyes encountered those of Jack, "My poor woman," said Jack, "go and seek food and shelter. How could you come to this fearful state, and not seek relief?"

"I have sought it," she said. "I have asked for bread, but met with insult. Poverty was enough to endure without that. Steal, I must not; beg, I dare not. But I ought not to be like this. I have no right to starve. But the poor can't get justice; that's only for those who can pay for it, not for such as me. But you—you have got a heart. You are not like—but, there! why should I tell my sorrows and sufferings to others? Thank you for this; and God bless you; though it will soon be gone. And then—why then, the pangs of hunger and the cold stones. Well, well! Perhaps justice may come in the meantime. Who knows?—who knows?"

The woman clutched his arm, and pointing down the street with her attenuated finger, said— "Do you see that house? The largest one, with the lamp in the fanlight." Jack replied in the affirmative. "There lives a man who calls himself my uncle. I was his ward; for my parents died when very young. He has robbed me of my just rights—the infernal miserly villain! Yes, that man—the owner of that house, withholds from me that which is mine by right; although he denies even himself almost the common necessaries of life. But for him, I should not be thus. But there, there! I am starving, and will seek some place where I can get food with this gold. God bless you!" And the woman hurried from Jack's side, and was lost in the distance of the dark street.

Jack took a good look at the house pointed out to him, shook his head sadly, and hurried away.

CHAPTER XXXIV.

JACK FORCES THE MISER TO RESTORE THE FORTUNE OF HIS WARD.

A THIN rushlight threw a dim, ghostly light around a well-furnished sleeping apartment in the large house, which had been pointed out to our hero by the starving woman the night before which we are about to pay it a visit, and lit up a large French bedstead, in which a man of about sixty years of age lay sleeping.

The hard lines on his face bespoke one of a grasping, avaricious turn of mind—one from whom the poor would find no relief and the debtor no sympathy.

Seldom, perhaps, did a man bear his character in his features to such a degree as did the owner of the house in question—one look was sufficient to turn a suitor away from asking a favour.

A hard, grinding man, indeed, was Jerard Scrivener, and so, to their cost, had many a poor fellow found when unable to meet his demands.

A rent-collector and broker had Jerard been till within a few years of the date at which we make his acquaintance, but latterly he was a money-lender in small sums to the poor mechanic or small tradesman.

Scrivener had never held house property of his own: he found it more profitable to collect rents on commission, and now, although able to do it, he never advanced as a loan a larger sum than five pounds.

"The risk was too great," he used to say, "and the interest too small; and people who wanted large sums generally paid punctually, while those who needed small ones did not; and consequently, for fines, letter-writing, and suchlike, he could generally depend upon getting forty to fifty per cent.; and if he did lose, it was very trifling."

But it was seldom, indeed, that Jerard lost— certainly not, if the borrower possessed any articles of furniture, let them be ever so old or humble. Goods or money was his motto, and not a few poor homes had he stripped of every vestige to satisfy his claims.

He had never married—that was an expense he never could incur; and as to keeping a cat or dog, the bare thought would make him turn pale.

Seven years before we introduce him to the reader, his only brother died, leaving a motherless daughter of fourteen to his care, and a sum of money sufficient to recompense him for trouble, education, and food; and also a thousand pounds to be handed over to her when she came of age.

Had Martha Scrivener's father died without means, her uncle never would have taken her to his home. A workhouse had certainly been her portion, but her uncle Jerard found, by calculation, that he could save at least fifty pounds a year out of the money left to keep and educate her, and have a servant to wait upon him for nothing, so he made no demur to being the guardian of his niece.

But Jerard never liked her: she ate too much, was extravagant in her habits, wanted clothes too often, and in fact wished to live as a girl should live, and consequently, as he dared not quite starve her, he came to the determination to reimburse himself for his great outlay by keeping the thousand pounds she was entitled to at the age of twenty-one, when his guardianship was supposed to end.

It was seven years of misery for poor Martha Scrivener, and she looked forward with hope to the day when the guardianship of her uncle should cease, and she could do as she pleased for herself.

She knew that she was entitled to a sum of money then, though she was not aware of the amount, nor possessed any deed or title thereto.

Her father was a generous-hearted, upright man, and looked upon his fellows as the same, so that it cannot be wondered at that he placed the fullest confidence in his own brother.

But that confidence was abused, and when Jerard's guardianship came to a close, he sent his niece adrift without a penny.

Entreaties were unavailing, and as time wore on, her stock of apparel, which had always been scanty, was disposed of for food, till at length she was reduced to absolute starvation.

How she had existed for months before our hero met her, it would have puzzled even herself to tell.

Appeals for assistance to her uncle had been made. At the workhouse she had been referred back to the miser, till ruined in mind, exhausted in body,' she only longed for death to come to put an end to her existence.

On the day following the night when Jack had relieved her necessities with a few gold coins, a gentleman had been making various enquiries about the neighbourhood with respect to the owner of the large house—large for that neighbourhood at least—and what he learned evidently did not give him a very favourable opinion of its possessor.

The rushlight, or rather half of one, was spreading its dim light through the sleeping apartment, when a tall figure, cloaked and masked, vaulted lightly through the window, and took up a position on the foot-board of the bedstead on which the miser lay.

It was none other than the gentleman who made the inquiries in the neighbourhood, and the hero of our story.

He had learned enough to know that the woman's tale in substance was correct, and he determined to frighten the miser, if possible, into relieving her necessities.

Hence it was that he was now in his chamber sitting on the footboard of his bedstead with the faint glimmer of the halfpenny rushlight, making his hideous mask and cloaked form looking more hideous than usual.

"Old men sleep lightly," he muttered to himself, "especially if their conscience pricks them, so it will take little to wake the miserly old villain."

He put his boot down, as he concluded, upon the ankle of Scrivener.

The old man half started up in bed.

His eyes encountered the strange figure at its foot, and a cry of alarm broke from his lips.

But he appeared powerless to raise his body higher or permit his head to fall back on his pillow.

Jack enjoyed his terror for several moments, then holding his hands out before his face, he said, in his assumed, hollow tone—

"Glad to see you, Jerard Scrivener."

"What—what are you?" gasped the old man, with difficulty.

"Oh! I'm the fiend that looks after misers, money-scriveners, brokers, and the robbers of the fatherless," said Jack; "and I've just paid you a visit to make you disgorge the money of which you've robbed your late ward."

"Money?" cried the old man. "Money! I've got no money; I'm now very poor."

"Jerard Scrivener!"

"Yes—yes."

"You're a wicked old liar."

A deep groan broke from Jerard's lips.

"Upon my soul, I'm poor—very poor. I don't know what to do for money, I'm so poor," cried the miser, his fear now being greater for his gold than for the supposed fiend, who sat in such a strange attitude at the foot of his bed.

"Jerard Scrivener!" said Jack, "you are a miserable, contemptible old liar, and I warn you not to attempt to deceive me. I know all your affairs as well as you do yourself, and I promise you if you do not restore willingly to your niece every farthing you have robbed her of, you shall not possess one coin when the sun rises over your dwelling to-morrow."

The old man's head now fell back with a heavy thud upon his pillow, and a groan, long and deep, rolled from between his lips.

"Oh, Lord! Have mercy upon me!" he cried.

"I'll have none, Jerard Scrivener," said Jack. "So come, if you would live and enjoy what you have gained by your other villainies, surrender that which belongs to your niece."

"She ain't got any—never had any!" cried the miser. "It's that girl that has been the ruin of me; she ate me nearly out of house and home!"

"Wretch! you starved her, and kept her money!" said Jack.

"Upon my soul, it's"——

"Hold! Don't attempt to play with me, old man!" said Jack, sternly.

"I don't want to."

"You had better not! Now, what did her father leave her!"

"Not a penny."

"Beware!"

"No, not a penny. I've brought her up for nothing, and this ruined me—quite ruined me— and me an old man."

SPRING-HEELED JACK BONNETS THE POLICEMAN.

Hard-hearted, unfeeling wretch," said Jack, "can you lay there and lie thus, in the hopes of retaining a few pounds that you can't take with you to the grave?"

"I'm not going to die yet—not yet," gasped Scrivener.

"How do you know?"

"I don't think I am."

"Perhaps you are nearer death than you think," said Jack, in an insinuating tone.

"Oh, no—oh, no!"

"I say, perhaps you are. Would you go to the grave with a lie on your lips, and the unatoned wrongs of your brother's child on your conscience? Wretched mortal, I have come to compel you to do her justice—and justice you shall do, or tremble for your obstinacy."

"You've come to the wrong man! I've got no niece!" cried the miser.

"But now you said she ate so much that she has ruined you!" said Jack.

"It was a mistake. I didn't mean it. You frighten me so that I don't know what I say," whined the miser.

"Now hear what I say, Jerard Scrivener, money-grubber miser, and home-destroyer, you possess some paper or deed by which your niece is entitled to a certain sum, at the expiration of your guardianship."

"No, no."

"Don't deny it."

"I must."

"It will avail you nothing," said Jack; "for I know of its existence."

That was false; but Jack believed himself justified in the falsehood.

"No, oh, no! I assure you it's true," cried Scrivener.

"No more words. Give it me, or I take it," exclaimed Jack, severely, and he made a motion as if to dismount from his position.

"No, no!" shrieked the old man, starting up in bed.

"Then get it."

"I can't."

"Why not?"

"I haven't got it."

"Where is it?"

"I never had it."

"Jerard Scrivener!"

"Yes, oh, yes!"

"Give me that paper without another word, or I not only take it, but leave you a beggar."

"Would you rob a poor old man?" cried the miser, in tremulous tones.

"No; but I would restore to the poor people you have robbed the ill-gotten gold in your strong safe," said Jack.

"Oh, it's all a mistake!"

"Is it?"

"Yes; I assure you it's all a mistake. You have been misinformed."

"Jerard Scrivener, I don't require information—I know all about it—all your villainous, hard-fisted dealings. Come!—quick! the money—the money, or the money's worth.

That's your style of business; only instead of goods and chattels, I take body and soul."

"Oh—h—h!" groaned the miser, every limb trembling till the bed fairly shook under him.

Still he clung to his darling gold, the only god he worshipped—the only thing till now he believed to possess the greatest power.

"Quick! decide!" said Jack; "for I have no time to lose. The midnight hour will soon pass, and I must then begone."

A look of joy passed quickly over the miser's white face.

Hope sprang into his breast.

Could he delay till the clock struck one, he could fail this fiend who pressed him so hard.

"Give me what I demand," said Jack, "or I take it."

"No, no; wait a bit," exclaimed the miser.

"I can't wait."

"Just a little while, so that I can collect my thoughts."

"Not an instant."

"Yes, yes; I'm trembling so, I cannot move. Let me recover myself, and I will do what you ask."

"I give you one minute," said Jack.

"No, no; say an hour—only an hour," pleaded the miser.

"So that you may defeat me," said Jack. "No, Jerard Scrivener, you cannot do that. If the fortune left to your niece, or the deeds to obtain it, are not placed in my hands by the time the clock strikes one, I bear you away from your gold to the dark and silent grave."

There was something so hollow in the tones of Jack, that the miser's heart almost ceased to beat, and the blood ran cold through his veins, while a strange sensation crept over his head as his scant grey hairs stiffened out in horror.

"Spare me!" he cried.

"I have said," replied Jack. "Come, the hour is near. Your niece possesses her just rights, or she inherits the whole of your hoarded gold! Quick, time's just up. The gold or the grave. Decide, or you are lost!"

Jack sprung up, his tall form reaching up almost to the cciling, as he flung open his cloak and extended his arms.

"You shall have the deed—you shall have it," shouted the miser, rising quickly in the bed. "I'm poor, very poor; but you shall have it. Yes, yes; only spare me. Spare the poor old man!"

The miser sprang from the bed to the floor, trembling in every limb, and Jack leaped to his side, to be sure that he made no attempt to escape from the room.

"Quick!" he said, in a hollow, hissing whisper, and laying his hand on his shoulder.

With a desperate effort, the miser opened an iron-bound box at the head of his bed, and took forth a paper, looked at Jack appealingly, and then made a movement as if to thrust it back again.

Jack tore it from his grasp, however, opened it, and permitted the light to fall upon it. A quick glance assured him that it was what he sought. So, thrusting the old man aside with his elbow, he blew out the rushlight, flung up the window, and bounded through it ere the miser could recover from his surprise.

CHAPTER XXXV.
THE PURSUIT—A STRUGGLE, RESCUE, AND AN UNPLEASANT POSITION.

JACK, however, had scarcely reached the ground when the miser awoke from the lethargic surprise into which he had been thrown, and the thought occurring to him that he had been made the dupe of a disguised robber and libertine, the fact of his ill-gotten gold tended to arouse the old man to immediate action.

"What a cursed old fool I am," he cried, "to suffer myself to be robbed by a clever villain. Robbed, too, of my gold—gold that I have plotted so to gain. But he shan't get off with it. No, no, I will have it back—I will have it back!"

Thrusting his head and shoulders out of the window, he shouted, loudly—

"Thieves!—help!—stop him!—stop thief! He's robbed me!—stop him!"

Jack heard the sound of his voice, and darted quickly along.

"Confound the old rascal," he muttered. "He'll certainly raise the whole neighbourhood. And though I am resolved he shall not deprive that wretched woman of her rights, I have no wish to fall into the clutches of the law. Hollo! There he goes again. I would not have given him credit for such lungs."

A hurried footstep came along the street.

Jack pulled off his mask, and thrust it into his pocket, at the same time moderating his pace, so as not to excite suspicion in the mind of the personage approaching him.

In a few moments a man walked close up to our hero, and looked scrutinizingly into his face.

Jack returned his stare indignantly.

"Well, sir?" he said:

"There has been a robbery," was the reply.

"A robbery?"

"Yes."

"That is no business of mine," said Jack. "Do you take me for the thief, that you stare in my face so rudely?"

"No, can't say I do. Only you see there's no one about besides you, and it was only natural that I should look at you," replied the man.

"Truly, there does not appear to be anyone about but you and I, so it is only natural that I should look upon you as the thief," said Jack, sarcastically,

"Me?" cried the fellow. "Why, I'm an honest man!"

"How do I know that?" said Jack. "Now, look here. You take me for a thief, so I take you for one. I heard a cry of stop thief, and as you are the only person about, I am justified, according to your way of thinking, in detaining you upon suspicion of having been guilty of some act against the law."

Jack made a motion as if to grasp the man's collar, when he uttered a cry, and took to his heels, tearing off along the street at a terrific speed.

Our hero stood gazing after him for some moments, and then with a smile at the fellow's fear he went on his way.

But he had not gone far before a chorus of voices broke on his ear, and the hurried tramp of many feet warned him that the miser's cries had sent several in pursuit of him.

He cast a hurried glance behind him.

Several persons were coming towards him.

Jack thought for a moment what was the best course to pursue.

To hurry forward would excite suspicion, and point to him as the person they sought, and to permit them to overtake him might also be fraught with danger to his liberty.

There was no place over which he could manage to spring and avoid those in pursuit behind coming up with him, as the houses were built in close rows, and opened directly on to the street, nor was there any break or turning for some distance.

While pondering in his mind the best course to pursue, a loud, exultant cry of—

"That's him! that's him!" broke upon his ear, and the little crowd in the distance appeared to receive a fresh impetus from the words.

Jack knew that it had reference to him, and he gathered the folds of his cloak in his hands, and bounded quickly away.

"Stop him! stop thief!"

Jack increased the distance easily between himself and his pursuers, and had reached the end of the street, when, turning the corner, he was caught in the arms of a tall, stalwart fellow.

The concussion was so violent that it nearly deprived him of breath.

Ere he could fairly realize his position, Jack was borne back against the houses, and pinned close to the wall.

"Hold hard, governor—not so fast!" said the man. "Don't you know you are wanted?"

This last remark had reference to the cries which now sounded nearer.

"Me!" said Jack, making an effort to free himself from his captor's grasp. "You are mistaken."

"Perhaps I am, and perhaps I ain't," said the man; "but I mean holding you till they come, and see whether I'm right or wrong: that's all."

The tones of the man's voice showed Jack that he was determined to keep his word.

Nearer came the shouts of the mob, which as it came gathered strength; and Jack summoned up all his strength to hurl off his captor's hold, he felt that if he could only succeed in getting from his clutches, he was all right, for there were few so fleet of foot as himself. So, suddenly twisting one arm from the man's hold, he struck him a heavy blow in the face.

The suddenness of the blow caused him to relax his hold, and Jack, taking advantage of the movement, tripped him up and bounded away, being full six yards from the man as he fell upon the pavement.

A few more leaps, and then he looked behind him.

The mob had come up with the fallen man, around whom they had gathered.

"Good!" said Jack, "that delay will, perhaps, enable me to leave this confounded locality."

But as he spoke, the crowd passed on again, yelling and hooting with all the strength of their lungs.

"They are bent upon capturing me," said Jack, "that's certain. But there's many a slip 'twixt cup and lip, and I may avoid them yet."

Every moment placed a greater distance between them, and Jack began to breathe more freely, when as he passed the door of a miserable-looking house, an arm was thrust forth, and before he could make the least resistance he was dragged into a dark passage, and the door closed behind him.

"Hush—don't speak—keep mum," said a gruff voice at his side. "I know what it is to be in trouble myself. The mob will go by, and when all is quiet, you can slope. It's hard lines if one cove can't help another when the peelers are after him. Been cracking a crib[41] and been bowled out—eh?"

Jack saw in a moment that the man who had offered him shelter and a means of escape from his pursuers was a thief, and was thereby enabled to understand the sympathy shown for a stranger.

Still, he felt anything but comfortable at being dependent upon such a character for security.

Ere the man had finished speaking, the tramping of many feet, and the tones of several voices sounded loudly as they neared the door.

"Hush, hush!" whispered the man. "You've doubled on 'em, but don't speak till they've gone clean off."

Jack took the man's advice, and remained perfectly silent till the sounds had died out in the distance.

"Well, old pal," said the voice at his elbow, "I reckon you ain't sorry for the little service I've done you?"

"I am indeed grateful," said Jack.

"Of course you are, and as one good turn deserves another, be sure you'll show your gratitude to one as ain't had a chance of doing a bit of business for nigh a month."

"You wish me to reward you for what you have done?"

"Well, don't call it that," said the man. "Share some of the haul you've had, that's better."

"My friend," said Jack, who saw that the man had no intention of parting with him without being paid for the service he had rendered, "I shall certainly make you a present for what you have done, but if you take me for a thief, you are much mistaken."

"What! ain't you in the profession?"

"Certainly not."

"Well, I'm blowed! and I've been fool enough to tell you I am," said the man.

"You need feel no alarm at that," said Jack, "for it is not likely I shall betray you."

"If I thought you would, I'd"—

The man had caught Jack's shoulder in a heavy grasp.

Our hero turned quickly, and struck up the arm of the man, then springing back, stood at bay.

The pitchy darkness of the place caused Jack some uneasiness, and the character of the man who was in that passage with him, and whom he could not see, was anything but cheering.

"Hark you," said Jack. "Whoever you may be, I mean you to keep your hands off. Taking me for one of your fraternity, you were kind enough to offer me a shelter from a misled mob, and I am not ungrateful for what you have done. You have, unasked, revealed your own character to me, and I assure you that you need have no fear I shall betray it. I have not seen your face, and hence it would be impossible for me to identify

---

[41] Robbing a house.

you. I am willing to pay you for the service you have rendered me, on consideration that you open that door, and suffer me to leave this place unmolested. But if you attempt to detain me, or offer me any violence, you will find that I have both the strength and the skill to leave you senseless on the floor of this place."

"What will you drop if I let you go?" said the man.

"Through fear, nothing," replied Jack. "If you think to wring anything from me by threats, you are mistaken. Open that door, and trust to my generosity."

"And suppose I refuse?"

"You will do so at your peril."

"Oh! you are coming the bouncible[42] now. You think you are safe," sneered the man.

"Will you open that door?"

"What will you give?"

"I will promise nothing while that door is closed," was the reply.

"And when it's open, you'll bolt like a sneak," said the man.

"Do not estimate my character by your own. Once more, will you open that door, and suffer me to leave this place?"

There was something in the tones of Jack that told his jailer he was not a man to be trifled with.

"Will you act fair and square?" he said, in a moderated voice.

"I do not understand what you mean," remarked Jack.

"Well, then, if I open the door, you won't sneak off without dropping something."

"I will make no promise as to that, but I will promise you this, that if you do not open that door immediately, I will drop something, and that something will be yourself. So, no more of this fooling. Open the door, or you will be unable to open it in another minute."

And Jack, whose eyes had now became accustomed to the darkness, sprang forward, and grasping the man by the shoulder and hip, flung him round and along the passage with such force, that had it not been for the wall he must have fallen.

"Curse you!" cried the fellow. "Is that your game?"

"It is," said Jack.

"Then look out."

The fellow sprang towards Jack, who, prepared for the onslaught, struck him a heavy blow on the mouth.

"Thunder me!" roared the fellow, "but I'll have your blood for that."

"No, you won't," said Jack, coolly; "but I'll have yours."

And lunging out his fist again, he lodged a heavy blow on the bridge of the man's nose, causing the blood to spurt out in a stream.

This seemed to have the effect of somewhat cooling the man's passions, and he retreated back out of the reach of Jack's arm, evidently having no desire to feel its force farther than he had done.

Jack ran his hand over the door in search of the fastening, keeping his eye strained through the gloom towards the man at the further end of the passage.

He was fearful lest the fellow might have companions in the house, and finding that he could not intimidate our hero, would call them to his assistance, and compel him to

---

42 Prone to boast; bumptious.

gratify their demands, be they ever so exorbitant.

At last he found the lock, and placing his fingers on the handle, to his horror, found he could not move it.

The man had secured the door, and he was a prisoner in that strange, dark house.

Jack was not a man to be easily frightened, but he could not help feeling uneasy at the position in which he found himself placed.

"Locked!" exclaimed Jack.

"You're trapped," said the man.

Jack sprang towards him.

"Unfasten that door, or I'll crush you," cried our hero.

"Stand off, or it will be the worse for you," was the reply.

And then the fellow whistled a low, shrill whistle.

Jack started.

His worst fears were realized.

There were companions of the fellow within call.

"You'll go without my leave, will you?" said the man. "We'll see about that."

The whistle was replied to by another, and a ray of light streamed through a chink in the stairs which ran up at the end of the passage.

"I must not be recognised," said Jack, mentally, and quickly pulling his mask from his pocket, he fixed it on his face. Then, stretching out his left arm, he seized the fellow by the throat, and placing his own back against the wall, held the ruffian as in a vice at arm's length before him.

"At the first attempt to interfere with me, I will beat that face of yours to a jelly," he said.

At this moment, from out of a small doorway under the stairs; a man, attired only in his shirt and trousers, issued, bearing in his hand a candle in a flat tin-candlestick.

"'What's the row, Joey; what's up?" he exclaimed, as his head and body, preceded by the candle, came through the doorway.

Then, catching sight of the masked face of Jack and his companion, he uttered a cry of surprise and terror, and permitted the candlestick to drop from his grasp to the floor.

The light was instantly extinguished.

But during the moment that it shed its rays along the passage, Jack had taken in every object, and felt that he now knew how to proceed to effect his escape.

And Joey, too, had seen more than he expected—namely, the hideous face of the man who held him in his grasp, and all his courage vanished on the instant.

"Bob! Bob!" he half shrieked, "come here!—oh, come here!"

But Bob, so far from complying, hurried back by the way he came, shouting out for Tom as loud as he could.

Taking advantage of the man's terror, Jack said, as he shook him violently—

"It's no use trying on any games with me. If you would have me spare you, open that door."

"Who the devil are you?" gasped the man.

"Perhaps you will find I am a devil if you do not comply instantly with my demand. You think you have caught me in a trap; but beware, or you will find yourself in one you will not be able to get out of."

Finding that the man did not return to his aid, the fellow, after making another effort to free himself, said—

"Let go, and I'll open the door."

"No," said Jack, fearing treachery. "Open the door, and then I'll let you go. I'll ask no more. Open at once, or fear the consequences."

He dragged Joey along the passage to the door.

"Now," said Jack, "delay no longer."

The fellow placed his hand beneath the lock, but made no attempt to undo its fastenings.

"Quick," said Jack, giving his head a bump against the panels of the door that made Joey's eyes fill with innumerable sparks.

"There, curse you!" said the man, flinging the door open. "Now, give us the money you promised."

"No," said Jack, hurling him back along the passage, and leaping over the threshold. "You thought to make a mark of me, but I have marked you in return. The punishment you have received was well-merited, and that shall be your reward."

And Jack pulled the door to with a loud bang behind him, as two men sprang into the passage from beneath the stairs, bearing lights in their hands.

CHAPTER XXXVI.

THE ESCAPE—A STRANGE FARE.

BUT Jack's difficulties were not quite over yet awhile, for as he sprang away from the door of the house, where he had been made prisoner, he ran full butt against a miserable, thin, shrivelled- up old man, who, bareheaded, was wringing his hands together, evidently in the greatest of anguish; and Jack being considerably the heavier of the two, drove the other, with no inconsiderable violence, into the kennel.

"My gold! Oh! you are he who stole my gold," cried the old man, struggling to rise.

Jack saw in an instant that it was Jerard Scrivener, the miser, who had hurried on as fast as he was able, after those who were in pursuit of our hero.

"Confound it!" said Jack; "this is out of the frying-pan into the fire."

And he was about to hurry on, when Jerard, by a desperate effort, clutched at the folds of his cloak, and dragged himself up.

"Oh! you villain! you robber!" cried Jerard, "where's that paper you have robbed me of, so that you may get my gold; all I have, all that's to keep the poor old man. Give it me! I'll tear it from you. Help—help!"

And so tenaciously did the miser cling to Jack's cloak, that he was unable to release himself from his frantic hold.

He had not the heart to strike the old man to compel him to let go, though he knew that every moment was fraught with danger to himself.

"You are no devil, but a man," cried Jerard, "and I will hold you till help comes. I will drag you to a prison—transport you. Villain, to rob a poor old man. But give me the paper, and I will let you go. Upon my soul, I'll let you go!"

"Hark you, old man," said Jack, in hurried and anxious tones. "'Tis you who are the robber, not I, for I would restore to the fatherless what you have stolen. Release your hold of my cloak, or I shall be tempted to forget that grey hairs should be respected by the young and strong."

"I won't let go—I won't let go!" shouted the miser.

"I would not harm you. Take your hand from my cloak; take your hand off, I say, or the consequences may be fatal to you."

And in his endeavours to release the miser's hold, he dragged Jerard several yards along the street.

"You shan't go! Help—help!"

"Confound you!" said Jack. "You will drive me to desperation."

"You are driving me to it. Give me what you have robbed me of. I'm a poor old man—very poor, and you shan't ruin me! No, you shan't go!"

Jack raised his hand threateningly, and then dropped it again to his side.

"Base as you are," he said, "your age shall protect you. By heavens! some one comes! Confound you! Release your hold!"

But the miser only clung the more tenaciously, and shrieked aloud for help.

"What's to be done?" thought Jack. "I can't strike him; and yet if I do not use force to release myself, I shall soon be surrounded by a yelling crowd. Ah! good!"

His eyes had rested upon the entrance to the cellar of a house close to where he stood, the flap of which was more than half rotted away with damp, leaving a large gap close to the wall of the house.

Dragging the old man close up to it, he stamped with all his force upon the remaining portion of the rotten covering to the cellar entry, and splintered it, driving the pieces down the orifice, and exposing an opening large enough for anyone to pass through.

Then grasping the hands of the miser, and using no inconsiderable force, he succeeded in releasing his hold of his cloak, and by a quick movement of his foot, he jerked the old man's legs down the opening, and holding him by the wrists, lowered him softly, but speedily, into the cellar.

The old man uttered a sharp cry of terror, as Jack, believing he would not have to drop far, let go his hold.

The form of the miser disappeared in the darkness, and Jack turned and fled in the opposite direction from whence the sound of the footfall he had heard proceeded.

But as he went, the cry of the old miser came loudly to his ears, and he knew that a short time only would elapse ere he would be discovered and released, even if he was unable to struggle out of the cellar himself unaided.

Jack hurried on, till he reached the Bethnal Green-road, and was congratulating himself upon meeting with no further annoyance, when a cry of "There he is! that's him!" saluted his ear, and two men sprang out of a doorway right before him.

Jack leaped back a few feet, and prepared to meet this unexpected surprise.

"Collar," said one, addressing the other. "We shall earn the fiver, after all, that Scrivener promised for his capture."

And as he spoke the man flung himself upon our hero; but ere he could fasten his grasp upon Jack's collar, a heavy blow upon the forehead sent him reeling back, and another planted between the eyes of his companion dropped him, as if shot, to the earth.

"So the old man has offered a reward for my apprehension," said Jack, as he darted off quickly. "But I don't believe he would ever pay it—the miserable old rascal. Well, the sooner I get clear of this locality the better. It's too hot to hold me till this night's work blows over."

He cast a hurried look behind him.

"They don't seem disposed to follow me," he said. "So much the better. I wish I could get a coach. Ah! that's one coming."

The sound of wheels had caught his ear as he spoke, and he darted forward to meet the vehicle.

The driver having pulled up, Jack got into the vehicle, and ordered the man to drive to Temple Bar.

"Certainly, sir," said the driver, who having had little patronage that day was going home rather dispirited, and looked upon this chance as a perfect God-send.

"Drive fast, for I'm in a hurry," said Jack, "and when we get to our destination, I'll give you a sovereign."

"You're a gentleman," said the overjoyed Jehu,[43] as he closed the door, and leaped on to the box of his vehicle.

"That's more than a good many say," mentally muttered Jack. "But different people take different views, and form different opinions of things and persons; and this fellow's opinion would alter, I'm thinking, if, at the expiration of the journey, I only pay him his fare."

Jack ensconced himself back on the cushions, and, the driver smacking his whip, he was hurried along the road.

When they had gone about a mile and a half of the journey, Jack pulled the check-string.[44]

The man drew up.

"Do you know a place, driver," said Jack, "where we can get a nice drop of brandy?"

"Indeed, I do, sir," was the man's reply.

"Then pull up there, for I dare say a glass will be acceptable to you."

"Ah! that it would!" said the driver, burying his chin in a thick roll of woollen stuff, which he wore round his neck, and smacking his lips at the bare thought of the liquor. "Gee-up, go along;" and urging his horses onward about half-a-mile further, he brought them up before a public-house, which was one blaze of light, despite the unseasonableness of the hour.

As the man got down from his box, Jack opened the left-hand door of the vehicle and leaped out into the road, taking care to close it after him as silently as possible, and as the driver opened the right-hand door our hero darted behind the carriage.

"Here we are, sir!" said the man. "I don't know a better house than this where spirits are to be had. Why, damn it—where's the fare? Blowed if I ain't been bilked!"

And the astonished Jehu drew his head out of the doorway of his vehicle, giving utterance to a deep sigh.

"Where the devil could he have got out?" he muttered, aloud. "It's a rum go, this—very rum. Cuss him! I hope he's broken his neck! to go and rob a poor man in this manner, the rascally snob!"

And the man closed the door with a loud bang.

"I'd like to lay hold of the humbug—I would. I'd show him how to bilk a poor fellow like me. Well, there! I must go home and tell the missus how I've been done by a fellow as I took to be a gentleman; and he promised me a sov., too! Oh, I'd like to let him have it, the mean-spirited runaway vagabond!"

---

[43] The Biblical King of Israel, known for driving a fast chariot, cf. 2 Kings 9:20.
[44] Cord for attracting the driver's attention.

And muttering maledictions, if not loud, at least deep, against our hero, he mounted his box.

Jack stole silently from the back of the vehicle, opened the door and vaulted inside.

"Gee-up!" cried the enraged driver, lashing his horse in utter vexation, and turning them round to proceed home.

Jack laid back against the cushion, and with difficulty suppressed his laughter.

"First I was a gentleman," he mentally ejaculated; "then a snob and a villain. Well, I'll let him go a little way, and surprise him a bit more."

Swearing at his horse, and smacking his whip furiously, the driver proceeded along, believing his vehicle was empty for about five minutes, when Jack again pulled the check string.

But this time the driver had not attached it to his person, and there was no reply to the summons, so Jack put his head out of the window, and called, loudly—

"Stop! stop!"

And stop the man did on the instant, turning his body round, and gazing at the head out of the window of his vehicle in unfeigned surprise.

"Are you not going the wrong way?" said Jack.

The man could not answer, he could only stare at Jack in the utmost amazement.

"I wish to go to Temple Bar, my good fellow."

"Well, I never!" cried the man.

"Did you not understand that to be your destination when I engaged your vehicle?" asked Jack.

"I can't understand it," said the driver, "blowed if I can, there!"

"My good fellow, I'm afraid you've been drinking," said Jack, in a serious tone, "and I begin to regret that I asked you to pull up at the nearest place where we could obtain refreshment."

"I did pull up," said the driver, "but blowed if I could find you."

"My good man, are you out of your mind?" said Jack.

"D——d if I don't think I am," said the driver, scratching his head, and speaking as if to himself, "for if the fellow could get out at the pace we went, cuss me, if he could get in! How the devil could I miss seeing him, when I pulled up at the public? I say, sir," he added, loudly, "I didn't see you when I pulled up at the Three Crowns."

"I am afraid," said Jack, "that it will be unsafe for me to proceed further in your vehicle. Your conduct is so strange that it alarms me, and I am a very nervous man. You must have been drinking, or else you are out of your mind. You have not pulled up anywhere. You only turned your horse round, and I have been unable to stay you with the check-string."

"Well, I never," said the driver. "I did pull up, and got off the box, and opened the door. I can't be mistaken in that. Surely, I ain't fell asleep, and dreamed it. I know I ain't drunk, and I don't think I'm mad. It's a rum go, and blow me, if I can make it out."

"Dare I trust myself to your driving?" said Jack; "or shall I get out and walk?"

"Oh! no, sir; don't do that. I'll drive you right enough; but I can't make it out—upon my soul, I can't. I suppose I must have fell asleep, and dreamed I pulled up at the Crowns; but I—blow it, it beats me, if. does! Temple Bar, you say, sir? All right! I'll take you safe enough; no fear of that. Well, it is a rum go!"

And muttering to himself, the driver turned his horse's head in the direction of the city.

"If you think you can drink a glass with safety, you may pull up at the Three Crowns," said Jack.

The confused driver waved his whip in answer, and once more the vehicle dashed on its way.

As Jack lolled back on the cushion he could with difficulty prevent laughing loudly at the continued mutterings of the man as he drove along.

The Three Crowns was soon reached, and once more the vehicle stopped before it.

Ere the horse could be fairly brought to a standstill, the driver had leaped to the ground, and flung open the door; but to his horror the vehicle was again empty.

He looked first at one seat, and then the other, and then lifting the frill of the cushion, looked under the seats.

Certainly, there was no one there.

The driver turned pale.

He staggered back, still keeping his eyes fixed on the interior.

He leaned against the wall, utterly dumbfounded, and gasping for breath for some moments.

Then he dived his hands into the capacious pockets of his great coat, heaved a heavy sigh, and cried—

"I'm damned if I ain't either mad, or that ere **vehicle is haunted. Now, no man could have got out of that this journey. It's the devil himself as must have got in, and in course he can get out anyhow; but no human creature could do it; and I'll sell that blessed horse and coach afore some harm comes of it. Yes, it's haunted, that's certain; and the sooner I gets rid of it, the better. It'll never do me any good now; and to-morrow I gets rid of it, if it goes for nothing."

And in a fit of desperation, the driver walked up to the door, flung it quickly to, and scrambled onto the box.

The moment he had closed the door, the one on the opposite side of the vehicle was opened, and our hero leapt in.

Again, the horse's head was turned towards the driver's home. Jack suffered the man to proceed about the same distance as before, when he put his mask on, and thrust his head out of the window, crying—

"Stop! Stop!"

The driver only whipped his horse to a gallop.

"Stop, I say!" Said Jack. "Don't you know there's somebody in the coach?"

The man turned his head just as they were opposite a gas-lamp, and caught sight of Jack's mask.

"The devil!" He cried. "I knew it was the devil I'd got for a fare; but I won't drive another inch. Curse me, if you shan't drive yourself."

And pulling the horse up quickly, he sprang from the box, and ran away down the road as fast as he could.

"Here, take your fare," cried Jack, leaping from the coach into the road.

"No, no!" cried the man. "I won't have anything to do with the money, or the coach either—stop, let me go—only let me go!"

Jack watched him till he was lost in the darkness, then drawing the vehicle to the side of the path, he flung a sovereign on the seat, and strode away.

CHAPTER XXXVII.
HOPES AND FEARS—THE POCKET BOOK

ANXIOUS to save her husband from a felon's doom, and wearied by the importunities of Ralph Grasper, which, despite the checks he had received at the hands of Spring-heeled Jack, he still continued with a persistency worthy of a better and nobler cause, poor Jane Slater, with a prayer to heaven for forgiveness, and having resolved never to look again upon her misguided partner, left her once happy home to keep the promise wrung from her by the heartless merchant, and proceeded towards the house where we first saw her, with tearful eyes and agonised bosom.

Poor woman! She knew the fearful wrong she was about to inflict upon him she fondly loved, despite all his failings—all the misery he had heaped upon her.

She knew, also, the enormity of the sin she meditated; but, then, she thought that alone would save her husband from transportation—and she could atone for it by death.

Yes, death—and at her own hands. For life—what would it be to her? A living misery—a lasting reproach—a fearful curse.

To save him, she would die! But, oh! How she wished death alone could shield him from the consequences of his rash and desperate act.

But that would not shield him from the penalty of his crime—Ralph would have no mercy.

She had pleaded—prayed—to that stony-hearted man—but all to no purpose. His results were fixed and decided.

She had hoped against hope, till despair took possession of her soul, and she knew that but one alternative remained, and to this she had at last yielded.

She wrote the letter, and placed it on the little chest of drawers, so that he might see it when he left the prison, and then, with the keenest and bitterest motions, she turned and left the house, with the intention never more to return.

"He will be saved," she sobbed, as she strode away into the darkness of the night. But at what a price!—Oh! What a price! I shall never see him more on earth. I have taken my last look at the man who alone possesses my heart. We must never meet again!—Never!—Never!"

With her head buried on her bosom, with the hot, scalding tears falling fast down her colourless cheeks, and her limbs trembling as if she had been seized with the ague, she tottered, rather than walked, in the direction of Islington.

No guilty wretch ever mounted the scaffold with feelings of such anguish, as did Jane Slater take her course to the house of the merchant.

Could she but have thought for one moment that her wretched husband was free, that he was hurrying to see her, and ask her forgiveness for the misery he had inflicted, how different would have been her feelings.

But she thought it not—knew it not; she thought of him only languishing in the cold prison-cell, waiting for his trial for forgery; and she kept on her way to save him, and to destroy herself.

She had promised to meet Grasper by mid-night.

She would not consent to go before, for fear that she might see anyone who knew her, and to this the heartless scoundrel consented, apparently to please her, but in truth,

because he had an appointment in the city, which would detain him until a late hour.

It was near one o'clock when she reached the Liverpool-road — silent, and deserted.

Never did the dreariness of a place appear so congenial to feelings.

But here she paused, and to proceed, not from a dislike of loneliness, but the knowledge of what brought her hither.

But the recollection if she turned back her husband was lost, again.

Slowly, with hands clasped upon her bosom to still the throbbings of her lacerated heart, she staggered on until she nearly reached the dwelling of Grasper, and then her limbs refused to carry her, and she sank down upon his on the gravelled pathway, and clasping her hands, and turning eyes to the star-spangled sky, she muttered— "Oh, God! Save me—save me!"

Was that prayer answered? Would the appeal of that woman be granted even when she was about to break the commandment of Him to whom she prayed?"

We shall see.

As that prayer floated upwards to heavenly support, the roll of wheels summoned her ears.

What was it that led to spring to her feet? and, instead of shrinking back abashed and fearful, as she had done several times on her journey, she seemed to welcome the sound, even strained eyes catch a sight of the coming vehicle. She knew not why, but there was something in the rumble of those wheels that seemed to whisper hope.

Louder and louder, and nearer and nearer, came the sound, and higher rose the new feeling in her breast.

She could not herself account for it, but to her it seemed as a good omen.

On the very edge of the curb she stood as it drew near her, and right before her it was brought to a stop.

The driver had caught sight of her figure in the gloom, and called out—

"Hi! Where's Cambrian-villas?"

The name of the place he mentioned caused a thrill of horror to run through her bosom. For it was the residence of Ralph Grasper.

Her tongue seemed to cleave to the roof of her mouth, and she was powerless to answer.

"Don't you know, then?" said the man. "Confound the place! I've got a fare here, more dead than alive, and am anxious to get rid of him. Do you know the name of Grasper?"

"Grasper!" almost shrieked Jane.

"Yes, that's the name of the fare. He is met with an accident of some sort, and has fainted, so I can't get out of him whereabouts he lives. He told me to drive to Cambrian-villas, and the devil himself couldn't find them in the dark, if he didn't know where they were."

If a wicked hope sprang up in Jane's soul then, surely she deserved pardon for it.

She hoped that Grasper was dead.

"Don't you know the name of the man nor the place?" said the driver.

"Yes—no," replied Jane, confusedly. "That is, I think, it's one of the next row."

"Oh, well, if it's one of them, I'm all right," said the man, as he urged his horse forward.

Jane Slater stood for a moment gazing at the vehicle, and then, clasping her hands together again, she mentally ejaculated—

"Oh! Has my prayer been heard? Has heaven shielded me from this fearful sin?"

The thought that if Ralph was to die what she would escape, and that her husband would have no one to press the charge against him, urged her forward, and she reached the gate of the house as the driver opened the door of the vehicle, after having assured himself that he had found the right place, to which Grasper had ordered him to drive.

"He ain't recovered," said the man, as he perceived Jane anxiously straining her eyes into the vehicle. "He's had a nasty blow somewhere. It's a fall, I expect, for his face is covered with blood. I wish he'd called someone else to bring him home. I don't like such jobs as this. I must get them to open the door before I left him out."

"Do you think he's dead?" asked Jane.

Jane knew it was wicked, but she felt that it would have removed a fearful weight from her heart had the man told her Ralph Grasper was no more.

Now she felt that her sufferings were only enhanced, and likewise those of her husband.

She heaved a deep sigh, and staggered against the railings, where she leaned for support.

The driver having succeeded in arousing one of the inmates, and informing the man who answered his summons of how affairs stood, returned to his vehicle.

"I must carry him in," he said, "for that chap's got to dress himself before he can come and help me, and I'll be only too glad to wash my hands of the affair. I suppose I'll get paid, or perhaps I'll have to come in the morning for my fare. Oh! I don't like drunken jobs nor accidents—there's always some bother with 'em."

While the man was speaking, he was lifting the bruised and insensible Grasper on to the footway, where he rested his burden a moment, and then lifting it in his arms, carried it through the little garden gate up to the door of the house.

The light from the candle, which the man who had answered the summons of the driver had placed on a table in the passage, fell upon the blood-stained face of Grasper, and as the eyes of Jane rested upon his harsh and bruised features, she shouted, and turned her gaze away with a sickening sensation.

Little did she dream who had inflicted such punishment upon the heartless merchant.

"Thank God for this respite!" she said. "But oh! Will he still persist in the sacrifice?— will he still pursue my poor husband with a relentless soul? Will he still persist in his demand or will pain and suffering point out a softer path to his heart?"

"Just give us his hat off the seat, will you, missus?" called the man, as he lifted Ralph into the passage.

Jane stepped up to the vehicle, and ran her still trembling hand over the seat.

It rested on a large pocket-book.

She was about to carry it to the driver, when a thought struck her.

A thought that sent a thrill of hope and to her heart. And she hastily concealed it on her person.

She knew that she did wrong. She knew that it was a theft, but she could not resist the impulse. Something seemed to whisper to her, "Thyself and husband are saved."

Eagerly she seized the hat which had fallen to the floor of the vehicle, and springing up to the door of the house, placed it in the driver's hand, who, having laid Grasper on the floor of the passage, took it from her.

Then she darted back to the pathway, her heart throbbing wildly, and her breast filled with emotions of hope and fear.

Her first impulse was to hurry away, but fearful of being suspected of possessing the pocket-book of the insensible man, she resolved to stay.

The person who had come to the door, attired only in his night-dress, now returned to the passage, having hastily put on some of his garments, and learning from the driver of the vehicle what he himself knew respecting Ralph, which only amounted to seeing him covered with blood in the street, being requested to bring him home, and his having lapsed into insensibility during the journey.

Being requested to call in the morning for his fare, and so to arouse the nearest doctor and dispatch him to the house, the door was closed, and Ralph Grasper was hidden from the sight of Jane, who gave relief to her heart with a profound sigh.

"It's always the way with these here sort of jobs, you see," said the man, as the gate closed after him. "Call in the morning for my money. Well, you have to pay me fer my time, that's all I know. Now I got to send a doctor to him; but, Lor' bless you! He ain't half so bad as he looks. When they washes the blood of his face, it won't be much to speak on, although it's a nasty knock he had somewhere. Which way are you going?"

"Towards the city," said Jane.

"Well, if you like to jump in, I'll give you a lift as far as I goes," said the man.

"No, thank you," said Jane, anxious to be alone.

"Well, just as you like. I don't want anything for it, and as it's a nasty road, I thought I'd offer it to you."

Jane hesitated a moment, then anxious to get back to that home she had made up her mind she should never see more, she said—

"If it would not be a trouble to you, I"—

"Trouble, be blowed. I shan't get a fare in this part to-night, and it won't hurt me, nor the horse neither."

"Then I will accept your kind offer."

"Pop in, then."

Jane obeyed, and was quickly on her way towards home.

A minute only did the vehicle stop before the residence of a medical man, announced by a red lamp in front of the dwelling, and as the clock struck to, she stood before her own home, her hand clasped to her bosom, and resting on the pocket-book of Ralph Grasper, which she had purloined from the cab, and which one moment caused her heart bound with joy, as she hoped it would be saving herself and her husband, and the next, sinking it to the depths of despair, lest its possession should only tend to enhance her misery, and place her even further in the power of that heartless and unscrupulous scoundrel, Ralph Grasper.

But she had reached her home now, and as her glance wandered up the front of the house, a cry of surprise broke from her lips at perceiving a light streaming through the blind of the window of the upstairs room.

What could it mean? Who was there? She gazed and listened, and then, as the tones of a voice fell on her ears, she clutched at the knocker, and fell fainting on the step, as the summons reverberated through the house.

CHAPTER XXXVIII.
The rival of Bristles finds himself in an unpleasant situation.

PEGGY MITTERN, the little maid-of-all-work, sat in the kitchen of the Misses Snookers Academy for Young Ladies, a picture of misery.

Her eyes were red and swollen with weeping, and she was endeavouring to choke the sobs which still broke from her bosom, by chewing the corner of her little white apron.

Peggy had got into trouble that day with two maiden ladies.

As we have before discovered, they had long suspected that something other than the cat had made free with the contents of their larder, and they kept a much stricter watch upon the cold food than Peggy had given them credit for.

They have several times hinted that Peggy must have given it away to somebody—the char-woman suspected of being the recipient.

This personage, upon being called into the parlour, stoutly denied the foul imputation upon her character, and consequently, while Peggy had gone out for a holiday, the two Misses Snookers had taken stock of the lower portion of their premises, and engaged the services of a young man to watch their servant narrowly when she went out to market, or for the usual supper beer.

The person employed to act the spy was a young fellow who was occasionally employed by the Misses Snookers to keep the little garden in order, and who, at one time, had endeavoured to win the affection of the pretty maid-of-all-work but failing in which, took every opportunity to insinuate that she was not a fit person to be trusted.

Hence it was, that when Peggy went for her supper-beer, carrying beneath her little cloak the leg of mutton bone, wrapped in an old newspaper, she was stealthily followed by the young gardener, and it was his footsteps which had been noticed by the girl and her lover.

Creeping within the shadow of the wall, he had seen and heard nearly all that transpired, and his jealous nature gloated in what he had learned, and the prospect of being avenged both upon Peggy Mittern and his rival.

So he crept stealthily back without being noticed, and when Peggy, with her beer in her hand, reached the gate of the Misses Snookers' house, he stood before her.

"Hallo! Peggy," he said, "I want to speak to you."

"Then I don't care to speak to you, John Grubber," she said, with a contemptuous toss of the head, and pushing open the gate to pass in.

"Don't you, now?"

"No, I don't; and I've told you so before," was the reply.

"I ain't good enough for you, am I?" said John, spitefully.

"No, you are not. I don't mean to have anything to say to you; and if you annoy me again, I'll tell missus, and you'll lose your place."

"Very well, Peggy Mittern," said John, drawing out the words, "very well; but mind I don't tell missus first about you."

"About me?" said the girl, firing up. "What can you tell her about me, I'd like to know?"

"Perhaps you would like to know, though. Oh! You ain't everybody, if you have got a policeman for a sweetheart!"

Peggy could have borne contempt towards herself, but not towards her lover.

"What have you got to say again him, I'd like to know? He's a man, he is—and that's more than you are. You clodhopping, nasty, contemptible fellow! Don't you say a word against him, for his little finger is worth more than your whole body; and if you dare to speak disrespectfully of him, he shall crush you, he shall—there!"

And the little infuriated damsel flounced away to the area in a high dudgeon.

"All right, Peggy Mittern," said John, as she disappeared. "You don't know what you've done. There'll be a shine in the house to-morrow, and then we'll see who'll lose their places. I should like to punch that Bobby's head, I should," he added, eventually, as he walked away.

Peggy went into the kitchen, and sat down, fixed and annoyed at the scene just past, but her feelings gradually calmed, and she proceeded to get her supper, when the bell rang, and she went to answer the summons.

The Misses Snookers wished the leg of mutton bone to be broiled, and brought up.

Peggy nearly fainted.

What was to be done?—What could she do?—How could she account for her inability to comply with the wishes of her mistresses?

There was but one way—a stale one, truly.

"If you please, mum, it's not in the pantry. That horrid cat must have stolen it while I was out for my holiday."

A severe look was in the eyes of the Misses Snookers.

"Peggy, if the cat stole it, he could only eat the meat. Where is the bone?"

This was a choker to Peggy.

She knew not what to reply, but thought it best to stammer out something.

"I don't know, mum, but that cat is the very Demon of a cat, mum, and is never satisfied, as you know, mum. I do believe he's eaten the bone, I couldn't find it when I looked."

"Preposterous!"

"I do think so, mum, I can't account for it anyhow. I'm sure I wish he was killed, for it's very unpleasant, it is, mum."

"This continual disappearance of cold food must be looked into. Very well, Peggy, you can retire. To-morrow we will see if we cannot fathom the mystery. Bones don't walk, that's very certain."

Peggy required no second bidding, but hastily left the room, and retired to the kitchen.

She had no relish for supper now, for she felt very uneasy in mind, and was only too glad when she heard her mistresses to bed, whither she went herself, and lay awake for some time thinking of the bother expected there would be in the morning.

The morning came, but nothing was said about the missing bone, and Peggy began to hope she heard the last of it; but towards the evening she was summoned to the parlour to confront not only the Misses Snookers, but John Grubber, the jobbing gardener.

As her eyes met his, she trembled and turned pale, for there was a strange twinkle in them, which seemed to say, "Proceed Peggy Mittern, now will I be revenged on you for slighting my advances."

"Peggy," said one of the ladies, in an austere voice, "have you found the leg of mutton bone?"

"Lor' bless you, mum, no!" cried Peggy. "That awful beast the cat has digested it by now, I should think."

"Peggy, the cat who had that bone is on two legs," said her mistress.

"Two legs, mum?"

"Yes, and wears a blue coat with metal buttons," said the other lady, fixing a penetrating glance upon the pale-faced serving maid.

"Oh!" gasped Peggy, starting back.

"You see, we have discovered the guilty animal, or at least John has done so. You have taken the mutton from the house, and"—

"Oh! Mum!" interrupted Peggy, "if that wicked man has said, he"—

And he drew his hand from behind him, and held up the identical portion of the joint which Peggy had presented her love with the night before.

"Can you dispute that evidence, girl?" said one of the ladies. "John watched you when you went to buy beer last night, saw you give it to the policeman on the beat, and this morning found it in the church, where it had been placed by him. We can keep you no longer. To-morrow you will leave the house, and we expect you will not have the assurance to send to us."[45]

And the lady waved her hand for the girl to leave.

John smiled grimly as the girl burst into tears of shame, and fled from the room to the kitchen, where she sat sobbing for some time, and biting the corner of her apron, and wondering what would become of her.

The fellow, not satisfied with what he had already done, was feasting his jealous heart by gloating over her misery.

So gratified was he with his revenge, that he could not refrain from congratulating himself aloud upon the victory he had obtained.

"He! He!" he grinned. "I've done it now. She wouldn't have me, and I've had my revenge on her. I hope they'll report Bristles, too, and get him out of the force, then perhaps he wouldn't marry; and as you get a character and the place, you might be glad to have it. But anyhow, I've paid her scorn, and I glory in it. Oh! He! He!"

And the fellow, with a stifled cry of horror, bolted back from the window as his eyes rested upon the phantom figure of Spring-heeled Jack on the top of the area steps.

Like most of his class he was easily alarmed by anything of an extraordinary character, and as Jack stalked down the stone stairs, John Grubber retreated backwards till his shoulders touched a cellar door, which flying open, he fell backwards into a dark apartment.

Jack instantly started forward, and the fellow, doubly alarmed, sprang to his feet, and hurried backwards further into the cellar, which extended under the footway of the garden to the footpath beyond.

On the threshold, however, Jack was, and grasping the door, pulled it quickly to.

The light from the kitchen window showed him a bolt on the outside, and he instantly shunted it into its socket, thus making a prisoner of the alarmed and jealous gardener.

Then he returned to the window and looked in upon the girl.

Peggy had risen, and was pacing up and down the window, her eyes fixed upon the floor, and muttering to herself.

Jack strained every nerve to catch the words, and succeeded.

---

[45] E.g. ask for a character reference.

"I shall never be able to get another situation," she cried, "for missus won't give me a character, and I can't get one without. Bobby[46] promised to marry me in three months, but what am I to do till then? I must tell him all about it to-night, and see if he can't get a home directly. I've got my last quarter's wages, and that'll do something towards it. It's nearly his time to go by, and I'll go out in the area and watch for him. I don't care now if missus does see me; and would I get him to give that John Grubb a thrashing—the nasty, jealous, mean-spirited, stinking cur. But I'll give it him yet, I'll let him see what I think of him."

She approached the door which led to the area, and darted to that which led to the cellar, and opening it, passed through, and behind him, as he came out into space before the kitchen window.

John Grubber, who had been striving to get out of the cellar, again started back in horror, when Jack opened the door, and gave vent to a groan, as our hero closed it behind him, and he found himself alone with him in that dark place.

"You're a pretty fellow," Jack said. "What have you been doing to cause that girl so much anguish?"

"I—I?"

Grubber could get no further, so great was his terror, and so violently did he tremble, that he could not articulate another word.

"You have been the cause of her trouble, have you not? Speak, sir," cried Jack, in a severe tone.

"Yes—no—that is, I"—

"You're a paltry, sneaking cur," said Jack. "I know all about it, so you need not lie."

"Oh!" groaned John, "it's the devil, then. I thought it was. Good sir! Kind sir! I"—

"Bah!" interrupted Jack, "you deserve a good ducking in a horse-pond. You will get your reward yet, depend upon it."

"Oh, good Mr."—

"Silence!"

"Yes, yes, sir!"

Jack had caught the sound of the girl's voice in the area.

"Oh, he comes!" she cried, as she detected the measured footfall of Bristles on the pathway, and hurried up the steps to tell him her sorrows and seek his commiseration.

Jack heard the footsteps of the girl over his head, as she ran along the stone slabs to the garden gate, and could tell thereby that the cellar went right up to the pathway.

An idea had entered his head that he might make Bristles the means of punishing his rival, and he felt about the door to see if there was any means of fastening it on the inside, and his fingers touched a small bolt.

It had not been used, and, consequently, required some strength to move it; but Jack, shielding his fingers with his cloak, succeeded at last in forcing it into its socket, and then moved along the cellar.

After he had taken eight or ten steps one hand touched the damp brick wall, but the other met with no obstruction, and he discovered that there was another cellar beyond that in which he was, and turning slightly he again went forwards and discovered that

---

46 Slang name for policeman, named after Sir Robert Peel.

he was in the cellar where the coals were kept—the one from which he had just issued being used for lumber, and had to be passed through for the coals.

A faint streak of light could be seen in the roof of this; and as Jack looked up at it he saw that it came through the sides of the iron plate which covered the coal-chute.

"As I expected," muttered Jack. "The hole is large enough for me to get through; and when this fellow discovers he is alone, he will believe the devil himself has paid him a visit."

Finding that the coals were heaped higher beneath the hole, and by ascending them he could touch the plate, Jack pushed it gently up off the surface, and giving a bound went through it; as he did so, nearly knocking over Bristles and Peggy, who stood beside the chute in earnest conversation.

An exclamation of surprise broke from the lips of Bristles, and a cry of terror from Peggy, at this sudden apparition.

"Bristles, if you would avenge yourselves on that gardener, you can do so. He is secreted in that cellar."

"Who are you?" gasped Bristles, while Peggy clung to her policeman-lover in terror.

"One who has learned the reason of this girl's terror—one who gave you a fright last night—Spring-heeled Jack."

"The devil!" cried Bristles. "And what did you do there?"

"Frightening the life out of Mr. John Grubber for reporting where the cold meat went. Now, if you wish to turn the tables on him, do your duty. He's in the cellar for some purpose, and I don't believe he's any right there."

"No, no!" cried the girl.

"Ain't he?" said Bristles. "All right. Cut it, Jack, because we've all got orders to take you if we can. I'll be one with John Grubber."

"Take me, if you can!" said Jack, with a laugh—"that will beat you, Bristles; but be a man, and take that poor girl for a wife, who has lost her situation through love for you, and may you be happy."

Then with a bound he sprang across the road, and was soon lost to sight.

"Now for satisfaction!" said Bristles. "Peggy, go and tell your missuses there's some one in the cellar, and call for the police."

The maid rubbed her hands together in glee, and hurried on her errand; for a few moments after the Misses Snookers appeared at the door in utmost trepidation, and Peggy called loudly for the police.

In an instant Bristles was by their side to hear that a burglar was concealed in the cellar; and Peggy, trembling with joy now instead of fear, held the light, while Bristles went, staff in hand, into the cellar to drag forth the intruder, which he did, not forgetting to prevent any resistance, to give him a blow on the head with his staff.

As he dragged John Grubber forth, the Misses Snookers retreated into the passage and closed the door, calling on the officer to take the villain to the station, an order which Bristles was only too glad to quickly obey.

In spite of the fellow's protestations, Bristles lugged him off along the garden, followed by Peggy, who sneeringly remarked, as she closed the gate behind them—

"John Grubber, who's got the laugh now? Mr. Bristles will know how to serve such a sneaking fellow."

CHAPTER XXXIX.
THE SEAMSTRESS AND THE JEW—A HARD BARGAIN—THE ISRAELITE MEETS HIS REWARD.

IT WAS EVENING, and Ellen Folder, now thoroughly recovered from the effects of her immersion in the water, and inhabited in a neat but pretty dress, sat in a well-furnished apartment in a pretty little villa residence not far from where the Victoria Park is situated, and to which the kindness and liberality of Spring-heeled Jack had consigned her.

Through him she had been able to satisfy the demands of Bill Jackson, her landlord, and had bidden adieu to the poor emaciated creature he called wife, and removed to the place in which we now find her.

Bill was puzzled to know how the poor seamstress had come by the money; and though he did not have the impedance to inquire, he could not resist making it known to many of his neighbours and friends that "something was up with that ere girl," a circumstance which told upon himself as well as Ellen.

The possession of a few shillings' ready money by Bill soon reached his landlord's ears, and brought him to the door with the greasy chord through its panel with the demand for his rent, or rather a portion of it, and this demand Bill had no excuse to deny, so he paid a portion of what he owed for the rent of the house, and bitterly cast his stupid tongue for wagging so fast.

The altered fortune of the seamstress soon reached the ears of the old Jew clothier, Mr. Abraham Levy, through the mouth of one of his workpeople, and his rage was furious when he also learned that Ellen had removed from the house of Jackson, and that he had not received the shirts entrusted to her to make up.

"Vere she get all de monish?" he asked himself, "unless she make away vid de property of her master. Dat's vere she get it; and by de beard of Moses! I will put her in prishon, de wicked, ungrateful Christian. And I took pity on her, and gave her such a lot of monish for her labour. But I will have an eye for an eye and a toofe for a toofe! She have my goodsh— I have her bodish! I won't be robbed by an ungrateful Christian!"

And Mr. Abraham Levy put on his hat, stroked his beard, looked around upon his shop shelves, heaved a deep sigh, and went forth to make inquiries where Ellen had gone, vowing that he would have his pound of flesh if he was ruined by it.

Time hangs wearily upon the hands of those who have nothing to do, and more especially where the poorest will has previously been the lot of the idler; and hence the hours hung heavily upon the hands of the young seamstress.

She had sat by the window, gazing out upon the fields in the distance, for the last two hours, and thinking of her altered fortunes.

Then she arose, determined to take a walk previous to seeking her couch, and asking in her evening prayer for the protection of heaven for her benefactor and friend, Spring-heeled Jack.

With her eyes fixed upon the ground, and her whole mind absorbed in thought, she walked slowly on till her small foot crushed the grass of the fields which stretched away before her.

"What a change!" she muttered to herself, as she raised her eyes from the earth and looked out before her on the green sward,[47] over which the shades of night were beginning to fall. "What a change is this in so short a time! But a few days ago I was toiling day and night at the Needle in a close room, without food or a breath of pure air, and now I am enabled to obtain even more than the common necessities of life, to inhale the balmy breath of unpolluted air, and wander over the green fields without the fear that to-morrow may see me the inmate of a workhouse."

"But it shall see you the inmate of a prishon, you wicked, ungrateful womansh," exclaimed a voice behind her.

Ellen turned with a slight scream, and stood face-to-face with her employer, Mr. Abraham Levy.

The poor girl turned pale as death, and almost gasped for breath.

The Jew's face flushed with rage, and stretching forth his hand, he seized the frightened girl by the wrist, and fixing his dark, piercing eye upon her, he exclaimed—

"Where's my goodsh?"

"Mr.—Levy," stammered Ellen.

"Where's my goodsh, I say? What haf you done with my property, you wicked womansh?"

"Sir—I—I have lost them," stammered Ellen, dropping her eyes to the ground.

"Don't lie to me! Don't lie to me! I know what you have done with them. You have pledged them—sold them."

"Indeed Mr. Levy, I"—

"Don't lie, I tell you!" interrupted the Jew. "Give me my goodsh! I will have my goodsh, or you go to prishon!"

"Mr. Levy, I am very sorry"—

"I don't want your sorrow," cried Levy; "I wants my goodsh, and I will have my goodsh."

"Oh, sir, believe me, I"—

"I won't believe you! Where's my goodsh? Where did you get the monish from to pay your landlord—to take your pleasure?"

"What is that to you, sir?" said Ellen, indignantly.

"To me! What ish it to me! I will show you what it ish to me, you tief of a Christian!"

"I'm no thief, sir."

"No tief, and yet you stole my goodsh!" said the Jew.

"I have not stolen your goods."

"Den give them to me."

"I cannot."

"Den you are a tief, and go to jail. I will have my property, or I will put you in prishon."

"Mr. Levy," exclaimed Ellen, "will you permit me to explain, ere you accuse me of an act which I would scorn to be guilty of. Poor and ill-paid as I was, I am still honest."

"Honest, honest!" cried the Jew, lifting up his eyes in disgust at the word. "An honest tief—ha, ha!"

"I will prove to you that I'm honest, and that my inability to return you the articles entrusted to me to make up, is no fault of mine."

---

[47] Meadow.

"Oh, no! Oh, no!"

"But, sir, I can if you will listen," said Ellen, striving to tear her wrist from his fierce grasp.

"I will not be robbed," cried the Jew. "My own peoplesh will not rob me, and a Christian shan't. I will have my goodsh, or I will punish you with all the severity of the law."

"If I had been guilty of wrong, I should deserve punishment; but, Mr. Levy, those shirts were lost through my endeavour to save them for you."

"Bah! Bah!!! exclaimed Levy. "You cannot make me believe your wretched lies."

"I will speak the truth, if you will but listen."

"I won't listen to anything till I get my property. Tell me where it ish—I will know where it ish."

"That is more than I can do."

"To be sure it is. But I will drag you to jail. I will have an eye for an eye and a toofe for a toofe."

"It is far from my wish that you should be the loser, Mr. Levy; although I assure you that the property was stolen from me."

"Vot you say?" cried Mr. Levy, at the expression of Ellen that he should not be the loser.

His grasp on her wrist somewhat relaxed in tightness, but he still did not release her wholly from his clutches.

"You shall not be the loser. The goods you were kind enough to trust to my care was stolen from me, and I am prepared to offer you their value, if not to restore the articles themselves.

"You are?"

"I am."

Mr. Abraham Levy's eyes glistened.

The severity of his countenance suffered down.

He looked almost admiringly on the pale, trembling girl before him, and he thought that there was a chance to him to make something out of her.

A keen eye to business had Abraham Levy. No man knew better how to turn a shilling into a pound, or a loss into a gain.

"You speak the truth? You will give me the worth of my goodsh?" He said.

"I have said so, and I am prepared to do what I have said," replied Ellen Folder, placing her hand in her pocket, and drawing for her purse, now well lined by our hero's doubtful hand.

Through its meshes, the eyes of Abraham Levy gloated on the coins it contained, and his back eyes twinkled, and his lips parted, in a broad grin of satisfaction.

"I ought not to take the moniesh," he said, "but drag you to prishon; but I am a poor man, and can't afford to lose my goodsh. I am too generous—much too generous. I pay too much for my work, and so I am kept poor by my too kind heart."

Ellen looked contemptuously at the grinding, avaricious Jew before her, and, opening her purse, took from it fifteen shillings.

"Mr. Levy," she said; "there were five shirts."

"Five," said Levy, pretending to think; though he well knew the girl had stated the number correctly. "Six; I'm sure there was six."

"No, sir, there were but five—five, shirts—which, when made, you sold at your establishment at two shillings and ninepence each—when you could get it; but more often at half-a-crown."

"God blesh my soul!" said the Jew, holding up his hands in faint amazement. "Those shirts fetch me five shillings each, and then I lose sixpence on every one of them."

"Mr. Levy!"

"'Shelp me Moses, I do," said the Jew. "But I don't want to be hard upon you, though I think there was six; and I'll take five shillings each, and make you a present of the six pieces I lose, though I know I ought to take you to prison instead."

And the avaricious old rascal held out his hand for the money.

Ellen looked at him for a moment, then dropped the coin back into her purse, and restored it to her pocket, much to the surprise of the Jew clothier.

"Mr. Levy," she said, "you accuse me wrongfully of robbing you, but now I accuse you justly of wishing to rob me."

"By the beard of Moses"—

"Hark you, sir," interrupted Ellen, firmly. "I am prepared not only to pay you for the material entrusted to me, but to pay the full value of the shirts, after they are made up; but if you think to frighten me into paying double, you are much mistaken. I will soon submit to be taken to prison, as I'm quite prepared to prove that so far from my having made away with them, I strove all in my power to shield them from the grasp of others. Now, sir, I am quite prepared to answer any charge you are base enough to bring against me."

And the girl moved away towards the inhabited part of the neighbourhood.

Mr. Levy's countenance fell.

He had thought to make Ellen's loss a good speculation for himself by playing upon her fears.

He was mistaken, and scarcely knew how to act.

Her willingness to meet the charge was what he did not expect, and certainly what he did not wish, since he had discovered that she had money in her purse.

Though his motto was an eye for an eye and a tooth for a tooth, he certainly preferred the value of the lost goods to the satisfaction of knowing that he had placed the girl in jail.

"What a fool I am," he thought, "to have only said they were worth five shillings each! Because if I bate I shan't get more than half; and if I had said twelve I might have got the five. Well, there's no help for it! I must come down in the prishe. Holy Moses, what a fool I am! But it's my kind heart that will keep me poor."

Then raising his head, he said, in an insinuating tone—

"Do you want to rob the poor old Jew gave you work and kept you from starving for** so long a time, and gave you more monish for the work than you deserved?"

"No, sir," replied Ellen; "I have ever striven to be honest and just, despite the fact that the paltry pittance I have received for my labours would scarce purchase food sufficient to keep soul and body together. I have no wish to cheat you now of your just due. There were but five shirts, which, at the utmost, would fetch twelve and sixpence. I have proposed to give you fifteen shillings to reimburse you for their loss, but I will not pay double their value under the fear of the threats of a man whose heart is as hard as the stones he stands upon."

"Vill you force me to send you to prishon? It vill go hard with you for robbing your trusting employer."

"I have an answer to the charge, and am prepared to meet it, and also to state that you were willing to take double the value for the goods and forego the prosecution."

Abraham Levy stroked his beard and shook his head at this. Then, turning suddenly to Ellen, he said—

"Miss Folder, only think of the disgrace."

"As I am not guilty of any crime I can feel none."

"Do not be so obstinate. But women are always obstinate, they are such fools. If it washn't for our kind feeling hearts they would suffer a great deal more than they do. Mine feels for you. I do not like to send you to prishon just as you have come into a little fortune, hut I must do it if you are obstinate, for I can't afford to lose my goods and my money; too I'm too poor—kept poor by my generous, feeling soul."

"I have offered you the money."

"But it ish not enough. I don't want to be hard on you, so give me five-and-twenty shillings and I will lose the rest."

I have offered you their value," said Ellen.

"God blesh my soul—the value! Holy Moses, hear her!"

And up went the whites of the Jew's eyes to the stars above, which began to peep through the dark clouds.

"Will you accept the money, and put an end to this scene?"

"There, to show you how tender my heart is, I won't be hard on you. I'll lose a lot more money. Say twenty-two shillings, and I'll let you go."

"Once for all—no, sir," said Ellen, determinedly.

"You won't?"

"No."

"You will force me against my will to send you to prishon," said the Jew. "But I can't bear the thought of taking a young woman like you to gaol. I'd sooner lose a good deal of my money, though I can't afford it. There, give me a pound, and I'll make you a present of the rest."

Ellen looked at him contemptuously for some moments, and then, drawing forth her purse again, she took from it a sovereign, and holding it between her finger and thumb, said—

"Mr. Levy, you are a cruel, base-hearted man, and rather than hold further conversation with you, I will consent to be robbed of eight or ten shillings. It will never do you any good, nor will the money wrung from your starving workpeople, I feel convinced. Take the sovereign, and I trust I may never see your face again."

She placed it in the outstretched hand of Levy, whose fingers closed over the coin with a nervous clutch.

"That's the way I am robbed," he muttered; "that's the way I am robbed. I am too kind hearted, and must alter, or I shall soon be a beggar. I'll make the people that work for me leave the value of the goods in my hands for the future, and I'll cut down the enormous price I pay. I'm too good hearted—much too good hearted."

Ellen turned from him with contempt, and a sigh, as she thought what would the poor wretches do if he performed his promise to allow them even less for their toil than he had hitherto done.

Dropping the coin into his pocket, the Jew clothier rubbed his hands together gleefully, and inwardly muttered—

THE FLIGHT AND TERROR OF CLAVERING.

"Holy Moses! but dish ish better than taking her to prishon, for then I loosh my goodsh and my monish. But now I got more than my goods' worth. He! he! he! Ah!"

A hand was on his collar, and he was swung round with great violence to confront the tall, strange figure of our hero, who for some time past had been an unobserved listener to all that had passed between him and Ellen Folder.

"You grasping, avaricious, blood-sucking old scoundrel!" cried Jack, indignantly, taking him by the beard and dragging him towards a small pond a few feet from where he and Ellen had parted; "but your villainy shall not go unrewarded."

"Father Abraham," roared the Jew, "look down upon the faithful!"

"Silence!" cried Jack, as Ellen, alarmed yet pleased, sprang to the side of our hero.

"Spare him!" she cried, quickly. "He is unworthy even of your scorn."

"Hark you, you dog of a Jew," cried Jack, "I intend to cleanse you of some of the dirty spots on your cheating soul, and mark my indignation of your conduct towards that poor, unfortunate girl."

And dealing the Jew a heavy blow, he sent him backwards into the pond, where Jack and Ellen left him floundering about and calling upon Moses and Abraham to save him.

CHAPTER XL.

THE FORGER'S WIFE AND THE SUICIDE—SELF-MURDER PREVENTED.

WHEN Jane Slater recovered from the insensibility into which the sound of her husband's voice had thrown her, and recollections of all that had transpired rushed upon her mind, the poor woman sprang from the door-step to her feet and looked up at the bed-room window with an eager glance, while her heart seemed as if it would burst its tenement, so violently did it beat against her bosom.

The light still shone through the blind, but all was silent now as the grave, and, as she looked, a cold chill stole over her frame and a shudder ran through her veins.

Hope, joy, love, all seemed in a moment to have vanished, and a presentiment of some fearful trouble weighed upon her soul.

She strained her ears to again catch the sound of that well-known, never-to-be-forgotten voice, but she listened in vain, and raising her trembling hand she lifted the knocker.

But ere she released it from, her hold she remembered that she had the key in her pocket, though she had resolved never more to return, and permitting the iron ring to fall softly back, she thrust her shaking hand into her pocket and. drew forth the key.

It was some time ere she could insert it in the lock, so violently did she tremble, but the task at length accomplished, she turned it and opened the door.

"He here—he—my husband!" she muttered. "But oh! how came he here? Can Grasper have relented—can his heart have softened? Can his better angel have triumphed, and prompted him to save both him and me? God grant it has been so; or has James broken from his prison walls, and—great God! that letter! He must have seen it—read it!"

She clasped her brow in one hand, and softly closed the door with the other, and then tottered along the passage to the stairs.

Still all remained silent, save the ticking of the little clock, and the beating of her own throbbing heart.

She clutched at the banister and dragged herself up the stairs by its support till she reached the landing.

The door of her bedroom was partially open, but no sound emanated from it.

Her suspense was terrible.

She longed to rush to her husband's arms—to clasp him to her throbbing bosom.

Yet she feared to move forward—feared to enter that room from which his voice had emanated

Why did she?

She could not tell.

Something seemed to hold her back.

Something seemed to whisper to her that in that room she would see that which would strike terror to her soul, and lacerate her heart deeper than it had ever been lacerated before.

She strove to call out her husband's name.

But her tongue refused its office.

The word came only through her lips in a hissing whisper.

She pressed her hand to her bosom.

It rested on the pocket-book she had taken from the cab.

The spell was broken which held her.

She took the book from the bosom of her dress, and sprang forward into the room with it in her extended hand.

But scarce had she crossed the threshold, than she fell with a bang to the floor, the sound mingling with the short, piercing shriek that escaped her lips.

Her eyes had rested upon the prostrate body of her husband as he lay upon the floor of the room.

A moment she stood gazing upon him with starting eyeballs and quivering lips, and then throwing her arms wildly above her head, she sank down upon her knees at his side.

"James! James! my own loved husband, look up. Speak to me. I—oh! my God—my God!"

She had grasped him by the shoulder, and raised his face from the floor.

The sight that met her gaze then almost drove reason from its throne, and called forth the exclamation in tones of the acutest agony and despair.

She did not faint now.

She knelt upon the floor by his side, holding his head in her hands, and gazing down upon the glassy eyes, pale face, and the pool of blood from which she had raised it.

Her heart, which before had throbbed so violently, appeared to beat no more.

Fascinated, appalled, she knelt thus for some time with bated breath, glaring upon the fearful sight before her.

Then the head grew heavier, till she could support it no longer, and she suffered it to fall back upon the blood-stained carpet.

Then her own head drooped lower and lower, till her bloodless cheek rested upon those of her dead husband, and the tears gushed to her eyes, and sobs shook her bosom.

"Dead! dead!" she cried. "Oh, God! am I dreaming, mad, or—but no, no; 'tis real—too real!"

And pressing his cheeks to her own, she swayed her body to and fro over that of her husband.

"James! James! my own dear James!" cried the woman, caressing his pale cheek and bloodless lips. "Oh! speak to—speak to me!"

But she called upon one who would never speak more.

She had heard the tones of his voice for the last time on earth.

"Oh, my God! what shall I do?" she cried, after a pause.

But the echoes of her own words alone answered her.

After a time she arose from her knees, and then her glances, through her tears, fell upon the note she had left.

"Oh, heaven! I see it all," she cried, staggering back and sinking into the seat her husband had occupied a short time previously. "I—I have murdered him. Curses on the hand that penned the lines which drove him to commit this crime. 'Tis I—I who have done this. I am his murderer."

Her agony of mind, if possible, became even more intense at the thought that what she had written had caused him to perpetrate the rash act, and she sprang to her feet.

"I had resolved to die," she cried; "why, then, should I live? He has gone to his last account. This hand sent him to the grave—a suicide's grave—and there—there will I join him."

She lifted the blood-stained weapon from the floor, where it had fallen from his powerless grasp.

"Yes, yes," she muttered, "this shall send me to the grave with him this has severed, and it shall join us, James, dear. James, you have gone but a short time before me. But I come—I come, my own—my husband!"

She raised her hand as she spoke, but dropped it to her side as. a crashing noise below saluted her ears.

"What's that?" she gasped, turning her pallid face towards the door of the room.

Crash! crash! and the street door was then flung violently back against the wall of the passage.

The weapon fell from her hand. She was powerless to retain it in her grasp. She could only glare upon the chamber door, and listen to the hurried tramp of heavy feet upon the stairs.

What could it mean?

She had no time to think, for the next instant a couple of officers bounded into the room, nearly overturning her as they did so.

One clutched at her arm, exclaiming—"Woman, where is your husband?—Where"—

His grasp relaxed, and he staggered back, pointing to the stiffened body which, as he spoke, met his gaze.

"Good heavens!" cried the other, "he is dead! "

"Ay," said Jane, "dead—dead!" And she dropped into the chair as she spoke, and her head fell upon her hands.

The officers stood gazing from one to the other for some moments, and then the one who had before spoken to Jane laid his hand upon her shoulder, and said in a choked voice—

"Woman, what is this? What does this mean?"

The other officer knelt down beside the body of the suicide, and placed his hand on the wretched man's heart.

"Cold and dead," he said, in a hollow, yet subdued voice. "Poor fellow, he has escaped us."

"Yes, we are too late," said his comrade; "he has cheated justice."

"Who are you? Why are you here? What do you seek?" cried Jane, scarcely knowing what she said.

"We came hither to seek this man, your husband, is he not he who broke from gaol a few hours since. Came to take him back, but"—

"But," said Jane, "he has foiled you—foiled that villain's malice, escaped the sneers of the world, the felon's doom, by self-murder. But curses on you both, why did you not delay another moment, then I—I had joined him."

She stooped to pick up the razor, but the man clutched her shoulder and held her back.

"Woman, what would you do?" he cried, forcing her down into the chair.

"Take the life that is wretched, worthless— lay with him in the cold and silent grave!"

"Poor thing!" said the other, commiseratingly, "poor thing! Take her down stairs. Take her from this fearful sight. Medical aid is useless here. You look to her, and I will go for further orders; but take her from this room. She must not be suffered to touch anything, nor left alone in her present state of mind. Carry her down stairs. Lift her gently, poor thing!—poor woman!"

The other strove to obey his companion's desires, but Jane struggled so wildly that the man could not raise her in his arms to bear her from the room.

"Let me go," she cried, "do not touch me; I will follow him. What have I to live for now he is dead? Let me go—oh, let me go!"

The officers tried to soothe her. Jane would not be comforted.

"Oh, let me die—let me die," she cried, struggling to fling herself upon the floor.

"Your grief is but natural," said one; "but be advised—leave this room and this horrible sight, and you will be more calm."

"Calm!" cried Jane, "oh! yes, I am calm— calm now. Believe me, I will be calm—I will be calm."

"Come, let me hand you down."

"No, no! I will not leave him—never, never! They tore him from me, but they shall not part us again! You shall not; I will find him in the grave!—oh, God! oh, God!

The efforts she made to release herself from the hold of the officer became weaker, and then her head sank upon his shoulder, and her eyes closed in insensibility.

Heaven was merciful to her.

For a time it shut out from her soul the fate of her beloved husband and her own poignant sufferings.

"Poor thing, she has fainted," said one.

"A good thing, too, both for herself and us," replied his companion.

"What do you think of this affair?"

"Suicide," was the reply.

"Not murder?"

"No. The fellow cut his own throat I should say. Poor devil!"

"Yes, I don't think she's done it for him."

"Not she; it's a safe case of suicide. I expect he made sure of being taken again, and so resolved to cheat justice of her due. He's a fool, though; it would have been time enough after he was committed. He should have stood his trial first."

The other shrugged his shoulder.

"Bear a hand here," he cried, "and help me to get the woman down. She's precious heavy, I can tell you."

The officer thus addressed stooped and raised the lower limbs of Jane tenderly, and his companion holding her beneath the arms, they bore her silently down the stairs to the little parlour, and placed her on the sofa.

"Better try and bring her to, hadn't we," said one.

"No, better let her keep as she is, as long as she will," replied his companion. "Poor thing! she'll wake up to her misery too soon, come to when she will."

Assuring themselves that she was not giving any immediate signs of recovery, the two men left her side, and proceeded to the bed-room.

"The fellar's dead enough," said one; "but we will call in medical aid, though all the doctors in the world couldn't bring back the life that's gone. What a gash! He'd made up his mind to do it effectually when he drew that blade across his throat. His hand didn't shake then, I'll wager."

"Where was his wife?" said the other.

"Out, I should think, seeing that she's got her bonnet and shawl on."

"A pretty sight to come home to."

His companion shuddered.

"Yes," he said; "but come on. I can't bear to look at him. I'm not over squeamish, but I shall see that face for a long time to come. Ugh! come on, don't let's stay here any longer; you look to the woman, and I'll go and send a doctor for form's sake, and then hurry off to the station to know how further to act. Don't let anything be touched till the coroner and jury have seen the place and body! What a fool the fellar must have been. But I can't help pitying him and his wife too."

And so saying, the man strode from the room on to the landing, followed by his companion, who turned the key in the lock, and then put it in his pocket.

Down stairs they went to the parlour and looked upon the still insensible Jane.

"She will be quiet enough, I dare say, when she comes to," said the man who had before spoken.

"I dare say it will lay her up, such a shock as she has had. But keep your eye on her, and see she don't do any mischief to herself. She's pretty desperate, and women are artful; you can't always be up to 'em."

"I'll be off and send the doctor, and make my report. Ugh! I don't want to see another such sight. Once in a life-time is quite enough for a scene like this."

And leaving his fellow-officer sitting watching by the side of Jane Slater, the man, shuddering, left the house to perform his duty.

CHAPTER XLI.

THE JEW CLOTHIER IN THE HANDS OF THE POLICE.

FRIGHTENED and alarmed, Ellen Folder gazed upon the Jew clothier, as the aged rascal struggled in the pond, and floundered about in the stagnant water, calling loudly for help.

But when the first shock was over, she turned her gaze appealingly upon Jack's face, saying—

"For heaven's sake, do not let him perish! Save him—save him!" And to this appeal the Jew added his own for mercy.

"Fear not," said Jack, in a low tone to the young seamstress; "the old villain will meet no greater punishment than a good ducking; for see, the water does not reach to his middle. Let him get out himself, and perhaps we will have learned him a lesson."

"So shall you," said a voice behind our hero, and Jack's collar was clutched tightly.

Ellen and Jack turned to find the latter in the grasp of a policeman.

"Attempted murder," said the man. "You'll get it for this."

"Take your hands off!" cried Jack.

"Steady now—steady, or I shall have to steady you with this staff," said the officer, drawing the weapon from his pocket, and jerking Jack along some little distance from the pond.

"Thank you," said Jack; "but had you not first better help that man out of the water?"

"And let you go? Oh, no."

"You'll have to let me go."

"Shall I?"

"Yes. There!"

And raising his hand quickly he brought it down on the shining top of the policeman's hat.

As that absurd head-dress happened to be somewhat too large for its wearer, it was driven over the man's face; and as Jack's hand had proved heavy, the policeman fell to the earth in a sitting position howling for help.

Ellen clung to our hero in terror, but Jack drew her gently away, saying—

"Let us hasten. There will be a riot soon. I've not hurt him, nor did I intend to. Come."

Together they hurried from the spot, while the officer was using every endeavour to force his hat up over his eyes.

Meantime the Jew had scrambled out of the pond, and stood the very picture of misery on its bank, trembling with excitement and cold in every limb.

Furious the officer sprang to his feet, and nearly overturned the Jew, who, to save himself, seized the policeman by the arm.

Scarce knowing what he did, the officer dealt him a heavy blow on the shoulder with his staff.

"Holy Moses!" roared the Jew.

"I beg your pardon," said the officer, perceiving his mistake, "I took you for that rascal Spring-heel'd Jack. Confound the fellow! he has given me the double. He sets the whole force at defiance."

"I will track him for this," said the Jew. "I will have an eye for an eye, and a toofe for a toofe!"

The officer looked around him, but the twilight fast deepening into night, he was uncertain whether or not an individual in the distance was Jack or not.

He was inclined to think not, as the figure which met his eye was alone.

"Officer, do your duty," said the clothier. "Pursue the villain—capture him, put him in prison, and I'll be very generous—very generous. I'll make you a handsome present—a very handsome present. I'll give yer sixpence."

The officer's eye, which had gradually opened in expectation, suddenly dropped to the ground.

"Sixpence," he said, "well, that is handsome!"

"Very—very," said the Jew. "I'm so generous—my good heart will ruin me. I must not be so kind as I have been—peoplish take advantage of my good heart—my kind heart—my generous disposition!"

"Your reward would be princely indeed! "

And the officer turned disgusted away.

He felt so amazed at the fellow's meanness, that he wished the Jew back again in the pond.

He had no right to expect any reward for doing his duty; neither did he; yet the offer of the Jew caused him considerable annoyance.

"Stop!" cried Levy, as the man went on his beat.

"What for?"

"That ish not the way the fellow went."

"I know that."

"Then what for you take the wrong way?" asked the Jew.

"Because it suits me!"

"Does it?"

"Yes."

"It don't suit me. I will have an eye for an eye, and a toofe for a toofe. That man must go to prishon for attempting to murder me," cried the Jew, gesticulating fiercely.

"Then you had better take him there yourself," said the policeman, "that is if you can catch him!"

"You must do that!"

"Must I?"

"Yes; I insist on your doing so."

"I am not going on any such wild-goose chase to please you or anybody else," said the man.

"You will not?"

"No."

"Am I to be treated in this manner, and the scoundrel allowed to escape?" said Levy. "You shall pursue the villain and take him to justice, or else I will have that coat off your back."

"Eh?" said the officer.

The Jew repeated his threat.

"Then I'll see you at the bottom of that pond first, before I'll move a step to arrest the fellow," said the officer, his face flushing as he spoke.

"You won't?"

"I won't."

"Then I'll see if you don't get punished for this refusal to do your duty. That coat shan't be yours long; I will have it off before you are many days older."

And the Jew laid his hand upon the officer's shoulder.

"Take your hands off," cried the man, dashing up the Jew's arm.

"I will take your clothes off, too, my fine fellow."

"Man, look here!" said the officer. "It won't be well for you to say too much to me. I know my duty; and don't want you to teach me, and so you shall find pretty sharp if you lay your hands on me again."

"You're a villain not fit to be in the force, and you shan't be, for I'll report you; I will take your number, and"—

"I'll take you where they'll keep you," cried the policeman, seizing the hand which the Jew again laid on his shoulder.

"Take me?"

"Yes, you!"

"To prishon?"

"To the police-station!"

"Holy Moses! What for?"

"Assaulting me in the execution of my duty— that's what for. I warned you, so it's your own fault if you have to pay for it."

"Father of Abraham!" gasped the Jew, "hear this wicked Christian!"

"Now, come on."

"I will not!"

"Won't you? I will see about that." And the policeman twisted his fingers around the Jew's wrist.

"Help!—oh, you'll break my arm!"

"Very likely," said the man coolly; "I shall do so, if you make any resistance."

"But you dare not"—

"Oh, yes, I dare."

"I'll—oh! Murder!"

The officer's knuckles pressed so hard into the flesh of the Jew's wrist, that the Jew could not stifle the cry called forth by the pain it caused him.

"I'll report your conduct—I'll write to—murder!"

The knuckles again sank into the bone of the Jew's wrist.

"You'll do well to come quietly," said the man, dragging the old Jew along.

"Mercy!"

Another pressure of the knuckles, and the Jew lapsed into silence.

He saw that threats were unavailing, one glance at the officer's face assured him of that.

Trembling now as much with fear as cold and wet, he walked on by the policeman's side for some time, then in the most abject and imploring tones, he cried—

"You are only in fun, my good man. I know it's only in fun, but I'm too wet and cold to play with you, so let me get home, there's a good fellow."

"Oh! dear, no; it's not fun, but real, right-down earnest, I tell you," said the man.

"It can't be; now let go my wrist, there's a good fellow."

"Let go?"

"Yes."

"Not exactly," said the man.

"You'll get yourself into trouble."

"You've done that, already."

"Now, look here," said Levy, "let the affair drop where it is and I'll give you a shilling."

"I mustn't take a bribe."

"I don't mean it for such."

"Don't you?"

"'Pon me soul."

"It is useless for you, sir, to say anymore. I have to do my duty. I'm paid for it, and I'm going to do it."

The heart of Levy sank lower.

He wished that he had accepted the first fair offer of Ellen and gone his way homeward. Bitterly he cursed his own greedy soul.

His hungry appetite had placed him in a very unpleasant position, which he had made doubly so by his offer to the policeman.

Of course, he knew that a small fine would get him off, but then the Jew clothier could not bear the idea of parting with his money.

"I shall have to pay at least forty shillings," he muttered inwardly, "and for only touching this man's arm. It's too much; it will ruin me, break my heart. I must not lose so much monish. What shall I do? Oh! I am a great fool! But I will ask him again to let me off, and offer him a lot more."

Then turning, to the officer, he said—

"Mr.—Mr. What's-your-name, I'm a respectable tradesman, and have done nothing wrong, but I know you will say I have. I ought to go to prishon so that I could expose you, but a tradesman's time is very valuable to him, and I will give you five shillings rather than go. It will almost ruin me, but you shall have it."

"No, sir."

"Yes; don't be a fool."

"Keep a civil tongue in your head, if you please," said the officer.

"Yes. I meant no offence—no offence, upon my soul."

"All right, then come on."

"Now do be wise."

"The least said is the soonest mended," interrupted the policeman.

"But, my good sir"—

"We are close to the station. If the inspector on duty feels disposed to let you go, all well and good; but, sir, in spite of all bribes or offers, I shall do my duty."

"And take me to the station?"

"Exactly."

"I will give—ah!"

The officer's knuckles sank so deep into the Jew's flesh, that Levy gave up in utter despair any further attempt to prevail upon the guardian of the peace to suffer him to go his way.

Inwardly cursing the girl, the shirts, our hero, and the officer, Levy suffered his saturated beard to fall on his bosom, and tottered with trembling gait alongside of the officer.

A short time brought them to the station, before which Levy raised his eyes to the policeman's face with an imploring look.

The man understood the mute appeal, but he only seized the Jew's wrist tighter in his grasp and hurried him over the threshold.

It did not take long for the officer to state his case to his superior.

The inspector, learning how affairs stood, offered to accept bail for Levy, and that personage having given the required sureties, was suffered to go his way.

So Levy hurried away from the station, and called a coach, with the driver of which, despite his saturated condition, he could not help waiting several minutes in bating down in his price; although the man objected for some time to take him at all.

At length, things being arranged, the Jew got into the vehicle, and was driven away.

The spot where the coach had pulled up was a very dark corner, Levy having taken advantage of that circumstance, thinking that if the driver had noticed the state in which he really was, with the green slime from off the surface of the pond, he would not get a seat in his vehicle at any price, consequently, when the Jew got in he could see nothing, and had sat himself down with a deep sigh, before he discovered that there was something bulky on the opposite seat.

When the vehicle had driven off, Levy extended his arm to discover what it was, and to his surprise found it moved.

He sprang up on his seat so suddenly at this discovery, that he struck his head a violent blow against the roof, which caused him to sink down again in an instant!

Then up before him on the opposite seat rose a tall human figure.

A glare of light being passed at that moment, lit up the interior of the cab, and revealed to Levy the masked face of Spring-heel'd Jack. He was about to give utterance to a sharp cry, when Jack's hand was placed upon his mouth.

"Silence, my worthy Israelite," he said, in a sharp tone.

"Help! Mur—"

"Peace, I say. I desire you to be silent. I thought you did not know me and intended to give you a fright; but as you do, and our roads be the same, we will travel together!"

The Jew sank back on the cushions, and trembled in every limb.

CHAPTER XLII.

THE ITINERANT DEALER AND MARTHA SCRIVENER— A BULLY PUNISHED—FLIGHT AND PURSUIT.

THE MOTLEY group of tradesmen who inhabited Monmouth Street, Seven Dials, something over a quarter of a century since, were thinking of closing their shops for the night, as not a few of the double-wicked oil lamps had exhausted their brilliancy, and were giving unmistakeable indications of going out.

Of course, at that period gas was not so much used as now, and from the houses of many of the inhabitants the stinking wicks extended their unpleasant vapours as they burned with a dull red glare from want of trimming.

Here and there was a brilliantly-lighted shop, but the generality of them were dingy and offensive to the nostrils.

The smell of old shoes, perhaps, after the lamps, was predominant, for in no locality in London were there so many persons who dealt in second-hand boots and shoes as there.

Old shoe shops were in abundance, still there were many other callings, and not a few stalls for the sale of vegetables, fish, and other commodities graced the kerb-stone of this thickly- populated locale.

"Now then, there!" cried the angry voice of a man who had charge of one of those fish- stalls, and supplied at a low figure bad fish to those whose poverty compelled them to deal in the cheapest and worst market. "Can't you see where yer are going to, or did yer want to nail that 'ere plaice?"

The person thus addressed, a poor-looking, thinly-clad female, with features pinched by want and suffering, turned, and stooping, picked up a not over-fresh member of the finny tribe, which in her hurried walk she had knocked off the barrow of the itinerant vendor of anything that bespoke quick profits and ready sale.

"I—I beg your pardon, sir," she said meekly, as the man savagely snatched the fish from her hand. "I am very sorry that I knocked it down in my hurry."

"Yer knocked it down in yer hurry? I'll bet a shilling you'd have picked it up in a hurry too, if I hadn't have seen you. Wanted a supper on the cheap, didn't yer? I know yer. You've been and spiled the look of it, so perhaps you'll buy it now you was bowled out in trying to pinch it."

A flush ran over the pale features of the woman thus addressed.

Her sunken eye kindled for a moment, but as quickly her glance faded, and the tears gushed forth.

Poor thing, sufferings had broken her once proud spirit, and the angry retort was stifled ere it could burst forth.

"I wish to steal it!" she half sobbed. "No, no; I never saw it till you called to me. I am poor and ill-clad, but I am honest."

"Gammon! Take in the flats with that. Now, ain't you going to pay for the fish after you spilled it?"

"I have no money."

"Of course not; shows you never meant to pay for it," sneered the man.

"I never wished to become its possessor," said the woman, moving away.

The fellow caught her thin shawl to stay her, and tore it.

"Here, hold on!" he said. "If you don't buy, I'll spoil you as you have spoiled this."

"Let me go, sir! How dare you insult me in this way!" cried the woman.

"Oh, you mean to come that dodge, do you?" said the man; "but it won't do with this chap. Now, shell out threepence for the plaice, or I'll show you up, I will."

"I've not got threepence in the world. I'm now going to see if I can sell my shoes for an old pair and a few pence to get bread with."

"Oh, you're a no-fly bird. Up to that dodge, and—but shell out, or there'll be a shine, I can tell you—threepence; and it's cheap at that. Threepence, I say, or a showing up!"

"For heaven's sake suffer me to go my way without further molestation!" said the woman. And once more she essayed to move along the pathway.

But the rough fellow's grasp detained her.

"Are you going to fork out?"[48]

"I cannot—indeed I cannot."

"All right, then," said the fellow, savagely, holding her shawl by his left hand and the fish up above his head by the right, and raising his voice to a loud pitch, he added—

"Hi! hi!"

This exclamation caused the keepers of the neighbouring stalls and several tradesmen to look in the direction of the gruff tones of the costermonger.

---

[48] Pay up.

JESSIE'S MAID CONFRONTED BY SPRING-HEELED JACK.

"Hi! look out for your goods and your pockets," he cried. "She's just been trying it on with a plaice. Show her up as she goes along, and mind she don't have you."

"Slap it in her face, Bill," called out the keeper of a cheesemonger's shop, directly in front of the stall.

"Here goes," said the fellow, thus encouraged by one who forgot he was, at least in form if not in soul, a man.

The fellow was about to strike the poor woman with the wet and unsavoury fish when his arm was caught in its descent, and the fingers of a tall, cloaked figure pressed into its flesh with a vice-like grip, and the tones of a man's voice hissed in his ear—

"Contemptible coward! "

The costermonger was about to retort to this in language of a forcible if not refined character, when the fish was torn from his grasp, and the words on his lips were stifled in the loud slap across the lower portion of his face which he received with the finny article of consumption.[49]

A moment the fellow stood cowed and terror-stricken, but the next he shouted—

"What did you do that for? I'll show you"—

"And I'll—that's what I'll do to such a mean-spirited, contemptible cur," said the other, striking him a couple more blows in the face with the fish, much to the astonishment of himself, the woman, and three or four persons who surrounded them. "You cowardly rascal, would you dare insult a woman by raising your hand against her?"

"She's a prig."[50]

"It's false," cried the woman.

"If she were, it is not for you to take the law into your own hands."

"She wanted to steal the plaice," cried the man, thoroughly cowed by the blows and the indignant bearing of his assailant.

"Oh! sir," cried the woman, turning to her protector, "I assure you I had no such intention."

"Yes, you did; and he's only one of your pals," cried the man.

"Scoundrel!" exclaimed the gentleman.

"No, I ain't," said the fellow. "I sell my things and buy 'em, too—not steal 'em, like other people."

"Hark you, fellow," said the other. "If this woman had attempted to rob you of your wares, there are proper tribunals to place her before. But I do not believe she had any such intention, and you are a cowardly, paltry fellow to attempt to strike her."

"I will, too."

"No, you will not, for here is an arm that will beat you to a jelly if you dare to raise a finger against her."

"Oh! you're her bully, are you?"

"No! but, I am a man who will not hesitate to punish one. Now, my good woman, go your way. He shall not molest you further."

"Shan't I?"

"No!"

"We'll see about that," cried the fellow. "Hi! here, mates; we can soon put down this

---

[49] i.e. the fish.
[50] A thief.

swell, can't we?"

"Not so quickly as I will put you down," exclaimed the other, releasing his hold of the man's arm, and striking him a terrific blow in the face with the fish.

"Oh!" roared the fellow.

"Oh!" echoed the cheesemonger, holding up his hands in dismay.

The blow had been dealt with such force, that the fish-dealer was knocked backwards by it, and fell fair into a chest of eggs beneath the window of the shop of the man who had suggested that the woman should have the fish thrust in her face.

A loud shout of laughter, mingled with the crash of broken eggs, from the bystanders, who witnessed the discomfiture of the costermonger and butterman, and a cry of recognition broke from the woman's lips, as Jack, turning his face so as to permit the light from the shop to fall upon it, looked down upon the bully at his feet.

That cry caused Jack to note well the woman's features, and he knew her to be the same whom he had met in the cold doorway, starving and homeless, and whose miserly uncle he had forced to give up the document which established her claim to a thousand pounds.

He had searched for her in vain for some time past, and had given up the task as hopeless.

He could scarcely help giving utterance to an exclamation of surprise and joy at this strange meeting, but he did stifle it, and made a motion for her not to speak just then.

"My eggs—my eggs—a whole chest broken," cried the cheesemonger. "You—you villain—you shall pay me for these, every one! Fetch a policeman, somebody—fetch a policeman."

But no one appeared willing to stir for that purpose.

They were too much amused at the figure cut by the dealer in fish, as he scrambled out of the box with considerable difficulty.

As he rose to his feet, be looked indeed a pretty picture, and instead of exciting sympathy and commiseration, called forth shrieks of mirth from the bystanders, who now were in considerable force.

His clothes were covered, at least the upper portion of them, with the liquid eggs; and his hair covered with the same glutinous substance, and suck a picture of misery and filth did he look, that the woman whom he had treated so harshly felt a pang of sorrow for him.

She, however, was about the only one in the crowd who did so.

The rough characters which surrounded him commenced to jeer and laugh at him, and this only added to the rage of the fisherman, who, goaded to desperation, turned upon a fellow-coster and struck him a blow in the face.

"What did you do that for?" roared the fellow, doubling his fist.

"What did you laugh at me for then?" roared the other, amid another shout of mirth from those around.

"Because you're a beauty, you are. Why didn't you hit the fellow that put you into the box?"

"Because he's afraid," said Jack.

"You're a"—

Smack went the fish across his mouth, and the remainder of the sentence was lost in the sound of the wet blow.

The man whom the fishmonger had struck, smarting from the blow he had received, called out—

"Bravo! governor! Give it him—give him another smell of his stinking fish!"

The punished bully could stand no more.

His blood was up.

He dared not turn upon the man who stood forth the champion of the poor pale woman. There was something in Jack's mien which cowed him, but he dashed at the fellow in his own sphere of life, and together they rolled to the pavement locked in each other's arms, swearing frightfully all the while.

Jack, flinging his finny weapon away into the road, as the attention of the whole mob became centred on the combatants, and seizing the arm of the woman, said in a low tone—

"We can get away now without difficulty. Follow me. I have something to communicate to you."

He moved away as he spoke, followed tremblingly by the woman.

But he had not taken two steps when the cheesemonger, who had been looking in vain for a policeman, sprang forward, and seized him by the collar.

"No, you don't go," he said. "Pay me for my eggs, or I'll lock you up."

"Take your hands off, my friend," said Jack sharply.

"I shan't. Pay me for the destruction of my property."

"At what do you value them?" asked Jack.

"Five pounds."

"Indeed!"

"Yes. They were all the best eggs, and I can't afford to lose them."

"Then, sir," said Jack, severely, "you are justly punished for your unmanly words."

"What do you mean, you scamp?" roared the tradesman.

"I will knock you down if you address such an offensive term to me again," cried Jack, the blood mantling his face. "'Tis you, sir, who are a scamp, or you never would have urged that rascal to strike this woman. Now, sir, I decline to pay you for those eggs, and perhaps their loss will be a lesson to you to treat the poorest female as a woman."

"You shall pay me. I won't be robbed—I won't be"—

"Take your hands off," interrupted Jack.

Then turning to the woman, he said in a low tone—

"Go, I will follow you."

"You shan't go, you thief—you villain—you robber! I'll have you dragged to prison—I'll lock you up. Police! police!"

"Here's another mill!" cried a voice, and the next instant the attention of the crowd was called from the costermongers to Jack and the tradesman.

"Confound it," said Jack, "I must put an end to this."

And exerting all his strength he raised the man from his feet, and by a dexterous thrust hurled him right into the box of broken eggs.

The fishmonger, who was struggling up from the ground at that moment, received so violent a kick in the eye from the cheesemonger as his head went down into the egg chest and his feet leaped into the air, that the stallkeeper fell backwards again as if shot.

"Bravo! Hurrah!—here's a lark!" shouted the crowd.

"Cut it—here's the police!" cried one.

"Slope, [51]" yelled another.

"Be alive, old chap; here's a couple of shiney-topped ones coming, so make yourself scarce."

Jack saw that he had now got the sympathies of the crowd of roughs, and after one hasty glance in the direction whence the two officers were coming, he said, hurriedly, to the woman—

"Fly, and meet me in an hour in front of the abbey. Quick! leave me to look to myself."

The woman cast one look upon his face, then turned and hurried away.

"Stop 'em—stop 'em! Don't let 'em go!" roared the cheesemonger, trying to struggle out of the chest; but, losing his balance, caught at the fishmonger, and falling back, pulled the man down on the top of him.

Jack gathered the folds of his cloak around him, and dashed away amid the cheers of the mob, who had witnessed the fracas.

But the cry of "Stop him!" soon rang in his ears, and casting a glance behind him, he perceived that the officers, with a troop at their heels, were in full chase.

"Come on," said Jack, with a smile. "But if there is no one in front to offer me any resistance, I fear not those behind."

Scarce had he given expression to this thought, than a man sprang out before him with extended arms.

Jack could not stop himself in time to avoid a collision, but he ducked his head, and went clean under the arms of the man, and shot along like an arrow, and the next moment his surprised and bewildered would-be-captor was hurled violently to the ground by the mob in whose way he stood.

This caused a check to the impetuosity of his pursuers, and Jack gained upon them considerably.

"I know this locality well," he muttered, "and must double on them by taking yonder court."

He made a dash at a dark entry, but ere he could turn down it, the ground seemed to give way beneath his feet, and he fell through a cellar flap on to a heap of old boots, shoes, and left-off wearing apparel.

In an instant he scrambled to his feet and looked around.

He perceived he had fallen into one of those cellars used as a shop and store-house by a dealer of second-hand clothing.

The stench of the fast-expiring wick of a suspended oil-lamp, mingled with the musty odour of damp clothes and mildewed leather, and Jack felt a sickening sensation steal over him as he tottered back from the opening, hoping to prevent being seen by his pursuers, and leading them to believe that he had given them the slip, by passing up the dark court.

A rush of feet along the pavement, and a hubbub of voices along the side of the house, told him that the crowd had taken the court, and, with a smile of satisfaction, he took a long and curious survey of the place in which he was.

There was no one but himself there, and this afforded him considerable gratification, as he thought that in a few minutes he could retire unmolested, and hurry on his way to keep

---

[51] Run away.

the appointment he had made with Martha Scrivener, in front of Westminster Abbey.

When all became still again above, Jack was about to scramble out of the cellar doorway, when he was met by a man coming down.

The comer was a dirty-looking fellow, and evidently scarcely able to keep his feet from the effects of the bad gin he had been drinking, and Jack, anxious to escape, hurriedly slipped on his mask.

Down staggered the man till he got to the bottom, and then, seeing our hero, he threw up his hands, uttered a loud shriek, and fell face forward among the heap of old boots.

"Now's my time!" said Jack, darting up the cellar flap. One look told him the coast was clear, and slipping off his mask, he hurried away towards the abbey, before which he arrived free from further molestation, and stood before the all-expectant miser's ward.

CHAPTER XLIII.
HUSBAND AND WIFE—INSULT HEAPED UPON INJURY—LOVE TURNED TO HATRED.

IN her splendid boudoir Jessie Clavering sat upon a satin-covered couch, a picture of grief.

Tears were streaming from her eyes, and trickling down her now pale, wan cheeks.

Her bosom rose and fell with emotions which shook her soul and lacerated her heart.

One month had she been the legal wife of Richard Clavering.

But her wedded life was more miserable than had been the latter part of her mistresshood.

She had forced the libertine to do her justice, forced him to lead her to the altar, and confer upon her the title of wife, because his coldness had wrung her heart, and under the belief that time would bring back the old love; but, alas! how had she been deceived!

True, she was now a wife in name, but that was all.

The coldness of Richard had now grown to positive hatred, and foiled in his attempt to destroy the proofs of their marriage, he strove all he could to make himself a widower by breaking the heart of her who had loved him with all a woman's love—sacrificed all for him.

Taunts, threats, and even blows—for the proud and wealthy libertine even descended to strike the woman he had sworn to love and cherish— brought not about that consummation so devoutly to be wished—the death of Jessie; and he determined to give her heart one pang more ere he shed her blood, for he resolved to rid himself of her, even at the sacrifice of his own peace of mind for ever.

He renewed his pursuit of the poor ballet-girl whom Jack had rescued from his unmanly violence, but learning prudence by the punishment he had received that night, he approached his intended victim in a different way, and sought to win her love through her mother.

He knew that the mother of the girl was poor, and that she consented to her only daughter taking to the stage because it kept them from the workhouse, and the wily rascal approached the old lady with words of commiseration for her altered circumstances, and anxious fear for her daughter's happiness, lest some one would take her from the boards, where he pointed out to the only too credulous dame that sin and shame abounded to such a degree as to preclude all hope of her child escaping its contaminating influences.

In Bridget Hendon he found a willing listener; the life her daughter led was distasteful to her, and every hour of her absence was but an age of misery and suspense to the anxious mother. She knew her beautiful Mildred was pure and innocent, but she dreaded lest that beauty she prized so much should prove a curse—become the means of luring her to that fate she so much dreaded. So the serpent-tongue of the libertine won the old lady's heart ere he again met the daughter, and she was as anxious that he should possess the affections of Mildred as he was himself.

And when at length he did meet the poor ballet girl in her poverty-stricken home, and Mildred turned from him in disgust and loathing, the wretch found a champion in the woman who would have lain down her life to shield her beloved child.

But the mother believed Richard Clavering all he professed to be—believed him the soul of honour; that he sought her daughter's love only that he might rescue her from a life so fraught with danger to her reputation and future peace of mind.

Mildred loved her mother, believed her the most far-sighted; and well knowing she would not say or do anything to harm her, she suffered her coldness and contempt to fade, and when in abject tones the scoundrel pleaded for forgiveness for the past, excused the warmth of his acts to his love for her, she placed her hand in his, and felt her heart warm towards him.

Never did spider lure the timid fly so artfully into the meshes of its web, as did Richard Clavering draw that trusting girl's soul to himself. He was rich, he was handsome, and the firm belief of the mother soon tended to cause the daughter to think he was honourable, and day by day her feelings grew stronger towards him; contempt gave place to respect, respect to love, and, anxious to secure for her aged mother, if not for herself, independence and comfort, she consented to become his wife.

Oh! had she known he was already married, how that blushing smile would have changed to a look of horror! How that head which rested on his bosom as she murmured her consent, would have drooped in shame and contempt!

Too well he knew that no less title than wife could make her his, and he had determined upon a mock marriage, when he sought the mother, should he succeed, for mistress Mildred would never be to him.

Oh! could that poor girl have realized the truth as her small white fingers trembled in his, and her timid eyes were raised to his face—could she but have suspected that his object was to ruin her and crush the soul of his wife, she would have died ere she uttered the words—"I am thine, Richard, thine!"

But she knew it not, thought it not, and was happy, while the heart-broken and ill-used Jessie sat in that sumptuous apartment, cursing the hour that she had ever listened to the tones of the betrayer, and regretting that heaven had not taken her from this world ere Richard Clavering had gazed upon her beautiful features—had seen the bright flower which he breathed on but to destroy for ever.

Gold will buy everything but happiness and a passage to heaven. It is the one great god which all men worship more or less. Its influence is almost unbounded. At its chink the heart throbs, at its sight the eye flashes, and at its touch the soul expands. Few, indeed, can resist its power. It is the talisman to all hearts. Nothing can resist it save the grave. There it is powerless—there and there alone.

Applied for good or evil, its power is greater than all else in the world. It can save the soul from sin, dry the widow's tears, ease the orphan's pangs, shed happiness and joy around, make the sad gay, feed the hungry, and clothe the naked; but when its possessor scatters it for evil, it can plunge more souls to perdition than all the hands in the world can save.

Richard Clavering knew this—knew that gold could purchase him accomplices in his wicked act—buy him a mock priest and witnesses for the sham ceremony, even though those who sold themselves to the guilty work knew that they were aiding a villain to plunge the soul of an innocent girl into a vortex deep as hell, and his own base soul to perdition. And not only could he buy their assistance, but their silence. Gold would do it all, and he possessed it.

So smilingly he went home, after pressing the innocent cheek, and murmuring how happy they would be in a few days—smilingly he entered the boudoir of his suffering and heartbroken wife.

Nor did the smile fade from his cheek, or the joy he felt at his success evaporate from his heart, as he looked upon the wreck he had made which sat before him.

Rather was he the more gratified, for he thought, one pang more and death will rid me of her.

The poor woman gazed mournfully up in his face.

It was then that a scowl darkened his brow.

"You have come, Richard," she said at length.

The libertine coolly drew out his cigar-case, lit a cigar, and took no notice of her remark. Jessie heaved a deep sigh.

Clavering puffed out a mouthful of blue smoke, and smiled again as he watched it curl upwards in fantastic wreaths.

That sigh would have caused another and better man a pang, but it only made him feel more happy.

It bespoke her sufferings, and her pain was his happiness.

"Oh, Richard," she said at length, "how you are altered!"

"Yes," he drawled out, "I think I am."

"Indeed you are."

"I feel more happy to-night than I have done for some time past," he said.

"I am glad to hear it."

"You!" he exclaimed, opening his eyes.

"Yes, Richard. I am."

"That's strange."

"Strange!"

"Why should you be glad?" he questioned, fixing his eyes upon her.

"Is it not natural that a wife should feel glad when her husband is happy?" she said.

Again the brow of Richard darkened till it was black as midnight.

He dashed the cigar from his mouth and sprang to his feet.

"Wife!—curse the word!" he cried, stamping his foot on the sumptuous carpet.

"Wherefore? Oh! Richard," sobbed the woman.

"It reminds me of my disgrace—reminds me of the fool I have been to make a wife of a"—

The woman rose to her feet and held up her hand deprecatingly.

"Richard Clavering," she interrupted him, "when you made me your wife you proved yourself to the world, at least, a man; but since you gave me your name you have been to me a wretch—a cruel, unfeeling wretch."

"I will be a devil yet," he exclaimed, "if not an executioner."

"Oh! man, what have you become!"

"A thing for my fellow-men to laugh and jeer at. Speak the word no more; lest in my fury I"—

He raised his clenched hand.

"Richard," she said, fixing her tearful eyes on his own fiery orbs, "your hand is powerless to inflict the pain upon my body which your tongue does on my soul. The pangs of a lacerated heart are more acute than those of a bruised skin. Strike if you will—a blow cannot inflict more suffering on me; but it will brand you as an infamous coward, as well as a contemptible villain."

"Woman, I say!"

"Would I could address you as man." she cried. "That title you have forfeited. Wretch you may be, but man you are not."

The ruffian bit his lips and ground his teeth together.

He longed to strike, yet feared to inflict the blow.

"Hold your taunting tongue," he cried, fiercely, "or I will still it for ever."

"You have the courage to break a woman's heart, Richard Clavering, but not to still its pangs. You can strike only with such weapons as leave no blood behind, and at such parts as are hidden from the gaze of mankind, for a dagger planted in my bosom, or a blow that would rid me of life hands you over to justice; but you stab at the inmost recesses of my soul with your forked tongue, and crush out my existence by your cruel contempt and cold indifference. Therefore I repeat, you are a coward. You dare not slay me by other means, lest you in turn should suffer."

Clavering rested his hand on the back of a chair, and, extending his arm, shook his forefinger in her face.

"Hark you, Jessie Bolton," he said.

"Clavering, sir. I am your wife—yes, the wife of a Clavering and a scoundrel—no proud name to bear; but as 'tis legally mine, I'll wear it," exclaimed the indignant woman, drawing her thin form proudly to its full height.

"Wear it," he cried fiercely, "but it shall not be for long."

"Will you slay me?—release me from this wretched life?"

"Ay."

"Then strike!"

"Fool! you are not worth the risk of the rope," he sneered.

"You can strike only with the tongue."

"But deeply."

"Indeed, yes."

"And with that weapon will I rid myself of your hated presence, and my name of the foul stain upon it," he ejaculated. "Hark you! Jessie Bolton, for I acknowledge you not"—

"I am your wife," she interrupted.

"Then, by heaven! shall you be my slave!" he cried, suddenly; "and the slave of those whom I respect. If you will persist in being my wife, you must admit you are to be obedient to my will."

"I have never denied it," she said. "Never, Richard—never."

"And never will?"

"No."

"Then, hark you, Jessie Clavering—I wonder the word does not blister my tongue as I utter it—I shall bring home a lovely and amiable girl in a few days—a charming creature who has won my love and reciprocates my affection. You will please to remember that it is the duty of a wife to obey her husband, and therefore my commands to you are, that you tend and wait upon her at every turn, humour her every wish, pander to her every desire, for my love for her is so strong you must deny me nothing. You hear me, Jessie Clavering?—and you'll heed me, wife!"

And he drew back a pace as he spoke, or rather hissed these words, and looked into her face with a look which only a fiend could conjure up.

Had a barbed arrow sank into the heart of that woman, it could not have caused her to start so fiercely, look so wildly, or thrilled her to the very marrow.

For a moment Richard's words prostrated her quite.

Her little strength appeared to be deserting her. Her limbs seemed to give way beneath her body.

Her brain became dizzy—reason appeared to be tottering from its throne—she felt she was going mad—that the climax to his cruelty had come.

But in a short time she shook off the feeling. By a violent and almost supernatural effort she roused herself.

The pallor fled from her face, and a blood-red flush stole over her cheeks.

Her trembling lips were compressed tightly together.

Her nostrils expanded.

The eye flashed with a fire he had never before observed, and her blue veins stood out like cords on her forehead.

A moment before she was the pale, trembling, spirit-crushed, heart-broken woman— now she was the injured and insulted wife—outraged in every sense and feeling by the man above all others who should shield and love her.

The look she fixed upon the mean-spirited wretch before her cowed his very soul.

His eye dropped beneath her steady gaze. His heart sank as she took one step towards him, and he almost shrieked with fear as her long white fingers clutched his wrist.

The tones of her voice cut like daggers through his ears, as in accents of such bitter contempt she cried—

"Dastard!—dog!—bound!—this to me!—me, your wife! Speak not this again to me! for the strength of fifty men are in my arms, and I will crush you—cur that you are!—crush you beneath my feet! Me, your wife!—the slave of—oh, God! shield him from my fury!"

She flung him from her as if fearful she would fulfil her threat, and anxious to shield her soul from the crime of murder.

Then, again, she was the meek and helpless thing his treatment had made her.

The paroxysm of rage left as quickly as it had seized upon her, and she burst into sobs, tottered along the floor as if under the influence of some powerful narcotic, and fell upon the sofa, helpless, hopeless, and despairing.

Burying her face in her hands she rocked her body to and fro, while her bosom rose and fell like a stormy sea.

She had suffered much indignity from the man before her—the man she called husband—but never such as this.

Never had her soul been so outraged—never had a pang so acute been inflicted upon her heart.

In spite of his treatment, she felt that she could still love and revere him if he would treat her with kindness. There had been a lingering hope, in her bosom that brighter days were in store for her.

But now hope had fled, and with it love. The words he had uttered had crushed out the last germ, and contempt and hatred alone found a home in her heart.

Had he gone down upon his knees before her, and craved her pardon for the cruel words he had uttered—had he sworn to love her with all the strength of a pure and holy love—had he laid the wealth of the world at her feet, she would have spurned him now.

Now and forever her heart was steeled against him. He had won her love, and she would have been content to be his slave; but the slave of another, and that other a rival in his affections, was too much for her to bear. Every feeling she had once possessed towards him had vanished, and bitter, lasting, undying hatred alone found a resting-place in that bosom that had beat alone for him.

CHAPTER XLIV.

THE TWO VILLAINS—THE AGREEMENT—THE LISTENER.

THE bully—for such in heart was Richard Clavering—felt his cowed spirit revive as he found the violent passion of his wife give way to despair.

His trembling limbs regained their wonted power.

His quailing eye rose from the carpet to the form of the suffering Jessie.

The look of terror gave place to one of triumph, and a smile stole over his quivering lip,

"Again," he thought, "I have quelled the fiery spirit—humbled her to the dust. I have added one pang more, and my revenge is almost complete; but one thing now is wanting to crush her stubborn spirit, and release me from the chain which binds me to her. Her fury is spent. She will do my bidding, and seal her doom, that doom I so long for."

He turned and left the apartment.

The smile of triumph still on his lips, hope in his heart—the hope that he had nearly rid himself of Jessie for ever.

"She shall tend and wait upon her rival," he muttered. "She shall feel what it is to force me to a hated marriage. Oh! I will be revenged— bitterly revenged!"

He glided into the drawing-room, and flung himself into a seat.

So absorbed was he with his own thoughts that he observed not the neat figure of Lizzie, formerly a housemaid, but now raised to the dignity of lady's maid and confidant of Jessie, spring quickly into a large closet, with handsomely-carved doors, at the further end of the room.

He saw not that the doors were just ajar, and knew not that eyes were watching his every movement, and ears were strained to catch his every breath.

"But for my anxiety for Jessie's death, I would not bring the beautiful and innocent Mildred Hendon hitherto. Poor fool! how she will be deceived when she learns—which she must do when I tire of her—that the ceremony was but a sham, a mockery—a means adopted to place her in my arms! Better had she not spurned my advances at first. But no matter, there is but one way to obtain her, and that by marriage. Ha! ha! She shall be married, but the tie which binds us can be easily snapped asunder. It will be a glorious revenge to humble her proud spirit, even as it is to humble that of Jessie's. But I have no time to delay. The licence is to be got, then minister and witnesses provided, for the day after to-morrow she has fixed for the ceremony—the day after to-morrow I have my revenge on her, and plant another thorn in the breast of her who calls me husband."

His back was to the closet door, or he must have seen the white face of Lizzie peering upon him.

He raised a small silver bell from the table, and shook it.

Its silvery tones rang through the room, and silently the watcher drew to the door of the closet, leaving only a little crack by which to see into the room.

The summons was immediately answered by James, the repulsed lover of the pretty Lizzie.

"If you please, sir, did you ring, sir?" asked the man, standing on the threshold.

"I did, James."

"May I ask your pleasure, sir?"

"Yes; come in."

The man took a step forward, then paused.

"Close the door."

"Yes, sir."

This order was obeyed by James, who looked somewhat surprised, and became half fearful that his master intended to give him warning for some dereliction of duty or other, of which he might have been guilty.

"Sit down, James."

James looked as if he could not believe he had heard aright.

"I beg your pardon, sir," he began.

"Sit down, man. You can sit, I presume?" said Richard.

"Yes, sir," stammered the man, now convinced that he had heard aright in the first instance.

Still he was surprised, both at the tones and condescension of his master.

He sidled into a seat close to the wall of the apartment.

"Come, sit here beside me," said Richard; "I have a question to ask you."

The man obeyed, half trembling, half proud at the familiarity.

"You have been a long time in my service, James, have you not?" began Richard, looking him in the face with a strange, keen glance.

"Yes, sir," replied the man; "and though I say it, sir, as oughtn't, I have always been a good servant, sir, and willing to oblige, sir."

"Yes, yes; but"—

Richard paused.

James's features fell.

He felt very nervous indeed, and shifted uneasily on his chair.

Lizzie strained every nerve to listen, while a look of contempt stole over her face, as she gazed through the crack at her quondam lover.

"But you are going to leave me, I hear," said Richard.

"Me, sir!—lor, sir. I hope not, sir," stammered the man.

"Hope not! Why, I should have thought the hour of your departure would have been the happiest of your life."

"The happiest, sir?"

"When a man is about to be married"—

"Married, sir! I'm not going to be married, sir."

"Not?"

"No, sir."

"You surprise me. I heard you were about to be married to Lizzie, Mrs. Clavering's maid," said Richard, looking eagerly at the man, and striving to discern the effects of his words.

James turned colour, and set his lips hard, as he replied—

"Nothing of the kind, sir."

"You love the girl?"

"Me, sir?"

"Yes."

"No, sir; I—I dislike her very much. She's so proud since she's been raised to her present position, gives herself airs, and"—

"Then you hate her," interrupted Richard.

"Well, sir"—

"Speak plainly, man."

"Well, sir, I do; for you see"—

"I have no wish to know your reason for the dislike. I simply wished to know if there was any truth in the report that you were about to wed her?"

"None at all, sir."

Richard leaned back in his chair with a smile, and fell into a hurried train of thought.

"This man," he thought, "is not likely to inform Lizzie of anything she would reveal to her mistress, and as the girl respects Jessie, this fellow doubtless detests her, for the ignorant are prone to dislike the friends of their enemies, albeit, they have done them no harm. I can judge from his looks and manner that he can be bought for any disreputable scheme, and gold shall bind him to my purpose. I must not place myself in other hands. He would answer my purpose, and I can depend upon his secrecy."

A decanter of wine stood on a side table, and this Richard commanded the man to place before him.

When this was done, the libertine poured out a couple of glasses.

"Drink, James," he said.

The man opened his eyes and mouth very wide, but raised the glass, and, bowing to his master, swallowed its contents.

As he placed it down, Richard filled it again on the instant.

"Come, James, another glass."

"Thank you, sir."

Another and another was forced upon the domestic, and then Clavering, leaning his elbow on the table and stretching his head over till it almost touched that of his servant, said—

"James, I can commiserate with you."

"With me, sir?"

"Yes. I know what it is to meet with scorn where I expected love—know the pang it causes the heart; in fact, I know nothing which engenders a feeling of revenge so quickly in a man's breast. And why should we stifle that feeling? Why should we not be revenged on those who have slighted our affection? Why not make the woman who has pained us feel the pangs she inflicts upon us?"

"You're right, sir," said James.

"You would like to be revenged on Lizzie, would you not?"

"Indeed I should."

"Then you can feel for me. Listen. But I can trust you, James?"

"Certainly, sir."

"You will be silent?"

"As the grave."

Richard scanned the man's face narrowly and half suspiciously.

But he saw nothing there to cause him to hesitate, and he continued, in a low tone—

"James, I have wedded a woman who despises me. The girl you loved, I believe, has had much to do with bringing about this coldness. Her tongue has been too glib, I fear, and a look—a word of mine has been enlarged upon to her mistress."

"Curse her," said James, over whom the wine was beginning to have an effect.

"Well, I may be wrong, but I don't think I am. However, it is enough for me to know that my wife hates me."

"Then I'd hate her, sir."

"You would?"

"Yes, sir."

"I do."

"And I'd be revenged on her, I would," said the man, his eyes becoming bleared, and his voice thick.

"I could, but"—

"But what, sir."

"It would require the aid of a friend, such a person as yourself, for instance, on whom I could depend—a man who, for past favours, would not mind straining a point in his conscience for a respected master, who in turn would reward him well."

"Eh?" said James, brightening up at the mention of a reward. "'Tis done, sir. I'd do anything for you—I wouldn't care what, for you've been a good master to me, sir."

"But suppose—mind you, I only say suppose—I was acquainted with a lovely girl who would love me as a man should be loved; but that the only way to possess her was by marriage, and if that marriage could be solemnized, I should be made the happiest man in existence."

"Then I'd have a mock marriage, and say nothing about it. I wouldn't lose the girl that did love me, if I loved her, because I was married to one that didn't care for me, not I. Let a woman domineer over me, would I—I'd see."

And the half-drunken James brought his hand down upon the table as he spoke.

"Look here, sir," he continued. "Your wife don't love you, and another girl does, but she won't have you if you don't marry her."

"Exactly."

"You can't, of course, marry two wives without a chance of getting into trouble, but how's the girl to know if you don't tell her, that it ain't all right. and if you don't tell her, she's none the worse; and I'm blowed, if I was like you, if I wouldn't do it somehow."

"Take another glass of wine, James."

"Thank you, sir—here's your health, sir. I'm very much obliged to you, sir; thank you, sir."

After bobbing the glass first against his chin, then his nose, he finally succeeded in finding his mouth, into which he emptied its contents in an instant.

Richard smiled, but he could not help a feeling of disgust at himself, in associating in such a way with his own servant.

But the man was necessary to him now, and he gulped down his indignation.

"James, I suppose you have not saved much money?" he said at length.

"About twenty pounds, sir."

"Twenty pounds! Now, a hundred to put to that would make a pretty little sum, would it not?"

"Splendid!"

And the fellow's bleared eyes glistened like live coals for an instant, then became dull as before.

"Now, hark you, James. You shall have a hundred pounds if you will aid me to secure that happiness I expected to find long since. Of course, as you say, the girl will be none the worse if she knows nothing of the cheat, especially as I shall treat her as my wife, and shower that affection upon her which the coldness of my wife repudiates."

"I'll earn them."

"You shall if you will."

"How, sir?" cried the man, eagerly.

"Assume the character of a clergyman, and perform the ceremony," hissed the libertine, in a loud whisper. "What's that?" added Richard, starting round, as a slight noise met his ear.

"What's what?" asked the domestic James, staggering to his feet.

"I thought I heard a noise."

"I heard nothing. Perhaps it was my foot against the pedestal of the table," said the man, seeing nothing, and anxious about the promised hundred.

"Very likely," said Richard, reassured, and again seating himself, little thinking that his words had caused a hidden listener to fall back against the panelings of the closet in surprise and horror.

"It was nothing, sir, depend upon it," said James. "As you was saying, sir, I could earn a hundred pounds by"—

"Playing parson, and joining me in a sham marriage to the only girl I truly love. Will you do it?"

"Do it?—rather."

"You can read, of course?"

"Yes."

"And write?"

"Yes."

"You would not permit hesitation or fear to cause suspicion?" said Richard.

"Lor' bless you, sir, no. I used to spout a good deal at school, and I could play the part as well as any minister, especially when I knew a hundred pounds were to be the reward for the service."

"And your lips would remain sealed ever after, James?"

"I dare not open them."

"Why not?

"From fear of the consequences. I should be equally guilty with you," said the menial.

"That's true."

"Quite," said James, now helping himself to another glass, and assuming a familiar air that caused the libertine to wince. "Come, drink, old boy—drink success to the job."

He pushed a glass near to Richard as he spoke.

For a moment, a look of indignation rose to Clavering's face.

He was about to resent the familiarity; but the recollection that he had made that man his equal deterred him.

He took the glass and swallowed its contents, as if anxious to perform a disagreeable duty as quickly as possible.

"The decanter's empty," said James; "ring for another."

"Hold," said Clavering. "It will not do for your fellow-servants to see us thus together."

"Fellow-servants," said the man; "well, yes, so they are; but I shall consider myself a little above them now. A confidential servant of the master of this house—eh? Well, let's to business. I'll get more wine after that is settled."

"Curse the fellow!" growled Richard between his teeth; "but I must put up with it till the service I require of him has been rendered, and then—ay, then shall I rid myself of him. Yes, I must, for I shall never feel safe with him about me. Another hundred would send him to America. But I need have no fear of him, for he will be equally guilty with myself."

Then turning to James, who was amusing himself by drinking up the dregs of the decanter through the neck of the vessel, he said—

"The affair, then, is all settled. The day after to-morrow you will personate a clergyman, and in the meantime you had better make yourself well acquainted with the ceremony. There must be no hitch—no hesitation—nothing to lead to the least suspicion of the genuineness of the affair. Your absence will be missed; you had better retire to bed. We meet, of course, in this house as we have ever done. Now go; and remember, silence places gold in your pocket, and makes you the friend instead of the menial of Richard Clavering." He rose from his chair as an intimation that the interview was ended, and James, taking the hint, staggered from his seat.

"Good night, old boy," he cried, staggering about, and placing his hand familiarly upon Richard's shoulder. "I'll do the job for you. I'll make you the happiest of men. Don't fear for me, there's none of your gossip, about me. I've said I'll do the thing, and I'll do it."

And so saying, the fellow staggered from the room, followed by Richard, who was anxious to see that he retired to his bed, instead of joining his fellow-servants.

When both were gone, Lizzie strode from the closet—her face, white as a spectre, with a look of pain and disgust on every feature, and hurried to seek her poor mistress in the boudoir.

THE SWEEP'S TERROR.

CHAPTER XLV.
MISTRESS AND MAID—THE REVELATION—THE SERPENT.

ELATED with the success of his nefarious plans Richard Clavering returned to the drawing-room, after having assured himself that James had retired to his bed-chamber instead of the servants' hall.

As he sat and mused over what had transpired that night, he could not, however, but feel disgusted with himself when he thought how he had descended to make one of his own menials his confidant and assistant in a scheme that was to add one crime more to the already overcharged catalogue of his guilt, and plunge a poor innocent, confiding girl to the uttermost depths of misery and despair.

But he drained glass after glass to wash down his indignation of his own conduct—and the fumes of the liquor soon steeled his senses against any such thoughts or feelings.

Meantime, Lizzie sought the apartment where Jessie reclined, sad, and broken-hearted, and approaching the couch, laid her hand upon her mistress's arm, ere the latter was aware of her presence.

Jessie looked up through her tears into the pale face of her maid and confidant.

"Weeping again, my poor mistress," said the girl, in a sad tone, her lips trembling as she spoke, and the tears starting to her own eyes.

"Yes, Lizzie, 'tis the only relief I can obtain to my sorrow, and a poor relief it is. Yet, but for the fountain of the eyes, my over-filled heart would break. Alas! I feel that it would be better were it to do so, for then —then"—

"Then what, madam?" asked the maid.

"This soul would be at peace—the grave would drown all my sorrows."

"Do not talk like this, it makes me sad," said the girl. "Do not speak of dying."

"For what have I to live?" asked her mistress, sadly.

"Yourself."

"Myself?"

"You are too young to die. You are not older than I am."

"In years, perhaps not; but in sorrow and"—

She paused.

Her face flushed.

Her head fell upon her bosom.

A deep, deep sigh escaped her, and she clasped her hand upon her heart.

"And what, madam?" asked the girl.

"Sin," was the deep reply.

"Sin?" echoed Lizzie.

"Ay, girl. I have been sinful—very sinful," said Jessie, "and now my sins are finding me out."

"Of what sin can you have been guilty that you should speak thus?" said Lizzie. "You blame yourself too much, and others less than they deserve."

"Indeed, no."

"But you do."

"Of what sin can you have been guilty that you should speak thus?" said Lizzie. "You blame yourself too much, and others less than they deserve."

"Indeed, no."

"But you do."

"Can there be any sin greater than disobedience?" said Jessie, looking up in the maid's face.

"To whom?"

"Those who gave you being."

"Your parents?"

"Ay."

"We are all guilty of such in a less or greater degree," was the reply.

"Mine has been great, indeed, to them, poor grey-haired, kind-hearted parents. Oh, Lizzie! had I but listened to their counsels—had I but heeded their prayers, I had been happy now— happy now."

"Do not take on so, madam; others have been more guilty than yourself—much more guilty they intend to be."

"Whom do you mean?"

The girl hung her head.

She did not like to reply, much as she wished to do so.

The question was repeated.

"Pardon me, madam, but I must speak—your husband."

"What of him?"

"Oh! madam; I know I have done wrong to play the eavesdropper, but it was more by accident than design I have done so."

"Go on," said Jessie, impatiently dashing the tears away from her long lashes, and sitting up on the couch.

"You see, madam, I had business in the drawing-room when master came in, and not wishing him to see me there, I slipped into the large closet, and heard and saw enough to chill my blood."

"Tell me all, Lizzie—tell me all," cried the woman, impatiently.

"I shall break your heart."

"Psha! 'Tis too hard, or it had broken ere this. I can bear anything if I can bear his cruelty and contempt, for nothing can be worse than that."

"Alas! madam, you have yet to learn the worst."

"Out with it, then, girl."

"It will pain you, yet I should be criminal were I to keep secret what I have heard this night. It will lacerate your heart, but I shall only be doing my duty by speaking."

"Keep me no longer in suspense," exclaimed Jessie.

The girl gazed a moment upon the pale suffering face before her and hesitated.

She almost wished she had not aroused the curiosity of her mistress.

She feared lest the communication she wished to make might be too much for Jessie to bear.

But then she thought how wicked it would be of her to know what she had learned and not tell her mistress, and she made the poor wife acquainted with all she had heard and seen while concealed in the closet.

Without a word of comment Jessie heard her to the end.

Not a sigh escaped her, but with her tear-bedewed face turned to the carpet, she drank in every word the girl uttered.

Lizzie felt alarmed at her silence; she dreaded lest reason should totter, and madness seize upon her brain.

She had expected to hear Jessie denounce her cruel husband in no measured terms, and when not a sound or motion escaped her, she became alarmed for her safety.

"And you heard this?" said Jessie, at length looking up.

"Every word that I have spoken."

"And that the day after to-morrow a false marriage is to be contracted, James acting as minister?"

"Such was the result of their conference," said Lizzie. "But, madam," she added, after a pause, "Mr. Clavering may never intend to be guilty of such a wicked thing."

"Lizzie," said her mistress, in a cooler tone, "Richard Clavering is my husband, but he is a villain. He has resolved to drive me from him or break my heart. There is nothing he so much desires as my death. A short time since, and I could pray for an end to this wretched existence, but now I will strive to live to thwart him. Villain, villain! And he seeks to have another victim by a mock marriage. I listened to his promises and found myself deceived. This girl must not fall. She must be saved—saved by her whose rival she has become unknowingly."

"That you might prevent so wicked a deed I hurried to make you acquainted with the plot," said the girl.

"You did right, for though your words have caused me a pang more, they have made a friend for that deluded girl. She must not—shall not fall. We will save her, Lizzie— save her from that bad man's machinations."

"Heaven grant we may; for though I know her not, madam, she is one of our own sex, and deserves our sympathy."

"Mine she shall have—mine she shall have. Speak not on this subject to a living soul. The day after to-morrow you said?"

"Yes, madam."

"Enough. Richard will have all in readiness, but we will spoil his plotting, rob him of his victim at the very hour of his triumph. Let no word or act of thine lead him to believe he is suspected of intending this wrong."

"It shall not."

"That is right. Now, come with me to my chamber, for I am weary, and would sleep if I can."

The poor wife walked across to the door, followed by her maid, and ascended to her room, where Lizzie assisted to unrobe her.

"Good night, Lizzie," she said, as an intimation to the girl that she wished to be alone. "Good night, and remember not a word or look to indicate the secret you have learned."

"I will be discreet. Good night, madam," replied Lizzie.

The girl slowly retired, and when the door had closed behind her, and her light footfall could be no longer heard on the stairs, Jessie clasped her hands upon her bosom, and sank down upon her knees at the foot of her bed.

"God of heaven!" she cried, in agonized tones, raising her eyes as she spoke, "have mercy upon me! I acknowledge the wrongs I have done— my wickedness—my sins. But, oh! am I not punished sufficient? Spare me from further pain—spare this poor lacerated and bleeding heart, and give me strength to save this poor wretch from the plottings of a villain! Give me power to shield her from the pangs I have been made to suffer—power to save one soul, in atonement for my sins, from perdition!"

Then she rose from her knees.

Her pale features seemed more calm.

As she drew herself up, she caught sight of the reflection of her figure in a large cheval glass:

Why did she start?

Why clutch at the richly carved bed-post, and glare upon her own image in so strange a manner?

Alas! the change was so great that she scarcely recognised the beautiful being who, so short a time since, had been the envy of dozens—the pride of her father's house—the flower of the village in which she was born and bred.

So great was the change—oh! so great, that she could scarcely recognise in the glass the once happy, smiling, free-hearted girl, full of innocent spirits, gay as the butterfly, frolicksome as a kid—her father's pride, and her mother's joy.

Then she was rosy-cheeked, bright-eyed; now she was pale as death, the eye sunken and lustreless, the tall form was bent, the gay smile gone, the features were pinched as if by want, and the glossy tresses gave indications of becoming prematurely grey, having lightened much in time, and lost that smooth and shining look her father so much admired and so often caressed.

"Does that glass lie," she muttered, "or have I indeed become so changed? Alas! the glass is true. 'Tis I who have altered—wonderfully altered, and in so short a time. They would not know me now. God forbid they should. I would not have them see me—me whom they loved so well, and who, setting their counsels and advice at defiance, sealed my doom by my own obstinacy. Poor painted moth! like thee I hovered around the flame till it burned me, and found, when too late, 'that all that glitters is not gold.' I was beautiful, and I knew it, hence I was vain, ambitious. Fool! had I been contented to live in the sphere in which my parents moved, I had now been happy. Why should I then repent the loss of that beauty which lured me to his arms? Had I looked then as I do now, would he have condescended to glance upon me? Would he have poured his poisoned words into mine ears—have tempted me with his riches? No! Then let me rejoice that it is faded, as well as curse the hours it existed. She must be beautiful, too—very beautiful, or he would not deign to smile upon her; but her beauty shall not fade beneath his upas breath.[52] No, no! I will save her, and foil him!"

She turned from the glass, and was about to retire, when she was startled by the entrance of Richard Clavering.

"You retire early, madam," he said. "I sought you in your boudoir, and finding you not there came hither."

Jessie made no reply.

She felt she could not address that man without betraying what her maid had told her.

She simply looked up at him from beneath her brows, and remained silent.

"I will not keep you long from your bed, madam," he continued. "I have but a few

---

[52] Upas, a tropical Asian tree, the sap of which was used as arrow poison.

words to say, which, perhaps, my absence in the morning might prevent. To-morrow evening you will please to be prepared to start for Devonshire with your maid. I may follow you immediately, or my business may detain me a few days in London. Anyhow you will please to start to-morrow, and travel during the night, as I wish you to see that my house is in order by the time I arrive."

Jessie heard him to the end, and then in low tone asked—

"Is it not strange you should have come to the determination of going to Devonshire so suddenly?"

"I have strange fancies, madam, and sudden ones, too," he replied, curtly.

"You have, indeed," thought Jessie, with a sigh.

"I shall doubtless bring some friends with me to spend a few days when I come," he said; "and hence my desire that you precede me, and have everything in order for their reception. You had therefore better make your maid acquainted with your journey ere you retire, as the girl may need some little time for preparation."

"I shall require more time than that, sir, for myself," said Jessie.

"Then you cannot have it."

"And why not?"

"Simply, because it is my will you go then," he replied.

"I'm not well enough to travel. Your unkindness"—

"Bah! a truce to your croaking. You were willing enough to travel at a moment's notice when I brought you away from your humble cottage."

"Would you never had!"

"Amen to that," he cried, insultingly. "There had been one curse to my life the less. Well or ill, you must go. You told me to-night you were my wife, and would never refuse to obey me. See that you do not in this case."

"Why cannot you go with me?" she asked, fixing a searching look on his face.

The eye of the libertine quailed before her ardent glance.

"Because I have business here for a day or two."

"Then why cannot I wait till you are ready?" she asked.

"I have given my reason. Suffice it to say I request you to go at the time I have named," he replied.

And, turning upon his heel, he left the room without bidding her good night.

"Oh! Richard Clavering," muttered Jessie, as the door closed behind him, and hid his tall form from her view. "Too well do I know the reason why my presence is not required here after tomorrow evening. I will pretend to obey you, make every preparation for the journey to your seat in Devonshire, but I will not go. You shall see me at the moment you least wish for or expect. Go to your pillow, and dream of the beauty you have won, and believe you will possess. Go, and hug yourself with the belief that your ill-used wife will be far from hence while you perpetrate a crime black as hell. Go, and think that my love for you has made me your dupe and slave, obedient to your every wish and look. But that love I once bore you, Richard Clavering, has turned to hate—deep, bitter, lasting hate; and you have no foe more implacable than her whose love you scorn for another!"

She tottered to her couch, and laid her head upon the downy pillow, but it rested not so easily then as it did on the hard bolster of the little chamber in her father's humble cot.

CHAPTER XLVI.

THE BROKEN HEART—FEARS AND PRESENTIMENTS.

THE day arrived—the day which was to make Mildred Hendon the wife of Richard Clavering—at least, so thought the lovely Mildred and her poor, but respectable widowed mother.

Of course, Richard Clavering had desired that the nuptials should be kept as secret as possible—not that he was ashamed, he said, to show the world his wife—her poverty made no difference to him; but that it would be better for Mildred if the wedding was as quiet as possible; she not being used to move in the sphere to which he was about to raise her, she would be timid, and he could the better tutor her how to meet his friends at a future time.

The poor deceived girl believed him actuated by the best of motives, and a desire to render her easy, and she was nothing loth to have the marriage kept a profound secret from all but her mother, and a female friend moving in the same position as herself.

Richard hugged himself too with the belief that the ceremony would go through without any interruption, although he intended that it should take place at his own house.

James had got well up in the service, and knew it almost word for word, and looked a very creditable parson in the suit of black purchased for him by his master.

It was not till the last moment, however, that Richard thought of the absolute necessity of having one male witness. He knew that as the ceremony would be illegal this could be dispensed with; but then would not Mrs. Hendon, if not her daughter, at once jump to the conclusion that all was not right, if he had no friend at all present?.

In this emergency he applied to James.

"I tell you how we can get over the difficulty, sir, and no one but ourselves be any the wiser," said the fellow. "I've got a brother who is insane. He will do anything he is told, but knows nothing of what he has done a minute afterwards. I will bring him here. He can act as groomsman, and you have no need to fear that he will speak of the affair, or even recollect anything about it an hour afterwards."

"Can you get him?"

"In less than an hour."

"Do so, and all will go as well as we could wish. I feared a storm with my wife, and her positive refusal to proceed to Devonshire, but she is more than half way there by this time with that maid of hers."

"Yes, sir, and my fellow-servants—miles on their journey as well to the same destination. We must not let anything stand in the way now of getting the affair over, and completing your happiness."

"Nor of placing the hundred pounds in your pocket, James."

The man smiled.

"Few ministers get such a fee as that."

"True, sir; but few ministers run such a risk of being lagged.[53] I beg your pardon, sir, I meant"—

"Never mind what you meant; see about your brother; and be careful not to put such

---

[53] Imprisoned.

words in the service, or there'll be a pretty scene."

"Where is the ceremony to be performed?"

"In the drawing-room."

"And at what hour is the minister supposed to arrive?"

"Eleven."

"It is now half-past eight. There is plenty of time. I'll fetch my brother and tutor him how to act, and then take another spell at the book. Upon my word, sir, I did not expect things would turn out so capitally. Mrs. Clavering off to Devonshire, followed by the servants! The girl's as willing as yourself for a quiet ceremony, and not a breath of suspicion as to your already being married. The job has been capitally arranged, and shall be as well finished."

The man hurried off, and Richard paced the apartment with quick and uneven strides.

"I have succeeded in throwing dust in the eyes of all who were in my way much better than I expected. Jessie and the servants are well on their road by this time, and there is nothing to fear from that quarter. The girl, too, being anxious for secrecy, has played into my hands. Good! I am not a man to forget or forgive. Jessie forced me to marry her, now I will force her to wait upon a mistress. Mildred scorned my suit, now I will plunge her to shame and misery. Two hours more—only two hours more. How shall I pass the time till then? Breakfast, dress, and a bottle of wine, for, by my soul, my hand shakes, and my nerves are somewhat unsteady. But a look at Mildred will charm all ills away, and render me the happiest mortal in existence. Curse the hour, I wish it was past!"

He strode out of the library, where he had been speaking with James, and proceeded to the breakfast-room, where James (now the only servant in the house, at least so far as Richard Clavering knew) had prepared the morning meal, and, seating himself, he proceeded to partake of the viands.

While thus occupied, two figures glided softly across the drawing-room to the closet in which Lizzie had secreted herself and overheard the conversation between James and his master.

They were Jessie and her maid.

The wife was pale but calm, and a look of determination sat upon every feature.

Lizzie was pale and nervous, and her eyes wandered furtively around the sumptuous apartment as if she half expected to see some one there whom she had no desire to meet.

"Where is he now, Lizzie?" said the lady, in a whisper, turning a sad look on her companion's face.

"In the breakfast-parlour, madam," was the reply, "eating as heartily as if his conscience was as clear as an infant's."

"And his confederate?"

"Who, madam?"

"James, his servant. Oh, how men lower themselves when they stoop to crime!"

"He's left the house."

"Ah! on what errand? Did you hear?" asked Jessie, anxiously.

"Yes, madam."

"What?"

"To fetch an idiot brother to act as witness to this wretched work," was the reply.

"And you say the ceremony is fixed for eleven o'clock in this room?"

"Such was the hour I think I heard stated; but fearful of being discovered, and thereby letting them know we had not gone away, I was compelled to keep a good distance from the library."

"Doubtless you heard right. Hush! is that some one coming?"

There was a footstep on the stairs.

"Quick, madam. It is Mr. Clavering coming up stairs."

And the maid, grasping the arm of her mistress, hurried her into the closet, pulling the door to softly but quickly after her.

The next moment Richard entered the room, and looked around.

"Strange," he muttered, aloud. "I fancied I heard subdued voices. Psha! I'm nervous. There's no one in the house but myself at this moment. A glass of brandy will set me to rights."

He shuddered violently.

"Were I superstitious," he said, "I should say that I was standing over my own grave. What a shudder! I wish James would return. The silence in the house is unpleasant, and a red film seems to float over my eyes. Bah! It's only the fact of knowing that the game I'm on is not exactly fair and square, and I'm trembling like an old woman who has seen a ghost. Away with such feelings! Brandy will soon dispel them. After that, the bright smiles and warm caresses of the lovely Mildred."

He left the room, and when he had been gone a few moments, Jessie and her maid came forth from the closet.

"You have given the directions to the servants," said the former, "to be within call, yet out of sight?"

"I have, madam."

"That is well."

Jessie seated herself on a magnificent lounge, and suffered her head to drop upon her hands.

Her maid stood before her, silent and sad.

"Lizzie."

"Yes, madam."

"I have a strange feeling here at my heart—a very strange feeling," said her mistress.

"You are worried."

"Ay, I am indeed. But I experience a strange feeling as if some ill were about to befall me," said Jessie.

"Shake it off, madam."

"I cannot."

"Try, madam."

Jessie smiled a sickly smile.

"Lizzie," she said, speaking in a hollow whisper, "did you mark Clavering well while we were in yonder closet?"

"His every movement."

"Did you perceive how he shuddered?'

"Yes, madam."

"And note his words?"

"I did."

"Such a shudder ran through my frame as he spoke, and I could not help inwardly catching his words."

"What? That you"—

"Stood over my own grave!" was the hollow interruption.

"My dear madam!"

"Lizzie, I cannot help thinking that some harm will befall me to-day—that something more than ordinary will overtake me."

"The knowledge of what is about to transpire, the grief under which you have been labouring these few days past, and a want of rest, cause this depression of the spirits."

"It may be so."

"Depend upon it, it is."

"It is near ten, is it not?" said Jessie, after a pause, and looking up at the beautiful timepiece as she spoke. "Past ten."

"I never observed that piece tick so loud before, have you, Lizzie?"

"Yes, madam. I hear nothing unusual in its ticking," was the reply.

"It may be my fancy."

"It is, madam."

"Hark, Lizzie."

"At what?"

"The clock. It seems to me as if its pendulum said at each stroke, 'for ever and ever,'" cried Jessie.

The girl looked at her mistress in alarm and surprise.

She began to think that her mind wandered—that the cruelty of her husband was driving her mad.

"You frighten me," she said. "Oh! do not talk like that."

"I know it is very foolish, Lizzie, very foolish indeed; but I cannot, though I strive to do so, make that timepiece say anything but the words I have uttered."

"Shall I stop it?"

"No; wherefore?"

"I thought if it annoyed you"—

"No, no; do not touch it. I know it is only fancy—foolish fancy, my good girl. But I am filled with fancies this morning. Do you know, Lizzie, I even fancy I shall not live throughout the day?"

The girl recoiled back a pace. Her pale face became even more white if possible than before.

"Why—why should you think this?" she asked, in a tremulous whisper.

"I cannot tell; I am powerless to explain," was the reply.

Then fixing her eyes upon the face of the maid, she said, in a low but impressive tone—

"Lizzie, I have told you where Clavering brought me from when he brought me hither."

"Yes—your father's home."

"But the place where that happy dwelling is situated?"

"Yes, madam."

"Do you think you could find it?" asked Jessie.

"Easily. I have been in that part of the country."

There was a few moments pause, during which time Jessie pressed her hands to her bosom, and a tear quivered like a dewdrop on her long, dark lash.

"Lizzie," she said, at length, taking the girl's hand and pressing it in her own, "will you promise me to go thither and tell those ever loved and never-to-be-forgotten parents that my last thoughts were for them—my last prayer invoking heaven's blessings on their heads."

"My dear madam"—

"Nay, interrupt me not, my good girl. I am sure that I shall never see them again—never more hear their loved tones, receive their warm kiss of affection. I have ill-repaid all their kindness to me, and would not, could not, ask their forgiveness, did I think that I should live. Start not, Lizzie; that strange inward voice for which none can account, whispers to me that my time has come."

"For heaven's sake, madam, do not speak thus," cried Lizzie.

"And wherefore not? I have no wish to live since life is to me a burden. Rather, then, let me welcome death, for it will still and rest the aching heart, and stifle the upbraidings of a guilty conscience. I tell you Lizzie, 'tis useless for me to attempt to deceive myself. The hour has come—the edict has gone forth. I must die?"

The girl clung to her mistress in terror.

Jessie threw her arm around Lizzie's neck, and kissed her cheek.

"My only friend," she said, "to you I confide my last request. Promise me you will fulfil it."

The girl sobbed hysterically.

"Hush, hush," said Jessie, "or he will discover our presence in the house, and the victim will fall. We must save her—I must save her, though in so doing, I destroy myself."

"What is it—whom is it you fear?" asked the girl.

"Nothing—no one," was the reply. "I have no fear, I only foretell my death, which I know is near at hand. Hark! there is my husband and James in conversation—another voice. They come this way. They come to prepare the pile on which this victim is to be sacrificed. Let us into the closet, Lizzie, to watch, and listen, and wait till the moment comes when, like a thunderbolt, I can fall upon him and denounce the guilty wretch to her, whom he would slay as he has me in peace and honour. Come, Lizzie—come. Oh! how I long for the moment when he shall stand exposed, confused before me! Then will be the hour of my triumph and my revenge—then shall the woman he has despised laugh at his shame and confusion."

Together they entered the closet and shut the door so close as only to leave a small chink through which they could watch and see all that was going on.

The voices below ceased for a time, and then were heard again; but this time the secreted females detected other tones than those of men, and Jessie clutched at the arm of her maid, as the silvery voice of Mildred Hendon broke upon her ears.

CHAPTER XLVII.

THE CEREMONY INTERRUPTED—THE EXPOSURE—
THE MURDER AND ESCAPE.

ABOUT a quarter of an hour of agony and suspense followed, during which time the two women strained every nerve to catch the slightest sound that might indicate their coming.

The subdued voice of the ballet-girl, mingled with the louder tones of the libertine, fell upon the heart of the poor wife with a weight that was almost crushing.

Setting her lips firm together, Jessie stifled the groans that arose from her bosom.

It cost an effort, and a mighty effort, too, to appear calm; but well did Lizzie know the emotions that raged so violently in her mistress's bosom, and the poor girl trembled from fear.

There was a footstep on the stairs now, a footstep which, despite the thick carpeting, both knew not to be that of Richard Clavering.

It was heavy. It was not the light elastic step of James, but it was of a strange, absent-looking individual, who immediately after entered the room.

"It is James's brother, I think, madam," said the girl, in a whisper; "the idiot that is to be a witness to this wicked work."

A pleased and childish smile played over the face of the man as he looked around the sumptuous apartment, and he exclaimed in wonder—

"Pretty—how pretty!"

At this moment James entered the room, and laid his hand upon his brother's shoulder.

The rascal was greatly altered, and, in truth, his appearance was more gentlemanly than Lizzie would have expected.

Habited in a superfine cloth suit and white neckcloth, he looked as much like a clergyman, and more, in fact, than many who mount our pulpits.

In his hand he carried a large prayer-book, from which he was to read the service.

"Now, you only do and say what you are told," he said, addressing the imbecile.

"Yes—yes, brother. What a pretty place— fine—nice!"

And with a stupid look the man stroked the satin back of the lounge.

"Fine bed!" he added, after a pause, dropping down full length upon the piece of furniture.

"Get up!" said his brother, dealing him a hearty kick.

"Oh! oh!" cried the idiot, springing to his feet in terror.

"Now behave yourself, will you? or I'll have to take you back to the asylum."

"No, no!" cried the man, trembling at the word; "I'll be good—very good."

"Then stand quiet, for the bride and the bridegroom will be here directly. I'll give you something to put a little life into you."

And the sham minister poured out a glass of port wine from a decanter, and offered it to his brother.

The man drew back.

"Take it, you fool, can't you?" said James, forcing it upon him.

"It's physic—nasty physic."

"It's wine."

"Wine?"

"Yes. It will put fire into you."

"Don't burn me," cried the idiot, imploringly, and pushing back the glass.

"You're a damned fool," said his brother. "If you don't drink it, I will. There!"

And he emptied the glass.

"Now stand here, and look as if you knew all about it."

"Yes, yes. I know all about it," said the imbecile.

"Do you? Hush! here they come." The scoundrel put on a look of such solemnity, that as he caught sight of his face in the large glass, he could not help grinning at himself.

Jessie clutched at Lizzie, and her form now trembled violently.

"Be calm," said the maid; "oh! pray be calm, madam."

"Calm!" said Jessie, in a hissing whisper. "I am calm—calm as the tigress when the hunters steal her young. Oh, I am calm!"

Richard entered the room, bearing on his arm the pretty and neatly-attired Mildred.

Behind them was her mother, and the young friend spoken of before, who was to act as bridesmaid.

As they strode into the room, the eyes of the ballet girl glistened with pleasure, and the mother, turning to her companion, whispered—

"What a magnificent room. Oh, how happy my poor child will be!"

Richard bowed with much respect to the sham minister, who, in turn, inclined his head to the libertine.

Their stations having been taken, and the licence placed before the clergyman, that worthy, anxious to end the scene as quickly as possible, opened his book, and in a solemn tone asked if there were any just cause or impediment to be shown why they should not be joined together in wedlock.

A momentary pause ensued. Richard stood looking in admiration upon the lovely and blushing girl beside him, when the doors of the closet were flung wide open, and Jessie, pale but stately, strode forward, exclaiming—

"Behold that man's lawful wife!"

Richard turned quickly—surprised, bewildered, and alarmed.

Mildred uttered a shriek, and clutched at her mother for support.

James dropped the book to the floor, exclaiming in a loud tone—

"Mrs. Clavering, by G—d!"

"Ay, Mrs. Clavering!" exclaimed Jessie; "the true, lawful, but ill-used wife of that scoundrel there!"

And raising her hand, she pointed her finger at the pale and trembling Richard.

"Liar!" he hissed, between his clenched teeth, and springing towards her; "you shall"—

He started back as Lizzie, grasping a cord in either hand, rang the bell violently.

"Villain!" said his wife. "You believed me and your servants miles away, but I learned your wicked purpose, and returned to expose a scoundrel, and save that poor girl!"

"Curse you!" muttered Richard; "but you shall suffer for this, I"—

He had raised his hand to strike her, but Mildred, recovering from her surprise, flung herself before him.

"Hold!" she exclaimed. The libertine fell back before her flashing eye and contemptuous look.

"Tell me," she continued, "is this woman your wife? Are you already married?"

He hesitated, and dropped his glance to the floor.

"Speak!" cried Mildred, imperiously.

"Ay, speak, wretch, if shame will permit you!" exclaimed Jessie.

With an effort to appear calm, the libertine said—

"Hear me, Mildred. I know I have done wrong in not telling you all. But the fear that I might lose you, held my tongue. This woman has been my mistress."

"And is now your wife," said Jessie.

"Is this so?" asked Mildred, with a sigh, and looking at him fixedly through her tears.

"No."

"Not your wife?" exclaimed Jessie.

"Not my wife!"

"'Tis false!" cried a loud voice, and the next moment Spring-heeled Jack bounded into the room, followed by the servants of Richard Clavering.

The libertine sprang backward as the other advanced

His features were convulsed with terror and passion combined.

He trembled as if attacked by the ague, and cold drops of perspiration broke out upon his brow.

Mildred uttered another cry and flew to the side of her mother, while James sank into a chair, and his brother, uttering a wild howl, flew from the room.

"You here!" exclaimed Mrs. Clavering, while Lizzie darted to his side.

The waiting-maid did not fear him now, and rejoiced in his presence.

"Yes, madam, I am here—here to see that justice is done to you—here to proclaim that thing—for man he is not—a scoundrel and a liar!"

"This to me!" shouted Richard, trying to assume a look and manner he was far from feeling.

"To you, rascal!—deceiver!—liar!—to you!"

"By heaven, you shall answer to me for this! Mildred, this is some plot concocted by a designing and cast-off mistress and that fellow yonder, to prevent the consummation of our happiness."

"It is a plot of mine to save that girl from ruin, and your black and craven soul from another and a deeper sin!" exclaimed his wife. "I am his wife, as this girl here can testify—his true and lawful wife!"

"Great God! how have I been deceived!" cried Mildred.

"Ay, girl," said Jack; "but better that you learn the truth now, than time hence. It may break your beating heart, but it will save your honour."

Mildred sank upon the lounge, buried her face in her hands, and sobbed aloud.

Her mother and friend bent over her, and mingled their tears with her own.

"'Tis false—all a lie!" roared Richard; "that woman is my mistress, not my wife."

"Behold the proof!" cried Jack, holding up a copy of the certificate. "Behold a copy of the register you burglariously entered the church to destroy. Look upon this, Miss Hendon, and then upon that man who would have done you so irreparable a wrong—who would have blighted your hopes and existence!"

He forced the certificate into her hand.

James sprang forward to tear it from her, when Jack dealt him a blow in the face, which sent him sprawling upon the carpet at his feet.

Richard also dashed forward to seize it, but Jack grasped him by the collar, and hurled him back across the room.

"Stand back, scoundrel!"

"Scoundrel in your teeth!" yelled Richard, passion alone now consuming him.

As he spoke he struck Jack a blow in the face.

Our hero, who wore his mask, paled with rage, and half raised his arm, but remembering that females were present, he suffered it to fall again to his side.

"Enough, Richard Clavering," he said; "you shall answer to me for that blow, though I feel how I shall degrade myself by fighting a liar and a villain."

"Too true—too true," gasped Mildred, letting the certificate fall from her hand.

"Wicked, unfeeling man," exclaimed the mother; "and I so believed him."

"And I, once," sighed Jessie.

Mildred rose, and placed her hand on the arm of Jessie.

"Madam," she said, "oh, what a wrong would I have done you! Forgive me—oh, forgive me!"

"I have nothing to forgive: you knew him not. Believed him, as I did, to be the soul of honour, but, alas! how have I been deceived! My poor girl, if I have pained your heart, I have severed you from a life worse than death—saved you from the villainy of a cold-blooded and designing villain."

"And glory in your triumph," sneered Richard.

"Ay, I do. By one cruelty and another have you sought to free yourself from the bonds which enchain us; but so long as life remains I will foil your hellish desires."

"Begone!"

"I will not obey you."

"Will not!"

"No."

"Begone!"

"I fear not your threatening looks, base man. As a wife, I know my duty is to obey you; but as an outraged and insulted woman, I set your authority at defiance. The love I once bore you, and which would have made me your slave, is turned to hatred. Richard Clavering, I now despise and defy you."

He strode towards her threateningly, his face livid with passion.

Jack stood before him.

"Stand aside," he cried.

"Not at your bidding."

"Stand from before her; she says she is my wife."

"And she speaks truly."

"Then stand from before me."

"She is a woman, Richard Clavering, and as such I protect her," was the calm reply.

"Shall she defy me?"

"Yes, if she pleases so to do."

"By heaven, she shall not! Begone—leave us. To your own apartment, or I"—

"Will show the girl you would have lured to your arms by a false marriage what a blackguard you are," said Jack, tauntingly.

"Furies!" roared Clavering.

"Wretched man," said Mildred, "what can you say in extenuation of the wrongs you have done me?"

"Ay, villain; what can you say to that?" echoed the mother. Richard was silent. He could find no excuse.

"Let us go from here, mother," said Mildred, taking her parent's hand; "let us go from here."

"Come, my child."

"Heaven forgive you for the crime you meditated," said Mildred, in a low, solemn voice, "for I cannot."

She led her mother towards the door, and burst afresh into tears.

Her woman's heart had been insulted and crushed.

Then turning, as she reached the door, Mildred extended her hand to Jessie, and looking with a painful and commiserating glance into the face of the wife, said—

"Heaven bless and protect you."

"Curse her! Let heaven protect her now!" shrieked Richard.

All turned towards the libertine.

He had taken a pistol from his pocket, and levelled it at his wife's head.

A cry of terror broke from every lip.

A look of horror was on every face.

"Hold!" cried Jack. "Man, would you murder your wife!"

"I would rid myself of a scourge and a curse! She has robbed me of my victim, let her take her reward."

Ere our hero could spring upon him, the libertine pulled the trigger.

There was a light flash, a loud report, a piercing shriek, a cry of horror, and the ill-fated woman fell to the floor.

The aim had been unerring; the bullet had entered the brain of Jessie, killing her on the instant.

With a groan Lizzie fell on her knees beside the body, and fainted.

Mildred clung to her mother, the servants gathered round their mistress, and Jack, springing upon Richard, tore the discharged weapon from his hand, and hurled him to the floor.

"Assassin! murderer!" he cried, placing his knee upon his chest, and pinning him down.

James stood for a moment horror-struck and paralyzed.

Then recovering himself, the sham parson sprang to the door, and, nearly overturning Mildred and her mother, fled down the stairs.

The turn things had taken warned him to seek his own safety in flight.

He hurried to the stable, and placed a saddle upon one of the horses, determined to be off as quickly as he could.

Meantime the servants had raised the bleeding and lifeless form of their unfortunate mistress in their arms, and placed her on the lounge.

The presentiment she had felt so acutely—the warning voice—had spoken but too truly.

Some, hurried for medical aid, others stood bewildered and alarmed; none were cool and collected in this trying moment save our hero, Spring-heeled Jack.

"Richard Clavering," he said, "you see now how one crime begets another. The first false step taken, and down to the gulf of perdition man must go. I will not upbraid you; your conscience must do that too acutely. I will not punish the deed; the laws of your country will mete justice out to you. The gallows looms before you, the executioner awaits his due, and may heaven have mercy on your soul!"

He rose from over the prostrate man, and turned to where the now lifeless form of Jessie reclined.

The instant he had done so, Richard leaped to his feet. One look he cast around upon the horror-struck assembly, then taking another pistol from his pocket, and levelling it at Jack, he cried, in a husky voice—

SPRING-HEELED JACK IN THE WINE CELLAR.

"Curse you! you have foiled me! but I'll have my revenge. If I must perish on the gallows, it shall not be for one victim!"

Jack turned. Richard fired; but his hand, rendered unsteady by passion, the ball flew wide of his aim.

"Foiled again, by G—d!" roared the libertine, hurling the weapon to the ground, and turning, fled down the stairs, as Jack and the servants sprang towards the door of the room.

CHAPTER LXVIII.
THE FLIGHT OF THE MURDERER—THE SPECTRE HORSEMAN.

WITH the report of the pistol still ringing in his ears, and with the speed of an arrow shot from the bow, the guilty, bloodstained, and wretched Richard Clavering sped down the stairs, and out of the house into the magnificent grounds which surrounded it.

To turn an angle of the mansion and reach the stables was but the work of a few moments.

Flight was his only idea now.

As he reached the door of the stable he met James coming forth, leading his roan mare by the bridle.

A cry of joy broke from Richard's lips, as he sprang forward and tore the bridle from the man's hand.

He was about to vault into the saddle when James, perceiving his object, and fearful of capture, grasped his arm.

"I have saddled her for myself," he said. "If you would fly, get another."

"Dog! do you talk thus to me! Stand aside!" cried Richard, thrusting the man back, and leaping into the saddle. "Away! another moment, and I am lost."

"So am I," cried James; "and, by G—d! I will have that horse!"

"Back, rascal!"

"Down, murderer!" shouted the other.

And seizing Richard, he dragged him from his seat.

"Curses on you, dog of a menial!" roared the other, dealing the man a desperate blow in the face which staggered him, and again essaying to leap into the saddle.

"Hell and fury!" shouted the servant, "you have led me into this scrape, and you shall help me out of it. I will have that horse to ensure my liberty, or you do not escape."

Richard turned upon him furious with alarm for his own safety, and seizing a stable fork, raised it, and drove the sharp prongs into the man's body.

With one piercing shriek the man fell, the iron prongs still in his flesh, one of them penetrating his heart.

"More blood—more blood!" cried Richard; "but the fool provoked his own fate. Ah! they come. Quick—quick! to cheat the gallows of its due!"

He sprang into the saddle, and striking the horse's flanks with his heels, urged it from the stable at the moment that Jack, followed by several of the domestics, emerged from the house.

"Stop him—stop him!" cried Jack, springing forward towards the mounted man, and grasping at the bridle.

But a blow from Richard caused the animal to rear and plunge, and Jack, to prevent being borne down, was compelled to release his hold.

Another blow, and the roan mare dashed forward, striking down a tall footman who stood in her way, and with terrific leaps bounded on towards the carriage gates, which were open.

The next instant she had disappeared from the sight of those who sought to stay her career, and bring the guilty man to justice.

"Escaped," said Jack, "but only for a time. The guilty may play with, but seldom defeat, justice. Ah! what is this?"

James, with the fork still sticking in his wounds, had caught his eye, and, with a shudder, our hero paused on the threshold of the stable-door.

The others gathered round him.

"Good heavens!" said Jack; "more blood has been shed. The villain has murdered his dupe. The rascal has received his reward in death. But what a death! My blood chills as I gaze upon him. Bad as he was, he deserved a better fate. This is too horrible!"

James was held in universal contempt by his fellow-servants, yet they could not help bestowing a look of pity on the wretch who had paid so fearful a penalty for his crime.

"Which is the fleetest horse in the stable?" asked Jack.

"The roan mare," said one.

"The animal which Richard Clavering has taken?" said Jack.

"Yes sir."

"The next best?"

"The gray horse."

"Yonder one?"

"Yes, sir."

"Those connected with this ill-fated establishment had better remain here to answer the questions of the officers of justice who will soon be here. I will saddle that horse, and start in pursuit of the murderer."

"I hope you'll catch him, sir," said one, "and bring him to justice."

"I fear you will never do it, with the start he has got of you," said another.

"Nothing here can touch the roan mare," said a third.

"I will do my best," said Jack. "I am a good horseman."

So saying, he assisted one of the men to saddle the gray horse, and leaping on its back, urged it from the stable.

"I beg your pardon, sir," said one, "but you'll doubtless be asked for. Who shall I say you are?"

"Spring-heeled Jack."

"That we know; but your right name?" asked the man.

"Lizzie knows it, and can reveal it if she pleases, though I would rather she did not. Still, if justice demands, justice must be obeyed."

And with these words he shook the reins, and galloped through the gate out into the broad road beyond.

The moment he had passed through the gate, he snatched his mask from his face.

"No further need of this," he said, "at this hour. Now, Richard Clavering, I am on your track, and it shall go hard with me if I do not bring you to the bar for the murder of your wife and that misguided servant, whom your gold lured to aid you in your villainy."

Away! with terror in his soul, and the brand of the first-born on his brow; away! along the high road with the fleetness of the wind, with his hair streaming wildly out, and the lappels of his coat floating behind him in the air; away! with that pale face in his mind's eye, and conscience pricking at his soul; away! from the scene of his crime! Away from justice fled the libertine and murderer, Richard Clavering.

The pedestrian paused in his walk, and stared after the fleeing man.

The horsemen drew rein, looked surprised, and puzzled, then galloped after him.

But so swift was the pace at which he went, that they soon gave up the chase, and wondered how the poor gentleman would fare with his runaway horse.

Many pitied him, but they knew not he was a wretch fleeing from justice, with the blood of his victim yet red on his hands—with the death-shriek of his murdered wife still ringing in his ears.

Had they done so, their looks of pity would have changed to glances of dismay— their tones of commiseration to those of horror.

So away he went unmolested and unsuspected, till the road narrowed and hedge-rows skirted his path on every side.

He looked behind him then.

A sigh of relief broke from his bloodless and quivering lips.

He was alone.

Not a soul was in sight.

He had thrown off his pursuers one by one, and he drew rein, fearful of too quickly wearing out his beast.

When he had brought the roan mare from a mad gallop into an easy canter, he began to review his position.

Truly it was a sad and dreary one.

Great, indeed, was the change which a few short hours brought upon him.

Now he was homeless, widowed, an outcast, and a murderer; with the hand of every honest man raised against him.

And as he rode, he confessed to himself that his desire to possess a poor innocent, confiding girl had been justly punished.

It was mid-day, and he knew that there were yet some hours of daylight, and fancying that every person who met him would read murderer in his face, he determined to hide himself and horse if possible, till darkness set in, and then again flee.

But whither, he knew not.

Still, to continue his flight in the open day was fraught with too much danger.

If none attempted to arrest, he would be recognised, and his course pointed out to the pursuing officers of justice.

While thus thinking, he neared a small wood. He knew it to be the private property of a gentleman of his acquaintance, and he determined to seek a shelter within its shadow till nightfall.

"If I am pursued," he muttered, "my pursuers will give me credit for placing a greater distance between myself and the scene of my crimes, and I may learn the route they take, and thus avoid them; though what I have to live for I know not. Still, to be borne to prison, and launched into eternity by the public executioner—Great heaven! the thought drives me mad! I must live!—live! I cannot—will not, die!"

Glancing along the road either way, and assuring himself that there was no one in sight, he plunged into the wood, and dismounting in the centre, tied his horse to a low branch of a tree, and sank down at the foot of its trunk.

Wearied with the furious gallop—a prey to the most agonizing and fearful thoughts—the guilty man suffered his forehead to fall upon his hands, and tears to gush to his eyes.

He rocked his body to and fro.

Groans escaped his bosom, and he struck his chest with his clenched fist.

"Fool!—fool!" he cried. "What have I done?—what have I done?"

The wind, as it rustled the leaves above his head, appeared to murmur the word "murder."

The guilty man sprang to his feet and looked upwards.

"Who spoke?" he gasped; "or was it only fancy—the taunting voice of conscience? It must have been, and yet how it has made me tremble! What a chill it has struck to my heart!"

He sat himself down again, and rocked his body to and fro.

For three long hours did the guilty man sit there, reviewing his past life, and present and future prospects.

For three long hours did he give himself to an agony of thought.

So absorbed had he been, that he heard not the clatter of a horse's hoofs on the road beyond the wood, nor through the interstices of the trees did he perceive the form of our hero galloping at full speed on the gray horse.

Jack had passed the wretched man, believing, as Richard had said his pursuers would, that the murderer would not dare to rest so short a distance from the scene of his crimes.

The shades of evening were falling when Richard Clavering arose from his grassy seat—arose with a wild and haggard look in his eye—a pale face, yet fevered brow.

His hair, ruffled by the wind, was matted about his temples, and this made him look even more weird than he would have done.

He sadly lamented the fact that he had no hat, as a man riding hatless along the public road was a circumstance sure to be noticed.

Still, there was no help for it, and so he went up to his horse, untied it from the branch, and leading it to a small pond of water, overhung and almost hidden by trees, permitted it to slake its thirst in the cool, refreshing liquid.

He stooped down and bathed his face and hands, then leaping into the saddle, urged the animal into the high road.

It was fast getting dark.

As the clouds of night floated up, the spirits of Richard Clavering sank lower and lower.

He dreaded to be alone in the dark, with the white face of his murdered wife in his thoughts.

The wind, too, moaned dismally, and the guilty man cast continual and hurried glances behind him.

As the night grew blacker, superstitious fear assailed him.

At one time he imagined he heard the death-shriek of the ill-fated Jessie. At another he saw her phantom form float past before his horse's head, and, with a stifled cry of terror, he reined in his steed.

Then dashed onward again, straining his eyes through the blackness, fearful of pursuit, and sometimes imagining that he could hear the sounds of voices in the wind, and the tramp of the horse's feet of those who sought to effect his capture.

In vain he struggled to shake off the feeling which took possession of his breast. The more he tried the less he succeeded, for darker and more dismal became his thoughts.

He had come to a portion of the road which was so narrow that it would scarcely allow two vehicles to pass each other, with high hedge rows on either side.

Not a ray of light broke from the clouds.

A pitchy darkness reigned around.

He shuddered as he reached this spot, and looked eagerly forward into the darkness.

Then he struck his heels into the animal's flanks, anxious to get again out into the broader road, which opened about a mile further on.

The horse had plunged into a gallop when Richard fancied he heard the tramp of another steed beside him.

He clutched nervously at the bridle, and abated his horse's pace, in order to be assured whether he was mistaken or not.

The sound came still to his ears, and appeared to come from the opposite side of the tall hedge on his right.

He shaded his eyes with his hand, and partially turned in his saddle.

He fancied he could see the head and shoulders of a man above the hedge a few yards behind him.

The next moment there was a break in the hedge, and, as the roan mare flew past it, the guilty rider perceived a dark figure on a white horse pass the gap on the other side, and he almost fell from his saddle as a loud, hollow voice exclaimed—

"Murderer!"

By an effort recovering from the shock, Richard Clavering struck his heels madly into the flanks of the mare.

Away flew the animal at terrific speed; and over the hedge, which now grew shorter and shorter, the guilty man saw the dark figure on the pale horse riding step by step by his side.

Richard felt all the blood in his veins running cold as ice through its channels. He could feel, too, his heart thump against his side, as though it would force itself from its prison-house. A cold sweat broke out from every pore of his skin, and he swayed like a drunken man in his saddle.

"Murderer!" again came to his ears, in an unearthly tone.

"My God! what voice is that?" gasped the frightened wretch, in tremulous accents.

"The voice of the dead!" was the reply. "Assassin, you cannot escape the penalty of your crimes! Justice will have her due; murder will out!"

"No, no!" cried Richard; "I will escape it yet—I will never die on a gallows!"

Madly he plunged his heels into his horse's side. Furiously the animal reared, and at a fearful pace bounded onwards with the terrified rider.

Richard looked again and again, but the pale horse no longer met his view.

"Gone—gone!" he cried. "Thank God! Again I am a man—again I am at rest."

"That you will never be!" said a voice behind him. "The murderer knows no rest in this world!"

Richard Clavering turned his head, and uttered a loud, piercing shriek, frightening the horse, and causing it to plunge even more furiously forward.

There, behind him on the roan mare, stood a fearful apparition—a skeleton head with a white hood, and a tall form enveloped in a black cloak. The repulsive face looked down upon his upturned and affrighted features, and from the fleshless eyes a ray of light darted down into his own.

"Your hour has come, Richard Clavering!" said the spectre, in a hollow tone. "The rope is spun—the gallows reared—the doom of the murderer is sealed!"

One wild, piercing cry broke from Richard's lips, he reeled in his saddle, and fell headlong to the earth.

CHAPTER XLIX.

MARTHA SCRIVENER'S JOY—THE ATTEMPTED ABDUCTION.

A LOOK of joy overspread the face of Martha Scrivener as Jack stood before her.

"Oh, I tremble for you," she said; "but, thank heaven, you are safe. I hope, sir, you do not think I was guilty of the act imputed by that man."

"Indeed, I do not," said Jack. "The scoundrel has learned a lesson, I hope, from the treatment he has received. Doubtless, you are anxious to learn why I desired you to wait here for me?"

"That I am, sir."

"Well, then, I have done so that I might place in your hands a certain paper, which I forced your unfeeling relative to give up—a document, I believe, which the possession of will enable you to better your circumstances."

The woman uttered a joyful cry.

"Oh, sir, you don't say that—?"

"Hush!" interrupted Jack, placing his hand on her arm to enjoin silence, as he perceived a man start suddenly, then slink quietly back into the shadow. "Hush! you will draw the attention of passers-by to us."

"I know I'm very foolish, sir; but your words so overjoyed me that I could not resist it," said Martha Scrivener.

"And I am overjoyed to be enabled to better your condition," said Jack, looking upon the wan face of the woman before him.

Then placing his hand in his breast he drew forth his pocket-book, and extracted from it the paper which he had frightened out of the old miser.

The woman's eyes glistened.

"There," said Jack, "take it – it will enable you to compel the aged rascal to do you justice."

The woman snatched eagerly at it.

"Mine, mine," she said, clasping her fingers tightly round the document. "Oh, thank you, sir; thank you. You have saved me from starvation, from death. But are you sure this paper will make my cruel relative give me that which he holds from me?"

"Doubtless."

"Oh, what can I say? How to express the gratitude I feel?"

"Say nothing, my good woman; only do not believe Spring-heeled Jack to be so bad as he is painted by his traducers."

"He is a man," cried Martha, "for he has a heart that can pity another's wretchedness.

Oh, sir, I never hoped for this. I had come to that place where you met me to-night in the hope of obtaining a few pence to buy food for another day; for it is hard to die, sir, and I was anxious to prolong my existence all I could. The coin you gave me so kindly had been all expended, and I had but a pair of boots which I thought I could change for a few pence and a pair of old ones, and then, after that was gone, I knew not what I should have done; but now—oh, sir, thanks to you—now I shall be enabled to get food and warmth."

"I would advise you to seek a respectable lawyer in the morning, and he will tell you how to compel your uncle to do that which is right and just."

"But can I not compel him without the aid of a lawyer?" asked the woman.

"You had better take my advice to spare yourself pain and trouble," said Jack; "and here are a few pounds to provide for your present necessities."

He dropped two or three gold coins into her hand.

The tears rose to the woman's eyes.

But they were tears of heartfelt gratitude.

"God bless you, sir!" she said. "I feel I never can repay you for your kindness; but night and day I will pray for your happiness."

She seized his hand, and raised it to her lips, and Jack felt the scalding tears fall upon it.

"Say no more," said Jack, in a husky tone, for the choking sensation rose to his throat. "I am rewarded quite enough by the feeling that I have perhaps been instrumental in saving you from starvation. Go now, and do as I advise you to-morrow."

He turned, as if to depart, when Martha seized his arm.

"Sir—sir! tell me who you are! You called yourself Spring-heeled Jack!"

"I am the individual who has earned that name."

"The terror of London."

"The same."

"But that is not your right name. Sir, tell it me, that I may treasure it up in my memory. But heaven forbid that I might use it to injure you!"

Jack hesitated a moment, then bent his head down till his face almost touched hers, and whispered in her ear.

The woman started back in surprise, exclaiming—

"The mar"—

"Hush!" interrupted Jack, quickly; "though to you I have revealed my name, never mention it."

"Forgive me."

"Say no more, but hurry home. The hour is getting late, and I'm fearful of your being molested by some midnight brawler. Good night, and farewell."

"Heaven's blessings on you, sir!" said the woman, shaking the hand of our hero fervently. "My prayers shall ever rise to heaven for your safety. God bless you, I say, and farewell."

A sob choked her further utterance, and Martha Scrivener turned and walked slowly away towards the bridge.

Jack followed her with his eyes for some moments, and then, drawing the folds of his cloak close around his form, he walked off in the opposite direction, muttering to himself—

"There is certainly something gratifying in the feeling that a man can do a good action.

The knowledge of the happiness I have given to that poor creature has made my heart as light as a feather, and I can almost forgive myself some of the pranks I have played. Well! well! I hope she will use the means she will now obtain frugally but generously. There are few in this world so poor that they cannot help a distressed brother or sister, and I do not think but she, when she has the power, will do so; but—hallo!"

He paused short, and turned quickly, as the form of a man brushed by him at a rapid speed, the momentary glance which Jack had at his face leading him to believe that he had seen the individual before.

As he gazed after the man, he endeavoured to refresh his memory, but was unable to recollect.

"I suppose I must be mistaken," he muttered, "for "tis seldom I forget a person I've had dealings with. Perhaps it was a face I saw in the crowd to-night, and if so, it is quite as well the recognition was not mutual. Now, whither shall I bend my steps in search of adventure?"

He stood thoughtfully for a few moments, when he fancied that he heard a faint cry in the direction of the bridge.

But so faint was the sound that it might have been caused even by the passing winds, so he strained every nerve to listen.

For a few moments all was still, save a heavy footfall on the pavement in the distance.

"I'm full of fancies to-night," he muttered; "and if I stand longer within the shadow of this old pile I shall be growing superstitions, I do believe. Ha! there again. There was no mistake this time. But it may only be the voice of some drunken brawler, staggering home from a debauch. Eh? by heaven, that was a woman's tones! and from the direction in which that poor creature has gone. Ha! can anyone have dared to molest her? By heaven! I recollect that face now. Yes, it was the features of the rascal who locked me in the passage when fleeing with the document I have just given her. And the shadow, too, of a man which I saw glide past us a short time since. I do not like the thoughts that crowd upon my mind. I will follow her. There is something wrong I feel, and that cry, I fear, was hers."

He hurried now, with terrific bounds, towards the bridge, which was then but dimly lighted by the round-bottomed, old-fashioned lamps, reared on the alcoves over the seats.

As he sped along he again heard the cry in a female tone.

"It must be her," he said; "I'm sure it must be her voice, and that scoundrel has something to do with it."

He readied the first seat, but those on either side were empty, and he darted on towards the second.

He heard no further cries now, and on finding the second alcove as deserted as the first, he paused.

"Surely, I could not be mistaken each time," he said. Then he added, in a quick, hissing tone, "Good God! the water."

He looked over the balustrade into the black depths beneath him, shading his eyes with his hands as he did so.

But nothing met his view.

Still he was not satisfied, and he scanned the dark stream more narrowly.

While thus engaged, the roll of wheels broke upon his ear.

He turned his gaze quickly from the stream to the road, and perceived a small two-wheeled vehicle pull up suddenly at the Abbey end of the bridge.

There was nothing particular in this circumstance, and he again turned his glance to the stream.

But with the same success.

He stood debating in his mind a few moments whether to proceed over the bridge, and endeavour to assure himself that Martha was safe and unmolested, or retrace his steps, when a smothered shriek caused him to start and look anxiously towards the vehicle. An exclamation broke from his lips as he did so, for by the dim light of the lamp near which it had paused he saw the forms of two men and one woman.

The former evidently were endeavouring to force the latter into the cart, as she was struggling violently.

One glance showed Jack this, and in a moment his mind was made up how to proceed.

Hastily putting on his mask, he bounded towards the spot.

Short as was the distance and swift his passage, he did not succeed in reaching the side of the vehicle before the two men had forced the woman into it and got in themselves.

As they were about to drive off, however, our hero sprung to the animal's head, and seized the rein.

By the light of the lamp the features of the two men were plainly visible to Jack, and in an instant he recognised the thief and the miser.

The features of the woman he could not then make out, for a large handkerchief was tied over her mouth and nose, but in the poor habiliments[54] she wore he recognised the miser's ward, Martha Scrivener, from whom he had parted a few minutes since.

In an instant the whole affair flashed upon him.

They had been watched and overheard by the two worthies, who, when they parted, had followed and overtaken the woman, whom they must have forced down the steps of the bridge, out of sight of any passer-by, till the arrival of the cart, which must have been ready at hand for her reception.

Finding a man at the animal's head, and doubtless recognising in an instant who it was, both Scrivener and his companion gave utterance to a cry half of terror and surprise.

"Cut him with the whip, Blodger—cut him down!" cried the miser. "It's the villain that robbed me! Cut him down, and trample him under the horse's feet!"

The fellow raised the whip to fulfil the injunction of the miser, when Jack exclaimed—

"Look you, my man; if you so much as touch me with that whip, I'll fling you into the river; and you have had good proof that I am no boaster. What are you doing with that woman?"

"What's that to you?" cried Scrivener. "Get away and let us pass, or I'll call for the police."

While this conversation was going on, Martha succeeded in tearing the bandage from her mouth.

"Save me!—save me!" she cried. "Oh! sir, save me!"

"They shall not harm you," said Jack.

"They want to say I'm mad, and take me to a lunatic asylum. Oh! don't let them. I am not mad!"

"She is mad—quite mad!" cried Scrivener. "Stand aside—molest us at your peril. I say she is mad!"

---

[54] Clothes

"And I say you are a wicked, contemptible old liar!" cried Jack, taking a knife from his pocket, and severing the traces,[55] so that the animal could not be urged forward. "Now, suffer that woman to descend from the cart."

"She shan't go!—she shan't go!" exclaimed Scrivener. "She is my ward, and she's stark, staring, raving mad! I'm her guardian, and will do what I please. Go away, or it will be the worse for you, you midnight robber!"

"Steady there, old man," said Jack. "You shall do nothing of the kind. The lady is beyond the reach of your guardianship, being over age. Now, sir, as I have neither time nor inclination to waste words in arguing with you, you will please to suffer that lady to get out of the cart, or I'll pull you out, and not very tenderly either, to enable her to do so."

"I'll call for the police, you ruffian!—you robber!—you"—

"You dare not do that, lest I give you into custody for seeking to deprive your niece of her liberty," said Jack. "Now then, out you come!"

And leaving the horse's head, Jack seized the old man by the arm with a vice-like grip.

"Blodger—Blodger!" cried the miser, "he—he'll kill me!"

"Very likely," said Jack; "for you are not fit to live. Now, sir, suffer that woman to get out."

"I won't."

"We'll see about that," cried our hero.

But as he put forth his strength to drag the man out of the vehicle, he received a blow on the head from the butt-end of the whip.

Martha had raised her hands to stay the intentions of Mr. Blodger, and had partially succeeded, or Jack would certainly have been stunned.

"Confound you!" cried Jack, his temper somewhat tried by the act; "but I'll punish you for that, my fine fellow."

Another blow descended, and to avoid this Jack released his hold of the miser's arm, and sprang backwards a few feet.

"Murder—murder!" roared Scrivener, who, losing his balance, brought his face right in the way of the whip handle, and received the blow upon the bridge of his nose, which sent him all of a heap into the bottom of the cart.

As he fell, Jack gave a bound and alighted beside Blodger in the vehicle.

"You confounded scoundrel!" he exclaimed, seizing the man by the throat. "But you shall suffer for this night's work. Now, Miss Scrivener, please to get out, while I hold the villain."

This the girl was not slow to do, and trembling and frightened, she leaped to the ground.

"Stop her—stop her!" cried the uncle, staggering into a sitting position. "I won't be robbed—I won't be robbed! Oh! Murder!"

Down he went again, as Jack, lifting Mr. Blodger from his feet, fairly hurled him over the side of the cart into the road, where the ruffian lay groaning from the pain caused by a dislocated collar-bone.

"Silence, you avaricious old villain," cried Jack; "or, by heaven, I will serve you the same!"

"Mercy! Oh, don't!" exclaimed Scrivener.

"Promise me, then, you will not seek further to molest this girl," said Jack.

"Yes—yes. I won't—upon my soul, I won't," cried the man, fearful that Jack was about to perform his threat.

---

55 Straps connecting the horse to the cart.

"Do not harm him, sir—oh! do not harm him," pleaded Martha. "He is a wicked man to seek to rob the orphan; but heaven, in its own good time, will punish him for his sins."

"He is, indeed, a wicked old scoundrel," said Jack, leaping from the cart to her side, "to seek to possess the little left you by your father, by wishing to bury you alive in a madhouse."

"God forgive him!" said Martha.

"The devil seize him, I say," cried Jack. "I would not have that man's feelings when he lays upon his death-bed for all the wealth of the world."

"I'm poor, very poor," gasped the miser. "It's not her money you would rob me of, but my hard-earned gold. I ought to be paid for my kindness to her. She eats such a lot she quite beggared me, and the money would not pay for a quarter of it. I'll never be generous again—never, never!"

Jack looked upon the old man with contempt, if not positive loathing.

"How debased must his heart be," he said, "when he could sell all his hopes of salvation for a few paltry pounds, when to possess that which is justly yours he could immure you in a living tomb. Old man, for shame, for shame! Already have you one foot in the grave. Can you take your gold there with you? Better will it be for you if you turn your thoughts to that God who alone has power to save, and not to that only god you have ever worshipped— gold."

Then, turning to Martha, he said—

"I fear to leave you, lest the old rascal seek some other means of securing the gold for himself; and yet to remain here is fraught with danger to me, for I can hear footsteps coming this way."

"Fly, then; do not endanger your own safety for me," said the woman, quickly and anxiously. "I should never forgive myself did you suffer for your kindness to me."

"I must see you beyond the reach of this man."

"He cannot follow me now."

And she pointed to the severed traces and the groaning form of Blodger.

"Whither will you go?"

"I will seek an asylum in Lambeth for the present."

"Then go at once, for in a few minutes this man will be found, and you must not be seen here."

"And you?"

"Oh, never fear for me. Do not stay. Away! We shall soon meet again."

He held up his hand to check her further utterance, and she sped away over the bridge in the opposite direction to the coming footsteps.

The miser stretched out his hand as if he would stay her progress, then reeled and fell backwards in the cart.

CHAPTER L.

A FRACAS ON THE BRIDGE—MR. BRISTLES AGAIN.

"HALLO! What's up?"

Such was the exclamation which caused our hero to turn from watching the fleeing figure of Martha Scrivener.

Two young men, belonging to that class vulgarly denominated "swells" by some, and "men about town" by others, were squinting through their eye-glasses at the recumbent figure of Mr. Blodger, as that worthy writhed in agony upon the cold stones of the bridge. Jack made no reply.

A contemptuous curl of the lip, however, bespoke the esteem in which he held the gentlemen just arrived upon the scene.

As the sound of their voices reached his ear, he quickly slipped the mask from his face and placed it in his pocket, so that when he turned towards them there was nothing striking in his appearance.

"Demme! I thay, Thir William, there's been an accident. Thome common fellow hath been flung out of hith vehicle. I thaid there'd been an accident, and thure enough there hath."

"Yeth, my noble friend, these rough fellows—the poorer clathes of humanity—are tho wewy wild, tho inconthithtent in their way, that I am often thurprithed they do not thuffer more for their daring. P'raps the fellow thought that his miserable stheed wath to be compared with the noble animals kept by uth gentlemen, and only found out hith mithtake when he was flung from hith dirty vehicle. But it will teach him a lethon, perhaps, not to think themselves or their horthes equal to the better clathes of thociety. Come away, my noble friend. It pains me to hear hith groans, tho awfully rough ith the tones of hith voith."

"Thall we help him up, Thir William?" asked the other.

"It would thoil my lavender kids.[56] I could not touch such a rough, ill-manneredly perthon."

"Thall we call the attention of the polith to the affair?"

"You had better not," said Jack, suddenly and sneeringly.

The man turned, looked at Jack in a contemptuous manner, and after measuring him from head to foot, said—

"And why not, pray?"

"Why not?" iterated Jack.

"Yeth; why not, thir?"

"I'll tell you, sir," replied our hero. "I see the police have orders to kill all puppies found straying about the streets."

The man started back.

"Confuthion! Thith to a gentleman of my respectability and standing? Do you hear that, my noble friend?"

"Thameful—dithgusting, the low scoundrel!" exclaimed the other. "Thome intholent pickpocket, doubtleth."

And the speaker fixed his eye-glass in his eye and contemptuously gazed upon our hero.

Jack coloured to the temples.

The insinuation pained and annoyed him greatly.

He clenched his hand and made a step forward.

"Sir," he exclaimed, "do you know whom you are addressing?"

---

56 Gloves.

"Thome ignorant fellow who hath the presumption to talk to a gentleman without knowing how to speak to one."

"You are talking to one, sir, who knows how to treat a contemptible puppy," said Jack, "and that is, by kicking him."

And raising his foot, our hero dealt the fellow a kick on the bottom of his back, which sent him reeling over the prostrate body of Mr. Blodger.

"Thcoundrel!" cried his companion, raising a small walking-cane threateningly.

"Take that," said Jack, tearing the weapon from his hold, and giving the fellow a smart rap across his knuckles with it, which made him cut a comical caper in the roadway.

"Oh!" roared the fellow. "Polith! Where are the polith?"

"Fortunately for you and your companion they are not at hand just now," said Jack.

"'Tis fortunate for you, for we would have you taken to prithon."

"On what charge?"

That of intholence and athault, you low, vile fellow."

"Well," said Jack, smiling, "you are certainly a pair of beauties—at least, in your own estimation."

"We are gentlemen."

"I doubt if you know even the meaning of the word," said Jack. "Gentlemen! What a burlesque upon the character! But take your cane, sir, and beware to what use you seek to apply it. If you must strike something, let it be of your own kind—puppies and mongrels." The man took the cane, muttering.

"I thay, fellow," remarked the other, coming up to Jack in a threatening manner, "how dare you kick me? I've a good mind to pull your noth, but I feel that it would be a dethecration of my fingers."

"Oh! I should never allow such a thought to deter me in the attempt," said Jack.

"Then I thould. I am sorry you are tho contemptible a perthon, which compels me to forego the gratification of my feelings."

"Hark you," said Jack, with some warmth in his tones. "There is a limit to the patience of most men, and I am no exception to the general rule. I therefore beg you will not address me again in the manner which yourself and companion have done. You are no gentlemen, though doubtless you are foolish enough to imagine you could induce some to believe so. However, you may rest assured I am of a far different opinion. You are a pair of conceited puppies, and as such you will most assuredly get treated if you offer any further insult to me, either by word or deed."

And so saying Jack turned away.

"You're obliged to go," said one.

"He's afraid to sthay," remarked the other, "in cathe we should chathtise him for his intholenth."

Jack turned quickly, and stretching out his hand, seized the last speaker's nose between his finger and thumb, and gave it so severe a twist, that the fellow shrieked aloud—

"Help me, Bill! Help—help! He's pulling my nothe off!"

"Bill is it, now, instead of Sir William!" said Jack, releasing his hold. "Well, now, Mister Bill, what have you to say?"

"Me? nothing. I"—

"You're a pair of contemptible curs," said Jack, again turning away.

THE ALARM.

"Oh, here's the polith—here's the polith," said the fellow, whose nose was as red as fire, and whose eyes watered as if he were crying. "Here, polithman—polithman!"

"Hallo," said an individual in the garb of a police officer, who had been summoned from beneath one of the alcoves by the tones of the would-be-thought gentleman, where he had been an amused spectator for some moments.

"Here, polithman, I give this intholent fellow into cuthtody."

"What for?" asked the officer.

"For inthulting and athaulting a gentleman in the public streets, doubtleth with the intent to commit a robbery."

"Scoundrel!" cried Jack, turning furiously upon the man; "dare you impute such a thing to me?"

The officer sprang before him to shield the man from Jack's vengeance, when the light of a lamp falling directly upon the face of both, Jack immediately dropped his upraised arm, and the police-officer opened his eyes and mouth very wide indeed.

Our hero had recognized in the policeman the redoubtable Bobby Bristles.

The policeman, of course, was not positive whether it was Jack who was charged, but he fancied, by the form and attire of the man before him, that it was so.

"Why don't you do your duty, polithman?" asked the fellow.

"Who are you calling polithman!" asked Bristles. "Policeman, if you please. Now, what's the row?"

"This intholent fellow—this ill-manneredly, inthulting—"

"Hadn't you better get your tongue cut, so as I can understand you?" said Bristles. "I tell you what, I think you had better go home and learn to talk properly, instead of making a row in the streets at midnight."

"Will you take the charge?"

"No, I won't."

"You won't?"

"No."

"Then you shall hear from my ethteemed friend, the Theeretary of Thate, and you won't be long in the forth, I can tell you."

"What do you say?" said Bristles, turning upon him. "Now, you move on, and sharp, too, or perhaps I shall move you."

"Thir Willim, do you hear that?" lisped the fellow.

"Dithgraceful," said the other; "but the polith, instead of doing their duty, only aid and abet the vile characters they should take into custody."

"Do they, now?" said Bristles.

"Yeth, they do; and you shall suffer for your neglect of duty."

"All right, old boy," said Bristles; "and you'll suffer if you ain't off. You know it's time you was in two hours ago."

"What does the fellow mean?"

"Why, you tailor's trotter, that your master has shut up shop two hours ago, and is waiting for you to go to snooze under his counter before he goes to bed. Now, go on; you know you are only a pair of counter-jumpers, for there's the yard measure sticking out of your pocket."

"The devil, there is!" cried the fellow, forgetting his affected lisp, and hastily clapping his hand to his coat pocket. Then, as if recollecting himself, he drew himself up, and, taking his companion's arm, said—

"Let uth go, my noble friend. This perthon shall hear more about this affair than he thinks. To inthult two gentlemen in this way ith dithgrathful—thocking—thocking!"

"Had you there, old boy," said Bristles "Think I didn't know you? Why, I saw you in the shop three hours ago. I say, you had better go, in case I should tell your master how you flash it of a night in the Haymarket. It don't look well for counter-jumpers—they can't afford it; at least, not out of their own money."

Jack, with difficulty, suppressed his laughter, as the two men slunk away arm in arm.

"Ha!" said Bristles, calling after them, "hadn't you better give this gentleman in charge?"

No answer was vouchsafed to this question.

"Don't forget to tell your friend, the Secretary of State, when you take home the breeches he's ordered!"

The two fops quickened their pace very considerably at this, and Bristles turned to Jack, who had clapped on his mask.

Bristles started, but recovering himself on the instant, he said— "Ha! I thought I knowed you, Jack."

"And, of course, knowing me, you will do your duty?" said our hero.

"What's that?"

"Take me into custody."

"Take you?"

"Yes."

"Not a bit of it. There's a good many men in the force would be glad of the chance, but Bobby Bristles is not one of them. You have given me a couple of frights, but I forgive you for 'em. But what's up here?"

"A poor devil had a fall and hurt himself, it seems," replied Jack.

Bristles laid his hand on Jack's arm. "A fall," he said, "or a throw?"

"Well, I will admit that I pitched him out of the cart, but the rascal deserved it. Together with an old man, who now lies insensible in the vehicle, he sought to carry off a poor sane girl to a lunatic asylum. Her cries for aid brought me to her side, a struggle ensued, and here's the effects of it."

"Where's the girl?"

"Fled, of course."

"Do you think he's hurt?"

"Stunned, perhaps; nothing more." Bristles stooped over the man, and shook his head; then rising, he said—

"Jack, help me to lift him into the cart. I must take him to the station, and then you had better make yourself scarce. It won't be safe for you, even if you did it in self-defence. Take my advice, and move on."

"Thank you," said Jack; "but had you not better take him to the hospital?"

"No, I'm not supposed to know he's hurt," said Bristles. "Of course not."

Jack aided the officer to place Blodger beside the old miser, who continued in the swoon, brought on either by the blow he had received from the whip, or chagrin at the escape of Martha.

"Now, you be off, Jack," said Bristles, "for there'll be another of our men here directly."

"I will take your advice; but first tell me, did you marry that girl who lost her situation through you?"

"Marry her?" said the policeman. "She's Mrs. Bristles now, bless her little heart."

"And the gardener, what of him?" asked Jack. "Got a month for being where he had no right to be, and consequently lost his place, and the confidence of the Misses Snooks."

"That's rather hard; but Mrs. Bristles was avenged," laughed Jack.

"So she was, sir, first-rate. Eh! they lost a good servant, they did, when they lost my Peggy."

"And they missed that cat, too, didn't they?" said Jack, slyly.

"Move on," said Bristles. "You hurt my feelings, upon my soul, you do."

"Ha! ha!" laughed Jack. "Well, if you've got a good wife I'm glad to hear it, and wish you all earthly happiness. Here's a sovereign to buy her a new bonnet."

"Move on," said Bristles, with pretended offended dignity, and turned his back to our hero as he did so.

Jack was about to request him to accept the coin, when he perceived Bristles had placed his open hand behind him.

Our hero dropped the coin into his palm, and the officer's fingers closed over it in an instant.

"We are forbidden to accept anything, sir," he said; "but, of course, if it's forced upon us, we can't help it."

"Of course not," said Jack. "Now, don't forget the traces are cut, and you will have to lead the animal."

"All right, sir. Good night! Here comes my sergeant, so please to move on."

"Quickly," said Jack, as the measured footfall of a policeman smote his ears.

In another minute our hero had cleared the bridge, and stood within the shadow of that ancient pile where the tombs of the great, the brave, and the learned mark the last resting-place of men whose names are emblazoned on history's scroll in letters of gold.

CHAPTER LI.

THE ATTEMPT TO DESTROY THE CHEQUE DEFEATED—THE STRANGE LOSS.

WITH a deep sigh, the poor wife of the forger and suicide awoke to consciousness— awoke to the real truth of her position.

Better would it have been had that lethargy never worn off—better that death had come to ease her of her sufferings, and still for ever the heart of her who never more would know peace in this world.

Her existence was completely blighted, and she cared not what became of her.

Still little more than a girl in years, she had known more misery in a few short months than fall to the life-time of thousands.

When she opened her eyes, they rested not only upon the faces of the two officers, but upon several, and two gentlemen of the medical profession, who had been called in to view the body of her husband.

For a moment or two she gazed with a bewildered look upon those assembled in the little parlour, then, as the whole truth flashed upon her brain, she sobbed aloud.

Looks of pity and commiseration were fixed upon her, and those men, used to scenes of misery and crime, spoke in husky voices to each other.

The human heart is not altogether callous, as could be proved by the wet eye of more than one present. Though emissaries of the law, they were men, and felt as such.

"Come, come," said one, who by his dress bespoke himself an inspector of the police; "you must not give way like this. Of course, you are pained by the unfortunate circumstances of the night, but you must be wise. If you go on in this manner you will lay yourself on a sick bed, and perhaps kill yourself."

"Why did they not let me do it?" she cried; "I don't want to live now that he has gone."

"It is wrong to talk thus, my poor woman. Remember that it is wicked to contemplate such a deed. Our life is not our own to take. Be more composed, and to-morrow you will thank heaven you were prevented from carrying out your intention. Where are your friends to be found?"

"Friends?" cried Jane.

"Ay."

"I have no friends."

"No friends?"

"None."

"Think—think. You must have some one who respects you—some who can counsel and sympathize with you in this trying hour. Come, give me their address, and I will send for them."

"I have none who would come to the forger's wife," said Jane, bitterly.

"The sins of your husband are not your own," said the inspector, "and it would be cruel to blame you for them. None could be so unfeeling as to refuse to come to you at such a time as this."

"I would not ask them."

"Why not? But there, I have no right to ask the question. You are not in a fit state of mind to be left alone. I will send for your friends if you like, but if you will not have it so, I must send some one myself."

"I need no one."

"Indeed you do. Your attempt upon your own life will not allow me to let you remain alone."

"As you please," said Jane, "I must submit, I suppose."

"Baintree," said the inspector, turning to one of his men, "you are a married man, I believe?"

"Yes, sir," was the answer.

"Would you object to your wife coming to this poor woman till the violence of her grief has abated, and she can with better safety be left alone?"

"Not in the least, sir."

"Fetch her, then."

The man turned, and left the room.

When he had gone the inspector took the poor woman's hand in his own, and in a kind and fatherly tone said—

"Mrs. Slater, do not think me actuated by any desire to wound your already lacerated heart. I have a duty to perform, and must perform it. You cannot under any circumstances be permitted to enter the room where your husband lies till after the jury have viewed the body to-morrow. So if there is anything you desire from that apartment, it shall be brought to you."

"Nothing," she said. Then suddenly she added quickly, "Yes, yes. I want a book—a pocket-book."

"Where is it, in the drawers?" asked the inspector.

"No, no; it lies on the floor by the door. Yes, it was there I dropped it when that fearful sight met my gaze."

"It shall be fetched," he said, and waved his hand to one of the men.

The man departed, and in a few moments returned with the pocket-book of Grasper.

Jane stretched out her hand to take it, but the inspector seized it, and moved her back.

"I must be sure," he said, "that there is nothing within it which you could use to attempt the destruction of your own life."

"Oh! no—no! there is not—there is not!" cried Jane, making an attempt to tear it from his hold.

Her tone and manner caused the inspector to fancy that there was, and he opened the clasp.

As he did so, a paper fell at his feet.

The officer stooped to pick it up, but Jane, uttering a cry, flung herself before him.

"You shall not touch it!" she cried. "It is mine."

"Let her have it, Simpson," said the inspector. "We have no wish to pry into any letter or such like. There is nothing here but a few papers, and therefore she can have the book."

Jane had secured the paper, and crumbled it up in her hand tightly, as if fearful it would be wrested from her, and when the book was offered her, she hastily thrust it into her bosom.

"Now, is there anything else you desire?" said the inspector.

"Nothing."

"Then, gentlemen," he added, turning to the doctors, "I believe there is nothing to keep us longer."

"No," said one. "I will send this poor woman a composing draught as soon as I get home."

The medical men turned upon their heels, and left the room.

"Simpson, you will remain till Mrs. Baintree arrives, and then report yourself at the station."

The man saluted his officer, and seated himself in a chair opposite to Jane.

"Again I ask you, ere I leave, if I can send for your friends, or be of any service to you?"

"No, sir—no."

"Then seek to compose yourself, and ask aid of heaven in your fearful trials. Anything that you wish for that can be done, shall not be denied you."

He turned from her with a sigh, and, beckoning to his men, strode from the room.

The door closed behind them, and Jane and the officer, Simpson, were left alone.

For some time neither spoke to the other. Jane was too much absorbed with her own grief, and the officer with watching her pale face and trembling form.

But the silence became painful at last to the young officer, and he remarked, not knowing what else to say—

"You was very anxious about that paper and pocket-book, ma'am. So anxious, that I did not think the inspector would have let you had it."

Jane made no remark in reply; she only tightened her fingers more tenaciously over the crumpled evidence of her husband's guilt, and sobbed aloud.

"Here—here," she muttered, inwardly, "is that which would have saved him. But too late—too late! Oh! is it not a judgment upon me for consenting at last to purchase his liberty. Why did I go—why leave my home, when, had I remained, he would still have lived? Oh! how cruelly have my hopes been broken—hopes that leaped to my bosom as my trembling hands touched that book. It contained the expected paper—contained that which could have transported him. Oh! but for that fatal letter I could have placed it in his hands—destroyed it before his eyes, and laughed to scorn the villain who has robbed me of my husband. But of what avail is it now! None—none. It cannot harm him, neither can it bring him back to life. What has it done for him—for me? Ay, what? Am I not a thief? Curses on it! It has plunged us both into crime. But no other eye shall see it. I will destroy it—hide it from men's sight for ever; but how? Would this man would go—would that I were alone!"

She raised her eyes and met those of Simpson.

She was anxious to dispose of the fatal evidence, but saw that to attempt to burn or destroy it would excite the officer's surprise and curiosity.

This she had no wish to do.

She alone knew her guilt now, and she resolved that none other should learn it.

"Perhaps if I feign sleep he will leave the room," she muttered; "if only for an instant, it will enable me to get rid of the forged cheque, if not the book."

She laid her head back on the pillow of the sofa, and closed her eyes.

But she could not stifle the long-drawn sighs and choking sobs which escaped her bosom.

The officer leaned his elbow on the table, and supported his head on his hand, but watched through his open fingers the form and features of Jane Slater.

A feeling of drowsiness stole over him, but he shook it off, fearing that if he suffered himself to sleep only for an instant she would attempt to rob herself of life.

The working of Jane's face as she murmured to herself excited his suspicions, and though he pretended to doze, he was watchful and wakeful.

He had no thought of what Jane contemplated, but he knew that she did not sleep, though he felt she would wish him to think so.

He was a young man, and young in the force, but he was an acute observer and deep thinker, two qualities which, in after years, raised him high in the police force.

For about half an hour both continued to be perfectly oblivious of the presence of the other.

Then Jane opened her eyes, and looked towards him.

His head still rested on his hand, and he appeared to slumber. Slowly she arose into a sitting posture.

Eagerly she strove to detect any sign or movement that might indicate he was aware of a change in her position.

None came.

Jane rose silently and stealthily to her feet.

Still Simpson moved not.

She opened her hand and noiselessly unfolded the crumpled cheque.

Holding it between her finger and thumb, she moved cautiously towards the table, on which the candle burned with a long wick.

She stretched out her hand towards it.

The paper was over the flame, which leaped up to enfold it in its embrace.

But ere it caught, her wrist was seized and her arm forced back, while, with the other hand, Simpson tore the cheque from her hold.

A scream escaped her lips, and she staggered back a few paces, then paused and gazed upon the tall form which had risen from its chair. .

For some moments she continued to gaze alternately at the officer's face and the cheque in his hand, and then, springing towards him, she cried—

"Give it me—give it me! You have no right to take it from me."

"Excuse me," he said, in a calm tone, "what would you do with it?"

"Destroy it—it is nothing," she exclaimed, in trembling accents.

"Then, why did you wait till you thought I slept, and then proceed in so stealthy and suspicious a manner?"

"I—I—oh, pray give it me. It does not concern you," she exclaimed, in a choking voice. "What would you do?"

"Simply my duty."

"But this is no part of it. You were left here to prevent me laying violent hands upon myself, not to take away any piece of paper I may wish to destroy."

"I am sorry to do anything which may pain your feelings, especially when they are already pained enough. But your anxiety to possess the paper when it fell from the book, and your strange proceedings during the last few moments, leads me to consider that I should not return it to your hands till I know what it is."

"It is a private"—

"If it is simply a private letter, its contents shall not be read by me. Ah!" he added, as he cast his eyes upon it for the first time, "a cheque!"

Jane uttered another scream, and staggered back to the sofa.

"A cheque," said Simpson, "drawn on the — bank; signed, Ralph Grasper."

He folded it over once, and looking at Jane, exclaimed—

"I should ill perform the duties I have sworn to fulfil, did I not place this in the hands of my superiors."

"You surely will not"—

"However painful it may be to you, I certainly shall do so. I am not the man to seek to harrow the feelings of others; but knowing what I do of the antecedents of your late husband, I will not part with this cheque. It may be nothing—it may be your own property. In either case no harm can come to you by its retention by me. I shall place it in the hands of my inspector, who, I am sure, will not make any wrong use of it. Doubtless you think me harsh and unfeeling, but you misjudge me if you do so. I simply wish to do what my conscience assures me is right; and therefore I shall retain this cheque till I arrive at the station, and then give it into the hands of my inspector."

"You shall not—by heaven, you shall not!" cried Jane, thinking for the moment only of the crime she had committed, and the triumph of Grasper, when it came to his knowledge she had been found out.

And springing upon the officer, she strove to tear it from his grasp.

But Simpson gently repulsed her with his left hand, and held the coveted slip of paper above his head, out of her reach, with his right.

"You cannot wrest it from me," he said; "nor shall any one else!"

As he spoke, the door of the room softly opened about half a foot, a circumstance which was not observed by the officer, his back being towards it, and an arm, with a hand more like the claw of some wild animal than aught else, was thrust through the crevice; and as the words left the officer's lips, the paper was torn from his hold, and the door again closed ere he could turn.

Jane sank back on the sofa, and covered her face with her hands. She had recognized the mask of Spring-heeled Jack.

CHAPTER LII.
THE CRUEL GUARDIAN—THE POCKET-BOOK.

WHEN Simpson turned and found his gaze only rested on the closed door of the room, his astonishment was even greater than at the sudden loss of the cheque.

For several moments he stood looking upon the painted panels—a circumstance which was favourable to our hero, for when at length he grasped the handle of the door in his hand and flung it open, the passage was deserted.

At first he only looked cautiously out into the passage, but seeing no one, he strode out of the room.

The instant he had gone, Jane drew the pocket-book from her bosom, and lifting up the swab of the sofa, thrust it under.

Scarce had she done so, when Simpson returned to the room.

The young officer's face was pale, and there was a nervous twitching about the muscles of the mouth which betokened that he had received a shock to his feelings.

Silently closing the door behind him, he looked beneath the table, and then, permitting the cover he had lifted to fall from his hand, he muttered— "Strange — very strange. I cannot understand it."

He fixed his eyes penetratingly upon the face of Jane Slater, as if he would there read a solution to the mysterious disappearance of the cheque.

But Jane kept her face partially concealed in her hands, and the officer sat down and turned his eyes to the door.

For several moments he made no remark either to himself or his companion, but it was evident that his thoughts were busy. At length he spoke. His tones were harsh and quick. "Mrs. Slater," he said," who stole that cheque from my hand?"

Jane hesitated ere she replied, then said—"No one."

He echoed her words.

"By some sleight-of-hand trick you have consigned it to your pocket."

"What?" he said. She repeated the words. The officer looked more puzzled than before.

"Indeed, nothing of the kind. But the affair is a mystery which must be fathomed, for I am the more certain that you have no right with the paper, and that some accomplice, though heaven knows by what means, has possessed him or herself of it."

"There is no one here but ourselves and my poor dead husband," said Jane, tears starting afresh at the mention of him who lay so cold and rigid above. "You say you have it not, and of course I shall not take the trouble to contradict you. If you will not restore it, I have no more to say than that I shall be glad when your presence is no longer needed here. I have enough to make me wretched without your insinuations."

She turned her gaze from him, and kept her face averted, till a knock at the door announced the arrival of Baintree and his wife.

A young woman, tall of stature, and not very intelligent in looks, was Mrs. Baintree.

There was something servant-girlish in her appearance, and Jane thought, the moment she entered, that she would be a personage of a very officious nature.

Consequently, the poor woman took a dislike to her at once.

Of course, now she had arrived, there was no further excuse for Simpson to remain, and he took up his hat to depart, beckoning Baintree to follow him.

In the passage, however, the two men paused to converse in whispers, and Mrs. Baintree was beckoned out of the room by her husband.

What the officer said to her, Jane could not hear, though she strove hard to catch the words, but she had no doubt it was to hear instructions to keep a sharp look-out on the actions of the suicide's wife.

She was not absent long, for in less than a minute she returned to the room, and the street door closed behind the officers, whose heavy tread Jane heard with pleasure pass the house.

The woman flung off her bonnet and shawl, and bustled about the room.

"Bless my soul!" she said, "how can you sit here by candle-light when its broad daylight?"

"I have other things to think of," said Jane.

The woman flung open the shutters, blew out the candle, suffering the long wick to smoulder and fill the room with an intolerable stench.

"There! Now I shall make myself quite at home," said the woman. "Where's the wood to light the fire?"

"In the coal cupboard, if you need it," said Jane, shortly.

"Need it, indeed! I should say I did, and a good cup of tea to warm me. I've been dragged out of my warm bed at a moment's notice, and I should think I did want a cup of tea. Some people have no thought only for themselves."

Jane sighed, but made no remark in return.

"You drink tea, I suppose?" said the woman, after a pause.

"I care for nothing now, but to be alone with my own sad thoughts," replied Jane.

"Ah! it's no use grieving for what can't be helped. You can't bring your husband back to life, if you cry your eyes out. Catch me grieving about a man who could do as he's done—not I."

"Unfeeling woman," said Jane, half aloud.

Mrs. Baintree caught the words, and turned almost fiercely.

"I've got as much feeling as most people, though I don't show it perhaps. It ain't them as sighs and groans and bellow most as feels most. Oh! dear no. The heaviest grief is the soonest over. Those as cries most at a death is generally the first to get married again. Ain't they now!"

"I am in no humour for conversation or argument," said Jane.

"Oh! no, of course not. Perhaps you don't think I'm good enough to speak to, because I'm a policeman's wife."

"Pray desist," said Jane.

"Oh! yes, certainly. I mustn't open my mouth—oh! dear, no; it ain't right I should; but I'm quite as good as—But there, I won't hurt your feelings—oh! no; I'm too tender-hearted for that."

Poor Jane! she felt as if her heart would break.

Surely she was wretched enough, without having her misery added to by this woman.

She rose from the sofa, and tottered towards the door.

She intended to seek privacy in the little back parlour, but Mrs. Baintree sprang up from the fireplace and opposed her passage.

"Where are you going?" she asked.

"What is that to you?" said Jane.

"Oh! it's a good deal."

"Is it?"

"Yes; I've got orders not to let you out of sight."

"Not to let me out of sight?"

"That's it."

"What do you mean, woman?"

"What I say. You can't go anywhere without I go with you."

"Am I a prisoner in my own house?" asked Jane.

"Well, I suppose you are. Now, look here; I've had my orders to watch you, and I mean to do it."

"To watch me!"

"Yes."

"Why should you watch me?"

"Oh! you know."

"Indeed I do not."

"Of course not. You don't know anything about any cheques, do you?" sneered the woman.

Jane started back.

"I've got my orders, I can tell you; and if you want to know what they are, this is them: I'm to keep a sharp eye on you, and see that you don't attempt to get rid of any papers or anything else as is in this house, as you are suspected of being as guilty as your husband was."

Jane's face grew gradually paler and paler, and the little strength she possessed deserted her.

She tottered back to the sofa, and fell, rather than sat down upon it; and a feeling of such wretchedness stole over her, that she wished death would come.

The woman gazed at her with a look of triumph in her coarse features.

Ignorant, she was very susceptible to the least slight; and that she had been snubbed by Jane Slater could not be denied.

But then her own self had been the cause. The poor woman's heart was lacerated with anguish, and she could ill brook the uncouth style in which she had been addressed.

Mrs. Baintree, however, could make no allowance for the other's feelings.

She felt hurt at Jane's manner, and a spirit of revenge took possession of her soul.

She had been requested to keep a sharp eye on Jane by the young officer, simply because he considered it his duty to tell her to do so. But the young virago went beyond her orders to gratify a feeling of revenge, called forth by the words of her she had been called upon to remain with.

Having been acquainted with the mysterious loss of the cheque, she had jumped to the conclusion that Jane was a professional forger as well as her husband, and that she would ill-become a policeman's wife if she did not look upon her charge as a dangerous and desperate character.

This feeling gained in strength when Jane, wearied and annoyed by her tones and words, requested her to be silent, and from that moment she was the enemy of the forger's wife.

There is an old saying, "That if you place a beggar on horseback he'll ride to the devil," and it may be added, "That if those who have been drudges are placed in a position above others, they will prove cruel and insolent overseers."

It was so with Mrs. Baintree.

What was it to her, that the poor woman she had been deputed to guard had lost her husband?—that her heart was almost breaking with the agony of grief she suffered?

Nothing.

The woman was weak, ill, and dispirited, and therefore her chance of showing her domineering spirit was the greater.

It was but a poor triumph after all, but it gratified her mean and paltry soul.

Jane made no further offer to leave the room, but sat silent upon the sofa.

The woman made the breakfast, but Jane partook of none; her heart was too full to eat or drink.

About mid-day several gentlemen, accompanied by the inspector, came to the house.

They were the jury, and the object of their visit was to view the body of the unfortunate forger.

A short time after this a shell was brought, and the remains of the guilty but unfortunate man placed therein, and removed to the little back room, and Jane was informed that her ingress to her chamber was no longer prevented.

Gladly did she seek it, but not till after Mrs. Baintree had spent nearly an hour above stairs.

What her object was Jane did not even care to inquire, although she fancied she could hear the drawers pulled open and closed more than once.

When she went up stairs there was no evidence remaining of the fearful scene which had been enacted in that room on the night before.

The pool of blood had been erased by the orders of the inspector, and everything put as smoothly as possible, out of respect to the feelings of the suffering wife.

As soon as she entered the room, Jane flung herself on the bed, and burying her face in the pillow, sobbed aloud.

"When—when will my sufferings end!" she cried. "Oh! why am I suffered to live this life of misery? Alas! the worst has not yet come, I fear, for I am more than suspected of being a criminal. That cheque I had so wished to destroy has been seen, will be spoken of, and I shall be traced as the thief who stole the hoary-headed villain's pocket-book. Oh! I have left it below. Will she find it? What if she does? What can it matter what becomes of me now? They may drag me to prison! Shall I suffer more than I do now? No. Let it remain then—let it be found—brought forward in evidence against me—I care not; for nothing can enhance my misery—nothing bring happiness again to this aching heart!"

She buried her face still further in the pillow, and, wearied in mind and body, at length sank to sleep.

Oblivious to all, she saw not, shortly after the shades of night had fallen, the policeman's wife-bending over her, and, by the light of a candle, assuring herself that Jane Slater slept.

"Now," said the woman speaking to herself, as she stole away from the side of the bed with a cat-like step, and silently closed the door behind her, "now to search for anything I can find that may prove her to be what I think her—as guilty as her husband. Who knows but I may search out something that mine may turn to account, and obtain for him a sergeant's stripes and a sergeant's pay. It won't be the first time a woman has raised her husband by her wit and perseverance. I feel certain that I shall find something. Yes, I feel quite certain of that."

She silently went down stairs, and commenced a search of the front apartment.

But nothing of an extraordinary character met her gaze.

Taking the candle in her hand, she was about to proceed to the back room, when she recollected she had not looked beneath the mattress of the sofa.

She turned and raised the swab, and the rays of the candle fell upon the pocket-book, hidden there by Jane.

She grasped it eagerly, placed the candle upon the table, and opened it with trepidation.

She was not much of a scholar, but she saw at a glance the name of Ralph Grasper on the first leaf.

With a chuckle she laid it upon the table, took up the candlestick, and walked towards the door, muttering—

"That's something. I'll find something else yet, or I'm much mistaken."

She pulled the door open, uttered a stifled cry of terror, and let fall the light from her hand, which was instantly extinguished.

In the doorway stood a tall figure, with a hideous countenance; a white cloak fell from its shoulders, and its arm was extended towards her, while one word only rang in her ears—

"Wretch!"

For some time she stood trembling in terror, then staggering to the mantleshelf she felt for a lucifer[57] she had placed there in the morning, hurriedly struck a light, and looked around.

The figure was gone, and so also was the pocket-book she had left upon the table.

---

[57] Match.

CHAPTER LIII.

THE SUICIDE'S GRAVE—THE VILLAIN AND HIS PUNISHMENT.

"FELO-DE-SE!"[58]

Such was the verdict of the jury who sat on the inquest on the body of the forger suicide.

James Slater was to be denied Christian burial.

He had usurped God's prerogative—he had taken that life which was not his own, and that, too, when in a sound state of mind, at least, so thought the jury, and he was to be buried like a dog at midnight, in the cross-roads.

What could it matter to that lump of inanimate clay where they placed his bones to moulder into dust?

Nothing.

He could rest as well in the cross-roads as in the consecrated ground.

To dust he must return. What mattered whether he mingled it with the road-side or the grass-bedecked mould of the churchyard, where sculptured stones with lying epitaphs rear their heads, and mark the last homes of many whose hearts were as black, and whose crimes were as great, as the poor suicide's, but whose failing had not been seen by the world.

But though to that dead man it mattered little where they placed his remains, to the living it was a bitter and lasting reproach.

What could be more painful to the feelings of those who loved him in life, revered his memory in death, spite of his faults?

'Tis those on whom the weight of such a verdict falls with crushing effect.

It was another blow to the already suffering heart of the poor wife—an overwhelming blow, and bitterly did she feel it.

But against that verdict there was no appeal. The fiat[59] had gone forth—James Slater must fill a suicide's grave.

But was it just?

On such a point there is always a difference of opinion among mankind.

Jane Slater felt that her husband had been driven to madness by the words she had written on that fatal night, and that in the height of his frenzy he closed his eyes upon the world, which had become hateful to him.

But the jury knew not this, and felo-de-se was their verdict.

The clocks of the various steeples were chiming the quarter to midnight, when the body of the ill-fated man was carried from that once happy home in a common black shell, and jolted along on the shoulders of four rough men, to where four roads met, about a quarter of a mile from the scene of the tragedy.

Half the world was bathed in peaceful slumbers, and thought not, cared not, for the end of him who, in an evil hour, had broken the commandments and his poor wife's heart.

There was but one who closely followed his remains to the grave, and that one was her who so ardently longed to lay by his side.

Weeping piteously, Jane Slater strode with trembling steps through the night air after the black box, heedless of the chilly atmosphere and the lateness of the hour.

---

[58] Literally "Felon of himself" – a legal term referring to the illegal act of suicide.
[59] Decree.

At some distance behind her, however, walked a tall cloaked figure, which, paused as the bearers rested, then silently pursued his way as they went on again. At length the spot was reached, and as the men placed the rude coffin upon the ground beside an opening in the road, the hour of twelve boomed out upon the night air, and another cloaked figure of shorter stature than the one before noticed stepped up beside the grave.

Absorbed by her own grief, Jane paid no heed to the circumstance; in fact, saw not the face, half covered with adhesive plaster, which was turned with a triumphant glance towards her.

Nor did she observe the tall cloaked figure steal silently up behind her, or notice that it held a fold of its long cloak up so as to hide its face.

It was a dark, damp night, not a single star shed a ray of light in heaven's canopy; but suddenly the red glare of a torch lit up the scene with an unearthly lustre.

Jane looked at the black hole and shuddered, then turned her gaze upon the box, and dropped her head upon her bosom, which rose and fell with the choking sobs she gave utterance to.

No other sound broke the stillness, for even those rough men appeared to become impressed with the awful scene.

They lowered the coffin slowly and silently into its last resting-place, as the shorter of the two men stealthily crept up to the side of the agonized wife.

When the shell had been deposited in its place, the silence was broken by the man who held the torch saying—

"Fill in quick. It's confounded cold!"

"No—no!" cried Jane; "not yet. Let me gaze upon him once more!"

She staggered forward as she spoke to the edge of the hole.

"Who is there left to care for me now?" she cried, as she tottered back. "None—none!"

An arm encircled her waist, and, in tones which made her blood curdle in her veins, the words in a hissing whisper saluted her ears—

"Yes, one—myself!"

Jane turned now to meet the ardent gaze of Ralph Grasper.

In an instant her form was drawn up to its full height.

Her tearful eyes flashed with a sudden fire. Her bosom swelled with emotions of insulted dignity instead of grief.

She hurled the arm from her waist, and, in a voice which showed how acutely she felt the insult, she exclaimed— "Wretch! you here?"

"Yes, I'm here, as I would be ever, at your side in moments of grief."

"Accursed villain!" cried Jane, pointing to the grave which the men were fast filling in; "look upon your work! Glory in your triumph over the poor heart-broken wife! Oh! how callous is the heart of him who could come here to insult me with his presence at such an hour! Begone, viper!—dastard!"

"Hold! Jane Slater, or you shall rue your words!"

"Away, I say!"

She stretched forth her hands and pushed him back.

"Again I say beware, or I will so embitter your life, that this moment shall have been the brightest in your existence! Viper! dastard! am I? But you are"—

"What?"

"Thief!" he whispered.

"Ah!"

"Oh! ah! that startles you, does it?" he cried, still in the hissing whisper with which he had carried on the conversation. "I lost my pocket-book—the forged cheque. They were stolen from a cab. I know the thief—and that thief is yourself!"

Jane staggered back, and nearly fell fainting to the earth.

"You will be less violent in your speech I think!" he hissed. "He who lies in that grave placed himself in my power, and felt the weight of my vengeance. Be wise, then, and make me your friend instead of your enemy!"

"Oh! heaven!" gasped Jane, "guide me how to act!"

"Be mine!"

"This to me, and at such a time and place?" cried Jane.

"Refuse, and"—

He seized her hand in his own, in a threatening manner.

"Coward as well as villain!" hissed a voice in his ear, as a vice-like grip fastened on his throat, and he was held at arm's length by the tall cloaked figure, whom neither had before noticed.

So tight was the grasp upon his windpipe, that Ralph Grasper could utter no sound; but a slight scream escaped the lips of Jane, as by the dim light she saw the masked face of Spring-heeled Jack.

Backwards our hero bore the ruffian towards the grave which the men, eager in their task, were filling in, and saw nothing of what was transpiring beyond, then exerting all his powerful strength, he hurled him from him into the hole.

"There, accursed, heartless villain, rest with your victim!" exclaimed Jack.

A cry escaped from Ralph Grasper now—a cry of pain and terror, then a shriek, that rang out upon the night air, and caused the men to pause in their work and fall back from the edge of the grave.

The ruffian's last cry had been called forth by a blow he had received on the head from the spade of one of the men as he fell backwards into the hole, and which, striking him upon the already injured temple, caused him excruciating agony.

A scene of confusion naturally ensued.

The cry of Grasper was echoed by that of Jane, who, half-fainting, fell upon her knees.

In a moment Jack was by her side.

He raised her to her feet.

"Be not alarmed," he cried; "the ruffian shall not injure you."

And he added, sinking his voice to a whisper—

"The pocket-book and cheque shall never be produced against you. They are both in my possession, and shall be buried in the grave of your unfortunate husband."

"Oh! my preserver"—

"Hush!"

The men assisted the half-stunned Ralph from the grave, whose bleeding and patched features looked truly hideous in the red glare of the torch which one of them held up before him.

"What's this mean?" said one.

"I will tell you, my friends," said Jack, advancing, but averting his face from the light, so that they should not see his mask. "This scoundrel has dared to insult the poor,

THE FATE OF CLAVERING.

heart-broken wife of the man you have buried, even at the edge of her husband's grave, and I flung the dastard into the hole."

"Serve him right," said the man with the torch, "if it's true."

"It is. And but that you were engaged with your labour you would have seen and heard what I have, and served him the same."

"It's a lie!" roared Grasper.

"It is true, you unmanly scoundrel!" retorted Jack; "and by heaven, if you dare molest this poor woman further, I will crush every bone in your body!"

"Get out, you old scoundrel!" cried the man with the torch.

"Serve him right to bury him," said another, as Jane, sobbing, came to Jack's side.

"The book and cheque," she said, in a whisper.

He grasped her arm with one hand, while with the other he dropped the pocket-book from beneath his cloak into the hole.

"They will be found."

"Never fear. They are hidden for ever."

And as he spoke, he hurled with his foot a quantity of the loose earth over the edge of the hole into the grave, and by the light of the torch saw they were covered from view.

A sigh of relief broke from her lips, and she tottered backwards.

"I say it's a lie," cried Grasper, who had become fearful of the threatening looks of the men. "He is a villain, who dares not show his face. If you are men, seize him. It is Spring-heeled Jack!"

"Spring-heeled Jack?" broke from each throat.

"Yes. The midnight marauder whom the police are seeking in every quarter, and for whose capture you will be well rewarded. Seize him—seize him!"

Jack turned quickly.

The torch-light fell on his hideous mask.

The men fell back startled, leaving Grasper alone.

"Yes, I am Spring-heeled Jack," cried our hero, "the terror of such hoary-headed old sinners as this—the protector of the weak and defenceless. I am he, and good cause has this ruffian to recollect me, for I have several times foiled his villainy. There is a reward offered for my capture; but take me if you can, or follow me if you dare!"

"I'll have a shy for it," exclaimed one of the men, springing forward with his spade upraised.

Jack saw his danger, and was prepared for it, but he did not take one of those terrific leaps backward which had so often saved him.

He seized Grasper by the arms, and as the man attempted to strike him, he hurled the rascally merchant forward, and the blow intended for himself fell upon the shoulder of Ralph, who instantly sank to the ground beneath its force.

"Oh, heaven! you have killed him, cried Jane.

"No such luck as that," said Jack. "My friend, you would have conferred a greater favour on society had you slain that man than you could do by effecting my capture."

The fellow, appalled at his own act, dropped the spade, and stood looking half frightened at the prostrate merchant.

The others, also, alarmed at their companion's rash act, flung down their implements, and raised Ralph from the ground, paying no heed to our hero.

"Return home," said Jack, in a whisper; "I will follow to see that no harm befalls you."

"But you are in danger. Seek your own safety, for now that I know that book is hidden there, I can defy him."

"Heed not me," whispered Jack, "but retire. You have paid the last respect to the memory of your husband, and this is no longer a place for you."

"Heaven help me! would I were with him!" sighed Jane.

"Come, come," whispered Jack, "do not gratify the feelings of yon villain by a sight of your grief. Go."

"No, you don't go," said Grasper, who had caught the last word. "You shall not go."

"Who shall prevent me?" asked Jack.

"This shall!" exclaimed Ralph, taking a small pocket pistol from his breast, and levelling it at our hero, as he staggered a few paces forward.

"No—no—no!" cried Jane, flinging herself between them. "You shall not harm him but through my body!"

"Curse him! he shall die!" exclaimed the merchant, furiously.

Jane flung herself upon him, and strove to tear the weapon from his hold.

"Men—men!" she cried, "will you aid a murderer?"

But ere either of those called upon made any reply, or Grasper could accomplish his purpose, Jack was upon him.

Seizing his wrist, he tore the weapon from his hand, and laid its cold barrel upon the heated brow of the merchant.

"Villain! why should I not blow your brains out?" he cried.

"Spare him—spare him!" pleaded Jane, turning quickly.

"Can you plead for him who slew your husband?" asked Jack.

"I would not have you his executioner. You are too good to stain your hands in the blood of such a base-hearted, unfeeling villain!" said Jane.

"Yes," said Jack; "he is even too bad to destroy."

"But you ain't, old fellow, now I've got you!" cried one of the men, seizing Jack by the shoulder. "Help, mates!—help!"

With a thrust, Jack freed himself, and springing backwards, levelled the pistol at his would-be captors.

CHAPTER LIV.

THE ESCAPE FROM THE PATROL—JACK SEEKS SAFETY ON THE HOUSETOPS.

THE man must be brave indeed who can unflinchingly stare into the barrel of a pistol when a desperate man's finger is on the trigger, and the weapon is loaded.

Certain it is, that among those who stood before our hero, there was not one endowed with the amount of courage necessary to perform the feat.

In terror and dismay they fell back, and Grasper slunk behind the man who had struck him.

A considerable distance was soon left between Jack and his would-be captors.

Jack could fairly have laughed outright at the figures they cut in the strange, dim light.

"Why don't you take me?" he said, at length. "Is not the reward offered for my capture sufficient? If not, I have no doubt that, to gratify his revenge, yonder cringing rascal will double it out of the sums of money he has wrung from those who have had dealings with him."

"I'll treble it," cried Grasper, "though it ruined me. I'll treble it."

"Kind of you," said Jack. "But hark you, Ralph Grasper; on the first attempt of either man to endeavour to avail himself of your offer, I'll send a bullet through your brain."

"Don't attempt it, then, my good men—don't attempt it," said the merchant, quickly, as one man made a step forward. "But he shall pay dearly for this night's work, and so shall she. I put her husband in jail, and there she shall go too. He broke it only to cut his throat, and there lies in his suicide's grave."

"Oh, unfeeling monster!" cried Jane.

"You shall find me so. You have robbed me. I have proof of it—proof from the police, and you shall suffer—bitterly suffer for it."

"Heed him not," said Jack; "he is powerless to harm you, other than by his cruel words."

"Think so—think so," he cried, joyfully. "But your hopes shall soon be annihilated."

"Look you, you scoundrel," said Jack, "it will be the worst day's work you have done yet —and you have done many—if you, by word or deed, cause this poor woman another pang. See that your villainy rests where it is, or it would be better for you we never met."

Then turning to Jane, he said—

"Go now, and fear not. This scene is painful in more ways than one. Let me beg of you to go home."

"Home?"

"Yes."

"What is home to me now?"

"A place where, at least, you will be free from the sight of that man's face and the sound of his voice."

"I fear lest he will follow me and again urge his hated proposals," said Jane.

"He dare not."

"Ah! but he is bad enough to do so," she replied.

"True; but not while I am near you," said Jack. "Besides, he is suffering too much from the treatment he has received to prevent you reaching home unmolested."

"Then I will go; but oh! be careful of yourself. Your kindness to me has made you many enemies."

"I fear them not."

"They are many—you are one."

"No matter. This weapon is a match for them; and if not, they could never overtake me," said Jack.

"God bless you, then. I shall never forget your kindness to me and him who has gone."

"Who?"

"My husband."

"Your husband?"

"Yes. Mrs. Baintree told me that a man in a mask aided him to escape, and I know it must have been you," said Jane, in a whisper.

"Hush! Who is Mrs. Baintree?"

"The woman who has been set as a watch over me."

"Her from whom I got the pocket-book, and gave such a fright?" asked Jack.

"I know not; for till now I knew not you had it."

"Do not mention that you know who aided your husband to escape, though I wish to heaven now I had never done so," said Jack.

"I will not."

While speaking, Jack kept his eyes fixed upon Grasper and the men, and observed that they were gradually drawing nearer to him.

"They intend to make another attempt," he said, quickly. "Away with you, and doubtless we shall meet again ere long."

The woman cast one more look towards her husband's grave, then turned and left the spot.

Jack also shifted his position a few paces back, and either from accident or design, the torch went out, leaving the place as dark as pitch.

Thinking it to have been designedly extinguished, so as to enable the men the better to effect his capture, Jack bounded away some distance further, and shaded his eyes with his hands, and looked towards the grave near which the men stood.

His eyes quickly becoming accustomed to the sudden darkness into which he had been plunged, he could perceive two of the men coming towards him.

"All right," thought Jack. "They are bent upon earning the reward, and placing me in limbo. They deserve something to recollect me by, and they shall have it."

He flung himself down upon his hands and knees, and waited for the men to come up.

He had only to wait a few seconds when they were close upon him.

Then up he bounded quickly, striking out his clenched fist as he did so.

The blow fell fair between the eyes of the foremost man, and sent him down as if shot.

The other made a grasp at our hero, but Jack cleared him, and alighted some seven or eight feet beyond him.

Turning quickly ere the man could recover from his surprise, he dealt the fellow a heavy kick in the back, which sent him sprawling over his companion.

"Have you got the villain?" cried Grasper, tottering up to near where Jack stood.

"To be sure they have," said Jack. "Here he is."

"The devil!" cried the merchant, retreating upon perceiving that Jack stood before him.

"No, sir; but what you are not—a man," answered Jack, thrusting him aside. "I'm off now. But mark me, do not further molest that woman, or our next meeting may be fatal to you."

So saying, he darted off in the direction where Jane Slater had gone.

He had not proceeded far, however, before he heard the sound of a horse's hoofs coming along the road at a quick gallop.

"Hallo!" he muttered; "who's this? It must be the patrol, and doubtless he has heard at the cross road I am about this quarter. I've no wish to fall in with the fellow; but there is no help for it."

In another minute a mounted patrol reined in his steed, as he called out, in a gruff tone—

"Who goes there?"

"A man, to be sure," said Jack.

"Yes; and the one I want, or I'm much mistaken."

"What do you want with me?" asked Jack, in a feigned tone of surprise.

The man urged his horse close up to our hero, and bending in the saddle, exclaimed—

"You're the man!"

"Me?"

"Yes."

"What man?"

"Spring-heeled Jack."

"Am I?"

"You are."

"How do you know that?"

"By your mask."

Oh! So you want me, do you?" said Jack, coolly.

"I do."

"What for?"

"To take you into custody."

"On what charge?"

"Several."

"That's a vague answer."

"Clear enough for you. But if you wish for a better, for nearly killing an old gentleman, and assaulting two men at the cross road engaged in burying the body of a suicide," replied the patrol, placing his hand on one of the large pistols in his holsters. "It's no use attempting to resist, Jack, and your jumping will avail you nothing. A bullet can leap farther than you can, and fly ever so much faster."

"Then if I attempt to get away, you will shoot me?"

"Assuredly."

"Will the law allow you to do that?" asked Jack.

"I think it will, if you resist it," was the reply.

"Then, of course, it would be madness for me to attempt to fly."

"It would."

"Well, I suppose I must give in."

"You had better."

"I surrender."

"That's wise of you, Jack. It's better to go quietly."

"Of course it is."

The patrol took his hand from his pistols with the intention of seizing Jack's arm, which he intended to fasten to the horse's trappings, when our hero stepped back and levelled his pistol at his head.

"Hold!" said Jack. "I'm a good shot, and if you attempt to place your hand on your holsters, I'll take off your fingers with a bullet."

"Ah!" exclaimed the man.

"You will cry 'oh!' if you do not take my advice."

"Do you resist?"

"Capture, do you mean?"

"Yes."

"Most decidedly. I have a great objection to being dragged to prison; I love freedom too much, my friend."

"You know not the consequences of such an act as this."

"You are wrong there."

"Then you must be mad."

"I should be to allow you to take me," said Jack, with a grin. "Be careful, now. The moment you move your hand to the holster, off go your fingers."

The man drew back his hand, and placed it upon the hilt of his sword.

As he drew it from its scabbard, Jack dealt the horse a kick in the stomach, which caused the animal to rear up so suddenly that the patrol was thrown violently to the ground.

Slipping the weapon quickly into his breast pocket, Jack bounded away along the road with the speed of an antelope.

He knew not whether the man was stunned or not by the fall; if not, he felt sure he would soon be in the saddle and in hot pursuit.

So Jack made the best of his time, and struggled hard to reach the inhabited part of the road, believing that he could the better evade capture there than in the open country.

"If I should be taken now," he muttered to himself, as he ran, "that villain, Grasper, would be persecuting this poor woman again, and I have every wish to shield her from his insults. What's that? By heaven, the fellow's in the saddle again, and in hot pursuit! I'll wager he has taken the precaution to take his pistols from the holsters this time; and if he has, that fall will have so incensed him that I cannot expect much mercy at his hands. Flight is my only chance now."

It was evident that the patrol was coming on at a furious rate, and Jack redoubled his exertions to reach the row of houses a short distance ahead, ere he was overtaken.

In this he succeeded, and bounding up he went over the garden wall of the first house, which was thickly covered on the top by broken glass bottles.

However, Jack cleared them easily, and alighted safely in the centre of a bed of choice plants.

"It's too bad," he muttered, "to destroy people's property like this; but then my life is of more value to me than a few flowers which can be replaced."

He heard the patrol pass by the next moment at a furious pace.

"Escaped this time," he said, as he looked around him as well as the darkness would allow him to see. "Hallo! we should never hallo till out of the wood."

This last remark was called forth by the sudden ceasing of the clatter of the horse's hoofs.

The man had reined in his steed, and had risen in his stirrups, and was endeavouring to look over the garden wall, believing that Jack had taken refuge beyond it.

Jack suspected this was what the patrol was after, and not wishing to be discovered, he hurried across the garden towards an outhouse he could discern through the gloom, and quickly got behind it.

Here he paused and listened.

In a few moments there was a loud knocking, and Jack knew that the patrol was arousing the inmates of the house, in order to obtain admission to the grounds.

"I mustn't stop here," said Jack, "and where to go puzzles me, for the whole neighbourhood will be aroused in a few minutes. In the road I shall stand little chance against the horse, and in these gardens I am pretty sure to be discovered. I have it. The roof, if there's a means of reaching it. The day will soon break, and a view of the rising sun from an eminence is worth seeing. Oh! there's a foothold there, and so I shall manage it easy enough, and my dark cloak will shield me from observation."

Without more ado, Jack clambered up on to the roof of the outhouse, and thence on to a window-sill. Then grasping at a water-pipe, he drew himself up by its aid, till he reached, the roof, and laying himself flat down upon the tiles, rested from the exertions he had made to reach it, and listened for any further sounds that might come to his ears.

CHAPTER LV.
THE SWEEP'S TERROR—A SCENE IN THE PARLOUR OF A SUBURBAN VILLA.

SLOWLY broke the morning—slowly from the east the light clouds drifted, chasing the dark vapours of night, which rolled on before the coming sun.

The feathered songsters, one by one, awoke, and, lifting their head from beneath their wing, carolled forth their hymn of praise for the coming day.

The lark rose from the grass, warbling its wild music as it took its heavenward flight; the rook, with flapping wings and discordant noise, started from its nest to seek the morning meal; and then streaks of burnished gold spread over the sky, and the bright orb of day threw its refulgent light over the earth.

Slumbering nature awoke.

Then streaks of smoke rose towards the clouds, the hum of voices broke upon the air, and the quick tread of the artisan was heard on his way to toil, and still Jack stood upon the housetop, gazing towards the east, watching the changing hues of the clouds, and almost lost in rapture at the magnificent sight before him.

Those who have never stood on an eminence and watched the rising sun have lost a treat indeed, and he whose heart could not be warmed by its beauties must be cold indeed.

The patrol, unable to discover our hero in the garden, had gone on his way, but when Jack had made up his mind to abscond and seek to get out of the locality, he perceived him returning in company with another mounted officer, and therefore concluded that it were better to remain where he was for the present.

Satisfied that he was still about, the patrol kept a sharp look-out in all directions, but made no attempt to arouse the inhabitants.

They evidently had no suspicion of his true whereabouts. They believed he was secreted somewhere in the garden, and that sooner or later he would make his way into the road, when he could be easily captured.

The hour flew by, however, and Jack still kept his position, gazing with admiration upon the scene before him, or turning a smiling look down upon the two horsemen as they conversed together in the street below.

At length the clock of a distant steeple chimed the half-hour after five, and the patrol rode slowly away.

Waiting a short time, Jack was about to descend, but resolving to take one more look upon the gorgeous scene, he sprang to the top of a high chimney-pot, and scanned the eastern horizon. A scratching kind of sound, which appeared to come from a neighbouring chimney, caused him to gaze towards it, and the next moment a brush protruded from a pot before him.

"A sweep!" he said; "I must vacate my post, or I shall be blinded with soot."

He was about to leap down to the roof, when the head and shoulders of a young sweep protruded from the chimney-pot, and Jack, ever anxious for fun, slipped on his mask, drew himself up to his full height, and extended his arms widely.

The lad turned, and his gaze falling upon the tall, ghostly figure and hideous face of our hero, he uttered a loud cry of terror, and, losing all power, slipped back down the chimney, never stopping in his course till he reached the room below, on the floor of which he rolled, screaming and bellowing with all the force of his lungs.

"The devil! the devil! the devil!"

His voice not only aroused the servant-of-all-work, who had risen to admit him, but also her master and mistress, and a young lady who rejoiced in the title of mistress's daughter.

The servant Mary, who at the time was preparing breakfast, rushed hurriedly into the room to learn the cause of the disturbance, and perceiving the little fellow rolling on the floor, at once came to the conclusion that he was in a fit.

The first thing she did was to scream, the second to shriek, and the third to rush like mad into the kitchen, where she nearly overturned the table and upset the coffee-pot.

Brought a little to her senses by this event, she hurried to the sink, and quickly filled a large jug with water.

With this she hurried back to the apartment where the puny sweep was.

The boy had scrambled to his feet, but the look of fright still remained on his features.

The moment Mary appeared in the doorway he burst forth with the cry which had before alarmed her—

"The devil! oh, the devil!"

"Poor fellow!" said Mary, seizing the jug by the handle, "so young, and such a sufferer!"

And then she flung the contents of the jug fair in his face, and darted back, calling loudly on her master and mistress.

The shock to his system caused by the cold water added to his terror, and the young sweep howled and screamed furiously, causing the maid to pull to the door of the apartment, and add to the confusion by loud cries of—

"Master!— Missus!—Miss Jane!—oh, do come down! He's mad, and we shall all be murdered! Mr. Pratt!— Mr. Pratt! Oh, do get up—do—do!"

"What's the matter, Mary?" cried Mr. Pratt, from his bedroom.

"The—the sweep, sir; he's gone mad, sir— he'll murder us all, sir. Oh, do come down, sir! Do, sir—do!"

Not only did Mr. Pratt hurry on his garment, but also Mrs. and Miss Pratt, a showy young lady of eighteen, who, flinging a morning wrapper around her graceful form, flung open her bedroom door, and hurried down the stairs.

"Goodness gracious, Mary! what is the matter?" she cried.

"Oh! miss! oh! miss! he's stark staring raving mad!" was the reply.

"Who?"

"The—the—Oh! he's so flabbergasted, miss, that I—oh! dear!—oh! dear!"

"What is all this about?"

"The devil, miss!"

"The devil, you silly girl?"

"Yes, miss."

"What do you mean?"

"The devil, miss! He says the devil!"

"Who?"

"The sweep."

"Do tell me what it's all about. There, don't shake like that, but tell me all about it—the cause of this disturbance, I mean."

"Yes, miss. You see, miss, I—oh! dear! I'm so frightened! "

Miss Pratt pushed the girl on one side, and entered the parlour, where she encountered the young sweep trembling like an aspen leaf, and looking fearfully at the chimney he had been commissioned to cleanse.

"What is the meaning of this noise?" she asked.

"Th—the de—de—devil!" cried the boy. "He's on the top of the house, looking down the chimney."

At this moment, a brick, loosened by the boy's descent, fell with a loud crash on to the stone.

"Here he is!—oh! here he is!" cried the boy. "Murder! Save me!—oh! save me!"

And he rushed up to Miss Pratt, threw his arms around her, and buried his wet sooty face in the clean folds of her morning wrapper.

"Go away, you nasty, dirty little rascal—go away!" cried the young lady, endeavouring to shake him off.

"Do—do—don't!—oh! don't let him touch me!" cried the boy, twining his sooty arms around her.

"Richard—Richard!" cried the young lady, endeavouring to shake him off. "Oh! make haste—make haste! The sweeper's gone mad!"

"No, I ain't mad! It's the devil!—it's the devil! He's coming down the chimney! Oh! save me, some one!" yelled the boy.

And in his terror, he clutched at Miss Pratt's dress, which he sooted from one side to the other, the soot smearing her all over, and, which being wet with the water which they had thrown over him, came off easily.

Mr. Pratt here entered the room, but stood transfixed with surprise the moment he entered the apartment.

"Get away, you nasty, dirty, little rascal!" cried the lady. "Oh! Richard, take him away, he'll spoil my wrapper."

Down came another brick clattering against the bars of the stove.

"Murder!" cried the boy. "Oh! don't let him come—don't, don't!"

And leaving go his hold of Miss Pratt he rushed at Mr. Pratt, whom he caught round the waist, and clung to like grim death.

Mr. Pratt had only waited to put on his boots and trousers, and the sooty hand of the sweep resting on his shirt-front, turned the spotless white linen front to the colour of a soot-bag.

"You young imp," growled the gentleman, "what do you mean by playing up such pranks as this?"

"Oh! sir, the devil—the devil!" was all the boy could say in answer to the gentleman.

"Are you mad?"

"No; I'm"——

"Take your hands off, you black villain!" cried the man, hurling the youngster off him, and sending him into the fireplace, where he floundered about among the loose soot which had fallen from the chimney.

"Send for a policeman," cried Miss Pratt. "Here's a state the little wretch has made me in. Only look at me; all this nice clean wrapper spoilt!"

"Oh! don't—don't," roared the boy, springing to his feet. "It ain't my fault, it's the devil's!"

"The devil take you!" roared Pratt.

And in his rage at the state the sooty little varmint had made him in, he rushed with upraised hand towards the boy.

"I'll kill you, you little villain," he yelled, "I'll kill you!"

At this juncture Mrs. Pratt entered the room, surprise and terror on every lineament of her features, and the boy, fearful of chastisement, and anxious to escape, ran full butt against her as she entered.

The knock caused her to roll over, and down on top of her went the young sweep, covering her with soot.

The lady screamed loudly, and so did the sweep, while Mr. Pratt swore as he never swore before, and Miss Pratt called loudly for the police.

A scene of confusion that beggars description now ensued.

Kicking, plunging, and screaming, the sweep endeavoured to scramble to his feet.

Yelling with terror, and not knowing what she did, Mrs. Pratt grappled with the sooty little rascal.

Mary rushed to the street-door, and yelled loudly for help, while Mr. Pratt had all his work to do in holding his sister, whom the excitement had caused to swoon away.

Meantime Jack, who had been a listener down the chimney, and who felt it was high time to reach *terra firma*, descended by the way he had got up, and springing over the wall, hastily slipped off his mask, and appeared at the front door at the moment that the maid-of-all-work called loudly for assistance.

"What is the matter?" cried Jack, in tones of surprise. "What is the matter?"

"Oh, sir—do come in, sir! There's a sweep gone mad, and he's rolling missus about on the floor! Oh, do come in, sir, I'm so frightened!"

Jack could well believe that, for the girl's face was as white as a ghost's, and she shook in every limb.

"I do not like to intrude," he said.

"Oh, don't mind that, sir—do come," cried the girl, catching him by the arm, and dragging him into the passage.

Nothing loth, Jack went into the parlour, and as he perceived how matters stood, he burst into a loud peal of laughter.

Covered with soot stood Mrs. Pratt, who had risen to her feet, holding by the hair of his head the young sweep, pinned firmly against the wall of the parlour, while Mr. Pratt was holding his sister, and in vain endeavouring to bring her to consciousness by fanning her face with a book which he had taken from a side-table.

Their faces, hands, and dresses besmeared with soot—the half-frightened, half-angry expression of their features, and the grotesque attitude of the little party was too much for the risibility of our hero, and, leaning his back against the doorpost, he laughed long and loudly.

At length he managed to gasp out—

"What, in heaven's name, is the matter here?"

"The matter?" echoed Pratt.

"This little villain"—began his wife.

"The devil!" yelled the boy.

"This wretch—this demon—this sweep," continued Mrs. Pratt, "is mad—quite mad! Look at him—see what he's done! Oh, sir, do get a policeman—send for his master—anything—so that we get him away from here!"

"Be calm, my good woman," said Jack, "and take your hand from the boy. The little fellow is alarmed—frightened."

"But he'll fly at us—he flew at me just now, and if he bites we shall all die of hydrophobia," cried Mrs. Pratt.

"I'll take care that he does not harm you, my good lady," said Jack. "Let go of him—you hurt the lad."

Thus addressed, the lady released her hold of the young sweep, and sprang quickly to the other side of the room.

"Now, boy, what's the meaning of this?" continued Jack, looking at him sternly.

"Oh—oh—oh!" was the only answer he received to his question.

Jack stooped, quickly adjusted his mask to his face, and raising his head, cried—

"Tell me at once!"

A yell of terror broke from the boy's lips, and he sprang across the room, and clutched wildly at Mrs. Pratt.

Slipping his mask off again, Jack turned to the lady.

"Oh, the devil!" yelled the boy. "Hide me—hide me! It's the devil—it's the devil!"

And in his terror he drew the light morning garment of Mrs. Pratt around him.

With a cry of mingled rage and terror the lady endeavoured to shake him off.

But in vain. Terror had lent him strength, and he only clung the tighter, yelling all the while—

"Oh, it's the devil!"

"He's mad," said Jack, "quite mad. We had better secure him, and then send for his master. Oh! here's his bag. It will answer as well as a straight-jacket. Put him in that, and secure it round his neck, and he can do no harm then."

He made a movement as if to seize the lad, when the young sweep yelled loudly, and, breaking away from the lady, dashed madly for the door, where the maid-of-all-work stood trembling and powerless to move, and against whom, in his eagerness to escape, he ran full butt, knocking her backwards into the passage, and losing his own balance in the concussion, rolled over her, yelling and screaming as if the devil himself had really got hold of him.

Struggling to his feet, he dashed along the passage, and out of the street-door into the road, leaving our hero to gaze upon as comical and curious a scene as ever he witnessed in his life, and, spite of all his endeavours, he could not prevent himself from shrieking with laughter.

Under the pretence of flogging the young sweep, he made his way out of the house, and, pulling the door to behind him, hurried on his way.

CHAPTER LVI.
JACK AND THE JEW—LEVY IN A FIX.

ON went the cab containing Mr. Levy, the Jew clothier, and our hero for some distance down the Mile End-road, before Jack again addressed the Israelite.

"Mr. Levy," he said, at last, "do you not think that you are a most confounded scoundrel?"

"Holy Moses!" groaned Levy, his teeth chattering more with cold than fright, "what a thing it is to be persecuted."

"Don't you think you ought to be prosecuted?" asked Jack.

"Our race have been persecuted for years, but the day of reckoning will come, when the Gentile"—

"Bosh!" said Jack; "you canting old humbug, when that day of reckoning comes, you will have a sad account to answer for. How many do you think you have robbed and cheated in your time? I am not particular as to the units, the tens will do. Now, how many?"

"Father Abraham."

"Never mind about him, but answer my question," said Jack.

"Not one!"

"That's a—but I will not be so rude, Mr. Levy," said Jack, "as to use such an epithet; but you speak falsely for all that. Come, now, Mr. Levy, make me your confidant. How many have you robbed directly or indirectly, legally or morally, in your lifetime?"

"Me rob! Holy Moses, it's myself that's being robbed daily, hourly; myself—yes, myself," groaned the Israelite.

"And yet you are a thriving, prosperous man, Mr. Levy?" said Jack.

"Me!"

"You."

"No—oh, no! I'm ruined—always being ruined by the hated Christians. I employ—I give them work, and they rob me. I pay them money, and they grumble. They are never satisfied, never—never!"

"Ah! Mr. Levy," said Jack, "it would be a sad thing for the poor devils who have to obtain their bread by labour, were such as you the only employers."

"Such as me?"

"Yes."

"They would thrive and prosper. I give too much for my work, for I've got a kind heart, and so I am imposed upon. First I'm robbed, and then I'm insulted, and when I ask for justice, I am smitten on the cheek, dragged to the police-station, and"—

"Honoured by a ride in a coach with Spring-heeled Jack," interrupted our hero. "Well, how do you like my company?"

"Not at all."

"You don't?"

"No."

"I'm sorry for that, because you see, Mr. Levy, I'm a first-rate fellow."

"You're a"—

He paused.

He did not like to finish the sentence, lest Jack should take umbrage at it.

"What am I, Mr. Levy?"

"Nothing."

"Oh, but you'll find you're mistaken."

"Shall I!"

"Yes, before we part."

The Jew heaved a deep sigh. He fain[60] would have called to the driver to stop, and have given Jack into the charge of the police, but be dreaded lest our hero might proceed to violent acts, so he concluded to remain quiet, and let matters take their own course. He crouched up in the corner of the vehicle, and inwardly cursed Jack, and every Gentile in Christendom.

They were nearing Whitechapel, when the Jew, putting his head from the window of the vehicle, called to the driver to pull up.

"Do you get out here?" asked Jack.

"Yes."

"Well, I don't think I shall let you," he said. "I wish to go to the West-end, and as you are such charming company, I cannot afford to lose you."

"But I must get out here. Stop! driver—stop!" he roared, leaning half out of the window.

"All right, sir," said the man, pulling up.

Jack pulled the Jew back into the vehicle, and thrusting his head out, cried—

"Go on, driver. Why don't you go on?"

The words and the change of voice caused the driver of the vehicle to look hastily round.

The Jew turned to the opposite window.

"Stop! stop!" he cried.

"Go on!" exclaimed Jack.

The man, puzzled, leaped from his box.

"What the dev—oh! I'm blow'd!"

He had got a glimpse of Jack's mask, and started back as if shot.

"Let me out!" cried the Jew, who had tried the handle of the door, but was detained by Jack, who had caught hold of his coat.

"Will you oblige me by driving on?" said Jack.

The man made no reply. He could only stand and stare in amazement and terror.

"Will you oblige me by moving your vehicle on?" said Jack.

"Who the devil are you?" cried the driver. "I didn't take you for a fool."

"My friend, it would be as well if you did not take my name in vain," said Jack.

"Your name?"

"Yes."

"I'm blessed if I know what you mean or how you got here, whoever you are."

"Then I'll tell you. I'm the gentleman you spoke of—the devil; and I've got a rascal here in my charge, whom I'm going to take"—

"To hell!" cried the man, springing back.

"I did not say so; but if you do not instantly mount your cab, and drive us to the West-end, I shall be under the painful necessity of taking you to the same place."

"That be"—

---

[60] Happily.

"Hush!" said Jack. "Remember in whose presence you stand."

"He's Spring-heeled Jack," cried the Jew; "don't be frightened—he's only Spring-heeled Jack. Let me out—let me out! Call the police—call the police!"

"Spring-heeled Jack!" cried the man.

"Yes, it's him—it's him! Let me out. I'll give him in charge—I'll"—

"No, you won't," said the man; "for curse me if he ain't the best friend to coachmen—you get your fare out of him. Where do you want to go, sir?"

"Let me get out," roared the Jew.

"Stay where you are, if you please," said Jack. "I've not done with you yet awhile, Mr. Levy."

"I won't be detained against my will."

"But you must."

"I won't, I say."

"We'll see. Sit down."

"I won't sit down. Police!—police!" cried the Jew, loudly.

"Now look here, Mr. Levy, if you are wise you'll be silent," said Jack.

"I'm in my wet clothes; I'll catch my death of cold."

"Very likely," said Jack; "and the sooner you die the better, for you are neither use nor ornament."

"Driver, will you let me out?"

"Certainly not," said Jack. "The driver is engaged by me, and for the time being is my servant."

"It's a lie; I engaged him."

"Will you pay him his fare?"

"Yes."

"What is your fare, driver? Don't be afraid to ask too much, as my friend is a very wealthy man," said Jack.

"It's false! I'm poor—very poor!" gasped the Israelite.

"Well, sir, my fare is"—

"Ten pounds," said Jack, interrupting him; "ten pounds, unless you made an arrangement before he got into your vehicle."

"Ten?"

"Yes, ten," said Jack, pointedly. "That is the sum I should give if the driver obeyed me in every particular; but of course, if he feels disposed to look upon you as his fare, I don't suppose he'll get more than ten pence. But you were not the person who engaged him—it was myself."

The driver of the vehicle scratched his head thoughtfully.

"Now then, driver, who is your fare—me or him?" asked Jack.

"Why you, sir, to be sure," said the man, with a grin.

"I engaged you, and this rascal"—

"Drive on! drive on!" said Jack.

"Where to, sir?"

"The devil, if you like," said Jack, unless you know where there is a good deep pond that you would not mind your vehicle standing in the centre of."

"A pond, sir!"

"Let me get out!" cried Levy. "Thieves! murder! police!"

"Hold that row," said Jack, "or I shall be under the painful necessity of gagging you."

The Jew sank back upon the cushion with a deep sigh.

"Oh, father Abraham," he groaned, "deliver me from the hands of the Philistines."

Jack touched the driver's arm.

"This is a painful case," he said.

The man looked surprised.

"Very painful," continued Jack, slipping a sovereign into his hand. "You see my friend is a little touched in the upper storey."

The man looked still more puzzled.

"He has attempted to commit suicide—the fact is, he is decidedly mad."

"Me mad—me mad!" cried the Jew.

"Be calm," said Jack. "Hark you, driver; my friend is now quite mad, and if you will drive us to Marylebone Workhouse the fare I mentioned shall be yours."

"I'll drive you to the other end of the world, sir, for that," said the coachman.

"No, you won't," gasped Levy; "I live just here; I won't go any further."

"You hear this poor fellow, how he roars," said Jack, pinching the coachman's arm, and giving him a meaning glance. "Drive us to the place I have named, and ten pounds shall be yours."

"Do you mean it, sir?" said the man, in an undertone.

"I do; and I suppose you are not above accepting it."

"No, sir, nor double, that."

Jack, still grasping the coat of Levy, so that he could not move, bent his head to the coachman's ear, and whispered—

"I will double it if you will aid me in this bit of fun."

"You mean no harm, sir?"

"Of course not."

"Then I'll do it."

"Mount your box, and drive on, then, quickly. There's a good night's work for you, and no fear of getting into trouble."

The man required no second bidding, but leaped at once on to the box of his vehicle, and gathering the reins in his hand, lashed the horse with the whip.

"Stop! stop!" said Levy,

"Go!" said Jack. "Silence, will you? I should be sorry to be compelled to use harsh measures, but if you utter another word I must gag you."

"Oh!" groaned Levy.

"You are quite mad. Poor fellow, it grieves me to see you thus."

"Me mad? Me!"

"Yes, you, Mr. Levy."

"It's a lie!"

"A very sad case."

"Mad!" gasped the Jew, in tones of horror.

"Quite. But do not let us converse upon so painful a subject."

"I'm not mad. I'm as sane as ever I was in my life."

"Poor fellow! how he raves," said Jack.

"My dear sir, I pray you be calm; now do— there's a good man."

Levy fairly gasped for breath.

"Mad!" he muttered. "Me mad!"

"As a March hare," said Jack. "No man in his sane mind would attempt to commit suicide."

"I never attempted to commit suicide," cried Levy.

"You did not?"

"No!"

"You mustn't say that now, when you are dripping wet," said Jack.

"If the man don't stop his horse, I'll leap out," cried Levy.

"Is that the act of a sane man, Mr. Levy? I tell you, you are stark, staring, raving mad!"

"It's a lie—it's a"—

"Be quiet."

"I won't."

"Then I must gag you."

"Help!—help!"

Jack flung his arms around the body of the Jew, and flung him down on to the bottom of the vehicle.

"I see there's no help for it," he said; "I must gag you."

"Murder!—mur"—

His further utterance was checked by Jack suddenly whipping his cambric handkerchief over the Jew's mouth.

Levy struggled, but Jack was a powerful man, and the Jew was but a child in his grasp.

He soon had the handkerchief securely fastened over his mouth, and tied at the back of his neck.

Then lifting him on to the seat, he said in a mocking tone—

"A clear case of confirmed madness. Every precaution should be taken to prevent his doing injury to himself. It's criminal to allow his hands to be at liberty. Better tie them behind his back. Poor fellow! what a sad affliction."

Levy strove to call out, but was unable to utter a sound.

In utter despair he suffered his head to fall upon his bosom, and Jack, tearing off the Jew's neckerchief, pinioned his arms behind his back.

"There," said Jack, "he cannot have brandy now. It's a hard case—a very hard case; but doubtless the doctors at the workhouse well know how to treat him for his malady."

Powerless to speak or move, the Jew leaned back against the cushions glaring upon our hero, who, with a smile upon his face—he having removed his mask—sat opposite to him.

The vehicle rolled quickly over the stones, and in the course of an hour drew up at the door of the Marylebone Workhouse.

"Come," said Jack, "we have arrived at our destination."

CHAPTER LVII.

INSIDE THE WORKHOUSE—JACK REVENGES HIMSELF ON THE JEW.

A TROOP of ill-clad, ill-looking, wretched beings, of both sexes, stood and sat huddled around the workhouse door, waiting to see whether the master's heart would soften, or the porter, without the orders of his superior, admit them for the night, when the vehicle which contained our hero and the Jew clothier drove up.

As the vehicle stopped before the door, and the driver dismounted from his box, inquiring and jealous glances were cast towards it by those who felt that though they could not themselves gain admission, the object in that conveyance, whoever it might be, would be able to do so.

Want and privation sours the temper, and the heart often swells with hatred where it should throb with pity.

A hungry stomach is not the thing to make men charitable, and cause them to look upon their more fortunate fellow-creatures with loving kindness. On the contrary, it excites envy and distrust, embitters their whole nature, and drives them to imagine that heaven's gifts are misapplied.

Angry glances then were darted at the vehicle, and low mutterings in discontented tones ran round the throng.

"Some bloke as can afford to be took where he can be paid for," said one.

"'Tis a shame," said another. "There's no pity for them as deserves it—oh, no. Them as can pay for coaches don't ought to come to workhouses and keep them out as can't."

A groan of contempt followed this remark, and the features of the hungry crew grew black as midnight when Jack leaped lightly from the coach.

"Hi!" called out the driver, "just knock at the door will you, one of you."

"Knock yourself," said a gaunt, half-starved fellow in rags. "We ain't a-going to knock for people to get in as can afford to pay their bed and grub, and we may knock till to-morrow before they'd let us in as ain't got nothing to eat, no, nor place to doss."[61]

"See that the Jew does not attempt to get out of the vehicle," whispered Jack, "and I'll drive this poor set of wretches away from the door."

"You'll get badly treated if you try, sir," said the man. "They're like tigers when they're hungry, they are."

"Do my bidding," said Jack," and you'll see."

So walking up to the door he looked round upon the ragged group, who had all risen to their feet, and said—

"Do you want to get in?"

"We don't want to stop here all night," replied one.

"Will the porter not admit you?"

"No."

"Why is that!"

"He says the house is full."

"Can you not procure another lodging?" asked our hero.

"How can we get a lodging without money? And if we'd got that, do you think we'd come here?" growled another.

"But if you had the money?"

"Certainly we could, or anybody else."

"I will give you money to obtain food and lodging for the night," said Jack.

The change that came over the haggard and careworn features of that group was something wonderful.

Where scowling eyes peered hatefully forth from beneath lowering brows, gleams of

---

[61] Rest.

joy shone brightly out, and on every lip hung the words, "God bless you!"

"Yes," said Jack, "you shall have the means to procure you food and shelter. I cannot believe it would be denied you here were it in the power of the authorities to admit you. Your sufferings fill your hearts with gall and bitterness towards those who often feel acutely for your pains. But there—take this, and this, and this, and get ye gone."

He placed a coin in each of the extended hands of the wretched throng, and felt, as he observed the bony fingers tighten over it, and saw the looks which accompanied it, that he was indeed doing good.

The thanks uttered were not loud and rough, as might have been expected from such as these; they were murmured in low tones, or only acknowledged by the grateful tear, which the swelling heart drove to the trembling eye, which gleamed brighter now through the salt drops than it did before.

Slowly, silently, each turned away from the workhouse door, and in another minute Jack and his companion were alone with the coach.

"Now, driver, look here," said Jack, who, of course, had removed his mask, but had substituted a thick pair of bushy whiskers, which gave him the appearance of being some years older than he really was—"look here, my friend. This poor Jew, through some affliction or other, has gone quite mad, and I feel it a duty I owe to a suffering fellow-creature to see that he is properly cared for. At this late hour it would be impossible to obtain admittance for him elsewhere than in the workhouse. Let me see, where did you take him up, you might be asked. At Eaton-square? Yes, Eaton-square, was it not?"

Jack gave the driver a nudge in the ribs with his elbow as he gave utterance to the last words, and the man, grinning all over his face, stuck his tongue in his face, and replied—

"To be sure, sir, if you say so."

"Of course I do."

"All right, sir, I'll swear to anything," said the man, "if well paid for it."

"No fear of that."

"All right, sir; shall I knock at the door?" asked the cabman.

"You had better."

The man sprang across the pavement, and raising the heavy knocker, let it fall with a loud bang.

A little hasp in the centre of one of the panels slipped back and the face of the porter appeared at the grated opening.

"Now, then, what do you want?" he asked.

"I want you to open the door."

"What for?"

"To admit an insane gentleman," called out Jack.

"Eh," said the man, "some one mad?"

"Quite."

"Better call the master."

"Be sharp, then."

The face disappeared from the grating, and the driver retired to the side of our hero.

"Don't you think, sir, you'll get into trouble for this. He'll swear he is not mad, and"—

"They won't believe him," interrupted Jack. "We will assert that he has attempted to destroy his life by drowning, which his saturated clothing will establish, and his rage at the treatment he has met with will but confirm our assertions. I wish to punish him for his greed, and a night in the infirmary will perhaps make the grasping old rascal a better man."

"Of course, sir, it's nothing to do with me; I'm paid for the job, and I've no right to say only what you tell me."

"Of course not. Hallo! there's the door open."

Poor Levy, who heard every word, but who was unable to speak or attempt to escape owing to his gag and bonds, almost fainted with excess of rage and terror, and commenced to kick and plunge furiously as the master and porter of the workhouse made their way to the door of the coach.

"What's this," said the master, a portly red-nosed gentleman, and who among the paupers must have made a strange contrast; "what have we here—a case for the insane ward?"

"The poor gentleman is mad, sir," said Jack. "Already has he made several attempts to destroy himself. But a short time since he nearly effected his object, and was only dragged out of a large cistern when life was almost extinct. See, his clothes are soaking, and this poor man's vehicle partially destroyed. A sad case, sir—a very sad case of insanity."

Levy struggled so hard to speak that a noise resembling a hideous groan penetrated the gag, and he kicked and plunged so violently that the master retreated back a pace from the vehicle, exclaiming, "He's raving mad; call up the doctor! Send two or three stout fellows here to carry him into the house. How he kicks! he'll break the coach to pieces. Be sharp, Dickson—be sharp. Mad! I never saw a fellow so mad in all my life. Who is he, sir?"

"A wealthy Israelite, of the name of Levy," replied Jack. "At times he believes himself to be a shopkeeper, and raves about being robbed by his workpeople, but of course that is only the workings of his diseased brain. Oh, here are your men. We will get him into the house, if you please. His violence will damage this poor man's vehicle."

Two stout paupers and the porter approached the vehicle.

"Lift him out, Dickson," said the master, "and you chaps secure his legs."

Levy was pounced upon, and dragged from the vehicle on to the footpath, where he was raised by his legs and arms, and hurried into the hall of the house.

"Stop here till I come out," said Jack, addressing the driver.

"All right, sir."

Jack sprang into the hall, and the door was closed behind him. The struggles of Levy now became of the most desperate character, and it was as much as the two men could do to hold his legs.

The kerchief, too, worked from over his mouth, and he screamed and yelled with all the strength of his lungs.

"Where's the doctor?" cried the master.

"Here, sir—here," exclaimed a voice, and a young man strode up to his side.

"Your services are required here, sir," said the master.

"Humph! Come for the insane ward?" said the doctor.

"I fear so, sir," said Jack; "there can be no doubt as to his being mad."

"Mad! None in the least, sir; none in the least," replied the doctor.

"I'm not mad," roared Levy. "It's a lie! I'm not mad."

"Poor fellow," said Jack.

"Mad people always assert they are sane," said the master.

"Always," said Jack.

"How long has he been in this state?" asked the doctor.

Jack appeared to consider.

"Let me see. Off and on for some time now, but never so violent as this."

"I tell you I'm not mad—I'm a sane man. My name's Levy. I live in Whitechapel. Send for Rachel! Oh, send for Rachel!"

"What Rachel does he mean?" asked the doctor, turning to our hero.

"Bless your soul, sir, he'll ask for Moses next, perhaps."

"Rachel's my wife," yelled the Jew. "I'm not mad. This is all a plot of that scoundrel, Spring-heeled Jack. Him—him—him!"

And the Jew nodded his head towards our hero, who shook his head with a sad and commiserating look.

"Spring-heeled Jack," said the doctor; "has he ever been frightened by that personage, do you know?"

"I think he has upon one occasion, for at times he believes every person who approaches him is Spring-heeled Jack."

"No doubt, no doubt; take him up to the insane ward. A straight-jacket shall be put on him, and his head shaved."

"Oh! Father Abraham!" shrieked Levy.

"It would perhaps be the best thing that could be done; the heated brain would be cooled thereby."

"Greatly, greatly," said the doctor; "we always shave the head in cases like this."

"And place a blister at the back of the neck, do you not, sir?" asked Jack.

"Yes."

"And apply mustard poultices to the calves of the legs, with ice-bags to the temples?"

"Such is the treatment I may find it necessary to adopt. But of this you may rest assured, sir, that everything shall be done for your friend which is necessary."

"Oh! oh! oh!" groaned Levy, completely overpowered with the agony of feeling, and suffering himself to be carried up a broad flight of steps to a long apartment known as the insane ward.

Into this he was carried by the three men, followed by the doctor, Jack, and the master of the workhouse, and flung on to a bed, and held there firmly by the paupers.

"You will put the jacket on him now more for fear that he should offer violence to himself," said Jack.

"As soon as his garments are removed," was the reply. "Take off his things."

The men proceeded to obey, and Levy once more finding strength to speak, yelled out—

"You shan't strip me! I'm not mad! Send for my wife—send for anybody. Everybody in Whitechapel knows me. I'm not mad. It's his work, that cursed Spring-heeled Jack! I'm not a wealthy Jew, but a poor shopkeeper. Touch me at your peril. I'm not mad—I'm not mad!"

"Off with them," said the doctor.

"Let me go—let me go! You shall repent this," cried Levy, struggling so desperately that he flung one of the men from him.

The doctor now advanced and aided them in the operation of disrobing the ready-made clothier, and after a little difficulty, he was stripped to his skin.

Jack stood at the foot of the bed with a look of feigned pity and commiseration on his features, but laughing inwardly at the trick he was playing on the poor Jew.

"Oh, you wretch—you wretch!" groaned the Israelite, catching his eye. "By the beard of Moses, you shall suffer for this!"

"Be calm, my dear friend," said Jack. "Be calm. It pains me to see you thus."

"You lie, you dog of a Christian! you lie! But I'll have your blood for this! I'm not mad —you know I'm not mad. Father Abraham, shower curses down, upon him!"

"Here's the strait jacket, sir," said one of the men. "Will you put it on while we hold him?"

"Yes," said the doctor. "Sit him up."

Levy, in spite of his struggles, was set up in the bed, and held firmly in that position while the young doctor proceeded to fasten the strait jacket upon his body.

"There," he said, when he had finished the operation, "he is powerless to injure himself or any one else; a composing draught and the razor will do much to relieve him."

"And the blister, sir?" said Jack.

"Will not be forgotten."

The doctor whispered to one of the men, who instantly left the ward, but returned in about a minute with the barber of the establishment, armed with scissors, razor, and lather pot, who approached the bed and looked upon the Jew.

When Levy saw him with the implements of his trade in his hand, the yell he uttered was something truly awful, and the feeling of horror which took possession of his soul was so acute that his head fell back, and insensibility stole over him.

Levy had fainted.

"Now," said the young doctor, "now's your time to get through your work before he recovers. We must keep his head cool, or there will be little use in any treatment we may adopt. Of course, it is a painful thing to do, sir," he added, turning to Jack, "but we must waive our own feelings for the sake of others."

"To be sure, sir," said our hero; "and I am well convinced you will do nothing but what is absolutely necessary in so distressing a case. I will remain to see the operation, and then retire after answering any questions that are necessary or in conformation with the rules of your house."

The barber set to work; and while the Jew lay in a state of insensibility on the bed, he cut away his hair close to his head, and then lathering his pate over with the soap, shaved it till it was as bare of hair as the palm of his hand.

CHAPTER LVIII.

JACK PLAYS A TRICK WITH THE SLEEPING DRIVER.—THE COFFEE-STALL AND ITS FATE.

JACK felt some little pricking of conscience when he gazed upon the bare head of Mr. Isaac Levy, but he felt at the same time that the Jew merited the punishment he had received for his wicked attempt to extort double the value of his property from, the seamstress whom he had employed and yet so badly recompensed for her labour.

By the time the operation of shaving was finished, Levy awoke to consciousness, and, worse still, the realization of the fact that every particle of his hair had been taken off his cranium by the ruthless implements of the workhouse barber.

Though he could neither see his head nor feel the same with his hands, he was certain of the fact that his hair was gone from the peculiar cold sensation of his skull.

A look of horror overspread his face. He rolled his eyes widely around. The muscles of his mouth twitched nervously, and a spasmodic gasping noise came from his mouth.

"Oh, inhuman wretches! "he cried at last, "to serve a poor man thus. Why am I brought here—why am I treated in this manner?"

"You will soon be all right, my good man," said the young doctor, soothingly.

"Right, right," said Levy. "Oh, sir, you don't believe this man; you know better—you know better."

"Compose yourself," said Jack.

"Villain! dog! you shall pay for this—you shall pay for this! You know I'm sane, but you wish to drive me mad. You have dragged me here—you have brought me here against my will, and caused all this; but I will be revenged —I will"—

"Raving, again," said Jack. "Doctor, don't you think the blister on the nape of the neck will allay the violence of his rage?"

"One shall be instantly applied. I will fetch it at once," said the doctor, moving away from the side of the bed.

"No, no, no!" roared Levy. "For God's sake don't. I'm not mad! Would you kill me— would you murder me?"

"You shall be well tended and cared for," said the doctor. "It will do you good."

"No, no! Let me go—take this thing off me. I will go quietly away if you will only let me go."

Then, turning quickly to Jack, he said "Is not your wicked nature satisfied?"

"My dear friend"—

"Friend! O, you viper!"

"You see, sir, he would not be safe were he shown any indulgence I fear it will be a long time, if ever he does recover."

"Skilful treatment, sir," said the master, "will make a great alteration in him, in a short time."

"Perhaps you are right," said Jack. "Even now he seems slightly altered."

"Altered!" cried the Jew, thinking of the loss of his hair. "Altered! Holy Moses! I am altered. Rachel wouldn't know me!"

"Has he a wife, sir, living?" asked the master.

"Bless your soul, no!" said Jack. "He's a bachelor."

"It's a lie!" roared the Jew. "Rachel's my wife! Oh! my poor Rachel!"

"See how wildly his eyes roll," said Jack, significantly.

"Fearfully."

"See how he grinds his teeth.

"Indeed he does."

"Do you think the doctor will consider it advisable to draw them,[62] sir?" asked Jack, with a meaning look at the old Jew.

"To draw his teeth, sir?"

"Yes."

---

[62] Pull them out.

"What for, in heaven's name?" asked the master, in surprise.

"To prevent him biting. I have heard that the bite of a madman is very dangerous."

"No doubt it is; but I never heard of their teeth being drawn," said the master.

"Haven't you?"

"Not that I recollect. No, sir, if he bites he must be gagged; that will effectually prevent him," said the red-nosed gentleman.

"Bite!" said Levy. "By the soul of Abraham! I'll bite if I get from this accursed place."

"You hear him, sir?"

"Yes—oh, yes."

"Shocking, is it not?"

"Very. How old is your friend?"

"About fifty."

"And how long has he shown symptoms of a deranged mind?" asked the master.

"All his life."

"Has he ever been under medical treatment?"

"Oh, dear, yes!"

"All lies—all lies! and it's Spring-heeled Jack that tells them. You fools! why don't you capture him?"

"Let him rave," said the master, "poor fellow! it cannot harm us. The doctor will soon return with the blister."

"Curse the blister! Curse you all! and let me go home," cried Levy. "I won't be kept here against my will. I—I"—

"Hold him down, men! hold him down!" said the master.

Levy had partially risen into a sitting position, but was instantly forced back on the bed by the two paupers, who laid across him to prevent him rising again.

"Oh! oh!" he groaned. "Thus are the children of Israel persecuted!"

The doctor returned with the blister, and, bidding, the men hold him, at once applied it to the back of the Jew's neck.

Levy cried and groaned, cursed and raved, but all to no avail.

The more he raved and asserted that he was sane, the more convinced all except our hero became that he was a dangerous lunatic.

Finding that no heed was paid to his ravings, he commenced to implore and appeal, when Jack, addressing the master of the workhouse, said—

"I can do no good by remaining; but, sir, if your rules will permit, I will call in the morning to see my poor demented friend. I am sorry to leave him, but I cannot help feeling that my presence, so far from allaying his excitement, is conducive to his rage."

"That is one of the principal features in madness," said the young doctor. "The lunatic invariably believes his best friends to be his greatest foes, and those whom in his sane moments he has the greatest cause to dislike he looks upon as his dearest friends."

"If your words required proof, sir, we have it, you perceive. He looks at me now as if he would fain fly at my throat, and tear me to pieces, does he not."

"I have observed the look of hatred with which he gazes at you. Your presence annoys or alarms him. It would be better, sir, if you retired, and left him to us. I know the anxiety you feel for the poor man, but rest assured that all that skill and kindness can do shall be done, equally in your absence as in your presence."

"I am convinced of that, sir. I will bid him farewell, and go," said Jack, stepping up to the head of the bed.

"Monster!" said Levy, glaring furiously upon him. "Oh! you wicked wretch!"

"Good night, my friend. I will come and see you in the morning. Try and compose your self, and submit with patience and resignation to the wishes of this gentleman. The mustard poultice will do you good—make you nice and warm."

"Go to hell!" roared Levy, flinging his body round on the bed, so as to bring his back to Jack. "You son of the devil! you—you"—

The doctor placed his hand on Jack's arm, and gently drew him from the bedside.

"Go, my dear sir—go! Your presence excites him too much."

"I will obey you; sir."

And Jack turned towards the door, followed by the master of the workhouse.

"If you will step into the office, sir, and answer me the necessary questions, that I may enter them in our book, I shall be obliged."

"With pleasure, sir," said Jack.

The master led the way into the office, and, opening a book, dipped a quill in the ink.

"Now, sir, if you please," he said; "the gentleman's name?"

"Mr. Isaac Levy."

"And yours, sir?"

"Captain Smith."

"Residence?"

"Eaton Square," was the reply of Jack, with promptitude and clearness.

Several other questions were asked, answered, and entered; and the master, who had formed a great opinion of our hero, accompanied him to the door, and politely bowed him out, closing the door himself behind him.

There stood the coach where he had left it, but the driver was nowhere in sight.

"Hallo!" said Jack, "where the deuce has the fellow gone to? This is a strange freak, to leave his horse and vehicle."

He looked up and down the street, but his gaze encountered no one; and, puzzled by the circumstance, he placed his hand on the window-frame of the coach to consider what course to pursue.

A loud snore from the inside of the coach caused him to look in, and, by the glimmer of the lamp near the workhouse door, he perceived that the driver was sitting inside his coach fast asleep.

"Well, he's a pretty fellow, certainly, or rather, I should say, a pretty stupid one. I might have gone off without paying him his fare. Well, I must rouse him up."

He was about to shake the man to awaken him, when he paused, and while a smile flitted over his face, he said—

"No, I won't. I'll punish him for not looking out better after his own business, He's sound as a top, and it's not a little jolting that will wake him in a hurry, I should say. But I'll first put the fare I promised him in his pocket, for the fellow deserves his due."

So saying, he took out his pocket-book, and extracted a note from a small roll, stealthily slipped it into the capacious pocket of the man's coat,—then, silently closing the door of the vehicle, leaped up on to the box, and seizing the reins started the animal, who, doubtless tired of waiting so long, went off at a good speed.

Jack turned his head ever and anon[63] and listened, and still the loud snore of the sleeping driver came to his ears.

"Sound as a church," said Jack. "I'll have a lark with him."

Jack urged the horse on at a pretty good speed, till he arrived close to the Harrow-road, at the corner of which was a strange-looking structure, with a sort of canvas hood or covering, and beside which, on the ground, was a rude iron pot full of round holes, and filled with live coals, which sent out a red glare over the pavement, and lit up the face of an old man who was seated beside it on a three-legged stool.

The structure itself was a coffee-stall, and the old man the proprietor, who was waiting anxiously for customers to purchase the dirty-water looking beverage which was contained in a tall, soiled tin-kettle on the top of the stall, and kept warm by a small charcoal fire beneath it.

Jack drew rein, and, leaping from the box, peered in upon the still sleeping driver, who continued to snore in so loud a key that it was a matter of surprise to our hero how he could possibly sleep through the noise.

"The fellow must have a light conscience," muttered Jack, "to sleep so soundly. However, I'll first light a cigar by that fire before I proceed any further."

So, advancing up to the fire on the ground, he took a cigar from his pocket, and, stooping, thrust one end through one of the round holes in the iron pot.

"It's a nice night, sir," said the old man, rising from his stool. "Allow me to give you a light."

"Thank you, my friend," said Jack, who found the heat to his fingers far from comfortable. "Well, how do you find trade?"

"Very bad, sir! very bad!" said the man, fumbling underneath the stall for a piece of paper, and flinging on to the path an heterogeneous mass of rubbish, ere he could discover the desired object.

Among the things thrown out was a piece of stout rope, and Jack, taking it up, said—

"Why, what do you want this for? To hang yourself?"

"No, sir; but times are so bad, it's enough to make a man hang himself, that it is. Why, lor' bless you, sir! where I used to take a shilling, I don't take a penny now. People don't patronize the stalls as they used to; there's so many night-houses open, and they thinks they get better served; but they don't, and only has to pay more for it. The gents used to stop and have a cup of coffee one time, but now they turn up their noses, and the only customers I gets now is the poor devils as can hardly find a penny, and comes here because they can get warm. Oh, sir, times is bad—very bad!"

"Why don't you try something else?" said Jack. "When one trade fails, you should take to another."

"Here's a light, sir," said the man, offering Jack a piece of lighted paper. "Take to another, sir? I can't, sir. You see I'm not a young man, and for an old one to do any good, he wants a pound or two to start with, and that ain't easy got, sir."

"But you could sell your stock-in-trade, and start afresh in something else."

"Why, lor' bless you, sir! that ere stall and chaney cost me about two pounds, but if I

---

63 Every now and then.

was to get any one to buy it, they wouldn't give fifteen shillings for the lot; and what could I do with fifteen shillings? Will you take a cup of coffee, sir?"

"Certainly, my friend."

"It's nice and hot, sir, and'll warm you. I made it myself, and I ought to know it's good."

So saying, the old man drew a cup of the black, steaming beverage in a vessel without a handle, and placed it on the board.

"I'll just pull my horse up a little nearer," said Jack, "before I drink it, for I think I should scald my mouth, by the look of it. How much is it, my friend?"

"Only a penny, sir."

"All right, I'll pay you directly. Just let me pull him up a bit," said Jack, darting to the side of the vehicle from whence the sounds from the driver's nasal organ still issued.

Jack drew the vehicle close up behind the coffee-stall as the old man again sat down on the three-legged stool, and held his hands over the fire.

"And so there is not much chance of your getting rid of the apparatus," he said, feeling in his pocket, from whence he took a couple of sovereigns, and wrapped them in the piece of unburnt paper the old man had given him.

"I wish there was, sir; for then, you see, I might do something in the day time. I'm getting too old for this nightwork. It wants a strong young fellow; for you see there's a rough 'un or two sometimes as comes and has coffee, and then won't pay for it."

"That's a shame," said Jack.

"So it is, sir; and they take advantage of it, threaten to overturn the stall, and break all the chaney.[64] I'm getting tired of it, sir, and would get rid of it to-morrow if I could only get something like a price for it."

"Can you oblige me with another light?" said Jack; "I have let my cigar go out."

"Certainly, sir."

The man found another piece of paper, and, while he stooped over the fire, to set light to it, Jack tied one end of the rope to one of the uprights of the stall.

"Here it is, sir."

"Thank you," said Jack, taking the paper, and holding it to the cigar, which still burnt with a red glow.

"Hallo! is that my horse moving? Confound him! He starts off at a moment."

Flinging down the paper, Jack sprang round the stall as if to stop the animal, and seizing the other end of the rope, quickly tied it to one of the springs of the vehicle.

"He's all right, sir, ain't he?" said the man.

"Yes, he's all right enough; but I know what he is, and am obliged to be cautious."

"Very right, sir."

Jack took up the cup, and made a pretence to drink; but as the man turned his face at the sound of a footfall on the pavement, our hero emptied the beverage into the road.

"Here, old 'un, just give me a cup of coffee," said a bleared-eyed fellow, coming up to the fire.

"Well, my friend, I'll be off," said Jack, springing to the box of the vehicle, as the old man commenced drawing off the required coffee for his new customer.

The old man shut the coffee off quickly, and laying down the cup on the board exclaimed—

---

[64] China.

KNOWN

"I beg your pardon, sir, but you ain't paid me."

"Right," said Jack; "I had forgotten. Here, catch."

Jack flung the coins, which he had wrapped up in paper, towards the old man, who caught them in his hands.

"Here, what's this?" he cried, thinking at once that Jack had wrapped bad money in the paper to cheat him. "What's this?"

A touch of the whip, a movement of the horse, and, with a smash and a crash, over went the coffee-stall, knocking down the bleared-eyed individual, and causing the old man to overthrow his pot of fire on to the pavement in his fright and hurry to get out of the way.

Away went the coach, and clatter—bash—crash went the stall after the vehicle down the Harrow-road.

Bump—thump—and at every yard leaving some portion of the wreck behind it, till only the upright, to which the rope was fastened, adhered to the coach.

Lashing the horse to its utmost speed, away Jack went, laughing loudly; while from the interior of the vehicle rang out loud cries of "Murder!" and behind him, in tones of grief, the old man shouted and raved like mad at the wreck of his stock-in-trade, and only means of a living.

CHAPTER LIX.
THE COACHMAN'S TERROR AND JACK'S DELIGHT—AN UNPLEASANT POSITION.

AWAY, with the vehicle swinging from side to side, and the upright of the old man's coffee-stall at every yard thumping against the panels of the back of the coach, went the vehicle along the Harrow-road.

The driver, awoke from his sleep by the crash of the old man's stock-in-trade, alarmed by the noise, and scarce knowing where he was, he did what might have been expected he would do, scream lustily for help, and hold on like grim death to the door of the coach.

Gradually the power of thought came to him, and recollecting where he last was, he came to the conclusion that his horse had ran away.

What was to be done?

That was the next idea that took possession of his mind.

It was a question he found it somewhat difficult to answer.

If he could get hold of the reins, he might stop the mad career of the animal, ere he dashed the vehicle to pieces; for he felt sure, from the continued thumping at the back of the coach, that a portion of it at least was a wreck.

But how could he get at the reins?

To attempt to leap from the vehicle would be worse than madness.

It would be suicide.

To remain was to be dashed to atoms.

He was sadly perplexed and bewildered, as well as frightened.

So he sank back on the cushioned seat of the coach, and groaned aloud.

Then he yelled for help.

But the noise drowned his cries, and in utter despair he resigned himself to his fate, whatever it might be.

Where was he? What part of the metropolis was he in? That was another thing he could not make out.

He could see through the gloom that wherever he was he was certainly not in Marylebone. He was in some sparsely-inhabited spot; but whether east, west, north, or south, he could not tell.

The speed at which the coach was carried along sent every object rolling past so swiftly that he could not trace with accuracy an individual thing.

"It's all owing to my being such a fool as to have anything to do with Spring-heeled Jack and his confounded games," he muttered. "I wish he had been at the devil before I accepted his offer to-night. Here I've lost my fare, shall lose my coach, and perhaps my life into the bargain."

And then he groaned aloud in his anguish, and clung to the window-frame in terror, as thump—thump, thump, behind him made him believe that the next minute he would be buried in the ruins of his vehicle.

Knowing the man was awake, Jack ceased his laughter, and applied the whip well to the horse's flanks.

"He's compelled me to be driver," he thought, "and I'll give him a ride. Well, the old man has got rid of his stock-in-trade, and doubtless will not regret its loss when he discovers what the paper contains. He was not hurt by the fall of his structure, I saw that; but I won't say as much for the hang-gallows looking dog I deprived of his coffee, and whom I saw go down among the ruins of the stall. Confound the fellow! how he's roaring. But there's none here to be disturbed by his cries. I wonder now whether he thinks Spring-heeled Jack a first-rate fare? but he'll forgive me, I know, when he finds the note in his pocket; but I must have a laugh for it, and then I do not mind paying for fun. Let me see. I know this spot well. The field past the white cottage,—yes, that's where it is situated, and no fear of doing more than giving him a good fright. Roar away, old chap. roar away!"

And giving the horse another cut with the whip, Jack kept a good look out for a white cottage, which he had often admired for its pretty look.

"Ah! there it is," he said suddenly, as he caught sight of a little cottage with a white front, and a tastefully-arranged flower garden before it. "There it is, and a few yards beyond the railings are down, and I can drive into the field. Yes, I can see the spot. That's it."

The cottage was passed, and, by a pull of the right-hand rein, he turned the horse on to the footway, and urged the animal into the field, and towards a clump of trees, which, spite of the gloom of the night, could lie plainly discernible about a hundred yards from the road.

Close to these trees was a large round pond, but very shallow, not being more than three feet deep in the centre, a circumstance which Jack had noted by seeing a boy wade across it after a toy boat which he was able to bring ashore. Towards this he urged the animal, while the driver, finding that the coach had left the road, called loudly for aid again through the window, to which he clung tenaciously.

Without pausing, Jack drove the animal into the pond, and pulled up at last right in its centre, where the horse, nothing loth to rest, bent its head and commenced to slake its thirst.

Jack turned on the box and looked behind him.

The cries of the man had ceased with the stoppage of the vehicle, and having no suspicion of where he was, and anxious to avail himself of the first opportunity to vacate his unpleasant position, he flung open the door, and, without waiting to look or think, leaped out, and fell with a loud splash into the water.

Jack quietly crossed his legs and puffed away at his cigar, which had not gone out, and gazed with a smile down upon the floundering driver.

"He—he—help!" cried the man, beating desperately at the water with his hands, and, in his struggles, clutching at the fore legs of the horse.

The animal evidently not relishing such treatment, began to kick, and down went the alarmed and bewildered driver once more beneath the surface. However, he soon became cognisant of the fact that he was in a place where he could stand upright with ease, and an exclamation of pleasure escaped him.

Having succeeded in again struggling to his feet he grasped the reins, and patted the horse's head as if to assure that quadruped that he had nothing to fear.

"Poor horse," he said. "Whoa—whoa," he added, as the animal again showed symptoms of going backwards. "Here's a pretty mess you've brought me into. What the devil did you run away for, and where are we? Whoa—whoa!" he continued, patting the animal, and gradually making towards the vehicle. "Let's get you out of this ere, and when I find the road, I'll tan your hide, I will for you, you varmint, for playing up such pranks." He had reached the fore wheel as he concluded, and placing his foot upon the step, raised himself up.

"Run away, will you—run away, will you? Let me get the reins in my hand, and you out of this mess, and war-hawks[65] to you, old boy. I'll knock the flies off your ribs with that little bit of whipcord, if it's in the socket. Oh! there —it—damn it, who are you?"

As he gazed up for the whip, and was about to spring upon the box, be caught sight of Jack's face, lit up by the burning end of his cigar.

"You're a pretty fellow," said Jack, "ain't you? There, don't come alongside of me in those wet clothes."

"Why, Jack, is that you?"

"Yes, and a pretty game you have been playing me," said Jack.

"Me!" said the man, still standing on the step.

"Yes, and if this is how you serve a good fare when you get one, you don't deserve another," said Jack, in a feigned tone of annoyance.

"Well, I'm blowed!" said the man, still more and more bewildered. "I can't make it out."

"Can't you?"

"No."

"Then I can."

"What is it?"

"What is it? Why, that you got drunk while waiting for me, and when I was ready to start, you was nowhere to be found. I got on to the box to wait for you, and the horse ran away with me, and never stopped till he got here; and you, I suppose, was all the while behind the coach inciting him to a fiercer gallop by thumping on the panels, so as to alarm the poor brute."

"Upon my soul"—

---

[65] Someone who advocates conflict.

"Now, I don't want any excuses. Your conduct has been too bad."

"Spring-heeled"—

"I won't listen to you."

"But, sir, I assure you I can't make it out. I waited for you so long that, being very cold, I got inside the coach and fell asleep, and never awoke till I heard the awful crash, and a bumping against the back panels, and found that the coach was being dragged along at a fearful rate. The moment it stopped I got out, and here's a pretty mess I'm in, for we're right in a pond or a river, I don't know which."

"Had you been looking after your business this would not have happened, and I should not have been carried so many miles out of my way."

"I'm very sorry, sir—I'm sure I'm very sorry," said the man; "and I suspect I'll have to suffer for it, for I expect the coach is nearly broken to bits."

"Well, say no more about it," said Jack, "and take your horse and vehicle out of this. Sit as far off from me as you can, if you please; I don't want to catch my death of cold."

The man proceeded to clamber up on to the box, when Jack, giving the reins, which he still held, a sudden jerk, the animal started forward, and the man, losing his balance, fell backwards into the pond.

In an instant he was up, cursing and swearing at the animal at a furious rate.

"Dear, dear," said Jack, "the man must be drunk, and I shall be very glad when I can get away from his vehicle."

"No, sir, I'm not drunk," cried the man; "the horse started, and threw me off; but I'll give his hide something for it."

And so saying, he scrambled up and took a seat beside our hero, who had dropped the reins.

Then the man gathered them up in one hand, and stretched forth the other for the whip.

As he was about to seize it, he recollected that he had lost his hat in the water.

"I've lost my hat," he said.

"Well, it is too dark to think of finding it," replied Jack, "unless you intend to stop here till daylight."

"Then I won't do that, if I can help it," said the man. "Do you know where we are, sir?"

"I've not the least idea."

"Haven't you?" said the man, in a disappointed tone of voice.

"No. I should say we must be somewhere near Kensal-green, but I don't know."

"Kensal-green!" said the man. "Curse Kensal-green! Gee up—go on, you old varmint," he added. "Give me the whip, sir, and I'll learn the beggar here to run away, I will."

"Do not hurt the animal. It is you who are to blame, not him, and if either has cause to complain it is the horse. There, I'll take care of the whip; you look to the reins, and get us out of this as quick as you can."

"He didn't back into this place, that's certain, so the best way will be to back out, and then turn round. Didn't you notice which way he came, sir?"

"I was too much alarmed," said Jack.

"Well, I suppose you was, for I know I didn't like it. Howsomdever,[66] sir, I'm very sorry, and I hope as you won't be vexed at what I couldn't help. Way back—way back,[67]

---

[66]Howsoever – in whatever manner.

[67] Back away.

will you."

And pulling the reins with all his might, the driver forced the animal to walk backwards out of the pond, and, as the bank was a gentle slope, it proved no arduous task to the horse, who soon stood on the grass.

"Turn round," said Jack, "I think I know where we are. Oh! yes; I recognise this place, now. Do you see yon white building?"

"Over there, sir?"

"Yes."

"Well, make for that, and you will find yourself in the Harrow-road. In my confusion, I did not think what place it was, but I know now. As soon as we get to that white house, I'll take my leave of you, and if you don't want a cold, I'd advise you to get home quickly to bed. Hello! what's that? I'll get down and see. You look to the horse. I'll see what it is that's knocking at the back of the coach."

Jack quietly dismounted from the box, and taking a knife from his pocket, severed the string which secured to the vehicle the portion of the coffee-stall, and then again sprang up behind the driver.

"What was it, sir?"

"Some one had tied a large piece of wood behind the coach."

"Blow 'em," said the man; "and I dare swear that's what frightened the horse, and made him run. He never did so before, sir. It's a shame. People don't know what harm they might do by such larks."

"It's too bad to play pranks," said Jack. "There, you'll find a bank-note in your coat-pocket to recompense you for your time and assistance, and, as I have no need to ride any further, I'll bid you good-night."

And Jack sprang from the box to the road, while the man thrust his hand eagerly into his pocket to discover whether or not he had been sold.

CHAPTER LX.
ISAAC'S WIFE VISITS THE WORKHOUSE, AND ISAAC LEAVES IT COMPLETELY CURED.

MRS. RACHEL LEVY had passed a sleepless night in the room over the shop of the ready-made clothier.

The lady, who, by the way, had once been a beauty, like most of the female portion of her tribe, had lost all the loveliness which had charmed the heart of her Israelite spouse in years gone by, and was now far from good-looking.

Still, if her husband honoured her not for her beauty, he did for her thriftiness and business qualities, for Mrs. Levy was second only to her lord and master in driving a hard bargain.

No one was ever known to purchase any article from that lady at its fair value. She looked upon the Gentile race as only fit to be made a mark of, and never failed, by plausible and false assurances, in obtaining considerably more for her wares than any Christian tradesman with a mercenary soul would have presumed to ask.

And, as to fitting a customer with any article of apparel, she was a perfect adept in the art; she could pinch a coat in at the back, and swear that she never saw such a beautiful fit, and that the garment could never have been made for any one else, whilst a man of twice the size could have leaped into it with ease: and so persuasive was her manner, that she never failed to secure a customer once she had looked in his or her face.

No wonder, then, that Mr. Levy was very fond of his wife; and this affection was returned.

So, when Mr. Levy did not return, and Mrs. Levy put up the shutters and put out the lights, the old lady began to feel very uneasy; then nervous, then alarmed, and finally went supper-less up to bed, wondering whatever could have become of her husband, and listening anxiously for any sound that might indicate his return.

One—two—three o'clock came, but no Mr. Levy. Four—five! and the old lady leaped out of bed, and paced the room with quick and uneven strides.

Six was struck by Whitechapel church, and Mrs. Levy, with trembling hands, commenced to robe herself, and in a quarter of an hour, with pale cheeks and quivering lips, she opened the shop door and looked out into the street.

But no Mr. Levy did she see, and so she sat down on a heap of clothing in the shop, and burst into tears.

Nine o'clock! and nothing but the front door of the shop was opened—a circumstance which created no little surprise in the neighbourhood; when suddenly a shadow fell upon Mrs. Levy, who, looking up, perceived a tall postman standing in the doorway.

"A letter for you, ma'am," he said, holding one out towards her. "Twopence, if you please."

"Twopence!" she gasped, drawing back the hand she had eagerly extended to grasp it. "Twopence!"

"Yes, ma'am."

"But ain't it paid for?"

"Shouldn't ask for twopence if it was," replied the man. "Be quick, ma'am, please, for I have other letters to deliver."

"Twopence!" she said, half aloud. "Twopence! I wonder if it's worth it."

"Now, ma'am, I can't wait all day," said the man, amazed at her resolution. "Will you take it or not?"

"Yes, yes," she said, fumbling in the pocket of her dress, and drawing out the required coins, which she placed in the hands of the man with a sigh, and took the letter.

"Twopence," she muttered, as she turned it over in her hands. "Twopence! there goes the profit on a shirt."

And thus giving vent to her feelings, she dropped down on the heap of clothing, and tore open the note.

Running her eyes hastily over the couple of lines which it contained, she suffered the letter to fall, and leaped quickly to her feet.

"Ha! ha!" she laughed; "I knew Isaac would not stop out all night, if it was not for something good. He's watching at the bedside of a wealthy relation who is dying in a ward of Marylebone workhouse, and wants me to go to him at once. I can't understand it, but Isaac does; catch him wasting his time and neglecting his business for nothing. Oh! he's too shrewd for that, much too shrewd. I'll lock the shop up, and go at once. I must have a coach—oh! what an expense—but we shall both profit by it. Isaac would do nothing that we did not profit by—oh, no. Oh, no, he's too shrewd for that."

The old lady went to the back of the shop, and hastily put on her bonnet and shawl, and then looking around her to see that all was safe, hurried from the shop and double-locked the door behind her.

Having satisfied herself that all was right, she hailed a coach, and after a long bargain with the driver, got in, and was hurried on her way to the workhouse.

Despite her anxiety to meet her husband, and learn more about what had induced him to send for her, she could not resist waiting five minutes in endeavouring to prevail upon the driver of the coach to accept less than the bargain agreed upon between them, and when she found that her persuasive powers had no effect, she paid the demand with a sigh, and a few bitter remarks upon the grinding propensities of the Christians, and walked up to the door of the house.

The large knocker fell from her hand, and the face of Dickson, the porter, peered from the little barred trap.

"Now, then," said the man, "what do you want?"

"My husband," was the reply.

"Who's he?"

"Mr. Levy."

"Levy—Levy! What is he?"

"A gentleman who—"

"Levy, did you say?" interrupted the man.

"Yes."

"Oh, the chap that was brought here mad last night, do you mean?"

"Mad!" gasped Mrs. Levy.

"Yes, that's the only Levy that I know of in the house."

"Oh, no; he's not mad."

"Then there ain't no other Levy here," said Dickson; "you've come to the wrong place." And he shut to the trap.

Rachel stood gazing at the trap for some moments with a perplexed look, and then, lifting the knocker, again summoned the porter to the peep-hole in the door.

"Now, then?"

"I'm sure I'm right. Here's a letter I had from my husband this morning, who has not been home all night, and he bade me come here to see him, as he could not leave the bedside of a wealthy friend and relative of his."

Dickson scratched his head.

"I know they called that mad chap Levy," he said, as if speaking to himself, "but I didn't know there was any one with him. I'll let you in," he added in a louder key, "but I must speak to the master before you can go up to the ward."

"Thank you," said Mrs. Levy.

The trap closed and the door opened, and Mrs. Levy walked into the hall.

"Stop here," said Dickson. "Oh, there is the master. Sir, this lady wishes to see a Mr. Levy, who is with the mad gentleman that was brought here last night."

The master, who had been thus accosted while crossing the hall, stopped, and measured Rachel with a surprised glance.

"There's no one there with him that I know of but the doctor. Who did you say?"

"Mr. Isaac Levy, the clothier of Whitechapel," said Rachel.

"Why, that's the person that the madman fancies himself," said the master.

Then, as if a sudden suspicion seemed to enter his mind, he added, quickly—

"What sort of man is your husband? What dress does he wear?"

In an instant Rachel described every particular feature and dress of the Jew clothier.

The master looked blank, then looked at Rachel, and afterwards at Dickson, then thrusting his hands deep into his breeches' pockets, balanced himself on his heels, and finally wound up by whistling a prolonged whistle.

"Wheu—eu—eu! The devil! But surely, it can't be. We can't have been imposed upon like this. Why, that's the very description of the man himself."

"What man?" asked Rachel, eagerly.

"The madman; the—but come this way, you shall see the only person that I know to be a Jew in the house, and his name's Levy. Come up here."

The master led the way up the stone staircase to the insane ward of the establishment, into which he ushered the lady.

The moment she entered the door, she was assailed with—

"Rachel! oh! Rachel! you have come to deliver me from the hands of the Philistines!"

As these words met her ears, Rachel's eyes wandered in the direction whence the words came, and she sprang forward with more agility than could have been expected in one bordering on sixty years of age, and paused opposite the bed from which the voice had come.

A look of blank surprise came over her face, and ere she could recover, Levy, whom the strait-jacket held powerless to rise, yelled out—

"Rachel, I am here—here, Rachel!"

"That voice!" she cried.

"They say I'm mad, but you know I'm not, Rachel; you can swear it. It's all a lie! They are killing me—murdering me! Oh! save me! Wife of my bosom—save me!"

Mrs. Levy looked wildly at the prostrate man, then uttered a loud scream, swayed about for a moment, and fell upon her knees beside the bed.

"My—my husband!" she gasped. "My Isaac!"

"Your Isaac!" he cried; "you know I am your Isaac—your husband"

The doctor at this moment came to the bedside.

"Is the fit on him again, sir?" he asked of the master.

"The fit be damned!" roared Levy. "You blood-thirsty devils, let me go away with my wife. I'm not mad! you know I'm not mad! Rachel knows I'm not mad!"

"Oh! oh! oh!" groaned Rachel. "Where—where's your hair—your beautiful hair!"

"They've shaved it off; blistered my neck and legs."

Rachel flung up her arms, gave a loud shriek, and, throwing herself on the bed, cried out—

"Murder! You shan't kill my husband! He's—he's—oh! you've ruined him and me—me! Oh! my Isaac—my Isaac!"

The master drew the doctor aside. "Sir," he said, "what do you think of this?" The doctor scratched his head, looked sheepish, and replied—

"I believe we have been sold—that the fellow is what he represented himself to be, and that he is no more mad than you or I am."

"You do?"

"I do."

"That's my opinion; but what's to be done?"

"Let him go away with his wife."

"But the disgrace. Your reputation, sir, as a medical man, what of that?" asked the master.

"Were he a Christian I should dread the bother that he would make," answered the doctor; "but, sir, as he is a Jew, I doubt not I can buy his silence."

"What! after shaving his head—laying his bald pate in ice—bleeding his neck—poulticing his calves—lancing his arms—leeching his temples—confining his body in a strait-jacket, and forcing a pailful of medicine down his throat! By my Soul, sir, if a Jew will sell his silence and forgiveness after such treatment, he'd kill his father, eat his mother, burn his children, sell his wife for a slave, and his own soul to the devil! I wash my hands of this affair, sir. My duty was to admit him into the house; yours to see that he was mad before you treated him as such."

And the master turned away, and left the ward and the doctor to get out of the mess as best he could.

The medical gentleman scratched his head, and looked anything but comfortable; Mrs. Levy groaned aloud, and Mr. Levy kept the lady company.

The other inmates of the ward, of which there were two, amused themselves in different, ways; one laughed, the other cried, and a more melancholy scene could scarce be imagined.

"I'll go to a magistrate," at length cried the lady, pushing back her thin hair from her forehead; "I'll see if they shall serve you like this, the inhuman Philistines. I'll let 'em see whether my husband is to be set down as mad, and treated in this shameful manner. I'll—I'll— oh, you villain!—you villain!"

And the old lady shook her clenched fingers in the face of the young doctor, and stamped her foot with vehemence.

"My good woman," began the doctor, anxious to appease her.

"I'm not a good woman," interrupted the lady, quickly and fiercely. "I'm not a good woman; but if I am a Jewess, I'd like to see the Gentile that would do as he likes with my husband. I'm not mad, nor you can't say I am, and I'll—I'll—oh you wretch—you wretch— you—you—you"—

The fury of the old lady's temper checked her further utterance, and she placed her hands on her hips, and shaking her head, looked savagely into the doctor's face.

"My dear soul"—

"Don't dear me—don't, now, or I'll tear your eyes out!" she yelled. "You monster, you wretch, you viper, you dog of a Christian, to hurt my Isaac in this way. Look at his head— look at his neck. Oh, you villain?"

The poor doctor looked anything but comfortable, and inwardly cursed himself for being imposed upon as he had been by our hero and Isaac's violence.

In vain he tried to think of some means to appease the old lady's wrath, and ensure the silence of her husband.

"Do you mean to tell me he's mad?" she cried, at length.

"No," said the doctor; "but"—

"But what?"

"The treatment he has received at my hands, instead of meriting your displeasure, should cause you to be grateful. Peace now, and listen to me."

And the doctor assumed a severe air, as he held up his hand to enjoin her to silence.

"As I said, your husband is not now mad," he continued.

"And never was," she cried.

"I beg your pardon. I say he was mad last night, and, but for the treatment he has received here, would be mad to-day. Fortunately, the means adopted have brought him to a rational state, and I was about to order the strait-jacket to be removed, when your violence prevented me. For shame, woman!" he added; "you ill-deserve to find your husband so far recovered. Had I ordered his instant removal to a lunatic asylum, I doubt much whether he would be so soon restored to your arms as he is now."

Mrs. Levy looked half-surprised, half-suspicious.

"I tell you he was not mad when he left me last evening," she cried.

"I have no reason to doubt you," said the doctor, "for madness comes on in a moment, and by timely treatment meets with rapid cure. This, I am happy to say, your husband has received, and now look with what effect. Instead of being to-day a chattering idiot, ready to tear the wife of his bosom to atoms, he is well enough to be suffered to go at large, and will doubtless remember with gratitude those who have done so much for him. Psha! woman, do you think if he had not been out of his mind we would have taken so much trouble with him? We have too many real cases of madness to attend to on this point, to wish to treat a sane man as a madman."

"But I was not mad," cried Levy.

"My good sir, you know nothing about it," said the doctor "Did ever a man admit that he was mad in his life? or is a madman competent to judge for himself? There, now, I'll undo the jacket, for there is now no further danger to be apprehended. A few hours ago, and you would have dashed your own brains out, but the fit is passed, and I sincerely hope it will never more return."

"And I, too," groaned Levy. "But I don't believe I was mad; curse me if I do."

"Don't think about it, or you will have a relapse. Endeavour to prevent a thought of it crossing your brain; for though you are, comparatively speaking, right now, the thought may prey upon you mind, and—oh, there's the jacket off; now let me lift you up."

"Oh! oh!" groaned Levy.

"What's the matter?"

"My neck—oh, my neck."

"Oh, that's nothing; see the relief that blister has given you. A little smarting, but that will soon go off."

"Damn the thing. I wish it had never been on."

"Don't say that," cried the doctor. "There, hold up your legs, and let me remove the poultices. What a wonderful deal of good they have done you. There's a virtue in mustard, that"—

"Blast the mustard! I'm sore up all my legs, and shan't be able to walk for a month. Take them off and let me go."

"The fit's coming on him again," said the doctor. "If he is not more calm, he must remain where he is, for it would be dangerous for him to be at large."

A change came over the features of Isaac Levy.

Those few words of the doctor made him fear that if he said anything further of an angry nature, he would not be suffered to depart with his wife, so he exclaimed, in a pleading voice—

"No, no! I'm calm now—quite calm. Let me go—do let me go with my Rachel."

"Oh, let him go, let him go," cried Rachel, in answer to her husband's imploring look.

"Of course, if the fit goes off. Perhaps it will as he gets dressed."

His clothes; which had been dried, were placed by his side, and, with the assistance of his wife, spite of the shaking of his limbs, he quickly robed himself.

In a few minutes he was outside the workhouse door with Rachel, not having uttered another word till he found himself in the street; but when the door had closed behind them, Isaac shook his clenched fist at it, and uttered a bitter oath, then slowly and painfully hobbled away with his wife.

CHAPTER LXI.
JACK IN THE CELLAR.—THE THIEF DISCOVERED AND TRAPPED.

"THAT'S a drop of good stuff, sir, and courses through the veins like a stream of pleasure. I've had that in my cellar for eighteen years. It sparkles like diamonds, and I don't believe if you search London through you could get a better glass of wine."

Such were the words addressed to our hero, who, having entered an hotel in the west of London, had ordered a bottle of old wine, and after the proprietor, who had waited upon him, had drawn the cork, was politely requested to take a glass, which he did, and after smacking his lips like a connoisseur, gave utterance to the above.

Jack sipped from his glass, and, placing it on the table, said—

"You are right, Mr. Larkin; it is, indeed, very fine. Have you much left of it?"

"Ah, sir, that's what grieves me. I have not much left. The fact is, sir, there's a thief about my establishment, and scarce a night passes but wine and spirits are purloined from the vaults."

"Have you no idea who it is?"

"Not the least."

"Do you not suspect?"

"I do not like to suspect anyone, and yet I suspect all."

"Do you keep no watch?"

"I have kept watch till I am tired, but without success," was the reply.

"Very strange."

"It is, indeed, sir; and if you only knew the extent to which I am victimised I'm sure you would pity me."

"And you can adopt no means by which to trace the culprit?"

"None, sir; and I am the more annoyed at not being able to do so when I think what an unpleasant thing it must be for the honest portion of my servants to feel that their every action is watched, and that they are open to suspicion."

"It must, said Jack, "be a very painful thing for them, and hence it behoves you the more to use every endeavour to bring the guilty to punishment. Surely something could be done— some trace must be left?"

The man shook his head.

"I would undertake to find out the culprit, I think," said Jack.

"If you could, sir, you would do more than me and the officers have been able to accomplish."

"Where is the entrance to your cellars?" asked Jack.

"Come this way, sir, and I will show them to you," said Mr. Larkin.

Jack followed him from the apartment down a flight of stairs, thence down a step-ladder into the vaults, into which a gloomy light just protruded.

"Do you see that bin yonder, sir?"

Jack strained his eyes through the darkness, and replied—

"Yes, I do."

"Well, sir, would you believe it? that out of thirty dozen of old port, over half have been emptied, and the bottles returned to the bin; and, I assure you, when I made this discovery, I didn't know how I felt."

"Doubtless you were very much annoyed," said Jack; "but, for the life of me, I can't see how it is possible for anyone to enter these vaults without being detected, if a watch is kept from above."

"It puzzles me, it does, sir; and, upon my word, I have sometimes been fool enough myself to think that the devil himself must do it."

Jack laughed.

"I think the devil has other occupations," he said. "Depend upon it, the culprit is in your establishment and your pay; and for the sake of those who labour honestly for their livelihood, I would leave no stone unturned to find him or her out."

"I'd give twenty pounds to anybody who would find it out," said Mr. Larkin; "for I am well assured that I should save that sum in a month."

Jack looked about the cellar, his eye becoming more and more accustomed to the gloom, and made himself acquainted with every corner of the place.

"Well, sir," he said, after a pause, "I sincerely regret your misfortune, and as sincerely hope you will soon be enabled to put a stop to such wholesale robbery."

And he turned to ascend the ladder.

"Ah! I must give it up for a bad job, I suppose," said Mr. Larkin; "I've tried all I can think. But, sir, I'm keeping you in a very dirty, gloomy place."

And motioning our hero to ascend, Mr. Larkin mounted the ladder after him, and together they returned to the apartment, where the decanter of wine was awaiting them.

Accepting the invitation to join him, Mr. Larkin sat down with our hero, and an hour passed pleasantly away in conversation on various topics, when Jack rose to take his departure, and was bowed politely to the door by the obliging, but much ill-used, proprietor of the hotel.

"Twenty pounds," muttered Jack, as he strode away; "and I believe Larkin would not hesitate to give that sum to anyone who would expose the rascal who thus systematically robs him. Now, thank heaven, I have no need of twenty. Providence has been bountiful to me, though I ill appreciate its blessings; still, though I don't want it, there are thousands who do. No man should be too proud to labour, and I will strive to earn that twenty, for well I know I can find many whom that sum would save from starvation or ruin. Well, I'll go to the club now, and, when the hour is later, return to the hotel. I have taken a good view of the place, and know the position of every object in it. Yes, I'll go; but none must know I'm there. Doubtless, I shall find the way into the cellars without being seen."

So saying, he went on his way, pausing ever and anon to drop a coin into the hand of a street beggar; for, with all his faults, among them could not be reckoned greed or unfeeling; he was generous to a degree, and few asked in vain for assistance at his hands. This redeeming quality often brought a blessing from the lips of those who at other times cursed him.

It was about eleven o'clock at night when Jack once more entered the hotel. He had watched from the opposite side of the way for the moment when the hall was empty, and he could pass through it without being seen.

Making his way noiselessly to the staircase, down which himself and Mr. Larkin had gone some hours before, he descended this, and felt for the step ladder which led to the vaults.

This he soon found.

When he had reached the bottom, he was in Stygian darkness; not a single ray of light penetrated the place; but, holding his arms extended before him, Jack made his way across the cellar to where he had noticed several casks, and then taking a phosphorus match from his pocket, he struck a light.

The faint glimmer which this threw over the place was sufficient for our hero, and he perceived an empty cask standing on its end close to him, and dropping the match into it, he saw that it was quite dry, a circumstance which evidently gave him satisfaction.

The place was again in utter darkness; but Jack drew his cloak around him, and seizing the top of the cask, drew himself up, and dropped his legs into it.

The top of the cask came up to about his middle, arch Jack gradually lowered his body till he found the rim of the cask would come above his head.

"This will do," he said to himself, as he rose again from his uncomfortable position. "I may have my trouble for nothing, but I somehow seem to think I shall not. At the first footfall or glimmer of light, I can crouch down into this vessel, and, all unsuspected, discover the culprit."

He took his mask from his pocket and adjusted it to his face, set the collar of his coat up, and drew on his claw gloves.

"The fellow, whoever he is, shall have a shock if I meet him," he muttered. "So now to await his coming."

He sat upon the edge of the cask, with his legs dangling inside the vessel, and waited for the least sound or glimmer of light which might make its way into the vault.

He had not to wait long.

A heavy footfall sounded overhead, and a glimmer of light shone down the steps.

"That's no thief," muttered Jack; "or if it is he is a bold one to come thus noisily. I'll draw back and watch."

He drew his body down into the cask as a pair of legs appeared on the steps.

Down they came, bringing a rather portly body after them, and then the head of Mr. Larkin.

The gentleman carried a candle in his hand, and taking two or three steps from the ladder held up the light above his head and took a long scrutinising glance along the vault.

"All right," he said, aloud. "It beats me, and I suppose I never shall find out the thief. I've had a new lock put on the door, and we'll see now whether I shall lose any more."

He turned, and walked back up the steps, and our hero heard a key turn in the lock of the door at the bottom of the stairs.

"Well," said Jack, "I'm a prisoner it seems. I never thought of being locked in. But never mind; we should never regret what we do in a good cause, so I'll await with patience what may transpire."

Jack is not the only man who ever said one thing and did another.

He found as time went on that his patience was getting exhausted.

His position was an uncomfortable one, his seat rather sharp, and his limbs became somewhat cramped.

Two o'clock had struck by the large timepiece in the hall, and Jack's patience fairly tired out. He was about to vacate the cask, when he fancied he heard a strange noise by the bin to which his attention had been drawn by Mr. Larkin.

Jack glared through the darkness towards it.

The noise continued.

It was very slight, but quite sufficient to attract his notice and excite his suspicion.

He almost suppressed his own breathing in order the better to make out what it could be.

Once or twice he fancied it might be caused by rats; but then, as it grew a trifle louder, the supposition was flung aside, and he strained every nerve to see and hear.

Suddenly a faint glimmer of light played around the bin.

Jack drew himself silently but hastily down into the cask, only permitting his eyes and forehead to protrude above it.

The ray of light became stronger, and then the figure of a man came from behind the bin.

He held a horn lantern in one hand and a jug in the other.

He nervously glanced around the vault, and Jack drew his head back quite into the cask.

"What a fool I am," the fellow muttered, placing the lantern on the ground, "to feel frightened, when I know old Larkin nor nobody else knows how I can get in here from behind the bin. He'll never find out the way; but I mustn't take any more of that wine yet, though the job pays me well. I'll just draw off a jug of whisky, and make a couple of bottles of it. Let's see—that's the cask. He won't miss any from there, I don't suppose; and if he does, he'll never find out who's had it."

The fellow strode up close to the cask in which our hero was concealed, and, falling upon one knee, placed the jug under the tap of a neighbouring vessel.

"This is the spirit," he said, as he laid his hand on the tap. "I don't think there is another spirit to equal it in the world."

"Behold me!" cried Jack, in a deep, hollow voice, springing upright in the cask, and extending his closed hand towards the man.

The fellow uttered a loud cry, and looked up.

The light from the lantern he had placed upon the ground fell upon the hideous face and spectre-like figure of our hero.

The fellow gasped, spasmodically. A look of painful terror overspread his face, and his very hair appeared to extend itself out upon his head. All power seemed denied him, for still he kept his kneeling position. He could only glare in horrified amazement upon Jack, whose body protruded from the cask before him.

"G-o-o-o-od Go-god!" gasped the fellow, "it's the—the de-de-devil!"

"Happy to make your acquaintance, my friend," said Jack, still in the hollow tone of voice he had before assumed. "I've been waiting for you for some time. I want you!"

The man let fall the jug, and sprang to his feet.

As he did so Jack bounded upwards, and out of the cask, right before him.

"Oh! oh! oh!" gasped the man. "D—d— don't."

And down he crouched upon the floor of the vaults.

Jack bent over him, taking good care to keep the rays from the lantern playing full upon his face.

"You're fond of spirits, are you not," he asked?

"No, no."

"Don't tell lies. What were you going to do?" asked Jack.

"No—no—nothing!"

"Lie the second," said Jack. "You came here that you might rob your master."

"Upon my soul—"

"Hush! What did you require that jug for?"

The man was silent.

"Rascal!" said Jack; "your peculations[68] are brought to an end!"—

"For God's sake"—

"Silence! don't mention that name in my presence."

"I—I forgot that you don't like to hear it. The devil never does," stammered the man.

"You know me, then?"

"Oh, dear! oh, dear, yes."

"Very good, then. You also know it would be useless to attempt to deceive me," said Jack, grinning under his mask.

"I won't try."

"You had better not."

"I won't—I won't."

"Now, then, to what extent have you robbed your master?"

"Robbed!—"

"Yes. No equivocation. It won't do with me," said Jack. "To what extent, I say."

"I don't know."

"Lie the third. Beware of the fourth," said Jack, taking a step nearer to the fellow, who crouched lower to the ground in his terror.

"A very great extent," he replied. "I can't tell you how much."

"Of course that don't matter, for I know," said Jack. "But how long have you carried on this game?"

"About six months."

"Does anyone assist you?"

"No."

"None of your fellow servants? Speak truly; it will be better for you to do so."

"Not one."

"You are alone guilty?"

"I am."

---

[68] Embezzlement.

LOST
A DOG
500
REWARD
SPRINGHEELD
JALK

"How have you managed to avoid discovery?"

The man hesitated to answer this question.

"Speak, or tremble."

"By the door behind the bin."

"Where does it lead to?"

"The coal-cellars and stables."

"And so out into the back street."

"Yes."

Jack had learned all he desired.

This would account for Mr. Larkin not being able, despite the watch he had set, to discover the robber.

"So," said Jack, after a pause, during which time the man had been tremblingly gazing upon him, but fearful to rise lest he should find himself in the grasp of our hero—"so, my fine fellow, I suppose you have made something handsome by your nightly visits to this place?"

"Not much—not much."

"Do you drink it all? But there I need not ask, only to see what a liar you are as well as a thief."

"No, I sell it."

"And what reward do you expect to meet with—eh?"

The man was silent.

"I'll tell you," said Jack. "A long term of imprisonment as a warning to others, and, finally, a warm berth in my regions."

"Mer—mer—mercy!" gasped the man. "Oh! I will never come here again. I will never do wrong any more. Mer—oh! oh!"

His further utterance was put a stop to by Jack giving the empty cask a sudden tilt, and sending it over the kneeling man. With such precision did he manage to fulfil his purpose, that the cask completely shut out all but the fellow's legs and feet from his view.

Then seizing the lantern, Jack held it high up above his head, and darted with it behind the bin, where he perceived a small door half open, and darting through this, closed it instantly, and found himself in a cellar used for storing wood and coals.

Looking hastily around him, he seized a large billet of wood, and planted it securely against the door, so that no ordinary pressure from the opposite side could force it open, and then looked about for another means of egress from the cellar.

CHAPTER LXI.

JACK MEETS AN OLD ACQUAINTANCE, AND BETTERS HIS CONDITION.

HOLDING the lantern above his head, our hero glanced around the cellar, and perceived a door which led into the stable.

"So, this is how the rascal has been able to carry on his pilfering without being discovered," he muttered. "It is hard for employers to be robbed like this by those who profess to serve them, and it is harder still for those who hold similar situations to be looked upon with the eye of suspicion, as one and all in this establishment must have been. I am not the man to desire to hand a fellow creature into the hands of justice, and be instrumental in branding him as a felon; but I certainly think, for the sake of his fellow servants, I ought to see that the rascal is discovered. Now, to get out of here the way that fellow got in. Oh! I see, that door leads out into the mews."

He strode across the stables, and placed his hand on the door.

It opened instantly.

"I will leave the lantern here," muttered Jack, "and remove my mask, and then consider the best course to adopt to make Mr. Larkin acquainted with the fact of the discovery of the thief."

He placed the lantern on the ground near the door, took off his mask, and passed out into the mews, when he was brought to a sudden stop by perceiving a miserable-looking object crouched in a small stairway that led up to the apartments above a neighbouring stable.

There was not much light yet, but still there was sufficient to enable Jack to make out the object before him, and to discover that the poor wretch was asleep.

His garments were ragged and dirty, and his whole appearance was that of the utmost wretchedness and misery.

"Poor devil!" said Jack, commiseratingly, as he gazed down upon the huddled heap of humanity at his feet. "What a blessing to such as him must sleep be. Those are the only hours of happiness such as he can know when slumber steeps the soul in forgetfulness. It is hard to arouse him to a sense of his wretchedness, but may I not awake him to joy. Larkin promised twenty pounds to anyone who would expose the thief. Twenty pounds to me is nothing, but what may it not be to this man!"

He bent lower down over the sleeping wretch, and, touching his shoulder, said—

"Wake up, here."

The man awoke and started to his feet.

"What are you doing here?" said Jack, as the man gazed half frightened in his face.

"Trying to get a bit of sleep," said the fellow; "but such as you, who have got beds to lay on, can have no feeling for them as ain't."

"You are severe."

"Am I?" growled the man. "I got cause to be."

"Doubtless," said Jack. "Have you no home?"

The man laughed.

But, oh! what a laugh! it was worse than any groan he could have uttered.

"Surely you are not compelled to lay about the streets like this?" said Jack.

"Certainly not," said the man. "There's the workhouse to go to."

"Then why do you not go there?"

"Why not?"

"Yes."

"Because I can't bear to," said the man. "Perhaps it's better than laying in doorways and on cold stones, but"—

He paused abruptly.

"But what?" said Jack.

The man looked hard at him for some moments, and then said—

"Nothing. We have met before. I know we have, though then I saw not your face. You were masked."

"Ah?" cried Jack.

"Aye, I know you," said the man, leaping forward, and grasping our hero's arm. "You are"——

"Who?"

"Spring-heeled Jack!"

"Ah! ha!" cried Jack, dashing the man's hand from his arm; "and who are you? But I recollect," he added, extending his hand, "you are the man, who, believing me actuated by some base purpose, sought to effect my capture, as I hurried to save a poor girl from a watery grave. You are the man who struggled with me near London-bridge some time since."

"I am," said the man; but not offering to accept the proffered hand of our hero. "I am the man who sought to hand you over to the police, and who would have done so, but that want had weakened my once robust frame. Spring-heeled Jack, I am poor and starving, and hence unequal to cope with you, or I would again detain you till"——

Jack placed his hand on the man's shoulder, and in a kindly voice, said—

"Why would you seek to deprive me of my liberty?"

"Why?"

"Aye, why?"

"Because I believe you to be a ruffian—because you roam the streets at night to insult and intimidate the peaceably-disposed—because you are guilty of actions which would place a poor wretch like me upon the treadmill—because"——

"Stop, my friend," said Jack; "I will admit that my love for adventure sometimes causes me to overstep the bounds of prudence; but you do me an injustice if you believe me guilty of wantonly injuring or insulting any one. You believed, on the night when we before met, that I was seeking to annoy the poor girl I was following, and acting upon that supposition you showed yourself a man. I had no such motive in view, and upon my sacred honour I saved that girl from a watery grave. You have heard only the dark side of my character, and I will admit that it is bad enough; but I am not the callous-hearted wretch you believe me. Gold will purchase immunity from many sins, but gold has never purchased me my freedom or exoneration from any guilty act. Your appearance bespeaks your poverty. I would aid you without seeking to know how you came thus. Take my hand. You need not blush to do so; it never yet harmed the innocent or the wretched."

The man looked at him, and still hesitated.

"Will you take it," said Jack, "and with it a trifle to aid you in your present necessities?"

The man took the preferred hand.

"I will take your hand," he said, "but not your money. I am too proud to seek a bed in a workhouse, and I am too proud to accept charity of you."

"Tush, man; I can well afford to help you, and to do so will give me pleasure."

"No, sir; I do not seek charity. I am willing to work for my bread if I can get it, but I cannot beg, neither can I steal."

"God forbid that you should!" said Jack. "The words you have uttered before this night are sufficient to prove that your heart is cast in the right mould. I will not again insult you by forcing charity upon you, but will give you the means of earning sufficient to better your condition, and all I ask in return is secrecy."

The man started back.

"Secrecy," he said, "about what? Nothing honourable requires secrecy."

"Listen to me, and you shall judge."

"Go on," said the man.

"You see that stable?"

"I do."

"It belongs to the hotel in the road."

"I know it does."

"I frequent that place when in this neighbourhood."

"Well."

"To-day the proprietor informed me that there was a thief in his establishment. His cellar was nightly robbed, and, in spite of all, the delinquent could not be discovered, and he promised the sum of twenty pounds to anyone who could give up the rascal. It was not the money, but the love of adventure which tempted me to seek to discover the thief, and unknown to anyone, I concealed myself in the cellar, and have now not only found the villain, but made him prisoner in the very scene of his delinquencies. Of course, I have earned the twenty pounds, or partially done so. That sum may be yours. Go to the hotel, arouse the proprietor, tell him to seek the thief in his cellar, and as he is a man of honour, ask him for the twenty pounds he promised for the discovery, and he will give it you. Only, say not that Spring-heeled Jack is the same man to whom he made that promise this morning."

"Is not this another of your tricks?" said the man.

"No; and if you will not accept a gift from me, do as I wish you, and receive the promised reward. I have spoken truly, and Mr. Larkin will hand you the money, and may it be the means of raising you from your present position."

"I do not think you are trifling with me," said the man, half-doubtingly.

"I am not, on my soul!"

"Then I will go. If you are playing me a trick—if you seek to raise hopes in my breast only to gratify a wicked feeling—heaven forgive you."

"Go and judge for yourself. If I speak falsely be my enemy for life. I am bad enough, as I said before, but I am not so unfeeling as to seek to embitter an already suffering heart. Farewell, now. We may some day meet again, and when we do, I hope you will think better of Spring-heeled Jack."

Our hero turned away as he spoke, and hurriedly left the mews; but he did not go far before he sprang into the shadow of a sunken doorway, from whence he could see the entrance to the hotel.

Here he stood and watched.

Presently he saw the man approach, hesitate on the steps, then slowly mount them and ring the bell.

A smile passed over Jack's face.

"Poor devil!" he said. "It will be a good night's work for him. Oh! the porter has admitted him. I will wait here and see what transpires," and taking a cigar from his case, he lit a piece of German tinder,[69] and puffed away at the weed, keeping his eye fixed upon the hotel door.

---

[69] Amadou: a spongy substance made from fungi. Extremely flammable.

The man, half doubting the good faith of Jack, found some difficulty in getting the porter to arouse his master with the information that the thief was secured in the cellar; but that pompous gentleman at length resolved to do so, and believing that if such was indeed the case, that the informant was an accomplice, took the precaution of locking the door and placing the key in his pocket, as soon as he had suffered the man to enter the hall.

He did not go and arouse Larkin himself, but summoned another servant from his bed, who came into the hall rubbing his eyes with both hands, an operation which he instantly desisted in when he perceived the miserable-looking creature who stood beside the porter.

At the latter's request, he proceeded to his employer's chamber, and soon made Mr. Larkin acquainted with his message, and that gentleman, as he leaped out of bed, requested all the male servants to be aroused, to accompany him to the cellar.

In a few minutes all was commotion in the hotel, and no less than ten persons were assembled in the hall.

Mr. Larkin looked around upon the surprised and half-sleepy faces of his employees.

"Where is Chambers?" he asked. "I do not see him here."

The man who had called the speaker from his bed, replied that he could get no answer, and that the man was not in his room.

Larkin shook his head.

"Then that's the thief," he said. "But follow me. No—some of you go first with a light."

Preceded by two of the men, and followed by the rest, the hotel proprietor made his way to the door of the stairs, which he unlocked, and thence down the ladder into the cellar where a cry of surprise and indignation broke from every lip, as their eyes rested on the crouching figure, and horror-struck face of the thief.

"At last," said Larkin, "the robber is discovered; but the man, where—oh, here he is," he added, as the man, who had been forced along by the domestics, stood forward. "How did you know he was here?"

The man told his story, but suppressed the fact that Spring-heeled Jack and the gentleman who had sent him were one and the same.

"Very well," said Larkin, when he had concluded. "Before you go I will give you the sum I promised the gentleman, who, of course, would be above accepting it himself. Take that fellow up to the hall," he added, "and send for an officer."

The thief was seized and born up to the hall, an officer sent for, and, in a short time, Jack saw him borne from the house a prisoner, shortly afterwards followed by the poor man, who clutched in his hand the means to buy bread and shelter; and then Jack flung the end of his cigar into the road, and strode away.

CHAPTER LXII.
THE STRANGE CAT.

IT was about ten o'clock when Tobias Johnson, a retired carpenter, sat in the kitchen of his little cottage, smoking a long clay pipe before the fire, and alternately watching the smoke curling upwards from the bowl and the fingers of an ancient dame, as she plyed the busy needle through and through the foot of a worsted stocking which she was darning. Tobias was one of those men who had always borne in mind the good old adage, that a penny saved is a penny earned, and though he was never anything more than a journeyman, he had at the age of sixty-five amassed a sufficiency to purchase a piece of ground, build a small cottage thereon, and leave himself and wife something like a pound a week to live on.

It was not much, certainly; still, with careful management, the aged couple managed to get along pretty comfortably.

Some of his neighbours looked upon him as a miserly fellow, but, in truth, Tobias was not miserly—he was simply careful. If he did not spend his evenings with his mates, while he followed his trade, at a public-house, he certainly did not deny himself his pint of beer at home; and there, cheered by his pipe and spouse, he laid the foundation of the little fortune which, at the age of nearly threescore, was sufficient to keep him from the workhouse.

Those who condemned him would have done well had they followed his example—an example which the youth of the present day would do well to follow; for, as Tobias used to say, pence grow to shillings, shillings to pounds, and in the course of time pounds furnish a home and independence.

With such feelings, it cannot be wondered at that Tobias and his wife, in spite of old age and growing infirmities, were very happy, far more happy and independent than many of their neighbours, who looked upon the old couple with scorn, for on either side of his house more pretentious residences had been built, and were mostly inhabited by those who preferred show to comfort, and lived considerably above their means, a failing that may be seen to a very great extent in the present day in the suburbs.

But Tobias was not a man to be frowned on by his neighbours because they wore fine cloth coats and white hats, and kid gloves, because their windows were dressed with fine curtains, and their passages sumptuously carpeted, and a poor little girl, who ought to have been at school, was made an hideous fright by a little white cap stuck on the back of her head, and kept, not only to open the door to all summonses, but made to do all the house-work.

No. Tobias had none of this; if he was independent he was not proud. He would sweep the front of his own house, clean windows, knives and forks, boots and shoes, and tend his own garden, despite the contemptuous curling of his neighbours' lips and the indignant tosses of the head of the little over-worked servant girl.

His wife, too, was made in the same mould. The good old lady did not hesitate to hobble to market, and return with her arms laden with meat and vegetables, or any other necessary—a circumstance which, in the shabby genteel neighbourhood, was looked upon with absolute horror by the be-bugled[70] and be-braided dames, who watched her from their parlour windows.

Tobias and his wife paid no heed to this. They saw no shame in what they did. They paid for what they had, and considered it better to only live up to their means than to go beyond them.

But if Tobias did not care for his neighbours, he did less for his neighbours' cats. He could shrug his shoulders and laugh scornfully at the airs of the former, but of the latter he had a perfect abhorrence.

With little to do, he had laid out, and kept in order, a pretty garden at the back of his

---

[70] Beaded clothing.

cottage, but the cats played sad havoc with his flowers, and if ever Tobias so far forgot himself as to swear, it was when he perceived the evidences of the destructive propensities of these feline creatures.

Here was a choice plant broken—there seeds were raked out of the earth; in another place, the ground had been torn up, and tufts of hair scattered about plainly gave evidence of a terrific battle which had raged during the night, or perhaps a bed of tulips or verbenas would be utterly destroyed, in a rough and tumble contest.

Tobias had taken a glance about his garden some few hours before the time at which we make his acquaintance, and had vented his indignation in no measured terms upon the confounded cats, and his rage was gradually cooling down under the influence of the pipe, and the busy fingers of the old lady.

But the circumstance could not wholly be forgotten, for, as the old gentleman knocked the ashes from his pipe on the bar of the stove and placed the long tube of clay in the chimney-corner, he exclaimed—

"Drat the cats!—drat the cats!"

"It's no use dratting them," said Mrs. Johnson, drawing the stocking over her arm which she was mending. "For my part, I can't see what people want with such a lot of dumb animals. It's them as ought to be dratted, not the cats. A cat's all very well if you've got mice, but the mice don't come where there's nothing to eat, and there can't be much where there's so much finery. I ain't got patience with people, I ain't!"

And the old lady slipped the stocking off her arm with a vengeance so expressive of her indignation of her neighbours; for, woman like, she was hurt at their scornful bearing towards herself and her husband.

"Well, as for that," said Tobias, "that's no business of ours. If people likes to keep cats, let 'em keep 'em; but I wish they'd keep 'em out of my garden. I shall get savage one of these days, and shoot 'em, I know I shall. Now, look at next door. There's three families in that house, and each family has got a cat—no, the kitchens has got two, so that makes four cats. It's shameful!"

"Yes, and I don't believe there's more than a ha'porth of meat taken in a day for the lot of 'em. If there was, they wouldn't be so destructive."

"Nonsense, wife," said the old man, with a smile. "You are too uncharitable. I don't care much for my neighbours, and look upon them with equally as much contempt as they look upon me; but I think you must be mistaken there. People who keep dumb animals seldom starve them; on the contrary, many rob their families for the sake of a tabby cat or dog. Still, as I said before, it is no business of ours what our neighbours do, so long as we are left in peace. It is only yesterday I saw Mrs. Sniggles in the garden and pointed out to her the destruction of which her cat had been guilty in my bed of tulips."

"And what did she say?"

"She turned up her nose, tossed her head, and flounced towards the house, saying—

"What disagreeable persons these common people are? My cat's quite as good as him, I know."

"What! that tailor's trotter's wife said that to you, a respectable retired mechanic!" cried the old lady bursting with indignation, and nearly cutting half the foot of the stocking away in her rage.

"She did."

"The impudent minx, I wish I'd heard her. I'd have given her a bit of my mind—I'd have—oh, the nasty, proud, stuck up, tall-dressed[71] hussy!"

"Hush! wife—hush!" said Tobias, deprecatingly.

"And what did you say—what did you do?" asked his wife.

"I smiled at her remarks, and I pitied her," he replied.

"Pitied!"

"Yes, wife."

"I'd have pitied her, I'd"—

"Yes, wife, I pitied her ignorance, pitied her for her want of self-respect. But I did more, for I was hurt at her remark. I told her that I had a blunderbuss, that I would load it and shoot her cat if it ever did more damage to my plants. Had she have only appeared to regret the damage I should have been satisfied. Of course the poor animal don't know any better; it's the nature of cats, I suppose, to scratch and tear, but it is certainly not the act of a lady to treat me as she did. Could I have so far forgotten myself as she did, I might have said to her that which would have pained her more acutely than her words pained me."

"And I would shoot them, too," said the wife, bursting with indignation. "I would shoot them if there was a hundred of them. We ain't so stuck up as them, and they think they can do as they like. I'd show 'em I was as good as they are, and better too. Load the blunderbuss, Toby, load it quite full, and when you see a cat in the garden just show 'em you mean what you say, and that you ain't afraid of no tailor's trotters nor jumped-up, would be somebody in existence. Common people are we—common people! Yes, we are common people, but we only eat and wear what's paid for, and that's more than a good many of such as them can say."

And the old lady severed the worsted with the scissors in such a manner as to lead her husband to think that it would have afforded her much gratification to have severed the head from the body of Mrs. Sniggles in the same manner.

"Anyhow, I'm determined I'll frighten the confounded cats, if I don't shoot them," said the old man, reaching down a blunderbuss from over the mantle. "I don't like to hurt the animals, but perhaps the start they'd get, would keep them away from my plants, and make their owners believe I'm in earnest."

The old man went to a cupboard, and, taking out a small tin canister, proceeded to load the weapon.

"There!" he said, when he had finished the operation, "I won't put any shot in it, I dare say it will have some effect on the brutes."

"Which brutes do you mean? The cats or their owners?" asked his wife, still smarting with indignation.

"Oh! both of 'em," said Tobias. "I'll hang the blunderbuss up again, and mind you don't touch it."

"Me touch it?—not for the world. It might go off."

"There!" said the old man, returning it to its place. "Now the first cat I see, or hear, there'll be a noise, I know."

"Quite right, Toby. We ain't a going to be put upon. Common people, indeed!"

And the old lady stitched away at a furious rate.

---

[71] Elegantly dressed.

Tobias took his pipe from the chimney-corner, filled it with tobacco, and was about to apply a piece of lighted paper to the bowl, when he dropped the light, and sprang to his feet.

"What's that—what is it!" asked his wife, dropping her hands on her lap, and looking questionably into her husband's face.

"What!" said Toby, laying his pipe on the table.

"Yes."

"Cats," he growled. "There! don't you hear 'em just outside the back door?"

Both listened intently.

"Mol—row—mol—row."

There was no mistaking the sound.

Tobias took down the blunderbuss, and his wife, rising to her feet, took up the candlestick.

"There's the beasts on the window-ledge, all among those pots of geraniums," said the old lady, as a scratching noise sounded plainly to the ears of both, and then, in loud and discordant tones just outside the back window, came—

"Mol—row—wow—whew—whew—whew—war—r—r!"

Grasping the blunderbuss in his hands, with a determined look upon his face, old Tobias stealthily neared the back door.

Close behind him followed his wife with the candle.

"Don't make a noise," whispered Toby, "or you'll frighten 'em away."

"Mol—row—mol—row—wow!"

"There's a dozen of 'em at the least," whispered his wife. "Oh, the brutes!"

The back door was reached, and the old man raised the latch as silently as possible.

But ere he opened it, his wife said—

"I think they're gone; wait a minute."

"Mol—row—mow—mol—row—wheu—war—r—r!"

"There they are!" cried the old man, flinging the door wide open, and springing over the sill into the yard. "Here—oh!"

He had come to a sudden stop—so sudden, that he trod on the toes of the old dame, who was close behind him, and who roared in pain, but quickly changed her tones to those of surprise and terror, as the fluttering wick of the candle she carried in her hand lit up the tall, cloaked form, and masked face of a strange-looking being, right before them.

"It ain't a cat—it's the devil!" gasped the old woman.

"Mol—row—mol—row!" came from the mask.

"Cat or devil!" cried Toby, recovering partially from his surprise, "he shall have the contents of this," as he brought the blunderbuss up and levelled it at Jack, who, overhearing their conversation, had imitated the cats.

"No, no, no!" cried his wife, springing out of the doorway, and clutching at the weapon with her disengaged hand.

But she spoke too late.

Toby, who had guessed who our hero really was, and knowing that the blunderbuss contained no shot, pulled the trigger.

With the loud explosion, mingled laughter, cries, and a loud splash, while sudden darkness shrouded the scene.

The concussion of the air caused by the firing of the piece had put out the candle, and the slight hold which Toby had of the weapon permitted it to kick, and the butt, striking the old lady on the waist, sent her reeling backwards into a large tub of water, just outside the back-door, wherein she sat and screamed lustily, while Jack made his escape, shouting with laughter, and old Tobias, the blunderbuss still in his hand, stood bewildered and unable to move.

It was not till Jack had cleared the little gate of the front garden, and gave utterance to a loud "Mol—row," that Tobias turned to assist his wife from her unpleasant position, and, as he led her, dripping wet, into the kitchen, he cursed the cats from the very bottom of his soul.

CHAPTER LXIII.
CLAVERING ATTEMPTS THE LIFE OF JACK, AND IS BORNE TO PRISON.

SIDE BY SIDE at the edge of the road grazed peacefully the grey horse and the roan mare.

The hides of both animals still reeked with perspiration, for they had run a furious gallop; but the sweet herbage quenched their thirst, and they rubbed their heads together and champed their bits with a feeling of satisfaction at the absence of the spur.

Both had nobly fulfilled their mission, and the steam rose from their haunches in a cloud while thus they browsed along the roadside where the grass had not yet been ruthlessly crushed into the sod by the traffic which now leaves few green tufts around London.

They were, doubtless, happy; but how was it some short distance along the road, where, stunned and bleeding, the murderer lay with the tall form of the avenger standing over him?

That spectre face and demon form had done its work. The libertine and the murderer, terror-stricken and powerless, had received a fall of such violence as to render him insensible, and the animal he bestrode had plunged forward with such rapidity that when Jack succeeded in springing from its back to the ground he alighted some hundred yards off, and completely out of sight of the fallen man.

Not knowing whether Richard Clavering was stunned or not by the fall, he made all the haste back which he could to the spot, and found him lying in the centre of the narrow roadway, bereft of all sense or motion.

Our hero stooped down beside him, and for a moment he fancied his earthly career had ended, and a feeling of satisfaction, if not of joy, took possession of him.

But on laying his hand on the breast of Richard, he soon became assured that he still lived, and he suffered a sigh to escape him as he rose to his feet.

"Perhaps it would have been better were he dead," he said. "Better had Providence saved him from the hangman. I have sworn to track him to his doom, and could with greater pleasure leave him here a corpse in the road than hand him over to the officers of those laws he has so basely outraged."

Richard gave signs of recovering, and Jack again bent down.

"Desperation," he muttered, "often lends to the weakest man a giant's strength, and unless I take every precaution he may yet escape me. I must secure him while yet he is powerless to offer resistance. It will be more mercy to him to secure him at once than for him to escape and daily, hourly be tortured with fears of capture. Oh! Richard

Clavering, whom I once called friend, how have you fallen! to what depths of misery and degradation have you sunk! to what a fearful doom have your violent and ungovernable passions borne you!"

He quickly unwound the neckerchief of Clavering from the guilty man's throat, and secured his hands together with it.

This feat he had scarcely accomplished ere the guilty man opened his eyes.

A moment or so the man glared about in the gloom, as if bewildered, and then, as his glance fell upon the white mask of Jack, he uttered a loud cry, and endeavoured to gain his feet.

His hands being bound, he was unable to do so, and, with a loud groan, he sank back again upon the earth.

"Here! here!—still here?" he gasped. "Oh, my God! what shall I do?"

"What have you done. Richard Clavering?" said Jack, in a low, impressive tone; "what have you done, guilty man?"

"What? oh, what?" gasped Richard.

"Murder!" said Jack.

"I was not myself when I did it," gasped Richard. "I was mad—mad!—driven mad by taunts and upbraidings! Who are you? Why do you stand there? Why do you look upon me thus? Go! for God's sake leave me!"

"Not yet, Richard Clavering; not yet."

"Who—who are you?"

"The avenger of your wife!"

"Mercy! and go, or madness will seize upon my brain. What do you seek with me?" he cried.

"I seek to hand you over to justice—to the gallows!" was the reply.

"The gallows?" gasped Clavering, with a shudder.

"Aye, the gallows!"

"Never! never!" cried Richard. "No gaping crowd shall feast their eyes upon my trembling form; no yelling voices shall clamour for my blood. I deserve to die, but I will die by my own hand. Thus—thus do I rob the howling mob of their pleasure, and the gallows of its due!"

He drew his body up, and flung it backwards upon the ground, endeavouring to dash out his own brains.

But Jack had grasped him by the hair of the head, and prevented the consummation of his wishes.

"Richard Clavering, would you add another crime to your already overcharged catalogue of guilt?" he asked.

"Who are you that ask? Man or devil, who are you?" cried Richard, as he endeavoured to again fulfil his fell[72] purpose.

"Once your friend; for then I believed you a true and honourable man; now the avenger of your ill-used and murdered wife—Spring-heeled Jack!" was the reply.

"And not a denizen of another world?" said Richard, in a tone of unbounded relief.

"I am"—

---

72 Sinister.

"Enough, I know you now. Curses rest upon you! You—you alone have brought me to this!"

"Shame—shame!"

"You have been the cause," said Richard. "Like a shadow you have hung upon my path. You forced me to wed a woman I hated; you stood before me when I would have possessed her I love. You"—

"Hold! Richard Clavering, hold!" cried Jack. "I would have saved you from crime, but your blackened soul would not be penetrated by words of kindness and advice. If I were instrumental in causing you to marry a woman who had sacrificed all for you, I was the friend of her and yourself. If I stood forward to prevent the consummation of the hellish design you had upon the poor ballet girl, it was to save you from another crime."

"And you did it," sneered Richard. "You goaded me to madness, you made me stain my soul with blood; and now you seek to hand me over to the tender mercies of the law, that you may glory in my misery, revel in the sight of my execution."

"I am not a man to rejoice over the sufferings of another," said Jack. "In handing you over to justice I seek no such motives. I would only do my duty as a man and a Christian."

"A Christian! Ha! ha! ha!" laughed Richard in a hollow tone. "But I will thwart you and justice yet!"

"Rather seek pardon for your crimes," said Jack, pained at the other's manner. "Seek mercy"—

"Where?" interrupted Richard.

"There!" said Jack, pointing upwards.

"And should I get it?" sneered the other.

"It is promised if sought," said Jack.

"What, mercy?"

"Aye, mercy."

"And you—you tell me this," said Clavering, bitterly. "You tell me that there mercy would be extended to me, and yet you would deny it. Oh! this is well—this is well. Ha, ha! tell me to plead there for mercy, and yet you stand guard over me lest I should escape. You can talk of mercy, but can you be merciful? Aye, answer that—answer that!"

"How would you have me answer it?" asked Jack.

"Release my hands; let me go free. You boast you were once my friend; friends are friends in adversity as well as in prosperity. Unbind my hands and aid me to escape the jackals of the law.

"Richard Clavering, for any crime less than murder I would do so," said Jack; "but the blood of your wife is warm upon your hands. I cannot, dare not, do your bidding."

"Will not?" cried Richard.

"No, I will not. I hear the tramp of horses' feet on the road. You and I will soon part, Richard Clavering—never more to meet, I hope, in this world; but ere we do, let me implore you to pray for forgiveness for your great crime, and may Heaven have mercy on your soul."

"And hell consume yours!" cried Richard, worked up to desperation by hearing the quick gallop of horses gradually drawing nearer and nearer to them. "Spring-heeled Jack, they cannot hang me at once—days must pass ere they can do that—ere the gaping crowd assembles before the gallows, and the bell tolls for my death. But I will cheat them yet. I will force my prison walls. Blood is upon my hands—my soul. I can die but once, and will yet be avenged. Look to yourself!—look to yourself!"

Jack made no answer to this wild raving, save by a look of pity, which he cast down upon the man at his feet, who had raised himself to a sitting position.

The tramp of the horses came nearer and nearer.

Richard heard them, and made violent efforts to free his hands—efforts which our hero did not perceive, as his attention was occupied by the new-comers.

The first intimation he received was by seeing Clavering leap to his feet, and ere our hero could recover from his surprise, his throat was clutched, and he was borne backwards to the earth.

So sudden and unexpected had been the onslaught, that he was powerless to make the least resistance, and the knee of the desperate murderer was planted firmly on his chest.

"Ah! ha!—ah! ha!" laughed Richard. "'Tis my triumph now, Jack—my triumph. 'Tis you who must sue for mercy, not me; but you will sue in vain. Blood is on my hands— fresh red blood. I cannot fall deeper by taking another life. I can hang but once. You shall die!—you shall die!"

With one hand still on our hero's throat, and his knee pressed firmly on to his chest, Richard Clavering sought his breast-pocket with the other, and drew from it a knife.

It was a clasp Spanish knife, and he placed the back of the blade to his lips, and opened the weapon with his teeth.

In spite of the darkness, Jack saw the gleaming blade, and summoning up all his strength he hurled the murderer from him, just in time to save the weapon from entering his throat.

The knife was buried deep in the earth, so fearful had been the violence of the blow which Richard Clavering had aimed; and as he strove to tear it out Jack clutched him in turn, and pinned him to the ground.

"Foiled again!" hissed Richard; "foiled, again!"

"Yes," said Jack; "you are foiled again, and here I keep you till assistance arrives!"

"Curse you!" roared the guilty man. "A bitter, lasting curse upon you—you"—

The fingers of Jack twined so tightly round his throat, that he could not articulate, and his knee was pressed on the back of the hand which strove to tear the knife from the sod in which it had buried itself.

"Yes, Richard Clavering," said Jack, after a short pause, "you are foiled again. Justice will have her due, and murder will out. Could I have been brought to pity you, that time has passed now and for ever. The gallows awaits its prey, and hither come those who will bear you to it. Fool! you struggle in vain. This is the last hour of your freedom."

He pressed his knees more forcibly upon the hand which grasped the handle of the knife, and twined his fingers more tightly around the neck of the murderer.

He had no desire to add to the pangs he knew he must already suffer, but he knew and felt that to relax in the least, was to lay himself open to a desperate and implacable foe.

Still the tramp of the horses sounded nearer, but the impatience of Jack became greater every moment.

He had no wish to be seen by the coming horsemen in the hideous mask he had worn, and yet he dreaded to relax his hold of Richard to enable him to remove it.

Gradually the pressure of his fingers told on the murderer, his struggles became less violent, and then Jack hurriedly tore the mask from his face, and thrust it into his bosom.

It was none too soon.

The next instant three horsemen were close upon them, and would have trampled them beneath the feet of their steeds, had not Jack called out loudly for them to stop.

They heard his voice, and immediately drew rein, questioning as they did so him whom they could scarcely distinguish in the dark.

"Who are you?" asked Jack.

"Officers in search of a murderer," was the prompt reply.

"Richard Clavering?"

"The same."

"He is here; dismount, and aid me. His soul is not yet sufficiently satiated with blood, for even now he has sought my life."

No second bidding did they require, but dismounted instantly, and assuring themselves that the prostrate man was the one whom they sought, they quickly slipped the handcuffs on his wrists, and mounting him on one of the horses, bore him towards London.

On the road they turned to question Jack, but, to their surprise, found he was gone.

CHAPTER LXIV.
THE ATTEMPTED ESCAPE AND DEATH OF RICHARD CLAVERING.

THE cold grey dawn of morning broke over the earth as the three horsemen, bearing Richard Clavering in their midst, drew rein before the sombre walls of Newgate.

Not a single word had Richard uttered during the whole of that long ride, but motionless as a statue had he sat before the centre officer—his head bowed upon his heaving chest, and his manacled hands resting despairingly upon the pommel of the saddle.

He had been baulked of his revenge, and the disappointment rankled in his soul.

Bitter, though silent, were the maledictions he heaped upon Jack as he was borne along.

He felt that his career must now soon be ended—that he could bid farewell to the world if he could only take the life of Jack.

To him he attributed his present position.

Toiled in his villainy, he blamed Jack for all that had transpired, instead of condemning himself—his own base, unbridled passions—and he vowed yet to be revenged.

The massive door closed behind him with a jarring sound, and he moodily followed the jailer to his cell, where he sank down upon a chair without uttering a word.

Now he was again alone, in silence, and the voice of conscience began its work anew.

Despite the growing daylight, the place was wrapped in gloom, and as he gazed round upon the blackened walls, and up at the barred window, he felt all hope of escape desert his bosom, and his heart sank within him.

The jailer came and brought him the prison fare, but he paid no heed to him nor the provisions.

Tired with his ride, his struggles, and his excitement, he at length sank to sleep in his chair.

But rest came not to his wearied brain.

The drawing-room of his magnificent house was again before him, and Mildred stood by his side; then the pale face of his wife rose before him, and he started from his sleep as the report of a pistol echoed around.

It was only the turn of the key in the lock of his cell, and the jailer, quite a young man, and not long in his office, shuddered as he gazed upon the pale, startled face of his prisoner.

Here's your dinner, Sir," said the man, placing the fare before him.

"Take it away; I do not want it," said Richard.

"You had better have it, sir."

"I have no taste for food; take it away— yet stay, I will have it: perhaps I had better eat."

"You had, sir."

Richard did not want the food, he could not eat it, but he perceived that the jailer had brought him a knife, and he hurried to countermand his order for the meal to be removed.

He had been searched, and every article taken from him, much to his chagrin; but the sight of the knife was joy to his soul.

When the man had departed, he arose and approached the table.

A sickening shudder passed through him as he gazed upon the viands,[73] but a glow of pleasure surmounted his face as he grasped the knife.

"One chance more," he said, in a hissing whisper; "one chance more to cheat the hangman!"

He gazed upon the blade, and felt its edges with his thumb.

It was very blunt, and a look of disappointment passed over his brow.

He stood twirling the knife thoughtfully for some moments in his hand.

"It is not sharp," he said to himself; "far from it; but it would let out the life-stream, and make a fool of the hangman. Why should I hesitate? oh! why?"

He flung it down upon the table, and paced the cell for some time.

"Why—why?" he continued, "when I feel that there is no escape but through the rope?"

He shuddered, and clasped his hands over his eyes.

"Oh, God!" he muttered, "even now I fancy I can see the upturned faces of the crowd—even now their shouts ring in my ears, as they pant for my death—even now I can see the hangman, and feel the rope upon my throat! Oh, God! I might have escaped but for him! Curse him! Oh that I could be revenged! I could die happy."

And the walls of that cell echoed the word happy, as if in mockery of the wretch who stood within them.

Richard looked around shudderingly.

"I cannot stop here alone when night comes," he said; "the fearful silence and gloom of the place will drive me mad. This cell will be peopled with shadows of those I have wronged. I shall see the bleeding form of my murdered wife and servant. I shall hear their dying groans, feel their hot blood upon my hands, and go mad—mad—mad!"

He flung himself into the solitary chair, and rocked his body to and fro.

---

[73] Food.

Suddenly he sprang up.

His face was pale as death.

His eyeballs were distended and bloodshot, and his lips were quivering.

"They do not keep so close a watch by day as night," he said. "Then now—now is my time to endeavour to escape from this infernal place. But how?" he added, after a pause, and looking up at the barred window. "Desperation will lend me strength. I may force these bars."

He sprang to the table, placed the dinner upon the floor of his cell, and listened.

All was silent.

Not a footfall broke upon his ears.

With trembling hands he lifted the table beneath the window.

Then he paused and listened again.

Still no sound came.

He took up the chair and placed it upon the table.

Noiseless was every movement.

"They will never think of an attempt to escape while daylight lasts," he muttered, as he took up the knife he had lain down, and mounted the table.

But now he fancied he could hear a distant footfall, and his blood ran cold in his veins as he listened,

Moments passed, and he became convinced that he was mistaken, and placing his left knee upon the chair, be looked through the bars of the window, and could see that a paved yard was at a short distance below him.

A ray of hope broke upon his soul.

For a moment he forgot everything but the idea of escape.

He turned his attention to the bars, and his heart again sank within him.

They were strong and massive, and he felt they could defy the strength of twenty men.

With a groan he turned and sat down in the chair, still holding the knife in his hand.

"No escape," he muttered, "no escape but death! and I, who have slain two, have not the courage to kill myself! Why do the words of Jack ring in my ears—'The rope is spun—the gallows reared—and the executioner awaits his victim!' Shall he claim me? Shall I be made the sport of a cruel, unfeeling crowd? Shall I die upon a scaffold, with a rope around my neck? No—a thousand times, no! This knife no—no; I cannot—cannot slay myself!"

His head dropped till his chin rested on his bosom, and hot tears gushed to his eyes.

They were not tears of remorse, but of bitter disappointment.

But he dashed them away with his hand, and again sprang to his feet.

"I will escape," he cried, in a hissing whisper. "They shall not detain me here. I will rend these bars asunder, if I tear my flesh from the bones to accomplish the task."

Placing his knee again upon the chair, he fixed the knife between his teeth, and grasping one of the bars in both hands, exerted all his strength to force it from its socket.

As well might he have tried to move the prison from its base.

Again and again he made the effort, but all to no avail.

The perspiration poured off his face in huge drops, and he bit his lip till it bled.

"Foiled again! foiled again!" he muttered, as he paused, exhausted from his futile labours; "and the gallows must—will have its due. But no! there is yet one hope—one.

I cannot force the bars, but I may remove one with this knife. All is quiet. I will try—I will try; and if that fail, then heaven have mercy on me!"

He forced the point of the knife into the lead, which had been run round the bottom of the bar to secure it into the stone, and as he did so the door of the cell was flung open, and the form of the young warder sprang into the gloomy apartment.

Richard turned like an enraged tiger at bay.

"Trying to escape?" said the man. "It's no use. Come down from there."

"Never!" cried Richard, all the passions of his nature aroused. "I will leave this accursed place ere night. Keep back! There is blood enough upon my hands already."

The man drew a pistol from his pocket and levelled it at the murderer.

"I must perform my duty," he said. "Come down, and give me that knife."

"To its hilt in your heart," said Richard, raising it above his head, and making a spring towards the young man.

The warder saw his danger and the desperate nature of Clavering, and, pulling the trigger of his weapon, fired.

The fall of a heavy body mingled with the report, and, as the smoke rose upwards to the roof of the cell, Richard Clavering, still grasping the knife in his hand, lay bleeding at the feet of the jailer.

The man shuddered as he gazed down upon the white, upturned, and distorted face of the murderer who was making frantic but ineffectual efforts to rise.

"Foi—foiled again!" gasped Richard, as he writhed in agony, and the red blood dyed his shirt-front; "foiled again! Raise me up—I am choking!"

The warder placed the pistol upon the table and dropped on one knee beside the wounded man.

The jailer's face was now as white as his victim's, and his limbs trembled as he stretched out his hands to raise the head of Richard.

"Foiled again!" gasped Clavering, as the young man raised him to a sitting position. "You have prevented my escape, but cheated the hangman. You have killed me."

"The fault was your own," said the man. "I have only done my duty."

"Then take your reward," cried Clavering, aiming a blow at the man's throat with the knife.

Fortunately for the jailer, he saw the act in time, and, releasing his hold of Clavering, the murderer fell back instantly, and the weapon struck only at the air.

The next moment it was torn from his weakened grasp by the jailer, and hurled to the other side of the cell.

The look which Richard fixed upon the man was something truly appalling.

So fearfully bitter in its hatred and malignity was it that the man drew back in horror.

"Foiled again!" gasped the wretch. "Yes, foiled again; but I, too, shall foil others in turn—the crowd—the hangman—the gallows. Ha! ha! ha! I have foiled them. Ha! ha! ha! Water—I choke. Water—give me wa"—

He turned his head rapidly from side to side over the floor of the cell as the jailer sprang to the pitcher of water he had placed there in the morning, and several of the officials, alarmed by the report of the pistol, hurried into the apartment.

No questions were needed to explain what cause had brought them there.

The chair placed upon the table beneath the window told all, and they turned their gaze upon the prostrate and bleeding man to whose lips the jailer held the pitcher.

The cool liquid revived him, and by an effort Richard raised himself upon his elbow and glared upon those now assembled with a wild and unnatural stare.

"Ha! ha! ha!" he laughed. "You have come to bear me to execution, but you can't—you can't. I have cheated the gallows. Let the crowd wait, and the hangman stamp with rage. You are foiled now—you"—

His further utterance was stopped by blood gushing from his mouth and nostrils, and his head again fell back upon the floor of the cell.

The jailer raised him, and wiped the sanguinary fluid from his lips, and, after a pause, he gasped, while his eyes rolled wildly round the cell—

"See—see! She is there! Hide me from her. Yes, she is my wife, and I killed her. Look how she glares upon me with her white, bloodless face. Keep her back—keep her back! Do not let her touch me. Her cold hand presses my throat—I cannot breathe. Take her off— I—I choke. Mercy—Jess—Jessie! Mer—mer –oh!"

His head rolled back on to the shoulder of the jailer, and the guilty soul of Richard Clavering had flown to meet that of his murdered wife at the footstool of the Supreme Judge.

CHAPTER LXY.
JACK LEARNS OF A PLOT, AND HAS A NARROW ESCAPE.

NOW THAT he had placed Richard Clavering in the hands of the officers, to be carried before the judges of his country to answer for his crimes, Jack felt no further desire to have anything to do with the business.

He had fulfilled his promise, and done what he believed to be his duty, in banding over a cold-blooded murderer to justice, and as soon as the sanguinary wretch was on his way to prison, Jack took the first opportunity that presented itself of bidding good-bye to both the prisoner and his guardians.

This opportunity was not long in presenting itself in the shape of a gap in the hedge which ran along one side of the road.

Through this Jack darted quickly.

Crouching down, he waited till the sounds of the horses' hoofs died away in the distance, and then rose to get once more into the road.

As he was meditating whether he would journey back on foot or endeavour to catch one of the horses, which till that moment he had quite forgotten all about, the sound of voices was borne on the wind to his ears from the opposite direction to that which the officers and their prisoner had gone.

Certainly there was nothing very strange in the circumstance of persons talking at that hour as they came along the road, but still Jack felt an interest to know who and what they were.

Perhaps the idea that, whoever it was, they might take the animals, finding them already saddled and bridled, prompted him to stay, such a thought having entered his mind.

So he retreated back through the hedge, and, crouching down beneath it, waited and listened.

The footsteps came nearer, but the voices did not grow more distinct.

This puzzled Jack a little.

Presently he could tell by the sound of the feet that there were several persons, and as they drew yet nearer to the spot where he was concealed he became aware that they were conversing in low tones.

Jack strained every nerve to listen, and as they passed the spot on the opposite side of the hedge, he caught sufficient of their conversation to make him acquainted with the fact that they were a gang of poachers, and their object was the robbing of the gentleman's preserves where Richard Clavering had rested and effectually put his pursuers off the scent.

Jack waited till they had got some distance down the road, and then, putting on the mask he usually wore when in search of adventure, and drawing his cloak closely around him, he slipped out into the road and followed.

The men were walking at a hurried pace, and Jack had to take quick steps to keep the same distance between himself and them.

After about an hour's walk he missed the footsteps, which ever and anon he paused to listen for, and was satisfied that they had entered the grounds he had heard them speak of.

Jack now went more cautiously along, and slackened his pace considerably, desiring to let the poachers get to work ere he entered the place, or attempted to give the inhabitants of the mansion notice of their presence.

Jack had no very great respect for the game laws, but he had for the owner of the preserves, with whom he was well acquainted, and on a footing of friendship.

And again, he set his face against those who preferred to rob their more fortunate neighbours rather than toil honestly for a livelihood. Had a poor, starving wretch been guilty of such an act as the trapping of a rabbit, he would have considered the act unworthy of notice; but when he saw men who evidently preferred such occupations to that of honest labour, his indignation was rather great. When he considered that the fellows had began their operations, he strolled leisurely into the grounds, and took up a position directly beneath the tree where Richard Clavering had sat a few hours before.

Presently a big, brawny, labouring-looking man came silently and stealthily towards the spot, and just as he got within a few yards of the tree, Jack leaped out right before him.

The suddenness of the apparition, the sight of the ghastly mask, and the consciousness of having no legal business there gave the fellow such a shock that he staggered backwards and fell upon his knees in terror.

Jack extended his arms over him, and in a low, hollow voice asked what he wanted there.

But the man was evidently so alarmed that he could only make some strange, incoherent noise between a groan and a sigh.

"What are you doing here?" Jack asked again.

The man only stared with open mouth and open eyes, and clasped his hands together in an attitude of supplication.

"Poor, ignorant devil," muttered Jack to himself. "If I had been a keeper with a gun in my hand the probabilities are the fellow would have done his best to have taken the weapon from me and beat my brains out with its butt end, but my mask has more terrors for him than a loaded musket."

Then, kicking with his foot a bag which the man had in his hand, he said, in a severe tone,—

"Is this some of the proceeds of your villainous expedition? Speak! or I'll"—

"Oh! be merciful to me, and I'll confess all," stammered the fellow.

"What will you confess?—but there, I know all about it; still, I should like to hear your confession. Go on, and speak truly."

"Yes."

"Go on, then."

"It's rabbits."

"I know that. Is that all you came here for to-night?"

"Yes—no."

"The truth and a lie together."

"It's all I came for—but"—

"But what?"

"Not all they came for."

"They—who? your vile companions?"

"Yes."   .

"And what have they come for? No falsehood. I can tell in a moment whether you speak truth or not," said Jack, beginning to think that after all poaching was not the only object of the men he had followed.

"To rob the house."

"Oh! to rob the house," said Jack.

"Ye—yes."

"Well. I know that. How many are there? Now, no lies, for I know," said Jack.

"Seven."

"Ain't there more?"

"No; six without me."

"And how do they intend to do that?"

"By forcing one of the windows."

"Where are they now?"

"Gone up to the house."

"While you were sent here to keep a look out, eh?"

"No; oh, no."

"Don't tell me a falsehood. It will be better to speak the whole truth."

"Yes-yes."

"I knew that; so what's the use of trying to deceive me." The man made no reply. It was very evident that he looked upon Jack as some supernatural being, for he could not keep a limb of himself still.

"They are bold men," said Jack, after a pause, "to expect to succeed in such an undertaking, where there are at least ten male servants in the place."

"There was," said the man; "but the family is in London, and there's only the housekeeper and the gardeners in the place."

Jack started and felt somewhat ill at ease at this information, which was news to him.

He felt that he was not much of a match for six strong men, rendered desperate by the fear of discovery; but still he resolved that his friend's house should not be robbed if he could prevent it.

But how to prevent it was the thing.

"And so you wish to have nothing to do with the robbing of the house," he said, after a pause.

"No, I don't; and I wouldn't ha'e come if I'd 'a known what they were up to," said the man.

"You wouldn't?" said Jack, doubtingly.

"No, I wouldn't. I don't mind snaring a rabbit, but I ain't a burglar."

"Then your sympathies are not with your companions in this business," said Jack.

"What's that?" asked the man.

"You do not side with them?"

"No, I don't."

"Then will you side with me."

The man stepped back.

"No, curse me if I sell myself to the devil; that would be popping out of the frying-pan into the fire."

Jack was about to assure the man that he had no pretensions to the title of that gentleman, but a moment's thought made him feel he had perhaps better let the rustic imagine he was that personage.

"Very well," he said, after a pause, "I shall have you all one[74] for that one of these days: Poaching is a crime; and I claim all criminals sooner or later. Now there is a means by which you may escape my power, but you do not feel disposed to adopt them."

"What be they?" asked the man, quickly.

"By doing right yourself, and preventing others doing wrong. By preventing this burglary you place yourself out of my influence."

"Should I?"

"Yes."

"But I don't see how I can prevent the lads doing it, seeing as how they've set their minds on the job. If I did, I expect they'd about do for I."

"Very well," said Jack. "Then I'll prevent it myself. Six, you say?"

"Yes."

"Will you for once take my advice and get off these grounds at once?" said Jack, as he moved away, "for if I find you when I come back you'll repent it."

"Then I'll be off at once, you may be sure," said the man. "I have no wish to see ye again in a hurry, I tell you."

And the fellow turned and darted away towards the road.

The mansion was about a quarter of a mile from where our hero stood, and was situated in an enclosed piece of ground which opened upon another road, and it was evident to Jack that the burglars intended to obtain access to this by scaling the wall which bordered the preserves.

Anxious to make the inmates acquainted with what he had learned, and also to preserve his friend's property, he hurried along across the preserves till he came to the wall, and, after assuring himself that no one was about, he sprang over it into the enclosure and hurried towards the house.

Just as he had reached it a cry broke from a man's lips; and a tall fellow sprang upon him.

Jack eluded his grasp, and trusted to his mask to scare the man; but he now reckoned

---

[74] Each and everyone.

without his host. The moment the fellow perceived it, he whistled, and the other five men were instantly at his side.

"It's Spring-heeled Jack," said the man, pointing to our hero. "He's discovered our game, and our safety must be purchased by his life."

Each man, at this, sprang towards him, but Jack took a terrific leap backwards, and, seeing how small was his chance of coping with the six desperate ruffians, he dashed madly towards the iron gates on the opposite side of the grounds to that from which he had entered.

"Kill him! kill him!" shouted the man who had before spoken, as one and all darted after him.

Jack trembled for his own safety, so close were they behind him, but he struggled on, and as he neared the gate, took one of his terrific leaps at the very moment that one of the fellows seized his cloak.

Fortunate was it for Jack that it was but insecurely fastened, for it came off his shoulders in the man's grasp, and Jack cleared the high gate in safety, and alighted upon the opposite side of the wall, whither his pursuers could not follow him, and at once set to ringing the bell with all his might to arouse the inmates and make them acquainted with their danger.

CHAPTER LXVI.

JACK PROTECTS THE CROSSING-SWEEPER, WHO IN TURN
PROTECTS HIM.

"HERE you are, sir. Don't walk through the mud, sir. Here's a nice, clean crossing, sir; swept it meself, sir. Drop a copper, sir."

"Get out, you young rascal. I don't encourage a set of lazy young vagabonds," was the reply of a tall individual, as he stepped across a portion of a muddy road which had been swept clean by a bare-beaded and bare-footed, ragged little boy, who followed the person across, trailing his broom behind him.

"Won't you drop us a copper, sir? See how nice and clean I keep your boots, sir; and what a lot of trouble I saves your servant, sir," said the boy, pointing to the shining top-boots of the man.

"Now, be off. I tell you I don't encourage such lazy young thieves and vagabonds as you are," was the cruel reply.

The lad looked in the man's face for a moment, as if he thought he could not have heard aright what had been spoken; then, drawing himself up, he retorted—

"I ain't no more a thief than you are, if you do wear a fine coat and top-boots."

"You insolent whelp!" cried the man. "I'll wring your ears off if you talk to me like that. Such young rascals as you ought to be sent to the treadmill instead of being suffered to annoy persons in the streets."

"I ain't annoyed you," said the boy, "unless you're annoyed because I took you to be a gentleman, which you know you ain't. If you don't like to patronise a poor crossing-sweeper, I wonder you ain't ashamed to patronise his crossing; you don't mind that, only the paying for a clean path you don't like. If I sees you crossing again, I'll sweep the mud over it."

The man raised his hand and struck the boy a heavy blow on the side of the head.

This was too much for the youngster, who, with a howl of pain and rage, struck his broom into the heap of sloshy mud which edged the crossing, and sent a shower of it flying over the boots, pants, and coat of the man, then, turning, made a desperate bolt to get out of the way.

With an oath the man sprang after him, and ere he had reached the opposite side of the road grasped him by his shoulder with one hand, while with the other he pulled the boy's ear so severely that a shout of indignation rose from the throats of two or three persons who witnessed the deed.

"Let the boy alone," cried one.

"Hit him in the face with your broom," cried another.

"For shame! sir," said a third, seizing his arm, and rescuing the boy from his grasp, "For shame! sir; no provocation from that lad, however great, can justify so violent an assault from a strong man."

"Hear, hear! Bravo!" cried one, while the boy, thus released, rubbed his eyes and cried lustily.

"Who the devil are you?" cried the man, turning upon the boy's champion, who, flinging his cloak back from his shoulders, stood proudly up before the enraged man.

"One, sir, who is sorry to see a man so far forget himself as you have done."

"Some swell-mobsman[75] or London pickpocket, I suppose," sneered the man, "and find these young vagabonds very handy in your profession."

The man stepped back on to the pavement; as he spoke, and Jack, for he it was who had come to the boy's aid, smarting under the gratuitous insult, bounded on to the flags after him.

"You are an insulting fellow," said Jack, "as well as a coward."

"Take yourself off," said the man, "or I'll serve you the same. Go and talk to your own kidney[76]—pickpockets and crossing-sweepers."

"Rascal!" shouted Jack, striking out fair from the shoulder, and planting a heavy blow between the man's eyes, which sent him staggering backwards till his head came in contact with a large square of glass in the window of a hardware-shop, which was shattered by the force of the blow.

"Jemery! crikey! hooray!" yelled the boy, commencing to dance an extempore horn-pipe in the mud, which he splashed about with his bare feet in the exuberance of his spirits.

A shout of laughter and approbation from the bystanders mingled with the crash of the glass, the fall of china, and the prolonged scream of a not very prepossessing-looking lady of questionable age, who stood behind the shop counter.

The crash caused Jack, as well as the others assembled, to start back in surprise and alarm, for certainly our hero had no intention of dashing the man's head through the glass.

His indignation at the insult he had received gave place to a feeling of alarm, and he sprang forward, not to again strike, but to extricate the man from his dangerous position.

"Hurray!" yelled the delighted boy. "Shove him right away through the chaney, master. Oh, Jemini![77] here's a lark! Take my broom and give him a hoist with it. I ain't afraid

---

[75] A smartly dressed pickpocket or swindler.

[76] Your own kind.

[77] A mild oath. Romans used to swear by the heavenly twins, Castor and Pollux whose forms

you'll steal it. Shove the muddy end in his waistcoat-pocket, and tumble him right through. S'help me tater! Hurray!"

And splash went his bare feet again in, the heap of slush, the young urchin not only sending the mud in showers up the legs of his own patched trousers but splashing it over the bystanders.

Jack of course paid no heed either to the words or actions of the young London Arab,[78] but, with, a look of pity on his face, caught hold of the shoulders of the punished man.

As he did so, other hands were stretched forward from the opposite side of the window, and the unprepossessing lady of the hardware establishment seized the hair of the imprisoned man, and twined her fingers among the clustering locks.

"You wretch! you villain! you shan't get away; you shall pay for the damage done to my property!" shrieked the lady, tugging at the man's head with all her might.

"Let go, my good woman," cried Jack, "or his face will be cut to pieces with the broken glass."

"Serve him right, the wretch! I won't let go, so that he can run away. I'll be paid for my property, or he shall go to jail."

"For God's sake let go!" yelled the man.

"I won't!" cried the woman.

"Hold him tight, missus," cried the boy. "Lay hold of his ears and pull-em half out as he did mine."

"Peace, lad!" said Jack angrily.

"Get out of the way, governor, and let's have a hit at him," said the boy, raising his broom. "Just one, that's all!"

"Stand back, boy!" said Jack, giving him a push; "the man has suffered enough punishment already."

The boy did as requested, but the woman could not be persuaded to release the hair of the man from her clutches.

On the contrary, she only pulled the harder, and the glass smashed from top to bottom. "Hallo! here; what's this?" was the first indication either Jack, the woman, or the bystanders had of the approach of a gentleman in blue, who, as he spoke, elbowed his way through the little throng to the window.

The boy set his broom down on the kerbstone, and, giving the arm of Jack a pull, exclaimed—

"Mizzle,[79] governor; here's a bobby."

Jack turned, and stood face to face with an officer.

"Spring-heeled Jack!" cried the policeman, in surprise.

"Sir!" said Jack, in an instant, perceiving that the man was one who had had good cause to recollect him.

"All right, Jack; up to your old games again; but you're nabbed now, my boy."

Jack sprang backwards as the officer stretched out his hand to grasp him, the little crowd giving way in surprise, and even the lady in the shop released her hold of the

---

make up the constellation of Gemini.

[78] Street children. So called because, like the Arabs, they are wanderers with no settled home (Brewer's Dictionary of Phrase & Fable).

[79] Get out of here.

hair of the man whom Jack had dashed through her window.

"Oh, jemini! Spring-heeled Jack!" cried the boy, flaunting his dirty broom; "mizzle-mizzle!"

Pushing aside the persons in his way, the officer strove to effect the capture of our hero, who eluded his grasp by a bound into the centre of the road.

"I call on you all to arrest that man," cried the officer, "or aid me in doing so."

"Come on, my friends," said Jack; "take me if you can."

"Blowed if they shall," cried the boy, placing his broom in the ridge of soft mud, and by a sudden jerk sending a perfect shower up over the face of the policeman, and for a moment completely blinding that worthy.

A peal of laughter followed this act, and the boy, springing to Jack's side, cried—

"Come after me; I'll show you how to double on 'em. Come on—come on."

So saying, he flung his broom over his shoulder and dashed away at a good speed.

A moment Jack hesitated, then hurried off after the lad.

"Stop him! stop him!" roared the officer, wiping the mud out of his eyes with the cuff of his coat. "Don't let him escape any of you, or it will be the worse for you."

And away he went, with smarting eyes, after Jack, followed by several of those who had been witness of the fracas, leaving the man to struggle through the broken window as best he could, and square accounts with the lady of the shop for the injury done to her premises and stock-in-trade.

"Come on," said the boy, taking the lead, and panting for breath at every step, "come on, sir, and they shan't take you."

"Where would you lead me?"

"Up here."

"Up there?"

"Yes."

"Look to yourself, my lad, I will get away from them somehow."

The boy looked behind him.

"Go it," he cried, putting out all his speed; "they're close behind us, and there's another policeman."

"Two of them?"

"Yes."

"Whew!" whistled Jack, looking behind him, "so there is."

"And there's another out there," said the boy, pointing right before them.

"Confound it! so there is."

"Never mind, sir. You've no need to be afraid of him, 'cos we'll hook[80] it down here."

So saying, the boy dashed across the road, and into a dark entry.

"Don't be frightened," said the boy. "I ain't a-going to hurt you."

Jack burst out laughing.

"Well, I've not much fear of that. Hallo! the hounds are in full cry."

"Stop him! down there—after him!" and such like cries came to the ears of Jack and his guide.

They were in a dark, covered entry, which Jack had no previous knowledge of, and hence he was compelled to trust entirely to the lad's guidance.

---

[80] To sling your hook, or to run away.

"Now, my man," he said, "as you got me into this scrape, you must get me out of it, for I don't know where I am."

"I do."

"Where?"

"Close to Mother Mokes's."

"Mother Mokes?"

"Yes."

"Who is she?"

"Don't you know Mother Mokes?" asked the boy in a tone of surprise, still running on by our hero's side.

"No, indeed."

"Well, I'm blowed! Everybody knows her," said the boy.

"Then I'm nobody, for I never even heard of the lady before."

"Lor'! you must be a ignorant chap, then. Why, Mother Mokes is Mother Mokes."

"Doubtless."

"Don't you know the old woman as sits at the corner of Davis-street with an apple-stall, and smokes a pipe?" said the boy. "You don't know her?"

"Oh! yes," said Jack; "I recollect the lady well."

"To be sure you does—everybody knows her, for she's a stunner,[81] she is."

"Well, but we are not near Davis-street," said Jack.

"Of course not, only the old woman lives down here."

"But how will that prevent my capture?"

"She hates the bobbies, she does, because they interfere with her sometimes, and she's a out-and-outer[82] to help anyone as wants to get away from them. I live with her, I do, and pay nine-pence a week for my lodging. She's a rum 'un, but she's a good 'un, she is. Mind how you come; here's the doorway. Mind, there's a lot of the floor broke there, and you'll get your foot in the hole, if you don't mind. There ain't no bannisters to the stairs, so you'll have to be careful, or you'll go pitching over 'em. Here, take hold of my hand, and don't be frightened. I won't hurt you, 'cos I like you for giving that chap a knock as nearly pulled my ears off."

The boy took bold of our hero's arm, and endeavoured to lead him forward.

The place was pitch dark, and an unwholesome odour pervaded it. Jack was not a man to be intimidated by trifles, but still he did not feel so much at his ease as he could wish, and hesitated whether to go any further in that rookery, or make his way back and trust to fortune to evade his pursuers.

While debating in his mind which course to pursue, several voices and the tramping of feet came plainly to his ears, and he knew that the officers and others had turned into the dark entry.

"Go on, boy," he said, "I will follow you, but if you lead me into a trap it will not be well for you."

"I ain't such a shoful[83] as that," replied the lad. "Mind! there's a step. No, I am only a poor crossing-sweeper, but I ain't a going to sell you after licking that chap for me. Joey

---

[81] Beautiful woman.

[82] Go to extremes.

[83] Counterfeit, false person.

Gibbons ain't a kid of that sort, I tell you. There, keep agin the wall. Mind! the next stair's broken; but what can you expect for ninepence a week? Now we are on the landing; up another lot, and that's Mother Mokes's room, where you can stop till the bobbies goes away, and then hook it."

""But what will Mother Mokes say?" asked Jack.

"She ain't there now; she's along of her stall."

"At this hour?"

"Yes, sir; it's as good a time as any in the day."

"The work's hard, or rather long hours, I should say," remarked Jack; "for I have seen her there early of a morning."

"Well, so all poor people does. I works the crossing from six o' clock in the morning till ten at night, and then does the cellar-flap business up till twelve."

"The cellar-flap business?" echoed Jack.

"Yes, sir."

"What's that?"

"Lor! don't you know—ain't you seen me? Why, stands on my head and dances on my hands, and plays the tune with my trotters."

"Your what?"

"Trotters—feet! But here's the door. It's jolly dark, but I knows where there's a bit of rushlight."

And the boy led Jack into a dark, unwholesome apartment, as a loud shout from below told him his pursuers had reached the house.

CHAPTER LXVII.

JACK DOES GOOD FOR TRADE, AND IS CURSED AND BLESSED IN A SHORT TIME.

JOEY the Sweeper closed the door quickly behind him as the shouts of those below reached his ears, and Jack felt the lad's hand tremble on his arm.

"I won't get a light, sir," he said; "'cos then they'll know somebody's here. I thought we'd have give 'em the double, for 'tain't many as likes to come up this alley, in case they don't get out safe again. Blowed if they ain't coming up the stairs! There!"

Jack listened, and could hear the tramp of boots on the worn and rickety staircase.

For a moment he began to suspect the boy had laid the trap for him, but the next instant he thought otherwise.

"They'll soon have this door down," said Joe; "for the panels is split all up, and a kick would send it in, and if you goes back they'll nab you."

"Is there any other way of exit besides the door?" asked Jack, hurriedly.

"There's the window."

And the boy led Jack across the room towards a frame minus several panes of glass, and through which the faint glimmer of a distant lamp came.

"Where does this look into?" asked Jack, hurriedly, placing his hand upon the dusty sash.

"Berker's-buildings."

"Not into the place from which we entered the house."

"No, sir; into a worse place than that."

"Worse?" said Jack, in a tone of surprise.

"Yes, a good deal; 'cos they're most all thieves as lives there; chaps as don't sweep crossings, nor nuffin."

While the lad spoke Jack had opened the window, and looked out.

He was about twenty feet from the ground of a dirty-looking court, and right beneath him was a heap of dust and vegetable refuse, but not a soul was in sight, and hurriedly placing a coin in the boy's hand he mounted the rotten window-sill.

"Now, boy, if you refuse to say which way I have gone I may get away."

"Quick, sir!" whispered the lad. "Here they are! Quick, sir! I'll hold my tongue."

There was a heavy blow upon the door, and rays of light streamed through two broad chinks in the panels.

Jack hesitated not a moment, but gathering up the folds of his cloak, leaped from the sill, and alighted safely on the heap of rubbish.

He gathered himself up, turned and gazed towards the window, as the boy hurriedly closed it behind him.

The next moment a flash of light from the window told Jack that his pursuers had entered the room.

"They cannot harm the lad," he said; "so I will get out of this confounded place as quickly as possible."

He was about to make his way out of the court, when he was suddenly confronted by a big, burly, bull-headed fellow.

The man stood right before him, and Jack started backwards, not in fear, but to place himself in readiness to resent any insult or injury that might be offered to him.

He had heard of that locality, though it was the first time he had been within it; and he knew that any person wearing a decent garb was pretty well sure to be molested.

"Well, sir, what is your business with me?" asked Jack.

"I'll soon show you. Tip up,[84] or over you go," was the reply.

"Tip up what?" said Jack, throwing back his cloak, and clenching his hands.

"Oh! you're green, ain't you? You'll be black soon, if you don't. Shell out! I don't stand any palaver, now. Let's have it, and sharp, too."

"Take it!" said Jack, throwing all his force into his arm, and dealing the fellow a blow on the mouth that sent him down as if shot, sprawling amid the heap of rubbish.

"Are you satisfied?" asked Jack, in a calm tone; "if not, I will accommodate you with the same dose again. You have mistaken your man, you bullying scoundrel."

"Strike me lucky!" yelled the fellow, scrambling to his feet. "Do you know who you are hitting on?"

"I can pretty well guess," retorted Jack. "A scoundrel who fancied he could intimidate, and then rob me with impunity—a bully and a cur!"

"I'm Jem Slogger, who has fought in the Ring, licked my man in five minutes, and come out smiling," growled the man.

"Had I been your man, you would have come out pummeled to a mummy," said Jack. "Stand aside, and suffer me to pass on my way, unless you desire another specimen of my skill in self-defence."

---

[84] Pay up.

"Curse me, if I do," growled the man; "for if I can't lick you myself, I can get a dozen to help me. You're a likely chap to have a few pounds about you, and I mean to have them. Whew-w-w!"

The man blew a long, shrill whistle, which Jack suddenly ended by another blow on the mouth, which again sent the fellow down, and, leaping over his body, Jack hurried towards the end of the court.

But he was not destined to reach it without interruption.

Another low, brutal-looking fellow sprang from a doorway, and flinging his arms around Jack's waist held him in a vice-like grip.

Jack, in turn, caught the fellow round the waist, and, lifting him from his feet, gave him a heavy back-fall, coming down upon the man with all his weight, nearly driving every particle of breath out of his body, and leaving him stunned on the ground.

Up he sprang, and again made for the entry of the alley; but he was clasped from behind by Slogger, and dragged backwards towards the rubbish heap.

"No, you don't," growled the fellow; "I hain't done so easy. I'll have what you've got afore you leave this place—oh!"

The hands unclasped themselves, and the fellow staggered with his head bleeding, while a shower of broken pantile fell around our hero.

In surprise, Jack cast his eyes upwards.

"Scamper, Jack! scamper!" cried a voice above him; "and if he touches you again, I'll let him have another tile bang on his head!"

Jack recognised the voice of Joey the Sweeper, and, with a grateful look at the boy, he sprang towards the entry of the Buildings, and out into the open street beyond, without further molestation.

He did not pause directly, deeming it best to put some little distance between himself and the place, and therefore drawing his cloak about him, he hurried along at a quick walk for some little time.

Meeting with no one whom he had any reason to fear, Jack slackened his pace, and sauntered leisurely along till he reached the corner of Davis-street, where, even at that late hour, a board, balanced upon a basket, leaned against the post at the corner, and an old lady, neither overclean in dress or appearance, sat beside it smoking a short black pipe.

"Well, Mother Mokes," said Jack, pausing in front of the dame, "there you are, enjoying your pipe."

The old woman removed the pipe from between her lips, and puffed out a mouthful of black smoke, as she laid it on the top of the post.

"Sure, honey, and it's the only enjoyment I've been afther knowing since Pat was laid in his coffin," she replied.

"And who was Pat?" asked Jack.

"Pat, your honour? Sure now, and Pat was Misther Pat Mokes, that used to come a-courting Biddy in swate ould Ireland, and that's meself, yer honour, sure."

"Your husband?"

"Bedad! an' it was the praste made him that same," said Biddy, polishing the rosy skin of an apple on the dirty apron suspended from her waist.

"And so he is no more, eh?" said Jack.

"Och! yer honour, he's been no more for nigh tin years—yes, it's quite that since his wake. It's the broth of a boy he was! and it's a mighty shame he didn't live longer; for then, your honour, it's selling apples I wouldn't be afther doing."

"You don't find it very profitable, I suppose?" said Jack, "do you, Mrs. Mokes? sitting here all day, and half into the night?"

"Och! yer honour, but it's thrue as my soul it's the loss I been living on and paying me rint[85] into the bargain for the last seven year."

"That's bad," said Jack, with a smile.

"Bad is it?" said Biddy. "Bedad! but it's worse than bad; for it's meself that can't get a glass of gin to warm me old heart widout taking it out of the rint."

"That is indeed a great misfortune," said Jack. "But I am afraid, Biddy, that you wouldn't be satisfied with one glass."

"Sure now, yer honour, and it's two or three I'd be afther liking better, though one is better than none at all," said Biddy, smacking her lips together.

"And you really can't get one?"

"Bejorah! but times is so bad, the devil of a shaddy of a quarthern[86] of one am I afther seeing at all, at all! Och! but it's hard lines for a poor lone widdy that was once married to a rale Irish gintleman who used to get stone blind drunk every night of his life, and smelt strong of the creature when they put him in his coffin, barring that they couldn't put him in at all, at all, but dropped him over the tother side on to the floor, widout hurting him, sure."

"And he was not at all angry at such treatment?" asked Jack.

"Angry, yer honour? Sure, an' the boy was as quiet as a lamb, and never said a blessed word," replied Biddy.

"But of course you felt vexed at such carelessness, Mrs. Mokes?"

"The devil a bit, yer honour. How could I, when they all sit down on the floor beside him, and trated him like a gintleman as he was."

"Treated him?" said Jack, in surprise.

"Sure and they did that same," replied Biddy, with a look of pride. "They poured the whiskey down the throat of the corpse till it couldn't hold a single drop more."

"Ha! ha!" laughed Jack, "and that's what you call treating him like a gentleman, Biddy, is it?"

"Bedad! an' I do, sir; and I'm sure it's yer honour thinks that same."

Jack did not, but he did not say so. If he had expressed his feelings they would have been those of disgust instead of approbation.

"So ever since you have been a vendor of fruit, eh, Biddy?" he asked, edging towards the corner of the stall.

"Sorry a bit, yer honour. Sure an' didn't they get up a friendly lead for me, and buy me a mangle?"

"And didn't that answer?"

"It couldn't spake yer honour," said Biddy, looking up with an air of surprise at her questioner; "barring it used to creak and groan like an evil spirit when it wanted oil.

---

[85] Rent.

[86] A shadow of a quartern (quarter measurement), i.e. a fraction of something that is already small).

Sure an' I never heard one spake at all, at all."

"I did not mean that."

"Sure, now, and what did yer honour mane?" asked Biddy.

"Could you not make it support you?"

"Sure an' it often did that same, seeing as I made the bed on the top of it, and barring that it was a little too high, it was as comfortable as any I ever had."

"Still you do not understand my question, Biddy. Could you not get sufficient work for it to enable you to live comfortable?"

"Och! that's it, is it?" cried Biddy. "Sure, now I know yer honour's maneing. The devil fly away wid me for a fool. Work, is it? Sure an' it was meself that had plenty of that same at a penny a dozen."

"Then why did you not keep at it, Biddy?" asked Jack. "I should think bad as mangling must be, it was far preferable to the life you now lead."

"Sure now, yer honour, it wasn't my fault, at all, at all, that I didn't kape it. You see, yer honour, turning a mangle is very thirsty work; and it was a little drop of the creature I used to take now and then, just to put strength into me elbow. Well, one day it was mighty busy I was, and I got Jem Flanagan's wife to come and help me. We had two or three drops, when Mrs. Flanagan made a mistake, and threw the bottle of the creature into a basket of clothes belonging to a laundress instead of some of the things, and the spirit ran all over them; and sure, yer honour, I didn't like to send them home like that, so I puts them in the fender to dry, when, bad luck to it! a large piece of coal, red hot, fell out upon one of them, and they was all in a blaze in a moment."

"And of course you lost the lady's work afterwards?"

"Bad luck to her! she wasn't satisfied with taking away the work, but she summoned me for ten pounds, and as I wouldn't be imposed upon by her, afther her things had nearly burnt me house and mangle, sure an' a lot of darty spalpeens[87] come and took the mangle away from me, and sold it, and gave her the money."

"And what did you do then, Biddy?"

"What did I do, yer honour? sure an' I acted like a dacent woman. I put a big stone in the foot of a stocking, and I smashed every blessed pane of glass in her windows as far as I could reach, and when I couldn't break any more I went into the door and broke her head with that same stocking."

"Certainly, that was the work of a decent woman," said Jack.

"Sure an' that's thrue yer honour. But I never could get justice, for as sure as I'm sitting here, if they didn't put me in prison for six months. Och! but it graves me sore when I think of it, for when I came back they had taken all the sticks for the rint, bad luck to them! and had left poor Biddy Mokes no home at all, at all. But Flanagan got up a raffle for me, and I bought this board and basket, and here I've been ever since."

"And I suppose if you had the money to purchase another mangle, you would not do so?" said Jack, after a pause.

"Bedad! but it's that same I'd do, for I gets rheumaticky sitting here."

"I'm afraid if you did get one you would upset bottles of spirits into the baskets of clothes, and again set them on fire."

---

[87] Scoundrels.

"Sorry a bit, yer honour. It's careful I'd be afther being that not a drop of the creature came into the house while the work was about. But it's a long time, I think, I'll be getting money for a mangle here, for I ain't had a blessed customer this two hours. Won't yer honour buy some of these nice apples? Sure an' they are as swate as sugar, and I'll polish them up beautiful with my handkerchief," said Biddy, taking from her pocket a piece of rag that certainly had not felt water for some time.

"It's only the colour, sir," she continued, as she began polishing the skin of an apple, after breathing upon the rind. "It was as clean as a new pin three weeks ago, and, barring that it's a nasty cold I've had on me through sitting here, it ain't been used much. There, your honour, sure an' ye could eat that apple with pleasure, I know."

Jack turned his head, with a shudder of disgust, as a voice exclaimed—

"Hallo, Mother Murphy! ain't you coming home to-night? There's been such a jolly lark. I'll tell you all about it."

Jack recognised the voice of Joey the Sweeper, but not wishing the lad to again know him, he hurriedly slipped on his mask.

"Such a jolly lark," continued the boy, springing up from the ground and clasping his arms and legs round a lamp-post, in close contiguity to the old woman's apple-stall, and taking up his position evidently there, while he intended to tell his story.

"Hould yer tongue, yer noisy spalpeen! " cried the old lady, "till I've served his honour; for sure it's one of my best customers he's going to be. How many will ye take, sir? Sure an' they're as swate as sugar, and will melt in ye mouth without biting."

"All the lot," said Jack, turning quickly, and placing his foot under the board, gave it a sudden tilt, which sent it off the basket, and all the apples rolling over the pavement into the gutter.

"Och! blue murther and botheration!" cried the old dame, springing to her feet. "The devil seize ye! Och! be jabez! it's the gintleman hisself!"

The old woman, who had sprung forward, suddenly paused, holding up her hands in surprise and horror, as she caught sight of the mask of Jack, on which the rays from the lamp streamed fully, and who, with one hand on his hip, stood pointing down upon the wreck of her stall, while the boy, with wide open mouth and eyes clung tenaciously to the lamp-post, to save himself from falling.

"Oh, gemini!" he gasped out, recovering himself. "It's Spring-heeled Jack!"

A portion of the old woman's terror subsided on the instant.

"Och! the blackguard, murthering villain!" she cried. "And it's yerself and not the devil at all, at all! What have you served a poor lone widow, without a husband, like this for, ye spalpeen?"

"Only to make good for trade, Mother Mokes," said Jack, with a laugh.

"Sure an' it's the ruin of the poor old woman you'll be, and may the devil fly away wid ye, you thaving robber! Bad luck to yer ugly mug, ye decateful deceiver!"

"Don't leave off yet, Mother Mokes," said Jack. "There's something so angelic about your voice when you are angry."

"Angry, is it?" cried the woman. "Bedad! but it's tear your ugly eyes out of yer head I could; it's a dirty spalpeen ye are! and it's meself that tells ye that same!"

"Much obliged to you," said Jack.

"Sure an' it's not much obliged I am to you, ye mane, deceitful spalpeen! An' I took ye to be a gintleman; bad luck to me! Och! sure an' it's ruined I am quite! ye wretch! ye villain! ye monster! ye fiend! ye black devil!"

"Well, Mother Mokes," said Jack, "I think by now you've had your say, and I'll begin."

"Go to the devil wid ye!" cried the woman, stooping to pick up the board.

"In another moment you'll fall to blessing me, instead of cursing me," said Jack, placing his hand in his pocket.

"Sorry a bit, ye dirty spalpeen! It's meself that will curse ye till ye die! Sorry a blessing ye'd get from me. I'd like to see your neck stretched, ye black-hearted thief!"

"Not when you turn the mangle again, Biddy," said Jack. "Here—at your time of life the streets is not a place to get a living—that will pay you for the damage, and set you up again in your old trade. Now, curse away Biddy as much as you like; only don't give way to drink, and again ruin your prospects."

He threw down several golden coins upon the board which she had again placed on the basket, and turned away.

For a moment the woman gazed at them in surprise, then hurriedly gathered them up and placed them to her teeth, while Joey dropped from the lamp-post, exclaiming—

"Oh, gemini! Here's a lark—hurrah!"

"And did I curse the gentleman?" cried Biddy, looking after Jack's retreating form. "The devil take me for doing so, for sure didn't I know he was a real gentleman? May yer honour live for a thousand years, and yer swate face never grow mouldy. May ye have a slathering wake, and meself be present. Och! it's a gentleman ye are; and may the devil fly away with the spalpeen as says ye ain't! Good luck to ye— good luck to ye!"

CHAPTER LXVIII.

GOOD ACTS MEET WITH BAD REWARDS—THE BURGLARY DEFEATED.

THE loud summons of Jack speedily brought to one of the windows of the mansion a night-capped head, possessed by the old housekeeper, who had tremblingly leaped from her bed to learn the cause of the violent ringing of the gate-bell at that unseasonable hour of the night, or rather morning.

As soon as Jack caught sight of the large frill at the window, he commenced to shout loudly—

"Thieves! thieves!"

"Oh, my gracious! oh, my goodness! What's to be done?" cried the lady. "The family are out of town, and there's only Gilpin the gardener in the house. Oh! we shall all be murdered! Oh, dear!—oh, dear!"

"Confound the stupid woman," muttered Jack. "She had better have held her tongue than revealed the absence of resistance to these villains."

At this moment a stone struck Jack on the shoulder, aimed by one of the men on the opposite side of the railings.

"Rouse the gardener, and have the dogs let loose," cried Jack, "while I go to seek assistance."

The head disappeared from the window, and Jack, fearful of being injured by stones thrown by the burglars, hurried away down the road as half-a-dozen missiles rattled on the iron gates.

"I've got the worst of that at present," said Jack, as he sped along. "But never mind, if I cannot prevent the place being entered, and obtain my cloak, I may be able to set the officers of justice on the track of the rascals."

The report of a fire-arm caused him to pause and turn, and look towards the house; then a loud cry broke upon his ears, and he knew that someone was wounded.

"Ah!" he said, "fired from that window? One of the rascals has fallen, I should think, by the noise he has made."

He hurried on again, well assured that he could be of little service in the grounds, and after about five minutes the sound of a horse's feet saluted his ears.

Jack listened a moment, and again hurried forward.

In a short time a gentleman on horseback came up, and Jack, tearing off his mask, sprang out into the road.

"Stop, sir—stop!" he cried, waving his hands above his head to attract the attention of the rider, who was urging his horse along at a gallop.

"Who are you?" cried the man, partially reining-in the animal.

"Sir, a rob"—

Whack came down the riding-whip with such force on Jack's head that he fairly staggered under the blow.

"A robber? Take that, you scoundrel, and don't try it on with me," cried the man, digging his spurs into his horse's flanks, and darting off at a furious gallop.

"Curse the fellow!" cried Jack, recovering from the shock. "But no—no; it's myself who is to blame—not him. For commencing my story as I did, he naturally took me for a robber. The fellow hits hard though, and a pretty bump I shall have on my forehead."

And Jack rubbed the sore place as he spoke.

"Egad! but my usual luck seems to have deserted me to-night," he continued, "for I get more knocks for performing a good part than I have ever done for a bad one. Well, it's the way of freaks of fortunes. One poor devil may struggle all his life to do good, and bad luck attends him; another will do bad, and his path is made as smooth as glass. I've half a mind to let things take their course, and yet it would be not only unmanly, but unfriendly to do so. Confound it! how that fellow has made my head ache."

And pressing his hand to his forehead Jack tried to think the best course to pursue.

While thus engaged, another report awoke the echoes of the place, and the deep growl of a dog saluted his ears.

"The dogs are loose," he said, in a tone of pleasure, "and as the burglars have evidently no fire-arms there is a prospect of their nefarious plans being thwarted. I'll go back now, for I may be of some assistance."

He turned and hurried back as quickly as possible towards the gates.

As he neared them he could hear the loud screams of help and murder from the housekeeper mingling with the deeper tones of a man's voice urging the dogs—then came a mingled cry of terror and pain.

"Take off the dog! take off the dog!"

Jack reached the gates, and as he looked through them he perceived a man attired only in his shirt and trousers, and armed with a blunderbuss, whilst beside him a large mastiff struggled with one of the burglars.

Jack was about to spring over the gate, when he recollected that the dog might attack him.

So he called out in a loud tone.

"Gilpin! Gilpin!"

The man turned.

"Gilpin!" cried Jack again. "I would aid you, but I fear the dog will seize me."

"Who are you?" said the man, springing towards the gate.

Jack whispered a name in a low tone, and the gardener uttered a cry of pleasure.

"Oh! sir, are you here?" he said. "Do come in, for there's three or four of the thieves, and nobody to tackle 'em but me and the dogs."

"I know it," said Jack; "but though you know me, the dogs do not."

"They won't touch you, sir, if I call 'em off," said the man. "But I must go and get the key, unless you could climb over."

"I can do that," said Jack, seizing the railings, and springing up to the top of the gate.

"Mind yourself, and look out the dog don't leave that fellow and take a fancy to me," said Jack.

"But you can't jump that, sir?"

"Can't I?" said Jack.

And before the words had died away he had leaped to the ground beside the gardener.

"Where's the other dog?" asked Jack, knowing that the man had said he had let two loose.

"He's followed the others out into the grounds, towards the other road. This chap couldn't get away quick enough, his foot caught in his cloak and he stumbled, and Boxer had hold of him in a moment. The other one there I've put a shot into, and so he can't do much."

And the man pointed to a dark object on the ground at a little distance beyond the house.

Meantime the mastiff who had been named Boxer had hold of one of the rascals by the hip, and despite the shower of blows reined upon him by the clenched fists of the alarmed and suffering man, he held on like grim death.

"For God's sake call off the dog!" shouted the man. "He'll tear me to pieces."

"Serve you right, too," replied the gardener.

"You have no business here," said Jack.

"Do call him off—do—do," pleaded the man.

"I'll see you d——d first," cried the gardener. "Boxer's got you, and may keep you. Sir, how that woman does keep a hollering," he added, looking up at the frilled night-cap at one of the windows.

"Ask her to be silent," said Jack, "and then call the dog off. The fellow don't deserve much sympathy, but the punishment he has received will teach him a lesson for some time to come."

"Hold that row, will ye?" cried the gardener. "Don't you see there's nothing to holler for now, and bring us down the double-barrelled gun in the library, and just mind it's loaded."

The head disappeared from the window.

"Call off the dog," said Jack. "He will kill the man."

"Stop a bit, sir. He can't do much harm while Boxer's got him, and this old blunderbuss ain't got a charge in it. When I get the gun I'll call off the dog, for who knows, he might have a shy at I as soon as he's got rid of Boxer."

"True," said Jack; "and prudence is the better part of valour. We may secure this fellow, and then go over the grounds with the dog in search of the others."

"That's just what I've been thinking on, sir. You see he can't make much resistance while you tie his hands and legs if I hold a couple of barrels at his head. But he knows this old thing ain't loaded, you see, sir, and might be obstropolous."[88]

"Very true."

"Gilpin—Gilpin! here's the gun," cried the voice of the housekeeper. "Make haste and take it. Oh! I'm so frightened."

And the old lady appeared at a lower window holding the gun in her hand.

The gardener, however, did not attempt to fetch it, but replied—

"Just give it to this gentleman, will you. If I come for it, the dog, perhaps, will turn on him,"

"Who is it?" cried the housekeeper. "Perhaps it's one of the thieves."

"No it ain't; I knows better nor[89] that," cried Gilpin, sharply.

"Ah! are you sure—quite sure?"

"Be not alarmed, my good woman," said Jack. "I'm the person who aroused you to a sense of your danger by pulling the gate-bell— a danger which, I'm happy to say, I think is over."

"Oh, lor'! I'm so terrified. I tremble all over. I can't keep a limb of me still. Only think of the family being away in London—only think of that, sir," cried the old lady, as she handed Jack the weapon.

"I cannot help thinking how foolish you must have been to have called out that circumstance from the window."

"Oh! I was so frightened."

"Well, go in and compose yourself, and I and Gilpin will see that all is right."

The old lady disappeared, closing the window quickly after her, and Jack returned to the side of the gardener.

"Just give I the gun, sir," said the man, sticking the blunderbuss between his knees. Jack did as requested.

"Now, sir, are you ready to prevent that Jack cutting away?"

"Quite."

"All right, then. Here, Boxer! Boxer! come here, boy, come here."

The dog let go his hold of the burglar, and turned at the sound of the gardener's voice, but as he caught sight of Jack he uttered a deep growl.

"Down! down!" cried Gilpin.

And the dog sank to the ground on the instant, crawling on its belly till its head laid at the feet of the gardener.

"He's as quiet as a lamb, and wouldn't bite a mouse now, unless I tell him," said Gilpin. "Now, you, sir, look here, both these barrels are loaded, and I be a pretty fair shot, so I give ye warning, if you attempt to resist I'll send both charges through your skull."

The man was too much weakened by his struggles with the dog and the loss of blood he had sustained to offer any resistance, and Jack, grasping his arms, pinioned them behind him, and holding them there with one hand, with the other tore off the large silk handkerchief from the burglar's neck, with which he secured them effectually together.

Then, by a sudden jerk, he thrust the burglar's legs from beneath him, and laid him

---

[88] Unruly or aggressive.
[89] Than.

on his face on the gravel walk.

"That be neatly done, sir," said Gilpin.

"Now I'll take my cloak," said Jack, picking up the garment from the ground where it had fallen.

"Your cloak?" said Gilpin.

"Yes, my friend. This rascal robbed me of it not long ago."

"Then I'm glad you've got it back. I wonder where the other dog be? Perhaps they got away from him, but be won't give up the chase now he's been set on. Here, sir, will you take the blunderbuss—though I don't know what use it be, as it ain't loaded, except to hit a fellow on the head with—and come over the grounds with me. There's none of them as know about the house; and the dogs."

"Certainly would," said Jack.

"Don't leave me here," cried the man; "don't leave me here with that dog."

"Ain't such a fool," cried Gilpin. "We're going to take the dog with us; we might want him to lay hold on one of your pals."

The fellow uttered a groan.

"Howl away, you won't be able to do anything else," said, the gardener. "Come, boy! come, Boxer!"

The dog leaped to his feet with a growl.

"Steady! steady, boy! Ha! Ha! you mustn't touch that gentleman. Down, sir! Down!"

The dog crouched down again.

He had showed unmistakeable indications of a desire to spring upon Jack, but the rebuke was sufficient, and our hero had now nothing further to fear from the brute.

"For God's sake don't go till you give me a drink of water," cried the man. "I'm choking with thirst."

"You may choke if you like," cried the gardener.

"Give the poor devil a drink," said Jack. "Ha! what's that?"

"'Tother dog, sir. Here he comes. Lay down, sir! lay down!"

With a whine, the beast crouched down beside its companion, and looked wistfully up in the gardener's face.

The man stooped over him, and examined his mouth intently.

It was covered with foam, but not a streak of blood was to be seen around it.

"The others have got clean off," said Gilpin, as he rose to his feet.

"How do you know?"

"There would have been blood on his jowl, if they hadn't, sir. The rascals have got clean off, that's certain; and perhaps, after all, it's as well they have."

"Perhaps so," said Jack. "Then you think it's no further use searching the grounds?"

"Not the least, sir. Towler's searched 'em enough, depend upon it; and so I'll leave the dogs here to look after these chaps, and we'll go and. get the water."

"I'll remain here."

"You had better not."

"Why not?"

"The dogs might get obstropolous when I'm gone, and then, sir"—

"True," interrupted Jack, quickly, "and I have no desire to feel their fangs."

"Look after them," said Gilpin, speaking to the dogs, and pointing to the two prostrate bodies.

A low growl was the response, and Jack followed the man towards the house, in search of water.

"I think, sir, that other one be dead," said Gilpin; "and I suppose I'll get into a row for doing my duty to my master."

"Of course an inquiry will be held into the cause of death, if he is dead; but no jury would convict you," said Jack. "Day is fast breaking, and we shall see how affairs stand."

The man obtained a jug of water, and together they returned to the man who had begged it.

"You don't deserve a drop, unless it be on the gallows," said Gilpin, kneeling down on the earth beside him; "but here you are."

The man made no sound or motion, and Jack, peering eagerly into his face, exclaimed—

"He has fainted; pour a drop down his throat, and over his face and forehead, and then let us see to the other."

Gilpin did as requested, then rising, approached the man whose body had received the charge of the blunderbuss.

His face was deathly pale, and his features rigid, whilst his fingers were clenched tightly into the palms of his hands, and his legs were stretched out straight.

Jack touched the face, and a shudder ran through his frame, as he hurriedly drew his hand away.

Then, after a moment's hesitation, he thrust his fingers into the bosom, and laid his hand upon his heart.

There was no pulsation, and Jack leaped to his feet, exclaiming—

"He will commit no more burglaries, for he is dead!"

"Good Lord! and I killed him!" cried the gardener. "Do you think the other's dead, too, sir?"

The burglar answered this question for himself, by giving utterance to a deep groan.

They approached him, and raised him from the earth, and placed the jug to his lips.

The man took a deep draught, uttered a prolonged sigh, and then, in a faint voice, asked—

"What will you do with me? Won't you let me go?"

"No," said Gilpin. "We'll take you to the house, and keep you there till the police come for you. You've done a pretty thing for yourself and I."

They led him to the house, and, after a time, Jack took his departure, and promised to send on the first officer he met.

CHAPTER LXIX.

JACK PLAYS A TRICK WITH A SCARECROW, AND ALARMS A COUNTRYMAN.

THERE is nothing more bracing to the nerves; or exhilarating to the spirits, than a sharp walk in the country at early morning, to see the sun rise above the tall trees filled with feathered life, and listen to the melody of a thousand throats, to gaze upon the lark winging its way homeward, or pause to examine the dew-drops which, like diamonds, glisten on every flower.

So green, so fresh, so luxuriant do the trees, the hedges, the grass appear, that we could almost chide the noon-day sun and dirt, that shall dull the freshness of everything around.

'Tis early morn, when the primrose, the clematis, and the climbing rose is sweetest—then that the honeysuckle sheds its loveliest fragrance. Certainly the country is ever beautiful, but never so fresh, so fragrant, as when the dew is on the grass, and the lark springs from the corn.

The dews of night have washed and cooled the parched vegetation, and given it, as it were, new life and stamina. The climbing plants which twine about the hedgerows are full of flowers—flowers that fade when the hot garish sun falls upon their petals, dulling their brightness, and curling around their many-hued cups.

But at the present period of the year the corn is only peeping through the ground, and the poppy dots not the yellow sea of waving blades. Still the lark sings, and everything is gay, fresh, and beautiful, and none could be a greater admirer of nature than our hero, Spring-heeled Jack.

It was broad day-light when he strode away from the mansion his timely warning had spared from being robbed, and the sun was rising amid a sea of red clouds.

Feeling that now there was no particular cause for hurrying, he slackened his pace after a short time, and listened to the song of the birds as he culled[90] ever and anon some wild, yet lovely flower.

Leaving the high road after a time, he struck across a freshly planted field, in order to take a nearer cut to the places where he intended to go, and, absorbed in a delightful reverie, he strayed from the beaten track without knowing that he had done so, and was trampling down the fresh blades all unconscious of the mischief he was doing.

The flight of a lark, filling the air with its melody, broke the spell which bound him, and looking up suddenly, he became aware of where he was going, and gazed about for the path which led across the field.

As he did so his glance lighted on a strange, ragged figure but a few paces from him—and a more miserable-looking object could scarcely be imagined.

At the first glance Jack almost shuddered, at the second, he burst out into a loud fit of laughter.

"A scarecrow!" he said, when his mirth had abated; "and if abject misery could afflict the heart of a crow, that object would certainly do it." He approached close to the stuffed effigy, and examined it curiously.

"Well," he muttered, after a pause, and having satisfied his curiosity, "it is certainly not a very prepossessing looking object, but I believe, after all, that there are many wretches who infest our courts and alleys of the great metropolis who could change garments with this thing advantageously to themselves. This is not the worst scarecrow I have seen in my rambles in search of adventure. Ah! it's a sad thing to contemplate, that in the wealthiest city in the world so much squalor, so much dirt, and so much poverty exists. The man who could find an antidote for this disease would obtain not only the blessings of the poor, but also of the wealthy. But, alas! I fear the day is long distant when that will be. Those who try it, however brave of heart and persistent of purpose, give up the task in despair: and why! because there are two classes of poor—the deserving and the undeserving, and the keenest observer is powerless to weed the good from the bad. A generous soul and a benevolent heart meet with inspiration at every step, and thus those who deserve

---

[90] Picked.

sympathy are more often overlooked than they would be. Ere poverty can cease to exist, the youthful mind must be trained, and taught to respect itself—education must do the work. The seeds of self-reliance and self-respect implanted in the mind of the child will make the man exert himself—struggle for a position with hand and brain, rather than wait in idleness for others to do it for him. Heaven helps those who help themselves; but while there are so many canker worms festering in the heart of society, the truly deserving are but ill-assisted. But I am moralising, and forget that I have encroached upon forbidden precincts. There's the path. Hallo! here's a chawbacon[91] coming this way. Confound it! the fellow will catch me among the corn! I don't think he has seen me yet, but he is sure to do so. I'll crouch down behind the scarecrow till he has gone, for I'm almost too tired with my night's work to care for a tussle with that raw-boned fellow, refreshed by a good night's slumber, and made strong by pure air, honest toil, and frugal fare."

Thus saying, Jack crouched down so as to permit the body of the scarecrow to conceal him from the path which the honest countryman was passing on his way to his daily toil, whistling gleefully as he trudged along with somewhat long strides.

"Honest labour is truly the source of happiness," said Jack, as he listened to the yokel's merry tune. "Hard worked and poorly paid as that fellow is, his heart is as light as the down that falls from the thistle. Work strangles care and laughs at misery. Be it ever so humble, the man that toils for his bread enjoys a happiness unknown to the indolent."

The man ceased whistling, and broke out into a song, in which, if there was no tune, there was something hearty in the way which he gave utterance to the words. One would think that perhaps he wished to drown the tones of the birds, so loudly did he carol forth his ditty:—

"To plough and to sow, to reap and to mow,

And to be a farmer's boy."

So long did he dwell upon the last word, however, that Jack slightly raised himself to get a glimpse at the man, and by so doing knocked over the scarecrow.

But in a moment Jack had it in position again, but not before its upset had been observed by the man, who instantly hushed his song, and paused in his walk, looked hard in the direction of the effigy, and scratched his head hard to enable him to account for its sudden fall, and still more sudden rise.

"Well, if that bean't[92] the first time I ever saw a scarecrow get up of itself after he'd tumbled down!" muttered the fellow. "It beats me, it does, and it doesn't take a little to do that."

The man walked a little further along the path, then paused to get a glimpse behind the scarecrow.

But Jack took the precaution also to shift his position, thus defeating the man's object of seeing whether there was anything behind it.

Still perplexed, the countryman walked back some distance, and paused, and looked again.

But again Jack shifted his position.

Still more puzzled, the man took off his battered billycock, and scratched his head

---

[91] Local, rural, bumpkin.
[92] "Be ain't", or "isn't".

with both hands, while he gave vent to a loud and prolonged whistle, indicative of nothing in particular and everything in general.

"That beats I!" he exclaimed, "dang it if it doan't! A scarecrow fall down and get up again of itself! Well, nobody would believe it, if I told 'em I saw it with my own eyes. I won't be beat. I'll know how it did it, if I tread down half an acre of corn. Dang it! it beats I, it does—it beats I!"

And the man forced his billycock on to his head, and stepped from the path in the direction of the figure and our hero.

"Confound the fellow!" muttered Jack, "there's no help for it now. I must be seen, and the man's doubts set at rest. I fain would have avoided him; but as that can't be done, I suppose I must give him a shook, and then take myself off."

He drew his mask from his pocket, and adjusted it to his face.

The man did not come on very rapidly, although the strides he took were of enormous length, doubtless so that he should hew down as little of the young corn as possible.

However, Jack did not have to wait very long before the man stood within a couple of yards of him, when he paused, and looked hard and curiously at the scarecrow.

"There be the stake that holds it," said the man, "fixed in it all right. It beats me, it does!"

So saying, he moved slowly round.

As he did so, Jack, still crouching so that his head should not come above the shoulders of the stuffed figure, kept hold of the ragged garments, and turned the effigy round, walking with it, and keeping the front of the scarecrow still present to the wondering gaze of the astonished countryman.

When the man had walked a perfect circle, with the scarecrow still moving round as well, he came to a full stop, and opening his eyes and mouth to a tremendous width, stood glaring upon the figure in utter bewilderment for some moments, then stepped back a few paces, paused, and looked again, and, finally, knocking his billycock on one side, scratched away at his rough head as if he would tear the skin off his pate.

"I seen some hundred of scarecrows," he muttered, after a time, "but I never seed one afore as could do that. If I doan't begin to think the dang thing's haunted by an evil spirit; and if it is, the crop will be a bad one. It'll be a bad harvest, I fear. It beats I, it does. The devil's in it; and if I bean't off pretty sharp, there'll be some harm come to I, I'm afraid. I'll go and tell farmer all about it, and let he come and see for hisself. Dang it! if I shan't expect to hear it talk another time, as well as see it move."

Anxious as Jack had been to avoid the man, he could not resist any opportunity for a bit of fun, and he called out—

"Don't go yet, chawbacon!"

The man no sooner heard this, than he gave a bound backwards of at least half-a-dozen feet.

"Lawks! alive!" he gasped. "There's an evil spirit in it."

"What's the price of hay?" asked Jack in a hollow voice, still keeping his head bent behind the figure.

"Ha—a—y?" gasped the man, in utter terror, and seemingly now powerless to move from his new position.

"Yes, hay, stupid. What is it a load? Mind what you are doing there, trampling down the corn. Don't you know I'm placed here to guard it?"

"Go—o—d gra—gra—cious!" cried the man. "I—it beats me. The—the devil's in it."

"That's true, chawbacon. How do you find yourself this morning?" said Jack, bobbing up his head over that of the scarecrow, and nodding at the countryman.

"O—o—h! oh! oh!" trembled on the man's lips, and he shook his hands before him, and his knees knocked together in horror.

"Glad to see you, my friend," said Jack.

"I—I bean't glad to see you," gasped the man. "Go—go away."

"That's unkind," said Jack. "I thought you would be happy to make my acquaintance."

"No—no—no!"

"I thought you would. I heard you singing so merrily that I quite took a fancy to you," said Jack.

And as he spoke, he drew up the stake out of the ground to which the scarecrow was fastened, and moved towards the countryman, still holding the effigy before him.

"Yes, I've taken a violent fancy to you," continued Jack.

This was too much for the man—and under ordinary circumstances he was no coward—for seeing the object approach him, he uttered a loud cry of terror, and turning, fled over the field, trampling down the young blades of corn in his course, at a terrific pace, yelling and shouting as he went with all the strength of his lungs.

"Measter! measter! here's the devil in the scarecrow! Here's the devil in the scarecrow, and all the crops will be ruined!"

Jack could not repress his laughter as he gazed after the man, who ran as perhaps he had never ran before, taking the shortest course over the field towards a farmhouse whose gables glistened in the morning sun.

Jack did not attempt to move away from the scarecrow till the man had got fairly out of the cornfield; then, forcing the stake into the ground, and taking a parting look at the effigy, he made his way to the path, taking care to do as little injury to the corn as possible.

Having reached this, he continued along it in the direction of a large and verdant meadow, where a number of cows were located, without any further interruption, smiling, as he went, at the game he had played upon the countryman, and wondering what would be thought of his story at the farmhouse.

CHAPTER LXX.

JACK ALARMS THE MILKMAID—A HARD RUN AND HARDER FIGHT—
TRAPPED IN HIS OWN TRAP—THE ESCAPE.

JACK soon reached the meadow, which, like a huge carpet of emerald green, stretched away for some distance.

From this he had a good view of the farmhouse, and its various outbuildings, but his attention was now more particularly attracted by a group of half-a-dozen cows, which had been called together to be milked.

At the side of one, seated on a three-legged stool, with a wooden pail between her knees, was a fresh-looking, ruddy-faced damsel, engaged in the operation of milking, lightening her labours with the burden of an old and favourite ditty, which rang out clear on the morning air.

We have said Jack was an admirer of nature, and human nature also came in for its share.

There was something pleasing to him in the sight of the young woman sitting at her morning task, and carolling away in a not unmusical tone.

He could not but contrast her fresh, rosy cheeks and robust appearance with that of some of the high-born dames of his acquaintance.

Certainly many of those had cheeks with the bloom of the rose, but then he knew it was artificial—not the natural glow of health.

True, many were beautiful—when not in déshabille;[93] but few could boast of the beauty of her on whom he now gazed.

With a form suffered to expand to its proper dimensions, and a carriage easy and graceful—not made so by the art of the corset maker—and with smooth, glossy hair parted over a broad, intelligent forehead, Jack thought her the beau ideal of that beauty intended by its Maker, and not to be enhanced by all those artificial appliances so commonly used by those of a higher station.

"Beauty unadorned is adorned the most," thought Jack, as, unobserved, he watched the movements of her fingers; "and I'd wager her manners are as prepossessing as her person. I'll beg a drink of milk from her, and if she gives it not with a smile and a blush, I am no judge of womanhood; and if she does as I am sure she will, she shall not lack the coins to purchase a holiday dress."

And thus muttering to himself, he made towards her.

So accustomed as he had become to wearing his mask, he quite forgot that he had not removed it from his face—a circumstance unfortunate for both himself and the blooming milkmaid.

With a light step he neared her, but occupied with her labours she neither heard nor saw his approach.

As he was about to make his presence known, the animal, which was submitting to the milking, shifted its position, and to avoid coming in contact with it, Jack stepped on one side, and when the cow became again stationary our hero was on the opposite side to the beast to that on which the girl sat, gazing down at the frothing milk in the pail, and singing in a pleasing tone—

"Dolly, she was the fairest maid,
That carried the milking-pail."

"I'll call her Dolly," muttered Jack to himself. Then, raising his voice, he exclaimed—

"I'm sure, Dolly, you will not let a thirsty stranger ask in vain for a draught of milk at your hands."

At the sound of his voice, the girl leaped up quickly, overturning the three-legged stool, and as her head rose above the cow's back, and her eyes caught sight of Jack's mask, she threw up her arms, gave utterance to a loud scream, and fell backwards into a sitting position into the pail of milk, splashing it about in all directions, and so alarming the cow that the animal bounded forward, leaving Jack standing gazing in great concern and evident surprise upon the milkmaid, who kicked and plunged and screamed, till finally the pail rolled over on the grass, carrying Dolly with it.

"What, in heaven's name"—began Jack. "Confound it! I have got my mask on, and frightened the poor girl out of her wits."

---

[93] Undressed or partially clothed.

He was about to remove it quickly from his face, when Dolly, scrambling to her feet, started off towards the farmhouse, screaming as she went in tones so shrill and piercing that Jack was certain they must be heard for a longer distance even than the affrighted milkmaid desired them to reach.

"What a forgetful fool I am," muttered Jack, annoyed at himself. "But there's no help for it, and the sooner I'm off the better, if I don't want a troop of farm-servants belabouring my bones with pitchforks and flails. Egad! here they come. Now, Jack, you'll have to run for it."

A number of men, and among them the yokel he had so alarmed in the corn-field, came hurrying from the house to meet the terrified Dolly

Jack cast a quick glance around him to see which was the best course to take, and decided upon running in the opposite direction from which he had come.

This course he considered best, as in that direction he perceived a small wooded enclosure, and thinking by making for that he might effectually baffle those who were making towards him, his mind was made up to try to reach it.

To do this he had to cross the meadow.

He was not a man to think twice before he acted, so away he sped at once, gathering the folds of his cloak around him as he did so.

By the time he had started, the men had reached Dolly, and heard her story, which happened to be the same as the yokel's—that she had seen the devil.

The farmer, who had also come out—being better educated than his servants, and having little faith in the supernatural,—persuaded his followers that it was only some person playing a trick, and exhorted them to follow him, and endeavour to capture and pay the rascal with a good beating for his antics.

Finding they had a brave leader, the men quickly armed themselves with pitchforks and other implements, and quickly bounding over the smooth meadow in pursuit of our hero, whose course could plainly be seen, from the absence of all shelter.

Wearied as Jack was, he felt that he would have to make great exertions to reach the preserves—for such was the little wooded spot he had marked out—and he struggled manfully to accomplish his object.

In spite of all, however, his pursuers gained upon him, and the gruff voice of the farmer came plainly to his ears as he urged on his men.

"Devil, or no devil, we'll teach him to play pranks on this farm! Come on, lads, and we'll have him, and make his bones sore before he's many minutes older."

"Thank you," said Jack; "but I won't let you, if I can help it." And exerting all his strength, he bounded on.

"I tell ye, it's the devil, measter, that was inside the scarecrow," gasped the countryman, panting for breath. "No mortal man could jump like that!"

"Come on, I tell you!" roared the angry farmer. "And the devil take me, if I don't teach him how to play pranks on my farm. Stop! you vagabond, stop! and have a taste of a yeoman's arm!" he added, calling after Jack.

"I should be happy to oblige you," muttered Jack to himself; "but I cannot possibly comply with your request just now, seeing that if I did I might get a taste of the strength of a dozen arms instead of two; and I don't feel exactly in right trim for that just now."

"Ah! you rascal, I've got you!" cried the farmer, making a grasp at him.

"Hold me tight, then," exclaimed Jack, taking one of his terrific leaps, which sent him half-a-dozen yards out of the farmer's reach.

"'Gad! If he were a horse instead of a man, he'd make an out-and-out steeple-chaser," said the farmer as he recovered from his surprise, and again bounded forward in pursuit.

"But he ain't a horse, and he bean't a man, I tell ye, measter," cried the countryman.

"Hold your row, you fool," roared the farmer, vexed that Jack had eluded his grasp.

The countryman was silent.

"Throw a fork at him, one on ye, will ye! and pin him to the ground," cried the farmer, as Jack reached the edge of the preserve.

Whiz-z-z came a pitchfork, which, fortunately for Jack, swerved from its course some five or six feet, as he dashed into the shadow of the trees.

"That's a pretty weapon to hurl at a man, certainly," said Jack. "The idea of those two prongs sticking in my back is not a very pleasant one. But I dare say I can dodge them now."

"Come on, lads! come on!" cried the farmer. "He's only got out of the frying-pan into the fire. He'll get his leg in one of the traps, or get a shot from the spring guns."

"Whew!" whistled Jack. "Spring-guns and traps are there. I did not think of that, or I should have been tempted to cross the corn-field, and make for the road, instead of coming here. There's danger whichever way I turn."

"There he be, measter," said one, pointing out Jack to the farmer.

"Hi, you, sir!" cried the farmer. "I tell you it be no good trying it on with us. Just you take my advice, and come here. We mean to have you, and give you a sound drubbing. So you better take it, and go quietly."

"You mean to take me, do you?" cried Jack.

"We do."

"Then come and do it, if you dare," was Jack's retort.

"That will I," cried the stalwart yeoman, dashing forward on the instant towards where our hero stood.

"Doan't, measter! doan't! He'll take thee," cried the countrymen, who could not believe that Jack could be other than his Satanic Majesty himself.

Jack suffered the farmer to approach him, but when he got within arm's length he struck out a heavy blow, which, resting on the farmer's cheek, brought him to a sudden stop.

Taking advantage of the confusion of the farmer, and the dismay of his followers, Jack dashed away, keeping a good look out for traps.

The yeoman, however, quickly recovered himself, and, smarting with pain and indignation, he immediately gave chase, calling out as he ran—

"Stop! you damned rascal, and I'll give you blow for blow. Stop! you coward, and give I a chance to lick you."

At the word coward, Jack stopped and turned; he could not bear the imputation on his courage for one moment.

"Look here, farmer," he cried. "If you will send back your men, I will give you satisfaction for that blow."

"I'll see you damned first, and I'll give you a drubbing in the bargain," exclaimed the enraged man, making a dash at Jack, and clutching him round the waist. "Now I got you; and, man or devil, I'll give you as neat a throw as ever you had."

But the farmer had counted without his host when he looked on an easy victory over

Jack in a wrestling bout, for no sooner were the words out of his mouth than he was lifted from his feet, and flung fair over the head of our hero on to his back.

A shout arose from the men, and one and all dashed towards him, brandishing their weapons.

"Hold!" cried the farmer, staggering quickly to his feet, and motioning them back. "He's gained the first throw, but there's not a man in the county can beat me."

"But he ain't a man," cried the yokel.

"I've beat every man as tried a bout with me, and if he be the devil, dang me if I don't beat him too."

Again he flung himself upon Jack, but passion had blinded him; and this time our hero, who was cool and collected, grasped him by the shoulder and the hip, and summoning all his strength, hurled the farmer several feet from him.

The yeoman did not fall, hut as he madly dashed forward for another trial, he was brought to a sudden stop, and the click of a trap mingled with a loud cry of pain from the farmer's lips.

"Trapped in his own trap!" cried Jack, who instantly perceived what had happened.

"Dang ye all! let me out!" cried the farmer, furious with pain.

His servants rushed forward to obey, and Jack, taking advantage of the confusion which reigned around, sprang towards the point where he had entered the preserves, and reached it ere anyone could intercept him.

"Stop him!" roared the farmer. "No—dang him! let him go. For if he warn't the devil I could have broken his back."

Such were the last words that Jack heard as he hurried away, and he was not long ere he had crossed meadow and corn-field and regained the road beyond.

CHAPTER LXXI.

THE BALLET-GIRL AND HER FRIENDS—THE ROBBERY.

THE season was over, and many of the disciples of the drama and the ballet were thrown out of work, which, to the greater portion of the profession, meant nothing less than starvation.

To the poor ballet-girl, the want of an engagement is often a very serious thing, though most of them follow some other occupation than pirouetting around the stage on their toes to the delight of thousands.

Seamstresses, ironers, bootbinders, laundresses, and such like, generally compose the ladies of the ballet—not the principal danseuses certainly, but their less accomplished sisters who fill up the stage.

There has been a great deal said against this class of females, but a good deal more than is either just or true.

Their detractors are many, and their friends few.

The respectable matron looks with disgust upon the skirts and fleshings, and there are few mothers of a family who would take into their service the unengaged ballet-girl; hence this class, when the theatres are closed, or the pantomime season is over, are compelled to resort to occupations which are terribly toilsome and sadly paid for.

So it was with Mildred Hendon, the unfortunate dupe of the libertine, Clavering.

The shock which the discovery of his perfidy had given her, though it did not lay her upon a sick bed, brought upon her a sort of dreamy melancholy, from which, at the slightest sound, she would start and tremble.

Every farthing she could scrape together had been spent in obtaining her wedding garments, but after discovering how basely she had been treated, this finery—the first she had possessed for years—had to be pawned for the means to obtain food for herself and mother.

Believing in his promises, and at the instigation of her deceiver, she had thrown up her engagement in the corps de ballet, and as her place had been instantly filled up, she found herself, before the season was more than half over, with no occupation.

Something must be done to provide food for herself and aged mother; and day after day she wandered through the streets of the great metropolis in search of employment, and night after night returned, sad, dispirited, and hungry, to her mother's abode.

"Still come back as you went, Mildred?" said the old lady, one night, as she placed a cup of weak tea before her fatigued daughter. "Still you can obtain no employment?"

"Nothing, mother—absolutely nothing. There are plenty of domestic servants required, but they will not take one who has figured in the ballet. Oh! you should see the looks of horror with which the ladies gaze upon me when, in answer to their questions, I tell them I have been engaged at the theatres. They turn from me with disgust, and leave me to go my way, saddened and tearful."

"I wish you had never had anything to do with the theatres," said the mother, sitting down, and clasping her hands on her lap.

"And so do I, mother; but you know why I did. It was the only course open for me to help to keep us out of the workhouse. I could not bear to see you go there."

"I know—I know, child," said the mother; "but I ought not to have been so selfish. I am too old to work, and have no right to be a burden to you."

"Oh, mother!"

"I should have gone," was the quiet rejoinder, "and then you could have got some domestic employment. Ah, me! that fatal stage! What has it done for you? Made you acquainted with a villain."

"Do not speak of him, mother. Heaven will punish his soul for his wickedness to us," said the girl, bursting into tears.

"If we were poor, we were at least happy," said Mrs. Hendon, "before he came hither to blight our peace. But we won't mention him. I have resolved to go into the workhouse, and then, perhaps, you will be able to get sufficient to keep yourself."

"No, mother. While you live I must be with you. You cannot—shall not go," cried the girl.

"'Tis hard to part, but it must be so," said the mother. "I have not the terror of the poorhouse which I once had. Want and suffering soon steels the heart, and makes us look more kindly upon those refuges which in our more prosperous days we turn from with a shudder."

"Oh! mother, I cannot let you go. We will starve together," said Mildred, sinking on her knees, and dropping her face, wet with tears, upon the clasped hands which rested on the old lady's lap. "It is always the darkest the hour before day, and heaven knows the darkest hour of our destiny has arrived. Do not despair, mother; something will perhaps turn up to better our condition."

The old woman shook her head.

"Yes, yes, mother, it will. London is a large place. There is plenty of employment—only I have not looked in the right place for it. Perhaps to-morrow."

"Do not hope it—do not hope it," interrupted Mrs. Hendon. "There is a stain upon your character—the stain of the ballet. 'Tis cruel, unjust, I know; but still it is a stain that blots you out of sympathy and respect."

The girl knew this—felt it. She had too much proof of it during the past few days. She had marked the look of disgust—observed the silk skirt draw hastily away for fear of contact with her form. And this was done by those of her own sex—those to whom she should look for pity.

But though the hearts of women are more tender than those of men, their prejudices are stronger.

A fallen sister seldom meets with sympathy from those of her own sex.

Let a spark of slander once fall upon an unfortunate girl, and those who should pity her most fan it to a flame—a flame that consumes her. Why is this? Alas! we know not.

After a time, Mildred rose from her recumbent position, and took up the bonnet and shawl she had not long thrown off. "Where are you going?"

"Out, mother."

"At this time of night? Why, it is eight o'clock, my child."

"I know it, mother."

"But where would you go?"

"To seek work."

"Work at this time — when all places of business are closed? You must be mad."

"I'm going to the theatre."

"But you know the season is over."

"Yes, I know that, but"—

"But what?"

"I'm going to ask the super-master if he can engage me."

"You can only dance."

"I can march on and off as others do. Of course, I should get hardly anything for it; but still, a few shillings will keep us from the workhouse, mother. And perhaps I may get something to do in the daytime, after a bit."

The mother shook her head, but said no more, and Mildred, wrapping her shawl closely around her, strode out of the house into the little dark street, and made her way towards the theatre.

Entering at the stage-door, she made her way to the super-master's room, and knocked gently on the panel of the door.

In answer to a gruff voice, she entered, and stated her mission.

"You know enough about theatres to know this is not the time to apply," was the remark which greeted her appeal.

"I know, sir," she said; "but in the morning I wish to seek for other employment, and thought you would not mind my breaking through the rules."

"I thought you went away to get married to a swell," said the man.

Mildred dropped her eyes to the ground, and the tears fringed her lashes, as she told him how harshly she had been deceived.

The man's manner softened as she concluded, and, with a pitying look, he said—

"Well, Miss Hendon, for your sake I'm sorry to say there is no vacancy; and business is too dull to allow me to add to the number."

"Then my last hope is gone," sighed Mildred, turning away with a sad heart.

She had passed over the threshold of the little room door, when Mr. Thomas, the super-master, called her back.

"What do you say to a ticket-night?[94]" he asked. "The manager, I am sure, will let you have one, and you can doubtless sell a good many."

"Alas! sir, I know but few. I have made no acquaintances."

"Well, you know best. But as I can't give you an engagement, I will induce the manager to allow you to send in tickets, if you like. Suppose you only sell a hundred, you will receive the price of fifty, and that may be some help to you till better times turn up. I am sure there are few of the company but will assist you to dispose of them; for, despite the cruel slanders hurled upon the profession from so many quarters, and from the pulpit especially, there are not a more kindly disposed class of persons in the world than those who tread the boards."

"I know it, sir," said Mildred. "Would that their traducers were so kindly disposed, so feeling, and so generous as they. I know, too, that to those in the profession the appeal of an unfortunate member is never made in vain, from the highest to the lowest. But, sir, I cannot avail myself of it, for I may as well speak the truth out. I have not, nor could I procure, the means to obtain the tickets."

"What! so down as that?" said Thomas sadly.

"Yes, sir."

The answer trembled on her lips.

"Stop a bit," he said. "Stop a bit. The curtain will fall in a few minutes, and then I'll see if I can't raise enough among the company to help you on."

"Oh, sir, I do not wish it," she said.

"Don't you? Then I do. You sit down there, and I'll see what can be done. I'll put a shilling down myself, and I dare say I can get you a few more. Why, a penny each will do it."

"I do not like taking from those who are almost as poor as myself," said Mildred.

"There is an old saying that many can help one: and if all the world would only acknowledge the truth of that, few would want. It may be painful to your feelings, Miss Hendon; but pride and poverty should not be suffered to go hand in hand. I can see no shame in accepting aid from others, for the day may come when you can extend it to them. Ha! there goes the bell."

The curtain had rolled down, and hidden the group upon the stage from the auditorium, and the actors hurried to their dressing-rooms.

Mr. Thomas left Mildred sitting in his apartment, and, with a strip of paper in one hand and a pencil in the other, proceeded on his mission.

On the top of that paper was written "Thomas, one shilling;" and without a word, he held it up before a gentleman who was absorbed in a deep draught of porter, which a boy in shirt-sleeves had just brought him in a pewter pot.

---

[94] Benefit performance.

The man glanced over the rim of the pot on to the paper, and after gulping down a draught of the liquid, remarked—

"Put me down the same. I'll give it you directly."

No question did he ask on the worthiness of the poor girl to sympathy. It was enough for him to know that a fellow-labourer in the same field as himself desired assistance to cause his heart to expand, and his fingers to roam to his pocket.

No painful or embarrassing questions—no insulting remarks—no annoying advice—the actor left that to those who grudgingly give, and insultingly advise.

To another and another went the ballet-master, and as he left each a coin jingled in his hand, and the point of the pencil traced the name of the donor, and the amount of his or her donation on the paper.

Slanderers of the votaries of the stage! if you would learn a lesson in true charity and benevolence, you may learn it behind the scenes of a theatre, and learn there, to your shame, how base are the lies daily uttered by the detractors of the poor actor.

From the leading man to the call-boy, the actor, the scene-shifter, all opened their hearts and pockets together, and where one had not a coin in his possession, he borrowed it of his fellow labourer, that he might be as charitable as he.

And this was done for one whom scarcely any of the company knew. It was enough, she was a dancer out of employment who needed aid.

She had asked it at their hands, and found it in their hearts.

In the course of half-an-hour Thomas returned to his room.

His slip of paper was written and figured on both sides, and the few last lines were cramped in.

A smile was on his face as he placed the paper in her hand, and, as Mildred gazed upon the pencil marks, her eyes filled with tears till she could not make out the names or figures.

"There, Miss Hendon." he said, "you will find one pound two and a penny. That will enable you to get a few hundred tickets printed, beside giving you a shilling or two to get along with. I can't tell you what night the manager will let you have it, but I should say about Wednesday fortnight."

"Sir, I know not how to express my gratitude," said Mildred, as a tear fell upon the paper in her hand.

"Never mind about that," was the reply. "Get your tickets done as soon as I let you know the night, which I will do to-morrow by note, and then, if you send me some, I'll push them out among the company, who will do their best with them, I am sure."

"I am sure they will," she replied.

"Yes, you may depend upon that. There is the money. It's nearly all in halfpence, but that don't matter, I suppose?"

"I am indeed thankful for them," she said, as she placed the coins which he took from his coat pocket in her handkerchief; "and I sincerely trust that those who have so kindly given them may never know their want. Sir, I would thank them individually, but of course I cannot, and I must ask you to do so for me."

"All right," said the man; "and I only hope you may be successful with your tickets. If we produce anything that will require a larger staff, I'll let you know; but I fear we shall not make any change just yet. There, mind the step. Good night."

He shook the poor girl by the hand as she crossed the threshold of his room, and as, with a grateful look, she turned away, he proceeded about his business without another thought of the matter.

With a swelling heart, Mildred hurried from the stage-door into the street, grasping the handkerchief which held the subscriptions in her hand.

She made her way out of the side street, and under the portico of the front of the theatre she paused for a moment to look at the bill hanging to one of the columns.

That stoppage was fatal to her.

As her eyes wandered over the lines thereon printed, a young fellow, of no very prepossessing appearance, stole up quietly behind her, and looking over her shoulder pretended to be reading the bill.

Mildred moved away, so as to permit him to obtain a better view, when, with a sudden snatch, he tore the handkerchief from her hand, and darting round the column, fled across the road ere she could give utterance to a cry.

For a moment she stood bewildered, then, dashing from under the portico in the same direction as the thief had fled, she called aloud—

"Stop him!—oh, stop him! "

But the words had scarce left her lips, than, with a heavy blow she was hurled to the ground, and a chorus of terrified voices rose on the air.

CHAPTER LXXII.
MILDRED FINDS A FRIEND IN JACK—SUSPICIONS AROUSED.

WITH the shout which rose from so many throats mingled the piercing and terrified scream of Mildred Hendon, as alarmed and horror-struck she found herself beneath the feet of a coach-horse.

The driver, powerless to pull up in time, for so suddenly had she sprung from the portico into the roadway, now struggled with all his might and skill to back the animal from over the body of the prostrate girl, and succeeded in preventing the wheels of his vehicle from going over her.

But Mildred was injured for all that. One of the animal's fore feet had seriously bruised her forehead, and its hind hoof had inflicted a wound on her hip; and it was with a groan of agony that she suffered herself to be raised from the earth by the many willing hands that were stretched forth to aid her.

In the confusion and alarm which naturally prevailed, the thief got off with the subscriptions of the employees of the theatre, no one caring to follow and endeavour to effect his capture.

Poor Mildred! misfortune seemed to have set in upon her. All her joy was turned into sorrow in the short space of one minute, and added to that she was now powerless to work even if she could obtain employment.

Carried in the arms of two men she was conveyed into a surgeon's, and placed upon a sofa in the surgery, where, on examination, it was discovered that one of the poor girl's ribs was fractured, and her instant removal to the hospital suggested by the doctor.

"Oh! take me home! take me home!" pleaded Mildred. "Do not send me to a hospital."

The doctor assured her that in those institutions she would be far better cared for than she possibly could be at home, but Mildred pleaded the harder to be taken home.

Finding that she had such an antipathy to a hospital, the surgeon desired a coach to be called, and when the driver made his appearance, he desired that his fare might be paid first, stating that he did not care for accident jobs.

"Alas!" said Mildred, "I have no money either here or at home. All I had was stolen from me, and it was in endeavouring to pursue the thief that I met with this accident. I can't pay you, and if some one will help me I must walk home."

"That is impossible," said the doctor.

"I will pay your fare, coachman," said a gentleman, who forced himself forward as he spoke. "Take the lady home, and there is your money."

Mildred looked up, and a cry of recognition would have burst from her lips had not the speaker motioned her to be silent.

"Do you know this person, sir?" said the doctor.

"Slightly," said Jack, for he it was who had spoken. "If you will aid me to lift her into this man's vehicle, I will myself ride on the box with him. Is she much hurt?"

"Bruised temple, and fractured rib. She had better go to the hospital," said the surgeon.

"Doubtless it would be better if she did so," said Jack. "But if she thinks she would be better cared for at home, I would not urge her. We have all our prejudices."

"Certainly—certainly," said the doctor. "Lift her tenderly, and do not clasp her waist so. That's it; you can carry her thus with ease, and without pain to her."

Jack raised the poor girl in his arms, and carried her from the shop to the coach, on the cushions of which he sat her softly down.

"I know where you live," he said; "and will get on the box and direct the driver. Truly, Miss Hendon, you're an unfortunate young lady."

Mildred sighed.

She felt she was indeed unfortunate; yet, when misfortunes were the heaviest, something seemed to turn up to help her.

She could not help looking upon Jack as something more than a friend. He had saved her from a fate worse than death, and though since that morning she had never set eyes on our hero till now, she had never ceased to think gratefully of him, and his presence at this moment was indeed comforting.

Thanking him in a weakly tone of voice, she sank back in the coach, and Jack, mounting the box, directed the driver the course to pursue.

"Who's to blame for that here job, do you know, sir?" asked the man, as he drove on. "But there, it's sure to be put on the poor driver, of course."

"I believe not," said Jack. "The young lady, in the excitement of the moment, hurried across the road as the vehicle came along—at least, as I have heard."

"That don't matter, sir," said the Jehu. "People won't never have it's their own fault they're run over. Why! bless your soul! I've seen 'em walk right under a horse's feet, and then swear it warn't their fault."

"Of course you sympathise with those of your own class," said Jack. "That is but natural; still you must admit there is a great amount of reckless driving in the streets of the metropolis."

"I know that; but still I say a man can't always pull up at a moment, and I'm only surprised there ain't more accidents than there are. If this here young gal says it's her own fault, I'm blowed if she ain't a curiosity as ought to be sent to the Museum—that's all I can say."

REWARD
1000
SPRING

Jack smiled.

"She certainly lays no blame upon the driver."

"She don't ?"

"No!"

"Then, just look here, sir. I'm a poor man, with a large family to support, but blow me if I charges anything for driving her."

"Why not?"

"Why not? 'Cos it will be something to say, that I have drove a female as was run over who said it was her own fault. Why, she's a natural curiosity, she is. I never knowed a woman as did anything wrong in her life, who didn't blame everything or somebody else; an' I'm proud of getting such a fare. and blow me, if I don't stick to what I said. I shan't charge nothing at all—no, not a penny."

"Then I can only say that you are the greatest curiosity I have ever come across," said Jack. "And I doubt very much whether any of your fraternity would believe there existed a coach driver who would take a fare for nothing."

The man stuck his tongue in his cheek and grinned.

"'Tain't many as would," he said.

"No, indeed; for they have a propensity to overcharge," said Jack.

"Well, sir, can you wonder at it?" said the man. "If we ask a fare a fair figure, he is sure to want to cut you down; and as for the women, oh! They're awful stingy, they are. Say you want five shillings, and depend upon it they offer you two. What's a man to do? It's not his fault if he sticks it on. If people would only deal fairly by us, we would do so by them; but they won't, sir, and I believe that one half think thank you enough for every ten miles."

"Well, perhaps to a certain extent you are right," said Jack.

"I know I am," said the man. "Down here, sir?"

"Yes," said Jack. And the driver turned his vehicle into the little dark street in which Mrs. Hendon resided.

"Pull up here," said Jack, as the vehicle reached the door of the house.

The man obeyed, and Jack leaped off the box, and opened the door of the vehicle.

"Miss Hendon, we have arrived at your home. Hallo! the poor girl has fainted," he added, "Knock at the door, and ask for a light."

This was done, and the aged mother opened the door with a candle in her hand.

Jack left the vehicle, and sprang to the old lady's side.

"Your daughter, ma'am, has unfortunately met with an accident; but do not be alarmed, as there is nothing to fear. If you will allow me, I will carry her to your apartments."

The old lady uttered a faint cry, and would have dropped the candle, had not the driver taken it from her hand to light our hero.

"Oh, dear! oh, dear!" sighed the old lady. "More trouble, more trouble. We are indeed unfortunate. What is it?—where is she hurt?— how did it occur?"

And wringing her hands, she tottered to the coach.

"Do not be alarmed; she has only fainted," said Jack, "and will tell you all about it as soon as she recovers. Take the light, and show me the way to your room."

The old woman obeyed, trembling in every limb. And Jack, tenderly raising Mildred in his strong arms, said, addressing the coachman—

"Do not go away. I will not be long, and then I will pay you."

"I said I wouldn't take no fare," exclaimed the man; "an' I'll be as good as my word."

"Nonsense," said Jack. "I promised to pay you, and I will do so. Wait till I come back."

And so saying, he bore Mildred into the house, and up the stairs to her apartment, where he placed her still insensible form on the bed.

As he turned, the old lady started.

"Surely you are no stranger to me," she said. "We have met before."

"We have, madam; and under very painful circumstances, I regret to say."

"At Clavering's'?"

"Yes."

"The villain!"

"Leave him to his Maker, before whom his paltry soul has flown," said Jack, "and look to your daughter. I may as well tell you that she has been knocked down by a horse, and that one of her ribs are stated to be broken by the surgeon into whose house she was taken, and who advised her removal to the hospital, but she preferred being brought hither. I was fortunately on the spot, and accompanied her here. Is there anything I can do for you ere I seek for a medical man to attend upon her?"

The old lady sank into a chair.

"I wish she had gone to a hospital," she said; "for heaven knows we cannot pay a doctor. We are very poor, sir. To marry that rascal, she gave up her engagement at the theatre, and she has been unable to procure any kind of employment since. We have struggled as well as we could with our poverty, but can struggle with it no longer. It is out of our power to employ a medical man. She must go to the hospital and I to the workhouse."

And the woman suffered her head to fall in her hands as sobs shook her bosom.

Jack placed his hand gently on her shoulder.

"Mrs. Hendon," he said, "do not let the expense of a doctor grieve you; and do not urge your daughter to go where she feels she would be wretched. I will send you a clever medical gentleman, and undertake to pay him myself."

The old lady started up, and dashed the tears from her eyes.

"Sir, I have no right to expect this kindness at your hands."

"Never mind that. I will do it, and ask no thanks for so doing. I can sympathise with your own and your daughter's misfortunes, and to alleviate them is now my wish. Take these few coins."

He offered her some money, which he took from his pocket; but the old lady drew back.

"Take them," said Jack, "for I can well afford them. They may obtain your daughter the necessaries she may require, and, with your permission, I will call upon you again in the course of a few days, when I hope to hear favourably of Miss Mildred's condition."

The woman still hesitated, but Jack insisted, by forcing them into her hand.

At this juncture Mildred opened her eyes, and perceiving her mother, cried—

"Oh, mother! mother! what will become of us now?"

"Rest content," said Jack kindly, "you shall be well cared for. I will go now and send the doctor. Keep a good heart, and all will yet be well."

He turned and hurried from the room ere the mother could inform the daughter of his generosity.

He had no wish for thanks. He knew they would be grateful, and that was sufficient.

He knew they were deserving, and he cared to know no more.

When he reached the street he found the coachman still there, and, getting inside the vehicle, ordered him to drive to the house of a celebrated and fashionable physician, near Piccadilly, adding—

"If you, then, charge me double fare for this journey, it will make up for the one you refuse to take for. I presume you have no objection to that?"

"Not the least," said the man, as he closed the door of the coach. "That's a rum chap," he added, as he mounted the box and gathered up the reins. "I wonder whether he does know that gal, or whether he's after no good. These swells ain't particular, when they sees a pretty face, how they scrapes an acquaintance. There's something in everything. And sometimes I'm glad them gals of mine ain't got much to boast of in the shape of good looks, for a pretty face is often the greatest curse a girl can have. Ah! it's a strange world, it is. Come up, will you?"

This last was addressed to his horse, who made a stumble, and at once put an end to his master's soliloquy.

The coach was not long in reaching its destination, and Jack, leaping out., offered the driver not only double his fare but considerably more.

The man looked at the money, and then at Jack.

"Do you know what you have given me, sir?" he asked.

"Perfectly well. Are you not satisfied? replied Jack.

"If I could get a fare like you every day, that old horse should have a little more rest than he does," said the man, as he pocketed the coin. "And all I can say is, that if you want to go anywhere else, I shall be glad to drive you for nothing."

"Thank you," said Jack; "but I have now no further need of your services."

"And thank you, sir," said the man. "And I hope, if ever you want a coach, and mine is about, you'll engage me."

"I shall do so; for I prefer riding in a vehicle driven by a civil man," said Jack. "So now, good night."

"Good night, sir," said the driver; "and I'll drink your health before I go much further."

Jack smiled, and bounded up the steps of the house.

To his loud summons an answer was immediately made by a youth attired in a tight-fitting green suit, covered with bright metal buttons, and who stood as upright as if he had been lashed to an iron bar.

"The doctor's engaged, sir, at present. Will you please to step into this room?" said the youth, opening a door that led out of the hall, and ushering our hero into a small apartment.

"Will he be long, do you think? My business is urgent," said Jack.

"I don't know, but I'll go and ask," said the youth. "Who shall I say?"

"A gentleman. Stay! here's my card."

The boy took it, and left the room, closing the door after him.

The apartment was warm, and Jack immediately opened the door about a couple of inches, and sat down beside it.

In about a minute, three ill-clad, evil-looking men passed on tip-toe along the hall towards the street-door, preceded as silently by the page.

Jack peered out of the crack of the door, and observed that the page looked up and down the street before he suffered the men to depart from the house, which they did, at a given signal, with great speed.

"Humph!" said Jack. "Strange patients, those. I should like to know a little more about them."

At this moment, with a smiling face, the doctor entered the room, and Jack turned towards him.

CHAPTER LXXIII.

THE BODY-SNATCHERS—THE DESECRATED GRAVE AND THE SCENE THEREAT.

HAVING stated his errand, and requested the doctor to attend upon the poor, unfortunate ballet-girl, Jack took his way from the house, anxious to learn who and what the strange characters were whom he had seen let out of the place so stealthily by the page, while he sat gazing through the chink of the little room door.

"Doctor Potters is not the man to have such patients," mused Jack, as the page closed the door behind him; "and their strange exit excites my curiosity to know more about them. Now, I would give something to know which way they went. To ask the page would not do, so I must trust to chance."

So muttering he turned to the right, and at a hurried pace continued for some distance along the street without seeing anything of the three men who had excited his curiosity.

But upon arriving at the corner of the street, he happened to cast his eyes into the open door of a public-house, and there, regaling themselves at the bar, were the three rough-looking men he had seen leaving the doctor's residence.

Jack, as he gazed through the door-way, examined the trio minutely.

They were a hang-gallows-looking lot, if ever there was one, and Jack felt sure they were neither of them likely to stop at trifles.

They conversed with each other in whispers, and, by the rapid looks which they continually cast around them, proved that they feared being watched, or were suspicious of listeners.

Jack entered the next compartment, and called for a glass of brandy-and-water, and endeavoured to overhear their conversation.

In this, however, he failed; not a sound was audible; and after about twenty minutes the fellows left the house.

Jack swallowed the beverage that had. been placed before him, and drawing his cloak around his form, did the same, only by another door, and a few moments afterwards.-

When he got out into the street he saw the trio at the corner, still in earnest conversation, and not wishing them to observe him, Jack passed by at a quick step.

As he did so, they bade each other good night, and separated, one going the very way which Jack had taken, and the other two turning off in different directions.

There was something, however, in the tone in which the "good night" was uttered that made Jack believe they intended to meet again. So he slackened his pace to permit the man who was going the road he had taken to pass him, and in a few seconds the fellow was ahead of him.

"I'll keep you in sight," thought Jack, "and see what business you are up to; and it strikes me, if I do discover it, I shall not find it to be the most honourable in the world."

It was now getting late, and few shops remained open. The number of pedestrians, too, lessened as the minutes flew by; and after keeping the man in sight for about half-an-hour, Jack discovered that himself and the fellow he was following were the only two about, and that they were then in a lonely locality, near Bayswater.

"If I go on much further, at the same distance between us, I shall excite the fellow's suspicion that I am following him," said Jack to himself; "so I'll turn off at the first opportunity, and come out into the road again further on."

He had scarcely made this resolve when a loud, peculiar whistle made him start.

The man whom he was following turned quickly round, and Jack shrank close up under the wall of a house which he was passing at the moment of the signal.

The man walked from the pathway into the road, and seemed to be looking back down the street as if to be certain that no one was about, then whistled in much the same way, evidently in answer to some preconcerted signal.

Jack drew still further back into the shadow of the building, and the next moment another man made his way into the road from a narrow lane, a short distance from where Jack stood.

"As I thought!" muttered our hero to himself. "It is one of those whom he parted from at the corner of the street, after leaving the public-house. They are on some expedition that will not bear too close an inspection, and I'll find it out. But I must be careful. This place is lonely, and two desperate men may do much. Hallo! there's another whistle."

This signal was answered by both the men in company, and directly afterwards they were joined by a third person, whom Jack at once leaped to the conclusion was the other whom he had seen at the doctor's. Then the trio pushed on along the road at a rapid pace.

Jack, as soon as they started on their way, also moved forward, but kept within the shadow of a tall hedge that now took the place of houses, and stepping lightly, quickened his pace so as to endeavour to come up with the men before him, and, if possible, strive to learn on what errand they were bent.

Keeping his eyes fixed upon the three forms, he gradually neared them, but suddenly they disappeared from his view, so suddenly indeed that Jack fairly paused in surprise.

On looking up, however, he saw, looming in the gloom, the tall spire of a church, and in an instant he came to the conclusion they had passed into the grounds of the sacred edifice, through which he expected there was a pathway—a circumstance not uncommon in the churchyards at the period of our story.

Starting forward again, then, Jack was not long in reaching the spot whence the men had disappeared, and which proved, as he had anticipated, to be a little gate leading into the churchyard.

But here he paused, and drew back a few steps, for the sound of voices reached his ears.

The tones, though subdued, were still audible in the silence which reigned around the precincts of the dead, and Jack strained every nerve to catch the words which were uttered, and succeeded.

"You got the sack, Bill?" said one.

"All right," was the reply; "and Joe's got the lantern. But are you sure you know the grave?"

"Am I a fool?" was the reply to this question. "Didn't I see the old boy chuck the earth in this morning on top of the box?"

"Well, you no need to be so humpy about it."

"Who's humpy?"

"Hold your jaw," said another, "and let's get to work. We must have the cold meat in the doctor's house afore long, or we'll stand a chance of being stopped with it."

"Hope it's got a fawnee[95] on its finger," said one.

"Jolly soon have it off," remarked another.

"Rather!" chimed in the third. "Would be fool to leave it there. But 'tain't many corpses as has got them ere things about 'em. Get on, Tom, and show us where the soft earth is. Fust I'll go and collar the old boy's spade. I told you I watched where he slummed it. Just in that corner, between the bushes."

"Well, go on, then; and look alive."

"Come with us."

"What for?"

"Oh, nothing; only you better come," was the reply, as the man moved over the mounds, followed by his companions.

"So—so," said Jack. "They are after exhuming the body of some poor wretch. Even the home of the dead is not sacred from the rapacious hands of such villains as these,—and Doctor Potters can encourage them in their unholy work. I am certainly deceived in him, for I thought him above such an action. I will endeavour to disappoint him, and these scoundrels too; and I do not think but I shall be able to do so, for 'tis evident one at least is afraid to tread this place without his companions follow in his footsteps. Rogues are generally cowards, and surely there can be no greater miscreant than a body-snatcher."

So saying, Jack took his mask from his pocket, and, adjusting it to his face, drew his cloak around him, and passed through the gate into the churchyard.

Stepping over the mounds, he made his way along till he reached the shadow of a tall stone, on which was recorded the virtues of some departed spirit, and taking up a position behind it, waited and watched for the further proceedings of the body-snatchers.

Presently they came back towards where he was hidden, but paused within a few yards of the stone.

"This here's the grave, I tell you," said the one who had been called Tom, sticking, as he spoke, a spade into the fresh turned mould. "Don't you see how soft it is?"

"All right, then, Tom. You set to work, and when you're tired we'll take a turn. Here's the sack, on this stone."

And the man flung the sack he had brought with him over the stone behind which Jack was ensconced, and which nearly betrayed his presence by knocking his hat from his head. Jack, however, caught it in his hands; and the fellows set to work without any suspicion that there was another beside themselves in that consecrated ground.

Spadeful after spadeful of the earth was thrown up, and the low thud of the iron blade as it entered the mould alone broke the silence for some time.

At length, however, Tom paused in his labours, and, wiping the perspiration from his face with his sleeve, said—

"Now, Joe, you give us hold of the lantern, and take a turn at the spade."

"Are you going to light up?" said Joe, as they changed implements.

"No, you fool; not till we get a little lower. What's to hide the glim from being seen in the road? When we get another couple of foot down will be time enough."

---

95 Fawnew, from Irish, a finger-ring.

Jack crouched down to the earth, and peered round the stone at them.

"Callous-hearted scoundrels!" he muttered to himself. "But you shall never disturb the remains of the being that lies there."

"What a thundering shame they bury 'em so deep," said Joe, as he laboured away with his spade. "It gives such a lot of trouble to get 'em out."

"If they didn't, they might take a fancy to look and see if they was nailed," said Tom. "Oh! lor', wouldn't the blokes as belongs to 'em holler, if they knowed we was after nailing it."

"They may holler, and be blowed to 'em, so long as we gets our price for it," said Bill. "And I must say the doctor comes down pretty handsome for a big un."

"He'll have you one of these days, I expect," said Joe. "You'd make a pretty corpse, you would."

"Stow it," said Bill. "I don't like such chaff in a place like this."

"Blowed if Bill ain't a-shivering with cold," said Joe. "Here, come and warm yourself at this fun, for blowed if I ain't tired."

Bill now took the spade, and leaped into the hole.

"I say, Tom, hadn't you better light the lantern? I can't see down here."

"'Tain't deep enough yet to hide the glim from the road."

"Yes, it is."

"All right! you can have a light, if you're frightened," said Tom.

"I ain't frightened. Only I can chuck out the earth better if I can see—can't I, you fool?" was the remark of Bill, uttered in a half-savage, half-frightened tone.

"Just mind you don't hit me with that spade," said Tom, as he knelt down beside the hole, and lowered a lantern into the grave. "There's a match; set it alight, and I'll hold the glim down while you work."

Bill struck the match, and applied it to the wick in the lantern, which was so constructed as to throw the rays of light only downwards, and was suspended to a stout cord which Tom held in his hand.

"Now, pull into it, good luck to you!" said Tom, as he moved the light so as to be out of the way of Bill's spade. "Chuck it out in barrow loads, and we'll soon have the box open."

"Never!" said Jack, setting his teeth firm, and rising from his crouching position.

"Hallo! what's that?" suddenly asked Joe, as Jack's foot slipped from the little mound on which he stood.

"What?" asked Tom and Bill in a breath.

"Didn't you hear something?"

"No. What was it like?" was Tom's question.

"I don't know."

"Stow it," said Bill, "I don't like joking in this place."

Jack could hardly suppress a laugh at the evident cowardice of the three ruffians.

He saw that it would take but little to alarm them. So, placing his hand to his mouth, he gave utterance to a deep, unearthly groan.

With a cry of terror, Tom let the lantern fall, and Bill dropped the spade from his grasp, while Joe clutched at Tom's arm, and looked around in speechless horror.

"What is it?" he gasped. "Oh, lor'! it's a ghost! I'm sure it's a ghost."

"Help me out! help me out!" cried Bill, in his fright, seizing hold of the coat of Tom, and pulling him head first into the grave on top of him..

The earth was soft—a rather fortunate circumstance for both of the ruffians; and grappling with each other they rose to their feet, and commenced scrambling out of the hole.

"Oh, lor'! what was it, I wonder?" said Bill, as he reached the side of Joe. "Tom, chuck up the lantern, good luck to you! chuck up the lantern."

The man handed the lantern to his companion, and was instantly by his side.

"Let's go. Don't let's have anything to do with the body," said Bill. "I don't like these noises. And I expect if we go on any further we shall see the ghost of the chap, as well as hear him groan."

"Behold him, here!" cried Jack, springing up, and alighting right before the body-snatchers. "Behold him, here! thou desecrators of the grave!"

With a shriek that was truly awful, Bill reeled backwards, and fell into the hole he had assisted to make, while Joe, completely overcome by his terror, fell upon his knees, and clasped his hands imploringly.

Tom seemed spell-bound, for he did not move till a well-delivered blow from Jack's fist sent him reeling over the loose earth and among the grass-covered mounds beyond it, where he rolled, shrieking aloud for mercy, and imploring his companions not to leave him.

Jack dealt Joe a kick on the chest, which made that worthy bend still lower, and then hurled over a considerable quantity of the loose earth with his foot upon Bill, who was making frantic struggles to get out of his narrow prison.

"Joe! Tom! help me out! Oh, lor'! Murder!—I—oh!"

Another lot of the loose earth was dashed into his face, half blinding him, and amid the confusion and terror, Jack quickly darted behind the stone.

The moment he had disappeared, Joe and Tom sprang to their feet, and tore off like mad towards the gate by which they had entered the churchyard, evidently not caring what became of their companion so long as they made good their escape.

As they disappeared through the little gate, Bill succeeded in scrambling out of the grave, and was about to rush after his companions, when Jack sprang out upon him, and, grasping him by the throat, hurled the terrified wretch on to the heap of newly turned-up mould, into which his body sank several inches. Placing his knee on his chest, Jack pinned him there; but ere a minute had elapsed, he discovered that the man had fainted with excess of terror.

CHAPTER LXXIV.

JACK PLAYS A GAME WITH THE BODY-SNATCHERS.

FINDING that Bill the Body-snatcher was unable either to offer the slightest resistance or attempt to effect an escape, our hero rose from over the prostrate man and considered what he should do to punish the rascal for the part he had played in the sacrilegious drama; for Jack had no idea of allowing him to escape as easily as his companions had succeeded in doing.

Casting his eyes towards the stone behind which he had secreted himself, he grasped the sack which had been thrown over it, and returned to the side of Bill.

"I'll have a game with him," said Jack; "and I doubt not he will be less willing another time to obtain subjects for a medical man. If justice were meted out to him, I should hurl his worthless carcase into the hole he has assisted to dig, and cover him in along with the body he hoped to make a few pounds by tearing from its last resting-place. But I'm not an executioner. I'll gag him, so that, when he awakes to consciousness he shall be powerless to make any noise, and then tie him up in this sack and leave him beside the grave, where I hope he will be discovered and punished."

Jack tore the yellow silk kerchief from the man's neck, and whisping[96] it round till it was not much thicker than an ordinary rope, he forced the centre of it through the clenched teeth of the man, and tied the ends securely at the back of his head.

"He won't halloo much now, I take it," said Jack, as he viewed his work, "But how can I secure his hands and feet to prevent his making his escape? Stay! a thought strikes me. His companions will not be long in recovering from the shock I gave them; and though they may not return here, they will doubtless await this fellow somewhere near the place. What if they could be induced to believe that he had, unaided, got the body out of the coffin into the sack, and left it for his companions to carry off, while he has taken his departure by another route, through some cause or other? It would certainly be a good trick, not only to play upon the rascals themselves, but upon the doctor. I'll put him in the sack; but first, I'll remove all his clothing but his shirt, so that he may appear as much like a corpse as possible."

So saying, Jack proceeded to unrobe the fellow in no very gentle manner.

While this operation was going on, the man awoke to sensibility; but finding the horrible figure still bending over him, he tried to shriek out, but of course no sound could emanate from his lips on account of the silken gag.

Terror now seemed to lend him strength, instead of depriving him of it, and he kicked and fought desperately.

"You struggle in vain," said Jack, as he pressed his half-nude body into the soft earth at the side of the grave. "You came hither to rob the dead, and the dead now will have vengeance upon you. You have assisted to open this grave, and it will be closed on top of you. Resistance is useless. You have made your own grave with your own hands, and with the dead, whom you have insulted, must you lay."

This was said in that hollow tone which Jack so often had recourse to, and he felt the limbs tremble as with the ague.

His struggles became less violent, and utter despair seemed to have settled upon his soul.

His chest heaved; every muscle of his frame quivered; and cold drops of perspiration started out in beads on forehead, face, and body.

Jack could just see the agonised look upon his face—a look that would have struck pity to the heart of our hero, but for the abhorrence he felt of the horrible deed that man and his companions had contemplated.

"His terror will soon deprive him of consciousness again," thought Jack, as he held the man firmly down with his hands and knees.

Jack was mistaken in his surmise.

A violent shudder ran through the man's frame; a fearful spasm passed over his face; his eyes closed; his limbs stiffened out, and scarce a pulsation existed in his frame.

---

[96] Twisting.

For a moment Jack dreaded lest the fright had deprived him of life, and he almost felt sorry for what he had done.

He placed his hand on the man's chest with no little anxiety.

The heart still beat, but very, very low was its throb.

Still, it assured our hero that he still lived, and he immediately recommenced the operation of disrobing the body-snatcher.

He had little difficulty in this, save when he came to his boots, which were laced up high above the ankles with thick, strong leather laces.

But these were off at last. And taking the laces from the boots, Jack proceeded to bind the wrists of the man together with one, and then the ankles with the other, so rendering him powerless to move hand or foot.

"Now for the sack," said Jack, leaving the side of the man, and searching round for the article he desired.

Having found it where he had placed it, after taking it from the stone, he opened its mouth, and raising the feet of the body-snatcher, drew the thick canvas over them, and gradually worked the sack up round the body of the prostrate man, till Bill's bare feet touched the bottom of the bag.

"He makes a pretty corpse," said Jack, looking into the pale face of the man; "only he wants washing and shaving to make him decent. Truly the face is an index of a man's mind, for there are few who could look upon this fellow and deny that all the baser passions of nature are to be found in his heart. However, let's cover up his beauty. I've seen enough of him."

And so saying, Jack pulled the mouth of the sack over the man's head, and, gathering it up in his hand, held it there while he considered what he could tie it with.

"I dare say there is a bit of rope in his coat-pocket," said Jack, as he drew that vesture towards him.

He was not mistaken. For, on diving his hand into the pocket of the fustian[97] coat, he discovered a good stout piece of rope, which he drew forth, and instantly secured the mouth of the sack with.

When this was done, Jack paused to survey his work, and a smile of satisfaction passed over his face.

"If he comes to, now," he muttered, "he'll certainly think he is in his grave. But I won't leave him here. I'll drag him to the little gate, and then search for his companions; for I doubt if one of them would be bold enough to enter this churchyard again to-night."

Gathering up the man's clothes and boots, Jack hurled them into the grave, and then, taking up the body by the shoulders, he proceeded to drag it along over the grass-grown mounds towards the path, first peering in that direction, to satisfy himself he was not observed.

Having succeeded in getting his burden into the pathway, his course became more easy, and he dragged the insensible man along the little flags till he reached the gate.

Here he laid it down, went through the gate, shaded his eyes with his hands, and looked along the road.

His glance failed to encounter any living object. And, opening the gate, and holding

---

[97] A heavy cloth woven from cotton.

it open with his foot, he dragged the sack and its contents through the wicket, and some little distance from the churchyard.

Then he placed it under the hedge, which skirted an adjoining piece of ground, took off his mask, wiped the perspiration from his face, removed his cloak, which he folded across his arm, and, taking a cigar from his pocket, applied a light to its end, and then hurriedly walked along the road in the direction whence he had come to the church.

He suspected that it was more than probable that the men who had made their escape would be waiting at the spot where they had met previous to entering the hallowed precincts of the churchyard, and he kept a sharp look-out as he took his way along the road.

Presently he saw the figure of a man crouching down under the hedge which bounded the garden of the house where he himself had paused to watch the body-snatchers, and he felt sure that it was one of the trio.

Appearing not to have seen the man, he kept on at the same pace, puffing the smoke from his mouth as if quite unconscious of the presence of a human being save himself.

As he passed the man, he said in a sharp tone—

"Good night."

"I say, governor, will you give us a light?" said Tom, for he it was.

"Certainly," said Jack, turning quickly. "You can light your pipe from the end of my cigar."

"Thank ye, master," said Tom, taking a little black pipe from his pocket, and holding it so as Jack could place the end of his cigar in the bowl.

"Draw up," said Jack.

The man commenced sucking away at the clay tube, and as the light from the end of the cigar played upon Tom's face, Jack saw it was deadly pale.

It took the man some time to light the tobacco, for his hand trembled so violently that he could not hold the pipe still. But at length he effected his purpose, and said—

"Thank'ee. I say, you ain't seen a man in a fustian coat along the road as you came, have you?"

"A man in a fustian coat, and a broad-brimmed, low-crowned hat, and a yellow silk handkerchief round his neck, about as tall as you?" said Jack.

"Yes, yes, that's him."

"I saw such a man a few minutes ago."

"Where ?"

"Just outside the little wicket that leads into the churchyards yonder."

"Thank'ee," said Tom. "I'm waiting for him."

"Then you may have to wait a little while," said Jack.

"Why?"

"Because when I saw him there he was dragging a large sack full of something through the wicket, which he laid under the hedge. I thought he was going to ask me for a light, as he came up to me, but instead, he said—'Governor, if you see two men on the road, just tell 'em I've left the sack for 'em to take to market, where I'll meet 'em.' But there, he said two men, so perhaps it ain't the one you are waiting for."

"Yes, it is," said Tom, quickly. "Thankee, sir. Good night, sir. Did you see anybody else about, sir?"

"No one."

"All right, sir."

Jack strolled away, but casting a quick glance behind him, he saw Tom joined by Joe, and the two men in earnest conversation.

A slight bend in the road here shut them out from his view, as Jack paused to see what turn circumstances would take.

Listening intently, he heard the footsteps of the two men receding slowly from him; and, springing up, Jack went over to the other side of the hedge, walked along after them, sheltering his form closely from observation by assuming a stooping posture.

The men walked slowly and suspiciously, and Jack was soon alongside of them without their having the least suspicion of his presence.

"Well, it's a rum go, Joe," he heard Tom say. That fellow must have seen Bill, or else how did he know he got a yellow belcher round his wizen?"[98]

"It was Bill, safe enough. But I'm blowed if I thought he'd got pluck enough to stop and nail the corpse, bring it out for us, and then go back again. Perhaps it's all a lie."

"We'll soon see, if we find the sack," said Tom, "an' if we don't find it, cuss me if I'll go into the yard after him."

"I won't."

"I didn't believe in ghosts afore."

"No more did I."

"But there is."

"Ain't we seen one?" said Joe. "Oh, lor'! I ain't a very frightened cove, but that awful thing licked me."

"Look out for the sack."

"There it is, s'help me never!" cried Joe, pointing to the object under the hedge.

"So it is; and blowed if the corpse ain't in it," cried Tom, touching it with his foot.

"True as death!" said Joe, feeling the body through the sack with his hands. "But where's Bill scarpered to? Blowed if he ain't the pluckiest of us now."

"Won't he brag a bit about it?"

"Rather! But I can't make out why he hooked[99] it?" said Joe, puzzled a little to account for the conduct of his mate.

"Perhaps he thought some one was after him?" suggested the other.

"That's it; and so he's doubled on 'em. He's a fly cove, an' no mistake, And the best thing we can do will be to hoist the sack on our shoulders, and take our hook with it. We shall find Bill waiting for us at the doctor's. That's what he meant by the market; just to blind that cove as give me a light."

In this the other coincided. And after looking up and down the road, the two men proceeded to lift the body on to their shoulders.

"It's a pretty heavy corpse," said Tom.

"Strike me lucky! it is," said Joe. "Just give another hoist."

As soon as the two men had got the sack, with its contents, into position, and were about to move off, Jack thrust his arm over the top of the hedge, and seizing the mouth of the sack, which was behind the men, gave it such a sudden jerk that it rolled from their shoulders, and fell with a heavy thud on to the pathway.

---

98 Throat.
99 Slung his hook; departed.

"Why don't you hold tight, you fool," cried Tom, furiously.

"It was your fault, you stupid!" cried Joe. "Why didn't you hold tight?"

"I did hold tight."

"I say you let go of it."

"You're a liar!"

"Why, I had hold of it," said Joe; "so don't call me a liar."

"Why not?"

"You'll see, if you do."

"Shall I?"

"Yes; you will."

"No cheek! I'm as good a man as you."

"And so am I."

"Shut up, then."

"I shan't, unless I like. I had hold of it right enough."

"Then what made it roll off?"

"Because you're a fool, and didn't hold tight, that's why."

"Oh, go to the devil," growled Tom, "and don't be so fast."

The other said nothing, but proceeded to raise one end of the sack.

His companion took the other, and once more it was raised to their shoulders.

"Have you got hold all right?" said Joe, gruffly.

"Yes. Have you?"

"To be sure I have."

"Go on, then."

Again Jack put his arm over the hedge, and, seizing the mouth of the sack as the men moved along, pulled it sharply, and with some force.

Both the men, however, kept firm hold of the sack, and the consequence was that they both lost their balance and fell to the ground, bringing down the sack on top of them.

In an instant Tom and Joe were on their feet.

Filled with rage at what each considered the other's trick, and muttering a bitter oath, each rushed upon the other with closed fists.

Tom, blinded by passion, struck Joe a blow on the cheek; and Joe, no less incensed, returned the compliment with one under the left eye of his companion; and a fight ensued which finally ended in their closing together and rolling over the body in the sack.

Jack crouched down behind the hedge, and fairly shook with suppressed laughter.

When the men rose to their feet, smarting from the punishment each had received at the other's hands, their passions were somewhat cooled, and instead of again resorting to blows, mutual recriminations took place, and the quarrel finally ended by Tom offering to fight Joe on Sunday morning for five shillings, the money to be staked as soon as obtained from the doctor as the price of that night's villainy

Having thus settled the dispute for the present they again raised the sack to their shoulders, and Jack, satisfied for the present with the game he had played upon them, suffered them to proceed on their way.

CHAPTER LXXV.
THE SCENE IN THE DISSECTING-ROOM OF DOCTOR POTTERS.

IN silence the two men now wended their way along the dark road with their still burden, for the blow which Bill had received upon his head, when suffered to fall from the shoulders of his companions, had been so severe that his returning consciousness was instantly annihilated, and he lay as if indeed dead—a helpless, inanimate mass.

Jack waited till they had got some considerable distance down the road, when he sprung over the hedge and followed them, but kept sufficiently far away not to be seen or heard.

After a walk of about a quarter of an hour, a waggon, partially loaded with vegetables, on its way to Covent-Garden market, was overtaken by the bearers of the sack, and a bargain was struck with the waggoner to carry the load of the body-snatchers for a quart of beer, and so Bill was placed on the tailboard of the lumbering vehicle, and Tom and Joe walked on beside the driver.

"I don't know that I can do any more," muttered Jack, as they neared the doctor's dwelling. "Still, I have done enough to-night in saving the body from being torn from the grave, to which it has so lately been consigned by sorrowing friends. I should like to see the surprise of these men and the doctor when the cheat is uncovered; but that of course is impossible, so I must forego that gratification. They have but little further to go, and as daylight will soon rest upon the earth, I'll go home with the conviction that the hours stolen from rest to-night have not been wholly wasted."

So saying, he drew his cloak closely around him, for the air was chilly, and turning off from the road, suffered the body-snatchers to proceed on their way without further molestation.

As the waggon would pass within twenty yards of the doctor's residence, there was little chance of the strange bundle exciting suspicion, consequently, with regard to that Tom and Joe had little misgivings.

Having given the promised reward to the waggoner, Tom left his companion and hurried to the doctor's house, where he announced his presence by a lusty pull at the night-bell.

The summons was quickly answered by the doctor himself, in his dressing-gown.

"All right," said Tom.

"You have got it?" said Potters.

"Yes. Leave the door open, so as we can come in quick."

The doctor winked and nodded, and Tom returned to the waggon.

"Come on; lend a hand," he said to Joe, who was by the side of the waggoner. The man obeyed, and lifting the sack from the waggon they bade good-night to the teamster and hurried with their burden to the house, without being observed by anyone.

The door was violently closed behind them, and the doctor, bearing a lamp in his hand, ushered them into his surgery.

"Place it on the table," he said, as he set the lamp down on a sideboard, "and I will fetch you your reward. But where is your companion?"

"He promised to meet us here," said Tom. "Ain't you seen him?"

"No."

"That's a rum go," said Joe.

The doctor left the room to proceed to his chamber for the purpose of obtaining the money wherewith to pay for the subject.

Although he did not hesitate to employ these men, he had no very great faith in their honesty. Indeed, he looked upon them as persons who would not hesitate to rob him of anything they could place their hands on; so he took the precaution, when he left the room, to lock the door behind him, and so prevent them, during his absence, from indulging in those little propensities he suspected them guilty of.

"Well, that here's a rum go about Bill, ain't it?" said Joe, when the doctor had departed.

"Can't tumble to it,[100] nohow," said Tom.

"Think he's nabbed?"[101]

"Don't know; but it's likely."

"What shall we do with his share, then?" said Joe.

"Stick to it," was the reply.

"Hope he is nabbed, then," said the other "'cos he'll only brag about what he's done."

"Sure to."

"Joe."

"Hallo!"

"What do you say to chissel him out of his whack?"[102] asked Tom.

"Shouldn't mind, if we could."

"It's easy done."

"How?"

"Swear we never saw the body. He don't know we found it through that bloke telling us about where he slummed it," said Tom.

"Of course not. And then we can swear he never took it out of the coffin."

"What do you say then?"

"We'll do it."

"You must keep mum."

"Of course I should."

"Yes, but when you are drunk you blabs a bit, you know."

"I shan't be such a fool as that."

"Then that's agreed to?"

"Yes."

"Wouldn't he holler if he knowed our little game," said Tom, after a pause.

A low moan, which seemed to come from the sack, made both men start and turn pale. "What was that?" gasped Tom. Joe did not reply, but made a dash at the door, and stood staring, with gaping mouth and eyes, at his companion when he discovered it was locked.

A prolonged "Oh!" now emanated from the sack, and the two men clung to each other for protection.

"It's the corpse!" gasped Joe.

"It's the dead 'un's ghost!" cried Tom, "and we are locked in. Call the doctor— oh! call the doctor!"

Joe was about to adopt this course, when his very tongue clove to the roof of his

---

[100] Can't work out what's happened.
[101] Been apprehended.
[102] Swindle him out of his share.

mouth in horror, and he grasped Tom so fiercely that he positively bruised his flesh.

The sack was moving on the table with a sort of rocking motion, and stifled moans came from within it.

Both now turned and made frantic efforts to open the door of the surgery, and were about to proceed to batter in its panels when they heard the doctor's foot descending the stairs.

A sigh of relief broke from the lips of both, and Tom gasped out in a whisper—

"He's coming, and it don't move now. Don't say nothing; but when we get the ochre[103] we'll slope quickly. Oh, lor'! I wish I hadn't gone out to the job at all."

Endeavouring to assume a calmness they did not feel, the two men awaited, with trembling limbs and throbbing hearts, the entrance of the doctor, who, turning the key, strode into the room, chinking five gold coins in his hand.

"Five pounds you want for this job, I think you said," remarked; Potters, as he stood before them.

"Six, sir. It's worth six to run such a risk," said Tom. "That's only two pounds each, you know."

"Very well. I suppose you must have it. But of course you will give your absent companion his share."

"As true as never we will, sir," said Joe.

"Then there is the money."

And he placed the required sum in Tom's hand, which shook so that he could hardly hold them in his grasp.

"Thank you, sir. Good night, sir. Come on, Joe," said Tom, now that he had got the gold, anxious to get away as quickly as possible.

"Stop! stop! You had better take your sack," said Potters, approaching the table.

"We'll call for it to-morrow, sir," said Tom, quickly.

"I had rather you took it with you now. I do not wish you to be seen here more than possible."

"We'd rather not wait for it now," said Joe, dreading that something fearful would happen the instant the doctor touched the corpse.

"Why?" asked Potters, suspiciously.

Neither replied.

"Nonsense! There's no necessity to give yourselves a journey for nothing. You can have it in a moment," said Potters, taking up a knife and severing the cord which bound the mouth of the sack.

"There! Catch hold of the bottom of it, and draw it off, while I hold the body."

Neither of the men seemed inclined to obey this order.

"Off with it!"

"You," said Joe, knocking his companion forward.

"No—you," said Tom.

"What are you hesitating about?" said the doctor, harshly, being somewhat annoyed at the strange conduct of the two men. "Are you afraid to touch a corpse any more in a dissecting-room than in its coffin. Hallo! what's this?"

The doctor let go the mouth of the bag, and leaped back from the table, holding his

---

[103] Money.

knife threateningly before him.

His exclamation of surprise had been drawn forth by perceiving the sack roll slightly on one side.

Tom and Joe had also observed it, and darted out of the room into the hall, nearly rolling over each other in their eagerness to escape.

Recovering from the shock, the doctor sprang after them, and threateningly presenting the knife he held towards them, cried—

"You confounded villains! what trick are you playing me? Go back into that room or I'll make a corpse of each of you on the instant."

"We ain't been playing you no trick," gasped Tom, in tremulous accents.

"Upon my soul we ain't," chimed in Joe.

"Go back into that room."

"I won't," said Tom.

"I shan't," cried Joe.

"Then, hark you, my fine fellows," said the doctor, who felt certain that he had been swindled out of six pounds by the two men, "if you do not obey me I will arouse my servants, send for the police, and charge you with sacrilege."

The jaws of the two men dropped in horror.

They saw that the old doctor was in earnest, and shivering in every limb they slowly walked back into the room.

"Now, draw off that sack," said the doctor, "and let me see what I have paid for."

The men, feeling that disobedience would avail them little, made a clutch both together at the bottom of the sack, and with a desperate tug led the burly form of Bill off the table on to the floor, and leaving the head and shoulders of their companion open to the gaze of themselves and the astonished doctor.

If fear had paralyzed the energies of the body-snatchers before, astonishment did so now, for they stood looking down upon the upturned face of Bill, still holding the bottom of the sack in their hands.

The doctor was the first to recover, and turning furiously to Tom and Joe, he said—

"Is it thus you wished to defraud me, who have ever paid you well for a subject?"

"Blowed if it ain't Bill," gasped out Tom, paying no heed to the doctor's words.

"Strike me lucky!" cried Joe. "Well, I'm flabbergasted all of a heap."[104]

"The varmint's been having a lark with us, or else it's the ghost, and blowed if I know which."

"Perhaps you will explain the meaning of this strange conduct?" said Potters.

"'Splain!" cried Tom. "S'elp me never, governor, we're as much licked as you are."

"Quite," said Joe. "And if anybody can explain at all, it's Bill—if it is Bill, and not the corpse that's changed itself into our old pal."

"There can be no mistake as to this being your companion, who has submitted to be stripped for the purpose of imposing upon me. I can well understand now why you did not care to wait for the sack. A well-concocted plan, certainly. And I suppose as soon as I had retired he would have let you into my house to rob it?"

"Stow it, governor!" said Tom, with a look of injured innocence. "I tell you, true as life, we thought it was the body I saw buried this morning. Upon my soul we did, and I

---

[104] Completely baffled.

wouldn't tell a lie, I wouldn't, for nothing. Ask Bill."

Bill, who had opened his eyes and was gazing in surprise and terror from one face to the other, here rolled his head backwards and forwards on the floor.

"Why, s'elp me never! he's got his belcher[105] in his tater-trap,[106] and can't say a blessed word," cried Joe, stooping down quickly and untying the kerchief.

Oh what a sigh of relief broke from the man's lips!

"Are you Bill, or ain't you?" asked Tom, still doubting the identity of his comrade. "Or are you a ghost? What the devil are you?"

"I'm Bill," cried the man. "Oh! untie my hands. How did I come here? Where's that awful thing we met at the grave? Oh, lor'!"

Joe and Tom at once set about getting the poor wretch out of the sack, and certainly their surprise was too genuine to allow the doctor to believe it assumed, and he instantly cut the leathern thongs which secured the hands and feet of Bill, and which had been drawn so tight as to cut into the flesh.

Bill tried to stand, but he could not; his legs were so swollen and cramped, and the doctor aided him to a chair, into which he sank with a deep groan.

"Where's your clothes?" asked Joe.

"Who tied you up like that?" inquired Tom.

"What, in heaven's name, is the meaning of all this?" asked the doctor.

To those questions, all asked at once, Bill could only reply by a puzzled stare and a shake of the head.

"His head is bleeding," said the doctor. "Have you attempted to murder him?"

"Good God! no!" cried both men, in a breath.

"There must be some solution to this mystery, and unless I learn it I will have the police called in," cried the doctor, placing his hand upon a bell-pull, and looking determinedly at the men.

Bill raised his head.

"Stop, governor," he said, in a faint voice, "and I'll tell you all I know about it."

"Go on, then, and speak truly."

"I will, s'elp me never."

The doctor took his hand from the rope, and waited impatiently to learn how Bill came to be brought to him instead of the corpse he had bargained for.

Placing his hand to his head, Bill, in a low voice, told how they had been alarmed at the grave—how his companions fled, and a horrible figure hurled him to the earth, and held him there till he became insensible—how he partly recovered, to find himself bound and confined in the sack, and how he was again plunged into insensibility by a blow on the head. He also said he had. heard voices, and strove to call out, while he lay upon the table, but he could utter no intelligible sound on account of the gag in his mouth; and finally wound up his story by stating that he firmly believed it was the work of the devil, who was angered at the business they were on, and swore he would never go body-snatching again, if one corpse would make his fortune.

To this Joe and Tom added how a stranger had overtaken them on the road, and told them of the sack; and how, believing it was the corpse, they had brought it on to the house,

---

[105] Neckerchief.
[106]Mouth.

and swearing never to tempt the devil again by engaging in such work.

Of course, a well-informed man like Potters had no idea that the devil or any super-natural personage had any hand in the business at all. He said that their errand had been discovered, and that a trick had been played upon them; and he could not help feeling that in his pursuit of science he was playing a desperate game himself, which he had better at once put an end to. So, procuring a suit of his left-off clothing for Bill, he told the men to keep silent about what had happened that night, made them a present of the six pounds, and bade them never more come near his house, and seek more honourable, if not more lucrative employment.

CHAPTER LXXVI.
THE BROKEN HEART AND THE SHATTERED BRAIN.

HOME! What memories, what recollections does not this one small word conjure up to the minds of the good, the bad, the true, the false, the rich or poor!

Home! There is a magic in its sound which sends a thrill through the hearts of all.

At the bare mention of this word the prodigal blushes with shame, the outcast sighs, and the alien's eyes dim with tears. There is a sound in the word which penetrates the heart of the most callous, and kindles with joy and pride the eye of the honest, just, and true.

The influences of home are doubtless greater than all else, for the memories of childhood are the dearest of all in life.

We look back to them with pleasure through the veil of years, and the fond remembrances of those days never fade wholly from the heart; those days of innocence and joy, when sin and sorrow was unknown, before the selfishness and deceit of the cold, unfeeling world had steeled our hearts, and bade us suspect all mankind ere we trusted and were deceived—ere we sought friends and found but foes.

There is no place like home to the feeling and true-hearted, whether constrained to leave it on business or pleasure; in hope or sorrow, home is ever the chief and dearest spot.

The exile dreams of home under the forest trees and on the bosom of the briny ocean; the felon pictures it upon the black walls of his prison-cell, and groans to think how his crimes have stained that holy spot; the young leave it with sorrow, and the aged turn back to it with joy.

Shattered indeed, then, must be the heart that can turn from home without a pang—lacerated the bosom that can leave it with pleasure; wretched the mortal who can turn his or her back upon it, hoping never to see it more.

And yet how many have done so; how many will yet do so; how many have and yet will look back upon it with a pang or a blush.

No happier home could have been found, humble though it was, than that of Jane Slater's; but a blight fell upon it, and the happy home became a wretched dwelling. Within its walls smiles had given place to tears, laughter to groans, joys to sorrows, and hopes to despair.

Now it was no longer home to her, but a spot where misery had raised its head, and sin and bloodshed had dimmed its lustre for ever, blotted out its influence, and blackened its dearest memories.

No wonder, then, that her footsteps faltered as she neared it, after parting with Jack at the grave of her suicide husband. No wonder, then, that she shuddered as she gazed upon it through the dim light of early morning. Never did the house look so wretched to her. Alas! poor woman! it was the same neat, clean little dwelling as ever,—the wretchedness and misery was in her own heart.

A cold shudder pervaded her frame as she stepped across its threshold into the dark passage, and the bang of the door, as it closed behind her, echoed dismally throughout the dwelling.

Cold and cheerless seemed all within, and in imagination the poor woman detected the odour of blood.

She entered the little parlour, and sank down upon the sofa with a sigh—that couch on which she used to sit side by side with her husband, and listen while he read from some book, or talked to her of their future prospects and hopes.

Alas! how had the one false step he had taken blighted them! how had his guilt shattered to their base the fairy castles then built!

A chaos had that happy home become—a very wreck of life, love, and hope.

So thought Jane Slater now, as she sat on the sofa in the dark room, and leaned her throbbing brow upon her cold, thin hand.

The last tie which bound her to that place was broken. She could remain there no longer.

She felt that to do so would be a disgrace to her honest and well-being[107] neighbours; and she also felt that she could not bear the gaze of those who knew her—their looks of pity, indignation, and disgust.

Would they not point her out to each other as a felon's and a suicide's widow? Would she not be the observed of all observers in that locality?

She must be—she was sure she must be; and therefore she must flee from it. Flee far, far away from the scene of her great trouble; flee anywhere, but God only knew where.

She had made every preparation for her departure ere the men had come who were to convey her husband to his unconsecrated grave.

It did not take her long to do so, for few, indeed, were the things she resolved to take with her.

A change of linen, and the likeness of her husband was all the stock; all else she determined to leave behind.

Long did she struggle against the temptation of even carrying with her the likeness of James Slater—that likeness presented to her in happier days; that likeness she had oft caressed ere the form it represented had been suffered to clasp her to his heart.

Not one other article would she remove—all else might become the property of strangers; for to her they were but so many memories of recollections she would fain forget.

Rising from her seat, after a time, she approached the table in the centre of the room, and felt for the little bundle she had placed upon it during the day; and, having grasped it, she turned towards the door, and placing her hand upon the side-post, she sobbed rather than said—

"Oh! thou spot so full of dear and cursed recollections! I now leave thee for ever, to go Heaven only knows where. Home! the dearest of all earthly joys, we must part. Farewell, for ever!"

By an effort she dashed the tears away that had sprang to her eyes, and, staggering

---

[107] Prosperous.

along the little passage, opened the front door, and passed out into the cold, grey twilight of the early dawn.

The cool morning air fanned her fevered brow and burning cheeks, and for a moment she paused to gaze up at the neatly-curtained window of that room where her husband had sent his soul, unbidden, to meet its Maker.

Her lips trembled, but she uttered no word. Then, pressing her hand upon her heaving bosom, she turned away, and with slow and tottering steps made her way towards the scene of her husband's burial.

Why she took that route she could not tell, but something seemed to urge her in that direction.

The light, fleecy clouds of morning floated up, and night's dark canopy rolled slowly away before them. The air became more fresh and warm, and the first golden ray of the rising sun glittered athwart[108] the cold grey vapours, spreading and widening its cheerful light, till it awoke Nature's feathered songsters to herald in its coming.

But the music of the birds found no response in the heart of Jane Slater; that heart was cold and passionless—hardened by grief, seared by sorrow—dead to every feeling of hope and joy.

Then, in its chariot of burnished gold, the orb of day rose in the horizon, and threw its golden beams upon her face and form, and kissed her pale cheek with its warm rays.

But it could not chase the pallor from her face, or drive the misery from her heart; and on—on she went, till she reached the cross roads, in the centre of which an oblong piece of new-dug ground showed her the last resting-place of him who had both cheered and crushed her confiding soul.

To this spot she tottered, and, sinking down upon her knees upon the yielding soil, clasped her hands and raised her eyes to heaven.

A look of the most unutterable agony swept over her face, and her bosom rose and fell like a heaving sea.

But no tear-drop dimmed her eye—the fountain of her heart was dried up, and madness was seizing upon her brain.

Tears alone could serve, and they were denied her.

A loud, hoarse laugh broke from her lips at length, but so unearthly in its tones that the birds upon the trees at the roadside hushed their songs in horror, and fled in dismay from the vicinity of the spot.

"Ha! ha! ha!" again rang out in unearthly tones upon the morning air as Jane, with glaring eyeballs, flung her arms wildly above her head. "You cannot harm him now, while I am near. Back! I say—back! He is my husband—my James. Who says he is a forger? You lie—you lie! He is too good, too noble, to be guilty of such a deed. Don't touch him, or I will kill you where you stand. Back! I say! Away! away! You shall not harm him! James, my own loved James! they shall kill me ere they touch you."

And thus wildly raving she flung herself flat down upon the yielding earth, and clutched at the sod with her hands.

"Cold, cold!" she continued, after a pause, and laying her hands flat upon the damp earth. "Cold as death! They have killed him! and he will never smile upon me more. Never more will his warm kiss thrill through my veins. He is dead—dead!"

---

[108] Across.

Her form trembled, but still no tears came to relieve the burning heart, or quench the consuming fires of the brain.

A maniacal gleam was in her eye. Madness was fast settling on her brain.

"Dead!" she cried; "but no, no! He promised to save him—he, Ralph Grasper, his master. Yes, he promised to save him if I would go to his house. I will go. He cannot deny my prayers—will not. Oh, no! Yes, I will away at once. Let me see. What did he say? Ah! I remember now. 'Come to me and I will save your husband.' He is a good man, and will keep his word. I will fly to him. Wait till I come back, and I will bring you pardon and safety, and all our miseries shall again turn to joy. Silence, James! Do not speak, do not go out, but wait till I return, then all will be well—all will be well!"

Slowly she rose from the earth. But, oh, God! what a fearful change was in that face on which the sunbeams now shone brightly!

There was a vacant expression in every lineament of her features, a lustreless look in her once gleaming eye.

Suffering had done its work at last. Villainy had shattered one of nature's noblest images. Jane Slater's reason had tottered from its throne—the wretched woman was a maniac!

Every rational sense she had possessed was now buried in the suicide grave of her husband, and she was alone in the wide world, bereft of all but life!

Of all the maladies which assail the human form, there is none so fearful as idiosyncrasy. The light of reason flown, life is but a painful shadow, a phantom of humanity.

One of the peculiarities of madness is, that the sufferer often shows the greatest abhorrence for their dearest friends, and an unbounded affection for their direst enemies.

With the loss of reason an utter change appears to come over the heart. The sufferer weeps where he should smile, and smiles where he should weep; hates where he should love, and loves where he should hate.

To this, poor Jane Slater was no exception. For when reason fell, and madness asserted its sway over her brain, she thought of the villain Grasper, who had brought all this misery upon her, as her best and dearest friend; and as if the king of hell, ever watchful for an opportunity to claim the soul of his victim, and inflict fresh pangs upon the heart of the good and true, had waited for this moment, the guilty merchant stood before her at the side of her husband's grave—stood there with the sunlight playing upon his disfigured face—stood there gazing with all a demon's joy upon the fearful wreck his guilty soul had made.

The miscreant saw at a glance the fearful truth, and his base heart bounded within his bosom.

He was no stranger to the fact that with the fall of reason the idiot forgot the persecutor—that madness would prove his best ally in his wicked schemes.

The wretch had followed the patrol, to whom he had given notice of Jack's presence, for some distance along the road; but not seeing anything of either, after a short time, had made his way slowly back to the end of the cross roads, and, unseen by Jane, had been a witness to all that had transpired.

Nay, he had even heard the latter part of her wild ravings, and then it was that he appeared before her.

Like a fiend as he was, he gloated upon the wretch before him.

She was alone, with none near to aid or advise her; she was alone with him on whom she now looked as her dearest friend; alone, without any other protection than heaven.

His glance was returned by Jane with a vacant stare for some moments. Then the lineaments of her face gradually expanded into a sickly smile, though no beam shot from the lustreless eyes of the demented woman.

"You are Ralph Grasper," she said, taking a step nearer to the wretch, and placing her hand upon his arm.

"Yes, Jane; and your dearest friend," he said, in a voice intended to be kindly.

And he hedged closer to her, and placed his arm around her waist.

She did not hurl it from her as she would have done before.

She did not spurn him with a look of indignation and loathing as in times gone by.

No. She placed her own arm around his neck, and looked with her expressionless eyes into his own.

Oh that she could have read there the passion which shone in them!

But heaven denied her that power, and the miscreant strained her to his wicked heart, pressed his fulsome lips to her colourless cheek, and murmured in low, soft tones—

"My own dear Jane!"

"You are my friend, the friend of my husband," she whined. "You will not let them tear him from me? They would take him to jail—kill him! But they shall not, for you are here."

"I am here," echoed the guilty wretch. "And I am happy that I am so."

"Yes, for you can save him and me. You will—you will," she cried.

"I can. But"—

"But what?"

"You must come with me," he said, leading her away from the edge of the grave, lest the sight of the soft earth should bring the recollection of the truth to her mind.

Unwittingly she suffered him to do so.

"Where would you have me go to?" she asked.

"Home with me."

"Home!" she cried.

And at the mention of that word the dull eye kindled for a moment, but the next it was leaden and lustreless as before.

Grasper observed the sudden light, and resolved to put a guard upon his words.

He felt that the long-wished-for, long-sinned-for triumph was at hand, and he resolved not to lose it by word or deed.

"You want me to save him," he said, after a pause.

"You can, and you will."

"To be sure I will," he replied. "But you must come with me, and I will give you that which shall defeat his enemies. Come."

He drew her still further away from the grave.

"You promised to shield him from the consequences of his sin, and you will be true to your word. I know you will be true."

"Yes; both to him and to you, Jane; for I know you love me," said the artful and designing villain. "Come. I will be your friend—your protector. You do not fear me, do you?"

"Oh, no!—oh, no! for you will be kind to me," she said, turning her vacant gaze upon his bruised features.

"And you will love me for that kindness, won't you, Jane?" said the man; "for you have a grateful heart—a very grateful heart."

She smiled vacantly, and leaned her head upon his shoulder in reply to his question.

The villain turned away his face to hide the look that rested upon his features.

The malignant and triumphant expression of a fiend was there, glorying over a lost soul. All the vilest passions of his nature were pictured there, and his heart bounded as he felt that now he could humble the proud woman who had defied him—that now she was powerless as a babe to resist his wicked schemes—that now he could avenge himself upon her for the scorn and loathing with which she had viewed him.

He resolved to place her in the first vehicle he met, and bear her to his home, where his base soul resolved to be revenged for the punishment his cruelties, insults, and oppressions had brought upon him.

Resistless and confiding as a babe, she suffered him to lead her along to her destruction.

Was there none to save her—none to shield her from a villain's wiles—a witless wretch like her? Was there no power on earth to prevent the wicked work?—no power to shield the innocent and punish the guilty? We shall see.

CHAPTER LXXVII.

THE MERCHANT AND THE MANIAC.

NIGHT had again thrown her sable mantle over the earth, and myriads of stars sparkled in the black canopy which hung like some huge spangled pall between earth and heaven.

Day's busy hum was hushed, and toil-worn humanity had sought its couch—sought that rest so much needed to enable it once more to grapple with the labours that produced its food.

The streets of the great metropolis were deserted by all save the prowling birds of night, the canker-worms[109] of society—the homeless, the outcasts, and the depraved.

The roll of the many vehicles which traverse the great metropolis during the day was no longer heard; the busy, jostling, ever surging crowd was dispersed, the flood of light which beamed from the thousand of shop windows lit not up the deserted streets, and the shadows of the lamp-posts, like spectre sentinels, alone appeared to guard the giant highways of London. A hundred iron tongues had boomed forth the midnight hour; a hundred bells of various tones had proclaimed to thousands that another day had passed on its way to eternity—had proclaimed to the sick man, whose pangs kept him wakeful, that the sands in Time's hourglass were swiftly running out, and that he was one day nearer the grave. To the strong and healthy it made known that nought could stay Time's resistless strides, and that the hours were last approaching when health and strength would be but things of the past.

Those iron tongues warned reckless youth to stay its mad career, and brought back to age the memories of days and nights of thoughtless pleasure—of hours wasted that never could be redeemed.

There is something solemn in the tones of those iron tongues, speaking in the still night, and echoing over a silent city; for it is Time making his voice heard in square and alley, hovel and mansion—Time speaking to all classes alike.

---

[109] Corruptors.

Yes, it is the voice of that fell destroyer of all things—of him who lays low the prince and peasant, who crumbles the stateliest edifice into dust, and scatters to the winds the ashes of kings. 'Tis the voice of him who laughs to scorn the ambition of the proud aspirants to fame; who smiles in contempt at the sculptured mausoleum, and who, with his foot, erases from all recollections and records all things. It is the voice of him who was at the beginning, and will be at the end—was at the creation of the world, and will be when chaos comes again. Time! resistless, boundless, impenetrable Time!

And yet how few give a thought to his warning voice—how few are called from their thoughtless pleasures by those musical tones!

Truly, if all mankind could be brought to weigh gravely the warnings hourly given by those iron tongues, they would pause ere they sought the gratification of their pleasures and passion. The course of the libertine would be stayed, sin would be unknown, and sorrow and shame exist but in words, and not, alas! as they do exist now—to such a degree as to fill our poorhouses, lunatic asylums, and gaols to overflowing.

But when the voice of Time's Master is treated with levity, no wonder that the voice of Time is unheeded.

Had he who lay back in a hackney coach, which rumbled through one of the large thoroughfares of London, but listened seriously to the tones of the iron tongues which boomed forth the hour of midnight, he would have ordered the driver to stop, or to turn his horse's head in another direction, rather than have continued on his way, with his blood fired with the lowest of passions, and his heart throbbing at the prospect of gratification and revenge.

The occupant of that coach was the merchant, Ralph Grasper—the persecutor of the forger's wife, poor Jane Slater.

We left him with the ill-fated woman near the grave of her suicide husband, anxious to obtain a coach to convey them home to his residence.

But as he walked along, he suddenly altered his resolves.

It struck him as probable that our hero had escaped the pursuit of the patrol, and that he would seek Jane at her dwelling, and, not finding her there, that it was likely he should seek to trace her out.

"He might suspect me of knowing her whereabouts," he muttered, "and pay a visit to my house. I am not the only inhabitant of the villa, or her presence there could be easily concealed. Besides, it would be bad policy. She must not go there. I will take her another road, and place her in the charge of someone whom gold will buy to any crime. Let me see—of whom can I think! Surely I should know a few whose scruples are easily overcome at the sight of a few coins. I ought not to be at a loss for one or a dozen such persons to suit my purpose, for there are few men who have more dealings with the callous-hearted than I have. There would be no fear of any punishment following their services to me in this case, for she is decidedly mad, and I doubt if she will ever be sane again. By heavens! fate seems to play into my hands, now, for nothing could be better for my purpose. Her greatest enemy she believes her dearest friend: her loathing has turned to love, and that love shall destroy her. But I am wandering from the present subject. To whom can I consign her? Ah! I have it— that's the fellow. He'd sell his soul for a crown, and no better locality could be found to suit my purpose. She has but one friend, I believe— this Spring-heeled Jack, curse him!—and he would never think to seek her there. Yes! there will I carry her. Bill Jackson dare not refuse to pander to my wishes, for he is in my power. Bah! the fellow will jump at the chance of obtaining money for drink,—no matter how it comes. That's decided, then. I'm glad I thought of it. That will entirely prevent all suspicion—all curiosity. Ah! ha! Master Jack! I shall outwit you yet, and the wife shall feel my revenge, as did her husband."

Vacantly gazing upon the ground, the demented young creature walked quietly along, resting upon the arm of the merchant as he thus plotted and planned. But as he turned his gaze upon her expressionless features she looked up in his face with a smile.

"Come along, Jane," he said. "I am going to be so kind to you."

"You are always kind," she replied. "Don't you remember, when first we met, I said I knew you would always love me?"

Grasper looked surprised at this remark, but quickly recovering himself, he replied—

"Oh, yes. That was"— He paused, for he saw that she evidently mistook him for someone else, and desired her to give him his cue where to continue, so as to humour her whim, and ingraft himself still more in her favour.

"Why, at my father's cottage. Don't you recollect the evening when you first came? How we sat in the little porch, where the climbing rose hung above our heads."

"To be sure I do. How can I ever forget that evening?" said Grasper. "Let me see. What did you call me then?"

"Why, James, didn't I?"

"Certainly you did."

"And you called me pretty Jane, and said you loved me so dearly, and asked me if I would not be your little wife. Oh! and didn't I feel the blood rush to my face, and could not say yes then, although I'm sure I meant it."

"Egad!" muttered Grasper to himself. "Better and better. She takes me for him who, with the brand of felon on his brow, lies beneath the gravel on the cross roads. She mistakes me for her husband. None but the devil could have turned her imagination that way. I must keep her mind in that vein, for nothing better could suit my purpose."

And the villain chuckled to himself as the poor wretch clung closer to his side.

"Ah! I knew that you meant yes, though you blushed deeper than the roses that hung around us," said Grasper. "My heart told me that you loved me, Jane, and so you did."

"I did—I did! And I was so unhappy when you were gone, and the days appeared so long after that, till you came again. Did they not to you?"

"Every hour appeared a year, dear Jane," said the wily rascal. "I thought of you all day, dreamed of you all night, and never was happy till we again met. And oh! what a meeting! was it not?"

"It was the happiest moment of my life," she replied, and for a moment her dull eye kindled.

But like the drop of grease let fall upon the lighted wick, the sudden brightness vanished on the instant, and, left the lustreless orbs more leaden than before.

That sudden gleam of reason was an arrow to the heart of Ralph Grasper; but as the eye deadened he became more at ease.

"It was the happiest hour of my existence," said Jane, after a moment's pause. "For it was then I promised to be your wife, dear James. And you swore to be true to me, and love me ever."

"And do I not keep my word?"

The woman sighed.

Ralph breathed less freely again.

"Why do you sigh, Jane?" he asked, almost tremulously.

"I will tell you," she said, pausing abruptly, and pressing her white hand upon his arm.

"Tell me, dear one," said the wily rascal, in tones as soft as he could possibly use.

Jane looked anxiously around her. Then, as if certain that there were none to hear her, she said, in a whisper so low that Grasper could barely catch the words—

"James, you have not been true to me or yourself. If you loved me and cared for me, as you professed, you would not have done what you have."

"What is that?" asked Grasper.

"Made me wretched, stained your soul with crime, forfeited your good name by—by"—

"By what?"

"Committing forgery!" she hissed, between her closed teeth. "Yes, forgery! He told me so, he, your master—Ralph Grasper!"

Ralph knitted his brows, but instantly taking her hand, he said—

"Jane, do not believe it; it's all nonsense. Someone has been playing upon your feelings. Do not let us dwell upon so foolish and ridiculous a subject, but talk of love."

Grasper feared if any mention was made of that thoughtless and illegal deed, it might tend to dispel the illusion under which the woman laboured, and defeat the object he had in hand.

No wonder, then, he was anxious to change the subject. The villain trembled lest his own villainy should become apparent.

But Jane would not immediately forego conversation upon that point, for she said—

"Are you not, then, guilty of the wicked deed laid to your charge?"

"Can you love me and think so?" asked Grasper, evasively and impatiently.

"I would not believe it, if you said it was false," she replied. "But if true, I would sacrifice my life to shield you from the consequences of your crime; for I am your wife, James, and in weal[110] or woe will cling to you."

"You are my wife—my true, kind little wife," said the hoary-headed[111] rascal. "But it is not true. Someone has been playing a silly prank upon you, because they know how happy we both are. There—let it drop. Don't think of it for a moment. Was not that a glorious sunset the evening we sat beneath the porch?"

"When?" asked the woman.

"You know that evening we met?"

"No. The clouds were leaden, and a storm was brewing," was the reply.

"Damn it!" muttered Grasper. "I'm wrong, and must be careful how I speak."

Then he added, quickly and aloud—

"To be sure they were."

"Then why did you say it was a glorious sunset?" asked the woman.

"Why?"

"Yes—why?"

---

[110] Prosperity.

[111] Grey or white haired.

"Can't you guess?"

"No."

"To see if you recollected the time as well as I did; that was all, my little wife—that was all."

Jane turned her dull orbs upon his smiling face, and shook her head, reprovingly.

"Can I ever forget it? Never," she said, "never, unless"—

"Unless what, dear Jane?"

"Some act of thine should drive reason and recollection from me; then I might, but not till then. Madness alone, James, could render me forgetful of those happy hours we have spent together; and I am sure I should go mad were you to bring shame upon us both, or I were to lose you, my dear, dear husband."

And as she concluded, that poor demented woman flung herself upon the bosom of the wretch who had caused her reason to forsake its throne, and buried her face upon his shoulder.

Were not the heart of Ralph Grasper callous to every feeling he would have sank in shame and remorse at the feet of her whom he now folded to his bosom.

But not one pang penetrated his adamantine breast—not one chord vibrated in his black and unfeeling heart.

To him pity and remorse were strangers— avarice and revenge alone found a home in his bosom.

A smile rested on his face—a smile of hellish triumph; and in that moment he forgot all the punishment he had received at the hands of Jack, and only thought of the wretched victim of his baseness.

He was suddenly aroused by the distant rumble of wheels over the hard gravel road, and raising the head of Jane from his shoulder, he said—

"I hear a coach coming. If it is empty, we will drive home, and have such pleasant talk about old times, and when I came courting you in the porch among the roses."

"Oh, that will be nice, James," she said; "for I love to think of those happy days, though, heaven knows! we have always been happy since. Haven't we?"

"Ah! happy as happy!" he replied. "But hush, now; for here is the coach. Oh! it is empty, for the driver holds up his whip."

Grasper motioned to the man, who had slackened the pace of his horse as he came near them, and the man drove towards them.

"Want a coach, sir?"

"Yes."

The man dismounted, and sprang to the door of his vehicle, which he flung open, and stood glaring in thoughtful surprise upon both Grasper and Jane, as the former hurriedly handed the latter into the coach.

"Where to, sir?" he said, as Jane seated herself, and Ralph turned towards him.

Grasper whispered the locality in Bethnal-green, where Bill Jackson resided, and then, ordering the man to drive quickly, leaped into the vehicle, and pulled the door to himself.

The man scratched his head, and mounted his box with the thoughtful expression still on his face—an expression which rested there long after he had driven from the spot.

"Drove that chap afore—certain of it," he muttered, as he whipped up the animal, "and her, too—but can't tell where. Don't like the look of him. Don't seem square.

Something's wrong. Tumbled her in too quick. Whispered where he wanted to go, as if he didn't want her to hear. She don't seem right. Can't make it out. No business of mine. Don't like it. It's queer—very queer—damned queer. Seen 'em both afore—not together. Know the cut of his gib[112]. Wonder if he ever bilked[113] me? No, 'tain't that. It's something. Can't tumble, but don't like it. Come up, will ye, you old rascal! Go along! Gee!"

And thus giving expression to his confused feelings, the man whipped up his horse, and drove with all the speed he could to Bethnal-green. And while he was thus occupied, Ralph Grasper sat beside the imbecile Jane, with his arm around her waist, giving utterance to sentences which he thought best calculated to feed the strange illusion which had fastened upon her brain—that he himself was none other than her dead husband, James Slater, the man whose death lay at his door, and for whose fearful end he would, one day, have to render up an account.

And he succeeded even better than he dared to hope he could. Still he was anxious and uneasy lest a dawn of reason should steal across her soul ere he could place her in the keeping of the ruffian whom he had marked out for her gaoler.

Once in the dwelling of Bill Jackson, he cared not whether she became again sane, although his dearest hope was that the strange fit would last for a long time, as it would the better suit his villainous purpose, and the easier administer to his revenge—a revenge he had long plotted, long panted for.

The course of the vehicle was, indeed, a swift one; but to the impatient Grasper it seemed to crawl, snail-like, on its way, and once or twice he nearly gave expression to his feelings, and only stifled his muttered curse upon his lips.

At length the vehicle was stopped, and the driver desired to know the exact spot he wished to alight.

To drive direct to the door of Bill Jackson's dwelling, Grasper felt, would cause an amount of curiosity among the neighbours, which it would be better not to incur, so he replied—

"We'll get out here." Then, turning to Jane, he added, "We will walk the rest of the way. Shall we, dearest?"

To this Jane gave a willing assent, and, handing her from the coach, he placed half-a-sovereign in the driver's hand, and hurried her along.

The man looked at the coin, placed it between his teeth, knitted his brows, and looked after him.

"I know you both, somewhere," he muttered, "and I shall know you again. I don't like the look of things, if it is no business of mine."

And, mounting his box, he drove leisurely along in the same direction as Grasper had taken.

In the course of a few minutes the merchant and the maniac stood before the dirty door with the greasy cord in the centre, and, in answer to a kick upon it, Bill Jackson flung it open, and stood glaring in surprise upon his visitors.

A look—a motion—and the ruffian drew back to suffer Grasper to enter the passage with his charge, which he did quickly, and the next moment the door was closed behind them.

---

[112] Know his type.
[113] Didn't pay the fare.

A whispered and hurried conversation ensued between Grasper and the pigeon-fancier, while meaning looks were ever and anon cast upon the pale and expressionless face of Jane Slater, who, apparently lost to everything surrounding, stood with her hand resting on Grasper's arm.

"I'll keep her safe, never fear. My old woman will be a mother to her. We'll put her in the room that that work-girl had, and she'll be all right. When will you come, did you say, sir?"

"Shortly after midnight," was the whispered reply. "Guard her as you would your life, and your reward shall be princely. Allow her to escape me, and a prison door closes upon your form."

And leaving her in the care of the pigeon-fancier, Grasper left the house, to return at midnight. And the vehicle which rolled through the silent city at that solemn hour bore him thither again.

CHAPTER LXXVIII.
WATCHED AND FOLLOWED.

THE driver of the coach, whose curiosity had been somewhat excited by his confused notion of having met before, and under somewhat unusual circumstances, with both Grasper and his imbecilic companion, having slowly followed in the same direction they had taken, drove his vehicle past the house of Bill Jackson, which he had seen them enter, and took a careful survey of that dirty tenement, fixing it indelibly upon his memory by the large pigeon-dormer that still disgraced the roof, albeit the birds had long since disappeared, not only from their old home but from sight entirely.

Bill had disposed of them the day after the fright he had received from Jack to a fellow fancier, who, after some day's confinement in a loft let them out for a fly, and, as a natural circumstance, instead of returning, they winged their way back to their old domicile at the top of Bill's house, where that worthy was not slow in discovering them.

Bill knew well enough that if he took them back to their purchaser that the birds would again return at the first opportunity, so he resolved to at once put an end to all chance of their doing so, and furnish a meal for his wife and children. So, bidding his wife send for a half-a-quartern of flour, he quietly twisted their necks, and had them cooked in a pie, which was greatly enjoyed by the whole family, even including Bill himself, who vowed he had never eaten a better or cheaper dinner in his life.

Of course the utmost secrecy was observed as to the fate of the birds, and a great many lies were told to their anxious and inquiring owner; but as no trace of the birds could be found—for Bill had burnt all the feathers—little more was said about them, and in a few days they were forgotten.

Bill had not again used his dormer, which was fast falling to decay; and its ruinous appearance did much to fix in the mind of the coachman the exact house into which his fare had gone.

Although the worthy Jehu kept muttering to himself that if things did look strange it was no business of his, he was unable to curb his curiosity. So, after having taken a good observation of the house, he turned his horse's head round and drew up at the "Pigeon Flyers," which he entered, and called for a glass of ale.

He did not immediately swallow the beverage, but stood thoughtfully toying with the glass and looking through the open door of the beershop, at the one with the greasy cord in the centre of the dirty panels, which suddenly opened to permit of the exit of Ralph Grasper.

Then the driver hastily swallowed his ale, and remounting his box urged his horse after the merchant, who, at a quick pace, hurried down the street.

The driver could soon have overtaken him certainly, had he desired to do so; but he had no such wish. In fact, had anyone asked him what his intentions were, he could not himself have told them.

In truth, he did not know. Something seemed to urge him to act as he did; but what that something was seemed beyond his conception. He slowly walked his horse along for some distance, keeping his glance rivetted upon the merchant, who had no sooner turned out of the street in which Bill Jackson lived, than he hailed another coach and got in.

The vehicle in which he had taken his seat dashed off at a grand rattling pace, and the driver who had been watching him now urged his horse forward, and followed it.

Over the stones went the two vehicles with a rattle and a clatter, keeping a good distance between them; the foremost driver conveying Grasper to his house, the hindermost swearing at himself for being a fool to be urged on by a curiosity, for which he could not account, to follow it.

On they went, till gravelled roads took the place of stone ones, and fields and hedgerows occupied sites where bricks and mortar now stand—on, till the first vehicle drew up before the villa in which the merchant resided, and then the second dashed past it along the road, the driver cursing himself for losing his time and making a fool of himself.

"Hi! coach!" cried a loud voice, as the man drove along, muttering imprecations, deep if not loud, upon his curiosity. "Are you engaged?"

"No, sir," he replied, quickly drawing up beside a tall, gentlemanly-looking man, from whose shoulders a long cloak fell in graceful folds. "No, sir, I'm not engaged—at least I've not got a fare inside."

"I asked you were you engaged. Are you on your way to pick up a fare?"

"No, sir. I was only engaged by my own foolery," was the reply. "I might have had a fare, I daresay, if I'd looked out for one, instead of looking after other people's business."

"You should always mind your own, and leave others to attend to theirs," said the gentleman.

"I know that, sir," said the driver, "and I can't account for why I have acted as I have. I took up a fare this morning close to the cross roads, where they buried a chap that committed suicide. There was nothing strange in that, certainly; but I've driven 'em both before and not together, and there's something about them that I can't make out. I feel it's not all right. Well, sir, I drove them to a dirty-looking house in Bethnal-green, where the old chap left the young woman; and I've been following the coach he hailed right down to those houses there."

And the man pointed with his finger to the row of villa residences, about a quarter of a mile down the road.

The man in the cloak had paid little or no heed to what the garrulous driver was talking about, till he mentioned the houses, and then he turned his gaze in the direction indicated by the man's finger.

"What! what!" he said, hurriedly. "You took up a fare at the cross roads, where the suicide was buried last night? drove to Bethnal-green and back again to those houses?"

"Yes, sir."

"What fare did you take up?"

"A wiry-headed chap about fifty, as had been a little bit mauled about the face, and a young woman, as seemed to me as if she had lost her senses. Why, lor' bless you!" added the man, quickly, "of course I know the chap now, well enough. Why it's the same man as I brought home one night that had been knocked down near the City, and had to go next day for my fare; and that woman is the very one I gave a ride back for nothing. Certainly, I recollect now. What a fool I am. Where shall I drive you to, sir?"

But Jack—for he it was in the cloak—did not reply. The words of the driver had set his mind at work, and his thoughts were busy.

He had leaped to the conclusion that the man was Ralph Grasper. But the woman, who was she?

He had been to the house of the suicide, but could obtain no admittance to his summons—a circumstance which had puzzled him much.

Had Grasper been there before him, and carried off Jane?

The thought struck him that such a thing was probable, and he turned to the driver to inquire what sort of a person was the woman who had been his fare.

The man described her particularly—her height, her dress; and Jack felt a strange pang as the man concluded.

"Did she speak?" he asked.

"Not a word," was the reply.

"Would you know this house again, where you set them down?" he asked, after a pause.

"Know it among a thousand," said the man.

And then he went on to describe it in every particular, even to the pigeon-dormer.

Jack recognised the house where the seamstress had lived, and he became more and more interested and perplexed, and instead of getting into the coach, he stood in the roadway with his hand upon the door of the vehicle, looking down at his feet, and knitting his brows.

The longer he thought, the more convinced he became that the fare the man had spoken of was Grasper and Jane Slater. But how came she in his company? Why did they go to Jackson's?

He was still puzzling his brains, when the vehicle which had brought Grasper home was driven by, and the driver called out—

"Ain't you got rid of your fare, mate? You kept pretty close behind me all along, didn't you? But you couldn't pass me, old boy."

This was addressed to the driver of the vehicle against which Jack stood, and caused Jack to start suddenly round and look at the speaker.

"You've got rid of yours, ain't you?" was the retort, half-sullenly.

"Yes, for the present."

"Oh, don't he live there?"

"Yes. But I got to pick him up at half-past eleven to-night, and drive him back from where he engaged me. There's a house a little lower down just open. If you like to come down when you've done with that gent, I'll stand a glass."

And with this, the man drove off.

"Hark you, my good fellow," said Jack, quickly, and getting into the coach as he spoke,

"I want you to drive me to Hyde Park-corner now, and pick me up on this spot at half-past eleven to-night."

The man opened his eyes wide at this.

"To take you where, sir?" asked the man.

"To Hyde Park-corner."

"But to-night, sir?"

"I will tell you there," said Jack, shortly. "Now, my good fellow, be sharp, for I'm in a hurry."

And Jack lounged back against the cushioned sides of the vehicle, and closed his eyes as an intimation that he desired no further conversation upon any subject whatever.

The man secured the door of the coach, and gathering up the reins, which he flung across the horse's back on dismounting, got on to the box, and drove off.

"Pick him up here at half-past eleven tonight. What for?" he muttered, as he whipped the horse on. "Is it to follow the other chap? Can't make it all out. There's something wrong—said there was—know there is. It's no business of mine, but can't help thinking things ain't going right, somehow. There's some mystery, but, as I said, it ain't no business of mine. All I want is my fare. Hyde Park now—where to-night, he wouldn't say. That's rum. Can't tumble,[114] blowed if I can; but I'll be here. Keep up, will you! Do you want to break your knees, you old varmint? Steady—come up!"

Jack kept his eyes closed as he lay back in the vehicle, but his thoughts were fully awake. A strange and unaccountable something seemed to whisper to him that he must follow the villain Grasper to wherever he went that night.

He could not help feeling that fate had thrown the driver of the coach in which he sat in his way, and that something more than he could at present see would come from what the man had told him, and he felt that he would find the hours pass tediously away till night came.

In the course of time, he was set down at Hyde Park-corner, and paying the man over his fare, he exhorted him to be at the spot where he had met him that morning at the hour named in the evening, or rather night; and drawing his cloak closely around him he strode away, resolved to at once seek rest, and refresh himself for the next night's adventure, be it of whatever kind it might.

The man promised faithfully to be at his post, and resolved not to work his animal further till the hour named. He immediately drove it to its stable.

It was exactly half-past eleven when Jack stood on the roadside, where he had hailed the coach in the morning, gazing at a vehicle standing in front of the house where Grasper resided, and anxiously listening for the roll of the wheels that were to announce the one he himself had engaged.

"The fellow is behind time," he muttered, "and I am resolved to track that villain. Surely the man will not deceive me, and thus thwart my intentions."

But no sound came indicative of the presence of any other vehicle than that which stood before the villa being in the neighbourhood.

"Confound the rascal!" said Jack, "for not being here. But I will not be baulked, if I ride behind yonder one. I will go where he goes, if it's to the devil!"

---

[114] Can't work it out.

And so saying, our hero drew his cloak around him, and walked towards the house of Grasper.

He had got within a dozen yards of it when a voice broke upon his ear, which he instantly detected as that of the merchant's, giving orders to the man to drive quickly, and the next instant the door of the coach was closed with a loud bang.

Keeping within the shadow of the houses till he was opposite the vehicle, Jack waited till the driver had taken his seat, and then sprang up behind, unobserved.

Away went the vehicle at a dashing speed, but Jack kept his hold. Away, off the gravelled roads on to the stones of the metropolis, rattling and rumbling and surging through the quiet and deserted streets, and almost drowning in its clatter the boom of the hundred bells that proclaimed the hour of midnight.

CHAPTER LXXIX.

ON THE TRAIL—FOUND OUT—THE VILLAIN CONFRONTED.

AWAY! with a roll and a rattle—away! with a bump and a swing, jolting and rolling our hero and its occupant from side to side, went the coach over the stones till it arrived at the end of the street, where Mr. Bill Jackson's tenement was located, where the driver suddenly pulled up, and Jack leaped down, aching in every limb.

Our hero gained the deep shadow of the houses ere the driver dismounted from his seat to let out the merchant; and, standing close up against the wall, he waited, and drew a long breath of relief.

His position had certainly been anything but a comfortable one for the last half-hour, and Jack was not at all sorry to be able to vacate his position behind the vehicle.

The jolting of the coach had rendered it necessary for him to hold on tightly, to save himself every moment from being hurled on to the stones, consequently his limbs were somewhat cramped and his hands benumbed, through the suppression of the circulation of the blood through his fingers.

He clasped them together, however, and a tingling sensation ran along each digit, and his fingers, in a few moments, were as pliable as ever.

While thus occupied, Ralph Grasper stepped out of the coach on to the pathway, and having paid the desired fare, bade the driver good night, and turned quickly down the street in which Bill Jackson lived, and where poor Jane Slater was a prisoner.

The vehicle was instantly driven away, and drawing his cloak around his form closely, Jack stepped from his hiding place and followed in the track of the merchant, with a light step but a beating heart.

The street was ill lighted, and the footfall of the merchant alone broke its silence.

Grasper did not once turn his head, but kept straight on till he reached the door opposite the Pigeon Flyers, which house of entertainment was shrouded now in complete darkness.

When Grasper stopped, Jack, still keeping well in the shadow of the wretched dwellings, hurried his pace, and even reached the next habitation to that of Bill's without being detected, ere that worthy answered the loud summons of the merchant, which he did by flinging the door open, and saying—

"Why didn't you pull the cord? Then nobody would have heard you knock."

"No matter; there is no person about," answered the merchant. "How is your charge?"

"Same as she was when you brought her this morning. Clean off her chump, governor," was the reply. "She's upstairs in the room the serving gal had. But come in, and I'll bring you a glim[115] to go and look at her with. My old woman says she don't like the idea of it; but I soon told her to shut up, or it would be the worst for her. I ain't a-going to refuse a chance of earning a pound 'cos she don't like it—not I. Let's shut the door, and I'll get you a light."

The door was closed, and Jack stepped out into the centre of the narrow pathway, shaking his head ominously.

"I can no longer doubt but that by some vile means or another this villain has obtained possession of the person of the young widow, and that he has secreted her here with this callous-hearted ruffian, the better to enable him to carry out his infernal designs. But I will baulk him yet. Thrice have I been her champion in the hour of peril, and I will be so again. Ah! Master Jackson, the fright I gave you has not, then, caused you to change your wicked course. You shall see me when you little expect it."

He strode out into the roadway and looked up at the rag-and-paper patched window, and the sill covered with oyster-shells, brickbats, and rubbish, which had been adroitly pitched there by certain little hatless and bootless specimens of humanity, whose school was the streets, and whose prospect was the gaol.

The room was in perfect darkness when Jack first cast his eyes towards it, but in the course of a few seconds a light gleamed within it; its lustre was deadened by the dirty panes of glass and the old worsted shawl that had been hung before them.

Jack knew, however, that Grasper had reached the room, and he listened for any sound that might indicate the presence of another than himself within it.

He fancied he heard a faint scream, but was not certain; and though he still listened, he heard nothing more.

"I will know who it is he has come to see," muttered Jack; "and I can do that without my presence being known, I fancy, unless the fellow has stopped up the opening in his roof, which once before gave me entrance and egress from the house. There is still that wretched building of dirty woodwork, so I doubt not all is as it was before. However, here goes to see."

Taking his mask from his pocket, he adjusted it to his face, and moved away from the spot.

About seven or eight doors past the one with the greasy cord and dirty panels was a small opening, leading to the back yards of the houses on that side where Bill Jackson lived.

This alley, if such it could be called, was greatly used during the day-time, albeit there was no house or habitation down it. But the costermongers and hawkers—of which there were several in that neighbourhood—found it well adapted for the passage of their barrows to their back yards.

It was not very wide, certainly, but still wide enough for the purpose named, and certainly saved the necessity of the wheels being removed from their carriages to enable them to be taken through the still narrower passages of the houses.

Some there were who ventured to leave them outside the front of their dwellings during the night; but these were few, as the risk was very great of their being stolen.

---

[115] Light.

It was to this entry, then, that Jack made his way, and he dived down it.

It was very dark. Not a single lamp, not a single ray of light, showed him where to step. But he had traversed it before, and passed quickly yet steadily on till he reached a low paling[116] that prevented encroachment upon the yards of the houses on either side.

For that locality the space of ground behind the dwellings was certainly more than would have been expected, or might be found in many a more respectable neighbourhood, being amply sufficient for a pretty little garden.

But flowers were very rare there. Dirty sheds, formed of old and rotten boards or crooked laths, took the place of greenhouses; and the only sign of vegetation was in the refuse of vegetable matter strewed about, and allowed to remain where thrown, mingling with dirt and ashes till it sprouted.

A more wretched and deplorable place it would have been hard to find than the back of the house in the street to which Jack had followed Grasper. Filth was everywhere, and the odour was far from pleasant.

However, Jack did not pause to gaze upon or ponder over the scenes around him, but lightly vaulted over the low palings into the yard next the court.

A half-starved, long-tailed, long-eared mongrel cur, who had taken up his lodgings in an over-turned soda cask, sprang yelping towards him, but which, as Jack raised his foot to give it a kick, slunk back, whining, to its kennel, with its long tail curled under its stomach, and gave him no further annoyance. So he vaulted over the next, and the next dilapidated row of low palings, till he stood in the yard attached to the house of the pigeon-fancier.

There was a dim light in the back room of the lower part of the dwelling, and as Jack looked towards it, he saw, through the glass, Bill Jackson sitting on a broken chair, smoking a short pipe, before the fire-place, and his wife sitting beside a deal table,[117] on which her elbow rested, looking the picture of grief and poverty.

There was no curtain to the window, and Jack had a full view of the wretched apartment, and, indeed, wretched it was.

Scarcely a particle of furniture did it possess, and that was old, broken, and rickety. On the walls were pasted, or held up by pins, some common engravings of sporting life, the margin of which were much torn—Bill having a propensity for stripping off pieces to light his pipe with.

The woman's face wore a troubled, care-worn look, while that of Bill's was clouded, for he knit his heavy brows as he puffed vigorously at the dirty pipe between his teeth.

Jack did not hesitate to draw near to the window, for he well knew that though he could well see them, they could not observe him, and he was anxious to hear what they were conversing about.

But several moments passed ere either the man or his wife gave utterance to a syllable that he could catch; but at length Bill, after thrusting the bowl of his pipe between the bars of the broken stove, and drawing it out with a hot cinder balanced on the top of the bowl, and taking two or three fierce draws through the stem, remarked—

"Now, look here. I'm master, and I'll do what I like. I've had enough of your jaw,[118] and I don't want no more."

---

116 Fence.
117 Low quality table.
118 Impudence.

"You'll suffer for it, if you don't mind, yet, Bill," said the woman, meekly.

"How would you like to have a gal of yours, if she went mad, taken to some place by an old scoundrel as ain't after no good."

"Well, I ain't got a gal as is mad," said Bill.

"But you might have."

"Perhaps I might."

"How would you feel, then, if some rascal of a fellow who had got a little money took her away for no good?" asked the woman.

"Why, I'd make him hand something over to me, that's all," said Bill. "He'd have to put a coutre[119] or two in my pocket, and that's what this bloke's promised to do, though the gal don't belong to me."

Jack involuntarily clenched his hands, and the features beneath his mask became suffused with a blush of indignation and horror.

"Oh, Bill!" cried the woman, as she shook her head, sadly.

"There, I don't want no more of your preaching, I tell you," said the ruffian. "I'm hard-up, and I'll make a pound if I can, anyhow. It's no business of mine if she ain't really his wife. She fancies she is, now she's off her chump,[120] and that'll do just as well for him, and for me too."

"But you know she ain't," said his wife. "You know she's some poor woman whom grief or misfortune has driven out of her mind, and you know that he is a hoary-headed villain who would take advantage of her imbecile, state to destroy her peace of mind forever, if she should again have her senses. You know this, Bill?"

"Perhaps I does, and perhaps I don't," growled the fellow, savagely.

"But you do."

"Do I?"

"Yes."

"Shut up, then."

"I can't shut up. I feel I must speak, if you won't let me do more to help her," said the woman.

"You better not try it, that's all," was the brutal remark; "for if you did I should be down on you like a sledge hammer."

The woman sighed, and was silent.

Poor, crushed, heartbroken thing! She knew what it was too well to feel the hand of the man who had sworn to love and cherish her fall with violence upon her person. She felt she could not say more without again exciting the villain to strike her, and so she buried her pale, wan face in her hands, and remained silent.

"Oh! how lost, how depraved must that wretch be," exclaimed Jack to himself, as he turned from the window, "when he can thus speak and act! He is but a man in form, a beast in soul, a brute in nature, a disgrace to the earth he inhabits, a foul blot on humanity—and yet he is but the type of many. Poor woman! I pity her, from my soul, for hers must be a hard fate to be allied to such a ruffian. And yet I dare venture to assert that the man who would stand forward to protect her from the violence of her ruffian husband would be assailed by her. In spite of his ill-usage she would cling to him, and him alone; protect him

---

[119] Coin, counter.
[120] Mad.

with teeth and hands as fiercely as the panther would protect its young, though she might feel that the next moment his ruffianly hands would again assail her. I cannot understand this trait in woman. Were I a woman, I imagine that I could feel nothing but contempt and horror for the wretch who could thus outrage all decency and self-respect. Well, it is indeed a strange world, this! and the more I see of it, the more it puzzles me."

Thus soliloquising, Jack vaulted on to a shed built up against the house, and composed of some old and rotten wainscoting, but which was sufficiently firm to bear his weight, but he made a great clatter among some loose pieces of board which were placed on the roof, two or three of which fell to the ground just beneath the window of the room in which Bill and his wife sat.

The noise alarmed both, and, taking up the candle, they came to see what it was.

Jack had no wish to be discovered just then, so he flung himself flat down upon the roof of the shed, intending to remain there till the husband and wife had again gone into the house.

"What was it?" asked Bill, peering, half-frightened, out of the back door into the yard.

"Why, the wind has blown down some of the boards on the roof of the shed," said the woman, as she stooped to pick one up. "We shall be having the windows broke with 'em some of these times."

"Oh! is that all?" said Bill. "Give it us, and I'll chuck it up again."

Jack at this began to fear lest he should get a knock with the missile as it came hounding on to the roof; but, fortunately for him, Bill flung it over the spot on which he lay.

"Here's another," said the woman.

Up came this one, falling with a clatter close to Jack's head.

"Is there any more?" said Bill.

"Don't see any," replied the woman, and the next moment the door was closed, and the light disappeared.

Jack rose to his feet, and cautiously stepped along the roof for fear of again displacing any of the loose timber, and catching hold of a stout piece of wood which had been driven into the brickwork of the house, to help support the weighty row of boards and laths which formed the dormer, drew himself up by it till he stood upon the tiled roof of the dwelling.

If he was cautious not to displace the loose timber on the shed, he was doubly so now not to pull down the loose tiles, for scarcely one was firm, the pigeons having so pecked away the mortar from between them that it was a wonder the wind had not hurled them into the street and yard below long before.

The dormer was fast falling to ruin. The door, by which he had entered it on his previous visit, was gone, so Jack found no difficulty in obtaining an entrance into the strange, cage-like place, and had the gratification of finding that the trap in the roof was still there, and unfastened.

He stooped and softly raised it, and peered down on to the landing, across the floor of which a thin streak of light shone as it penetrated a crack in one of the panels of the door of the room over that occupied by the poor seamstress.

Jack did not immediately descend, but, leaning over the trap, listened intently.

He heard the low, subdued tones of Grasper, as he spoke in persuasive accents, and then the blood ran cold and chill through his veins as, in a louder key, the tones of Jane Slater's voice reached his ears.

"'Tis her! 'tis her!" he gasped. "Oh, God! am I too late?"

He thrust his legs through the trap, and seizing the sides of the hole with his hands, lowered himself gently to the floor of the landing.

He clenched his teeth, and his breath came quick and short as he placed his eye to the crack in the door.

On a table, in the centre of the room, a thin candle burned with a long wick, and cast a sickly ray upon the features of two persons who stood near the window—the persons of Ralph Grasper and the imbecile Jane.

The villain's arm encircled the waist of the idiot, who, with a vacant stare, gazed up into his face, evidently as unconscious as a new-born babe that she stood in the presence of her deadliest foe.

The blood in Jack's veins ceased to run through its channels, and his heart seemed to stand still for a moment. Then, as a pang of indignation and horror pervaded his frame, he softly placed his hand upon the knob of the lock.

It was fastened.

A cold sweat broke out upon his forehead, as through the chink he perceived the head of the imbecile drop upon the bosom of the merchant, and the smile of triumph that played over his face as, like a fiend, he gazed down upon the form he held in his arms.

Then the life-fluid coursed like molten lead through its channels. The momentary fear had passed, and Jack was a man again—a man filled with indignation, horror, and disgust.

Taking one step backwards, he hurled his stout body against the panels of the door, shivering them to splinters, and forcing off the lock. Then, with a bound, he sprang into the apartment, and stood before the surprised and alarmed Ralph Grasper.

CHAPTER LXXX.

GRASPER DEFEATED—RESCUE OF JANE SLATER.

HAD a thunderbolt dropped at the feet of the merchant, he could not have been more terrified.

His horror was literally speechless, and, dumbfounded, he stood glaring upon Jack's hideous mask and cloaked form drawn up to its full height before him.

His arm fell from the waist of Jane Slater, and dropped powerless to his side. He seemed to have become fixed in his head, and, like a statue, he stood powerless to move hand or foot.

"Villain!" hissed Jack. "Base, despicable, designing villain! Providence has guided me hither to thwart your accursed designs. Man! fiend! devil! why should I not strike you dead at my feet?"

Jane, who had looked upon his sudden entrance, first shrunk back from him, but as his tones fell upon her ears, a sudden light sparkled in her eyes, and she sprang towards him.

But recoiling on the instant, she clasped her hands together, and sinking into a sitting posture on the floor, murmured, as she swayed her body to and fro—

"Poor James! poor James! Do not harm my husband. He is not guilty. He has told me he did not forge the cheque, and he would not lie to me, whom he loves so dearly. Do not harm my James—my husband!"

Jack had raised his clenched hand, and the power of a giant seemed centered in that arm; but as the imbecile's words fell upon his ear, he suffered it to fall by his side, as a sigh broke from his manly bosom.

"Mad!" he said. "Powerless to know right from wrong—powerless to discriminate; and he can take advantage of her fearful malady. Great heaven! can it be murder to slay such a wretch as this?"

"Murder! murder! Who talks of murder?" cried. Jane, springing to her feet. "Murder! blood! See! see how it runs along the boards from that gash in his neck! Look! red, red streams of fresh, warm blood! 'Tis his—his! James! Oh, my God! my poor, poor James!" And flinging her arms wildly above her head, she again sank upon the floor at Jack's feet, and covered her eyes with her hands, as if to shut out the imaginary sight.

A moment Jack stood gazing upon her with pity, swelling his heart almost to bursting. Then turning quickly, he sprang forward and clutched the panic-stricken Ralph Grasper by the throat, and holding him at arm's length, hissed between his clenched teeth—

"Are you human?"

For the first moment, since Jack's unexpected entry, the wretch seemed to possess life, for he uttered a gurgling cry for mercy, and franticly grasped at the arm that held him powerless as an infant in the hands of a giant.

The pressure upon his throat was fearful, and the fingers of Jack sank deep into the flesh of his neck, compressing the windpipe, and causing the eyes of the wretch to start from their sockets, and his tongue to protrude from his mouth.

In vain he struggled to free himself from that fearful clutch; in vain he tore at the hand that held him; and, believing his last hour had come, he sank upon his knees, and clasped the legs of Jack, imploringly.

"Wretch!" cried Jack, hurling him violently to the floor, and spurning his body with his foot. "I cannot longer desecrate my fingers by keeping them in contact with your contemptible form. You are not worth the rope that would hang you. Such an accursed scoundrel would disgrace even the gallows."

And, in his indignation, he again spurned the merchant's body with his foot, hurling it across the room to the door.

"Mercy!—help!—mercy!" cried the affrighted man.

"What's the matter—what's the matter?" cried the voice of Bill on the stairs.

"Oh! there's murder, Bill; he's killing the gal! I know'd some harm would come of this," exclaimed the wife, as she followed her husband up the stairs.

The noise of the broken door had first alarmed them; but Bill, believing it to have been caused by a struggle between Grasper and the imbecile, would not permit his wife to go upstairs, nor yet go himself; but as other sounds succeeded, he himself became alarmed, and hurried from the room, followed by his wife, to learn the cause of the disturbance.

"Oh! come and help me!—come and help me!" cried the merchant. "I'm being murdered! For God's sake, come!"

By the time the words were out of his mouth, he had with difficulty struggled to his feet, and Bill and his trembling wife reached the landing.

"Who's a murdering you?" asked Bill. "What! can't you tackle that girl?"

The merchant pointed into the room, and Bill started, as he perceived, for the first time, the cloaked figure of Jack, then uttered a howl of terror as our hero turned, and he caught sight of the mask which concealed his features, and, turning to flee, the cowardly bully ran against his wife, hurling her to the ground, and knocking the candle from her grasp, which was instantly extinguished.

At any other time Jack would have burst out into a loud laugh, but his heart was too full of indignation to permit him to do so now; and, springing out upon the landing, he grasped with one hand at Bill as he rose, and with the other he hurled Grasper back into the room.

"Oh! it's the devil come for me! The devil! the devil!" cried Bill, in tones of the most abject terror. "Oh! Poll! save me! save me!"

And the rascal shook like a feather in the wind, as he thus appealed for succour to his ill-used and insulted wife.

Mrs. Jackson, however, rose to her feet, and hurried down the stairs, screaming as loudly as she could scream, and wringing her hands in utter dismay.

"Oh! my Bill!—my Bill!" she cried. "What shall I do? Oh! my Bill—my Bill!"

Jack could not help pitying the woman's grief, and thinking how ill her husband deserved her.

"Is this," said Jack, shaking him by the shoulder, "how you keep your word—your promise to me, by suffering a callous-hearted scoundrel to bring hither, for a base and wicked purpose, a wretch whom sorrow and misfortune has deprived of reason."

"Forgive me! oh! forgive me!" gasped Bill, falling on his knees and clasping his hands. "Oh! pray do forgive me, and I'll never do wrong any more."

"Good is not in your nature," said Jack.

"Yes, it is," quickly gasped Bill. "Oh! do give me another chance, do!—do! good Mr. Devil; do!—do!"

And the ruffian, overpowered by his fears, caressed the feet of our hero.

"Devil!" said Grasper, who began to gather courage at the presence of a third party. "It's Spring-heeled Jack, for whose capture a reward is offered." Then, dashing past Jack on to the landing, he cried, "Send for the police! Arouse your neighbours! Capture him, and put gold in your pockets. He's Spring-heeled Jack!"

Bill leaped to his feet with a cry of joy, for a weight had been removed from his heart. Oh, such a weight!

And so did Jane leap to her feet, as his name fell upon her ears.

She sprang up from her crouching position, with the light of reason once more beaming in her eye.

"Spring-heeled Jack!" she cried. "Oh, God! my preserver! Ha! ha! ha!" and with a wild laugh she flung herself upon his bosom.

The left arm of our hero encircled her form, as with his right hand he drew from his bosom a pistol, exclaiming—

"The first that moves I will lay dead at my feet! Bill Jackson, call your wife here. But stir not, or you are a dead man. Ralph Grasper, my capture is not so easy as you imagine. Utter one sound more, to bring you assistance, and that sound is your last. Call your wife—she has nothing to fear from me, for I have not yet fallen so low as to harm or insult a woman."

The attitude, the tones of Jack, convinced both Grasper and Bill that it would be unsafe to play with him, and the former remained silent, while the latter called out—

"Poll! Poll! come up here. It ain't the devil. Come up here, I say, directly, or it'll be the worst for us all. Do you hear, Poll? Come up stairs, and hold your frightened jaw."

Tremblingly, the woman obeyed, and slowly she made her way up to the little landing.

But there she paused, as if fearful to move another step.

"Come hither, my good woman," said Jack. "You have nothing to fear, for I know that you have done all you could to persuade your rascally husband not to permit this villain to seek to outrage this poor creature."

Bill began to tremble again, and the impression that Jack must be indeed the devil once more took possession of his breast.

If he was not, how did he know what his wife had done—how did he know the girl was there?

He was not quite sure yet that he would be permitted to exist any longer on the earth he disgraced.

Still, he thought the best thing he could do to shield himself would be to obey implicitly the orders of the strange being, and he said—

"Why don't you do as the gentleman asked you? Go in."

The woman, shaking in every limb, and pale as a corpse, tottered into the room.

"Take this poor creature," he said, "she has fainted, and do your best to revive her. Ralph Grasper," he added, turning to that worthy, who stood gnawing his nether lip, "I intend to take her away from here. I warned you to beware how you sought to annoy or insult her again, when, you stood by her husband's grave this morning, and I feel that if I did what was right I should send your black soul to hell this instant. But I will give you another chance, and, now, heed me well. Much as I should despise myself for condescending to slay such a callous-hearted, contemptible villain, if ever again, by act or deed, you seek to molest or annoy this poor suffering woman, as I hope for salvation, not even the fear of the law shall stay my hand; but, like a worthless cur, I will rid society of your accursed presence. I have but a few more words to say, which I sincerely trust will be the last I shall ever utter to one for whom I feel such unbounded contempt and loathing, and they are these: I desire to depart with Jane Slater from this neighbourhood, and I warn you not to seek to prevent me. You know who I am, and you have felt my power. Beware, then, what you do! I am not to be played with. You have felt my grip upon your throat to-night, and will feel it for some time to come. Beware you do not feel it there again! Attempt to seek to prevent my departure, or to again obtain possession of that woman, and you had, indeed, better rouse the passions of the devil himself than mine. Now, scoundrel, let these words be the last between us."

"I will not interfere with her or you again," said Grasper, "but at once go home."

He moved towards the landing, as he spoke in a low tone.

"Stay!" said Jack.

Grasper bit his lip deeper, and stopped suddenly.

His object was defeated.

He thought to deceive Jack, but he was mistaken. Our hero read his intentions on the instant.

"You will remain here till after we have taken our departure. I am not to be captured to-night."

"I do not seek your capture," said Grasper, grinding his teeth together, in suppressing the rage he dared not openly show.

"Don't add liar to your other base qualities," said Jack.

"I assure"——

"Silence!" interrupted our hero.

Grasper slunk back in terror.

The glaring barrel of the pocket-pistol flashed before his eyes, and fear taught him prudence on the instant.

"Now, Mr. Jackson, I have a word to say to you," said Jack. "Take my advice and mend your ways, or one of these days you will find, to your sorrow, that your black deeds have brought misery upon you, your wife, and children. You have lent yourself to as great a piece of villainy as was ever planned, and laid yourself open to a punishment as severe as it is just. Be careful, or you will yet find yourself in a felon's dock, which, perhaps, after all, would be the best thing that could happen for your family. Mend your ways, I say; and if you can have no respect or feeling for others, strive to have some for yourself. You will find it more to your interest to aid me to take this poor demented woman away, than to seek to help that villain to detain her and effect my capture; and, if you are wise, you will do so."

"I will, upon my soul I will!" cried Bill, quickly.

"That was what you said when you promised to reform on our previous meeting," sneered Jack.

"But I mean it, I do," said Bill, who felt certain even now that Jack was something more than human.

"You do?"

"Yes, sir. I'll do anything you wish—anything, I don't care what it is," said Bill.

"Will you prevent this man giving any alarm when I am gone?" asked our hero.

"If he does, so help me"——

Jack held up his hand, deprecatingly, and the ruffian stifled the oath on his lips, then added—

"If he tries to prevent your getting off clear with her, I'll give him a Whitechapel uppercut as'll lay him down for a month."

And Bill Jackson turned back the cuff of his fustian coat as he spoke.

Grasper looked as if he could not believe the evidence of his senses, when he perceived that Bill was anxious to take sides with the man who had nearly frightened him out of his life.

But he was too cautious to say anything; and inwardly he cursed both him and Jack from the deepest recesses of his unfeeling and unscrupulous heart.

"Enough," said Jack, "I will trust you."

"You may," said Bill, growing half-a-dozen inches taller in a minute. "Say the word, sir, and I'll settle him now at once."

"Hold!" said Jack. "I have, I think, pretty well settled him for the time being. It is after my departure from this house that I depute you his keeper. Well, Mrs. Jackson, is she coming to?" added Jack, addressing the wife of Bill, who was chafing the hands of Jane.

"Yes, sir. Oh! I'm so sorry all this happened. I'm sure I wish that man hadn't brought her here. There, my poor girl, you're all right. Here's a nice, handsome gentleman come for you. Come, come, you're better now. There, you'll soon be all right," said Mrs. Jackson.

Jane opened her eyes, and glanced wildly around her.

"Where—where am I?" she asked. "What place is this I—who are you? Great heavens! how came I here? Oh! that villain, Grasper!" she screamed, as she clung to the woman in terror. "Do not let him come near me. Oh, heaven! how did I come here?"

"Fear not, Mrs. Slater," said Jack. "That rascal is powerless to harm you while I am near."

At the sound of Jack's voice, Jane looked towards him, and, breaking from Mrs. Jackson's arms, with a cry of joy, sprang to his side.

"You here? Then I am safe, my good, kind friend. But what place is this? how came I here? Am I awake, or dreaming? or have my sufferings driven me mad?"

"I will tell you all about it some other time," said Jack. "Will you trust in me?"

"As in heaven," replied Jane, to whom, in that faint, the light of reason had returned. "You are the only friend I have on earth, now that he is gone."

"Then leave this place with me, and woe to him if he put forth hand or voice to prevent our departure. Bill, remember your promise, and one day you will have your reward. Grasper, beware we meet not again, or the day of reckoning will have come."

Jack drew the arm of Jane through his own, and, with the pistol still grasped in his hand, led her from the room.

CHAPTER LXXXI.

THE ATTEMPTED RE-CAPTURE—JACK ALARMS THE NEIGHBOURHOOD.

THE door, with greasy cord and dirty panels, had closed behind them, and Jack and Jane stood in the dark and silent street, in the cool air of the night, and beneath the starlit canopy.

Perhaps never in his life before did Jack feel such a pang of relief as he did when he found himself and companion once more in the open air; but he did not pause an instant. Drawing her arm more firmly within his own, he hurried her along in the direction of the Mile End-road.

He believed, that Bill, rascal as he was, would keep faith with him; yet he could not completely stifle a feeling of uneasiness—a dread that Grasper would endeavour yet to suffer him to escape.

He was anxious to place Jane Slater in security. He had no fears for himself, but many for her.

He knew the unscrupulous character of the man who had brought her husband to an untimely grave, and herself to misery; and he well knew that he would leave no means untried to prevent him getting her away safe, if any chance presented itself of his so doing.

"You have said you will trust in me," remarked Jack, as they went along.

"I have, and I will," she replied. "But do tell me how I came in that place with my bitterest foe, for I remember nothing since I stood at the cross-roads this morning."

"I will tell you all I know another time. At present, I am all anxiety for your safety. In that house you have just left, some time since resided a poor girl who struggled to keep body and soul together by slop-work. I pitied her and assisted her, and she resides about two miles from here, in a pretty little house, overlooking the green fields. She owes me a little debt of gratitude, which I know she longs to repay, and would be glad to receive you. Will you go there? for I fear your own home would be but a poor refuge against the wiles of that villain Grasper."

"Oh, I will go anywhere but back to that fatal spot. I cannot bear to look upon it more."

"Then there will I take you. Ellen, I know will receive you kindly, and be to you a sympathising friend; for she has known suffering and poverty: and those who have suffered themselves can best feel for the miseries of others."

"Is she your wife?" asked Jane.

"Wife?" cried Jack, in surprise at the unexpected question. "Bless you, no! I am not yet married."

Jane looked up in his face with an inquiring glance.

Jack thought he divined the question thus mutely asked, and said—

"Ellen Folder is no more to me than any other woman for whose sufferings my heart can feel. She was poor and friendless—I, rich and thankful. She required aid, and I willingly extended it to her, seeking as my only reward the justification of knowing that I had helped one who could ill help herself. She is a kind, virtuous girl. Were she otherwise, Spring-heeled Jack would not ask you to take up your home with her."

"Forgive the cruel thought," said Jane. "I fear I have wounded your generous heart."

"No," said Jack; "for as the world goes, the thought was natural enough. Hallo! what's that?"

A murmur of voices floated to their ears from a distance behind them.

They paused a moment to listen, and our hero started as he heard his own title distinctly uttered.

"Confusion!" he exclaimed. "They have given the alarm. The whole neighbourhood has been aroused, and are in pursuit of me. Quick! We must reach the open road, where we may be fortunate enough to procure a coach. Were you in safety, I could enjoy some fun with this yelping crowd; but I dread lest you should again fall into the hands of that ruffianly merchant."

"Oh, heaven! Anything but that—anything but that!" cried Jane. "Oh! let's run—let's run!"

Together they hurried on, the sound of voices swelling louder every moment on the night air, and mingling with the tramp of many feet.

They reached the Mile-end-road, Jane panting and breathless, but not a vehicle could be seen either way along the road.

Jack's anxiety every moment became greater for the safety of his trembling companion, and a feeling of uneasiness stole over him, lest this new trouble should again affect her weakened brain.

"There is no vehicle to be had. I must conceal you somewhere while I lead this ruffianly lot in another direction. Here," he added, taking some coins from his pocket and forcing them into her hand, "take these, and if a coach should pass, order the driver to take you to Holly Cottage. There ask for Ellen Folder, and say I sent you, and I will come after you. Do not fail to do as I bid you. Now, go into this garden, and crouch down behind those bushes, so that you cannot be seen from the road by any one. If we keep on together, they will overtake us, and you will be torn from my protection. I will go back, and draw this mob in another course, so that you can escape. If you can get a coach, do so; if not, remain concealed here till I return. Do not fear for me. If I stay longer, that fiend may yet triumph."

Leading her into the garden of one of the houses, he left her, and hurried back to the street, up which he had come to reach the road, and arrived at its corner just as a crowd of about a dozen persons came bounding along.

Jack turned, so as to permit the light of the lamp to fall on his mask, and such a howl broke from the lips of the mob as was sufficient to arouse the neighbourhood.

"Here he is! That's him! Spring-heeled Jack! Stop him!" and other exclamations broke the silence of the night as Jack bounded away in the opposite direction along the road to that where he had left Jane concealed.

Jack cast a hurried glance behind him to see if Grasper or Bill were in the throng, but neither met his eye.

Still he was certain that one or the other had given notice of his presence in that neighbourhood.

Nor was he wrong in his suspicion.

As soon as the street door had closed behind himself and Jane Slater, Ralph Grasper attempted to leave the room, but Bill doubled his brawny fist, and stood, threateningly, before him.

"No you don't, governor," he said. "I said I'd keep you here while they got off, and I mean to do it."

"You do?" said Grasper, whose rage was in no way abated at the treatment he had received at the hands of Jack, and the loss of his intended victim at the very moment of success.

"I do," was Bill's firm reply.

"Then hark you, Bill Jackson," said the merchant. "I know I am no match for you in physical strength, but I can punish you for all that. You recollect I employed you as a porter at my warehouse, and that you robbed me, don't you?"

"Well," said Bill, "you sacked me for it, didn't you?"

"Yes. But I can still do more than that. I can transport you," said Grasper.

Bill staggered back.

All his bravado was gone in an instant.

"Why, you forgave me for it," he gasped.

"Because I thought I could make use of you to help me to carry out any plan I had on hand. But since I find you are unwilling to aid me, over the seas you go, as sure as your name's William Jackson. You can keep me here as long as you like, but the longer you keep me the warmer I'll make it for you when you stand in the felon's dock on the charge of robbing your employer. What do you think of that? It's a pleasant prospect, ain't it?"

"A damn sight too pleasant," growled Bill. "But what will you do if I let you go now?"

"Take no further notice of the affair, at least if you will arouse your neighbours and the police, and set them after this Spring-heeled Jack."

"But if I do, he'll make it go hard with me some day," said Bill, dreading punishment whichever side he went on.

"That's nothing to me," said Grasper; "you should not have suffered the fellow to enter the house."

"I didn't know he was here. He gets into the place without opening a blessed door," cried Bill; "and I'd advise you to let him alone, or it will be the worse for you."

"I'll track him down," said Grasper, furiously, "if I spend a fortune to do it, and lose my life in the attempt. So, let me pass, and go and arouse your neighbours. Five pounds, the reward I promised you, if you do; the felon's dock and transportation, if you refuse."

The mention of the five pounds had a great effect upon Bill—a much greater effect even than the threat of imprisonment—and he buttoned up his coat and stood back from the doorway.

"Tip us the tin, governor, and I'll have the whole street out of bed in the twinkling of an eye. It don't take the blokes as lives about here very long to look over their wardrobe."

Grasper took from his purse the gold, and gave it to Bill.

"Now, go," he said, "and arouse your neighbours, while I seek for the police. I observed from the window the way they took, and if we are smart they will soon be taken. Once he is in custody, the girl will soon be in my power again, and there will be a chance for you, Bill Jackson, earning a like sum to that you hold in your hand."

"Don't have anything to do with it, Bill," said his wife. "Don't, there's a good fellow."

"Hold your row, woman," said Grasper. "Your husband, I presume, is master."

"Aye," said the woman, bitterly, "and I am the slave!"

And with a sigh she left the room.

"Now, there's not a moment to be lost," said Grasper. "Hurry! hurry! for I will triumph yet, in spite of Spring-heeled Jack or the devil himself!".

And catching up the candle, Grasper hurried down the stairs, followed by Bill.

In a few minutes ten or a dozen persons were aroused from their beds by Bill Jackson to give chase to Spring-heeled Jack, whom he asserted had broken into his house, and Grasper, having succeeded in finding a watchman dozing at the corner of the street, aroused him, and he immediately joined the half-dressed throng who were assembled around Bill, who was relating things he had neither seen nor heard, but swearing fearfully that it was all true.

Urged by Grasper, they were soon speeding along the street. But Bill, after running with them for a few yards, suddenly dropped back, and returned home.

Intent upon again getting Jane into his power, Grasper did not miss him, and when, in about half-a-minute, he found himself left far behind, he came to the conclusion that Bill was ahead with those whom he had aroused from their beds to go in pursuit of our hero.

They caught sight of Jack, as we have noticed, as soon as they reached the end of the street, and struggled hard to come up with him.

But Jack dodged and doubled on them, and, by degrees, led them away from the locality where Jane was, and finally darting down a side street, effectually eluded them.

Still, he was anxious to draw them as far as possible from the high-road, on account of Jane, and while he was thinking how best to effect this object, a hand was placed on his shoulder from behind, and he turned, to see a watchman, rattle in hand, at his side.

"Hallo! Spring-heeled Jack. I've got you, have I?" said the man.

"Hold me tight, then," said Jack, making a grasp at the rattle, and at the same time putting his foot behind the man's legs and toppling him over.

"This will draw them down here," said Jack, "and leave the road clear for me to get Jane safely to her destination."

And, swinging the rattle round with all his force, he sang out at the top of his voice—

"Thieves! Murder! Police! Watch! Help! help! Thieves! thieves!"

The watchman scrambled to his feet; but, with no great violence, Jack pushed him down again; and the next moment windows were raised, and the tramp of those who had given him chase was plainly heard hurrying in the distance.

"My purpose, I think, is served," muttered Jack, flinging the rattle away, and bounding with the speed of an antelope away from the spot, and fairly getting out of sight before the crowd had reached the watchman, and all asked at once what was the matter.

Down one street, and up another, went Jack, till he reached the high-road again, and sought the garden where he had bidden Jane Slater secrete herself, and where he now found her, half dead with terror. A few words, however, reassured her, and they started again on their way without any fear of further molestation.

CHAPTER LXXXII.

THE TRAMP AND THE WAGGONER—JACK OFFERS ASSISTANCE.

A FINE team of horses were slowly walking along a country road a few miles from London, dragging behind them one of those lumbering, large-wheeled waggons, common enough some thirty or forty years ago, but now seldom met with, and which was being driven by a ruddy-faced yokel attired in a long smock and a billycock hat, and who whistled loudly as he trudged along, with the brass-hound whip over his shoulder, either to cheer him on his way, or dispel the silence which reigned around at that early hour of the morning, or else to keep awake the animals, who, judging from their slow pace, were drowsy and tired.

A thick canvas, supported by broad wooden hoops, formed an awning over the waggoner, and which was wet with the heavy night dew.

Suspended inside the waggon from the centre hoop was a large horn lantern, which threw a dim light on to the numerous tubs and bushels and quantity of loose straw which the interior of the vehicle contained, and also played fitfully on the red face of a hearty-looking youth, who snored loudly among the goods.

This was the waggoner's mate, who, having had his spell at the driving, or rather minding the team, had turned in for a snooze till the vehicle reached its destination—London.

The horses had been on the road for many hours, and were worn and jaded, and were only kept in motion by the continued "gee-wut," "mether way" of their driver, who was as anxiously looking forward for the end of the journey as they were.

But they had still some miles to go ere the city was reached, and the hard turnpike roads gave place to the stones of the metropolis.

There was a bright moon, which reflected the shadows of horses, waggon, and man, on the dry road; and as the waggoner whistled, he amused himself by trying to step on the legs of his own shadow—a feat not only ridiculous, but impossible to perform.

While thus engaged, a figure suddenly rose up from under a hedge by the roadside, and in a pleading voice, said—

"Are you going to London, sir?" The sudden appearance of the stranger in his path caused the waggoner not only to desist whistling, but to spring backwards in alarm.

"If you please, sir, are you going to London?" was the question again asked by a poor, miserable-looking youth, whose pale face and shabby attire bespoke him no stranger to want and suffering.

The waggoner recovered from the sudden shock which he had experienced by having his reverie broken in upon so unexpectedly, and in a surly tone, replied—

"What's that to thee?"

"If you are, sir," said the youth, in a tremulous tone, "would you kindly give me a lift in your waggon?"

The driver of the lumbering vehicle eyed him for some moments, and then sneeringly remarked—

"What for should I give ye a lift?"

"Because I've walked many miles, and am worn out with hunger and fatigue. Will you, sir, if you please?"

"I bean't a 'sir.' I'm Roger Stokes, that's all," said the man.

"Then, Mr. Roger Stokes, will you be kind enough to let me get in your waggon, and ride to London?" said the youth.

"An I bean't a 'mister' neither," growled the man; "and I bean't a-going to let you get in the waggon."

The youth heaved a sigh, and drew back as the surly words were spoken.

"I suppose ye be some darned, lazy skulk," said the waggoner, as he flung his whip over the neck of one of the horses. "Gee-wut! Mether way!"

And with this the waggoner commenced to trudge on again beside his team.

"I hope you may never need a lift over a hard road, and meet with any one as unfeeling as yourself," said the youth; "and I thank heaven that it has forced poverty upon me rather than an unfeeling heart."

"Ye bean't a preacher, be ye?" said the waggoner, turning his head.

"No. Nor are you a Christian."

"Bean't I?"

"Indeed, no, or your tones would be more kind to one in distress."

"I tell 'e what it is," said Roger Stokes, speaking as he trudged along. "There be a darned sight too many of you lazy varmints, and I bean't a-going to give a lift to the loikes of you. I don't starve, because I work; and if you were a mind to do the same, you needn't neither. I see too many of you chaps, and I knows your game."

The youth, who had started on the road, now came up alongside of Stokes, and looking in his face, said, in a tone half indignant—

"You know me, but do you know any harm of me?"

"Well, can't say I do, but I guess you're after no good," was the reply.

"Oh, you Lunnoners are very, green, ain't you? but I been had once before, and I bean't a-going to be done again. Gee-wut!"

And as if memory had brought some unpleasant recollections to his mind, Roger slashed the middle horse of his team across the neck so violently with his heavy whip that the startled animal fairly reared up.

"Mether way! Steady, will ye, ye rascal?"

And down came the whip again on the neck of the offending horse.

"So, because another may have injured you," said the youth, sorrowfully, "you must be uncharitable and insulting to all."

"And so I mean to be," said Roger. "It'll be a long while, I know, before I give anyone a lift on the road again."

"If you have resolved not to help a tired wretch on his way, you might at least speak civilly," said the youth.

"Oh, yes, I'd be civil certainly. I'd be civil to the fellow that served I the trick, if I met him. He was just such another looking chap as you, and I let him get in my waggon and lay down among the straw, because he said he were tired and hungry, and just as I got into Lunnon I found he had broken open one of the boxes and stole what was in it, and got clean off, without I ever seeing the shadow of him. Do you think it's likely, after that, I'd give anyone a lift on the road? Think I be civil to any as axes[121] me, after that? Not I. I be a darned sight more inclined to lay my whip about his shoulders, just to give him a warning not to try it on again."

"And so you take me for a thief?" said the youth, his pale face flushing as he spoke.

"Ye look a sight more like one than an honest man," said the driver, with a sneer in his rough tones, "and I don't think I'd be far out of my reckoning if I said you were one, too."

The flush on the youth's face became deeper as he eyed the burly form of the waggoner with a meaning look.

"Don't say I am a thief," he cried, in a suppressed tone, "or, big as you are, I'll resent the insult."

Roger paused in his walk, and looked with ineffable contempt upon the stripling.

"Ye be a cheeky sort of chap, I take it," he said, "to threaten I. Why there bean't enough of ye to make a meal for a dog."

"There is enough of me," said the youth, bursting with passion, "to defend my character when assailed, or to show a coward and a brute that I am not to be insulted with impunity."

"Ye be a little cock to crow so loud," said Roger, "and, darn me, if I don't change your crowing to crying with my whip, if ye don't take yourself off."

And as he spoke the waggoner raised his heavy whip as if about to strike the wan-looking youth.

The young man grasped at the thick thong and secured it, and, by a sudden jerk, tore the whip from the waggoner's grasp; but the next moment, and ere he could use it as a means of defence, the infuriated yokel dashed upon him, and seizing his weakened frame in his strong arms, hurled him to the ground, and savagely tore the whip from his hands.

"There, ye darned thief, what do you think of that, eh?" he asked, as he stood over the prostrate lad. "Ye took I for a green 'un, didn't you, and thought to come some of your Lunnon bounce[122] over I? But ye'll have to eat a few more hard dumplings afore ye can stand up against Roger Stokes. How d'ye like that fall, my bantam cock? I reckon I've larned ye summut this time. Don't 'e come near I again, or I'll break thy ribs for thee, thou Lunnon thief."

Hesitating a moment whether or not to give the prostrate youth a cut with his whip, Roger turned to look after his team.

The drowsy horses had gone a few paces down the road, when finding that their driver was not at their side had come to a dead stop.

Starting them on again with voice and whip, Roger fell into his accustomed long, heavy stride, and never once deigned to look behind him at the poor weak young man he had left lying upon the rood.

In the course of a few moments the youth rose to a sitting position, and gazed after the team and the heavy lumbering vehicle which they conveyed along.

Heaving a deep sigh, he suffered his head to fall upon his hands, and, in a melancholy voice, he muttered—

---

[121] Asks.

[122] London impudence.

"Heaven knows poverty is hard enough to bear, but insult—oh that I were not so weakened by want and suffering! But, alas! I have not the power to protect myself. My limbs are bruised by the fall, and now my prospects of reaching London are farther off than ever, and my poor mother may die without ever again seeing me. Oh, Fate! Fate! why am I so hardly—cruelly dealt by?"

Slowly he staggered to his feet, and tottered to the thick-set hedge on the road side, against which he leaned for support.

"Fifteen miles from London," he continued aloud, "and a dying mother anxiously waiting to give me her last blessing. I shall never see her more in life—never, never, for I cannot reach her side unaided, and heaven seems to have deserted me in this trying hour. Weak, friendless, and alone, God help me!"

At this juncture a large dark object passed clean over his head, and fell on the road before him.

The young man uttered an exclamation of surprise as a tall, cloaked figure rose up in the bright moonlight, and stepped towards him. "My sudden and unexpected appearance has somewhat startled you, young man," said the cloaked figure; "but be not alarmed. You are evidently in distress, and I can aid you."

At this the youth took a step towards the speaker, but recoiled back to the hedge, as his moist eyes rested on as hideous a face as he had ever imagined.

"Who are you?" he gasped.

"A friend to all good men, but a foe to bad ones. I heard your lamentations but now, and knew you required aid. Speak plainly; can I aid you?"

"First tell me who you are, for I confess your looks alarm me," said the youth, gaining courage as he spoke.

"I have alarmed a great many in my time. But in reply to your question, and to set your doubts at rest, I am known as Spring-heeled Jack."

"Ah! I have heard of you."

"Doubtless. You are weak and ill."

"I am, indeed; but the treatment I have just received has rendered me almost powerless to move," said the youth.

"What treatment?" asked Jack.

The young man told our hero of his request to the waggoner, and stated, truthfully, everything that occurred between them.

"Why are you so anxious to reach London?" asked Jack, when he had concluded.

"That I may see a dying mother ere heaven takes her from this world," said the youth, trembling as he spoke.

"You cannot walk?"

"No, I cannot; I am too weak. I have not tasted food since yesterday morning, and am footsore, weary, and in pain. I have already tramped fifty miles, but the remaining fifteen I cannot go, and she will die without giving me her blessing—die, believing I am callous-hearted and unfeeling."

Jack felt pity for the lad before him, and drawing from his coat-pocket a small flask, offered it to him.

"Drink the contents of that," he said. "It will put fresh life into you. 'Tis brandy."

The young man accepted the flask with thanks, and placed it to his lips.

"No conveyance can be obtained here," said Jack, "to convey you to your destination, or I would willingly aid you to reach it. The waggon was your only chance, and the driver must have been an unfeeling rascal to refuse to help you on the road."

"All men have not hearts like yours," said the youth, handing back the flask to Jack, "and Robert Blackthorn will not forget your kindness, sir, though I doubt if he will ever be able to repay it, save by thanks."

"Never mind," said Jack, "that's sufficient for me. I do not ask more. Indeed I have not yet earned them. Your condition excites my sympathy, and your objects my determination to aid you to obtain them. Sit down there under the hedge, and I will see if I cannot induce this waggoner to convey you to the metropolis."

The youth shook his head.

"It would be useless, sir. You would only meet with insult or outrage at his hands," said Blackthorn.

"I have little fear of that," said Jack, with a smile, which his mask hid from the other.

"Do not try, sir, for I am powerless to aid you should the ruffian assault you, as he did me," said the youth.

"He will not dare attempt such a course with me; for, thank heaven! I have sufficient strength to protect myself. Do as I request you, and rest assured I will induce the man to turn his team back to pick you up."

The youth obeyed, but shook his head, doubtingly, as he did so; and Jack, gathering the folds of his cloak around him, sped away along the road after the waggon.

The slow pace at which it went rendered it an easy task for Jack to come up with it, which he soon did.

Roger Stokes had resumed his whistling, and with his eyes fixed upon his shadow on the ground before him, he neither heard nor saw the approach of our hero, who, gliding up behind the lumbering vehicle, seized the tail-board with one hand, while with the other he parted the thick canvas awning, so as to admit the passage of his body into the vehicle.

The next moment he had sprung lightly up, and dropped in upon the loose straw that covered the floor of the waggon.

As he alighted, however, his foot rested upon the large, brown hand of the slumbering youth inside, who, with a howl of pain, started up, awake, into a sitting position.

But no higher could he rise.

The dim light of the lantern played upon the form and mask of Jack, and the yokel's jaw dropped in utter terror and dismay, and he sat glaring at our hero, with his large goggle eyes, like one bereft of reason.

Jack looked down upon him for some moments in silence. Then, seating himself upon a large hamper, right before the youth, he said, in a deep, hollow voice —

"You're a nice-looking youth, but if you open your mouth much wider, your head will drop off."

"Eh! he! he!" shuddered the boy. "Ye be the devil!"

"So you know me, do you?" said Jack, "then the best thing you can do is to be silent, or"—

Jack did not finish the sentence, for the alarmed youth, springing to his feet, made a bolt at the parted canvas at the back of the waggon, and, tumbling over the tailboard of the waggon, ran away down the road, shrieking loudly—

"The devil!—oh! the devil!"

CHAPTER LXXXIII.
JACK ALARMS THE WAGGONER, AND COMPELS HIM TO DO THROUGH FEAR WHAT HE REFUSED BY ENTREATY.

THE boy's cries, ringing out loudly on the night air, alarmed the driver of the team, and the whistle of that worthy was instantly hushed as he started round to see the boy fleeing down the road at a speed he never could have given him credit for, and which, in fact, he would not have believed possible had he not observed it with his own eyes.

"Dang it! what be up now!" he exclaimed, scratching his head, and looking with a puzzled expression after the retreating figure of the youth, whose fears led him to place as great a distance as possible in the smallest space of time between his ungainly form and the lumbering vehicle. "Wey! wey! Jem! Jem! where the devil be ye going to? What be the matter with ye? Come back, I say, or I'll horsewhip thee."

The horses certainly obeyed his orders, and came to an instant standstill, but Jem either did not or would not heed his words, but continued his flight till a turn in the road shut him from his companion's sight.

"What be the meaning of this?" muttered Roger. "Has the dang boy gone mad? Why, I thought he be snoozing sound enough in the waggon. It be a rum go; but I'll tan his hide for him when he comes back, the dang rascal! I will."

By the time he had uttered this, and the horses had come to a quiet stand, Roger Stokes stood by the tailboard of the vehicle, and casting his eyes upon the canvas that fell from broad hoops to the panelling of the waggon, he staggered back as if he had been shot, for there, peering from the opening in the centre of the covering, was a hideous face, on which the bright moonbeams played.

Roger Stokes was a man possessing great physical strength and power, and no ordinary amount of brute courage, but the sight of the hideous mask, lit up in the pale, spectral light of the moon, drove the very blood from his heart, and, for a time, completely deprived him of all power to speak or act.

Jack enjoyed his terror for some few seconds, then, extending his claw-gloved hand towards him, he said—

"Roger Stokes!"

At the mention of his name the man staggered still further back, and, if possible, his terror increased.

Surely, thought the countryman, he must be some supernatural being, or how could he know his name?

Jack had learned it from the sickly youth, who had learned it from the waggoner himself in their conversation.

His hand shook so that he could scarce hold the whip, his knees knocked together, and his teeth chattered loudly.

"Roger Stokes!" said Jack again.

But Roger Stokes could not answer.

He could only look with a fascinated yet frightened stare upon the face in the centre of the canvas.

"Come here," said Jack.

Roger obeyed, by retreating still further; and the clattering of his large teeth rang out clear and loud on the night air.

"And this is the fellow," thought Jack, "whom the poor young man dreaded would assault me. Why, he hasn't the courage to raise his hand."

Flinging the canvas back, Jack made a pretence of leaping from the waggon.

This action had the effect of arousing Roger.

He uttered a whining cry and essayed to fly, but his limbs refusing to carry him a single step, a deep groan escaped him, and he sank down upon his knees in abject terror.

Jack saw that he would have little difficulty in doing as he liked with the countryman, but he resolved to make the fellow believe that he was certainly not a human being he had to deal with.

"Roger Stokes," he said again, looking down with contempt upon the affrighted wretch, "you are a callous-hearted scoundrel."

A groan from Roger's throat followed this remark, and a supplicating look from Roger's eyes was fixed, pleadingly, on Jack's mask.

"Yes, Roger, you are a hard-hearted, unfeeling rascal. Well fed, healthy, and strong, you ought to feel pity for the weak and hungry; but instead of so doing you insult the wretched and assault with your brute strength the powerless and careworn wretch who asks aid at your hands. Roger Stokes, you are no longer fit to live; you must give place to better and more feeling men. You must come with me."

Again Jack pretended to get out of the waggon.

"No—no—no!" cried Roger, fear lending him strength now, and leaping to his feet as if the point of a sword had been applied to his back.

"You must come. You are not fit for this earth. You must go with me—you know where."

And Jack pointed downwards as he spoke.

"Oh lor'! oh lor'!" groaned Roger. "What shall I do to be saved?"

"Saved?" said Jack. "Why, you are worthless."

"Oh no, doant'e say that, measter devil— doant'e say that. I bean't a bad man. It be some mistake—some mistake."

"I never make mistakes," said Jack. "I say you are a cruel, unfeeling rascal, who can refuse to a poor, weak, half-starved fellow-creature a lift over the road he is powerless to travel from illness and want. So no more words. Better men must take your place here, and you must come with me."

So saying, Jack sprang out of the waggon, and alighted right before the terrified waggoner, who, with a shriek, tottered back several paces along the hard and dusty road.

Another spring, and Jack was by his side, and his hand on the other's arm.

"Murder! murder! Oh, lor'! oh, lor'!" cried the man. "Do—oan't! Oh, doan't!"

"Why should I spare you, Roger Stokes?" said Jack:

"I—I thought he was a thief," said the man. "My waggon's been robbed afore, and my measter's made me pay for it. I thought he would have robbed me, upon my soul I did! or I'd have given him a lift. I bean't a hard-hearted man, sir."

"Well, hark you. The lad lies down the road on the spot where you threw him—a cowardly act for a powerful man like you. Go back with your team and pick him up, if you would escape me. Carry him to London in your waggon."

"Yes—yes. I will—I will," said Stokes, quickly.

"And hark you! Hurry on your horses, for he is anxious to get to the metropolis."

"I will."

"Pick up your whip, then, and do my bidding, or it will lie the worse for you," said Jack, pointing to the whip which had fallen from the man's nerveless grasp.

"I'll do as you wish, so as you don't interfere with I," said the man, as he raised his whip from the dust.

"You must," said Jack. "And what's more, I intend to see it done. So go to your horses."

The waggoner obeyed, walking backwards, so as to keep his face to Jack, whom he feared would pounce upon him.

Roger turned the animals, and as the lumbering vehicle swung round on its heavy wheels, our hero vaulted lightly and unseen again in at the back of the vehicle, and suffered the canvas to fall into its place.

Roger looked about for the cloaked figure, and seemed as much surprised as gratified to discover it had gone.

But whither?

That puzzled him.

He looked about and down the road, and on either side, and finally drew a long breath of relief, and muttered—

"Gone! oh, lor'! Gone! It was horrible. And I won't drive the waggon no more—no, not if measter give I another shilling a-week to do it. It must have been the devil himself, for he knowed my name, and all about I. I wish I hadn't have seen him, for he's give I a shock I shan't get over for some time to come, and Jem, too. I wish the boy were here now, for I'm blowed if I don't feel skeered being all alone."

Jack, who had passed along the waggon and out at the front of it, now dropped down on to the back of the shaft-horse.

"I'm with you, Roger," he exclaimed. "You are not all alone."

Roger turned round, and a cold perspiration broke from every pore.

He felt he must say something, so, with an effort, he exclaimed, in tremulous tones—

"I thought you'd gone, sir."

"Oh, no. I wish to enjoy the cool, night air for a short time."

"It's very warm down where you live, sir, ain't it?" said Roger, feeling that he must speak.

"Well, rather," said Jack, "seeing that I never allow the fire to be put out for a moment. But you'll know all about it one of these days. You can bear the beat pretty well, I should think, Roger Stokes."

"Oh, lor'! no, sir," stammered Roger. "I can't bear the heat at all."

"Well, that's unfortunate, Roger."

"Unfortunate, sir?"

"Yes, because you will feel it more than you might do if you could well bear heat at all times," said Jack, slyly.

"I hope I'll never have to bear it," said Roger.

"I daresay you do."

"I do, indeed. And I mean to be a good and kind-hearted man, so as I shan't," said Roger.

"You'll have to alter very much, then, Roger," said Jack, "and not refuse a lift to the footsore and weary."

"It bean't my fault."

"Whose, then?"

"Measter's."

"How's that?"

"He told I never to let anyone get into the waggon and ride," said Roger.

"He told you not to?"

"Yes, sir."

"Why?"

"Because it was robbed once," said the man. "And if he knowed I did it he'd give I the sack."

"So you only obeyed his orders?"

"That be all."

"No, it's not all. You did more," said Jack.

"More?"

"Yes."

"What more?"

"You insulted and assaulted the poor fellow who wished you to let him ride."

"He were cheeky."

"He was weak, and you were strong. Your insulting words and tones naturally caused him to retort warmly. Roger, take my advice, and always keep a civil tongue in your head. If you won't aid, don't insult; for greater pain is often inflicted by the tongue than by the fist; and always be sure you are right, before you accuse another."

Roger, trembling and ashamed, walked on at the head of the centre horse, and Jem said no more, but sat astride the shaft-horse, shaking the animal's mane.

In this way they kept along the road for some distance, when Jem sprang from the shadow of a hedge to Roger's side, exclaiming—

"Oh, Roger! oh, Roger! Where are you going? Did you see him? It was the devil. He's burned a great hole in my hand, and if I hadn't have run he'd have took me away—I know he would. Oh! what have you come back for?"

"Hush!" whispered Roger. "Doant — doant!"

"I tell you it was the devil that made me jump out of the waggon. Oh, dear! Is he in it now?"

And the lad seemed ready to start off again, if his question was answered in the affirmative.

"Don't talk like that, I say. You'll offend him," said Roger, still in a whisper.

"Is he inside?"

"No."

"Where then? Has he gone?"

"No."

"Where is he? Oh, tell us. I'm so frightened," cried the boy, quickly.

Roger nodded his head backwards.

The boy looked behind him.

"I don't see him," he said.

"On the shaft horse."

Jem looked again, but saw nothing on the animal indicated that was at all unusual.

"No he ain't."

Roger looked over his shoulder at this, and, to his great surprise and relief, discovered Jack had vacated his seat.

"He's in the waggon, then," whispered Roger.

The boy was about to dart off, when the waggoner seized his arm.

"Stop! stop!"

"I can't. Let me go."

"Don't leave me," said Roger. "Don't, Jem— don't, there's a good boy. If he wants you, he'll have you, wherever you are; and it will only make him vexed. Do stop, there's a good boy —do stop, now."

The lad's teeth chattered as he looked back again at the canvas-covered vehicle.

"Where are you going, Roger? What did you turn back for? Wouldn't he let you go to Lunnon?"

"No."

"Oh, lor'!"

"He made me turn back to pick up a chap I wouldn't let ride. But he won't hurt us if we do as he wants us to," said Roger.

"Oh! I won't come with the waggon again—I won't," said Jem.

"No more will I. But don't talk so loud, or he'll hear you."

"I'm not deaf, my friends."

Both boy and man uttered a loud cry, and turned quickly.

There stood Jack behind them.

The boy sprang to the hedge, and Roger staggered along till his horse's head would not allow him to go further.

"Come, urge your team to a quicker speed," said Jack; "for I must see this unfortunate youth safely ensconced in your vehicle before we part."

The waggoner urged on his horses, and the rumbling vehicle went along quickly, rolling and jolting loudly in its course.

Jack kept a look-out for the young man, and, in a short time, he perceived his attenuated form reclining in a sitting position against the hedge.

"Halt!" said Jack.

The waggoner brought his team to a stand right opposite the young man.

"Look at him," said Jack. "Are you not ashamed to possess the heart that could refuse assistance to one so ill and wretched? Does not your conscience smite you for using violence to one so powerless to defend himself? For shame! If you would atone for your utter want of feeling, raise him gently and lay him tenderly in your waggon, help him on his road, and freely extend to him all the aid in your power when he reaches the metropolis; and, above all, remember, that dark clouds at times obscure the brighter skies—affluence smiles to penury—health gives place to disease—plenty, to want. Your turn may come some day to need assistance such as he does now. Turn not, then, from another, when it is in your power to aid him, lest he, in time, turn upon you. A kind word and a good act cost nothing, whilst it gratifies the heart with the knowledge that it has done right. Now, lift him up."

The boy let down the tailboard of the waggon, and Roger, taking up the youth in his strong arms, laid him gently on the straw.

In a minute more the heads of the team were turned towards Loudon, and the yokels looked round for Jack, but he was nowhere to be seen.

CHAPTER LXXXIV.
THE DYING WOMAN—THE CONFESSION.

IN a wretched apartment of a wretched-looking house, situated in a narrow court in the neighbourhood of St. Giles's, upon a wretched pallet in one corner, reclined the attenuated form of a woman of about fifty years of age.

The dim morning light, as it forced its way through the dirty panes of glass in the small window, revealed the miserable objects scattered about the apartment.

Three old rush-bottomed chairs, a small deal table, a broken washstand and a small box was all the room contained, save the thin, small flock bed which rested on the floor, and on which the woman reclined, covered by an old blanket and dirty patchwork quilt.

The head of the suffering woman lay almost flat with the bed, for a thin bolster alone propped it up. Her scant grey locks fell over a face pinched with long want and suffering, and an almost fleshless arm lay upon the coverlid, while her lustreless eyes were fixed, with a longing stare, upon the door of the apartment.

"Another night has gone," she said, "and yet he comes not. Must I die without seeing him? No—no. I can't leave this world till he comes, and I tell him all,—how I have deceived him— how I have wronged him and his sister. Will he curse me, or will he forgive me? No, I dare not hope it. But why does he not come—why does he stay, and he knows I am dying? Oh, God! let me live till he comes; let me make atonement for my great sin; then—then, with his bitterest, direst curses ringing in mine ears, I can go from this world happy. Happy, did I say? Happy? Ha! ha! ha! I have not known happiness for years, long, long years. Never shall, never shall! for after death comes punishment, as if I had not suffered enough in this world for what I have done! But let me not think of that now. Let me only think of him and his sister. Would I knew where she was! whether she be living or dead. Will he never come—never! and the secret die with me, and that villain still possess his wealth? No, no. Great God! save me till he come—for he will come yet—he will come!"

The head which had been raised, while she thus muttered in low, weak tones, fell back on the low pillow, and the lids dropped over the lustreless eyes, while a spasm seemed to shoot through her frame, and a look of intense pain crowned her features.

For a time she appeared to slumber, then up she sprang, wildly, in the bed, and clasping her thin hands together, rocked her body to and fro.

"Richard! Richard! will you never come? Oh! will you never come? And shall the ungrateful libertine still keep from you your wealth and station? Oh! how quickly the hours roll away! Three days gone—three! and yet he does not hurry to my bedside. Fool! he knows not what I have to tell him. No, no, I will not call him fool—poor, deceived boy! What can detain him—what can keep him from me? He loves me as if I were indeed his mother. He must be ill, or he would have been here long ere this. I cannot last much longer. Death's icy fingers are upon my brow, and I am going fast— fast—to answer for my great and wicked sin. Oh! how I tremble lest he come too late. I had died ere now, had he been here. But can I hold out much longer? Can I battle longer with the grim phantom? But I must—I will. He shall know all—all!"

Exhausted, she again sank back in the bed, and the hollow cough that shook the clothes above her form spoke but too plainly how near she was to the grave. But the sun-ray that stole in at the top pane of the window crept down to the second square of dirty glass, and still the door remained closed on which the dull eye of the woman was fixed with an anxious gaze.

"Not yet—not yet; and still the sands run quickly out," she said. "And my eyes grow more dim, and my pulse more feeble. Not yet —not yet!"

Lower and lower down the window crept the sun-ray, and over the carpetless floor of the apartment towards the bed, and finally rested upon the white face of the sufferer, who, by an effort, rolled her head back upon the bolster to avoid it, for it dazzled her vision as she gazed at the door.

"Nine o'clock," she said. "Yes, 'tis nine o'clock. That streak of light has been my only time-piece for years, and never yet deceived me. It has reached the mark on the wall, and it is nine o'clock; and still the boy does not come—still he does not come. Yesterday I thought when the ray of light rested where it does now I should have relieved my overburdened heart, and have taken my departure from this cold, cruel world. But I am deceived. Alas! how have I been deceived for years! But I am past deceiving now. The grave will not deceive me. Oh! no—no! Oh, no! I am hurrying to it. Oh that he would come!—ere its portals open to receive me—ere it is too late for him to learn the truth so long hidden from him—ere it is too late to atone for the terrible wrong I have done him—ere I can unfold to him my own wickedness, and the bright future that must open upon him! The light creeps up the wall, the moments fly swiftly by, death draws nearer and nearer this wretched pallet, and yet he comes not—he comes not!"

And the woman sighed heavily.

Hark! there is a tottering footstep on the stairs.

It reaches the invalid's ears.

The woman summoned all her strength, and raised herself upon her sharp elbows in the bed.

The lids are extended wide open, and the lustreless eyes start forward as she fixes them with intense anxiety upon the panels of the door.

Her breath comes in short gasps, and her haggard face lightens up with the momentary excitement of hope.

Up comes the step.

The footfall is louder as it nears the room.

It pauses on the landing before the door. A hand is run over the panels, and the woman, clasping her hands together, shouts in her weak tones—

"Richard! Richard! My boy! my boy!"

The excitement is too much for her weakened frame, and with a sob she sinks back upon the pillow as the door is flung open, and a young man staggers into the room.

His face was pale as that of her who lay, with clasped hands and closed eyes, on that wretched pallet; his eyes and cheeks were as sunken, and his lips as thin and white. Illness, want, and misery were stamped there; and the woman, as she opened her eyes and looked towards him, uttered an exclamation of surprise and pain.

The young man staggered forward towards the wretched bed, and dropped on one knee beside it, exclaiming—

"Great heaven! Mother! is it thus I find you! Alone, ill, and in want? Fate has indeed been cruel to us both—very cruel."

He pressed her shrivelled hand in his, and, placing one arm beneath her head, raised her tenderly up, and gazed with a look of anguish in her wan face.

"Mother," he said, "I could not reach your side earlier. I started the instant I received news of your illness. I had no money for conveyance, and had to walk nearly the whole way. Oh! what a thing it is to be poor, especially at a time like this, when you want so much!"

"I want nothing now, Richard, that you are here," she replied, looking from under her half-closed lids into his face. "The wish to see you ere I died has alone kept me clinging to life. Thank God you have come! and the last prayer of the guilty, dying woman has been granted."

"Guilty, mother?" cried the youth.

"Ay, boy. Guilty—very guilty."

"Of what? Towards whom?"

"Towards you and"—

"Me, mother?"

"Ay. But call me not mother, Richard; call me not by that endearing name," cried the woman, in a low, yet impassioned tone.

"Not call you mother!" said the youth, gazing upon her in surprise.

"No, boy—no."

"Wherefore not? You have ever been to me a kind and tender parent."

And as he spoke he bent his head down and kissed the pale, thin cheek.

"Because, Richard"—and her voice was husky with emotion—"because, boy, that title belonged to another. I am not your mother."

The youth sprang to his feet.

His pale cheeks became bloodless white, and his lips quivered.

For a moment he stood gazing upon the form which, losing his support, had again sank back; then, in a whisper, he hissed, rather than spoke—

"Not—my—mother!"

"No, Richard. One who is now an angel in heaven gave you being. I am but the guilty wretch who substituted my own babe for hers—who robbed you of your birthright, that a villain might enjoy it."

"Mother, mother! you are raving! You know not what you say. Your mind wanders. Want and misery have brought you to this. I will go for a doctor, who will give you something to calm your mind and cool your burning brain."

And he hastily picked up the hat he had flung from his head on entering the apartment.

"Hold! Richard!" cried the woman. "No earthly aid can save me now. Death has set his seal upon me, and the unknown world opens before me. Stay, I say! for I have not long to live. But in the moments there are yet allotted to me, I have an act of justice to perform—a reparation to make. Come, kneel beside me; for my voice is weak, and my tones must reach your ears. Then, when I have told you all, curse me, and let me die."

"Curse you, mother! Oh, never, never!" cried the youth, as he flung his hat on the little deal table, and sank on his knees beside the bed once more.

"Now, give me your hand, Richard," she said, "and bend your ear down to my lips."

"Let me raise you up, mother?"

She smiled her assent, and the young man raised her into a sitting position, and supported her with his arm.

"Now, listen; for these are the last words I shall speak—words of shame to me—ay, bitter, bitter shame!"

She paused, and pointed to the table on which a yellow jug stood, and motioned him to reach it.

He did so, and held it to her lips.

"Water!" he said. "Oh! would it were wine!"

"No matter now," she said. "Wine and water will soon be alike to me. Are you listening?"

"Yes, mother."

"You will never call me that name again. Boy, how old are you?" she added, quickly.

"Twenty-one," was the reply.

"Twenty-one. Ay, so you have been led to believe, and so have others; for you were ever an effeminate child, and looked not so old as you are. Richard, you are twenty-four—yes, twenty-four. I cannot mistake, for I have never forgotten—not for a moment—when you were born. Oh! too well, even now, do I remember that fatal month! I was a pretty young woman then! so pretty that months before I excited the notice of the rich and handsome Sir Giles Clavering. I was flattered by his attentions, made vain by his notice; and, in an evil hour, I fell a victim to his wiles. I had flattered myself that the poor servitor would become his wife. But alas! how soon was the dream dispelled! for in less than a month he married another—a beautiful, accomplished lady, moving in his own sphere. Bitter was my disappointment! overpowering my grief! But my love for him was strong as ever. But it was gall and wormwood to my proud soul to feel that another's offspring would inherit the broad lands I had fondly hoped one day would be the property of mine."

She paused, and then continued—

"But I must be brief, for the moments fly, and my soul pants to leave its earthly tenement. Time went on, and wife and mistress gave birth, on the same day, each, to a son. As I pressed my little one to my bosom, and impressed a mother's kiss upon its brow, something whispered to me that I should yet see my babe the inheritor of its father's wealth. From that moment I planned and plotted, matured my schemes, which the devil himself must have aided me to carry out successfully. Are you listening?"

"Yes!" gasped the young man in a choking tone.

"The young wife, less fortunate than I, was seized with a fever, and great were the fears entertained for her life for more than a month. Consequently, her babe had to be taken from her. When she recovered, and asked for it, an infant was placed in her arms. And never shall I forget the loving way in which she ever gazed upon it. But, Richard, that babe was not hers—it was mine. I had vowed it should inherit its father's wealth, and changed them—I taking the real heir to my bosom, she clasping to hers the offspring of sin and shame. Three years passed on, and the deceit was never. discovered, and then a daughter was born to Sir Giles. Day by day he became more cool towards me, and though he never suffered me to want, he turned his back at last upon me. Whether shame at his own conduct prompted this, or a dislike to me, I know not. But it made me mad! and I vowed to embitter his happiness as he had embittered mine. One night his baby girl was stolen from its little cot, and he never saw her more."

"By whom?" asked the young man, his lips quivering as he spoke.

"By me. But I did not harm her, as you know. Together we lived in peace and content for years, till want and suffering drove her from me to seek bread by her needle. Then the boy went miles away to work, and I was left alone. In my solitude I reviewed my past life, and regret stole into my heart. Sir Giles died a few years after his wife, and I was again happy for a time in the knowledge that, after all, my boy came in for his wealth. But I had grown poor, and needed assistance. I sought it at his hands, and he spurned me, called me liar, impostor, and had me hurled from his door. It was but a just reward for my sins; but as I had raised him up, I resolved to hurl him down, and do justice at last to you, my poor, kind Richard. Curse me, if you will; but I could not die without divulging the truth. You are Sir Richard Clavering, and the libertine who enjoys the title is the offspring of my illicit love!"

"Is this—can this be true?" gasped the young man.

"As true as heaven! As true as the grave now waits to receive my body, and hide for ever a guilty, heart-broken wretch."

"But I never can claim my right. The libertine known as Sir Richard Clavering is"—

"Dead!" exclaimed a voice behind them. And, looking up, both beheld a tall, cloaked figure in the doorway.

"That voice!" cried the woman. "That voice is—is"—

"Spring-heeled Jack's!" said our hero, advancing into the room.

The woman fell back, and, pointing to the box we have mentioned, gasped—

"There, in that box, are the proofs of my crime and your birth. Secure them. My boy dead, your claim cannot be disputed by him. When—how did he die? Where did he die?"

"In Newgate," said Jack.

"My sins have found me out," gasped the woman. "I am justly punished. Curse me, boy! Curse—cur"—

Her lips moved for an instant, and then were still—and Jack and Richard gazed upon a corpse.

CHAPTER LXXXV.

THE DRUNKEN WATCHMAN, AND HOW JACK SERVED HIM.

"PAST twelve o'clock, and a moonlight night!"

Such were the words which emanated from the mouth of a tall man, about fifty years of age, attired in a great coat, ornamented with large pearl buttons, and a short cape, knee-breeches, striped worsted hose, and shoes fastened by strap and buckle. A billy-cock hat graced his head, which was fast becoming bald on the top, and in his left hand he held a lantern, which he swung to and fro, as if to keep time with the words he uttered.

His gait was far from steady, and instead of walking in a straight line, he swerved from side to side of the pathway, and occasionally striking the toe of his shoe against a stone, uttered an exclamation, and ran on two or three steps in a stooping position.

"Past twelve o'clock, and a moonlight night!"

In this he was wrong, for the hour of three had struck, and a drizzling rain was falling—a rain which the sensible costume of the watchman could well bid defiance to, but which, falling upon the garments as worn in the present day, would have penetrated them in a very short space of time.

Not a star was visible—thick black clouds hung overhead; and, as for the moon, if it shone at all, it was only in the confused imagination of the guardian of the night.

The light of the lantern flashed its rays in his eyes as he staggered along, with his head bent low; and this circumstance might have led him to believe that it was the moon's beams which lit up his sleepy face.

"What's the time, watchman?" suddenly exclaimed a voice above him, as a night-capped head protruded from an open window of the second storey of the house he was passing. "What's the time?"

The watchman looked up, but in the opposite direction to that where his questioner awaited an answer, and replied—

"Past twelve o'clock, and a moonlight night!"

"Zounds! What are you talking about? It's pouring of rain, and black as pitch."

"Eh?—eh?—what!" cried the watchman, holding his head back, and, losing his balance, rolling against the wall of the house. "Rain! Black as pitch! Why, so it does rain, I declare; but the moon is shining as bright as day."

"I tell you what, old Kimber, you're drunk!" exclaimed the man, putting his night-capped head still further out of the window. "You're a pretty watchman, ain't you? My wife says it's past three, and she stuck a pin in the rushlight,[123] so she knows the time. You're drunk, I say, and ought to be ashamed of yourself."

Down went the window with a bang, as the white mystery disappeared; and Kimber staggered off the kerbstone, on which he had balanced himself a moment, into the roadway.

Having reached the centre of the road, the watchman steadied himself, and, looking up at the wrong window, exclaimed—

"Come down here, and I'll take you up. What do you mean by interfering with me in the execution of my duty? Call me a liar, will you? tell me I'm drunk! I'll lock you up, you scoundrel, for disturbing the peace of the neighbourhood. Hallo! Where the devil has he gone? Ain't that the window? Why, there's nobody there. Never mind, I'll be even with him, that's all. Burns a rushlight, does he? What right has anybody to have a light but me. Lights ought not to be allowed at night, for fear of setting the house on fire. No one ought to have a light but a watchman, who knows how to take care of it. Eh! why there's two lights burning in my lantern, by jingo! Who put t'other candle there? I'll swear I only lit one. Somebody's been playing a lark with me, while I took a nap in my box for five minutes. Yes, that's it, that's it! and I only wish I knew who it was."

Staggering out of the road on to the pathway again, he lifted the lantern up, and placed the right forefinger on the piece of curled tin to open it.

"Wilful waste makes woeful want," he muttered. "I don't want two lights to see to do my duty by, so I'll blow one out."

He opened the door of the lantern after two or three ineffectual attempts, and stood looking at the roll of tallow within it, in unfeigned surprise.

"Eh! what? Why, dang me if there ain't only one candle now! Where the devil's the other gone to?"

And he looked down at his feet, to see if it had fallen out on his opening the lantern door.

Of course, his search was unavailing, and he had to shut the lantern quickly to prevent

---

123 Cheap candle.

the light being extinguished by the wind, which was blowing pretty freely, and hurling the small drops of rain along before it, as it swept down the street.

But no sooner had Kimber closed the lantern than to his confused vision there again appeared two lights.

"Well! this beats all I ever did see, and I've lived fifty years in the world come next Michaelmas," said the man. "There's something wrong somewhere, to-night. The moon was shining splendid a minute ago, and putting the light of the lantern into the shade—now the lantern's put the moon out—and one minute I've got one candle, and the next, two. Yes, there's two lights there—nobody can say different. One—two—yes two, or else I am drunk."

He held the lantern up before his face, and gazed for some time upon the glass, a proceeding which eventually caused his eyes to fill with water.

Raising his hand to his right eye, which naturally closed as that member approached it, when lo! there appeared but one light again in the lantern.

The hand was dropped, the closed eye opened wide, and again two lights appeared, burning brilliantly.

Kimber became more and more confused, if not positively alarmed. Here was a phenomenon, for which he could not account.

Again he placed his hand to his eye—only one light—removed it, and two were visible.

He shifted his lantern into his right hand, and placed the left to his right eye, and the same effect as before was apparent.

He placed the lantern on the ground at his feet, and leaning his back against the front of one of the houses, dived his hands into the capacious pockets of his great coat, and shook his head ominously.

"I won't touch the darned thing agin, and yet it's the best lantern I ever had. There's something queer about it, or—No, no, I know what it is now—I'm drunk, to a certainty, and see double. Yes, that's it! and I suppose I may as well own to it. It was the hot rum-and-water at the Feathers as did it, and I had better go back and have a snooze in my box till morning. Past twelve—damn it! What is the time, I wonder? Oh, Kimber! Kimber! you are a pretty watchman."

"Hi! Watch! Watch! Thieves! thieves! Watch!" shouted a female voice in the distance.

"Hallo! what's up?" cried Kimber, making a sudden dart forward, and, losing his equilibrium, went sprawling along the pavement. "I'm down, blessed if I ain't," he added, as he tried to grasp his lantern and regain his feet. "Lord! how very slippery it is tonight. These paths are all on the slant, and a fellow can't keep his footing."

"Watch! Police!"

"There she goes again," muttered Kimber, as he rose, and again fell. "Curse the path! I can't stand on it. Hallo! What's the matter?"

"Who calls? Where are you!"

"Thieves! Watch! Police!" came again in a shrill female voice from the farther end of the street, and the noise of one or two windows hastily thrown up mingled with the sound.

Once more Kimber was on his feet, and drawing his rattle from his coat pocket, swung it round and round with all his force, each turn of his arm threatening to hurl him on to his back.

"What's the matter, watchman? Is the house a-fire?" asked an old lady, as she protruded a red face encircled with a monstrous frill, over the window-sill of the house opposite which he stood.

"Oh, dear!" cried another. "Who's murdered? Anybody killed?"

"Kimber's drunk," said the man who had before asked the time, and who now again appeared at his window. "There's nothing the matter, only the watchman ought to be lugged to prison. He's drunk, and don't know what he's doing."

"I'll take you up, you scamp, if you take my character away," cried the watchman, angered.

"You never had one—go home!"

"Thieves! Watch! Police!"

"Somebody's calling for you down the street, why don't you go, watchman?" cried an old man from a neighbouring window, "instead of annoying people with that row."

"Mind your own business," answered Kimber, "or I'll teach you."

"Teach me! you don't know your own," retorted the man, "and you shall be reported for this unseemly conduct."

"Go to the devil!" cried Kimber, giving another swing to his rattle, to drown the voices of his questioners.

"Watchman," said a tall man in a cloak, who had come along the street at a hurried pace, "you are wanted yonder. They have been calling for you some time."

"Mind your own business," said Kimber. "I know my duty."

"You are a saucy knave," said the man. "But, of course, if you do not choose to answer the call for you, it is no business of mine." And so saying, the man was about to turn away, when the old gentleman at one of the windows asked—

"What is the matter, sir? That was a woman's voice that called out for help, I think."

"Yes."

"Is it a robbery, sir? or is she being ill-used?"

"Neither, I believe. She has been alarmed by Spring-heeled Jack."

"Spring-heeled Jack!" echoed on all sides.

"Yes. Such I have learned to be the case," said the man in the cloak.

"Spring-heeled Jack!" said Kimber. "I should like to take him. I've been looking out for him for some time, and I'll have him yet."

"Then why don't you go?"

"What's that to you?"

"I see, you are afraid of him."

"Me afraid?"

"Yes, you."

"Don't say that again."

"Why not?"

"Because don't. I ain't afraid of nobody," growled Kimber. "But I'm not going to hurry myself for nothing. He'd be clean off before I got half way there. No, no, I ain't such a fool as that. But let me get within arm's reach of him, and I'll stop his springing and his liberty at the same time."

"You will, eh?"

"I will."

"You think so."

"I know so. I don't think anything about it. He ain't such a fool as to get too near Paul Kimber, I can tell you. He'll keep away from me, as far as he can."

"Humph!" said Jack—for he it was, "That's your opinion, is it?"

"To be sure it is."

"Well, keep it."

"I mean to, and keep him when I get hold of him," said Kimber.

"Perhaps you may find your mistake out before long."

"And perhaps I mayn't. Let him come within reach of that hand, and it's all up with him for some time—the vagabond!"

"Why don't you go and see if you can catch him now?" asked the old man.

"Because I don't choose."

"Then, perhaps, you'll choose to take yourself off, and let honest people get a little sleep."

"I shall do as I like about that," said Kimber, "and shan't ask you what I shall do."

"It will be a good job when you are all superseded by the new police, for you are a set of incompetent old fools, all of you," said the man at the window.

"I'll mark you for that, my boy," exclaimed Kimber, filled with rage at the laugh which rose on every side. "I'll catch you drunk one of these nights and then I'll"—

"Pick me up, eh?" interrupted the man.

"No. I'll knock you down first, and pick you up afterwards. I won't forget you, see if I do."

"Nor I either," muttered Jack, as he drew his cloak collar up over his face, and hurried away. "You wish to have me within arms length, and you shall be gratified; but I shall certainly be disappointed if your boasted courage is not all moonshine. I should have liked to have discovered myself to him, but it would not have been good policy to do so. However, he'll know who I am time enough, and if I don't prove a better antidote for drunkenness than all the seidlitz powders[124] in London, why Spring-heeled Jack is no reader of human nature.

After submitting to a good deal of chaff[125] from the persons assembled at the different windows, Paul Kimber staggered away from the spot, swinging his lantern in one hand and his rattle in the other, lounging occasionally against the fronts of the houses, and slipping off the kerb into the roadway.

Still, the watchman was fast recovering from the overpowering fumes of the liquor of which he had partaken a considerable quantity during the early portion of the night—the rain not a little tending to sober him.

But for all that, his gait was unsteady, and his brain confused, and the taunts he had met with had not a little soured his temper, which, by the way, was at all times anything but a very pleasant one.

So, as he strode along, he muttered maledictions and threats against those who had angered him, and vowed vengeance upon the heads of one and all who had so offended his dignity and jeered his courage.

"I wonder who he was that dared to say I was afraid of Spring-heeled Jack?" he muttered. "Me afraid?—me, Paul Kimber, who has had more charges in one month than any dozen watchmen in a year! I wish the fellow had given me a chance of locking him up. I wish he had. Me frightened? I'd show him, or a dozen like him."

---

[124] A laxative.

[125] Teasing.

And Paul swung his rattle over his head, and brought it down upon the top of a post, while the gleam in his eye bespoke how much he wished the post had been the head of Jack.

"Well, I'll go into my box and have a snooze," he muttered, after he had thus given vent to his passion, "and I shall be as fresh as a daisy in an hour. Hallo! what's that striking? One—two three—four. My eye! what a sleep I must have had! Well, I'm getting sober now. I suppose some of those meddling fools will try to make some harm out of my having a drop too much; but war-hawks to 'em, if they do. I'll be down on 'em like a hammer. I'll watch 'em like a cat does a mouse, and when I get a chance, grab and off with them to the station. Let 'em try it on— only let 'em, and Paul Kimber won't forget it."

He had readied his box, and pulling the upper half of the door open, he uttered a loud cry, and staggered back, exclaiming—

"Who the devil is here?"

"Hallo! old fellow," cried Jack, leaning over the lower part of the door. "So you have come, have you, at last? I've been waiting for you this half hour."

"Who are you?" cried Kimber, holding up his light, so that it came full on the mask of Jack, which it no sooner did than Kimber let fall his rattle in terror, and stood as if transfixed to the ground.

"I am the man you said you would take to gaol. I am Spring-heeled Jack!"

"The devil!" cried Kimber, completely sobered by his fright, and turning to flee as he spoke.

Jack flung open the lower part of the door, and, ere the watchman had taken two steps, was upon him, enfolding him in his arms, and lifting him from his feet, carried him, resistless, into his box. Seating Kimber on the seat, he slammed the door to upon him, and then, grasping the sides of the box, he exerted all his strength, and hurled it to the ground. The wooden edifice fell with its door next the ground, and completely prevented Kimber from getting out till assistance should arrive.

CHAPTER LXXXVI.

THE COUNTRY BOY AND THE LONDON MERCHANT—A FORTUNE MADE—IN SEARCH OF A WIFE.

MR. TOBIAS BACON was a little man in stature, but with a great mind—that is to say, he had large ideas—he made large ventures, and great successes invariably followed.

He began life as a farmer's boy; but ambition had crept early into his heart, and the belief that one day he would be a very great man induced him to pack up his wardrobe and tramp from Devonshire to London, in search of the fortune he was sure was there awaiting him.

It was a foggy November morning when he entered the metropolis, minus his wardrobe, which consisted of a striped shirt, a pair of knitted woollen hose, and a well-patched pair of leather breeches, which he had found it necessary to sell for money to obtain food.

Like many others before and since his time, he had miscalculated the distance and time it would take to reach the metropolis, but although when he did reach it, without a coin or article of apparel besides what he stood in, the boy did not become disheartened.

He saw the vast city stretching away before him, and though he was unacquainted with a single person within it, his heart was light and his spirits buoyant; for surely in such a place there was no lack of employment for those willing to toil.

Tobias had not started for London with the idea that gold was to be picked up in the streets, but that it must be earned by hard work—that he must toil, early and late, six days out of every seven.

If he built castles in the air, he at least built them with solid materials, and he felt certain in his own mind they would not crumble into dust.

Fatigued as he was, he at once set about seeking employment; and, ere he had been in London three hours, obtained a situation in the warehouse of a large cheesemonger's.

This was the first step towards the possession of that wealth he coveted. And honest, sober and industrious, he rose, not only in the estimation of his employer, but, in the course of ten years, to the highest position in the firm.

Few would have recognised in the gentlemanly manager of the extensive cheesemonger the rough country lad who had tramped from Devonshire, in search of work, ten years before; and few indeed whom fortune has favoured with smiles have so wisely appropriated her blessings.

Tobias longed to amass money. Not that he might live a life of idleness and gaiety—not that he might hoard and gloat over it, but that he might possess a whole farm in his native country.

This view he even had from the moment he started for London, and every penny he put by for this object caused him to rub his hands, and smilingly remark to himself, "Another foot of land."

But although his wages were good, and his expenses moderate, after ten years' service he had amassed but little towards the large amount he required for the fulfilment of his darling object. Three hundred pounds was the amount he had accumulated, and he wanted something like five thousand.

He. knew that it was a large sum—that his present salary, though liberal, would never allow him to amass it; but he knew also that money makes money, and that many had made colossal fortunes on less than that.

He did not, however, rush headstrong into speculations, but waited and watched for an opportunity to enable him to invest his savings to good advantage.

This opportunity came at last, and from a quarter where he least expected it—from his own employer.

Difficulties had arisen—creditors were pressing—the cheesemonger was in dread of a failure, unless he could weather the storm for another month, and Tobias saw a prospect of being out of employment.

The affairs of his employer were known pretty well to himself. He knew how he stood in a commercial point of view, and boldly made the offer of his savings to ward off the threatened blow.

The offer was accepted. Tobias's employer weathered the storm, and Tobias himself became a partner.

Shrewd, careful, and minutely just, every year the firm became larger and more prosperous, until Mr. Fisk, the former employer but now senior partner, died, and, for a time, plunged the affairs into difficulties; but Tobias was not long in settling all satisfactorily and making himself sole proprietor of the establishment where once he had been the lowest servant.

With the business qualities he possessed, the dream of his boyhood was soon realised; but he continued to toil on, till, at the age of fifty, he had amassed no less a sum than thirty thousand pounds, and finding the fatigue of the business too much for him, he sold the warehouse, and resolved to marry and purchase a farm.

"A cheesemonger can do without a wife," he said to himself; "but a farmer cannot. Besides, I can well afford to keep one now."

We have said Tobias was a shrewd, clever, man—in business, he certainly was—but in love he was completely out of his element.

He had made no acquaintances—had kept no company; consequently, he had no circle of friends among whom he could choose a partner. But believing that his usual good luck would attend him in his new pursuit, he resolved to visit a fashionable watering-place, and trust to chance for a presentation to some beauty who would not object to his advances.

What if he was fifty years of age? Did he not possess thirty thousand pounds? And where was the female heart could resist that, even though it had only beaten for twenty or five and twenty years?

So, his mind made up, he started for Brighton in the height of the season—resolved to find some fair creature who would love him for himself and his gold, ere he returned to Devonshire, and settled down as a gentleman farmer.

"A good wife is worth a thousand," he said to himself, as he picked up his things for the journey; "and that amount I will spend in the search for one, and no more."

Poor Tobias! He was doomed now to learn that all a man's shrewdness is no match for a woman's cunning. He could judge the quality of a cheese by a glance; but his perception was greatly at fault in judging of the female human race. At the first party he attended he was smitten by a lovely damsel with auburn hair, pale blue eyes, and rosy-tinted cheeks. Her soft tones thrilled his blood; her smile made his heart leap within his bosom; the touch of her hand— oh, ecstasy!—and she was not yet twenty.

No sleep for Tobias that night. Through the long hours the face of the auburn-haired damsel haunted him, and he turned upon his pillow, unable and unwilling to shut out the bright vision.

He had bribed a servant to obtain her address. And, when the morning was well advanced, with a beating heart, he made his way to the hotel, where she was staying with her brother, to inquire after her health.

She met him with a smile so winning, so charming, that he could have fallen at her feet, and poured out his whole soul, but that he was prevented by the entrance of her brother— a tall, gentlemanly-looking man, habited in the very height of fashion—who paused on the threshold to take a somewhat impertinent stare, through a gold-rimmed eye-glass, at the would-be suitor.

"My brother—Sir Timothy Tumberlain," said the young woman, in a bland tone, and with a bewitching smile. "Mr—Mr— I forget your name."

"Bacon," said the ex-cheesemonger, in a faltering voice.

"Ah! a very hoggish sort of name," said the fop, permitting the glass to drop from his eye. "Nothing very aristocratic in the sound; but there, we are not so proud as many in our high position, and, therefore, I am glad to see you, Mr. Hog—Bacon, I mean—excuse the mistake; and am much obliged for the consideration you entertain for Miss Florentine's health. A retired merchant, I'm informed. Pray be seated—no ceremony—we are not proud."

And Sir Timothy, as he called himself, motioned Tobias to a chair.

"I am sure, sir, I am very happy to make the acquaintance of yourself and charming sister," said Tobias, as he fell into a seat; "and should feel highly honoured by your accepting an invitation to a party I intend giving at the hotel where I am staying."

"Oh! I shall be delighted!" cried Florentine.

"Stay, Florentine," said Timothy. "We must first be assured that none but the *elite* will be present. There are so many snobs in Brighton at this season, who palm themselves off as members of the aristocracy, that we cannot be too careful. Does Lord Dunfred honour you with his company, or Lady Ticklem, or"——

"Neither, sir. In fact, my whole life has been passed in business, and my acquaintance is very small," interrupted Tobias, blushing. "But I hope to have the honour of knowing both the persons you mention. Perhaps you would be kind enough to bring them with you?"

"All! well. Lord Dunfred is a good fellow, and——eh, Florentine, what do you say?"

"Oh! I should be delighted to meet his lordship at our new acquaintance's," was the quick reply.

The eyes of Tobias fell, and his chest rose, while a change came over his features that were not lost on the two—a change which both instantly divined the cause of.

A quick glance passed between the pretended brother and sister.

"Ah! talking of his lordship, Florentine, have you heard of the alliance he has formed with Lady Ticklem? The wedding is to take place early in the winter."

A deep sigh of relief broke from Tobias Bacon, his little form was again erect, and his sad expression gave place to one of unbounded joy.

He became every moment more and more at ease, and in a few moments was conversing without the least restraint with Florentine and Timothy.

At length he rose to take his departure, when the young swell, placing his hand upon his arm, remarked—

"Mr. Bacon, you will not leave yet, I hope. You are such charming company, and as I have an engagement with Count Flaskiwaski at three, and shall be compelled to leave my sister, may I hope that you will remain till my return in the evening? She is a young lady of somewhat nervous temperament; and doubtless, being left alone, you will favour me, I am sure, by staying."

"I shall be delighted," cried Tobias. "My dear Sir Timothy, I shall be delighted, if—if the charming lady will not think me"——

"Bless your soul! it will be the greatest pleasure in the world to her," interrupted Timothy, with a quick glance at Florentine.

"You see, my dear sir, your presence here will keep her from the intrusion of a set of young nobodies, who are ever anxious to force themselves upon the notice of the aristocracy. There now, I shall be able to go without feeling any uneasiness on Florentine's account. Ta, ta, sir, I shall return early. Be gracious to our new friend. But there, I need not ask you, for you cannot be otherwise, yours is such a noble nature. Ta, ta! But, bless my soul! what a thoughtless fellow I am, to be sure."

"What's the matter, Sir Timothy?" asked Florentine, with apparent concern.

"Dear, dear! How very annoying, to be sure," said Timothy, pretending to be addressing himself rather than anyone else, and drawing a gold repeater from his pocket, and consulting its dial. "I am vexed beyond measure, and such a very pressing engagement, too, my dear Florentine. But doubtless, you can help me out of my dilemma."

"What dilemma, Sir Timothy?" asked Florentine. "If I can aid you in any way, you know you have but to ask me, and it is granted."

"I am well assured of that, Florentine. The fact is, though I ought not to tell you, I promised to lend the count five hundred pounds till his return to London."

"Well, Sir Timothy, you can easily do that, or five thousand either," said Florentine, with a sly wink, which was not intended for Bacon to see.

"Yes, certainly; or even double that amount would not put me to the least inconvenience. But the fact is, sir, my secretary obtained my permission to visit the metropolis this morning, and I omitted to tell him to fill up a cheque before he went. I am a stupid fellow, for the count needs the money today."

"Can't you fill it up for yourself, Sir Timothy?" asked Florentine.

"Yes, I could, of course. But to do so, I must have possession of my cheque-book, must I not? and that is in the keeping of my secretary."

"No matter. I daresay I have as much by me, Sir Timothy, and you are welcome to it."

"I only want it till tomorrow. He will be back then."

"I'll fetch it you."

"Thank you. Don't be long, for it is getting near the hour I promised to meet the count. Under ordinary circumstances, I should not hurry myself, but when we wish to assist a friend over a pecuniary difficulty, we cannot be too particular not to wound their sensitiveness by a show of delay. Are you not of my way of thinking, Mr.—Mr."——

"Bacon, Sir Timothy."

"Yes, Bacon—wise name—something relishing in bacon when a fellow's hungry. I'm very fond of bacon—very."

Tobias did not know whether to look pleased or angry.

"Oh, don't mind my rudeness," said Timothy. "You see I always think the best way to make a fellow feel at home is to be very free. Where there's restraint, of course there is an uncomfortable feeling. I have taken a fancy to you, and wish to make you stand on as little ceremony as possible with us. Oh, here she comes with the five hundred. Very awkward for a gentleman of my position not to have such a flea-bite of a sum by me at any moment—is it not? I must insist upon my secretary leaving my cheque-book where I can obtain access to it at any moment."

"But, sir, as you are doubtless well known at your banker's, a written cheque would serve your purpose," said Tobias.

"Well, no, it would not. I'll tell you why. A fellow in my service once had the audacity to write out a cheque for a thousand, present it, and obtained the money; and I gave my banker to understand that he was never to cash a written order for any amount purporting to come from me."

"Very wise."

"Yes, I think so. Oh, Florentine, I am so sorry to trouble you."

"And I am sorry, Sir Timothy, that I cannot oblige, you. I find I have only two hundred and thirty pounds by me, but you are welcome to that, my dear brother."

"Not quite half. Well, the count must wait till to-morrow, that's all, though I'm very sorry to disappoint him, for he's a very worthy fellow. Confound that sec. of mine; but there's no help for it, so he must wait."

"Hem! hem!" coughed Tobias, wriggling about on his seat in a very uneasy manner, appearing anxious to speak, yet fearing to do so.

"I beg your pardon, sir. What did you please to observe?" asked Florentine, suddenly turning to the ex-cheesemonger with an inquiring glance.

"I was about to say—that is—I hope I shall not offend"—

"Oh dear, no; we are such homely people. Do not for a moment think you will offend me," cried Florentine. "Anything you may desire to say will be listened to with pleasure."

"Then, my dear miss—madam, I should say"—

"Oh, don't stand upon ceremony, Mr. Bacon," said the girl. "Address me as you please."

"Then, if I may be pardoned for such a thing, I should be most happy to lend Sir Timothy the sum he requires for his friend, till he can give me a cheque for the amount."

"My dear sir," cried Sir Timothy, "I am extremely grateful for your kind offer, but really I could not take such a liberty."

"Oh, no liberty at all. I am sure I should be most happy—nay, feel highly honoured by your accepting the loan of the sum you require for the immediate use of your friend."

"Oh, Florentine! How could I accept his generous offer?" said Timothy, turning to his sister; "much as I should be delighted to oblige the count, and though only required for so short a time, yet I cannot be so familiar—so"—

"Sir Timothy, you begged I would stand on no ceremony with you, and I hope you will stand on none with me. You are unable to get at your cheque-book. I have mine in my pocket. I beg you will accept a cheque for five hundred, which sum you can pay into my bankers on the return of your secretary. Nay, do not refuse me. I shall feel honoured by your acceptance."

"You are so very pressing, my dear sir, that, much as I dislike to do so, I fear I must allow you to prevail upon me to accept your cheque, or I shall give offence. But really I am sorry I mentioned the subject in your presence—such a slight acquaintance, too."

"Tut, tut," cried Bacon, drawing his cheque-book from his pocket; and, taking a pen from an inkstand on the side table, commenced filling up a cheque for five hundred pounds.

CHAPTER LXXXVII.

TOBIAS BACON MAKES A FOOL OF HIMSELF IN MORE WAYS THAN ONE—THE CONFEDERATES.

OH Mr. Tobias Bacon! where was that shrewdness now which had changed the poor country lad into the wealthy London tradesman?

Had a woman's smile caused this change?

It must have been so, or with that perception of character so keenly acute hitherto you had not been so deceived.

The ex-tradesman had turned his back upon Timothy and Florentine while, with a shaking hand, he traced the words on the cheque, or he would, perhaps, have observed the glances which they cast upon each other and himself—glances which bespoke not only their pleasure but their contempt.

But so anxious was Tobias to engraft himself into the good opinions of the brother and sister that he forgot all his prudence, and was led to commit the first foolish action of his life.

"Fool!" whispered Florentine, pressing the arm of her companion.

"A chicken worth plucking," was the low-spoken rejoinder. "The old idiot is smitten with your charms. Play with him as a cat does a mouse."

"Never fear, Tim. I know how to manage him."

"And wheedle him, eh?"

"I'll wheedle all the money out of the old idiot's pocket." But here she held up her finger, and wreathed her lovely face in smiles, as Tobias laid down the pen and turned towards them.

"There, Sir Timothy," he said, "is the cheque for the five hundred pounds."

"I can hardly bring myself to accept it, my dear sir," said Timothy, as his fingers closed upon the paper.

"There—there, don't say any more about it. Why, if we can't oblige each other we are not fit to live."

"It shall be paid into your bankers the instant my secretary arrives," said Timothy; "and now you must excuse me or the count will believe I have no intention of keeping my appointment. I leave my sister in your charge, Mr. Bacon. She will be delighted with your company."

"And I with hers, Sir Timothy."

"Good morning, sir."

"Good morning, brother. Do not be late," said Florentine.

Tobias wished he might be very late, although he had taken a strong fancy to him.

The adieus uttered, Sir Timothy left the room, and Florentine sank, with graceful ease, on to a couch beside her visitor.

Bump—bump—bump, went Tobias's heart in his bosom, and he blushed like a school girl as the eyes of Florentine were fixed upon his own.

"Ah me!" sighed the young lady.

A responsive sigh burst from the lips of the old gentleman.

Then a silence reigned for several moments, while both looked at the gaudy patterns of the carpet on the floor.

Another sigh, and Tobias shifted his position nearer to that of Florentine.

The girl moved not, and Tobias moved again.

Then there was another awkward pause—awkward, at least, to Tobias.

He wished to break the silence; but, somehow or another, he could not tell what to say.

He felt nervous and bashful, and finally summoned up courage to cough.

"Are you asthmatical?" asked Florentine.

"Good heavens! No, my dear madam!" cried Tobias, quickly, anxious to dispel such an idea on the instant. "I am neither asthmatical, rheumatical, or any other atical. I enjoy the best of health, I am happy to say."

"What a pleasure!"

"Yes, it is, indeed," said Tobias, once more gaining courage. "But what is health, wealth— aye, even life itself, when—when"——

"When what, Mr. Bacon?"

"We are compelled to enjoy it alone," he gasped out, by a mighty effort, which caused the blood to suffuse his face, and his eyes again to fall before the glance of Florentine.

"It must be very dull to be alone," she said, in a soft, low tone.

"Very—very."

"Are you a widower, Mr. Bacon? as you speak of being alone."

"No. I am a bachelor."

"Oh, my! how nice!" said the lady. "And you have never been married?"

"Never!"

"And I suppose you never intend to be, now?" said Florentine, fixing a look upon him that caused his pulse to throb.

"Well—I—that is—I don't know," stammered Tobias, confusedly.

"Don't know?"

"You see, I've hitherto had little time to think of a wife, business having absorbed my whole attention," said Tobias. "But, now that I have retired, and have nothing to occupy my mind, I think I should like to—to"——

"Marry, sir?"

"Yes, marry!" said Bacon. "I am still a young man, or at least in the prime of life. I possess good health, a moderate fortune, and flatter myself that I could make happy the woman who would ally herself to me."

"Cannot you find such an one, Mr. Bacon?" asked Florentine.

Their eyes met.

Oh! that look! There was a fascination in it which even Tobias Bacon was powerless to resist.

The couch seemed to slide away from under him. He felt himself slipping down.

"Yes, my dear Florentine!" he cried, coming down with a bump on his knees on the floor, and catching frantically at the little jewelled hand which rested on the skirts of the pink silk dress. "Yes! I can! I have! You are that woman! I love you to distraction— to madness! Oh! turn not away those bewitching eyes! I must speak—must tell you what I feel—must lay bare this heart of mine to you. Say, Florentine! oh, do not be offended—do not—do not!"

With pretended surprise and alarm, Florentine tore her hand from his grasp, and rose to her feet.

"Mr. Bacon!" she exclaimed, "you—you alarm me! "

"Oh, say not so," he cried, making a snatch at her hand, and clutching it. "Oh, deign to look upon me with favour—deign to smile upon one whose only hope—only happiness—is the possession of your love. Oh, Miss Florentine, do not turn from me in anger—do not repulse me. See me at your feet, your devoted slave."

"Mr. Bacon, this declaration is so sudden, so unexpected, I—I"——

"Say that you return my love—reciprocate my affection. Oh, say that, and make me the most blessed of men! I am some years older than you, but what of that? Oh, look mercifully upon me. Say, say you love me."

After a little show of resistance, a faint attempt to turn herself from him, the artful woman sank back on the couch, with a deep sigh.

"Oh, say the word that is to make me the happiest of mortals!" cried Bacon. "I am wealthy. I will lay all that wealth at your feet. I will be a husband to you. Nay, more, I will be your slave. Oh, keep me not longer in suspense—lacerate no longer this beating heart— but make my soul bound heavenward with the sweet responds of love."

"How romantic!" muttered the lady to herself, as she turned aside her fair head to hide the look of contempt on her features, but which Tobias believed was done to conceal the blush his words had called forth.

"How can I prove my devotedness— how"——

She turned her gaze upon him, and, in a voice so low that he could scarce hear it, murmured—

"Dare I believe you love me with the passion you would have me think? Dare I imagine, after so short an acquaintance, that you"—

"You may—you may," interrupted Bacon. "I swear I love you to madness! and that if you spurn me from you, I—I shall die of a broken heart. You can save me—you alone. Be merciful, my own sweet Florentine."

"This is so sudden, I know not what to say— how to act," said the girl.

"Let me tell you—let me advise you," cried Bacon.

"In this case I must judge for myself. I—I"——

"Oh, say you love me!"

Florentine suffered her head to drop on his shoulder, as she sighed out—

"I do—I do!"

Bacon sprang to his feet as if shot. "You do?—you do?" he almost yelled with pleasurable excitement.

"Why should I deny it?" she replied. "Why should I seek to deceive my own heart? I know that maiden modesty should prompt me to be less frank, that I may lower myself in your estimation by the candid avowal I have made."

"Never! never!" said Bacon, enraptured. "Lower yourself in my estimation? 'Tis impossible. Then you do love me? Your heart does respond to mine? Oh, joy! joy! This is indeed the happiest moment of my life!"

He raised the hand he still held in his own to his lips, and covered it with kisses, while Florentine, unable to suppress her smiles, turned her face away.

Tobias was fairly beside himself with joy, and his little form trembled with emotion. He could hardly keep himself still, so inclined did he feel to give vent to his exuberant feelings by dancing about the room.

The staid, methodical man of business and the now happy Tobias Bacon were vastly different persons. His whole nature seemed to have become changed; and had any of his London acquaintances seen him then they must have thought him deranged.

And so he was. Love had turned his brain, as it has that of many a man beside himself. A woman had made a fool of him, and he was not the first.

He had been a clever man. But what availed his cleverness with such a bewitching creature as Florentine? He was but the mouse in the paws of the cat, and the wily woman knew well how best to treat him.

With apparent confusion, she implored him to suffer her to retire for a short time to compose herself. The affair had been so sudden, so unexpected—had taken her so by surprise. The confession had been wrung from her ere she could think how rash she had been to reveal the affection she bore him; she was ashamed of her boldness—nervous, trembling. She must retire for a short time to compose her feelings.

With a lingering pressure of the hand, he suffered her to depart, and, with a throbbing heart and heaving bosom, he watched her till she had disappeared from the apartment.

"Mine! mine!" he cried, as the door closed behind her stately form. "Oh! I am the happiest man in the world. Tol-de-rol-liddle- lol!"

And the little man capered about the room with a step as lively as a boy's of fourteen.

In the excitement he heard not the low, sarcastic chuckle outside the door—the suppressed titter that broke from the lips of the lovely woman as she was met on the landing by no less a personage than Sir Timothy Tumberlain.

"Well, Flor, what success?" he asked.

"The old fool came to the point at once," was the reply.

"You don't say so?"

"Yes. You had scarcely gone out of the room when he was down on his knees," said the girl, "pouring out such a rigmarole, that I had the hardest trouble in the world to prevent laughing in his face."

"Good!" said Timothy. "Keep him up to it, and we'll soon have all the yellow-boys[126] in his banker's hand. But I say, Flor, I must be off to town now."

"What for?"

"To get that cheque cashed the old stupid was so eager to draw," was the reply. "By jingo! but we'll cut a dash, I reckon, now. I was drained out completely, and was beating about for a chance of getting some ready.[127] That wasn't bad of you, Flor, to come down with two hundred and thirty!"

"He! he!" laughed the woman. "I thought he would take the bait. I wonder what he is worth?"

"He's precious warm, I expect; but we'll cool him before we've done with him, eh, Flor?"

"Rather!"

And the woman winked her eye mischievously.

"So, he's head over ears in love with you, is he, Flor?"

"Adores me."

"Then put the strain on his pocket at once, without seeming to do so. Jewellery, you know, Flor, is very handy to raise a few pounds on when hard up."

"But I don't intend to be hard up just yet," said Florentine. "Lor'! I wonder what sort of a look the old boy would give if he knew I was your wife?"

"Or if he knew that I was only Timothy Brown, blackleg and swindler, and you had been lagged for shoplifting—that our aristocratic acquaintances are kite-flyers,[128] mat-drawers,[129] parlour-jumpers,[130] mumpers'-stags,[131]" etc., etc. And, with a grin, Timothy stuck his tongue in his cheek, and turned away.

"Are you going to London, directly?" asked Florentine, following him down the stairs.

"Yes."

"When will you be back?"

"To-morrow."

"What excuse shall I make to the old boy for not seeing you again to-night?"

---

[126] Gold coins.

[127] Ready Money, cash.

[128] Card cheat.

[129] Counterfeiters.

[130] Housebreaker.

[131] Beggars.

"Any you like."

"Very well. Good bye!"

"Ta—ta, old girl. Don't fail to hang on to him like a leech. Now's your time to tog up swellish.[132] Mind he don't slip away. Keep him in tow; and when you have got all you can out of him, me and Jemmy—the count, I mean— will have the rest."

"Let you alone for that, Tim. What a pity you weren't born a gentleman," said Florentine, looking admiringly upon Timothy as he stuck his gold-rimmed eye-glass in his eye, and laid back his shirt-frill.

"A gentleman! Humph! I am one as the world goes. If I had been born a gentleman, it ain't likely I should have picked up with you. It's quite enough that fools take me for one— that is, those who look upon the coat as the badge of gentility. The snob is the man who is flattered, and favoured, too. A gentleman! Why, what an unpretending, unostentatious being I should be. True gentility would not agree with my disposition."

"Well, never mind, Tim. You are not the only humbug who apes[133] the gentleman."

"Not by a few thousands," said Tim, with a laugh. "Only to those who know me, Flora! I am willing to admit what I am. It does amuse me sometimes to see the jumped-up jackasses try to make those who know better believe they are what they so ridiculously caricature. Anyone with a grain of sense can see through the flimsy covering of the snob, if he'll only take the trouble to look. But one half of the world is blind, and, for my sake, I hope it will keep so—at least, till I have made enough to live on out of the idiots who cannot tell the difference between black and white. Goodbye, old girl. Play your cards well, and our fortune is made."

And with his eye-glass in his eye, and his forefinger hooked in the large gold watch-chain, Timothy Brown strode gracefully from the hotel, while Flora, alias Florentine, went back to the room where she had left her admirer so anxiously awaiting her return.

Timothy walked slowly along, his left hand toying with his watch-guard, and his right holding his white kid gloves, peering through his eye-glass at the people who thronged the way, when suddenly his glance rested on a young man just ahead of him, who appeared to be lost in deep thought, so intently did his eyes seem fixed on the ground.

Timothy quickened his pace, and in a few moments was by his side.

The young man did not raise his eyes, nor did Timothy lower his; but they continued to walk on side by side for some distance, as if each was unconscious of the other's presence.

Having reached a spot more deserted than any over which they had travelled, Timothy, without moving his head or eyes, exclaimed—

"Well, Jemmy, what luck this morning, old boy?"

"One ticker,[134] one locket, two wipes,[135] one scent-bottle, and all told," was the reply, with eyes still fixed on the earth.

"Jemmy!"

"Hallo! Tim!"

"That game don't pay. I've got something on hand as will turn in the money quicker,"

---

132 Dress up smartly.
133 Imitates.
134 Pocket watch.
135 Handkerchief.

said Timothy. "I got a first-rate haul this morning."

"What is it?"

"A cheque for five hundred."

"Strike me lucky! you don't say so. Who from?" exclaimed Jemmy, raising his eyes, but dropping them again on the instant.

"An old bloke who has fallen in love with my Flor. He's got plenty of the ready, and can be had to rights.[136] I'm off to London now, but will be back to-morrow. Give a call about six, and I'll leave word I expect Lord Dunfred. You tumble,[137] don't you?"

"To rights!"

"There's money to be made in Brighton this season, old boy. But don't let's be seen together now. Tog up when you come, and bring Emma with you—Lady Ticklem, whom you are about to marry early in the winter. Large names make people look large, you know. Fly your kite, and don't forget to-morrow evening."

As he spoke, Timothy slackened his pace, while Jemmy redoubled his, and they parted company, without causing anyone who might have observed them the least suspicion that they had been in conversation together.

CHAPTER LXXXVIII.

AT THE FARM—THE CONFEDERATES AT WORK— THE DICE—JUST IN TIME.

NOT far from Barnstable, in Devonshire, was situated an extensive farm, known as The Hollies.

It had once been owned by one of the most thriving men in Devon, who had laid out upon it a considerable amount of money, and for miles around it was looked upon as the best farm in the county.

But, unfortunately, no sooner had the proprietor effected every improvement he could upon the place than he was seized with a severe illness and died, and his widow advertised the estate for sale.

Tobias became its possessor for a sum considerably below its value, and now the dream of his boyhood was fulfilled.

But he did not enter upon it at once. A matrimonial arrangement being in course of formation with Florentine Tumberlain, a wealthy London lady, was stated by the gossips to be the cause. But the servants were kept, and the work of the farm went on under the superintendence of a bailiff whom Bacon had sent to superintend it.

Entranced, enraptured with Florentine, whose beauty had so won his heart—fearful of losing her, yet anxious to get settled and retire to his farm—Tobias urged her to name an early day for their nuptials, and at length got from her a promise to become his wife in a month.

The month flew by, and Florentine was taken suddenly ill, so the wedding had to be postponed for still another month.

Bitter was the disappointment of Tobias. But there was no help for it, and he was

---

[136] Makes a good target.
[137] Understand what to do.

forced to submit to the delay.

Meantime, Sir Timothy commenced to play the game he had intended from the first—namely, to seek to obtain the hard-earned wealth of Tobias for himself and companions, and soon Bacon was well in the toils of the pseudo lord and count.

Pretending to feel for him the greatest commiseration, sympathising with him in his disappointment, and appearing to be anxious to make his unwilling stay in Brighton as pleasant as possible, they prevailed upon him to join them at the theatre, the parties, conversaziones,[138] lectures, and every amusement of the fashionable watering-place.

So Timothy invited him, night after night, to join himself and friends at a game of cards or billiards, and appeared, in every way, to seek to make his stay as happy as possible.

So much consideration caused the heart of Tobias Bacon to warm towards them, and, ever anxious to be near his beloved Florentine, he soon fell a victim into their hands.

Small sums were played for, only to make the game interesting, and the usual luck of Tobias followed him in play as well as in work, and he never left their hotel to return to his own without finding himself a winner of several pounds.

Little did he imagine that, to obtain the money he had won, Sir Timothy had pawned the trinkets which he himself had presented to Florentine at different times.

With success, Tobias began to cherish a love of play.

The others noted this, and exchanged significant glances.

As time wore on, higher sums were played for, and Sir Timothy and his companions found it necessary to put their wits to work to obtain money to pay their losses, for they had no desire to win yet awhile.

The second month wore away, and still Florentine's health was so bad that her medical adviser insisted some weeks must elapse ere she could enter a church and undergo the ceremony.

Tobias was in despair.

In vain he pleaded. The brother would not hear of his sister contracting a marriage in the state of health in which she was. He had too much consideration for her. These delays pained her as much as Tobias. She longed to consummate his happiness, but must abide the orders of her medical adviser.

What could he do but again submit.

A happy thought struck him.

A change of air would be beneficial to the lovely invalid.

He proposed she should be removed to his farm at Barnstable.

Sir Timothy's eyes gleamed fiercely at this suggestion, the count looked black, and Lord Dunfred sneered.

What would the world—the aristocratic portion of it—think of such a thing? Florentine become an inmate of the farm before marriage—reside under the same roof as Tobias? Look at the slander! It could not be. Her character would be irretrievably lost.

"Not so," pleaded Tobias, "if you go with her as her guardian. Whilst under the protection of her brother, who would dare defame her character?"

That was quite another thing, but unfortunately Sir Timothy had arranged that his

---

138 Literary or artistic gatherings.

two friends were to remain with him till the wedding of Lord Dunfred and Lady Ticklem, a period of some two months.

Here was another difficulty, but Tobias resolved to surmount it.

Would they all take up their abode at the farm, till such time as Florentine's health would allow her to enter the marriage state?

Many objections were raised to this, but eventually Tobias succeeded in his object, and it was decided that all should take up their abode at The Hollies.

Tobias was to precede them by one day, so that everything might be in readiness for their reception; and, in good spirits, Mr. Bacon started on his journey, after an affectionate interview with his beloved.

True to their promise, the others followed; but their real desire was not that Tobias should precede them by a day, so that all might be in readiness for their reception, but from a fear that he might become acquainted with the fact that they left their hotel without paying their bill.

However, they were clear off ere any suspicion was excited, and not one of the party was more gay on the route than the pretended invalid, who laughed and jested on the plots and plans laid by her companions to possess Bacon's wealth.

But on arriving at The Hollies her spirits immediately became dull. The smile vanished from her face, and the journey had so prostrated her, that she had to be carried to her chamber, which was to be shared by Lady Ticklem.

Tobias's face wore a proud look as he showed his friends about the farm, but when evening came, the whole party seemed to grow weary.

"You are dull, Sir Timothy," said Tobias.

"Oh, yes, rather. This is a very dull place— no life, no amusements, nothing to kill the *ennui*[139] to which we aristocratic members of society are so addicted. Suppose we have a rubber at whist, to break the dullness?"

"With all my heart, Sir Timothy. But what are we to do for cards?"

"Have you no cards?"

"No."

"Lor'! Whoever saw a house without cards? My dear count, did you?"

"Never, Sir Timothy."

"No cards?" chimed in Lord Dunfred. "What a strange thing!"

"No billiards, neither?" said Timothy.

"No."

"However do you intend to pass your time when we are gone?"

"In domestic pursuits."

"Domestic devils! But really we must find something to amuse us, Mr. Bacon."

"I should be most happy."

"What can we think of, count?"

"I'm at a loss to suggest anything, Sir Timothy, unless"—

"Unless what?"

"We have a throw or two at the dice."

"Dice! oh, well, yes."

"Dice!" said Bacon. "I never play with dice."

---

[139] Boredom.

"Don't you?"

"No."

"Well, that is strange. Capital things! There's so much excitement."

"Oh, I've often thrown for a thousand pounds at a throw," said Lord Dunfred.

"Have you, indeed?" said Bacon.

"Bless you! yes."

"Are you fortunate with dice?" asked Bacon.

"Bless you! no—quite the reverse. I generally lose, or at least I lose two out of three throws. I'm a confounded unlucky fellow."

"Just like me," said Timothy; "and if I didn't possess a very large fortune, I should have been ruined over and over again."

"And yet you are willing to play," said Bacon.

"Bless your soul! what does it matter how a man sets his money afloat? If I didn't lose it that way I should spend it some other. Besides, what's a few thousands to me—a mere flea-bite."

Bacon felt his fingers itch. He had imbibed a love of play as we have before observed. He had been lucky hitherto, might he not still be fortunate; and these men did not mind losing a few thousands.

"Suppose we have a few throws, then, for small amounts?" said the count, after a pause, during which, unobserved, he had passed his full glass towards Bacon, and withdrawn his empty one.

"With all my heart," said Bacon.

"But first let us drink the health of our worthy host," said the count, filling the empty glass.

The three adventurers rose and drained their glasses.

When they had sat down, Bacon rose, glass in hand, to thank them for the compliment, and drank theirs in return.

The moment the glass touched his lips, strange glances passed between the others. Then, every eye turned towards the glass which Bacon had placed empty upon the table.

The old gentleman had no suspicion of anything wrong, and the smile still wreathed his face.

"Now then, Dunfred, you have a set of dice, have you not?" asked Timothy.

"Yes, in my travelling trunk. Shall I fetch them?"

"Do so," said Bacon, "and let us see if they will help us to kill time."

"They will at least give us a little amusement," said Timothy.

"I hope so."

"So do I," drawled the count; "sincerely do I hope so."

In a few minutes Dunfred returned to the room, and, placing the dice upon the table, walked towards the window.

Timothy was by his side in an instant.

"Well" he said, in a whisper.

"Capital," was the reply. "Flor and Em have found out where the old man keeps his ready cash, and I have a pretty weighty bag of gold in my pocket now. We must fleece him all we can to-night, and be off before morning."

"Yes. You see the count put the drug in his glass?"

"I did."

"He will be a child in our hands in another hour. We must lead him on, then clean him out. Take cheques, notes—anything, for we can cash them ere he can prevent us. Did you tell Flor to keep her eyes open?"

"All right. She has taken stock of everything before this."

"Be careful. The old fool must not only lose his wife but his money. Flor's beauty has turned his head quite, I do believe. I did not think the man who could make a fortune by work could be so easily gulled[140] to lose it. Pass me some of the old boy's tin[141] to make a show with."

"Hem! hem!" coughed Dunfred, as he observed Bacon approaching them. "Change for a fifty? oh yes. How will you have it—all in gold?"

"It will be more handy as we are going to play for small amounts," said Timothy.

"Oh, do you stake the money?" said Bacon. "I will get some gold. I have nothing but notes about me."

And he moved away as he spoke.

"No, no; don't trouble—don't trouble," cried Dunfred, quickly catching his arm.

"But I have plenty upstairs," said Bacon, "and will get it in a minute."

"There's no necessity, my dear sir," said Timothy.

"But I would rather."

"I beg you will not trouble yourself. You are so lucky, that you will not require it. Besides, if you lose you can pay your losses when we are done."

"Very well," said Bacon. "I will keep fair account."

"We are sure of that."

"Are you ready?"

"Yes."

"And your friends?"

"Quite."

"What shall be the first stake?" said Bacon.

"Oh, something small, as we play more for amusement than anything else. Say ten guineas—will that do?"

"Yes."

"Then the highest number clears the table of thirty pounds."

"Forty, you mean."

"Ah! wins thirty, certainly. There's my ten."

"And mine," said the count, who had received it of Dunfred.

"And mine," cried Dunfred.

"I must take up ten," said Bacon, "and place this note of twenty down as my stake. Now, I have gold for the next ten."

"Just so," said the count, shaking the dice. "Eleven! Now, Dunfred."

"Eight!" cried Dunfred. "Go on, Sir Timothy."

"After our worthy host. Then I shall know my fate. He is so lucky."

"Twelve!" cried Bacon, gleefully.

"Just as I said," remarked Timothy. "Six! It's Bacon's. He has the devil's luck and his own too. Shall we double this time?"

---

[140] Cheated or fooled.
[141] Money.

This was agreed to. The dice were again thrown, and Timothy won.

The next time the stakes went down to ten, and Bacon won. Another ten, and still he won.

The old gentleman was getting excited, his face was flushed, and his eyes rolled over the table and from face to face of his guests.

He laughed uproariously ever and anon, as he won, and at length suggested that the stakes should be a hundred pounds.

The others consented.

Bacon cleared the table, and offered to double the stakes.

This was agreed to, and he lost.

Still his excitement increased, and the stakes were proposed at a thousand.

Again he lost.

"I will keep account," he said. "I am unlucky now, but my luck will soon turn."

"To be sure it will. It's time it did," said Sir Timothy; "quite time."

And he looked round upon his companions.

Bacon's manner became more and more excited every moment, and a thin white foam gathered round his lips.

The narcotic was working, and his blood was on fire.

"I will make a fortune to-night," he cried, at last, "or I will lose one. Ten thousand pounds. Have you the courage to venture such a sum on one throw of the dice?"

"Oh, that's a mere nothing," said the count. "I'll make it twenty, if you like."

"No. Ten—ten is all the available money I have, the rest is invested in the farm."

"Well, ten be it," said Timothy. "Ten thousand each, and he who wins has got forty; a pretty little sum for some people, but nothing to me. Well, let it be ten, then. Of course, we can't stake so heavy a sum, but the acknowledgment is sufficient among gentlemen. Who'll throw first?"

"I," said the count. "Six! That's lost."

Dunfred threw next—eight. He shrugged his shoulders, and turned away.

Bacon grasped the box, and shook the dice furiously ere he flung them out upon the table.

"Eleven!" he shrieked. "Eleven!"

"Capital throw! No beating that," said Sir Timothy. "It's hardly worth while my attempting it. But I'll take my chance, of course."

He stuck his glass in his eye, and coolly shook the dice. Then, flinging them out upon the table, he cried—

"Seventeen! How strange! I never thought it; but positively I've won—yes, won!"

"No, rascal, you have lost!" cried a voice.

And the next moment the hand which held the dice-box was grasped tightly, while another hand rested on his shoulder, and he turned to confront a man whose features were hidden beneath a hideous mask.

The others started back in surprise and alarm, while Timothy, with one hand resting upon the table, stood as if paralyzed.

"Who are you?" he gasped, at length.

"Your servant, Spring-heeled Jack; and in the next room are the officers who have come to bear you and your companions to jail. Old gentlemen, it is fortunate for you we arrived so soon, or these cheats and robbers had wrested from you the wealth you have toiled so hard to amass. What ho! there. Officers, do your duty."

CHAPTER LXXXIX.
THE ROOM OF DEATH—THE PROFFERED ASSISTANCE AND THE GRATEFUL HEART.

SLOWLY the sunbeam which penetrated the dirty panes of glass glided up the wall against which the wretched bed of the guilty woman was placed, and played upon the white, rigid face and skeleton arm, which was all that remained uncovered by the patchwork quilt, while a silence, broken only by the breathing of Jack and the consumptive-looking youth, as they gazed down upon the inanimate mass of clay, alone broke the silence of the room.

For some moments both continued to gaze upon the form which lay so still and motionless—a form that never more would feel the pleasures or woes of this world— a form which, now the spirit had fled its earthly casket, would fast return to that dust from which it had sprung.

"Dead—dead!" sobbed Richard, at length, falling on his knees beside the mean and wretched couch, and slowly drawing the quilt over the pale features.

"Ay, dead!" said Jack, in a solemn tone. "She has gone where her sins will meet their just reward—gone before that Judge whom eloquence cannot turn, gold cannot corrupt—gone to that judgment-seat where justice is administered to all alike, and meted out to the prince as to the peasant—the worldly rich as to the poor. May she find mercy there, and the repentant's sins be forgiven."

"Amen!" exclaimed the young man. "For she was good to me—oh, so kind. No mother could be kinder."

The young man rose to his feet, and, dashing away the tear which shamed not his eye nor degraded his manhood, said—

"But how, sir, came you here? Did you know her?"

And he pointed to the bed. "No. At least, I have met her once, and interposed between her and a ruffian who had her turned from his house."

"Sir Richard Clavering?"

"No; but he who assumed that title. I knew him well, and once esteemed him as a friend. But no matter now. He has gone; and be it not my tongue to utter bitter words against the dead. Still, I will explain my strange appearance here at such a moment. Resolved to compel the waggoner to carry you to the metropolis, I kept close to the vehicle without being seen, and when you vacated it in the broad daylight, I was so struck with the resemblance you bore to one for whom I entertain the greatest respect, that I resolved to follow and learn more respecting you. Not wishing to appear dogging your footsteps, I followed at some little distance, but suddenly lost sight of you as you entered this house. On passing the open door below, I thought I caught sight of you on the stairs. But ere I could reach your side you had entered this wretched apartment. I was about to make my presence known by a tap on the door, when her voice met my ears. And I know not what could have induced me to pause and listen, unless it be that strange feeling which sometimes comes over us and prompts us to do that for which we can find no possible reason. Well, I stood outside on the landing and listened, and when I heard the name of the libertine, Richard Clavering, I entered, unannounced—and you know the rest."

"And he is dead?"

"Yes. His evil passions goaded him on from crime to crime, till murder stained his soul, and he died in Newgate."

"And till now I had no knowledge that his wealth and title were mine," said the youth, musingly. "Fain would I not know it now. Better had she died with the secret unrevealed."

"Wherefore?"

"Because what hope can I have of ever making good my claim—of ever being acknowledged as the legitimate son of Sir Giles?"

"You forget the proofs."

"Oh, in the box?"

"So she said."

The youth stooped, and placed his hand on the lid to raise it, but paused suddenly and looked hard at Jack.

"Sir," he said, "last night on the dirty road, footsore and weary, sad and almost heartbroken, and feeling that I had no friend in the wide world, a strange figure stood before me. Kind tones cheered my drooping spirits, and generous hands aided me. As I lay in the waggon I wondered whether I should ever again meet you, and certainly never expected to see you here, for of course I recognise you without the mask you then wore. I have heard strange stories respecting you, but still I felt my heart warm towards you. It does so now. I need a friend more at this moment than ever I did when, faint and smarting, I lay in the roadway. Nay, I look upon you as a friend. Dare I"—

Jack stretched forth his hand, and placed it on the other's shoulder, and, looking kindly into his face, said, in a soft tone of voice—

"Sir Richard Clavering, could you trust the man whom the world speaks so ill of?"

"I could. For can I not give the world the lie? Have I not found you a kind and feeling man?" exclaimed the other.

"The greatest villain hides his rascalities under the cloak of religion, sometimes," said Jack.

"True. But you are not one of those who would cover their sins with the cloak of kindness."

"You think not?"

"I am sure."

"And you feel you could trust me?" said Jack, with a smile.

"Implicitly."

"Then fail not to see whatever you may require at my hands, for it shall be ungrudgingly bestowed," said Jack. "If you wish for gold, it is yours."

"'Tis not that I would crave of you," answered the young man, quickly.

"What then?"

"Your friendship."

Jack grasped his hand. "It is yours."

"Your advice."

"As far as I can give it."

"Thanks!—a thousand thanks!" said the young man, joyously, grasping fervently at Jack's hand. "Now for these papers."

He flung back the lid of the box, and looked in.

A small roll of papers was all it contained, and those he seized eagerly.

He was about to untie the cord which bound them, when, casting his eyes upon the bed, he hesitated, and said—

"Not now—not now. When she is buried, not till then. But oh! how—how can I obtain for her a decent funeral?"

"Let not that grieve you."

"But it does, sir."

"Why should it?"

"I have no money."

"I have."

"But"—

"Tut! tut!" said Jack; "seek out some respectable undertaker. I will settle his bill."

"And if ever I get my rights I will repay you," said Richard.

"I know that, and if you do not, I will freely bear the expense myself."

"How can I thank you?"

"By saying no more upon the subject," said our hero.

The young man fixed a look of gratitude upon his face, then turned his gaze upon the packet he held in his hand.

"What shall I do with these, sir?" he said. "I do not wish to leave them in that box, and fear that if I carry them about with me I may lose them."

"As you ask my advice, and are willing to take it," said Jack, "I would place the packet as it is, unopened, in the hands of some respectable solicitor."

"A solicitor?"

"Yes. And he will act upon it as he may think best."

The young man looked down thoughtfully, and a low sigh escaped his bosom.

Jack was not slow to divine his thoughts, and a smile played upon his lips, as he remarked—

"I know a very worthy member of the law who would undertake to guide and advise you in the business, and one who would not put you to an enormous expense to seek to obtain that which you may, perhaps, have no claim to after all. Or I will place the papers in his hands myself, if you will trust them with me."

The young man held the packet towards him, saying—

"Willingly."

But Jack did not take it.

"Your confidence is great, young man," he said, "very great. You forget that I am a stranger to you."

"Still I cannot doubt your honesty and candour," was the remark

"You should doubt all men till you have proved them."

"Not you."

"And why not me?"

"You ask me a question I cannot answer. But something tells me I may place implicit trust in you, sir."

"You may," said Jack, taking the papers and placing them in his bosom. "Spring-heeled Jack will not play you false."

"Pardon me, but that is not your only name," said the young man.

"Certainly not," said Jack; "but it is the only one I care to be known by to the world."

The young man bowed his head.

He felt that even to him Jack cared not to reveal it, and though he felt he would have been glad to know the real name of his new-found friend, he forbore to ask it.

"If I refuse to tell you who I really am, I fear your confidence in me will undergo a change," he said, after a pause.

"Believe me, no."

"Then, for the present, I prefer withholding from you who I am."

"I shall esteem you none the less for that," said the other.

"I am glad to hear you say so."

There was another pause, during which the young man continued to gaze upon the heap of rags in the corner which covered the remains of her who had died that morning.

"You have a sister," said Jack, suddenly.

"Yes. Oh yes; but I do not know whether she is living or dead, or where to seek her," said the young man. "I wish I did—I wish I did."

"Her name?"

"Ellen."

"Yes; but her surname, or rather the name she has been known by," said Jack. "But I need not ask—Folder, is it not?"

The young man started.

"Do you know her?" he cried, eagerly.

"I think I do."

"Oh, sir"—

"Be calm, my friend. After all, the Ellen Folder, to whom you bear so striking a resemblance, may not be your sister."

"She must—it must be her. We are so much alike."

"The likeness is indeed great."

"Tell me where I can find her—where I can seek her, to make her acquainted with her mother's end—at least, with the death of her who, notwithstanding her great sin, has ever been, all in her power, a mother to us."

"You shall go with me to where she is to be found," said Jack.

"Oh, thank you—thank you!" cried the young man, snatching up his hat, and placing it upon his head with trembling hands.

"But not now."

"Not now?"

"No."

The young man looked disappointed and grieved.

"Be advised," said Jack, "by me. You are weak and tired, and need rest. Besides, there is much to be done here, and I myself have need of rest, and am ill-fitted for the journey. Seek out a respectable undertaker, and have that poor woman's remains placed in a coffin. Then obtain a lodging, and go to bed; and at this hour to-morrow morning I will meet you here and accompany you to where the Ellen Folder of my acquaintance is to be found. If you exert yourself too much now, you will be laid up."

"Sir, my anxiety must be my excuse for appearing so eager. But I will take your advice, and trust implicitly to you."

"Believe me, you may, for I seek only your happiness," said Jack. "Now, refuse not, from any false pride, this purse. It contains sufficient for your present necessities, and to secure the services of those who do the best offices for the dead."

The young man took the purse with a look full of gratitude.

"Sir," he said, in a choking tone, "I cannot find words to thank you."

"I do not ask thanks. You will do as I suggest; and in this room, at this hour to-morrow, meet me here."

"I will, sir."

"Very good. And I shall then doubtless inform you that the papers you have entrusted to me are in the hands of one who will be better able to judge of their merits than myself, and who, I am sure, for my sake, will do all he can to obtain for you your just inheritance."

"God bless you, sir! My heart is too full to say more."

"It is not often that blessings are asked on my head."

"People do not know you, sir," said the young man, looking through the tear that glistened in his eye upon our hero's face.

"Nor do you, my friend."

"I feel I do—yes, I feel I do," said Richard, placing his hand on his heart. "This tells me that I do know you."

"Well, well," said Jack, "we will not converse more now, for you have much to do, and need rest and refreshment. So I will take my leave of you, and return hither in the morning, when I hope to see that form in its coffin."

He looked down at the bed, and then, taking the hand of Richard in his own, and holding it there for some moments, he said—

"It is always the darkest the hour before day —the sun breaks through the darkest cloud. If I may judge from your words and appearance, yours has been a hard struggle of late. But I sincerely hope brighter days are dawning."

"God knows it has!"

"Hope, then, that your sorrows are over. Hope for the best."

"I do."

"Farewell, then, till to-morrow."

"God bless you, sir!"

They shook hands, and Jack turned with a sort of melancholy pleasure from the room of death, and slowly took his way down the narrow staircase out of the house into the fresh morning air.

As the door of the room closed behind him, Richard sank down upon his knees beside the wretched bed, and, covering his face with his hands, wept aloud.

Now that he was alone he felt he could weep—that he could relieve the heart so bowed down with suffering and want.

For some time his sobs echoed through that chamber of death, and when relieved and comforted, he rose to his feet. The sunbeam had crept up the wall, and marked that the hour of eleven had arrived.

"Not my mother!" he said; "not my mother! But I loved her as if she were, and will respect her memory as deeply as though she had died with that secret unrevealed. And she called on me to curse her with her last breath! She asked me to curse her. Me! me! Oh, God! would she had lived but another moment that she might have heard my blessings on her head! But they shall rise to heaven after her soul, and, mingling with her prayers at His footstool, ask His mercy and forgiveness for her one great sin!"

Then seizing his hat again, which he had removed from his head, he went out to find an undertaker, and commission him to provide a coffin for the woman's remains, and, in a few minutes, had discovered the object of his search.

Arrangements were soon made. A deposit paid to ensure the coffin being supplied immediately, and leaving the whole arrangement of the funeral in the man's hands, he retired and looked about for a place where he could obtain a bed, and seek strength, rest, and refreshment.

Of course, he need not look far for what he desired, and entering a quiet-looking public-house made his wants known; and ere twelve o'clock had struck, he had partaken of a hearty meal—a luxury he had not known for some days—and retired to a neat and clean little chamber which had been provided for him while enjoying his repast.

He laid his head upon the pillow, and sleep, the soft healer of all human ills, stole over him; and for a time he forgot, in sweet, refreshing slumber, the joys he fondly hoped were in store for him, and the anxieties and miseries he had so lately passed through.

CHAPTER XC.
THE WIFE AND WIFE-BEATER—GRASPER PLANS AGAIN.

BILL JACKSON no sooner saw Grasper and the neighbours whom he had aroused in full pursuit of Jack than that worthy turned back, and reached the door with the greasy cord in the centre.

On the threshold he encountered his trembling wife, who was inwardly muttering a prayer that Ellen and her preserver might escape.

"Nammus, [142] Poll," said the burly ruffian, giving her a push, which drove her back into the passage, and against the wall, with such force as to bring down several pieces of the broken mortar, "Let me get in."

"Have they caught him?—oh! have they caught him, Bill?" cried the woman.

"Don't expect they ever will, do you?" growled Bill. "'Tain't natural to think as how anybody could take him, if he warn't a mind to be took. He's summut more nor a man, or he couldn't have took all the pluck out of this hinfant twice, I can tell you."

"But Grasper, where's he?"

"Gone off arter him, cuss him! I hope as he'll get a topper as'll put him out of the way."

"Oh, Bill!"

"Now, what are you arter? When it comes to 'Oh, Bill!' there's sure to be some of the penny-gaff[143] sentimentality behind. What's your game, now?" said the fellow, as he followed his wife into the back room.

"I wish he'd never come here."

"Who?"

"Who?"

"Yes. Who?"

"Why, that hoary-headed old villain of a Grasper, to be sure," said his wife.

"Do you, now?"

"I do, indeed."

"Well, so do I," said Bill, "for one thing, and not for the other. You see, Poll, if he

---

[142] Run away.
[143] Cheap.

hadn't a been, I shouldn't have got the five couter.[144]"

"It will never do you any good, Bill, never," said his wife.

"Won't it? You'll see. I'll have a stunning good lush on to-morrow at The Flyers."

The woman heaved a deep sigh.

"What are you groaning at?" cried Bill, furiously. "Curse you! you never did care to see a fellow enjoy hisself."

"Enjoy yourself, Bill. Oh, what enjoyment? what enjoyment?" cried the woman, sorrowfully.

"Now, look'ye here, Poll. Don't you come for to try on any of the penny-gaff heroine with me, 'cos I tell you it won't take. S'help me never, it won't! I got the chips, and, of course, I means to make myself comfortable with 'em among my pals."

"Oh that you had never seen them or the villain either!" said the woman, who pretty well knew what she had to expect after Bill had enjoyed himself at The Flyers. "He'll do you some harm yet, the hoary-headed old rascal. It would have been a deal better for you if you had had nothing to do with him."

"Perhaps it would, and perhaps it wouldn't," said Bill.

"He has you in his power."

Bill winced.

"So has the other chap," said Bill. "That man's a devil, and that's the reason I came back, for I knew if he'd seen me after him, he'd make it hot for me."

"I'm afraid trouble is coming on us again, Bill—very much afraid it is."

"Oh! you're afraid of anything, you are," sulkily replied the man. "You should be plucky like me."

"Like you?"

"Yes, me."

"God help me!" said the woman. "I'm bad enough as it is."

"What do you mean? Do you mean that I'm a cur?" said Bill, waxing wrath.

The woman made no reply.

We said that the way things had turned out that night had annoyed Bill, and that he only wanted some excuse to vent his displeasure on her.

"What do you say?" growled Bill, finding his wife did not speak.

"Nothing. I said nothing," replied the woman, timidly.

"Then, why don't you? When I ask you anything, it's your place to answer, ain't it? You want to get up a row, don't you?"

"No, Bill, no."

"Yes, you do, I say. You ain't had enough of 'em lately, I suppose?"

"God knows they have been none of my seeking," said Mrs. Jackson.

"Of course not. Nothing's ever of your seeking. Oh no! certainly not."

"Are you going to bed, Bill?" said the woman, fearful that the storm was about to burst forth.

"No, I ain't."

"Then I am, for I am too tired to sit up longer."

"Certainly, you're tired. You always are, though what you've got to make you so would puzzle the devil himself to tell. Of course you're tired. I should like to know when you

---

[144] Pounds.

warn't. If I'm ever at The Flyers, it's 'Bill, are you coming home? I'm tired.'"

"You forget, Bill," she said, in a meek tone, "that I have not only you and the children to do for, but that I work hard to get a few pence as well."

"Oh yes! you work, and a mouthful you make of it, don't you? But you don't say 'Bill, you're tired,' when I work. Oh no! And if you do try to get a few halfpence, so do I; and then the moment I get 'em, you begin to preach and palaver, and—There, don't say no more to me, for I ain't been put in the very best of tempers to-night."

The woman was silent, and remained so, spite of the remarks which Bill continued to make, in the hope of causing her to give him some excuse to vent his rage upon her.

Bill—like too many a paltry villain of the present day—vented the passions he dared not show in the presence of his own sex upon his poor wife, and planned and plotted hard for some excuse for his unmanly conduct. For who ever knew a wife-beater who was not the most injured male in the world, instead of the most contemptible.

Bill Jackson was but the type of thousands, not only in the class of which he himself was a member, but of that which boasts of education and refinement.

If there could possibly be any excuse for a man raising his strong arm against the weak form of a woman, surely it could alone be found in the very lowest grades of society, among those whose brute passions have never been tamed by education or example; in those slums where filth abounds, and the light of reason has not penetrated; and yet even there the excuse must be weak indeed.

But the man who can boast of education, whose daily and hourly intercourse is with men possessing those abilities which stamp them superior to the grades with which such men as Jackson claim kindred—the intellectual working-man or tradesman—who can descend to disgrace his manhood, by striking his wife, is a thing so utterly contemptible, that no term too base can be used towards him—no punishment that could possibly be inflicted be too severe. He is a man without manhood—a disgrace to his sex, an eyesore to society, and a shame to humanity.

And yet, how many are there who walk daily among their fellow-men with head erect, without one feeling of shame? Alas! they may not be counted, they are too numerous, as, heaven knows, the reports of our police-courts show to the reading public. Not one-hundredth part of these rascals are brought to exposure or justice, or held up to the scorn and loathing of their fellow-men, and why? Ask their victims—ask the poor ill-used wife, and she will say, "I cannot hurt my husband," and so the wretch, in return for mercy, plays over and over again the brutal and degrading part of woman-beater. Forgiveness to such a wretch is mistaken mercy. His back should be made to feel the cat, wielded by women's hands and women's will.

But we forget Bill and his wife, who were suddenly startled by the ringing of a policeman's rattle in the distance.

This had the effect of putting an end to all further taunts for the present from Bill, who went to the street door, and peeped out.

A trampling of feet, and several voices, all speaking at once, told him that his neighbours were returning.

Closing the door silently, he went back to his wife, and, laying his hand on her arm, he said, in a softened tone—

"Look here, Poll. It won't do for us to offend either Spring-heeled Jack or old Grasper. If Jack has been collared, he'll be down on me some day, if he lives. I had my hand in setting the slops[145] after him, and if he's got off, which I believe he has, and old Grasper finds I hung back, he'll be getting me lagged, and then, what will become of you and the kids? I tell you what you must do. If he comes back here, and he's pretty sure to, say I haven't come in yet; that the last you saw of me I was a tearing like mad with the others. D'ye hear?"

"Yes," said the woman. "But oh! Bill, don't have anything more to do with him."

"All right. You do as I tell you."

"Very well."

"There's a lot of 'em gone by, home," he said, as several footsteps passed his door. "If I hear a knock, I nammus out at the back, over the gardens, and come in after a little while, as if I'd been the last to try to collar Jack. That'll keep the old man from mischief, do you see, and I shan't offend Jack, neither; but, upon my soul, I don't believe he's a man, after all."

There was a loud thump at the door.

Bill started, and his wife turned pale.

"Shall I go, Bill?"

"Wait till I get out of the way," said Bill, hurriedly lighting his pipe, and darting out of the room.

Thump—thump—and then the door flew back, as Bill reached the garden, and, puffing and blowing, old Grasper staggered into the dark passage.

"Who's there—is that you, Bill?" asked Mrs. Jackson, nervously.

"It's me!"

"Who's me?"

"Bring a light and see, woman!" exclaimed the angry merchant.

"Oh! is it you, Mr. Grasper?"

"Yes, it is. Have you no light?"

"I'll bring you one, sir."

"Be sharp!"

She entered the back room, and hurried back into the passage with the candle.

"Is Bill with you, sir?"

"Who?"

"Mr. Jackson—my husband?" she asked, in some trepidation.

"No, he ain't," was the curt reply. "Ain't he here, woman?"

"No, sir; he has not come back. Did he capture the—the"—

"The damned scoundrel, you mean!" said Grasper, placing his hands on his sides, and panting heavily. "No; the fellow's got clean off. But I'll hang on him like a shadow, till I bring him to justice."

The woman made no reply. She was wondering how Bill was getting on.

"So your husband has not been back, eh?" continued Grasper.

"No, sir."

"That's strange! Everybody else gave up the chase long since."

"Bill would follow him as far as he could, I know," said the woman.

"I don't know so much about that," said Grasper. "I have not got much faith in him."

"Oh, sir!"

---

[145] Police.

"No, I've not. He will sell himself to the highest bidder," growled Grasper. "if he had stood by me, that fellow could have been made prisoner in this house, and the woman would have still been in my power; and she shall be again ere long. Haven't you got any better place than this passage?" he added. "I intend to remain till your husband returns."

"Perhaps he won't be back yet, sir," said the woman, hoping that Grasper would go away.

"Then I'll wait till he does."

"As you please, sir. Will you sit down here? I haven't got a very nice room to ask you into. That's the best chair, sir. Take that."

"What a smell of tobacco," said Grasper, as he flung himself into the chair. "Phew! it's enough to make one sick."

Mrs. Jackson trembled.

She expected Grasper to give her the lie about Bill not having been home.

So used to the tobacco herself, she did not think that even if some had been smoked in the house that day Grasper would have discovered the smell of the weed on every article in the apartment.

"So this Spring-heeled Jack has paid you a visit before, has he?" said Grasper, suddenly.

"So my husband says; but I did not see him. Do you think he's a man, sir?"

"A devil of a one," growled the merchant.

"Bill says he thinks he's the devil in disguise;" said Mrs. Jackson.

"When did he say so?" And Grasper looked suspiciously in her face.

"When, sir?"

"Yes. You said you had not seen him since he left with me. When did he say so, then?"

"Lor'! sir, a long while ago."

"Oh!"

And Grasper relaxed into silence. A quarter of an hour flew by, during which time the merchant sat with his eyes apparently shut, but scrutinizing the woman's face closely, and Mrs. Jackson sat looking into the grate at the cold embers.

All of a sudden the silence was broken by the street door being thrown back against the wall, and the rattle of the falling mortar on the floor of the passage.

"There's Bill."

"Now, then, missus, are you gone to bed?" cried Bill, as he banged the door behind him.

"No, Bill. I'm here."

"I couldn't catch the fellow," said Bill, pretending to be out of breath; "and I've been looking everywhere for Mr. Grasper, but I can't find him. I wonder which way he went. I ran too fast for him, and lost sight of him before I got out of the street. It's given me such a bellowsing,[146] it has. Oh! you are here, sir?"

This last sentence was uttered in a tone of assumed surprise by the ruffian as he entered the room.

"Yes. I have been waiting for your return. Where have you been to?" said Grasper.

"Just let me get my breath first, and I'll tell you."

Bill panted, as if fearfully distressed, for some moments, and the impatient Grasper rose from his seat.

"How far did you follow him?"

"Oh, a long way."

---

[146] Left him out of breath.

"And the girl?"

"Ah! I don't know what he did with her. She wasn't with him when I see him," said Bill.

"You saw him, then?"

"Yes. I laid hold of him, but he gave a spring, and was out of sight in a moment," said Bill.

"No fooling."

"Who's fooling?"

"Why, you are. The man can take terrific leaps, I know; but as to being out of sight in an instant is all nonsense. However, that's neither here nor there. He's given us the slip, but only for a time, and the girl, too."

"Clean gone, and I hope I shall never see him again," said Bill.

"Then I hope I may, hanging on the gallows," cried Grasper. "But send your wife to bed. I want to speak to you."

The woman looked at her husband, as much as to say, "Bill, mind you have nothing to do with him."

But Bill merely pointed to the door, and, in his usual gruff tones, exclaimed—

"Poll, take your hook; and if I catch you listening, it won't be well for you."

The woman sighed, and left the room; and Bill kicked the door to with his foot after her.

"Now, then, governor, she's gone. What do you want?" asked Bill.

"Your assistance."

"What for?"

"To get that woman again in my power," said the merchant.

"Better let her alone. That's a downy cove,[147] and war-hawks to you[148] the next time he collars you up to anything," said Bill.

"I do not want your advice, but I require your assistance. I have made up my mind to possess that girl, or woman, or whatever you like to call her, and I will, if it cost me a fortune, and end in my destruction. As you are well aware, you are in my power; still, if you aid me to effect my purpose, I will pay you well. We have little to fear from that man, if we are silent and secret in our actions. But ere I retire home to seek some rest I must know whether you will aid me or not."

"If you pay well, yes," said the ruffian; "but I must, and will be paid, and well, too."

"You shall."

"Then I agree."

"But say nothing to your wife about it," said Grasper, quickly.

"Not a word."

"Well, then, I think we may succeed in discovering where he has taken or sent her," said Grasper, "if we mind how we go about it."

"How?"

"By learning who were the coachmen on the Mile-end-road to-night. For he would be certain to place her in a conveyance," said the merchant. "That could be done, could it not?"

"It might."

---

[147] i.e. Jack is a sharp fellow.
[148] i.e. Grasper will suffer.

"By you, I mean."

"Yes. I think I could learn from Bob Dickson."

"Who is he?"

"A bloke as keeps a lot of pigeons, and drives a hackney."

"He could, doubtless, inquire for you."

"Daresay he would, if"—

"If what?"

"He got something for it."

"How much would he require?"

"A couple of pots of beer."

"Give them to him, and if he is successful in putting us on the right scent he shall have a sovereign."

"Ah! that's the way to talk."

"Now, when will you see him?"

"He's sure to be in The Flyers to-morrow morning, afore he goes out with his coach."

"Very well. Proceed cautiously, learn if a gentleman and lady, or a lady alone, took a coach in the road about the time he left here. Find out where he drove to, and let me know. Then I can proceed for myself."

"And you won't want me any more?" said Bill.

"That will depend on circumstances. It's more than probable I shall. But if I do, you will be paid well for your services," replied the merchant. "But, above all, do not go rashly to work, but quietly."

"I'll take care of that."

"Then, I have nothing further to say now, and will set out for home. Mind how you attempt to play with me, for I have still the power to punish you for robbing me. You had better remain my friend than attempt to become my enemy. Good night."

Grasper took up his hat, and moved towards the passage.

"Of course you'll pay all my expenses, governor," said Bill.

Grasper flung a couple of sovereigns on to the table without a word, and hurried out of the passage into the street, ere Bill had placed them, with a grin, in his pocket.

Day was dawning as the merchant strode away; but night was in his heart—black night in his soul!

CHAPTER XCI.

JOY AND SORROW—BILL'S DISCOVERY—THE MERCHANT'S GLADNESS.

AFTER having effectually baffled his pursuers, and quieted the fears of Jane Slater, Jack, as we have before observed, proceeded with his companion in the direction of Holly Cottage, situated near where Victoria Park now stands. After a walk of some minutes, without meeting with any cause of alarm, the rumble of wheels on the deserted road caused Jack to pause and listen, and he soon discovered that the vehicle was coming towards them, and he judged from the sound that it was a hackney coach, and an empty one, too.

Anxious to arrive at the cottage as speedily as possible, and likewise to prevent any possibility of discovery, he resolved to await the approach of the vehicle.

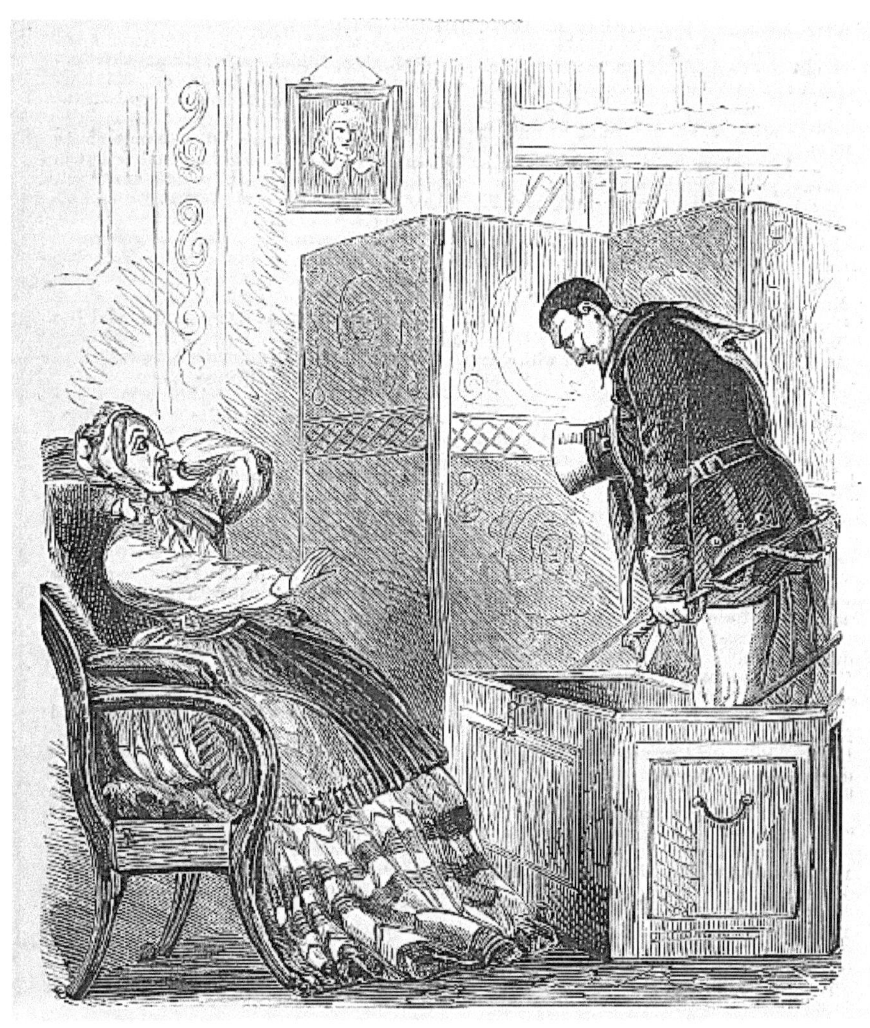

He had not to wait long ere it came up, and Jack instantly hailed the man on the box.

As he had expected, the vehicle was empty, and, placing Jane inside, bade the driver to proceed to Holly Cottage, and drive quick.

The man obeyed this injunction to the letter, and in a short space of time the vehicle drew up before a small detached cottage standing about twenty feet from the road, and surrounded by a small but neatly kept flower garden.

Having dismissed the driver, and waited till the coach had rolled away, Jack pulled the bell at the side of the little gate. Then, turning to his companion, remarked—

"Would you like to live here?"

Jane sighed as she looked up at the pretty little dwelling; then, turning her gaze on Jack's face, she said—

"Were I happy, there is no spot on earth I could crave for more than this. But"—

"But what?"

"Can you ask? The cross-roads."

And the woman burst into tears.

"Do not grieve so," said Jack. "Time, if it will not obliterate the sad past, will tend to soften your sorrow. 'Tis, I know, easy to preach, but hard to practice; and those who advise, seldom take it. But strive, for your own sake, to think less of your affliction. In the society of the fair girl who lives here you will doubtless find much relief to your sufferings. I fear I have alarmed her by this unseasonable summons."

A light appeared at one of the windows, the sash of which was gently raised.

"Who is there?" asked a soft, sweet voice, which Jack recognised as that of Ellen.

"It is me—Jack."

"At this hour!" said the girl. "My good friend, what brings you hither at such an unseasonable time?"

"The desire to assist an unfortunate fellow-creature, Miss Ellen," said Jack, "and introduce to you a poor lady whom I am sure you will receive with kindness, for my sake."

"I see you are not alone."

"No; or I had not come here at this hour," said Jack, in a tone which bespoke his willingness to do anything but cause a breath of slander to fall upon the fair occupant of the cottage.

"I will hurry down and give you admittance," said Ellen, disappearing from the window.

Jane had felt a thrill run through her heart as the tones of the poor seamstress fell on her ears.

There was something in the soft accents which seemed to assure her that Ellen possessed a kind and gentle soul, and she longed to press her to her bosom, and pour out all her sorrows in her ear.

Not long did Ellen keep them waiting.

In the course of about two minutes those outside heard the door-bolts withdrawn, and saw a sylph-like figure hurrying along the little gravelled path towards the gate.

"My good, kind friend," said Ellen, placing the key in the gate-lock with one hand, and extending the other to Jack, "I am delighted to see you."

"At this hour," he said, "and after, perhaps, arousing you from some pleasant dream, I think I ought to apologise for thus breaking upon your slumbers. But I am sure you will forgive me when I tell you for what I have come. But we won't talk here."

And taking the arm of Ellen, the three went into the house, and entered the little parlour where Ellen loved to sit and pray to heaven to reward Jack for his kindness to her.

A few words from our hero explained the motive of his unseasonable visit, and when he had concluded, Ellen turned to Jane, who stood gazing abstractedly on the floor, and flinging her arms around the young widow's neck, drew her to her bosom and burst into tears.

The sight of Ellen's grief opened the fountains of Jane's heart afresh, and, locked in each other's arms, they mingled their tears together. These two fair creatures, whom Fate had so frowned upon—who had suffered so much, and who, though so young, had drank deeply of sorrow.

It wanted not words to express to each other their feelings. Their tears told it more eloquently than words could have done. Their hearts yearned towards each other. Suffering and misery bound them, in an instant, in the firmest friendship.

Jack stood aside, a silent spectator, nor did he attempt to stem the torrent of their tears. He knew that they would relieve the overloaded hearts of the poor girls, and that they would find relief by suffering them freely to flow.

But he also felt an inward gratification at being the means of saving both these poor women from great suffering and death, and in that feeling he found his reward.

Grief, however violent, cannot last for ever, neither can tears continue to flow—the well-springs of the heart sooner or later dry up.

Their violent sobs gave place to softer sighs, and then the tear-bedewed faces were turned towards Jack; and, though no word was uttered by either, the look they fixed upon him, as each extended her hand towards him, was quite sufficient.

The outpourings of grateful hearts were in those moist eyes, and Jack almost felt that, had he been called upon to speak, a choking sensation in his throat would not have permitted him to do so.

But this feeling wore away in a few seconds, and, placing the hand of Jane in that of Ellen, he said—

"For my sake, love and befriend each other. For my sake, seek to be happy, and bury the past in oblivion; and let me feel that, by aiding you, I am atoning for some of my ill-deeds; for though I am wild and reckless, my heart is not all stone. And the feeling that I have done some good is a joy to my bosom which I can appreciate—a something to dwell upon with pleasure. Strive, then, to be happy, and by so doing make me the same. Be to each other as sisters, and to me as a friend. I know you will, for your hearts are tender and kind, and can feel for those sufferings many have never known, and, I trust, may never experience. But I forget that I have roused you, Ellen, from your couch, and that Mrs. Slater is tired and worn out; so I will make my stay no longer, but go home with a glad feeling here that many a better man might envy."

He took up his hat to depart, and moved towards the door—his hand upon his heart.

Both sprang towards him, and, raising their hands to his lips, he strode hurriedly from the house, as if he would fain go to hide the teardrop that rose to his own eye.

It shamed not his manhood—it was a greater tribute to his soul than aught else could have been.

No, Jack; that small tear, as it trembled on the lash and rolled swiftly down your cheek, washed away many an indiscretion in its course,—atoned for many a thoughtless deed of thine.

And while the cool morning air fanned his brow—while he walked along slowly, meditating on the scene he had witnessed—while Bill Jackson puffed away at his short pipe, and jingled the gold coins he had received from Grasper in his pocket—and while the merchant wended his way, full of bitter and revengeful thoughts, those two young creatures who had known so much suffering and misery knelt down beside the white-curtained bed, and asked heaven's blessings on the head of one who, let his sins be what they might, possessed a heart soft as a woman's, and ever anxious to alleviate the pangs of the unfortunate.

Time, as Jack had said, would soften the grief of Jane Slater; but, aided by all the influences of a genial heart, the poor woman soon came to feel far more happier than she had done for some time past.

Of course the fate of her husband was ever apparent in her mind, and knowing this, Ellen was ever on the alert to keep her thoughts in another channel, and when a week had worn away, poor Jane, if not happy, was far from wretched.

They had received several visits from Jack, and our hero could not but remark the change in Jane's appearance; but, of course, he forebore to make any mention of it.

He had taken his departure one evening, and while the two females leaned over the little garden-gate, watching his retreating figure down the road, Ellen caught sight of a form slinking along behind him, which she fancied she had seen before, but when and where she could not at the time call to mind.

When it had disappeared from her view, in the turn of the road, it had likewise disappeared from her thoughts, and was entirely forgotten.

She had made no mention of it to her companion, but she would have been ill at ease had she known that the figure she had observed following our hero was that of her late landlord and persecutor, Bill Jackson.

The ruffian had followed the injunctions of Ralph Grasper, and ferretted out the fact that a gentleman and lady hailed a coach in the Mile-end-road, and were driven to Holly Cottage.

This learned, Bill was set to watch the place, as Grasper resolved to be certain this time of his victim.

Day after day Bill hung about the cottage, and the locality in which it was situated, but without seeing any person resembling Jane, whose features, of course, he would well know again.

On the evening we mention, he had come to the decision in his own mind that Jane was not there at all, and had determined not to watch any longer; in fact, he was about to leave the spot and return home when he caught sight of Jack, whom of course he did not know, but ere the casual glance he had cast upon him, as he came through the little gate into the road, had been satisfied, he had caught sight of one whom he little expected to see—Ellen Folder.

Ere his surprise had died away, another figure stood by her side, and Bill Jackson fairly staggered.

It was Jane Slater!

Shrinking back into the shadow of the wall of a neighbouring garden, Bill watched them as they bade our hero good night, and when Jack had gone some distance along the road, Bill wedged half the contents of his iron tobacco box into his mouth, and followed after him in high spirits.

"Found at last," he muttered. "By jingo! but I'll have another night at The Flyers, for Grasper will come down like a prince."

And so he did. For after Jack had hailed a coach and driven off, Bill retired to the low beer-house, and, in the exuberance of his spirits, stood lots of beer to the company, who marked their gratitude for his liberality by hinting to each other that he had stolen the money by which it was paid for.

But of course Bill did not hear the foul imputation on his character; it would have been better, perhaps, if he had for Mrs. Jackson, as he might have been goaded to show his pugilistic powers at The Flyers instead of at home, for Bill, after being turned out at the close of the house, mad drunk, commenced a furious onslaught on his wife the moment he stumbled into the passage—his excuse for so doing being that she had not stood prepared to save him from knocking his head against the wall, and held the door, so as to prevent it slipping from his hand.

Having thus finished up the day, he retired to bed, without undressing, and awoke in the morning with a bump on his forehead, a filthy taste in his mouth, and a feeling of gratification in his heart at the discovery he had made, and instantly commenced to bully his wife because his breakfast was not ready, swearing that he had told her he wanted to go out early.

Of course the meek, frightened woman busied herself to provide the meal, and in an hour Bill was on his way to Grasper's to communicate his success, and receive the reward of his services.

The merchant was in high glee at the intelligence, and paid the rascal liberally for his dirty work, and when he had gone, he set himself to thinking the best course to pursue to inflict fresh pangs upon that heart he had already made suffer so much and so cruelly.

CHAPTER XCII.
SURPRISED BY SAD NEWS—ON THE SEARCH.

SLUMBERING London had awoke, and poured forth its thousands of toilers into the streets, and the busy hum which broke the silence that had reigned throughout the night aroused from a refreshing sleep the young man whom Jack had induced the waggoner to carry to London—Richard Folder, or, as we may now call him, Clavering.

The good meal of which he had partaken the night before—a luxury which to him had been a stranger for some days—had tended greatly to strengthen his weak frame, and he leaped from his bed, with a glow upon his cheek, and without that languid feeling so common to him.

Having breakfasted, he went to the house in which the body of Mrs. Folder lay, and he had not been there more than ten minutes, when the coffin he had ordered on the day before was brought into the apartment by two men.

The corpse was placed within its last house, under his immediate superintendence, and when the undertakers had taken their departure he sat himself down in one of the old chairs, and awaited the arrival of his new-found friend.

Punctual to the moment, Jack arrived; and even if he had not done so, no doubt would have entered the mind of Richard as to his honesty of purpose.

There was something which seemed to draw him towards our hero.

It was not only the fact of his having befriended him on the road, or his asserted knowledge of his sister's whereabouts, but a something which he could not describe to himself, one of those peculiar feelings which will cling to us despite all we do, or any argument we may use, to upset.

He sprang up, with a smile, as Jack knocked upon the panels of the door of the room, and extended his hand, as he crossed the threshold.

Our hero grasped it warmly, and reverently raised his hat as his eye fell upon the black object resting upon tressels, and extending nearly across the room.

There is a feeling of awe which pervades the bosoms of even the most callous-hearted, when in the presence of soulless clay,—the voice is hushed in the room of death, the footstep is noiseless, the movements slow, as if fearful of awaking that which will never more awake in this world,—and it was in a whisper that Jack spoke, as he greeted the young man.

"You have been anxious, doubtless, for my arrival," he said, after a moment's pause, and looking at the young man as if he would read in his face the answer.

"Yes,—and no," replied Richard.

Jack smiled at so strange a reply.

"I was anxious for your coming, because I wish to see my sister; but had you not come, I should have felt assured other and more pressing business alone caused you to break your appointment with me."

"And not a doubt of my honesty?" said Jack, half suspiciously.

"Indeed, no."

Jack looked hard at him.

The young man stood the scrutiny.

"I believe you," said Jack.

"You may, indeed."

"But have you no questions to ask me?" said Jack,

"Questions?"

"Yes."

"Respecting what, sir?"

"The packet you entrusted to my care," said our hero.

"I am sure you will only do what you deem best."

"I am glad of that," said Jack. "And you shall have no cause to alter your good opinion of me."

"I am certain I shall not."

"I may as well inform you that yesterday I placed the papers confided by you to me in the hands of an eminent solicitor of Lincoln's Inn, and begged him to give me an opinion as soon as possible."

"I am obliged for your kindness," said Richard.

"And he did not fail to do as I desired. For, last evening, after a careful perusal of them, he informed me that he had little doubt but that your claim could be established," said Jack.

The young man's heart bounded joyfully in his bosom.

"Yes. He doubts not but that you will obtain possession of the title and estates, now held by a cousin of the late supposed Richard Clavering, who died in Newgate."

"Oh, I am so delighted! But"—

He paused quickly.

"But what?" asked Jack.

"Though I can be nothing but happy at the prospect of such an unexpected and unlooked-for fortune, sir, I feel a pang of sorrow at the disappointment of the present holder."

"He is nothing to you," said Jack.

"Only the same as I am to you," said Richard—"a fellow-man."

Jack looked up from beneath his brows, and a smile of gratification stole over his face.

"Richard Clavering," he said, "you are a noble-hearted fellow."

"I must say the same of you, Spring-heeled Jack."

"It's more than many would."

"That may be. But I speak as I find; and, having found you to be a noble-hearted man, I can do no less."

"Well—well," said Jack, "let us drop that subject. We will bandy compliments some other time. Now to business."

The young man bowed.

"You are anxious to meet with your sister?" said Jack.

"I am."

"Very well. But do not buoy yourself up with the certainty that the lady named Ellen Folder with whom I am acquainted is the person you seek. There are many Folders in the world, and resemblances are often strange. The Ellen Folder of my acquaintance may be the veriest stranger to you, my friend, after all."

"I hope not."

"So do I. But still you had better look forward for disappointment in your hopes. Have you breakfasted?"

"Yes."

"Then we will go at once."

"With pleasure," said Richard.

Jack took up his hat, and moved towards the door.

The young man followed him down the stairs into the street.

Jack took his arm, and together they moved along.

But Richard showed some evidence of wishing to hang back—a circumstance which caused Jack some surprise, and called forth a remark that brought the warm blood to the young man's cheek.

"Sir," he said, in answer, "I would rather walk behind. I should be sorry to disgrace you."

"Disgrace me?" cried Jack, in surprise. "What do you mean?"

Richard turned his eyes from Jack's face on to his own person with a meaning glance.

"I am so shabbily attired, sir, that I am"—

"Tut, tut!" exclaimed Jack. "I care not a fig for the coat; 'tis the man I look at. A gentleman may be robed in rags as well as broadcloth; and he is still a gentleman, whatever his attire. My dear friend, you will not disgrace me nor yourself."

"But, sir, should you meet any of your friends," said Richard.

"They would treat you with the same respect as myself," was the answer. "The case might be different were I in the company of one of those self-conceited, overbearing, pompous individuals of which this country can boast a very great number. I mean that class who have no qualification for gentility, and by a show of dress, jewellery—everything, in fact, but common sense and common decency—wish to be thought by their fellow-men their superiors."

"And are generally their inferiors," said Richard.

"Yes. So no more about disgracing me, if you please. Though, doubtless, it would be more congenial to your feelings to change your well-worn coat for a better garment, only I trust that, with the change of garb, there will be no change of heart and soul."

"Never!" said the young man, fervently.

"Oh," said Jack, "if there is, you will not be the first. Many a good heart has been changed to a bad one by a stroke of fortune."

"Mine never will be."

"I believe it," said Jack.

Placed at his ease by the remarks of Jack, Richard Clavering walked on beside our hero for some minutes, when Jack hailed a coach, and bade the driver proceed to Holly Cottage.

The morning was fine, and the ride pleasant, for although the thoughts of Richard would turn to the room of death, and fill his heart with sadness, yet Jack was so affable that he could but be gratified and often amused.

Having discharged the coachman at the gate, our hero looked around the tastefully arranged garden, in search of Ellen, and, not finding her there, a sudden thought seized him that she was ill.

Certainly, she could not always be in the garden, for the domestic duties must be attended to; but still Jack could not banish the presentiment that had laid hold of his heart, when he found her seat, beneath a large alder, where she invariably sat at work in fine weather, vacant.

He, however, kept his thoughts to himself, and hurried along the little gravel walk to the door, at which he knocked.

Scarce had his fingers been taken from the knocker than the door was opened, and the tearful face of Jane Slater met his gaze.

There was no mistaking that the poor woman had been weeping long and violently, for her eyes were swollen and red, and her cheeks bore the traces of tears.

"Mrs. Slater," cried Jack, springing over the threshold, "why—why do I find you in grief?"

"Oh, sir! oh, sir!" sobbed the woman; "I am so unhappy, so unhappy; but perhaps you know all about it?"

"About what?" said Jack.

"Miss Ellen!"

"What of her? Is she ill? Tell me, quick, is she ill?" exclaimed Jack, in the utmost concern.

"I don't—oh! I don't know."

"Where is she?"

The woman shook her head.

Jack started back in alarm.

"For heaven's sake, what has happened?" he asked. "Don't keep me in suspense."

He had taken the woman's hand, and was looking into her face with an appealing glance.

Checking back her sobs, Jane raised her tearful eyes to his, and gasped, rather than spoke—

"Oh, sir! she's gone."

"Where?"

"Heaven knows!"

And, unable longer to control herself, the woman suffered her head to fall on his arm, and sobbed as if her heart would break.

Jack curbed his impatience, and led her into the little parlour, and, seating her on the sofa, awaited till the violence of her grief had somewhat abated.

"Now tell me what all this means," he said, at length.

Jane dried her eyes with her handkerchief, and said—

"It was the night after you were last here that Ellen went out to make a purchase, about nine o'clock. She said she would not be gone more than five minutes, as she was only going to the shop at the corner of the road. As she did not come back shortly, I began to be alarmed, and went to the gate to look for her, becoming more and more anxious every moment, and when I heard the clock strike ten, and she did not come, I could not bear the suspense any longer, so I put on my bonnet, and went to the shop, to see if she was there."

"Well?" said Jack.

"When I got there, the person who keeps it was shutting up, and, in answer to my inquiry, he told me that she had not been there that night—nor, indeed, had he seen her for two or three days. Of course, I became more and more wretched, and hurried back to see if she had come home during my absence. But she had not, and I could not rest. So I threw on my shawl, and went out again."

"Go on, go on," said Jack, as the woman paused.

"Well, sir, eleven o'clock—twelve o'clock came, and no Ellen. But a little after midnight the patrol rode by, and I told him of her strange disappearance. He promised to look out for her, and advised me to go to bed; but, of course, I could not. I was so unhappy, so I sat up all night; and next day—yesterday—I searched everywhere, but no one had seen or heard anything of her, and I have been so wretched ever since. I could not write to let you know, for I did not know where to find you. But I am so glad you have come, for I am sure you will do all you can to find out where she is."

Jack looked down thoughtfully and sorrowfully, then raised his eyes to the young man's face, over which a painful expression had spread itself.

He had listened eagerly to every word, but had made no remark; and now, as his eyes met Jack's, a deep sigh escaped his lips.

"Gone!" said Jack. "There is something strange, very strange in this."

"Yes; for I do not believe she meant to go," said Jane.

"No. She has been detained against her will," said Jack.

"But how?—where?—by whom?"

"I cannot think," muttered Jane.

"Nor I," said Jack, thoughtfully tapping his foot on the carpet.

"There is no villain Grasper to insult and annoy her," remarked Jane.

"No. But"—

"What?" asked Jane, eagerly.

"Isaac Levy might. But the idea is preposterous," muttered Jack. "The old Jew would never seek to be revenged upon me by harming her."

"The man for whom she worked?" said Jane, who had heard of the affair at the pond.

"The same."

"I should not think he could be the cause of her strange disappearance."

"Not for a moment," replied Jack. "The idea is too absurd. No; the cause I cannot understand. Could she have been taken ill, and carried to an hospital or poorhouse?"

"The patrol told me last night that he had made inquiries, and no such person had been admitted to either."

"I am more and more puzzled," said Jack, rising and walking about the room with uneven strides. "I know of no one who would tear her away from her home. She has never spoken of any persecutor to me."

"Nor to me," said Jane; "and we have no secrets from each other, I think."

"Strange—very strange!" muttered Jack; "but I will fathom this mystery some how or other."

"Oh! do sir, do," cried Jane. "I will leave no stone unturned to do so—spare no expense—lose no time," said Jack. Then, turning to Richard, he said—"I can feel for your disappointment, for it must, indeed, be great; for should this young woman be your sister, her strange disappearance prevents not only your meeting, but learning the sad and happy intelligence you have to communicate."

"I feel that she is my relative," said the young man.

Jane, who had scarcely observed his presence before, now looked hard at the speaker.

"Ellen's brother!" she exclaimed. "Oh! how like her, you are."

"You think so?" said Jack.

"Yes. Do not you?"

"There is a likeness."

"A striking resemblance," said Jane. "She has often spoken of her brother, and wondered how he was getting on in the world, whether he was dead or alive. And now you have come to see her, she is not here!"

"I am pained—deeply pained—at what I have heard," said Richard. "Can she have gone to any friends, and be remaining with them?"

"She has told me she has but one friend," replied Jane.

"And who is that?" asked Jack, turning quickly at the words.

"Yourself!"

"Her only friend! And she may be in trouble, and I unable to assist her," mused Jack. "I know not what to think!"

"Nor I," said Jane.

"Nor I," echoed Richard.

"I am loth to believe she can have met with foul play at the hands of anyone," said Jack, after a pause; "and yet"—

"What?" cried Jane, her face becoming pale as death.

"Alas! there are wretches base enough for any crime in this world; beings—for men they are not—who would plunge their souls to eternal damnation to render another wretched in this life."

"Indeed—indeed there are!" said Jane, "and well do I know it."

"The man who would dare harm my sister," exclaimed Richard, clenching his hand, and drawing his form proudly up as he spoke, "had better meet an enraged tiger than her brother."

His eyes sparkled as he spoke, and his nostrils dilated.

"Or me," said Jack. "And though Miss Folder is no more to me than a friend whom I deeply respect, the ruffian who would so debase himself as to insult her, by word or deed, would rouse a devil here that could not easily be quelled!"

He placed his hand upon his heart as he spoke, and continued his rapid and thoughtful walk about the little apartment.

Suddenly he paused before Jane, and asked—

"Has she ever hinted a desire to leave this place?"

"Never."

"The question I felt was unnecessary," said Jack, "yet something prompted me to ask it."

"On the contrary, she has said she never was so happy as she has been here."

"Has anyone ever been here to see her?" asked Jack, after a pause.

"None but yourself."

"Has she made any acquaintances?"

"No. I never heard her speak of any. In fact, I am sure she has none."

"Something must be done to solve this mystery," said Jack, after a long and thoughtful pause; "but what? There I am at a loss."

"I can think of nothing."

"Well, do not grieve so much," said Jack, as Jane began to cry again. "You may be sure that if she can be traced out she shall, and weeping will only serve to make you ill. I will set forth at once and make inquiries, and I sincerely hope they will tend to elucidate the mystery.

"Heaven grant they may!"

"Amen to that," said Richard.

"I have inquired everywhere I can think of," said Jane.

"About this neighbourhood?"

"Yes."

"I will try the one from which she came, and those who know her. The rascal in whose house she lived may throw some light on this strange affair, perhaps," said Jack, as he thought of Bill Jackson.

But he did not think that he had had any hand in Ellen's disappearance, for what had Bill to gain by it? Still, he knew her, and those who had often seen her while living in the locality where he resided.

So Jack made up his mind to go at once to Jackson, believing the fellow would not recognise him in his ordinary attire, and minus his mask; and, under the pretence of having work for her to do, seek to learn if he knew ought of her whereabouts.

Should this fail to put him on Ellen's track, he resolved to seek the aid of the police; and exhorting Jane to be of good cheer and hope for the best, he prepared to take his departure, accompanied by Richard, whose sudden good fortune had been so unexpectedly damped.

Dispirited and disheartened the young man took his leave of Jane Slater, and silently walked on by the side of Jack in the direction of Bill Jackson's dwelling.

Jack's face wore a gloomy expression. He knit his brows thoughtfully together, and walked at a rapid pace, and seemed to be unconscious of his companion's presence till Richard, struck by a sudden thought, placed his hand upon his arm, and, in a sort of hissing whisper, said—

"Do you think she is dead?"

Jack paused, looked at him for a moment, shook his head slowly, and again continued his rapid walk.

CHAPTER XCIII.
SCENE AT THE LAWYER'S CHAMBERS—A STRANGE DUEL.

A WEEK passed, and no clue could be obtained of the missing Ellen, in spite of the exertions of Jack, Richard, and Jane Slater.

Bill Jackson knew nothing of her, or certainly the offer of a sovereign would have bought information from him.

Mrs. Folder had been conveyed to her last resting place, followed by Richard, who, in spite of her wish that he might curse her, dropped tears upon the coffin-lid as he took his last gaze upon the box which contained her remains.

Though Jack's principal anxiety was to discover Ellen, he still found time to pay a few visits to Mr. Brief, the lawyer, who, at his recommendation, had undertaken to seek to get the property for Richard, now held by a Charles Lorain, a cousin of the libertine whose base deeds had brought him to a fearful and degrading doom within the dark walls of Newgate.

The lawyer had given notice to Mr. Lorain of his intention to dispute his right to the title and estates enjoyed by the unhappy murderer; a notice which he first treated with contempt, then looked upon with fear.

At the advice of his solicitor, he accompanied that gentleman to Mr. Brief's chambers, and while there Jack made his appearance, and was introduced as the person who had placed the papers in the lawyer's hands, and upon whose recommendation Mr. Brief had undertaken the case for his client.

Jack, of course, had no personal ill-feeling towards Lorain, and although at a glance he read the character of the man, treated him with the utmost respect and courtesy.

Lorain was a young man about seven-and-twenty years of age, tall in stature, and proportionately well-made; but there was a something in his movements and expression which stamped him at once as a man of violent passions, of an overbearing spirit, and a cruel and designing nature, and Jack could see on the instant that however just might be the claim of Richard, it would not be yielded without a struggle, and with a bad grace, by his opponent.

He bent his head coldly to Jack, in reply to his courteous greeting, and, with a supercilious curl of the lip, turned to his solicitor, who was conversing with Mr. Brief.

"Well," he said, in an assumed tone, "have you persuaded the old gentleman that none but a fool would undertake to dispute my right to the title and estates of my late lamented cousin?"

"Mr. Brief and myself will, doubtless, understand each other in good time, sir," said the person addressed, somewhat sharply, evidently angered at the other's manner.

Lorain bit his lip at the rebuke, and frowned scorningly upon Jack, who was observing him keenly.

"Who the devil are you staring at?" he asked, suddenly.

"Not at a gentleman, sir," was the retort of our hero.

"What do you mean by that?" cried Lorain, becoming perfectly bloodless in the face with passion.

"Simply what I say."

"That I am no gentleman. Is that what you would infer?"

"Really, sir, your conduct makes me doubt your claim to gentility, equally as much as your right to the estates you now hold," said Jack, in a calm, cool tone. Lorain measured him from head to foot with his eye; then, taking a step forward, he said, in a voice choked with rage—

"You're a scoundrel!"

Jack smiled contemptuously.

Without altering his usual cool tone of voice, he remarked—

"Were you a gentleman, I should say you were mad; but, as you are not, I say you are a liar!"

Lorain raised his arm, and struck Jack a smart blow on the cheek, which caused the others to look round, and Jack to colour to the temples.

"That's how I serve the dog who calls me a liar!" cried Lorain, trembling with passion.

By an effort, Jack retained his calmness, but the blow was more than he could tamely submit to.

For a moment his eye swept up and down the form of the man before him. Raising his arm, he struck Lorain a blow in the face, that instantly felled him to the floor.

"And that is how I chastise the puppy who presumes to bark at me!" said Jack.

"Gentlemen!—gentlemen!"—exclaimed Mr. Brief.

"I beg your pardon, sir," said Jack, coolly. "If your words have reference to us, they are misapplied. You speak in the plural, instead of the singular. Mr. Lorain is no gentleman; and I have to apologize for almost forgetting, in my indignation, that I am one."

Lorain leaped to his feet.

"I'll have your blood for this!" he said, furiously.

"I warn you," said Jack, "not to tempt me to forget myself again. Keep your distance, sir, or, rather, a distance which takes you out of the reach of my right arm, or you may fall again."

The look which accompanied these words had the effect of causing the angry man to step back a pace.

There was a dangerous gleam in Jack's eye, despite the calmness of his tones; and, grinding his teeth in rage, Lorain said—

"You claim to be a gentleman?"

"I do."

"Then you shall give me the satisfaction one gentleman has a right to demand from another!" cried Lorain.

"All the satisfaction a gentleman has a right to demand from me, he shall have," said Jack.

"Then, sir, we must fight!"

"You are not, then, satisfied with the blow I gave you?" said Jack, sarcastically. "I am sorry for that, as I have no wish to strike you again."

"Gentlemen," began Mr. Brief.

But he was interrupted by Lorain.

"Hold your row!" he cried; "and don't interfere with me."

"This is my office, sir."

"It may be the devil's for all I care!" roared Lorain.

"You are excited, sir."

"Damn it! Am I to take a blow tamely from that fellow?" roared Lorain. "No; curse me, if I do! We must fight!"

"I will have no fighting here, sir, in my place," said Brief.

"Who the devil wants to fight here?"

"You do, seemingly," said Jack.

"No I don't."

"Oh, I thought you did. Well, I'm glad you have altered your mind, like a sensible man," said Jack, with a smile.

"But I've not altered my mind—nothing can alter it!" roared Lorain. "You have struck me, and I'll have your blood!"

"Do you desire to murder me?"

"I will put a bullet through you—yes, sir, a bullet. I demand satisfaction, and I will have it."

"Will you, indeed?"

"I will, or I will brand you as a coward—yes, as a coward! You—you—damn it! who are you?" roared Lorain fiercely, foaming at the mouth.

"One who can keep his temper, converse like a rational man, and treat a stranger at least with common courtesy."

"By calling him a liar."

"Yes, if he asserts I am a scoundrel."

"So you are."

"Beware you do not goad me to knock you down again!"

"Sir, I beg you will have some respect for me," said Mr. Brief, laying his hand on Jack's upraised arm.

Jack's arm dropped to his side, and he bowed to the lawyer.

"I regret, sir, that I should have dropped in to see you while this person was present," he said; "and as I dread further insult, I will take my departure."

"Like a cur," snarled Lorain.

"What does that mean?" asked Jack.

"Why, you'd sneak away. You are too great a coward to meet a gentleman with a gentleman's weapon," cried Lorain. "You fight only like a costermonger, with your fists, but dare not face a bullet."

"You would never have the courage to pull a trigger," laughed Jack.

"You have not the courage to meet me with a pistol in my hand. I thought you were a cowardly snob, now I know you to be one."

Jack's face was again crimson, but the retort on his lips was not uttered.

The appealing look of Mr. Brief caused it to die away ere it was spoken.

Fixing his eyes upon Lorain, he said, in a low, calm voice, but in a tone of firmness—

"Mr. Lorain—for I deny your right to any other title—I do not fear to meet a gentleman with any weapon he may choose, and give him the satisfaction he desires. If I meet you, I meet a blackguard, who should be either kicked or horsewhipped. But a man of your stamp cannot be made to understand that a gentleman does violence to his own feelings by placing himself as your equal. Still, since you so ardently desire to place a bullet in my chest, I will give you an opportunity of trying to do so. I will bring myself to your level, and meet you when and where you please."

"I'll have you both arrested," said Brief, "if you dare meet for such a purpose as a duel."

"You mind your own business," cried Lorain, darting a scowling look at Brief.

"Let him have his way," said Jack, "for he has not long to live."

"A braggart," sneered Lorain.

"As you please," said Jack. "But to-morrow will show whether I am right or wrong. You will never hit me."

"No. For you will not dare to stand before me, I expect," sneered the other.

"You have but to fix the time and place," said Jack, "and I will be there, never fear. So decide quickly, if you please, as I should be glad to retire till you have gone."

"Oh," sneered Lorain, "I can see your drift."

"Indeed!"

"Ay, well."

"And pray what is it?" asked Jack, quietly.

"Get me to name time and place in the presence of Mr. Brief, so that you may be arrested, and save yourself from my vengeance by the duel being prevented," was the reply.

"Humph!" coughed Jack.

"I can read through you," sneered Lorain.

"No such idea entered my thoughts," said Jack. "But since you imagine it did, the best way to keep our place of meeting a secret from the gentlemen of the law will be for you to send me word one hour before the affair is to take place where you would like me to meet you. That will be plenty of time for me to provide myself with a friend, and reach the place of rendezvous, providing it is not more than three miles distant from this spot."

"Agreed!" said Lorain. "You will hear from me to-night or to-morrow."

"Your own convenience will suit mine," said Jack.

"But where am I to send to?"

"Beecher's hotel, Piccadilly."

"And to whom? For Mr. Brief simply introduced you as the friend of the madman who disputes my claim to my inheritance."

"Oh, Mr. Brown."

"Brown?"

"Yes, sir, Brown! Have you any objection to the name?" said Jack.

"I don't believe it is your name."

"Well, you don't want to shoot my name, do you? I thought it was me you wished to perform that kind office for."

"And so it is."

"Then, what matters it my name?"

"Because I should like to know who you really are."

"You shall be gratified, never fear," said Jack, pointedly.

"When?"

"When we stand face to face, with weapons in our hands," was the reply.

"Ah! but shall we?"

"If you wish it."

"I do."

"Then, fear not that I shall refuse to be at any place you may feel disposed to select as suited for the purpose. I do not admire duelling, but I do not fear to become one of the principals in a duel."

"My wounded honour shall be—must be, appeased!" said Lorain, tragically.

Jack shrugged his shoulders, and turned towards the door, with a smile on his face.

"Let this foolish quarrel end here, gentlemen," said Mr. Brief.

"It cannot," cried Lorain.

"My dear friend, let me beg"—began Lorain's solicitor.

"Silence!" cried the young man, in a tone that made his adviser leap back, and cause him to let fall the eye-glass he held between his finger and thumb. "The fellow has insulted me. My feelings are wounded, and—and, why, damn it! I'll wound him, or he shall me."

"I shall be sure to do that, if I do not kill you outright," said Jack, with a sly look at Mr. Brief.

"Or I will you."

"There is too much talk about it, to come to anything, it appears to me," said Mr. Brief, turning to his fellow lawyer. "It is an old saying, that those who talk most do least."

"So I believe," said Jack, pointedly, staring into Lorain's face.

Lorain bit his lip, and was silent.

"You will not forget? Mr. Brown, Beecher's Hotel, Piccadilly," said Jack.

"No!" roared the other, furiously. "Nor will you forget me—at least, not as long as you live to recollect me."

"It will be long after you are dead and gone," said Jack. "Poor young man! poor young man!"

Lorain could have strangled him as he stood with his hand on the handle of the door. To be struck, and then taunted, was hard enough, but to be pitied was unendurable.

"I will see you again, when this gentleman—person, I should say—has retired," said Jack, addressing himself to Mr. Brief.

That gentleman bowed, and, respectfully saluting Lorain's solicitor, he opened the door, and stepped over the threshold.

As he drew it to behind him, Jack turned his gaze upon Lorain, saying—

"I shall await your message."

Then the door closed behind him, and silence reigned in the lawyer's office for some time.

At length, the consultation between the two solicitors came to an end, and Mr. Brief bowed Lorain and his lawyer out.

The young man walked on with his companion in moody silence for some time—a silence which the lawyer did not seem inclined to break, and from which Lorain argued all was not so well as he could wish.

"Well," he said, impatiently, at length, "what do you think of that madman's claim, Mr. Tomlin?"

The lawyer shook his head.

"My dear sir, it is impossible to say what evidence may yet be brought forward to disprove those papers placed in Mr. Brief's hands. But, to tell you the truth, I would rather be the madman's solicitor in this case than yours."

"The devil!" cried Lorain. "Then, do you really think he has any claim whatever?"

The lawyer looked hard into Lorain's eyes, and then whispered—

"Mr. Lorain, I don't think."

"Don't think?" echoed the other, turning very pale as he spoke.

"No, sir. I know."

"That he has?"

"Yes."

"Then I'll kill him before he shall have it!" cried Lorain, furiously, and stamping his foot as he gave utterance to the words. "No doubt but he will be the second of the rascal I am going to fight; and if he is, I'll pick a quarrel with him and shoot him. Yes, sir, shoot him dead!"

"But you forget Mr. Brown may shoot you first," said the lawyer, coolly. "How then?"

"Why, then," stammered Lorain. "Well, that is awkward, ain't it? I ought to have sought the fellow who calls himself Richard Clavering, and goaded him on to a meeting— that is how I should have acted. But he shan't have it!"

"You cannot prevent him—you cannot defy the law. Besides, if Mr. Brown shoots you, it won't matter who enjoys the titles and estates —at least, not to you."

"And so you think I shall lose them?" said Lorain, becoming more calm.

"His claim is a good one—a very good one. Proofs abundant—evidence plain—convince any jury, unless"—

"Unless what?"

"They are rebutted by stronger proof on the other side—and that, I think, is impossible."

"Curses on it all!"

"Mr. Lorain, you should strive to curb that violent temper of yours. One day it will lead to your ruin," said the lawyer. "Already it has placed your life in danger."

"I don't care. For if I have to give up my wealth, I'd as soon die as live," said Lorain, bitterly.

A few moments after, they separated.

It was late in the evening when Jack sat smoking a cigar in the hotel he had named, when one of the servants of the establishment placed a note in his hand, informing him that the bearer waited an answer.

Jack opened the paper, and a smile broke over his face as he perused the lines written therein.

Slowly folding the note up, he said—

"Tell the person who brought this that I will not fail to be at the place at the time named."

The man hurried to perform his errand, and Jack, placing the letter in his pocket, lolled back in his chair, and puffed away at his cigar, watching the blue wreaths of smoke as they curled upwards towards the ceiling.

"So the fellow is in earnest," he muttered to himself. "He intends to make my heart a receptacle for a bullet, if he can. I thought that when he cooled down he would think better of it. Well, I must go, though I do not like the idea of killing a fellow-creature, or being slain myself. Perhaps it will come to nothing, after all, and so much the better if it does not. However, I must be up early; so I will just drop a note to Richard, to request him to meet me here at six in the morning, and then get to bed. No games to-night, for the head must be cool, and the hand steady when engaged in such business as this. He insists upon my promise being kept of divulging who I am. He feels it less honour to fight Mr. Brown, perhaps, than he would to slay the————Spring-heeled Jack; though, to my thinking, it is as great a crime to murder one man as another. Let's hope the affair will end in bluster and smoke—without fire and lead. But if it must be, why, it must. I shall not flinch."

Jack flung the end of his cigar into a spittoon, and taking a sheet of paper, hurriedly scribbled a note to Richard, which he despatched by the hotel messenger, and then retired for the night, after desiring to be called at the early hour of five o'clock, much to the surprise, if not absolute disgust, of the person to whom the request was made.

Punctual to the hour stated in the note, Richard Clavering was ushered into the chamber of our hero, whom he found attired for a journey.

After the ordinary salutations had passed, Jack told his young friend that the object of his sending for him so early was to accompany him a couple of miles to meet a person who wished to have the honour of slaying Spring-heeled Jack.

Of course, the young man's surprise was only equalled by his fears for our hero's safety; but Jack treated the matter lightly, and, after a little conversation, the two sallied out of the hotel, and took their way westward.

Three-quarters of an hour's walk brought them to the spot selected by Lorain—a field lying back some distance from the high-road, and sheltered from observation by a tall, thick-set hedge.

Here they found Lorain awaiting them in the company of a gentleman about his own age, who advanced to meet Jack as he entered the enclosure, and who demanded to know if any apology would be tendered by him to his friend.

Jack's reply was a scornful laugh, and a request that the preliminaries might be arranged as quickly as possible, as he had business to attend to, and was anxious to shoot his man without any delay, and have the trifling business disposed of at once.

Lorain's cheeks paled when he learned how his friend had been received by the man he had challenged, and bitterly cursed himself for having insisted upon the duel. He had never thought that Jack would be at the spot. But, finding his mistake, he began to think how best to save himself from the consequences of his rash temper. He had soon resolved how to act. He determined not to wait for the signal to fire, but to aim at his opponent the moment he had taken up his position.

The preliminaries being arranged, each was led to his corner, and then Jack, slipping on his mask, turned to inform Lorain that he was Spring-heeled Jack, if it was any gratification for him to know it, when that worthy levelled his weapon, and placed his finger on the trigger.

As he pressed it, the sight of the mask caused him so much and so sudden a surprise, that he started back—thus bringing the barrel of his pistol up, and the ball flew several yards above the head of our hero.

In a moment Jack realized the other's treachery, and, bounding forward, he seized him by the throat, and laid the barrel of his weapon against Lorain's brow.

"Villain!" he cried. "Coward! assassin! But 'tis my turn now."

"Mercy! For God's sake, mercy!" cried the man. "It was an accident. I could not help it."

"Liar!" exclaimed Jack, hurling him to the ground. "But you are safe from my vengeance. I cannot slay you. You are too contemptible."

Flinging the weapon on the grass, he took Richard's arm, and left the field, never once looking back on the wretch who had fainted from excess of fear.

CHAPTER XCIV.
MARRIED AT LAST.

SPRING-HEELED JACK sat in the smoking-room of his hotel, thoughtfully watching the blue wreaths of smoke that curled upwards from the glowing end of his cigar.

He had laid aside the paper he had been perusing, and lolled back in his cushioned chair, and his face wore a thoughtful expression.

"Why, Jack! Jack!" he muttered, half aloud, as he watched a ring of blue vapour widen out, as it ascended towards the beautifully corniced ceiling of the apartment, "if you go on much longer in this way you will become the most romantic and sentimental individual in the metropolis. You donned the mask and cloak for fun and adventure, that you might afford your mischievous mind the gratification of frightening people out of their wits; but instead you find yourself acting the part of the Good Samaritan on all sides—serving by kindness, rather than killing by fear."

He puffed away at his cigar, and took up the paper again; but his thoughts would not permit him to read. So, flinging it down upon the table in disgust, he lolled back in his chair, stretched out his legs, and began to smoke furiously.

"I feel something like the Irish gentleman who grew mouldy for the want of a beating," he muttered; "for, in truth, I am getting melancholy for the want of some amusing adventure. Here I am, running over the country protecting ill-used females, when I had made up my mind to send a few into hysterics—playing the part of a philanthropist, instead of a devil. I want food for laughter, and I seek that for grief. Egad! Jack, you will have to lay aside mask, cloak, gloves, and boots, if you go on much longer this way, and turn hermit, or get married. Egad! I don't know which would be the most sensible proceeding of the two. If I turned hermit, I should go mad; and if I got married, why I should send my wife mad, to a certainty. Ah, Jack! you are a sad fellow; but I suppose it's all for the best. Ah! thinking of marriages, let's see if any of my acquaintances intend to sow their wild oats!"

He took up the paper, and turning over the leaves, glanced, with a smiling look, over the announcements of births, marriages and deaths.

"Eh!" he cried, "what's this?"

His eye had swept over the marriages, and rested on a little paragraph at the bottom of the column, which ran as follows; —

"We learn that the accomplished and beautiful sister of Sir Timothy Tumberlain is soon to be allied to a retired and wealthy merchant, named Tobias Bacon, who has become the possessor of the magnificent farm, called 'The Hollies,' in Devonshire, where the lady, now suffering from ill health, has taken up her residence with her brother and a select circle of friends."

Jack read and re-read the paragraph, slowly folded up the paper, and thoughtfully tapped the compressed sheet on the table.

"Sir Timothy Tumberlain!" he mused. "Why, to my certain knowledge, he is now in Italy with his sister, a confirmed cripple, poor girl, and a mere child in years. There's some mistake, or"——

Jack paused, opened the paper, and again carefully read the paragraph.

"I cannot understand it," he mused. "The affair is a canard.[149] Oh, by fate! here is an explanation of the matter."

His eye had caught another paragraph, which stated that a person, supposed to assume the. name of Sir Timothy Tumberlain, had filched a hotel-keeper at Brighton, and was supposed to be in league with others who had left their hotels without paying their bills.

Jack threw down the paper, and sprang to his feet.

"Whew! here's some gigantic swindle on," he said, "and my name's not Jack if I can't read through it. Some rascal has assumed the name of my friend for the purpose of gaining an introduction to those he intends to dupe, and if this retired merchant, now farmer, is not one, I'm much mistaken. Now, I don't know that it is any business of mine, still it may afford me some gratification and amusement to be instrumental in exposing the rascal whoever he be that assumes the title of my old school-fellow. A run out of town will do me good, and a change of scene drive away the melancholy that is settling upon my heart. I'll go to Devonshire, and start at once."

Having made up his mind to go, Jack was not long in making preparations. In fact, in less than half an hour he was being wheeled out of the metropolis as fast as a post-chaise[150] could carry him. As he had himself said, the fresh air of the country would do him good, and as he progressed on his journey his spirits rose, and his whole frame seemed invigorated with fresh life.

It was towards the evening of the second day that Jack arrived at Barnstable, and put up at the principal hotel.

He could not but observe that he was an object of considerable interest to several persons, and he was not long in discovering that they were officers.

Jack had a way of engrafting himself into the confidence of others, and in a short time he not only had stated his own reason for coming there, but likewise learned more of those who had been so intently watching him since his entrance into the town, which was none other than the arrest of a gang of swindlers whom they had traced thus far.

Jack soon entered into a league with the officers, and after partaking of refreshments set out in their company for The Hollies, and having, surrounded the farm, our hero soon found a means of making himself acquainted with all that was transpiring within.

An entrance was gained, and Jack, leaving the officers outside, entered the room at the moment the pseudo Sir Timothy was claiming to be the winner of the heavy stakes.

It was the intention of that worthy and his companions to have got the cheque for the amount from Bacon, and then, during the night, to have taken their departure for London, and great was the surprise and terror of the confederates when Jack entered the room and announced the officers whom he had been instrumental in bringing there.

The surprise of Timothy soon gave place to fear, which, in its turn, was usurped by desperation, and the swindler struggled hard to free himself from Jack's grasp.

But our hero held him as if in a vice; and two officers entering at his summons, the mock nobleman found his wrists encircled by a pair of handcuffs before he could utter the least remonstrance.

His companions, after the first shock, turned to fly.

They did not succeed, however, in making their escape out of the room.

---

[149] An unfounded rumour.
[150] Light open carriage.

Met by another of the officers, they were immediately made prisoners.

Old Bacon stood glaring upon one and the other in bewilderment.

The words which Jack had uttered had completely destroyed the power of the drug which had been administered to him, and he was sober on the instant.

Still he was confused by the events.

He could not speak, but his eyes questioned for an explanation.

Seeing which, Jack immediately gave it.

"And I have been in the hands of sharpers?"[151] he said, at length. "Oh, how I have been deceived!"

"You had deceived yourself in the first instance," said Jack.

"How?"

"By imagining that a young lady of good birth and position would ally herself to a man of your age. Your brain has been turned by your foolish passion, and you have been made the dupe of designing men. You may congratulate yourself, sir, that you have got off so easily; for, had we not arrived as we did, the rascals would have been off with your ten thousand pounds."

"And they are not gentlemen?" cried Bacon.

"I knows 'em," said one of the officers, who had been scrutinizing them closely. "This is Tim Brown, as used to do the thimble-rig[152] and garter fakement. This is Jack Snooks, the kite-flyer, begging-letter dodger—you know. And this chap is Jem Baker, the pickpocket. Why, I've had 'em all in the jug, and can swear to 'em!'

"It's false!" cried Timothy. "I'll have you punished for this vile assertion, you base scoundrel!"

"Stow yer chaff!"[153] said the man. "We want you for nammusing with the things from the hotel at Brighton."

Timothy pulled a long face.

"The game's up!" said the fellow who had passed as Lord Dunfred. "But if we'd had another hour, we'd have done you."

"Daresay you would," said the officer. "But we've done you now, and you'll have to do a little harder work for a time."

"I'll do all that on my head," said the fellow. "But look out when my time's up."

"What for?"

"I'll pay you."

"Will you?"

"Yes. Oh! oh!"

The officer had twisted his hand into the fellow's coat collar, and, as he gave utterance to the threat, dug his knuckles into his neck with such force as to draw forth the exclamation.

"Don't say that again," said the officer.

The fellow thought he had better not, and remained silent and crest-fallen.

"Now for the woman!" said Jack.

"The woman?" replied Bacon.

---

[151] A person who cheats to win money.

[152] One who presents false papers to obtain cash or credit.

[153] Stop talking.

"Yes. Your bride that was to be, but this gentleman's wife that is,—the fair Florentine and her companion. Why, old gentleman, if you had married her you would have made a strange alliance, for these gentlemen inform me that she is a shoplifter."

"A"—

Bacon could say no more.

He held up his hands in astonishment and horror, and sank into a seat. "Sold!" he gasped at last.

"You have bought common-sense dearly," said Jack. "Now let me give you a word of advice."

"What is it?"

"Marry your cook, and settle down comfortably for the rest of your life. Avoid gambling, and let this teach you a lesson—teach you that old men with one foot in the grave need a nurse, rather than a young girl for a wife. Oh! here they come."

Two of the officers, who had left the room, now returned with the two females, who looked anything but happy.

"Oh, Florentine!" said Bacon, as the young woman was pushed somewhat rudely into the room, by her captors. "Oh, Florentine!"

"Flora Brown, you mean," said the officer.

"Oh! how could you deceive me thus?" cried Bacon, in tender tones.

"Because I saw you were an old fool," said the woman, savagely.

"A fool!"

"Yes, a stupid old fool."

"I'll be careful for the future," said Bacon.

"And marry your grandmother," said Flora. "Cheer up, Em, don't cry, we shan't get above a year, and we can laugh at that."

Jack shrugged his shoulders, and turned away in disgust.

"We'll first know what you've got about you, before we go," said the officer. "Turn out your pockets."

They knew resistance was useless, and the women took various articles from their dresses, which belonged to Bacon, and showed immediately to that gentleman that his boxes and trunks had been opened.

"Take them away," he said. "I will not charge them with anything, for I cannot bear the idea of prosecuting—but take them away!—take them away!"

He moved his hand towards the door, and the officers led the confederates out, and as the last disappeared, the old man sank in his chair.

"What a fool I've made myself," he cried. "Oh, what a fool!—and at my age, too."

For some time he sat looking ruefully at the table on which the dice had been thrown, and then, suddenly springing up, he muttered—

"I have been foolish, very foolish; but I will be so no more. What could an old man like me want with a young wife, unless it was to annoy me, and make me jealous of her? I don't think I should have cared for her long, I'm sure I shouldn't. She is not so beautiful as I thought her. I was deceived. What a fool I must have been not to have seen she was not what she pretended to be, and that paint only made her more lovely than she really is."

Sour grapes, Mr. Bacon, sour grapes! But he would not acknowledge that.

"Marry my cook!" he muttered, after a pause. "A very pretty suggestion, truly! Marry my own menial—a woman so far beneath me in station—preposterous! And yet I don't know; she is a woman not near so old as I am. She can't possibly be more than forty. She is not bad-looking either, and when I come to think seriously, I do not know but after all she would not make a bad partner. If I still live a bachelor, I must give up the farm, and to become the possessor of one has been the whole aim of my life. No; I won't do that. I'll keep The Hollies, and I'll get married, and settle down. I have been very stupid, but I'm not the only one. I'll be more careful in future. I feel now that, at my age, I had no right to look for a girl to become my helpmate; and I have been punished for my presumption— punished by the loss of a good deal of my hard-toiled-for cash, and the ridicule that is thrown upon me. Well, never mind, Tobias, you must live and learn. Older men than you have been duped, so make the best of a bad job. Think no more of Florentine, and turn your attention to the cook. The Hollies will be dull without a mistress, and what better wife can I have than one who, like myself, is not too proud to labour!"

Having thus given vent to his feelings, Tobias retired to bed, and rose early, as was his wont, the next morning—rose, with the form of his cook—a respectable, homely-looking woman of five-and-forty—in his mind, instead of the lovely Florentine, who had so long usurped his heart.

"Where there's a will, there's a way," you know; and the way to the affections of the Widow Greaser was sooner found out by the will of Mr. Tobias Bacon,—ay, and even before he breakfasted that morning; for Tobias was not a man to dilly-dally, as we have seen before. "Strike the iron while it's hot," was his motto, and strike he did to the purpose.

But one thing he did not—that was, he scorned to go down upon his knees to Mrs. Greaser, as he had to Florentine; although had he been guilty of such an absurdity, he would have knelt to a better woman than before. No; he was satisfied with a quiet expression of his love, and an equally quiet assurance that he was not detestable to his new charmer; and so, in less than a month, there was a wedding in Barnstable, and Mrs. Greaser became Mrs. Bacon.

CHAPTER XCV.
JACK HORSEWHIPS THE SQUIRE.

HAVING seen the disreputable gang of swindlers lodged safely in gaol, Jack returned to the house at which he had put up, and partook of supper. He had no wish to be seen further in the business, and resolved to start for the metropolis on the following morning, intending to walk several miles through the country, ere he engaged a post-chaise to take him home.

Accordingly, at an early hour, much to the surprise of the keeper of the house, he called for and settled his bill, and took his departure. It was a beautiful morning, and the warm sun streamed down upon the dusty road over which he travelled.

Jack had no particular object in view, and sauntered along as if the flight of Time was the greatest indifference to him, pausing ever and anon to examine some object, or listen to the birds as they carrolled on the boughs.

A rustic now and then came trudging along the road, looked at him with an ignorant stare, growled out "Good morning," and passed on with his long, heavy strides, or a shoeless urchin would look up from his task of keeping off the crows, flap his clappers[154] as if in honour of his presence, and express a hope he wouldn't go further without finding him a copper.[155]

"Talk of the beggars of London!" muttered Jack, as he passed on after flinging a small silver coin to one of these little wretches, which, by the way, the boy seemed half afraid to pick up from the grass at his feet, after it had been given him, "they are numerous enough, and importunate enough, heaven knows! but nearly every person you meet in some parts of the country are beggars to a lesser or greater degree."

And so they are: but what makes them so? The wages they receive for their labour is so small, that when they come near a person evidently better situated than themselves, they cannot refrain from asking assistance.

There is very little pride among the agricultural labourers; and, to a certain extent, they look upon the better favoured as a legal prey.

It has often been remarked by the country gentry that the cottagers pay their rent one day, and beg it back the next. Certainly they have a hard struggle to keep soul and body together on such little means; still, the want of self-respect and self-reliance makes them greatly the beggars they are.

There has been a good deal said and written about the hardships of the agricultural labourers, and their hardships are many, there can be no denial; but it is doubtful whether they are not overdrawn—whether the symptoms sought to be excited for them might not with greater benefit be excited for those who struggle with poverty in the hearts of the great cities—men, whose wages are little more than the farm labourers, and are yet expected to appear respectable, and give their children an education—men, who are trusted with thousands, and whose honesty and faithful services are rewarded by perhaps a guinea a week.

There are not a few of this class in London; and it is doubtful whether Hodge and Roger would not lose by the change, were they induced to accept it.

Hodge, with his little cottage and vegetable patch, and his numberless little presents of milk, meat, etc., and in the enjoyment of pure air and twelve or thirteen shillings a week, is not so bad off after all as the city porter or under clerk.

Still, Hodge is not paid as he ought to be; and, when he gets a chance, he often pays himself by stealing a hurdle,[156] a few turnips, and such like, to make up for his bad wages.

To a well-to-do farmer, the loss of a few turnips or a hurdle is a mere nothing; but then, if Hodge and his companions take hurdle after hurdle, and turnip after turnip, it becomes a serious matter, and the farmer finds it necessary to make an example of the delinquent by sending him to prison for a week—a proceeding, by the way, which is pretty sure to call down upon his head a fearful storm of anathemas, both uttered and printed, and find for Hodge a number of commiserating friends. Another proof how fortunate is the country labourer, when compared with the city one,—for not a voice would be raised, nor a word uttered of sympathy for Thomas Smith, if he so far forgot himself as to abstract a shilling from his employer's desk or till, albeit his wage is no better than that of Hodge, and the temptation ever so much greater.

---

154 Two pieces of wood. used to make a noise to scare the birds.

155 A low denomination coin.

156 A fence panel.

It would be cruel to assert that country labourers are not so upright as they should be; but it is no libel to assert that there are many who look upon various things belonging to others as legal spoil, and the consequence is, that landowners and farmers are often robbed to a fearful extent by their poorer neighbours, and, driven to desperation, at length the sufferer has either recourse to the law or violence.

Now, the latter ought never to be tolerated. An aggrieved man has no right to be his own judge, because, smarting under an injury, he is apt to inflict a punishment greater than is merited. Yet it cannot be wondered at that men, after being robbed continually, having sought the assistance and protection of the law, finding themselves badgered and bullied on all sides resort to other means than a court of justice to avenge themselves on the offender.

Still, such a course is objectionable. And so our hero thought as in a few minutes after his musing, he came in sight of a gentleman on horseback, lashing furiously a cowering rustic with a heavy riding whip, at each blow of which the countryman yelled and capered to an almost ridiculous degree.

It was evident to Jack, as he hurried forward, that the horseman had lost all control of his temper, so furious were the blows which came down upon the shoulders of the yokel.

"Oh, sir! I'll never do it no more, sir," cried the countryman, in tones so loud and pleading that they might have been heard a mile off.

"You cursed, thieving scoundrel!" roared the horseman. "I'll take care you don't. I'll not be robbed, day after day, in this manner. If I put you in gaol there's a bowl about justices' justice,[157] and such like; so I'll take the law in my own hands, and protect my property with my whip."

And down it descended upon the rustic's shoulders, raising a weal at every blow.

The countryman wriggled and ran, but the horseman spurred his animal alongside of him; and, raising himself in his stirrups, beat away with all his might, one blow falling across the man's face, as Jack hurried up.

The man's cheeks were cut by the thong, and he covered his blood-stained face with his hands, and yelled in agony.

The horseman, who appeared to have lost all control of his temper, raised his whip again, but, as it descended, Jack caught at the thong, and held it firmly.

"Hold, sir!" he cried.

The man rose still higher in his stirrups, and, casting a quick glance at Jack, yelled out, in tones furious with passion—

"Who the hell are you, sir? Let go the whip, or, by heaven! I'll lay it over your shoulders as well."

And as he spoke he strove to tear the whip from Jack's hold.

"Sir, you are either drunk or mad," said Jack, "or you would not so unmercifully lash this poor fellow, or address me in such terms."

"Who are you, I'd like to know?" retorted the man, in the same angry tone of voice, and the same furious look.

"You may know sooner than you wish," said Jack, indignantly. "Pray, who are you?"

"That's my business."

---

[157] ie. full punishment will not be carried out.

GROCER
RETAIL
REWARD
DOG
LOST

"He be Squire Hepworth, of the big house out there," said the countryman. "That's who he be."

"You scoundrel," roared the squire, turning to the man.

"For shame, sir," said Jack, "to lower yourself thus. You have beaten this poor man in a manner that must excite the indignation of anyone with the least feeling."

"Curse him! I'll kill him," roared the squire. "The—the—Damn' it, sir, let go my whip, or it will be the worse for you."

"Have a care, sir," said Jack. "I am not in the habit of submitting to threats."

"Let go my whip."

"I will not."

"Not?"

"No, sir," said Jack, calmly. "I will not let go the whip until you have gained a sufficient command over your temper, to know how to use it."

"Confound you!" cried the squire, tugging with all his force to tear the whip from Jack. "Shall I submit to be dictated to by you—a stranger? You had better release your hold, or I'll ride you down."

And, failing to get possession of the weapon, the squire turned his horse's head round upon Jack.

"He'll be over ye, measter," cried the countryman. "Look out! he'll be over ye!"

And so, in truth, he would, but for the coolness of Jack, who, still retaining his hold of the whip-thong with one hand, grasped the bridle with the other, and, using all his force, drove the animal back several yards.

The squire was furious.

Jack was cool and collected. The countryman was in raptures. "That be the way to serve him, measter," he cried. "Bravo!"

"Furies!" roared the squire, plunging his spurs into the animal's flanks.

The horse reared and plunged, and Jack was compelled to let go his hold of the whip, and use both hands to the bridle, to prevent being hurled to the earth and trampled on by the goaded steed.

"Coward!" cried Jack, indignantly.

"Meddling fool!" yelled the squire, "take that, for your pains!—and that!—and that!"

As he spoke, he struck Jack three blows across the shoulders with his whip.

They were not light ones, either, and Jack ground his teeth together at the pain they inflicted.

"You shall suffer for this," he cried, "Squire Hepworth. You shall find a different person to deal with than you expect."

"Stand aside!"

"We have a little affair to settle first, squire," said Jack, still retaining his hold of the bridle.

"Stand aside, or I will trample you to death!" roared the squire.

Grasping the bridle firmly in either hand, Jack forced the animal back still further.

"Curse you! your blood be on your own head!" cried Hepworth, plunging in his spurs again, and at the same moment cutting at Jack's shoulders with his whip. "Go, mare— over him! Trample him down into the dust! Curse you, for a fool!"

But Jack's hold of the bridle was too firm. The animal could only go backwards.

Maddened beyond measure at Jack's obstinacy and the triumphant howl that broke from the countryman's lips at his discomfiture, the squire rose in his saddle, and, grasping his whip furiously, was about to deal a terrific blow at our hero, when Jack suddenly released his hold of the bridle, and seized the squire by the leg.

The horse, thus released, plunged forward, and the next instant Hepworth lay in the centre of the dusty road, while the animal bounded on at a furious gallop.

Jack could hardly suppress a smile as the fallen man rolled over in the thick dust, and the countryman fairly shrieked with pleasure.

If Squire Hepworth had been enraged before, he was doubly so now.

With a curse, loud and deep, he sprang to his feet.

The blue veins stood like ropes upon his forehead, and his breath came in short gasps from between his clenched teeth.

His face was blood red, and his whole frame trembled with passion.

A moment he looked upon our hero, who stood calmly before him, and then he swung his whip aloft.

"Hold, squire!" said Jack. "If you suffer that whip to touch me again, I will thrash you as you have thrashed that man. I've warned you, so beware!"

"To hell with you and your warning both," cried the squire. "I beat that hound because he robbed me. You interfered, and shall have your pay."

"Beware! I say. You will find me no idle boaster—no squire-fearing man—but one who will keep his word. You know not whom you threaten, or you would pause ere you let fall that whip."

"Who are you?" sneered the squire. "I'd like to know the man who can terrify me?"

Jack slipped his hand hurriedly into the breast of his coat, and, drawing forth his mask, fixed it in a moment to his face.

"I am Spring-heeled Jack!" he cried. "And now you may be well assured what you will get if you perform your threats."

Hepworth gazed upon him for several moments in silence.

"I have heard of you," he said. "Heard of you as a scoundrel who can only annoy women and frighten children. A rascal"—

"Hold, sir."

"A rascal, I repeat," cried the squire, "whom every honest man should lash from his path as I do now."

As the squire spoke, the whip swept a circle round his head, and descended with a with a whizzing sound upon the shoulders of Jack, but not with such force as it was intended, for our hero had sprang forward and clutched at the throat of Hepworth, and bore him to the ground.

"Rascal in your teeth!" cried Jack. "You have had your turn, now it is mine."

Planting his knees on the breast of the squire, he pinioned him to the dusty road, and twisted the whip out of his hand.

"Coward! Would you strike me?" cried Hepworth.

"Not while you are powerless," said Jack, taking his hand from his throat. "If you think my nature is like your own, you are mistaken."

He rose from over the prostrate man, and drew back, so as to permit the squire to regain his feet.

This Hepworth was not slow in doing.

Up he jumped, furious and foaming with passion, his hands clenched, and his chest heaving.

"Villain!" he cried.

"Silence!" said Jack. "As I told you, Squire Hepworth—for such, I believe, is your name—I intend to soundly thrash you with this whip you have so cruelly handled. It is but meet that you should know the amount of pain it inflicts, so that you can judge what force to use when you desire to again apply it to the shoulders of any poor devil who may merit your displeasure."

"You will not dare," cried the squire.

"Oh! yes," said Jack.

"At your peril."

"I'm a man of my word, Squire Hepworth, and always keep a promise made," said Jack, with provoking coolness, playfully tapping his boots with the whip.

"Remember, sir, I am a justice of the peace," said the squire.

"Indeed!" sneered Jack.

"Yes, and you will touch me at your peril."

"Doubtless. But, justice or no justice, I shall keep my word," said Jack.

And the whip curled above his head.

"I will put you in jail."

"Bah!"

"I will commit you to prison."

"You are not talking to yonder rustic," said Jack, jerking his head towards the countryman, who forgot his own pain in the pleasure he derived from the squire s defeat.

"Go, fetch the officer, Hodge," he cried. "Go! or it will be the worse for you."

"He bean't at home," said the man.

"Then, I charge you, help me to secure this man."

"I can't move my arms, squire; you've made 'em sore with your whip," was the answer of the exultant rustic.

"Villain! Seize this man, I say! or I'll—I'll"—

"Now, squire, I think I've given you good time to get your breath after your fall," said Jack. "So, now to business."

"Hodge, in the king's name, I command you to help me," cried the squire.

"In the devil's name, I mean you, Hodge, not to stand between us," cried Jack. "Now, squire, how do you like that?"

The whip descended, and curled round the shoulders of Hepworth, who uttered a mingled howl of rage and pain, and leaped backwards.

"Bravo! measter—give it him!" cried the yokel. "That's just how he served I. Give it him, measter!—there be no one coming; and, dang me, if I help him! Lay it on hard, measter; don't hit him as if you only wanted to cut a wasp off!"

Again the whip flew in the air, and again the thong encircled the squire's shoulders.

Calling loudly for help, the man danced about at every stroke, and tried to close with Jack, who, springing backwards and forwards, kept him off, and let every blow of the whip tell with great force on the squire's body.

"Ruffian! villain! scoundrel!" he yelled. "You shall pay dear for this!"

"All right, squire!" said Jack in a tone of the most provoking coolness. "How do you like that? and that?"

"Hodge, help me—help me!" he pleaded.

"Can't move, squire."

"'Tis a lie! I'll ruin you—you villain! I'll —oh! oh!"

The whip was again round his shoulders and arms; then it twined around the calves of his legs, causing him to leap about in the most grotesque manner.

"Ha! ha! ha!" laughed. Hodge. "I say, squire, how d'ye like it? Stings, doan't it? Ha! ha! ha!"

"Ay!" hissed Hepworth; "but not so deep as I'll sting thee, my fine fellow. Spring-heeled Jack, for every blow you have struck, I'll strike two, if it cost me a fortune, and take me a lifetime to do it."

"Take that, to keep you in remembrance of your promise," said Jack, once more whirling the thong around his head, and bringing it down upon the squire's shoulders.

"I will remember it, by hell!" roared the beaten man, and, with a look so full of malice, that Jack fairly started back. Never had he seen so diabolical an expression on a man's face; and, before his surprise had fairly died away, the squire had sprung beyond the reach of the whip, and the next moment Jack and Hodge watched him as he ran at full speed down the dusty road.

CHAPTER XCVL
JACK GIVES ADVICE TO ONE, AND A FRIGHT TO ANOTHER.

IT was not till a turn in the road hid the squire from his sight, that Jack turned to gaze upon Hodge, who was pressing his hands on his sides, and laughing uproariously.

"Dang it!" he cried. "Dang it, zur, but that does the heart of Hodge good; and he doan't care the licking he's had now, not a bit. Won't I be telling 'em all at the village alehouse how ye whipped the squire, and how he ran off like mad, and won't there be a jolly lot of happy faces when they hear it. Why, zur, there bean't hardly a man in the village, but he's sent to jail, for just taking a few turnips, or breaking down a hurdle. It wur only last week he committed Roger Williams for trapping a hare on his estate."

"And quite right, too," said Jack. The rustic opened his eyes and mouth to their full extent, and glared into Jack's mask, as if he couldn't believe the evidence of his senses.

"D'ye say it, serve him right, zur?"

"To be sure, I did."

"What! for only taking a hare?"

"Yes."

"And he have plenty of them?"

"What of that?" said Jack.

"Eh? Ah! I doan't know, zur," grinned Hodge.

"Look here, Hodge," said Jack. "If you were to save a few shillings out of your wages, and some person came and stole them from you, what would you do?"

"What wud I do?"

"Ay."

"Why, zur, I'd give him a darn licking, if I could," said Hodge.

"And if you couldn't?"

"Why, zur, I'd take him afore the justice."

"And get him sent to prison?"

"To be sure I would."

"For what?"

"For robbing I."

"Then, you do not think that anyone has a right to rob you?"

"Why, no; certainly not."

"Then, why should the squire like to be robbed?" asked Jack.

"Why, that be only a hare."

"No matter what it be," said Jack. "It was the squire's property, and the man who trapped it was as much a thief as he who took your money."

"Oh, no. I can't see that."

"You can't?"

"No."

"And shall I tell you why you cannot, Hodge?" asked Jack.

"Eh! eh!" grinned the man; "if you can."

"Then, it is because you are an ignorant dolt, friend Hodge."

Hodge's features drooped.

The idiotic grin faded, and he stood before Jack with open mouth and eyes.

"Yes, Hodge. It is because you are too ignorant to discriminate what belongs to the squire. No man has a right to take without his permission—no more than has the squire to rob you. Now, I daresay you would set Squire Hepworth down for a thief, if he was to steal your potatoes."

"Certainly, I should."

"Then, what is wrong in one is equally wrong in another. But why did he horsewhip you so unmercifully?"

"Why, zur? I hardly like to tell ye."

"Out with it. Have you been robbing him?" said Jack.

"Lor' bless you, zur! I pulled down some of his fence for a bit of firewood."

"Only a bit of his fence?"

"Yes, zur."

"How much?"

"A couple of boards."

"Only a couple?"

"Yes,—this time."

"And how many before?"

"Well, I can't say 'zactly; but not more 'an twenty, altogether," replied Hodge.

"And you don't think there is any harm in that, eh?"

"None at all, zur."

"Hodge, I am afraid you are a very dishonest man," said Jack.

"Doan't say that, zur. It warn't many I took."

"Granted. But if you had taken ten shillings out of his pocket, it would have been no worse."

"That be hanged!" cried Hodge. "Oh, no. That won't do for I."

"Stop a bit," said Jack. "Now, look here, Hodge," continued Jack, tapping the rustic's arm with the handle of his whip. "The squire, if he would keep his grounds private, must have that fence mended."

"In coorse he must."

"Very well. And to mend it, wood must be bought."

"That be right."

"And a man paid, for putting it in order."

"Ees, that be right, too."

"The wood would cost seven shillings?"

"Quite."

"And the man would want to be paid three, for mending the fence?"

"Ees, he would."

"And that makes ten," said Jack, "does it not?"

Hodge counted on his fingers, and looked up with a grin.

"Ees, that makes ten."

"Which the squire would have to find, of course?"

"Of course."

"Now, if that fence had been permitted to remain whole, as it was, the squire would not have to pay for wood or labour to repair it; so you see, Hodge, that you might as well have taken ten shillings out of his pocket. You stole money's worth, if not the actual coins, and are a thief in every sense of the word."

Hodge looked very downcast, and his eye fell before the look of Spring-heeled Jack.

"I tell you what it is, Hodge, the squire, and, in fact, most persons of property in country places, have to submit to a great deal too much of this kind of pilfering, and I trust that you, for one, will desist from so disreputable a practice, and urge your fellows to do the same; or, depend upon it, one of these days you will find yourself in a more unpleasant position than you were a short time since. And, bear in mind also, that the man who disgraces himself by an act of dishonesty, disgraces his friends; and his family are the greater sufferers, for not only does the law punish him, but the thief inflicts a fearful punishment on the innocent by leaving them to beg or starve. Now, go to your work, or your home, whichever you are on your way to, Hodge, and think over what I have said, and try not only to become honest yourself, but urge others to be the same."

Hodge scratched his head, and turned silently away, ashamed to look into the eyes that glared down upon him, and convinced, for the first time in his life, that the squire had good cause to be angry.

Jack stood gazing after him as he strode along with his awkward step, unconsciously tapping his foot with the squire's whip, and with a feeling of mingled pity and contempt, and finally muttered, half aloud—

"And that is a man. Well, in form he is one certainly, and not a bad specimen. He has muscle and strength, but thought and discrimination, where are they? Pinch him, and he feels the smart; but if he pinches another, he cannot imagine the same pain is inflicted. Selfishness is natural to an ignorant mind. He is a mere machine, and must be worked by the intellect of others. Sad—very sad! But such as he are their greatest enemies. Persuade him to send his child to school—persuade him that the child will benefit thereby, and he would not believe you. He has not the power to look forward. He lives but for the time; works while strength remains, and dies in a poorhouse. He has no ambition, no pride, no self-respect. He considers his best advisers his enemies, and makes foes where he could secure friends. Doubtless, to-morrow, if he saw a loose hurdle, he would take it home for firewood, despite what I have said; for I verily believe he will think no more of the lesson I have read him, unless it be to make light of it at the village ale-house."

And still tapping his boot with the whip, Jack continued his walk musingly down the road, quite forgetting that he still held in his hand Squire Hepworth's property.

He kept on for about a mile further, when the yelping of a dog caused him to look off the high road to the right, and, perceiving a silvery stream meandering its course along amid bushes and tall trees, Jack resolved to turn out of the high road, and follow its course for a short distance.

He had no particular object in view, but the cool, smooth waters looked so tempting that he could not resist the temptation of a stroll along their banks.

He reached the edge of the stream, and stood looking into the clear waters for some time, thinking over his adventure with the squire, and gazing down at the reflection of his own figure, when he started, from a small dog sniffing round his legs, and, giving the animal a gentle cut with the whip, turned and walked on.

On passing a large tree, which stood upon the bank, he paused, and nearly laughed outright; for right before him, on the edge of the stream, stood the tall, attenuated figure of an aged gentleman engaged in fishing.

So deeply was he absorbed in his occupation that he observed not the presence of our hero; and Jack drew still nearer, and, pausing close by his side, took an inventory of this disciple of Walton.

He was a man between fifty and sixty years of age, and thin almost to attenuation, his long, slender arms supported a long, slender rod; and, as if unable to bear the weight of his long body, his long, thin legs were bent at the knee, giving the old gentleman a half sitting attitude. He was habited in a surtout coat,[158] plaid trousers, low, broad-brimmed hat, and gaiter boots, an enormous frill stuck out from his bosom, and a terribly stiff stock encircled his thin neck. He wore an eye-glass in his eye, and a look of such comical anxiety sat enthroned on his features as he gazed at the float bobbing up and down on the surface of the stream, that Jack thought he had never before seen such a strange looking personage.

At his feet was a green painted tin can, the lid of which was perforated with holes, and which was intended to receive the fish when caught, but which apparently contained nothing at present.

Jack edged up close to the old man's side.

"A fine morning, sir?" he said.

But the angler took no notice of him.

The words were repeated.

Still the same result.

The old man either did not, or would not, hear; neither did he turn his gaze from off the float, bobbing about by the action of the wind or water.

On that his very thought and sense appeared to be centred.

Jack stood silent for some moments, and then, in a louder tone, remarked—

"Have you had good sport, sir?"

---

[158] Overcoat resembling a frock coat.

But Jack might as well have spoken to the tree by his side, for he received no answer.

"The old gentleman is deaf, I suppose," thought Jack, "but surely he can't be blind as well? How intent he gazes upon that float—how motionless he stands. He might almost be taken for a statue, only statues don't wear frilled shirts, or carry eye glasses; at least, I never recollect seeing one that did. If he won't look or speak, I wonder if he can feel? I'll first touch him to make him acquainted with my presence."

Jack stretched forth his hand to touch the old gentleman's shoulders, but paused as the angler gave vent to the half grunt, half laugh of satisfaction.

"Got a bite?" said Jack.

No answer, but the old man commenced to talk to himself.

"Oh!" he exclaimed, in a half whisper, "I shall have him yet; he's been hovering round the bait these three hours, getting a nibble now and then; but he'll have a taste too much—he'll bite too deep. There he goes—there he goes—now he comes back—he's close to the bait. Eh! the rascal!—he's artful. No—yes— there—confound it! but I'll have him yet, the rascal—I'll have him yet."

"Who will you have, old gentleman?" asked Jack, feeling assured the angler must see him now.

"The devil!—eh, the devil! he's gone for another swim," cried the old man.

"Does his satanic majesty indulge in aquatic sports?" asked Jack, smiling.

"There he is, flapping his tail," continued the old gentleman, never once moving a muscle of his face, or taking his eyes from the float. "Down he goes. No; up he comes. He can't resist another taste. Ay!—no—yes—no, he don't. Confound him; he's off again. Them jacks[159] are perfect devils—so full of fun—so confounded artful. Now, only think one should be close to my rod all this while. But I'll have a hook in his gills before I go."

"Which Jack does he mean, I wonder?" smiled our hero. "But there can be no doubt of that, for his attention is so wrapped in the jack down there, that he will not bestow a glance on the one up here. Well, if that is patience, it is a virtue I do not possess, I must confess. Three hours' standing in one position, and gazing upon one object, is something beyond me."

"There he goes!" muttered the old gentleman, again bursting forth. "Now, back again— closer—closer! Now he smells it—now—now! No, damn it! it ain't a bite after all. Never mind! Never mind! If they bit at once, there'd be no sport; and this is capital! capital!"

Jack shrugged his shoulders, and thought otherwise.

"Hallo! he's back again! Steady!—oh, oh! Now—no—yes—yes! A bite! hurrah! a jack at last!"

Wonderful was the change, in an instant, in the old man's face, as he gave the line a jerk, and hooked the fish he had so long watched and toiled for.

"Right in his gills he's got it. Eh! eh! Master Jack; it's right in your gills."

And the old man, leaping backwards, caught our hero a blow under the chin with his rod, screaming out at the same time, "A jack at last—a jack at last!" but, turning at the obstruction, the sudden joy vanished from his face—the rod fell from his grasp, and he tottered backwards to the very edge of the stream.

---

159 Freshwater pike.

"Do not be alarmed, old gentleman, cried Jack, taking a step forward, "I am only"—

"The devil!" cried the old man, making an attempt to retreat still further back, and losing his balance, rolled over the edge of the bank into the stream, where he commenced to flounder about and make frantic efforts to grasp at his rod, which hung partially over the water.

Jack laughed outright at the comical figure he cut, but instantly rushed to his aid; but the old gentleman had floundered out of his reach, so, taking the rod from the bank, he held it towards him, and the angler, nothing loth, grasped at the other end. Jack drew him in till he could take him by the hand and land him on the bank, where he stood, a most comical picture to behold, dripping wet and smothered with mud, glaring upon one Jack and then upon the other!

CHAPTER XCVII.
THE ANGLER AND OUR HERO—A BAD TEMPER AND A SUBMISSIVE HUSBAND.

JACK could not refrain from laughter, although he felt sorry at the misfortune of the old gentleman, and his sensibility was not a little enhanced when the aged angler, in his anxiety to secure the fish, which seemed of more importance to himself than anything else, received a severe bite on the finger from the voracious jack, as he attempted to take it from the hook.

"Who the devil are you, sir?" cried the old gentleman, angrily. "Confound you for a fool, sir. There's my finger half off, and all through you, sir. Do you know you are trespassing, sir? —do you know that, sir?"

The old gentleman had unhooked the fish and slipped it quietly into the tin can.

"You ask too many questions at once, my ancient friend."

"Ancient!—who do you call ancient! I'd have you to know, sir, that I am only sixty-five, and a young man at that, sir. I'm not so strong as I was, sir, twenty years ago, or I'd—what do you think I'd do, sir?"

"Positively, I cannot say," replied Jack.

"Then, I'll tell you, sir," said the old gentleman, fiercely.

"I should be happy to hear?"

"I'd—I'd—yes, damn it, sir, I'd fling you into that stream, sir, and make bait of you for the fish, sir—that's what I would do."

"You are very kind, certainly," said Jack. "I am very glad indeed that you are twenty years older; for, upon my word, old gentleman, I should cut a sorry figure after I got out, with the mud and the slime clinging to me, as it does to you. But, don't be angry. Take my advice, and go home. A change of dress would not be out of place, I am sure."

"Go home!" cried the old man. "And my day's sport spoilt by an idiot who walks about with a mask on his face."

"Surely, you had no intention of remaining at the end of that rod all day?" said Jack.

"Yes, I did; and your confounded fooling has robbed me of my sport," said the old gentleman, sadly.

"Believe me, sir, I sincerely regret"—

"Bah! What's the use of that? Now I must go home, and a pretty scene there will be with my wife," said the old gentleman, despairingly.

"Never mind, sir. A woman's sympathy"—

"A woman's fiddlestick," growled the other. "Mrs. Tomkins is not the woman to sympathize. No, sir, her tongue will go thirteen to the dozen, I warrant you. I'd as soon meet the devil himself as meet her in this state. And yet, how can I avoid it?"

"So the old lady has a tongue, has she?" said Jack.

"A tongue? Yes, longer than my fishing-rod. I shall never hear the last of it—never."

And the old gentleman's face became more gloomy as he spoke, and he looked despairingly at his soaked and soiled habiliments.

"Perhaps she don't admire fishing?" said Jack.

"Confound her, no. What woman does? Angling, sir, requires an amount of patience that no woman in the world ever yet possessed. No, sir, not one of them from the time of Eve downwards."

"And many men, too," said Jack. "But have you far to go home?"

"About half a mile," said the old gentleman, "and here's a pretty figure to move along the high road!"

"Certainly your appearance has not been improved by your ducking."

"Improved! Damn it! sir, I look like a drowned rat, with my things clinging to me. My appearance"—

"Is laughable, at least," interrupted Jack; "but no one will see you."

"No one see me!"

"No, sir—not if you will take my advice," said Jack, with a smile.

"What is that?"

"Hide yourself behind your fishing-rod."

"Eh!—what? What the devil do you mean by poking your fun at me, sir?" said the old gentleman, turning very red in the face.

"Indeed, you might escape a deal of observation by so doing," said Jack. "Your usually attenuated frame is so much thinner since your misfortune that, if you will only walk in the shadow of your fishing-rod, I am sure you will not be seen."

"You rascal, you!" cried the old man, unclasping the first joint of the rod, and raising it above his head threateningly, "I've half a mind to lay this over your shoulders."

"So long as the other half inclines your mind not to attempt it, I don't care," said Jack, "But come, old gentleman, don't let us be bad friends, for I sincerely regret your ill luck."

"Then what the devil did you pop on me so suddenly for?"

"I stood beside you for some time ere you saw me."

"Then why didn't you speak?"

"I did more—I positively bellowed, to attract your attention," was Jack's reply; "but you were so intent upon the capture of the jack in the water that you would neither see nor hear the Jack on shore. Your whole mind was so absorbed in the sport, as you term it, that you had neither eyes nor ears for anything else. Come, sir, lower your rod, and let us be friends."

"Friends! I've a good mind to bide you[160] as long as I can stand over you. But there, I— well, there—I won't be angry!"

And the old man lowered the upraised cane, and extended his hand to Jack, who shook it warmly.

---

160 Remain with you.

"I seldom travel without a flask of brandy," said Jack, placing his hand in his pocket, and drawing forth a leather bottle. "Take a good pull out of this. It will save you from catching cold."

The old man's eyes twinkled, as he grasped the flask.

"If there's anything I take a pleasure in besides angling, it's brandy," he said.

"Oh! you are partial to it, are you?"

"Very; but my wife won't let me have it."

"Perhaps you indulge too deeply?" said Jack, with a mischievous twinkle of the eye.

"No, sir, it's not that, it's"—

"What?" asked Jack, as the other hesitated.

"Mrs. Tomkins is so fond of it herself, that she is afraid if I drank it, there wouldn't be enough for two of us," said the old man, winking over the flask he placed to his lips.

"Oh, that's it, is it?" said Jack.

"Yes, that's it. And if she has had a drop this morning, her tongue will go enough to drive a poor devil mad. Only give her an excuse for talking, and when she begins there's no knowing when she'll stop; a pretty fine excuse she'll have now, when she sees me in this pickle. Confound it! I wish I could get in without her seeing me."

"You should not allow her to indulge too freely in her favourite liquor," said Jack, "if it makes her bad tempered."

"Well, you see, sir, I am passionately fond of fishing, and she don't like it; so, in order to have my way, I let her have hers," said the old gentleman, confidentially.

"Oh I see," said Jack. "So, by mutual consent, you humour each other's failing."

"That's it. I enjoy my passion, and she hers, and things run smoothly enough, unless something upsets her."

"And you fear she will be upset now?"

"I'm sure of it."

"Perhaps not."

"But she will. Why, bless you, I know what it will be. She'll see me coming towards the house, off she'll pop to the big box in the back parlour, just behind the screen where she keeps her bottle of brandy, take a good swig to nerve her for a rumpus, and then— oh, then, you should hear her!"

"It would afford me much pleasure to"—

"Not if you had as much of it as I have," interrupted Mr. Tomkins, quickly.

"I was about to observe, but you interrupted me, that it would afford me much pleasure to save you from the expected scolding, not that it would be gratifying to me to hear this lady's voluble tongue."

"I wish you could, but I tell you what, sir, I don't believe it is in the power of any living man to do it."

"She must be a perfect virago, then."

"She is worse than that, sir."

"Did you know her temper before you married her, Mr. Tomkins?" said Jack.

"What a question!"

"Well, I must confess it is a rude one," said our hero.

"As if any woman in the world ever showed her true temper till after the bait had taken, and she had hooked her fish," said the old gentleman, wiping the moisture and mud from his shirt-frill with his wet pocket-handkerchief.

"Then you were deceived in her, Mr. Tomkins?"

"I was caught—hooked as clean as that jack. Confound him!"

And the old gentleman looked mournfully at his bitten finger, which the voracious fish had fastened its sharp teeth into.

"Well, I suppose you have pretty well got used to it by this time?" observed Jack, after a pause.

"Used to it, oh yes; but that makes it none the more pleasant, does it?"

"Certainly not."

"I have been used to it for quite six years now—yes, six years," said the garrulous old gentleman. "It's as near about that time as possible."

"Then you had many years of uninterrupted happiness?" said Jack, playfully tapping his boot with the squire's riding whip.

"Not with the present Mrs. Tomkins."

"Oh! I see. She is your second wife?"

"No; she is my third."

"The others were not such scolds?"

"Bless you, no. They were angels, sir—angels of tempers. Never said a word against my passion for angling. Never objected to my killing a cat now and then, so that I could have a good stock of gentles[161] whenever I required them. Never said the fish I caught were stinking, and they could not think how I could make such a fool of myself by standing all day on the bank of the stream watching the float bobbing up and down as this one does. Never threatened to break my rod over my shoulders, or wished I might hang myself with my line. No, sir, they used to praise me for my patience; but times is altered now, sir, very much altered, indeed."

And Mr. Tomkins raised the flask again to his lips, and drowned the sigh that swelled his chest, in a deep draught of the fiery liquid.

"Ah, sir! it's a bad thing to have a scolding wife," he continued, handing back the flask to Jack, with a look of the most comical grief; "and you would say so, too, if you knew her as well as I do; and yet no one could tell by her looks what a passionate temper she has got. Why, if you was to see her now, coming along, you'd take her to be the most amiable creature in the world. But see her at home, and"—

"Mr. Tomkins! Mr. Tomkins!" cried a voice, in the distance.

Mr. Tomkins was packing up his fishing-tackle, as the voice fell upon the ears of Jack, and, with a look of utter dismay on his face, he dropped the rod to the ground, and turned in the direction whence the sound had come, exclaiming—

"That's her! that's her!"

"Mrs. Tomkins, do you mean?" said Jack.

"Yes, sir, my wife. She'll see me! Oh, dear! there will be a row."

"Then I had better be off," said Jack.

"No, no, don't! Do stay, there's a good fellow," cried the old gentleman, in a pleading tone.

"Really, I cannot longer intrude."

"No intrusion, believe me," cried Tomkins, his long thin legs trembling as he spoke.

---

[161] Maggots for fishing bait.

"I could not think of being a witness to your affectionate interview, my dear sir," said Jack. "So I will bid you good morning."

"Mr. Tomkins! Where are you?" came a shrill voice.

"Now, don't go, there's a good fellow," pleaded Tomkins, "and I'll introduce you to her."

"Some other time," said Jack. "I do not feel equal to the task of confronting the lady."

"I beg—Oh, lor'! here she is. I'm booked!"

Jack glided quickly away behind the tree, against which the old gentleman had stood, and Mr. Tomkins turned to confront a tall, ill-tempered looking lady, who at that moment appeared in the bend of the path.

"Oh, you are there, are you?" she exclaimed, as soon as she caught sight of the old gentleman.

"Yes, my dear," answered Tomkins, meekly.

"And I to wait all day long for you coming home to dinner. Oh, goodness gracious! there's a pretty mess you are in!"

And the lady held up her hands in horrified amazement.

Tomkins stood trembling before her, in speechless terror.

"You nasty, vile, wretched, disreputable, unfeeling"—

"My dear."

"Don't dear me, sir. How did you get in that state? What have you been doing?"

"My dear, I"—

"Don't dear me, Mr. Tomkins. I'm not your dear, or anybody else's. Was ever a poor woman compelled to put up with such a stupid dolt? Mr. Tomkins, your goings on is enough to vex the temper of a saint. There's a state! there's a—Oh! you villain!"

And Mrs. Tomkins, overcome with her feelings, shook her hands in Mr. Tomkins' face, and stamped her foot upon the rod.

"It's all owing to this stupid fishing. But I'll put a stop to it! I'll break every rod, and burn every line. Oh, you dirty, unfeeling man! Look at yourself, ain't you ashamed of yourself! There's a sight for a poor unfortunate woman to look upon! Mud and filth, and soaked to the skin! But you may clean yourself, and wash your own clothes, Mr. Tomkins. I'll not do it, nor shall the servant. If you will fall into the water, in your stupid eagerness for fish catching, you may suffer for it."

"So I do, my dear. But"—

"Don't 'but' me, Mr. Tomkins! Don't speak to me—don't look at me! I'm ashamed of you, sir! I'm disgusted at you! I'm—I'm —oh dear! oh dear! Why did I ever become Mrs. Tomkins?"

Whether it was the words of his spouse, or the brandy of Jack that roused the meek spirit of the old angler, it is hard to say; but when the old lady, for want of breath, came to a pause, Mr. Tomkins drew his lank form up, and, looking into his wife's face, exclaimed—

"I'll tell you, ma'am. It was because"—

"What, you vile man?"

"Because you couldn't get anybody else fool enough to have you," cried the old gentleman. "That's why you became Mrs. Tomkins."

"Oh!" gasped the lady, as if the explanation had fairly taken her breath away. "Oh, you old wretch! You—you tell me this!"

"I do," said Tomkins.

"Because I couldn't get anybody else!" shrieked Mrs. Tomkins. "Oh, I shall faint! I know I shall die!"

"I wish you would," said Tomkins, in a loud voice.

"You do, you villain, do you?" cried his wife. "Yes, I expect you do. You have long tried to kill me with your unkindness. You would murder me, only you know you dare not. But what can I expect of a man who wastes half his time catching poor little fish—makes sport of their sufferings? Why, that tells what you are—that tells what you are, Mr. Tomkins!"

And Mrs. Tomkins took out her handkerchief and held it to her eyes—a proceeding which seemed to cause Mr. Tomkins a certain amount of uneasiness; for his tall body shrank some inches, and the look of indignation he had summoned to his face gave place to one of the utmost concern.

He put one of his long arms forward, and with his thin hand gently drew the kerchief down from her face.

"My dear Mrs. Tomkins," he exclaimed, "don't take on so! Pray, don't, for my sake. I can't bear to see you weep—to hear your"—

"Go home, sir! go home at once!" cried the lady. "Don't speak to me! don't pretend to feel for me! It's all hypocrisy, sir! You care for nobody, you unfeeling man! I'm a poor, neglected woman! I'm a—. But I won't talk to you here, sir. Go home, and make yourself decent, and then I'll talk to you; then I'll let you know what I think of your conduct! Don't stand there looking at me, but do as I bid you. I'm not equal to the task of making you acquainted with my feelings here. But go home; and then, sir, you shall know what I think— what I feel—what I mean."

And the lady flounced away, leaving poor Tomkins to gather up his tackle and follow her, which he did with a very trembling hand and woe-begone countenance, and slowly followed in the track of his wife.

As he left the spot, Jack came from his concealment, and, shrugging his shoulders, followed after them.

CHAPTER XCVIII.

THE ANGLER AND THE WRANGLER—JACK IN THE BOX.

THE wrathful Mrs. Tompkins never once turned her head to gaze upon the dripping and muddy form of her spouse, as she lead the way along the banks of the stream to the high road.

Still, if she kept her gaze before her, she threw her harsh squeaking tones behind her; and with suck volubility did she talk, that the poor angler could not get a word in edgeways, and, at length, gave up the hope in despair of reconciling his wife.

Jack kept on behind them, at the distance of some yards, greatly amused at the scene he was witnessing, without his presence for a moment being suspected.

But, if he was amused, he also felt pity for poor old Tomkins, who bore his scolding meekly; and, if ever Jack felt inclined to be rude to a lady, it was then.

Nothing would have given him greater pleasure than to have given her a shock like her husband's, and for her to have experienced the same results—namely, a good ducking.

"The lady must certainly have been indulging rather freely in her favourite beverage," thought Jack, "for she never could keep up such a running fire of words. They say drink loosens the tongue, and here we have proof of it. I think, certainly, she is not inebriated now, but I doubt much if she would not be with another taste, and if this is the treatment poor old Tomkins gets when she is sober, heaven defend us! what must it be like when she's tipsy? It's a sad thing to see a respectable man's wife give way to such a degrading vice—very sad; and, if I were Tomkins, I'd forsake my favourite sport to keep a watch upon her actions, and see that she did not have too much. I daresay it vexes her to see a man stand hour after hour looking at his own shadow in the water— a shadow, by the way, which, if a true likeness of his form, must be somewhat attenuated. Still, she forgets the respect due to herself when she forgets that for her husband. Egad! but it's a strange world, and the longer we live and the more we see, the more strange it appears."

By this time the aged lady had reached the high-road, followed by Tomkins carrying the tin can in his hand, and the fishing-rod under his arm; his long, thin legs looking even longer and thinner than usual, so tightly did his wet garments cling to his limbs.

Here Mrs, Tomkins turned for the first time since she left the spot of meeting with her husband.

Jack saw the movement, and shrunk back into the shadow of a large lime.

"There's a picture!—there's a picture!" said the lady, measuring her trembling spouse with her eyes, and pointing derisively at his wet garments with her forefinger. "Ain't you ashamed to go along the road in that state, or have you lost all shame, Mr. Tomkins? Have you drowned all self-respect and common decency in the water you are so fond of dabbling in! What will people say if they meet us? They'll say—and rightly too— what a fearful affliction that poor woman has to bear, by being tied up to a dirty, disreputable old man; and well they may, Mr. Tomkins—well they may."

Tomkins drew back terrified, as his wife stopped in her walk; but now, as she gave indications of starting on again, Tompkins hitched the rod higher under his arm, and, with some show of boldness, remarked—

"Hold! I'm no older than you are, ma'am."

Mrs. Tomkins stopped dead short.

A blush of wounded pride suffused her rather coarse features.

"Not older than I am! You good for nothing aged mummy!" she shrieked. "You are old enough to be my grandfather, and you know you are. Me, old! me! Don't you raise my temper, Mr. Tomkins; now don't. I'm cool as a cucumber now, despite your conduct; but don't tease me, Mr. Tomkins; don't make lying assertions, or you'll find I can get in a passion; yes, Mr. Tomkins, in a passion!"

"Of course, you are not in one now?" said Tomkins, in a meek tone.

"No, sir! I am not, sir! You never saw me in a passion, sir; though, heaven knows! you are enough to make a saint boil with rage. No, sir, I'm calm, and you know it; but I won't be answerable for myself if you goad me too far. Don't throw out such insinuations about my age, when you know you are an old man to me."

"I know the clerk put down fifty on the register when we were married, and that's only six years ago," said Tomkins.

"Mr. Tomkins—Mr. Tomkins!" gasped his wife. "Oh! you vile man!

"Fifty! And you know I ain't forty yet. No, nor thirty-five, either."

REWARD

"Oh! you—you"—

Mrs. Tomkins did not finish the sentence, otherwise than by a stamp of the foot, a flounce of the body, and a quick turn of her back upon him.

Tomkins grinned. He saw that he had got the best of it this time.

"Only thirty-five, ma'am?" he said. "How strange—very strange, when that scapegrace[162] son of yours is thirty-six."

Mrs. Tomkins fairly screamed.

"Yes, ma'am, thirty-six! So you see if you are not telling a lie, he must have been born before his mother," said Tomkins, his lank legs fairly trembling at the pleasure he experienced in being even for once with his scolding wife.

"Oh! was ever a poor woman allied to such a monster!" groaned the lady. "Mr. Tomkins, I'll drown myself, if"—

"Do, there's a good creature, do!" cried Tomkins, quickly. "You'd make fine bait, and I'd fish all over the spot where you went down. Lor', how I should enjoy the sport—rare sport —fine sport there'd be! Do, Mrs. Tomkins, do, and there's a good soul. Roach, dace, carp, jack! Oh! what a splendid haul!"

And the old gentleman positively looked radiant with the idea.

Mrs. Tomkins stood looking at the thin figure before her, as if she could not believe the evidence of her senses.

Was that shadowy form Mr. Tomkins?

Was that him—always so meek towards her—who expressed a wish that she would consign her body to the stream to bait fishes, and so enhance the pleasures of his favourite sport?

Could it be his tongue that gave utterance to such a wish?

It must be he. And yet she could hardly believe it.

But there was no mistake now. And Mrs. Tomkins drew herself up, furious in her wrath, before the attenuated man she called husband.

If a look could have slain him, he had been dead at her feet.

But it could not.

And so Tomkins returned her stare, and waited for what was to follow, swinging the tin can backwards and forwards in his hand.

It was a long time coming, however.

The lady's indignation and horror were so great that she could not articulate.

The words seemed as if they had to be torn up, and when they did come it was with a perfect burst.

"Mr.—Mr. Tomkins, I—I—oh!"

Overpowered with her feelings, she could say no more.

But the look she fixed upon him was quite as eloquent, and as much to the purpose as ever words could have been; and the old gentleman read there, in her red face, what he would have to expect when he got home.

He knew his dinner would consist of tongue, and plenty of it, too—the tongue of Mrs. Tomkins.

He dropped his eyes to the ground, and moved on with a very desponding cast of

---

162 Rascal.

countenance, thoughtfully swinging the tin can in which was the poor jack that had occupied Tomkins the whole morning to catch.

"I'm in luck's way," thought the old man. "Sport's been dull. I'm in a pretty pickle; and I expect—damn it! what a thing it is to have a scolding wife."

And he relapsed into a train of melancholy thought.

Mrs. Tompkins, however, could not remain silent till they reached their dwelling; and she paused yet once again when they got in sight of a pretty little villa that lay slightly back from the road.

"Mr. Tompkins," she said, in that hushed sort of whisper that tells, but too forcibly, of the effort to keep down the smouldering passions, "we are just at home, sir. Your words—your conduct have so unnerved me that I do not feel equal to the task of saying to you what I would say. No sir; but thank heaven! my shattered nerves will soon be repaired— this hysterical feeling will soon pass away, after I have sat down a moment to compose myself. And by the time you have made yourself decent, Mr. Tomkins, I shall be prepared to let you understand, in plainer language, what I think of your vile conduct. Now, sir," she added, pointing to the house, "go in, sir; let the servant see the beast you have made of yourself, sir. Go in before me, sir, and don't disgrace me, sir. You are the laughingstock of the whole parish, sir; you are a villain, sir—a wicked, cruel, unfeeling old rascal! Me fifty-six! Oh! I shall faint at the thought! I must take something to save me from going into hysterics."

"Go to the devil, if you like!" said Tomkins, dashing past her, and entering the little green gate of the garden which surrounded the white walled villa.

"The base creature!" cried Mrs. Tomkins, looking after him. "But he shall learn who's master, him or me. Oh, I'll let him see, I'll let him see. The fif— What a blessing it is I've got a little of the best brandy in the box behind the screen in the back parlour. That will give me nerve, that will open my mouth. Go to the devil, eh? No, I won't, Mr. Tomkins; but I'll go to a spirit, for all that, and then you'll think the very devil's in me, see, if you don't."

And shaking her hand at the little green gate, the passionate woman kicked it wide open, and bounced through the orifice into the little garden.

As she glided along the narrow walk, sweeping the box edging on either side with her dress, a rather strange-looking face peered over the top of the green paling, and twinkling eyes watched her form till it entered the house, then Jack's merry laugh rang out on the still air.

"What an angel of a temper," said our hero. "Poor old gentleman, I pity him. What's independence, luxury, to a man with a Mrs. Tomkins for a wife? I suppose she pays her first visit to the back parlour. Egad! but I will meet her there, if I can make my way up to the house without being seen. I'll just take a survey."

Jack again looked over the paling towards the house, and minutely examined the place.

"It won't do to try it from this side," he muttered, "for there is nothing to break the view from the house; but, if I mistake not, the thing can be easily enough done from the back. Yes, that little hedge of thorns will do nicely."

Chuckling to himself, Jack retraced his steps about twenty yards, and stood at the end of the row of green palings and the boundary of Mr. Tomkins' garden.

Here commenced a piece of land, used for nothing in particular and everything in general, for the stunted grass was here and there decked with a piece of broken china or brickbat and articles of rubbish, which Jack more than suspected had been flung over the palings by the happy couple at different times.

Entering this, after taking a survey both up and down the road, Jack kept close along the fencing of the garden till lie bad passed one house, and then he stretched up his head and looked over.

The vegetation at the back of the. house was thick and rank. Small trees had grown straggling for the want of cutting, and a general air of neglect was about the place.

Tompkins was too much engaged with his fishing to attend to his garden, and the lady of the house paid little heed to anything but the black bottle kept in the large box behind the screen in the back parlour.

The boughs intersecting each other formed, an unbroken hedge in front of the paling, and Jack saw at a glance that there was little prospect of his being seen from the house, as the undipped branches rising high above the wooden boundary would effectually shield him from observation.

Rolling the ample folds of his cloak up around him, so as to prevent it catching on the top of the pales, where the ingenious but not less cruel heart of man had driven several iron spikes, he placed his hand upon a spot where some of these rusty pieces of iron had rotted away, and giving a spring, went clean over them, and dropped on the other side between the paling and the bushes.

"So far, so good," said Jack, placing his hat straight on his head, which had been knocked away by a straggling twig of whitethorn. "Now to get to the back parlour—that's the thing."

He looked through the interstices of the branches, towards the window of the room in question.

One side of the window was partially opened, and by slightly shifting his position, Jack was enabled to see into the room.

All he saw there at present, however, was a tall screen, covered with pictures, and which was opened half across the room.

"Good again!" said Jack. "For, if the old woman is there—really, I beg her pardon for calling her old, though I would rather swear she was sixty than thirty—she will not see me, especially if I keep along behind the hedge as far as it goes. That will take me almost to the side of that window, and then one step places me behind the screen."

Having decided on this course, Jack was not long in making his way to the side of the long window. One hasty glance to see that the coast was clear, and he passed through it into the room.

Keeping close to the screen, and as much on one side of the window as possible, Jack listened.

Not a sound.

He raised his head, and peeped over the screen.

There was no one in the apartment.

But his eye fell on a large oak chest, just on the other side of the screen; and he passed round, and examined it minutely.

It was very large and very massive, having two large iron handles on either side, and an immense lock, with a key in the wards, in the front.

"If I were Tomkins, I should feel disposed to stop the old lady's tongue by shutting her up with her brandy," mused Jack. "The trunk is large enough to hold her."

At that moment the harsh voice of the lady addressing the servant saluted his ears.

"Mary, take Mr. Tomkins's plate away. I will dine alone today. If he wants any dinner, let him cook and eat his fish by himself. He shan't sit down with me."

"Yes, mum. The dinner's a spoiling, mum," said the maid, from another part of the house. "Shall I take it up, mum?"

"Yes," replied the lady. "I shall be ready in a minute."

Then Jack heard her footfall approaching the room, and was about to get behind the screen, when a thought struck him, and, hastily flinging up the lid of the large box, he stepped into it.

It contained nothing but a few black bottles, and as the lock of the room door clattered in the fingers of Mrs. Tomkins, Jack took off his hat, and sunk all of a heap in the trunk, pulling the lid down on top of him.

He had scarce done so, ere the lady entered the room.

"Oh, dear me!" she exclaimed, as she closed the door softly behind her. "Was ever poor woman tried like me? I declare, if it was not for the good a little drop of brandy does me, that man's conduct would kill me outright. He don't deserve to have a good wife, he don't! But, there! it all comes of marrying an old man. I should have been wise, and looked out for a dashing young fellow, after my poor dear Samuel died! But women are such weak and confiding creatures, so easily imposed on! But there's one comfort—a little drop of spirits will ease their pains, and I'm never without a drop in the box."

She had approached the box, and her hand rested on the lid.

"Ah!" she sighed; "what a blessing it is that there's such a thing as brandy! When one's spirits is down, another spirit raises—oh! Oh! Murder! Tomkins! my dear Tomkins, save me! save me!"

To the unspeakable horror of Mrs. Tomkins, the lid of the box flew out of her hand, and up sprang the gaunt figure of Spring-heeled Jack right before her, who, as the old lady fell backwards into an armchair screaming lustily, placed his hand upon his heart, and made a low obeisance.

"You are fond of spirits, madam," he said, in his hollow tone. "Permit me to introduce your humble servant—the devil!"

CHAPTER XCIX.

THE HOUSEHOLD IN AN UPROAR.—THE FLIGHT THROUGH THE
GARDEN, AND HOW IT CAME TO AN END.

FOR some moments the old lady lay back, half-fainting with terror, with her head hanging over the back of the chair, and, in her fright, terribly crushing her bonnet, which she had not removed since she had entered the house; and our hero, with the brim of his hat pressed against his chest, with his head bowed and body bent, looked up from under his brows at the terror-stricken woman.

After her first cry of terror, the lady's voluble tongue apparently became paralyzed.

The organ on which she played so furiously, to the dismay of her spouse, here became tuneless—not a note could she get out of it—though it was evident from the motions of her almost bloodless lips that she tried hard.

But the shock had silenced her.

Yes, Jack had done more in one single moment than poor Mr. Tomkins had been enabled to accomplish in six years—more, in fact, than he ever hoped to accomplish in the rest of the days allotted to him.

Certainly it was more than Mrs. Tomkins herself would have given any man credit for—she would as soon have believed a babe could stop the roll of the ocean than anything short of death prevent her having her say.

With her head laying on the back of the arm chair, and her eyes fixed on the figure in the box, Mrs Tomkins at length succeeded in giving vent to a sort of hysterical sob.

This was followed in rapid succession by another, and another; and then the feet began to beat a strange tattoo on the floor of the apartment.

Quicker and quicker became the movement, and then a wild, half laugh, half cry escaped her, and Jack knew that the lady had gone into a fit of hysterics.

"That's more than Tomkins could do, I'll wager," said Jack, stepping from the box; "and I think he owes me a debt of gratitude for so befriending him as to possibly prevent the old lady indulging her scold for a little while. Hallo! here's either the old man or the maid coming."

A footstep had reached his ear, and he quickly darted behind the screen. In another moment a slatternly-looking young woman entered the apartment.

"Did you call, mum? Oh, lor'! Master! master! missus has gone in high strikes,[163] and is a trying to beat her brains out on the back of the chair! Master! Mr. Tomkins! Oh, sir! Do come down, sir!"

And the maid sprang out of the room in the greatest alarm.

"What's the matter?" cried Tomkins, from the landing.

"Oh! missus is a screeching and a knocking so sir, in the back parlour," answered the maid. "Do come down."

"I can't; I'm undressed."

"Oh! make haste, sir, I'm so frightened."

"You must wait. What's she knocking for?" said Tomkins.

"And she can't help it, sir. Oh, do come, sir."

"You must wait till I'm dressed," cried Tomkins. "I can't come down in my shirt."

"Oh, don't stop for anything, sir," cried the girl, in her alarm.

"You look to her. I don't suppose it's anything, after all," growled Tomkins.

He was a lucky fellow, that Mrs. Tomkins did not hear him.

"Oh, yes, sir, she's in high strikes, sir, and she's a smashing her bonnet awfully."

"Eh!" cried Tomkins, in quite a different voice. "Doing what?"

"A smashing her bonnet, sir."

"I'll be down directly, Mary. Smashing her bonnet! There's something wrong to a certainty, when a woman smashes her own bonnet."

And with this the old gentleman proceeded to hurry on his clothes in the utmost trepidation. Indeed, so eager was he to get them on, that he thrust his long legs through the sleeves of his sparrow-tail coat, and did not discover his mistake till he found he was unable to button it round his loins.

In his eagerness to remedy the error, he drew on his trousers over the coat; then, giving vent to a curse, tore them right down one of the legs, in his eagerness to get them off again.

---

[163] Into hysterics.

To add to his confusion, were the loud cries of Mary, the maid, as she clung to the bottom rail of the bannisters, and begged him to make more speed, for she was afraid to go to the room by herself.

The girl had seen and heard so much of her mistress's temper, that she had no desire to be alone with her in the state she was then in.

Meanwhile, Jack and Mrs. Tomkins were left to themselves in the little parlour, and when the former found that there was but little prospect of either the master or maid entering the room immediately, he stepped out from behind the screen, and approached the hysterical lady.

He looked at her for a moment, curiously; then went to the large box, and, taking out each of the bottles, placed them behind the screen, leaving it perfectly empty.

"If I could shut down the lid of the box, there can be but little fear of hurting the old dame, if I try it on her," he muttered; "and it will afford me some amusement to see the surprise of old Tomkins and his servant when they enter the room. Come on, my dear young lady—only thirty six. Ha! ha!" but Jack lifted the insensible woman from her chair, and bore her gently to the box; hesitating for a moment, he placed her within it, and satisfying himself that she would in no way be injured by the lid when closed upon her, he took one of the bottles, forced it in her hands, and placed its neck to her mouth.

He looked down upon her as she lay in the trunk, for a moment, and then closed the lid upon her.

"It's too bad, I know," muttered Jack, as he took up his position behind the screen; "but I can't resist the inclination to punish her for her nagging at the old gentleman; and perhaps it may have the effect of breaking her of the vice to which she is evidently greatly addicted—at all events, I don't believe she will ever keep her brandy in that chest again."

The maid still continued to importune the old gentleman to hurry himself; and, at length, attired only in the torn trowsers and shirt, Mr. Tomkins made his way down the stairs.

"Oh, sir! Oh, sir!"

"Hold your tongue," cried the old gentleman. "Why didn't you go in and see to her. It's only her violent passion, I expect, that has sent her off."

So thought the girl, and hence her reason for remaining in the passage.

Both at once they entered the room, and both at once they came to a dead stop just inside it.

Both looked hard into each other's face, and both at the same moment exclaimed—"Oh!"

The chair in which the old lady had sat was empty, and no Mrs. Tomkins was to be seen. Tomkins looked furious—the girl alarmed.

One was frightened and the other amazed.

The maid leaped to the conclusion that her mistress had rushed out at the window, without knowing what she was about, and the master instantly fancied the girl had been fooling him.

"What does this mean?" asked Tomkins.

"What can it mean?" asked the girl.

"My wife's not here!" cried Tomkins.

"My mistress has gone!" cried the maid.

Then both looked at the other again, and then at the window.

"Mary!"

"Master!"

"I'm"—

"So am I, sir."

Another pause, and another look round the room.

"Who told you to fetch me down in this state?" exclaimed Tomkins.

"Nobody, sir—that is, sir—oh! my, sir! Where's she gone?"

"Girl!"

Tomkins had caught hold of the maid's arm, and his tones were more severe than ever she had known them before.

"Yes, sir!"

"Look at me."

"Yes, sir!"

"I'm annoyed."

"So am I, sir!"

"I say, I won't submit to it."

"What, sir?"

"What!"

"Yes, sir!"

"I'll tell you what, Mary. If I'm compelled to submit to the goings-on of your missus, I won't submit to be annoyed by her servant."

"Sir, I"—

"Go to the kitchen, and never presume to"—

"Oh, sir!" interrupted the girl, bursting into tears.

Tomkins' heart became soft in a moment. Tears—he could bear anything but tears. He could remain indifferent to the scolding of his wife for hours; but when, at length, tears came, Tomkins could bear no more.

Many a bonnet had Mrs. Tomkins got through tears; many a draper's bill had been paid without a murmur, when sprinkled with tears; and even the maid herself could have got her wages rose, without a doubt, if she had only shed tears in asking for the advance.

"What are you crying for?" asked Tomkins, in a milder tone. "There! there! I forgive you. I know it was your mistress set you to make a fool of me, and, of course, you didn't know how to refuse her. But don't do it again, there's a good girl."

"I ain't a-making a fool of you, sir. Upon my word and honour, sir, I heard missus a screeching out, and came up to see what was the matter, and then I seed[164] her a sitting in that chair, a rolling her bonnet over the back rail, and beating the floor in a fit of high strikes, and I called you, sir."

"Where is she now?"

"Gone."

"But where? Did she go out at the door, or out at the window?"

"She never came out of the door."

"Then see if she is in the garden." The girl hurried across the room out of the window without perceiving Jack, who was crouching close to the screen, and concealing himself

---

[164] Saw.

in its folds.

"Hysterics!" growled Tomkins. "Don't wonder at it. What else can she expect, when she lets her passion almost drive her crazy, then she adds to it by drinking brandy. I suppose that's what she came here for now. Hallo! she's left the key in the lock."

The old gentleman looked anxiously towards the garden.

"Don't see anything of her," he continued, "so I'll just take a drop myself before she comes, just a little drop. Never knew her leave the key in the lock before. He! he! I wish she would leave it. All right, she won't know I've had any. Lor'! if she was only to see me take a drop, what a row there would be; but she won't see me, and so here goes."

The old gentleman cast one more look towards the window, then flung up the lid of the chest.

The howl of surprise to which he gave utterance on perceiving his wife lying within the trunk, with a bottle in her hand, and the neck of it to her lips, positively made Jack start, and had the effect of rousing his wife to instant sensibility.

The lady opened her eyes, and so did Tomkins, to such a width they had never been opened before, and both glared upon the other in unfeigned surprise.

Mrs. Tomkins was the first to thoroughly realize the truth of her novel position, and, taking the neck of the bottle from her mouth, in the course of a few moments, she hurled it, with all her force, at her husband, shrieking out at the same time—

"You—you villain!"

Fortunately for poor Tomkins, the missile went wide of its mark, and was shattered into a thousand pieces against the wall of the apartment.

"Mrs. Tomkins!" gasped her husband, "you are mad! Mary! Mary!"

"Mad—mad!" shrieked the lady, struggling to get out of the trunk, and treading on her skirt, in her eagerness, pitched out head foremost on to the floor.

Tomkins stood like one in a dream, while the lady scrambled to her feet, and, in all the fury of an enraged woman, stood before him.

"You villain! You viper! You assassin! Oh, you wretch!"

"Mrs. Tomkins!"

"Don't speak to me—don't! I see it all. You've long been tired of me. You can't get rid of me, and you have tried to murder me!"

"Good heavens! she is quite mad!"

"No, I'm not mad—you wicked, vile man, though you have tried to drive me so for a long time. Oh, yes—I see it all now! You tried to drive me mad by getting someone to frighten me, and then you put me in that trunk to suffocate me; and I should have been dead in a little while if I had not, fortunately, recovered. Oh, you monster! you monster!"

Tomkins stood dumbfoundered.

There was no mistaking his look of genuine surprise. And even Mrs. Tomkins at last began to alter her opinion.

"Me!—me put you there!" gasped Tomkins. "Me! Why—oh, she's quite mad, poor thing. Mary! Damn it! Where's that girl?"

If Tomkins was alarmed before, he was doubly so now.

Assured in his own mind that his wife had gone mad, he dreaded personal violence to himself.

So, keeping his eyes fixed upon her—for he had read somewhere that insane people quail before a steady glance—he shuffled towards the window in the hope of getting assistance.

He reached it, and, with one bound, went clean through it into the garden.

Terror had taken twenty years off his age, for he ran like a young man, shouting lustily for Mary, leaving Mrs. Tomkins standing in the middle of the room gazing after his retreating form.

As Tomkins disappeared, Jack sprang from behind the screen right in front of the bewildered woman, and the howl of terror that escaped her caused poor Tomkins to rush like mad out into the high road to seek the aid of some passer-by to place under restraint his afflicted wife.

As Mrs. Tomkins screamed, she shrank back, but the next instant she made a furious rush at the window.

In her eagerness to leave the room, she shattered a couple of panes of glass, the clatter of which brought Mary round the house, just as she sped away across the garden, screaming loudly to her husband.

Mary no sooner caught sight of Jack, as he, too, passed through the window, than she joined her cries to those of her mistress, and dashed away in the same direction.

Jack gave chase, and the maid, coming up with the mistress, seized her by the arm, and clung frantically to her, and, in unison, they both shrieked aloud for help.

In their terror they ran across the garden beds instead of keeping to the walk, and just as they approached a large cucumber frame, both turned their terrified gaze behind them.

Another shriek, louder than its predecessors, broke from their lips as they perceived Jack within a few yards of them, and, in their blind eagerness to escape, both mistress and maid ran full butt against the frame, staggered to regain their balance, lost it, and both fell headlong through the glass top, clutching frantically at each other.

Such a smash of glass—such a chorus of shrieks, Jack never heard before; and, feeling that the game he had played upon the old lady had been carried far enough, he first cast one glance on the two women as they rolled among the shattered glass and broken plants, and then, drawing his cloak around him, and pressing his hat over his brows, he glided quickly behind the hedge, and vaulted, unseen, over the paling, and, in another minute, was quickly strolling along the high road.

CHAPTER C.

AN OLD CHARACTER IN A NEW PART.

WHEN Bill Jackson waited upon Ralph Grasper, with the welcome intelligence that he had discovered the whereabouts of Jane Slater, that disreputable worthy made no mention whatever of the fact that the wife of the deceased clerk was residing with another female— one like herself, who had suffered much persecution from unfeeling man.

Had he done so, a strange mistake might possibly have been avoided.

Having learned the exact position of Holly Cottage, and obtained all the information he thought necessary, Mr. Grasper rewarded the dirty labours of Bill Jackson, and dismissed him.

Bill had expected further employment, but Grasper, fearful lest the man's terror of Jack might bring our hero down upon him when least wished for, resolved to employ someone else in the little bit of business he had on hand.

The merchant was not to be kept from the purpose of his heart by the chastisement he had received on more than one occasion from Spring-heeled Jack, he certainly was afraid of him, and knew that if he again fell into his clutches, it would go hard with himself, but he determined to risk all in again obtaining possession of the poor, insulted, and broken-spirited woman.

Defeat and resistance only seemed to add fuel to the fires of his callous heart. He was a man of firm resolves, and when he had once set his mind, he would go through with the work.

Grasper's was a nature which would not succumb to difficulties; indeed, the greater the obstacle, the more determined his purpose to surmount it.

Had Ralph Grasper possessed the heart and soul of a man, instead of that of a devil, he would have been an ornament, where he was now a curse to society.

As we have seen from the moment that his eyes fell upon the wife of his clerk, he had resolved to persecute her. He had done so and suffered greatly for it, but he was not deterred in his base purpose.

So, when Bill Jackson left him, clinking the gold coins in the pocket of his corduroy breeches, and thinking of the glorious "drunk" he would have with his disreputable associates at the Pigeon Flyers, the merchant sat down calmly to think over and mature his plans.

"Humph!" he coughed. "Let me see. Holly Cottage. Yes. I'll make a note of that. Pretty name for a decent dwelling. I know the locality well. It's where I once thought of lending a speculating builder some money on the carcases of a few houses, but unfortunately for me the fellow got hold of a more tender-hearted mortgagee, or I should have ruined him to a certainty. Well, Holly Cottage, where this Jane Slater is hidden, is out there, is it? Now, the best way to get her from it? I must not go rashly to work this time—no rash ventures—the speculation must be certain; and then, where's the goods to be consigned, that's the next point. Not to Bill Jackson's. Oh, no, that will never do. That confounded scamp of a Spring-heeled Jack will keep an eye on him. To send her to a foreign port won't do. I can't afford to let pleasure altogether interfere with business. A prolonged absence from home would be remarked—a few days at a time would scarcely be noticed. I have it! I'll take her to Brighton. Now, who can I get to assist me? That's the thing, and the principal thing, too."

Grasper leaned his head on his hand, and puzzled his brain for a solution to his own question.

"There are thousands," he muttered, at length, "in this vast city, who would sell their souls for a guinea, and surely I ought to have no difficulty in procuring an accomplice out of the vast number whom want or crime has rendered callous to the sufferings of others or their own situation. Could I proclaim aloud my wishes, legions would answer to the call. To the just man, what a sad contemplation; to the unprincipled, like myself, how gratifying is the thought, that thousands are as bad, if not worse, than myself. There are few men whose hearts are not naturally prone to evil, and the poor sin through want, the rich through their passions; and yet, with this knowledge of the world, I dare not cry aloud for the aid I require. Still, I must not suffer that to deter me from my purpose. Jane Slater must and shall be mine, even if I tear her from her concealment unaided!"

He struck his clenched hand on the table as he finished speaking, and bounded from his seat.

"Yes. In spite of a thousand Jacks, I will yet humble her pride, break her haughty spirit, make her a thing loathsome even to herself. I swear to do so, and I will keep my oath, not that I have more respect for an oath than the ground on which I tread, but my mind is made up. And those who know Ralph Grasper, can assert he never broke his word, where his own interest or gratification was concerned. It was love which first prompted me to obtain this woman, but now 'tis hatred and revenge."

He paced the narrow limits of his room for some time in meditative silence, knitting his heavy brows together, and twisting his massive gold watch-guard round his finger, with a fierceness which threatened to snap their links asunder.

"Yes, tonight!" he muttered at last, "I will tear her from her retreat—from her place of fancied security, and hear her miles away where I need fear no rescue by that rascal, whom the walls of a gaol should keep from her protection. This night—this very night! There shall be no delay, I am resolved, if I have to bear her in my arms the whole distance. Curses upon the hand that tore her from me! But she shall be beyond its grasp—far beyond it— beyond all aid."

He seized his hat, and was about to leave the room, when a gentle knock at the door caused him to change his severe look, and utter, in a calm tone—

"Come in."

The door opened slowly, and an aged lady stood on the threshold.

Grasper measured her with his eyes, and then, somewhat gruffly, exclaimed—

"Well, madam, what do you require?" With a simpering smile, the lady curtseyed, and entered the room, and Grasper recollected that he had often seen her before.

It was none other than Miss Frump, the mischief-making old maid whom Jack and the young cashier had so sadly plagued, for her garrulous and unfeeling nature.

But the poor lady did not seem to be quite so lively as she used to be, a circumstance which may be accounted for by the following conversation:—

"Oh! it's you, is it! Miss—Miss"—

"Frump, sir. Yes, Miss Frump," interrupted the lady. "You recollect me, sir—one of your neighbours!"

"Yes, slightly," said Grasper. "And, pray, to what am I indebted for this visit?"

"Well, sir, the fact is," said the lady, first looking up, and then down, and toying with the fringe on her shawl, "I have called"—

"Yes—yes! Be quick, if you please; for it is time I was at my office," said Grasper, rather testily.

"Well, sir, the fact is"—

Miss Frump paused, raised her eyes timidly to those of Grasper, and heaved a deep sigh.

"Is what?" said the merchant.

"Why, sir, you see, I'm a lone woman, who has always done my best to keep myself respectable, and never interfered with anybody or anything that didn't concern me. I've always kept myself to myself, and, in consequence, I've been grossly imposed upon and persecuted."

"What is that to me, ma'am?" growled Grasper.

"Nothing, sir; only, as I was a saying, being a lone woman, as keeps herself to herself, and minds her own business, I've been made a victim of by cruel, unprincipled people. I have got a little income, but it ain't much; and so, to be able to be respectable, I took a house— you know it, sir, down the road—and let furnished lodgings to respectable aged gentlemen. Well, sir, one went away without paying me at all, and the others—oh! it breaks my heart to think of the base ingratitude of cruel, unfeeling men!"

"What has all this to do with me, Miss Frump?" said Grasper, quite out of patience.

"You shall know, sir; but it ain't everybody I would speak to as I do to you. The other lodger, the deaf gentleman in the parlour, has left me under the most painful circumstances. Of course, I don't mind telling you of his cruelty, the wicked deceiver. We were going to be married, when all at once he lacerated my heart by refusing to lead me to the altar, and packed up his traps and started, even refusing to pay me for the last six months' board, lodging, and attendance—and now my house is empty."

"But, Miss Frump, I cannot possibly see what your misfortunes have to do with me, a stranger to you," said Grasper, putting on his hat, as a hint to the lady to take her departure.

"I'll tell you, sir. I've come to the determination to give up keeping house for myself, sell my furniture, and go into service."

"Well, ma'am, I should advise you to seek a situation at once. Good morning."

"That's what I'm doing, Mr. Grasper," said the lady, taking no notice of the hint.

Grasper opened his eyes.

"You see, sir, knowing that you was a nice gentleman, without any incumbrances, I thought, perhaps, that a respectable, middle-aged single lady might be just the sort of person to suit you."

"Suit me!" cried Grasper. "What the devil do I want with an old woman hanging about me? I have my health, and I hope it will be a long while yet before I shall require a nurse."

"A nurse! Lor', sir! I could never descend so low—a housekeeper."

"Well, I don't want a housekeeper. I can't be bothered with a house."

"But, sir, as I was saying, I thought, perhaps, as you were a single gentleman, who must find it very unpleasant living in lodgings, that if you could meet with a respectable, middle-aged, domesticated person like myself, you might feel disposed"—

"Miss Frump, I don't feel disposed to listen to you any longer. If you wish to give up housekeeping for yourself, and do it for someone else, you can do so, but it will not be for me. I am very well suited as I am; and if I was not, I do not think I should engage any person of your age to look to my house."

"My age, sir," said Miss Frump, her face scarlet, either with blushes or indignation.

"Yes, ma'am, your age. You are seventy, I suppose, and would be ill-fitted to look after the house of anyone."

"Sir, I'm not. But you are jesting, Mr. Grasper; you are such a nice, merry-hearted man, I used to often say to my back parlour lodger when I saw you pass the house. Yes, sir, I used to often say what a nice-looking gentleman Mr. Grasper is. Why, if I was ever to go into service, I don't know where I should so like to go as to his house."

"Humph!" coughed the merchant.

"Yes, sir. You don't know how often I used to say so. Lor' bless you, sir, I can tell a man the moment I look at him; and if my back parlour lodger had only been such a one as you, I should never have given up housekeeping, and Miss Frump would have been Mrs. Duppy."

"I'm much obliged to you for your good opinion of me, I'm sure; but I can only say that I'm not likely to require the services of any person like yourself," said Grasper.

"Ah, me!" sighed the old lady. "I'm so sorry, for I am sure you would like me very much."

"Perhaps so, ma'am; but I'm not very partial to old ladies."

"Oh! you sly, funny man!" said Miss Frump, appearing to feel pleased, but, in reality, feeling as if she would like to pull his iron-gray whiskers out of his face. "I see you would like a young housekeeper. Perhaps you think of getting married?"

Grasper frowned, and bit his lips impatiently.

"Ah! I can see! I can see!" said Miss Frump. "Oh, you men! What strange creatures you are, to be sure. So, you are really going to get married, Mr. Grasper. I can tell by your blushes."

"Bah!" cried Grasper. "And if I were, what of that?"

"You might still require someone to keep house to the lady, young sir."

"What lady?"

"What lady? There now. Why, you know you can confide in me," said Miss Frump, in a wheedling tone.

"I have nothing to confide, nor anything further to say, than that you must excuse me, as I wish to be off to business."

So pointed was the tone of Grasper, that the old lady could not pretend to misunderstand its meaning, and she rose from the seat she had taken unbidden, and moved towards the door.

"I'm very sorry, I'm sure," she said, "that you do not require a housekeeper, or something of that sort, as I know I should suit you. I don't chatter other people's business, you know, as some do. I can keep a secret, and am not very particular."

Grasper had moved impatiently to the door, but paused suddenly, and looked the lady in the face, with a fixed and penetrating stare.

"You can keep a secret, can you? and are not over particular?"

"Bless you, I can do anything for a man I like."

"Suppose I were to offer you the charge of a young woman, whose mind has been shattered from childhood, would you undertake to look to her—keep her from escaping from the house, and only heed her wild ravings as the source of a diseased brain?"

"I should be delighted with such a position."

"Could you take charge of her at your own house?"

"Yes."

"And keep her both from the sight and hearing of your neighbours?" said the merchant.

"To be sure I could, and there's nobody in the house but me."

"Then listen to me, Miss Frump. I have a young relative whose madness is of the strangest character, although there is nothing to fear from her, for she is gentle as a lamb, but the strange illusion under which she labours, is that her husband was a clerk, who committed suicide, and that I am the greatest enemy she has got in the world."

"How strange!"

"Very, is it not? Now, if I could be sure you would take care of her—not suffer her to leave the house, pay no heed to her words, and not tell anyone about her being with you, I might be induced to place her in your charge, and well reward you for your care and fidelity."

"You can trust me, Mr. Grasper, and I'm sure I would fulfil all your wishes to the letter, even if the person you speak of was not a relation of yours, and only the wife of your guilty clerk, who committed suicide, and was buried at the crossroads."

"Ah!" cried Grasper, springing back. "Do you know Jane Slater?"

"Oh, dear, no!" said Miss Frump, with a peculiar look. "I only know a young woman who has sneered at the old maid named Miss Frump—the lady that is a mad relation of yours, and who it would be both my duty and my pleasure to keep from all eyes and all ears, but my respected employer, Mr. Grasper."

Grasper glared at the woman before him for several moments. Then, laying his hand upon her arm, he said, in a hissing whisper—

"Dare I trust you?"

"You may," said the other, "for I detest her. She jeered me upon my maidenhood, once, when I called her a chit to be a wife. I have not forgotten her sneers, and never shall."

"Enough," said Grasper. "Expect me tonight at your house, for you shall be revenged as well as I."

CHAPTER CI.

GRASPER AT WORK—THE ABDUCTION.

IT was nine o'clock at night, when a small, covered vehicle, driven by a man whose form was enveloped in a large cloak, and whose features were concealed by the broad brim of a slouched hat, pulled down low over his brows, drew up about twenty yards from the little cottage where Ellen Folder and Jane Slater resided.

Throwing a horse-cloth over the back of the animal, the man dismounted from the box, and, opening the door of the carriage, gazed within it.

It was empty; and it was apparently to satisfy himself that such was the case that the man did so, for a growl of satisfaction escaped his lips as he pushed the door to again, after having closed up the blinds.

He took off his hat, and wiped his face with a white cambric; and as the dim light fell upon his features, and the iron-grey hair that stood almost upright on his head, it revealed the countenance of Ralph Grasper.

His features were paler than usual, and it was evident that a nervous anxiety had taken possession of him; for, as his trembling hand passed over his brow, he cast half-fearful looks behind him.

No one was about; and, after patting the animal's neck in a coaxing manner, he replaced his hat, pulling it even lower down over his brows than before, and walked stealthily towards the cottage.

Standing before the little gate, he looked up at the window, then along the neatly-gravelled walk, and listened attentively.

Through the drawn blind of the upper room a mellow light stole out into the street, and Grasper's heart beat almost audibly as he gazed upon it.

"This is the house," he muttered to himself; "for there are the holly trees that Bill Jackson spoke of. I cannot have mistaken the place, for there is no cottage similar to this about here; and besides, I know the neighbourhood well. Still it would set all doubts at rest if I could but hear her voice—that voice that so charmed me when first she called at my office to see her husband. Ah! there's a shadow on the blind. 'Tis hers—it must be hers!"

He placed his hand upon the gate, and, leaning upon it, watched the shadow till it disappeared, together with the light, from the blind.

"Coming down stairs," said Grasper. "Will she come out? I must be prepared, and there must be no bungling this time!"

He took the cambric again from his pocket, and also a small phial, drawing the cork from which, he placed the handkerchief over the neck of the bottle, poured some of its contents upon it, and then hastily replacing the cork, placed the phial in his pocket.

"That will stop her cries, and prevent all resistance," he muttered. "A better assistant than Bill Jackson will this chloroform be, or I am much mistaken. This kerchief placed to her face, and she is powerless to escape me. Now to summon her to the gate."

He searched about for a bell-handle, for the little wicket[165] was fastened, and while thus engaged he heard the door of the house open.

He fell back from the gate, and listened—half fearful lest it might be someone else.

But the tones of Jane's voice came to his ears.

"'Tis her—'tis her!" he gasped, pulling his hat still lower, and grasping the handkerchief tightly in his hand. "Oh! ho! She is again in my power, and none to save her!"

Still further back from the gate he drew, as a footfall echoed on the little gravel walk; and crouching into the shadow, awaited with abated breath.

"She must not see me till she has passed through the gate," he muttered, "or I may yet be foiled. Foiled!—never! Ralph Grasper never was, and never will be foiled in any undertaking he had set his mind upon. I have sworn to humble her pride, and crush her spirit; and I will do so, though it hurl me to destruction!"

Still further back he drew, until he seemed to be a part of the dark boundary that skirted the road; and the next moment the footsteps ceased, and a key was turned in the lock of the gate.

Another moment it swung open with a creaking sound, and the next a female figure passed out into the dark street.

Grasper held his breath, but his heart beat so fiercely, that he fancied she must hear it.

The woman passed him without even seeing him but she had not gone a couple of yards before, with a spring, the old rascal was upon her.

He flung his left arm around her neck, and drew her head back. At the same moment, he placed his right hand, which held the handkerchief, firmly over her mouth and nostrils.

A short hysterical sob broke from her lips, her body drooped, and she lay a dead weight in his arms.

"Ha! ha!" chuckled the merchant, as he withdrew the kerchief, and hastily thrust it into his pocket. "I have found you—possess you again; and, when I lose you, it shall be of my own free will. Now, Spring-heeled Jack, I think I have outwitted you this time!"

He raised her in his arms, and bore her quickly towards the vehicle, after casting a hurried glance around him, to be sure his actions were not observed by anyone.

To reach the carriage was but the work of a few moments, and, lifting her inside, he laid her back on one of the seats, and was about to close the door, but hesitated.

"I must make assurance doubly sure," he said. "It has never been my motto to sink a ship for the unwillingness to pay for a pennyworth of tar. Things should be done well, if done at all. She is quiet enough now, but the dose may not be strong enough to keep her so till she is out of the way of all prospect of a rescue. It won't do to let her escape me now. No, no. Safe bind—safe find. So I'll give her another smell of the opiate."

---

[165] Small gate.

He held the kerchief to her face for a moment, then, with a self-satisfied smile, he closed the door of the vehicle and locked it.

Mounting the box, he drew his cloak around him and his hat almost over his entire face, and, gathering up the reins, urged on the horse. The vehicle moved away, and soon was out of the dark street, and whirling along the high road to London.

"Why, this is better than ever I dared hope for," he thought, as he plied the whip to urge the animal to greater speed. "If you want a thing done properly do it yourself, is a good old maxim; had I trusted this job to Jackson, the fellow would have bungled over it out of his fear for Spring-heeled Jack, or if he had indeed succeeded, I should have placed myself in his power, and he would have been a continual drain upon my pocket. I did well to have nothing to do with him in this venture. He knows nothing, and therefore can say nothing. So I have nothing to fear from him. When Jack finds the girl gone, he will doubtless have his suspicions of me, but there will be no Bill to blab, and suspicion is not certainty, so he will search in vain. Ha! ha! Master Jack, I have done you this time. You are a clever fellow, but not so clever after all as old Ralph Grasper."

And the hoary-headed ruffian chuckled in high glee.

So elated was he at the presumed success of his mission, that he could not refrain from lashing the sides of the beast, which struggled nobly along the road.

Had Ralph Grasper seen for an instant the features of the woman he had placed in his vehicle, it is doubtful whether he would have felt so happy in his mind. He had only seen the form of the female, but that was enough for him at the time. He was quite satisfied with himself.

Off the smooth roads on to the London stones rolled the covered carriage, and rattled along at a speed that caused more than one pedestrian to look up in surprise, mutter a curse at his furious driving, but Grasper heeded neither the one nor the other. He was too anxious to arrive with his captive at their destination—the house of the old maid, Miss Frump.

And there, in the course of time, he did arrive safely, pulling up before the door of the shabby-genteel house as the clock struck ten.

He had little fear of exciting much curiosity there, for it was a quiet neighbourhood, where the inhabitants generally retired early to rest, being principally composed of that portion of the community who have to toil hard and keep themselves respectable on very low salaries, and whose means would not permit them to keep late hours or enjoy much company.

The moment the vehicle stopped before the door of Miss Frump's residence, it was opened by that lady herself, who had been waiting eagerly its arrival, and making her way through the little fore-court, stood before the horse. "Is that you, Mr."—

"Hush!" said Grasper. "All right!"

"Inside?" asked Miss Frump, pointing to the carriage and nodding her head towards it at the same time.

"Yes."

"Then I'll get a light."

She was about to go back into the house for that purpose, when Grasper, leaping to the ground, caught her arm.

"We don't want a light, woman," he exclaimed, in a whisper. "Do you think I want anyone to see her?"

Thus rebuked, Miss Frump pursed up her lips, and waited his orders how to act.

Grasper looked up and down the road and listened, then turned his gaze to the windows of the neighbouring houses.

Having satisfied his scrutiny, he proceeded to unlock the door of the vehicle.

"Oh! you locked her in," said Miss Frump; "that was wise."

"There was no necessity."

"None?"

"No; for she could not escape," said Grasper, with a grin.

"Not while the carriage was going along?"

"Nor while it was still. I took good care of that."

"How?"

"Gave her chloroform."

"Chloroform?"

"Yes."

"Lor'! Ain't you frightened?"

"No."

"It might kill her."

"Too much might, but I took care of that," said Grasper. "Now, get in, and I'll carry her into the house."

Miss Frump obeyed, and Grasper proceeded to lift the insensible form of the female from the carriage.

Her dead weight was sufficient to tell him that she had by no means recovered from the effects of the drug she had inhaled.

Drawing her from the vehicle, he lifted her in his arms, and followed Miss Frump into the passage.

"Now, woman, shut the door!" he exclaimed the moment he had crossed the threshold.

"But, Mr. Grasper"—

"What?"

"We are in the dark."

"What of that?"

"Oh, nothing."

"Then, shut the door, and you can bring a light. Can't you?"

"Yes."

"Be quick, then, for she is heavy."

"Heavy! and she was so delicate," said Miss Frump, closing the door.

"There, sir. Now, if you'll wait here, I'll get a light. But hadn't you better take her upstairs to her room?"

"To be sure, I had."

"You don't think she will remain insensible long, do you, sir?"

"No."

"I'm glad of that, because"—

"What?" growled Grasper.

"I should be so frightened. Chloroform is such a dangerous thing."

"That's nothing. Now, then, the light, or tell me which room to take her to, and I'll find it in the dark," said Grasper.

"It's the first floor back; but I'll get a light in a moment."

Grasper did not wait for the light, but walked along the passage, and half up the first flight of stairs, ere the old lady returned to the passage with a lamp in her hand.

"The first floor back, Mr. Grasper," she called out, as she followed him up the stairs.

"All right, ma'am, I have not forgotten," said Grasper. "Oh, I see, the door is open."

"Yes, sir, and everything got ready for the poor, mad lady."

Miss Frump's tone was rather sarcastic. Grasper observed it, but made no remark, except to himself, which was—

"Sane or mad, I care not—now I have her." He entered the room, which was certainly neatly and cleanly furnished; and, making his way to the bedside, placed his captive upon it, then, turning to Miss Frump, he said—

"Now, ma'am, I'll leave her in your charge, and take home the carriage; she is still insensible, but you will know the best means to bring her to, I dare say. When she recovers, you will take good care that she does not escape. It would be better that she wholly recovered ere she sees me. So I will not return till tomorrow."

"At what time, sir?"

"That I can't say. I always make a point, Miss Frump, of coming and going among those I employ at all hours. No stated time for me; for then I am prepared for—"

"Are you afraid to trust me, Mr. Grasper?" said the lady, a little nettled.

"I make a point of trusting no one, ma'am," said Grasper.

"Oh, indeed!" said Miss Frump; "then I wonder you brought her here."

"Tut, tut," said Grasper. "I daresay you will act according to promise. But recollect that, if you do not, you will get punished as well as me. Now, look to your charge, and as you act towards me, so will I towards you. I am a man of my word, ma'am, and hope you are a woman of yours."

"Of course I am, sir."

"I do not say you are not. But I must go. The vehicle at the door may excite surprise or curiosity, if left longer unattended to. Good night, ma'am. Your charge will be all right soon, with a little attention, and tomorrow I hope to see her and yourself both well."

So saying, the old rascal, without looking towards the bed, stalked out of the room.

Miss Frump followed him down the stairs with the light, and in a few moments heard the vehicle driven off.

"I don't like his nasty, sneering manner," she muttered as she turned to go up stairs again. "But never mind, I'll make him pay me well for my trouble. I've had bad luck with my lodgers, but this one shall pay me for all."

She entered the room, and approached the bed, holding the light up, so as to throw its rays full upon the face of the unconscious woman, then staggered back, exclaiming—

"Why, it's not her—what can this mean?"

CHAPTER CII.
MISS FRUMP EXCITES SUSPICION—TOM BEDFORD AGAIN.

MISS FRUMP knew not what to think.

She had expected to look upon a face that she had seen before—a face that had lured away one of her best back-room lodgers many months before, when James Slater was an honest young man, and the most trusted clerk of Ralph Grasper.

Great then, was her surprise when she looked into a face she had never before seen— a pale, beautiful face of a female, about Jane's age, that, in the pallor of insensibility, looked angelic in its sweet serenity.

"Who can it be?" she said, at length, placing the lamp on the table. "Where did Grasper get hold of her? Why did he deceive me? But I'll know all about it in the morning. He pretended to trust me; and he shall, or it won't be well for him! If I am a lone woman, I am not to be put upon. Confidence for confidence. And I'll have it, or he shall take her away from here! Lor'! how faint I do feel again, to be sure! I've never been myself since that arch deceiver, Duppy, lacerated my poor confiding heart, and basely turned from the pure soul that yearned towards him. Oh, man! man! how cruel you are to us maidens!"

And Miss Frump, in the agony of her soul, wiped her eyes with the corner of her apron and sighed heavily.

The remembrance of the way in which the deaf old lodger had slighted her advances was more than she could find spirit to bear with, so she shed a few tears of bitter regret, and then sought relief for her sufferings in a little cupboard in the corner of the room.

There she kept the panacea for all her ills— the only medicine that could relieve her— a medicine kept in a little leathern bottle that smelt strangely like gin.

A few drops, and Miss Frump was herself again—the wounded heart was healed, and the tear was dried.

Her calmness restored to her, the old lady set about endeavouring to restore to consciousness her beautiful charge.

This she did in her own way, which was by forcing the neck of the little bottle between the lips of the poor girl, and turning it bottom upwards.

But the firm-closed teeth resisted the liquid, and it ran out of the mouth and over the cheeks and neck of the senseless woman, filling the room with the odour of a gin-palace.

"Dear—dear!" said the old lady. "What a pity—what a sin to see so much good liquor wasted! There is nearly half-a-quartern, and not a drop has gone down her throat—the very best Old Tom,[166] too! Dear—dear! how sinful! If I had not been a fool, I should have kept it for myself, and given her water; for I'm sure to feel faint before the morning, and I can't go out tonight to get any more."

And with a sad look, Miss Frump placed the empty bottle in the little cupboard, and had recourse to the water-jug, which stood by the side of the bed.

"Water don't cost much," she muttered, "so she may turn it all out if she likes, though I don't want the pillows soaked for all that. Lor'! how tight she does keep her teeth together."

---

[166] A brand of gin.

Finding that she could not force the water into her mouth, Miss Frump eventually became alarmed, and, bending lower, placed her ear to - the lips of the insensible woman.

Not a breath fanned her cheek.

Miss Frump turned pale, and the glass she had filled from the water-jug shook in her hand and scattered its contents over the bed.

Tremblingly, she placed the glass on the table.

Nervously, she laid her hand on the bosom of her charge.

With a look of terror, she drew back; and, with extended eye-balls, glared upon the form before her.

There was no discernible pulsation.

Was she dead?

Miss Frump uttered a low cry, and sank, half swooning, into a chair.

The thought was horrible.

If the woman was dead, what fearful consequences to herself might arise! How could she account for her death? What excuse could she make for her being in that house?

None.

She must tell the truth, and then—oh, horror!

The old lady's hair stood on end.

That is, a peculiar sensation pervaded her bald pate, and seemed to lift her wig from her head.

What could she do?

She looked towards the little cupboard for relief, and sighed heavily when she remembered the bottle was empty.

"Oh! I shall be ruined—undone—transported—hung, or something worse. Oh, why did I suffer myself to be tempted to have anything to do with this business. Oh, Mr. Duppy, Mr. Duppy! but for thy unfeeling heart I had never —— But I'll go for a doctor. No, I won't; I'll run away, and never come back again. No, I mustn't do that. I'll—I'll go to Grasper. Yes, I'll go to him, and tell him to take her away. Oh, dear! what an unfortunate, ill-used woman I am!"

Miss Frump hurried on her bonnet and shawl, frantically grasped at the leathern bottle, and left the house, forgetting, in her nervousness and anxiety, to take the key with her, in order to obtain access on her return.

Through the dark road towards Grasper's dwelling she hurried along, till she reached the corner public-house—where we have before seen her—and, diving into the side entrance, had her bottle filled, and partook of two glasses of gin in rapid succession, then darted out of the house, pale and trembling.

"I say, Mary, the old maid likes her gin," said a young man, who stood smoking a cigar in the next compartment, winking at the pretty barmaid as he spoke.

"What's that to you, Tom Bedford?" said the girl, with an arch smile. "It's the only comfort she has got, poor thing. Perhaps I shall like my gin when I get as old as her."

"Not you, Mary; you'll like me better," he said.

"Oh! go along with you."

"Now, you know you love young Tom, and I'm sure you'll like old Tom. You be like her, why I'd drown myself if I only thought you would."

"There, hold your tongue," said the girl, laughing, as she turned to another portion of the bar to serve a fresh customer.

Tom Bedford strolled to the door, and looked out after Miss Frump, and, to his surprise, perceived her going in the contrary direction to her own home.

"What's the old girl after?" he muttered to himself. "She seemed terribly nervous, and I could not but remark that strange trap and driver at her door tonight when I looked through the blind. He seemed very anxious not to be seen, as he took that large parcel out of the vehicle. I wonder what it could have been; it was very large and heavy, but I could not make it out. I don't know that it is any business of mine, still I should like to know, for, somehow or other, I don't like that woman. But what is she going that way for at this hour?—there's no shops up there, and she is hurrying too much for the mere taking of a walk. Egad! if I don't follow her. See you before you shut up, Mary." And the young man stepped into the street, and hurried along after Miss Frump, overtaking her just as she reached the gate of Grasper's house, into which she turned.

Her hurried walk, her anxiety, and the spirits she had imbibed, had worked the old lady up to such a pitch of excitement, that she neither saw nor heard Tom as he passed at the gate-post; and, without hesitation, she knocked loudly at the door of the house.

In an instant it was opened.

"Mr. Grasper!" she said, in a tone which came clearly to Tom's ears.

"Not in, ma'am. Any message? Be glad to take it. The gentleman has been out all the evening."

"Oh, dear!" said Miss Frump. "I want to see him very particular. Ain't he been in lately?"

"Not since seven o'clock."

"How provoking!"

"Will you leave any message?"

"No—yes; say that a lady called."

"Yes, ma'am—Miss Frump —down the street. We know, ma'am."

"Know what?" cried the woman, quickly.

"Your name, ma'am. Our little boys have pointed you out to us—that's how we know, you see. Anything further, ma'am? for it is very uncertain when he'll be home."

"No, never mind! It's nothing particular!" said Miss Frump.

But her tones belied her words, and set Tom thinking.

"Good night, ma'am."

The door was closed, and Tom slunk back into the shadow of the stone-work as the old lady turned towards the street.

"Dear, dear," she muttered aloud, as she passed through the gateway; "not at home, I'd better wait about to see him. I don't know what to do. I'm afraid the girl will die if I don't get a doctor; and then if I do, how am I to account for her being in my house. Oh, I wish I'd had nothing to do with it, and let him take her somewhere else. She's had too much chloroform, I'm sure she has, and I'm afraid it will be the ruin of us both. Oh, dear, I wish he'd come; but I won't go home without seeing him, if I wait all night. He won't be long—I dare say he's only gone to take the carriage home."

And the old lady paced nervously up and down before the villas.

"Whew!" whistled Tom. "There's something up, and something wrong, too, between her and Grasper. It was him I saw with the vehicle, was it? and the bundle was some girl, who has had a strong dose of chloroform. Don't like the appearance of things, old gal's afraid she'll die, too, from an overdose. I'll learn a little more of this business, or my name's not Tom Bedford. Jack found a way into her house out of my window, so can I, and while she is looking out for this stern-looking, hang-gallows fellow of a Grasper, I'll take the liberty of making myself acquainted with the interior of her domicile."

Tom let the old lady place about a dozen yards between them, and darted to the opposite side of the road, and turned towards his house, merely exciting a passing glance from the lady as she looked over at the sound of his footfall.

Arriving at his dwelling, Tom let himself in with his latch-key, and locking his bedroom door, so that the people in the house might imagine he had retired to bed, softly raised the window and got out, as Jack had done before him, into the out-building.

Drawing himself up, he looked in at the window of the room where the light still burned, and through the little slip left uncovered at the side by the blind not being lowered straight, he could just see the bed on which the woman lay.

The lamp-light fell full upon her face, and Tom saw that the lovely features were pale as death, and motionless as marble.

"Good heavens!" he said, "what can this mean? Is she dead? There is some villainy here. What shall I do? Why, act like a man, and see if I can save her, to be sure."

Tom tried the window; it was fastened.

He hesitated a moment, then broke the centre pane of glass, and slipped back the latch.

He thrust the blind aside, drew himself up still further, and vaulted into the room.

As he did so, a low sigh escaped the form on the bed, and, with a beating heart, Tom sprang towards it.

CHAPTER CIII.
THE FACE IN THE PORTRAIT.

JACK had not got more than half a mile down the road from the house of Mr. Tomkins when the clatter of horses' hoofs caused him to look behind, and he saw several horsemen coming along in a cloud of dust, at a good speed.

At the moment, Jack thought nothing of the circumstance, but suddenly recollecting the squire's threat, he fancied it was probable that he had obtained the assistance of others, and was bent upon his capture.

He looked back again at the approaching horsemen, and imagined that he could trace, amid the cloud of dust, the tall form of the horse-whipped squire.

"Egad!" muttered Jack; "if my suspicions are correct, I had better make myself scarce. I have no fear of the squire, but I should stand a poor chance with a dozen mounted men. So, as prudence is the better part of valour, I'll be prudent, and get out of the high-road as soon as possible."

Looking around, he perceived a cluster of houses to the right, and saw that a broad, winding lane, a short distance from where he stood, led down to them.

In an instant he had made up his mind to go that way and wait till all was quiet. So, hurrying along, he struck off into the lane, and went along it at a good speed, till its bend took him out of sight of the high-road.

Louder sounded the clatter of the animals' hoofs, and then the sound of voices reached his ears.

Jack paused and listened.

"As I thought," he said. "There's the squire's tones."

The voice of the squire was loud and indignant as he vowed vengeance upon our hero, and urged his friends forward to his capture.

Then there was a pause in the clatter of the horses' hoofs, and by the cloud of dust, which rose high into the air, Jack was certain they had drawn rein at the end of the lane.

"Whew!" exclaimed Jack. "This is out of the frying-pan into the fire, I fear; for if they turn down this lane my prospects of escape are very small."

In anxious suspense Jack listened to the chorus of voices as each spoke at once, and advised at the same moment.

"I will keep the high road with half of you," said a voice, which Jack recognised as the squire's; "and the other half go down this lane, and meet us a couple of miles down the road. We shall thus be certain of him."

The proposition was agreed to, and Jack took to his heels with all his speed.

He knew his only chance was in obtaining a hiding-place in one of the houses some distance down the lane—a chance that was certainly augmented by the lane winding about, so as to prevent one person seeing another at a distance of a hundred yards.

The voices of the men, and the sound of their horses' hoofs, told him the troop was again in motion; and he pushed on as fast as his legs would carry him, and was fortunate enough to reach the cluster of cottages ere he had been sighted by his pursuers, whose eagerness for his capture had become somewhat relaxed since parting with the squire.

Jack did not hesitate a moment, but cleared the fence of the first at a bound; and, perceiving a side door standing wide open, entered without ceremony the little hall at the moment the first horseman—a sturdy, farmer-looking man—came in sight.

Jack was about to close the door to prevent being seen by the horsemen as they rode past, who had doubtless a good description of his person from the incensed squire, but fearful that the act might bring their gaze that way, he opened a side door, and entered a small room, containing no other furniture than a side table and a chintz covered easy chair and ottoman.

In the centre of the room stood a painter's easel, with the canvas stretched upon it, and covered with a long cloth.

Several pictures adorned the walls, and in one corner a suit of armour, sadly out of repair, was reared against the wall.

Jack took the whole in at a glance, then turned his gaze to the window, muttering—

"Humph! A painter's studio. Well, if he requires a subject, in faith! here is one. Ah! there go my would-be captors. I had a hard run for it, but I have eluded them, and as soon as they are out of sight I'll be on the road again."

He flung himself down on the easy chair, and looked half abstractedly at the covered easel.

"So this is the house of an artist, eh?— talent in an out-of-the-way corner, surely, in this place. It is certainly a pretty retired spot to nourish art in; but I expect it is ill paid for in a place like this. Well, so it is, as a rule, everywhere. In this strange world there are strange doings—fools thrive well, and worth is passed by unheeded. But perhaps I am praising one who possesses no claim to be styled an artist. Let's see!"

Jack rose and lifted the covering from the easel, and gazed upon the portrait of an old lady, not badly executed.

"Humph!" said Jack. "Not badly done. I'll wager but the dame for which this is intended to be the representative doubtless thinks herself better looking than the picture. The features are coarse, and what woman ever believed her own to be so? Now, what will he get for that, I wonder? I am curious to know. Ten guineas, perhaps, or about a third of what, it is worth; for I'd almost swear the possessor of a face like that is not troubled with a benevolent heart. Hallo! here's someone coming! Now, Jack, you are in for it!"

He let the covering fall quickly before the easel, and darted behind it as the lock in the door clicked.

The next moment the door opened, and a tall woman, between fifty and sixty years of age, entered the room, followed by a young man attired in a brown holland[167] blouse, secured at the waist by a leathern belt, and a red skullcap surmounting locks of raven black, which curled around his neck.

"The artist," muttered Jack; "and, as I live, his model!"

"No more sittings, madam, will be necessary," said the young man. "The portrait requires but a few touches now, to render it complete."

"But do you think it is like me, Mr. Delain?" said the lady.

"Most certainly; but of course it would be better if you asked the opinion of some other person than the artist. I believe it to be one of the best my pencil has produced. Your glass, madam, will tell you how like it is."

"Don't you think it is a little too old?" said the lady.

The artist smiled.

"You desired a true portrait, madam. I did not presume to act otherwise than from your orders."

"Yes, yes," said the lady. "Of course I desired a life-like portrait; but I think, sir, you have been at fault in some parts. The features are too large, the expression harsh, and, in fact, it would almost seem I had been very ill when the picture was painted, and I never looked better."

"You look at it with a prejudiced eye, madam," said Delain. "Please glance at it again, and then at yonder glass, and I am sure you will admit the resemblance to be strikingly true."

The young artist uncovered the picture by drawing the cloth on one side, and the lady sitting down in the easy chair, raised her glasses to her eyes, and looked criticisingly at the portrait.

"Now, madam, if you will please look into that glass," said the young man, pointing to a mirror hanging against the wall, "you will favour me."

The lady's face had been growing black, and it was in no very good humour she rose to comply.

It was evident she did not admire the portrait.

"Why," thought Jack, "does she think it too good, or too true to life?"

Such was the case, but the lady did not acknowledge that she thought it too old; and, like poor Mrs. Tomkins, wished others to believe her younger than she really was.

She turned from viewing herself in the mirror, and beckoned the young artist to her side.

Delain suffered the cloth to fall over the picture, and obeyed.

---

[167] Linen.

"Oblige me, sir, by looking at the reflection of my face in that mirror."

The artist bowed and complied, and while they both looked into the polished glass, Jack took his penknife from his pocket, and drew the blade over the canvas on which the portrait was painted.

"Now, really, Mr. Delain, you cannot say the face you see in that glass is like the face on that canvas?" said the lady.

"Madam, I assure you it is the very counterpart," was the reply.

"Is my nose so long and broad?"

"It is."

"And my mouth so large."

"Madam, shall I measure it?"

"No, sir. But do you wish to make me believe that my lips are so thick and coarse, my brows so lowering, my neck so short, my forehead so heavy?"

"I can only say, madam, that if any person who will speak conscientiously can assert the portrait I have painted is not a life-like and speaking picture of yourself, at your present time of life, I will paint it out, and do it again for nothing," said the artist, evidently grieved at the tones of the lady.

"Don't be angry, Mr. Delain," she said, "we are none of us right at times—we are all of us liable to err, but you must allow me to be the best judge of my own portrait. I say it is not like me, at least, not so like as it ought to be, and I think I can point out to you where it is wrong."

"If you can, madam, I shall be happy to learn."

"Then, sir," said the lady, trying to get up a blush, "it is too old, many years too old."

"Madam!"

"Make the picture ten or twelve years younger, and then, I think, it would be as good a portrait as ever was painted," said the lady.

"Madam, had you desired the artist to flatter you, he could certainly have done so, but he would have belied his art. If anything, the colouring is in your favour. The hair, too, is not really so silvery as your own."

"Sir!"

"I beg your pardon: but I speak truly, as here is proof I do. Look upon these tints. If you will be seated, you will see these better, and I will explain what I mean."

The lady dropped into the chair with a very bad grace, and the young artist again, drawing the cloth from over the portrait, said, placing his finger upon the forehead of the likeness—

"To do you justice, I should have placed a deeper tint here."

"And what effect would that have had?"

"To throw out the wrinkles on the forehead, and"—

"Make me as ugly as"—

"The devil!" cried Jack, thrusting his head through the canvas.

"The devil!" shrieked the lady, letting fall the glasses she was about adjusting to her nose.

The startled artist sprang backwards, and the cloth, falling from his grasp, shut out the canvas and the face of Jack from the affrighted gaze of the old lady, who had sprang from her chair and stood glaring in terrified amazement upon the hideous mask and ears of our hero.

The moment the face was no longer visible, the woman made a rush for the room's door and if years had dimmed her beauty, it would appear they had done little towards robbing her of agility; for the next moment she was out of the house, and tearing down the lane with all the speed of a young girl.

CHAPTER CIV.
THE PAINTER REWARDED—A DRUNKEN WOMAN PUNISHED.

RECOVERING from the surprise into which so strange an incident had thrown him, the young artist darted behind his easel, and stood face to face with our hero.

"Happy to make your acquaintance, Mr. Delain," said Jack.

The artist measured Jack with his eye from top to toe for several seconds.

"And who the devil are you, sir, I'd like to know?" he said, his voice choked with passion, and his face red with indignation.

"One who trusts you will forgive the little trick played in your studio upon the old lady who wished to be thought young, and was unwilling to acknowledge your talents. You have heard of me, doubtless—a sad scapegrace— Spring-heeled Jack!"

"Ah!" said the artist, stepping back, and again measuring our hero with his eye, as if he would read the strength of his muscles and the probabilities of success should he seek to effect his capture.

"Yes, sir, I have the honour to be your servant, Spring-heeled Jack!"

"What do you do here, sir?" cried the indignant artist.

"Seeking to cultivate the acquaintance and friendship of a man of no mean talent," was the reply.

"And this is how you go about it!"

The artist pointed to the canvas.

Jack bowed.

"By ruining me, insulting my patrons, and destroying my labours," said Delain, bitterly.

"Pray don't be hard upon me," said Jack, "What was the worth of the portrait?"

"Ten guineas."

"Ten?"

"Yes."

"Then fifty will pay for it."

"Fifty pay for it? What do you mean, sir?" said the artist.

"That, being willing to patronise talent, I will give you fifty for it," said Jack.

"But it's spoilt."

"I know that."

"Look you, sir," said Delain, clenching his fist, and advancing in a threatening attitude; "you may play your pranks where you like, but not with me. I am not the man to tamely submit to insult or injury in my own house."

"I'm glad to hear you say so. But, come; we will not quarrel. Take this."

He drew out his pocket-book, and placed a small roll of notes in the other's hand.

"You will find fifty pounds there, the value of the picture I destroyed."

The artist looked at the little packet, as if he could not believe the evidence of his senses. He turned them over in his hands several times, then gazed up in the smiling face of Jack.

"What does this mean?" he asked, in a puzzled tone.

"Well, I will tell you. You must know, in the first place, that I had occasion to horsewhip a rascal who grossly insulted me. He obtained the assistance of friends and sought my capture, for you are, doubtless, acquainted with the fact that a reward has been offered to any person who will lodge me in gaol. To avoid him I made bold to enter this house. Here I overheard your conversation with the lady, and, feeling assured that she would never take the picture, or else pay you nothing equivalent to its value for it, I resolved to give her a shock—destroy the painting, and pay you its worth."

"But—fifty pounds!"

"Is it not enough?"

"I am not a robber!"

"I did not say you were."

"But I should be, did I take this sum. Ten will satisfy me," said the artist.

"But not me,' said Jack. "The portrait was a work of art, and you set too mean a value on your talents, besides this freak[168] of mine may be the means of your losing patronage; so I pray you accept the money, and let us part friends."

"With all my heart," said the now delighted artist, extending his hand, which Jack grasped.

"As the road is clear, I will again set forth on my journey. Some day I may ask you to paint my portrait."

The artist looked hard at him.

"But it must be a life-like picture, mind you."

"To be sure. I should be happy to do it now," said Delain.

"Thank you; but I have not yet sowed my wild oats. When I have I will put aside the mask, and then you shall do it. I promise you, at present, I have little care that my face should be seen or recognised. I have not yet learned enough of the world."

"And you seek to learn it in this disguise?"

"Yes; for I am neither a poet nor an artist. I would know it—as it really is, not as imagination may picture it. But I have trespassed too long, and if we ever meet again I trust you will not have formed a bad opinion of Spring-heeled Jack."

He shook the artist's hand, and gathering his cloak about him, walked out of the house, leaving Delain in the middle of the room gazing alternately upon the shattered canvas and the banknotes which were to recompense him for its injury.

It was drawing towards evening, and Jack felt that he must hurry on if he would reach the next town by nightfall, where he resolved to hire a post-chaise and return to London.

He had yet five or six miles to go, and he put his best leg foremost, as the saying is.

He kept a sharp look-out on the road for the squire's party, whom he thought it was probable he might meet, but saw nothing of them, and, as the night closed over the earth, he came in view of a little thriving town, the lights of which he could see far over a mile ere he reached it.

Making his way to the principal hostelry, he ordered refreshments, and asked to be accommodated with a post-chaise.

The landlord could not reply with his request then, but stated that one would be home before midnight, if he would delay his journey till its arrival.

---

[168] Whim.

To this, Jack assented, as it was either journey on foot or to wait, and as the second pleased him better than the first, he adopted the alternative.

Having finished his meal and partaken of a glass or two of wine, he lit a cigar, and left the hostelry with the intention of having a walk through the town, to pass away the time till the chaise was ready to start.

The town consisted of about six hundred houses, about seventy of which were shops, many of them fitted up in the London style, and adopting all the London schemes to get patronage.

Jack strolled about, observing all that was to be observed; and feeling somewhat tired, he leaned against a post, and amused himself by reading the notices in a grocer's window.

While thus engaged, a slatternly-looking young woman, with a basket on her arm, stood between him and the window, where she proceeded, by the aid of the lights which streamed therefrom, to count over a few coins she held in her hand.

Jack was about to turn away, lest he should excite in the woman's breast a suspicion that he was watching her, when she muttered to herself—

"Yes, I can get a little less of each, and save sixpence for myself. I don't see why I shouldn't. He won't know whether I get the right quantity or not, and if he won't let me have money for a little drop when I want it, I'll have it some way, I will."

And thus muttering, the woman walked into the shop.

Jack watched her through the glass, and shrugged his shoulders contemptuously, as he read in the besotted features of the young woman her true character, that of a drunkard—a woman degraded to a beast, who would sell her soul for drink.

The words, too, she had uttered he was not slow to comprehend the true meaning of.

They denoted that her husband, cognisant of her degrading passion, doled out the money for absolute necessaries as they were required, hoping by that means to save her from the worst of all vices.

"You cannot outwit a woman," muttered Jack, "be her station what it may. 'Tis evident her husband deems it best to keep her without money, so that she cannot obtain her favourite beverage; but get it she will, even if she starve herself and children to obtain it. A man can have little pity for such a being as that. Egad! when a woman is inclined to be bad, she is bad indeed! There is some hope of redemption in the male sex, but in the female none, none, I fear," and Jack shook his head sadly.

"She will save enough out of her purchases to get a drop, which I should like to prevent her obtaining; but I don't see how to do her that kind action, unless it is by giving her a fright, and perhaps making her forget her insatiate longing for a time. It might have that effect certainly, so I can but try it."

Jack slipped on his mask, and, leaning his chest on the top of the post opposite the window, waited for the woman to come forth from the shop.

In a few minutes, out she came, clinking a few pence in her hand, and with a look of satisfaction on her bloated face.

"Just enough for a glass," muttered the woman, as she passed before the window. "He's to be done, though he does keep the money. I'll have a glass, in spite of him, whenever I want it."

"And send your soul to the devil," said Jack, turning his face towards her, and suffering the lights to fall upon his mask.

The woman uttered a loud shriek, and, suffering the pence to fall from her hand to the pavement, staggered backwards in terrified amazement.

"And plunge your soul to perdition," said Jack, "by indulging your insatiate thirst for drink!"

He made a motion, as if to advance towards her, and the terrified woman sprang back towards the shop-door, evidently with the intention of rushing inside; but, having her gaze turned towards Jack, she stumbled against a chest of eggs, and, losing her balance, fell backwards among them, smashing them beneath her weight.

Her cry was echoed by the shopkeeper, who hurried to the door; and Jack, hastily tearing off his mask, turned and strolled away towards the hostelry, where, a few minutes after, he stood listening to the most outrageous accounts of the affair, and just before midnight took his seat in the chaise that was to carry him to London.

CHAPTER CV.

JACK AND THE JACKSONS AGAIN.

"WELL, here I am again, in London!" said Jack, flinging one leg over the other, and toying with his cigar-case, on the evening following the morning on which the post chaise drew up safely at the hotel door.

"The little jaunt in the country has done me good, I believe, for I feel as fresh as a lark, and particularly larkish, too. The fresh air has revived my spirits, and I feel half inclined to bid farewell to London for some time, and lead a quiet and respectable life among the green fields, till some of my pranks in the metropolis are forgotten, and less anxiety is exhibited to place me between the cold grey walls of a prison cell. I don't like the look of those large bills, which meet my gaze at the corners of the streets, offering a reward for my capture, they show that my little games are becoming intolerable in this vast emporium, and that well-intentioned people are no longer willing to be haunted by the fears of meeting one in the dead of the night. I know, as well as anyone, that this conduct ill becomes a gentleman; but I did not make myself, and it is a part of my nature to frighten people half out of their wits. It's growing too hot for me here. My very name has become a terror in London; and so, for a time, I must bid it farewell, if I would not stand unmasked in a court of justice."

Jack lit a cigar, and sank into a deep reverie for some time; then, starting, he brought his open hand down upon the table, and muttered, half aloud—

"Yes, I must put an end to these midnight pranks for a time, as soon as I have discovered the poor girl whom I promised to protect, and have seen the true Richard Clavering in possession of his just rights. To leave the metropolis now, would be to leave them both to ruin; once they were happy—then Jack drops the mask and takes a spring out of the noise, the smoke, and dirt of London. But this girl—this Ellen, where can I look for her? Her brother is brokenhearted, and not even the prospect before him can make him forget the sister he has scarcely known. To restore happiness to him and to her is all I seek now, and I will not rest until I have accomplished my wish."

He rose, and flung his cloak around him, hesitated a moment, then threw it back on to the chair.

"I will not encumber myself with it," he muttered, "the evening is warm enough, and I will order a servant to take it to my room; my belt, too, may keep it company," he added, taking off the broad leathern band he was wont to wear at his waist. "There, now I feel comfortable; so here goes to seek Ellen."

Without any decided course in view, Jack left the hotel, and sauntered quietly through the lighted streets till he arrived at Charing Cross; then, hailing a coach, bade the driver take him to the east end.

"I'll try this fellow once more," he said to himself, as he reclined back in the vehicle. "He is a cruel and cunning rascal, but gold will open his mouth, if he really does know anything respecting Ellen. Stay! it would be better to endeavour to see his wife. I may learn from her what her blackguard husband would not tell. Yes, that will be the best plan of action."

Arriving at Whitechapel, Jack dismissed the coachman, and proceeded along the Whitechapel-road at a good pace till he neared the street in which was the residence of Bill Jackson and his wretched spouse.

It was about a quarter to eleven when he turned into the dark thoroughfare; and, making his way to the Pigeon Flyers, he boldly walked into the beer-house, and ordered a pint of ale at the bar.

The Pigeon Flyers was full of customers, and burly forms shifted on their seats, and bleared eyes looked up and winked knowingly at each other, as they looked, in surprise, at the gentlemanly attired man who had ordered the pint of ale.

Bill Jackson, with a short pipe in his mouth, sat leaning his elbows on the edge of a barrel before him, on which stood a pot of beer, puffing a perfect cloud from his lips, and speaking to his companions in a tone of voice that already showed he had drank a goodly quantity that day.

"Who's that bloke, I wonder?" said the man who sat next him, nodding his head towards Jack, who sipped at his ale, and pretended to be taking no notice of anyone. "A shoful,[169] a slop,[170] or a"—

"Shut up," said another, giving the man a dig in the ribs with his elbows, and putting an immediate stop to his sentence. "He don't look like neither. He's a no-fly cove[171] as ever dropped in here for a drink. He don't look a bad sort neither. Wonder if he'll sport a tanner[172] for a ticket for Slogger's lead?"

"Ask him," said Bill. "Tell him the bloke's in trouble, and, perhaps, he'll come down with the dust."[173]

The man took his pipe from his mouth, rose, hesitated, sat down, and rose again.

"Go on, you fool," said Bill. "You ain't half a cove."

Thus urged, the man sidled up to Jack, and laying on the counter a dirty piece of cardboard, said, in a husky voice, without once looking up in Jack's face—

"I say, governor, you see there's a chap as uses this house has got into trouble, and, in course, as we used to have a pint together, and knowed me for a long time, we are going to raffle a silk handkerchief for the benefit of his gal. Perhaps you wouldn't mind taking a ticket, seeing as he's a deserving bloke as would do the same for you? It's only a tanner, and that won't break you, I know."

Jack read the card as it laid before him, and, turning his head, so as not to inhale the

---

[169] Base person.
[170] Policeman.
[171] A man who is unaware.
[172] Sixpence.
[173] Cash.

breath of the man, which smelt strongly of beer, tobacco, cheese, and onions, he replied—

"I do not want your card, but I have no objection to give you a shilling towards assisting a fellow creature. But what's his trouble?"

"Why, you see, we have a little ratting[174] here now and then, and"—

"Hold your jaw, will you, you fool!" roared Bill jumping up.'

"What for," said the man, turning quickly. "Just you mind your own business, while I'm talking to a gentleman, as is going to give a bob[175] to Slogger and stand a pint to me."

"I shall interfere if you go jawing about what you oughtn't, now then."

"Then I shall give you a top aside the head as'll shut you up," retorted the other.

"You will!" cried Bill, staggering to his feet, and flinging his pipe on to the top of the barrel among the wet rings of beer, with which it was marked all over, and doubling his large fists threateningly. "You give me a top aside the head."

"Yes, me."

"Do it."

"So I will, if you're cheeky."

"I am cheeky," said Bill, staggering round the barrel, "and if you think you can take the cheek out of me, do it. I'll fight you or any man in the Flyers for five bob now, and stake the money."

"I ain't got five bob, you know that, or I'd jolly soon stake it."

"I will stake it for you," said Jack.

"You will?" said the man.

"I will; there it is."

Jack laid the sum on the bar.

"Cover it, Bill," cried two or three in a breath, and every man rose to his feet.

"There's my five bob," said Bill." Now, come into the skittle ground, and see how soon I'll polish him off."

"Easier said than done," retorted the other. "Come on, governor, and see who's the best man."

"I will follow you directly," said Jack.

The whole party of ruffianly-looking fellows, most of them more or less inebriated, now left the bar, and hurried towards the skittle-ground at the back of the house, showing the greatest eagerness for the fight—swearing terribly, and offering bets of pots of beer on their favourite man.

"Good," said Jack, as he found himself left alone in the bar. "I can make sure the fellow won't go home now for some minutes, and can talk to his wife without any fear of the ruffian hearing my business. I should be sorry for her to suffer, whether she can give me any information of Ellen or not."

He cast one look over at the house opposite, and left the Flyers.

He knocked at the door with the greasy cord in the centre of the panel, and the shouts that reached his ears from the beerhouse while he awaited an answer to his summons, convinced him that the affray had begun.

He had to knock a second time before anyone came, when the wife of the pigeon fancier stood before him.

---

[174] Informing.
[175] Shilling.

"Mrs. Jackson!" said Jack.

"Yes, sir, I am Mrs. Jackson."

"I wish to speak to you."

"Yes, sir," said the woman, evidently half fearful of her gentlemanly visitor, and seeming to hesitate whether to shut the door in his face, or not.

"Do not be alarmed," said Jack; "I wish to ask you a plain question, and all I require in return is a truthful answer. I know that your fear of your husband might withhold it, but rest assured, he shall never know of this meeting; and, if you give me the information I require, I will, in return, give you five pounds. It can do you no harm to speak truly, nor shall it harm your husband, even if he has had any hand in the strange affair."

"Oh, what is it, sir? Has Bill been up to anything?" said Mrs. Jackson, tremulously.

"You can tell me that. Now, some time since, you had a young woman living here, named Ellen Folder?"

"Yes, sir."

"Where is she now?"

"Lor' bless you, sir, she went away one night, and we've never seen her since. I'm sure I couldn't tell you, if you were to give me a mint of money."

"Have you heard of her from your husband, or anyone else?"

"Not a word."

"Remember, any information you can give of her places five pounds in your hand," said Jack, rattling the coins in his pocket as he spoke.

"I wish to heaven I could tell you," said the woman, "I do, indeed."

Jack was convinced that the woman spoke truly.

The tones of her voice told him that.

"Then you cannot earn the five pounds?" said Jack

"No, sir. I wish I could; for little Bill havn't got a shoe to his foot, nor Sally a gown to her back. Oh, I only wish I did know; for five pounds, unknown to my husband, would be a fortune to us. Oh, that it would—quite a Godsend," said Mrs. Jackson, sighing heavily.

Jack saw that to press the woman further would be useless, but he hazarded the remark—

"I suppose you could think of none who could give me the information I desire?"

"Not a soul, unless Isaac Levy, the Jew clothier; he might know. She used to work for him before she went away so strange, like. I think the poor gal committed suicide—I do."

"Perhaps," said Jack. "However, I won't detain you longer, since you can neither give me any clue to Miss Folder, or change the five pounds from my pocket to your own."

"God knows, how willing I'd be to do so," said the woman; "but I won't rob you by telling you a lie, sir, much as I want even a shilling."

Jack looked at the woman a moment, and saw by the light which streamed from the window of the Pigeon Flyers full upon the doorway, that tears were in her eyes.

"One more question," said Jack. "Do you know a man named Grasper?"

"The old villain!" cried the woman. "I do know him."

"Has he been here lately?"

"Yes—no! I don't know."

"I intend no harm to you or yours, Mrs. Jackson; so tell me, has the man Grasper been here since the night he encountered Spring-heeled Jack in the room above?"

"Good heavens! no, sir. But how did you know"—

"No matter. I believe you have answered me truly, and you shall not suffer for your candour. Here are five pounds. Keep the gift unknown from your husband, who would but squander it in that low beer-house; and now goodnight!"

The woman took the money with a bounding heart, clutched her fingers tightly over it, and looked half-frightened into Jack's face.

"Oh! thank you—thank you; but who are you, sir, who give me this? Who are you that seek Ellen Folder, and know the character of my husband so well?"

"Can you keep a secret?"

"Yes—oh, yes!"

"We have met before, Mrs. Jackson."

"Where, sir?"

"In your front room, upstairs."

"Then you are"—

"Spring-heeled Jack!"

The woman staggered back aghast, and when she sufficiently recovered herself, the doorway was empty, and Jack was gone.

CHAPTER CVI.
THE FATAL FIGHT—THE END OF BILL JACKSON

IN the meantime, the fight in the skittle-ground continued to rage between the two intoxicated men; and the shouts of the onlookers, mingled with the disgusting oaths of the combatants as they struck, and closed, and fell, in the dirty, sawdust-floored apartment of the skittle-alley—rat pit of the Pigeon Flyers.

The confusion reached the ears of the wife as she stood in the doorway, clasping the coins Jack had given her in her hand, and thinking how she could prevent Bill knowing anything about them.

But she thought nothing of it—the drunken howls being of too frequent an occurrence in that disreputable place of refreshment.

She was still wondering what she should do, and how she should act, when the burly form of the landlord appeared in the doorway of the Pigeon Flyers.

The gaslight played on his besotted[176] face, and showed it pale as that of a corpse—a circumstance very much to be remarked in features naturally so red and bloated as his were.

In an instant he was joined by one of his customers, who spoke to him in a low tone; but low as it was, Mrs. Jackson heard the words, and uttered a loud shriek.

"Bill's a goner, sure enough. Pappy hit him slap under the ear, and it's done for him."

Such were the words the poor woman heard; and, after giving utterance to the cry, she suffered the five golden coins to fall from her hand on to the floor of the passage, and staggered back against the wall, where her heart seemed to stand still, and all power to be denied her, save that of hearing, which now was horribly acute.

"It'll damn up the Flyers," said the landlord. "There'll be an awful row, now! What can be done? If we send for a doctor, it'll be as bad as not sending for one. There'll be

---

176 Drunken.

an inquest, and we'll all be getting lagged, see if we don't! You go and tell his old woman, and we'll get him took home. Better have all the shine over there."

"What shall I tell her?"

"God's truth! tell her what you like, only let her get him out of my skittle-ground. We mustn't have a row here, for the police have had an eye on this crib for a long time, you know."

"Blowed if I like to go! You do it. You can patter better nor I can."

"No, you go, and I'll give you a pint. Strike me lucky! there she is at the door!"

"Call her over."

There was no need for this; for Mrs. Jackson, recovering from the momentary prostration, uttered another cry, and sped over the way to the Flyers, her face pale as death, her limbs trembling, and a choking sensation at her throat.

"Bill! Bill!" she cried. "Oh, where's my Bill?"

"Don't make a row, Mrs. Jackson," cried the landlord. "Bill's got a knock, that's put him out of time; but if you get him home, it will be all right."

"Don't deceive me!" cried the woman. "Bill is—is"—

"Hush! Don't speak so loud; for we don't want the police here," said the man.

"I will speak!"

"Be quiet, and have a drop of beer."

"No!" cried the woman. "Let me go to Bill! Let me see him! Where is he?"

"In the skittle-ground."

The woman pushed the man aside, and rushed through the house into the yard where the skittle-alley was situated, and, hurrying into the place, saw a number of men standing round the form of her husband, who lay in the sawdust, with his face turned upwards.

With a shriek, she sprang among them, and, dashing them on either side, flung herself on her knees.

"Bill! Bill!" she cried, grasping his shoulder, and looking into his blood-stained face. "Bill! speak to me! It's Poll, your wife!"

She paused, as if for an answer; looked round upon the assembled men; then shrieked aloud—

"Oh, my God! He is dead—he is dead! Who killed him?—who? Show me the man! I'll hang him! I'll—oh, Bill! Bill!"

Her feelings overpowered her. For, brutal husband as he had been to her, she loved him with all that rough devotion which was as sincere as the more tender love of those whose natures are more kind and gentle; and in that moment she saw only the father of her children —the man who had won her heart in days of happiness.

No thought of his cruelty—his neglect—his harshness, then crossed her mind. She looked only upon the corpse of her husband—not the brute who had caused her a life of wretchedness and want.

"Don't make a row about it," said the landlord, entering the ground with a pot of ale, and offering it to Mrs. Jackson. "It's an unfortunate affair; but it was his own fault. He would fight Pappy for five bob, and got a knock under the ear."

The woman dashed the pot of ale from his hand, and, turning round, glared upon Pappy, who shrank back before her.

"Wretch!" she cried, "it is you, and such as you, who have kept him from his home, made him spend the money which should buy his children bread, and left me to starve, while he drank all he got with you. See what you have brought him to! Oh, this cursed place! I knew it would be his ruin. But I will ruin this place! You are all guilty—you have all helped to murder my Bill, and I will have justice. Oh, Bill! Poor Bill! Oh, the poor children! what will they do now?"

"Don't be so hard on a cove," said Pappy. "You know as I wouldn't have hurt Bill, who was always a pal of mine. We was only a larking."

"Is murder a lark?" cried the woman. "Is it a lark to make me a widow, and my children fatherless? Is it a lark to bring your own neck to the rope? This cursed place should have been burned down years ago. It has been a curse to the neighbourhood—a curse to every woman who lives in it. It has dragged the men from their homes—the bread from their mouths. But this shall destroy it. I will fetch the police, I"—

She was hurrying to the door as she spoke, when the landlord placed himself before her.

"No, you don't," he said. "You'll take that fellow away; I ain't a-going to have no scenes here."

"Let me go out, said the woman, or it will be worse for you."

"You slope, Pappy," said the landlord, "while you've got a chance."

"He shall not escape," cried the woman, turning, and catching at the shirt-sleeve of the man.

"Let him go!" roared a chorus of voices.

"He shall go to gaol," said the woman. "He murdered my Bill, and he shall suffer for it."

"Let go of me, will you?" said Pappy, "or I'll chuck you over!"

"I will drag you to gaol, you murderer. You shall not go. Help! police! help!"

"Curse you! Take that, then!" said Pappy, striking her on the lips with his open hand, but with sufficient force to draw blood, and cause her to release her hold and totter back.

"Now, nammus," cried the landlord, "and perhaps we can settle the job with her. Sling your daddle[177]—quick!"

"By God! he shall not," cried the woman, furious at the blow, and seizing the pot, which the landlord still held in his hand.

"Get out of my way," said Pappy, who really began to fear the woman. "I don't want to hit you; but I shall, if you interfere with me."

And he strove to pass the landlord, and slip from the skittle-ground.

Mrs. Jackson again faced him, grasping the pewter pot by the handle.

"You shall suffer for this!" she screamed. "You shan't escape! You killed my Bill, and you shall not go, only with the police."

"Get back, or I'll serve you the same!" said the man, pushing her away from the door, which he grasped in his hand, and opened quickly.

But not quick enough for his own safety.

Mrs. Jackson uttered a cry, raised the pewter pot above her head, and before anyone of those assembled could prevent her, she brought the sharp rim down upon the bared head of Pappy, cutting it fearfully, and felling him at the feet of the astounded and terrified landlord.

With flashing eyes, she glared around her.

The men fell back from before her as from an enraged tigress, and even the landlord retreated hastily from her side, leaving her standing alone with the man who lay stunned

---

177 Shake hands.

and bleeding beside his victim.

"Don't come near me," she cried, in a husky, voice, "or I shall kill you if you do. I am mad. This cursed hell has made me mad, and I will tear it down. But for this den he would have been a good man; but for the cursed poison he drank here he would be alive now. Don't come near me, I say, for my blood is up, and there will be another murder. If you do I will not be silent. I will rouse the neighbourhood for miles round. None shall escape— not one— not one!"

Brandishing the pot, she rushed out of the skittle-ground, through the bar, into the street, shrieking aloud—

"Help! Police! Murder!"

Her cries soon brought a number of persons around her, and among them our old friend, Bobby Bristles, who had his beat in that neighbourhood for the first time, and, hearing the cries of Mrs. Jackson, and perceiving her flourishing a quart pot in her hand at the door of the beershop, immediately leaped to the conclusion that she was drunk.

So Bobby quietly walked up behind her, and, making a sudden snatch at the pot, deprived her of it.

"Now, then—now then!—what's all this row about?" he cried, as he pitched the pot into the bar, so that it should be out of the way.

"Oh, my Bill! my Bill!" cried the woman.

"Go home with you," said Bobby, "and don't be making this drunken disturbance here, or I shall have to take you where you won't find a feather bed to lay on."

"I'm not drunk—I'm mad!" cried Mrs. Jackson, clinging to Bobby.

"I should think you was," said Bobby. "But the best thing you can do is to go home without showing any of your mad tricks."

"She ain't drunk," cried an attenuated[178] woman in the crowd. "Poor cretur, she don't get enough to get drink with, like me. Catch Bill letting her have the price of a pint. He wants it all for his own inside—he does. What's the matter, Mrs. Jackson?"

"Oh, my Bill! my Bill! he's"—

"Been slogging into[179] you, again?" interrupted the woman.

"No! he's been murdered—murdered in the skittle-ground of this hell here!"

"Eh, what?" cried Bobby, whipping his staff from his pocket. "Murder!—did you say murder?"

"Murdered!" echoed the crowd.

And, without waiting for an answer, the crowd passed into the bar of the Pigeon Flyers.

"Oh, they've murdered him!" cried the woman, turning to Bristles. "He lays dead in the skittle-ground! Don't let them go! Hang them! They've killed my Bill!—they've killed my Bill!"

"Show me where he is," said Bristles. "Go on, woman!"

"This way—this way."

And the excited woman, clutching the arm of Bristles, led that model officer through the bar into the yard.

"They are all in there," she cried, pointing to the door of the skittle alley.

A rush was made for the door by those who had been brought to the scene by the

---

[178] Thin.
[179] Beating.

cries of the poor wife; but Bristles majestically waved them back with his staff, and, rough fellows as they were, they retreated at the command.

Bristles pushed at the door, but could not open it.

It had been secured inside.

"Open the door! In the name of the law, I demand this door be instantly opened!" cried Bristles.

There was no response.

"Break it open!" shrieked Mrs. Jackson.

"They'll nammus out of the window into the next yard," said a bystander; "that's their game."

There were several pieces of solid wood lying about, and, pointing to these, Bristles ordered the people assembled to batter in the door with them.

In a few moments the old dirty panels were split into a dozen fragments, and egress gained to the skittle-ground, which had been plunged into darkness. Bristles, however, turned the slide of his lantern, and suffered the stream of light to fall into the place.

There were two bodies lying on the ground, but no one else was there.

"Gone!" cried Mrs. Jackson; "they've got away."

She pointed to the window on the opposite side of the alley, which was wide open.

"Some of you go for a doctor, and call at the station, and ask the inspector to send down a couple of men?" said Bristles, as he sprang over the prostrate bodies, and looked from the window into the next yard.

Two or three immediately started off, while Mrs. Jackson sat down beside her husband.

"Oh, Bill, Bill!" she cried; "they shan't escape!—they shan't escape!"

"Not if I knows it," said Bob. "There's one! I'll have him."

He clambered out by the window as he spoke, and dropped into the next yard; but his feet had scarce touched the ground, when his staff was torn from his hand by the landlord, who dealt him a heavy blow with it upon the forehead. Then, throwing the weapon down, he was about to continue his flight, when he was grasped from behind, and the next instant a couple of officers leaped the wall of the house beyond to their brother's assistance.

Lights flickered from different windows, and floods of light danced into the dirty yards of the wretched dwellings, which were now filled with police, seeking the capture of all who had been present at the fatal affray, not one of whom but was taken ere he could make good his escape.

And while this transpired, Bill was carried home, followed by his weeping wife, and Pappy was borne to the hospital to have his wounds dressed.

There was no hope for Bill; his wretched life had come to a close, and poor Mrs. Jackson, if she had lost a husband, had also got rid of a cruel monster.

CHAPTER CVII.

JACK RENDERS TWO HAPPY AT A CRITICAL MOMENT.

AS Jack could learn nothing, after paying a visit to Jane Slater, he returned to his hotel about two o'clock in the morning, and retired to rest, little dreaming that the ruffian who had been the source of the girl's abduction had paid the debt of nature, and died as he had lived, drunk, and with an oath upon his lips.

The next morning he paid a visit to Mr. Brief, the lawyer, where he met young Richard

Clavering, whose sorrow at his sister's absence had made him quite ill.

But Jack bade him keep a good heart, and Mr. Brief endeavoured to assuage his grief by telling him that, his affairs assumed so cheering an aspect that it would only be a matter of form to carry them into court.

Mr. Lorain, too, was convinced, at, length, that he had no chance of contesting the other's right, and had made, through his solicitor, an offer not to oppose the claim if ten thousand pounds were given him, with which he offered to go to America, and never return to England.

This offer was refused by Richard, who desired to have the case settled in such a manner that there could be no after proceedings; but added, that if he obtained the estates, he would give that sum to the man who would be compelled to forfeit them.

Jack admired this resolve, and invited the young man to meet him in the evening, and assist him in the search for his sister; and, with a stronger attachment to each other than ever, they, parted.

Jack's was a nature which must be ever busy. He was not a man to loll in an easy chair, and yawn half the day away—he must be doing something, even if that something was discreditable to himself.

So, after a late dinner, he once more strolled out into the air, sauntered slowly through the parks, and, without heeding whither he went, found himself, just before dark, in the Edgware-road.

Suddenly recollecting his appointment with Richard, he took his watch from his pocket, and consulted its dial—he had yet two hours to wait for the time agreed upon.

"Two hours yet!" he muttered. "Well, how to pass them is the thing. I suppose I had better count the flag-stones; for, by my faith, I know not how to kill the time. He is a happy fellow who has to labour for his daily bread—always providing there is no lack of work, and it is well paid for. But to a man like me, who never soiled his hands—albeit, I have often stained my conscience—time drags so heavily, that he knows not what to do to keep his mind employed. I'll count the flags. It is not a very artistic occupation; but I shall learn something thereby, more, I'll wager, than the man who laid them down. I shall know how many of these stones it took to pave the road; however, that is worth knowing—so here goes."

Jack commenced counting the flags, amusing himself, at the same time, by trying to place his foot, at each step, in the centre of the stone; but the slabs being of different widths, he gave up that portion of the task, for fear that the persons who were near him should imagine him to be intoxicated, from the unevenness of his strides.

Still he continued to count; and to do so, of course, kept his eyes fixed downwards, when suddenly he pounced on a small object glittering on the stone at his feet.

It was a pin, and a good sized pin, too. There was nothing of an extraordinary character in the little object—it was nothing but a common brass pin.

Still, Jack stopped to look at it—then stooped and picked it up, held it between his fingers, and, finally, stuck it in the lappel of his coat.

Many persons would have done the same with the little piece of brass wire, and thought no more about it; but Jack never recollected doing such a thing before, nor could he tell what prompted him to do so now. He had often observed a pin on the ground, but never condescended to stoop to pick it up. What induced him to do so now, he knew not; but something did, and that something he was not philosopher enough to understand.

He continued his walk, counting the stones, and, over and anon, looking at the round shining head of the pin, as it stuck out of the dark cloth into which he had inserted its point; and had nearly reached the Harrow-road, when he overtook two young persons, who were sauntering slowly along, with their eyes fixed like his own, on the flags, and evidently in no very good humour with themselves or each other.

They were a young man and woman between twenty and twenty-five years of age, and evidently belonging to that class which have but little means, yet strive to appear decent and respectable upon them.

"I verily believe they are engaged in the same occupation as myself," said Jack to himself, "counting the stones, or are they looking for pins, I wonder; or is there a little cloud stealing over the sunshine of their love. Ah, that's it!"

And, with a smile, Jack slackened his pace, and kept as close behind them as possible, without exciting their suspicions that he was following them.

"I tell you, Milly," said the young man, at length, "it is cruel of you to play thus with my feelings. You have led me to think you loved me, and now that I would make you mine, you will not agree to become my wife. It is true I am poor, but I will be kind and true to you."

"I know you would, John," said the girl, in a voice that caused Jack to start, "but I will never marry."

"Never!"

"Ay! Do not ask me why. I have my reasons. I cannot bear the thought of marrying. I will own I love you, but can never become your wife."

"Then you love another?"

"Indeed, no!"

"Why this strange resolve, then?"

"Do not ask me."

"But I will know."

"No you will not, and if you love me, you will not seek to know. I have my reasons, John. Do not question them."

"Mildred Hendon, I must—I will," cried the youth, pausing in his slow walk.

"John, I have said I will not give them," was the firm reply.

"Then, we must part for ever," said the young man.

"Do not leave me in anger, John," pleaded the girl. "You would not, did you know my heart."

"I am not angered. I shall leave you in sorrow. I had hoped to make you my wife, but find I have been but following a shadow that glides from my touch when I extend my hand to grasp it. Not in anger will I leave you, Milly, but in sorrow."

Jack at this moment passed them, and, as he did so, he took the pin from the lappel of his coat.

They neither of them observed him, and after looking in the girl's face as she kept her eyes fixed on the ground, he turned and passed them again as they stood close together, their hands locked in each other's, and their eyes both fixed on the ground.

As he did so, he pinned the skirt of the girl's dress to the coat of the youth, and waited for her to speak again.

"He shan't run away from her," he muttered. "I know her reason, and so shall he. I like the look of him, and if I can prevail upon the girl to forego her resolve, I will do so."

"John," she said, at length, "it is hard for me to drive you from my side; but we never can be united."

"Farewell, then, Milly. May we never meet again," said the young man, shaking the trembling hand, and turning quickly.

He took but one step ere he discovered, by the pull upon his coat and Milly's dress, that they were secured together; and while both looked at their extended skirts in some confusion, Jack said—

"Why, my friend, you are already united, you see!"

The young man darted a fierce look at Jack, and Milly, turning, uttered a little scream.

"How dare you, sir!" cried the youth.

"I was resolved that you should not lose the prize you seek; so don't be angry, young man."

"This insolence"—

"Oh, do not; he is my friend," cried Mildred, extending her hand to Jack.

The young man looked as if he would slay our hero on the spot.

He saw, or rather fancied he saw, the true reason of Mildred's refusal to become his wife.

She loved another, and that other the man who had dared to pin them together in the public streets; and had it not been for the presence of the girl he so fondly loved, he would have struck Jack to the earth.

Our hero read what was transpiring in the young man's mind; so, turning to Mildred, he said—

"Miss Hendon, I am happy to see you here, recovered from your accident; and shall be more happy still, if you will introduce me to your intended husband. Nay, do not blush. You owe me a favour, I think."

"Indeed—indeed, I do, my noble benefactor and kindest of friends!" said Mildred.

"Then forego your cruel intention, and be happy with this young man, who, I am sure— for I read a man's nature in his face—will be to you a kind and indulgent husband, who will take you from that profession to which few, indeed, cling from love, and where fewer still are kindly looked upon by the unfeeling world. I guess the reason which has prompted you to refuse him your hand; but let me ask it as a mark of respect—gratitude, if you will, to me— to gainsay the words you have uttered."

Mildred looked blushingly to the ground.

"You love him?" said Jack.

"Yes, I will not deny it," was the soft response; "but"—

"But—but what? You are a silly girl," said Jack, "and if you do not like to say yes to his pleading, I will say yes for you."

"No—no!"

"Then, speak the word yourself. I know it will make you happy as well as him; and I am sure it will be a source of great pleasure to me to know that you are comfortably settled— no longer compelled to make the theatre a means of obtaining bread for yourself and aged mother. Now come, Miss Hendon, it is an old friend who joins his appeal to that of this young man, and I am sure you will not turn a deaf ear to our pleadings."

"My good, kind friend," said Mildred, raising her eyes to those of our hero's, "I can deny you nothing."

"Not even this little hand," said Jack, taking the taper[180] fingers of Mildred in his own and holding them tightly. "Not even this little hand, to bestow upon our surprised friend here."

"Do as you will," said Mildred. "If you wish it, I will consent."

"I do wish it, if you love him; but not else," said Jack, quickly.

"I do love him!"

"Then I must respect him. There, my friend, that little pin which almost brought your hand on my head, has got you this hand, and the heart with it. And now, Mildred, tell me his name."

"John Harkwright."

"Then, Mr. John Harkwright, I am happy to make your acquaintance; but will leave you now, to talk over affairs to yourselves."

"But not before you tell me who to thank," said the young man in tones of surprise and pleasure, as he drew Mildred towards him.

"Certainly—Spring-heeled Jack! Farewell!"

As Jack spoke, he took one of his tremendous springs, and disappeared over a garden wall, beside which they had been standing.

CHAPTER CVIII.

JACK AT HIS PRANKS. GOOD NEWS AT LAST.

THE exclamation of surprise which broke from John Harkwright in the street was echoed by an elderly lady in the garden into which Jack had fallen, among a beautiful bed of geraniums, which the aged female was denuding of their dead leaves at the moment that our hero alighted on his feet right before her.

She was a strange-looking personage, this old lady—for old she certainly was, despite the flowing black curls that fell over her wrinkled cheeks and twined around her shoulders.

Her face was pinched, although her cheeks were rosy, but it was not the natural that of health and youth, but the free application of rouge, which gradually peeled off the yellow, wrinkled skin as her terror caused the blood to stagnate around her heart.

The moment Jack discovered he was not alone he clapped his mask to his face, and bending over the old woman, exclaimed, in a low tone—

"Silence!"

There was no need for the demand; for the moment the old lady's eyes rested on his upturned features all power of speech was denied her, and from a stooping position she sank into a kneeling one, rolling her eyes in terror from side to side, and trembling in every limb.

Jack stood gazing upon her for some time, while a scornful and pitying smile stole over his face, and a feeling of contempt pervaded his heart at the absurdity of a woman near seventy years of age trying to make herself appear as young as a girl of twenty.

---

[180] Slender.

Jack cast a look around him, to satisfy himself that there was no one at hand, and then, turning to the terrified lady, exclaimed—

"Pray, madam, how old are you? It certainly may not appear a very polite question on the part of a stranger; but curiosity is so strong within me that I must yield to its demands, even at the risk of being thought rude."

"Go—go away, you naughty, ugly man," gasped the lady. "You have no right in my garden."

"Naughty man!" said Jack. "Come, that's better than usual. Most people, at first sight, have taken me for the devil; but this lady is a more acute observer of human nature, and has discovered on the instant that I am only a man.

"I should not have intruded," continued Jack, "had I expected to meet so charming a creature. Pray, get up; you will catch cold kneeling there on the grass. Allow me, madam, to assist you to your feet."

He extended his hand, but the lady uttered a cry, and sprang up unaided.

"What an agile frame!" said Jack. "Would you believe it, madam, I positively took you, at first sight, to be an old, decrepit specimen of humanity, with one foot and a-half in the grave! and I positively discover you to be a charming creature of more than ordinary beauty. Such rosy cheeks! such pearly teeth! such sylph-like movements and graceful carriage! such beautiful eyes and hair! Such—Hallo! who the devil's this coming?"

Jack turned quickly round, and perceived a servant-girl tripping lightly along the garden walk towards them.

The girl no sooner perceived him than she uttered a sharp cry, and turned and fled towards the house.

The old lady, as soon as Jack's back was turned towards her, took advantage of the circumstance, and darting through the splendid bed of geraniums, hurried away, calling, in a squeaking tone—

"Mary—Mary! go for the police—go for the police!"

"Whew?" muttered Jack; "that won't do, for I have got an appointment with young Clavering. No police tonight. I haven't time to play with them."

So, leaping over the bed of geraniums, he caught the old lady by the arm, and brought her to an instant standstill.

"Call your maid to your side, do you hear me, madam? If she give any alarm, it will be the worse for you, I assure you."

"What business have you in my garden? How dare you come here, sir?"

"I dare do anything that pleases me, madam. Call back the girl," said Jack, in a threatening tone.

"I won't. She has gone for the police lo take you into custody. You rude man—you robber—you"—

"Madam!"

"I am not afraid of you," said the woman, suddenly bridling up, and showing some spirit.

"I would warn you not to suffer that girl to enter the house."

"You warn me?"

"Yes, me!"

"Who are you?"

"People call me Spring-heeled Jack!"

"Oh!" shrieked the old lady, her former terror returning on the instant. "Murder—thieves—fire—help —police!"

"Silence!" cried Jack, placing his hand over her lips.

"Murder! mur"—

The rest of the sentence could not force its way through Jack's fingers.

"Call back the girl. Call her, I say, or"—

"Yes, yes. Oh! dear. Mary—Mary, come here," cried the lady, in tones of abject terror and dismay. "Oh! clear, to think that I should live to see the monster. Oh! dear—oh! dear. I shall die. I shall faint, I know I shall. Mur— no, Mary—Mary! oh! come here, it's only Mr. Spring-heeled Jack!"

"Silence!" said Jack.

"I can't."

"You must."

"Go away. Oh, please, go away."

"I intend to."

"Do—do."

"When your maid comes to your side."

"She is coming."

"I see she is."

"Then go."

"Come here, girl, to your mistress. Don't be frightened. You have nothing to fear."

The girl hesitated, and kept some yards off.

"I will not harm you, I assure you," said Jack. "Your mistress simply wants you to tell me her age."

"Seventy," said the girl.

"Oh!" cried the old lady, "It is false!"

"Certainly it is," said. Jack. "I saw that at a glance."

And, making a sudden snatch at the old lady's black glossy ringlets, he tore them from her head.

Oh! the look of consternation—the cry of anguish that escaped the lips of the old lady! It was something horrible, and Jack almost dropped the cluster of false hair from his extended hand as she sank down on her knees among the geraniums, and, clasping her hands together, fixed on her false locks a look of the most comical despair.

"Oh, mercy!" cried the girl, holding up her hands in amazement and terror, "she is"—

"Shorn of her beauty, girl—is she not?" said Jack. "Here—take her wig and put it on, for her bald head is enough to frighten anyone out of their wits, and let me give you a bit of advice, old lady, before I go. Don't try to make yourself what you can never be— young again! You may excite contempt by such proceedings, but never admiration. Age is honourable when borne with dignity; but contemptible, when made ridiculous by such stupid things as this."

He threw the wig to the girl, and, with a contemptuous smile, sprang upwards and on to the top of the wall.

No person was close at hand on the other side; so, taking a parting look at the old lady, who still knelt among the geraniums, he leaped down, and was making off, when a cry caused him to turn, and he saw a young man running towards him.

"Jack—Jack—Jack!"

"Who the deuce is that?" mentally asked Jack of himself, as he looked hard at the man.

"Don't you know me?" cried the young man, coming up, and extending his hand to our hero.

A smile broke over Jack's face.

"Mr. Bedford?"

"Yes, it's Tom Bedford."

"I did not recognise you at the moment."

"Nor should I you, if I hadn't caught sight of you as you leaped down from that wall. I know there are few men can take such a leap so easily."

"Well, I am glad to see you, Mr. Bedford."

"And I am more so to see you. In fact, I have been endeavouring to find you out for some days."

"Ah! For what purpose?"

"You know old Mother Frump?"

"The old lady we"—

"Yes, yes. Well, about a week ago I saw there was something wrong about the old woman, and didn't like the appearance of things in general, so I took the liberty of paying her house a visit, after the manner you did that night, and discovered there, lying insensible, a young girl about"—

Jack clutched so fiercely at Tom Bedford's arm, that a cry of pain put a stop to his story.

"I beg your pardon," said Jack. "But go on—go on. A young lady—yes!"

"She had been taken there against her will by that fellow Grasper, at the villas, lower down; and, of course, I knew it could be for no good. So, while the old gal was out, I made bold to steal her charge, and carried her to my own rooms, fetched a doctor, and, after a long while, she just recovered sufficient to murmur your name."

"Mine?"

"Yes. So I leaped to the conclusion that you must know something of her. She has not spoken since, for she has been mad with brain fever. I have tried to learn where I could find you, and had given up the task in despair when I saw you leap from that wall."

"Tom, God bless you for your news! I do indeed know her; but why Grasper could have taken her there, I know not. But come with me; this is no place to talk over the affair. Believe me, nothing could be more welcome to me at this moment than to learn where Ellen Folder is to be found."

CHAPTER CIX.
THE FATE OF RALPH GRASPER.
(conclusion.)

GREAT, indeed, was the consternation of Miss Frump and Ralph Grasper when in company they entered the chamber where Ellen had been left by the latter to find it empty; and but one conclusion could be arrived at, and that was that the girl had recovered her consciousness, and made good her escape; and, muttering curses loud and deep upon the head of the old maid, Grasper insultingly flung a shilling upon the table, as a reward for the trouble she had had, and refused to have anything further to do with her; and Miss Frump, not altogether sorry, placed the coin in her pocket, and, in not over choice language, ordered him to leave her house, and seek someone else when he wanted them to aid him in his dirty work.

Filled with rage, Grasper left her to smother her ruffled spirits in a draught of her favourite liquor. He returned home, obtained a coach next morning, and drove to the east-end, resolved to find out, if possible, whether the woman had gone back to Holly Cottage; for the constant checks he received only served to make him the more determined to ruin poor Jane Slater.

Here, to his great surprise, he saw Jane standing at the gate, weeping, and thus satisfied as to where she was, he resolved to wait a few days ere he again attempted to carry her off, feeling that she would now be upon her guard, for he had not the least suspicion of his mistake.

Day after day he hung about the vicinity of Holly Cottage, occasionally catching a glimpse of his intended victim; and on the evening in which we have seen Jack and Tom Bedford together, he had fully made up his mind to wait no longer the consummation of his desires, and bear her off to his own home.

"I will trust none but myself," he muttered, as he alighted from the box of the same vehicle which he had used to carry off Ellen. "The woman has not been at all scared, it seems, by her late abduction; for every evening she has sauntered out, and doubtless she will do so again tonight. No Bill Jacksons and no Miss Frumps shall be called into requisition now. I will myself be both her gaoler and lover; and if I let her escape me this time, may I never live to see her again."

Scarce had he given utterance to these words when Jane Slater emerged through the gateway out into the dimly lighted street, on her way to the police-station, to see if she could learn any news of her absent friend, which she had done every night before retiring to rest; but she had not got twenty yards before a couple of arms were thrown roughly around her, and Grasper's voice sounded in her ears.

The tones of that man instantly paralysed her, and before she could recover strength to cry out, a handkerchief was stuffed into her mouth and tied behind her head, and she was thrust rudely into the darkened coach, her hands were secured behind her back, the doors of the vehicle closed and locked, and she felt herself being carried away at a great speed.

She did not faint, for her terror was too great; but she sank down upon her knees and sobbed aloud.

Furiously, Grasper whipped the horse, and as the animal galloped away, the merchant muttered through his clenched teeth—

"Tonight I will crush her proud spirit or perish. No chloroform to plunge her into insensibility, and delay my long-wished-for success. Once more she is in my power, and not one moment will I listen to her pleadings. I will not delay my triumph an hour lest accursed fate baulk me of my prey. Tonight— ay, tonight! and nought but death shall save her from me now!"

In an incredible short space of time the vehicle was brought to a standstill before his residence, which, strange to say, was in complete darkness, for not a light gleamed from any one of the windows.

The inmates had not all retired to rest, as the darkened place would have suggested, but had gone to the theatre—a circumstance which coming to the knowledge of Grasper, had decided him upon making the attempt that night to again get Jane into his power.

Dismounting from the box, the merchant hurried to the door, unlocked it with his latch key, then returned to the vehicle, and lifting Jane out, bore her into the house and up the stairs to his own apartments.

Without uttering one word, he set her down upon the sofa, and retiring from the room locked the door behind him, leaving her in the dark, and took home the vehicle from whence he had borrowed it.

Having settled the demands of its owner, Grasper hurried on his way back in a state of great excitement, and dreaming of his revenge, which now it seemed must be consummated, he observed not a tall, cloaked figure steal out of a front garden a short distance from his residence, and follow, with noiseless footsteps, in his track.

He reached the villa, unlocked the door, and strode into the dark passage; and as he crossed the threshold a cold shudder pervaded his frame, for which he was unable to account, but he paid little heed to the circumstance, and closing the door behind him, hurried to the room where he had left Jane Slater.

As the bang of the door echoed through the house, the cloaked figure gave utterance to a low whistle, and two forms stole out of a neighbouring garden and approached him.

They were Tom Bedford and Richard Clavering!

"Well, Jack," said Tom, addressing the man who had followed Grasper, "was it the old scoundrel?"

"Yes, it was him. Now, Richard Clavering, I intend to know what induced him to bear off your sister, and to punish him for the unmanly act."

"Let that be my task," said the young man. "Poor girl! She may yet die through his conduct. I could scarce believe her the same I left so long ago, when I went forth to seek for work and bread."

"The shock has done her much harm; but she is gradually recovering," said Tom.

"Thanks to you, my friend," said Richard. "I shall ever owe you a debt of gratitude. But I am the most injured of us three; therefore, be it me to chastise the villain, and avenge my sister's wrongs."

"Not so; you remain here with Tom, and if I require your aid, I will whistle. Besides, you cannot get at him as I can."

And as Jack finished speaking, he leaped on to the top of the wall which bounded the forecourt, from thence on to the balcony of the first-floor, hesitated a moment, and then took a leap which placed his hands within reach of the coping-stone, to which he clung as we saw him in the early part of this story.

Hanging thus for a moment, he managed to place his feet on the sill of the second-floor window, and then grasping the water-pipe, which ran close beside it, he gradually lowered himself, and paused for breath.

While thus engaged, a light flashed from the window, the curtains of which were looped back, and Jack saw the form and face of Grasper as he placed a lamp upon the table.

But the next moment he almost lost his balance, as a female form rose up from a couch and confronted the merchant; for, despite the kerchief which was fastened over her mouth, Jack recognised the features of Jane Slater.

For a few moments, surprise held him powerless, and caused a dizziness to float through his brain; but the voice of Grasper roused him, and he was himself again.

"So! Jane Slater, you are again in my power! Time after time have I been foiled in my purpose. I have sworn to crush your proud spirit, and blight your happiness! Looks, tears, prayers are in vain! I will have no mercy now! Mine you are now! Mine, this very hour! and nought but death can save you!"

He sprang towards her, as she fell back in horror, but paused as Jack darted from the window and sprang into the room.

A cry of joy escaped Jane's lips, a shout of horror broke from the guilty man, and he turned and fled from the apartment.

"Hold, ruffian!" cried Jack. "The hour of vengeance has indeed come. You have spoken truly, Ralph Grasper. The hour has come at last!"

As he reached the landing, Jack seized him by the shoulders; but the terrified man made a frantic effort, and tore himself away, and dashed up the narrow flight of stairs, which led to the attics, closely followed by Jack, who again grasped him as he dashed through the doorway of the front chamber.

"Mercy—mercy!" shrieked Grasper, and terror lending him strength, he again succeeded in breaking from Jack's hold, and, dashing across the room, he sprang out of the attic window on to the coping stone.

In a moment Jack was beside him, and, shrieking aloud for mercy, the guilty wretch ran along the gutter till he stood on the very corner of the coping stones, when he turned and sprang at Jack's throat, perceiving he could fly no further.

That moment was fatal to him, for Jack, dashing his arm aside, Ralph Grasper lost his balance, swayed for a moment like a drunken man, then fell backwards into the street below.

Jack, seeing his danger, made an effort to grasp him, but in vain, and the next moment Ralph Grasper lay, with his neck broken, on the flags before the door of his own dwelling.

The fall of the body startled not only Tom and Richard, but a watchman who was passing. He shouted lustily for help, and as Jack, with Jane Slater, emerged from the house, he was violently seized by the watchman, and in his endeavour to throw him off, Jack's mask slipped from his face, the light from the adjacent lamp flashing upon his features he was recognised by the man who held him, and who, in his younger days, had been a servant in his father's family.

"Spring-heeled Jack!" he shouted. "The Mar"—

A heavy blow on the mouth from Jack's fist stifled the word, and released him from the watchman's hold.

"Richard—Tom!" cried Jack, "look to this woman, befriend her for my sake! This unfortunate discovery renders my presence in England dangerous to my safety. I must fly. To your protection I commend Jane Slater!"

Away went Jack, and after him followed a goodly crowd, headed by the watchman, who had recovered from the stunning effects of the blow; but Jack gained upon them, and obtaining a coach, drove to his hotel.

But well he knew he could not now remain there in safety.

So, hastily securing his cheque-book and a few valuables, he left the hotel in a post-chaise, after making inquiries where he could obtain a vessel bound for Spain.

One had dropped down the river that morning, and would be lying off the coast for a couple of days; and Jack promised the postilion[181] a handsome reward if he made all the speed he could.

Night and day he travelled, and the next night he dismissed the chaise; and after partaking of some refreshment, went down to the beach, and engaged a boatman to go off to the vessel, and learn if the captain would take him on board; and while the men got their boat ready and sped over the water to the ship, Jack leisurely strolled up on to the rocks that rose in weird and picturesque masses on all sides.

In the beauty of the scene before him—for the moon had risen, and was tinting the waves with silver—he did not observe the approach of three men, who were stealing cautiously over the rocks towards him; nor was it till one of them exclaimed, in a loud tone, "On, lads! 'tis Spring-heeled Jack!" did he know of their presence.

Jack started round at the mention of his name, and that one look assured him they were officers.

"Spring-heeled Jack, we arrest you in the name of the sovereign!" cried the man who had before spoken.

Jack cast an anxious look towards the sea and saw the boat returning quickly to the beach "In the name of the law we call on you to surrender! You have taken your last leap, Jack!" cried the man, springing towards him.

"In England, for some time, I have, my friend," said Jack. "Good bye! Give my respects to all I leave behind."

And as the man was about to lay his hand on his shoulder, Jack sprang out over the rock into the glistening sea!

Over the dancing waves the vessel bounded for sunny Spain—glided like a thing of life; and the white cliffs of England faded from the view of him who trod her deck with a heart sad at parting, yet bounding with joy at his narrow escape.

And while her sails filled with the wind, and she threw the spray high up over her bows, Richard Clavering told the story of his fortune to his fast-recovering sister, and made her happy with the prospects before them, and hinted that when some few months had passed, a wife would share his title, his name, and wealth—for he had learned to love Jane Slater, and she to love him.

And months passed, and the law decided in his favour; and Richard went, with his sister and wife, to reside in the mansion which was justly his own, and where happiness reigned, and grateful hearts anxiously looked for the time to come when they could welcome back their best and dearest friend—SPRING-HEELED JACK, THE TERROR OF LONDON!

THE END

---

[181] Man who rides one of the horses pulling a carriage, in order to guide them.